ZACHARY GOLDMAN PRIVATE INVESTIGATOR

CASES 1-4

P.D. WORKMAN

ISBN: 9781774681367 (KDP Print)

ISBN: 9781774681374 (IS Paperback)

ISBN: 9781774681381 (IS Hardcover)

pdworkman

SHE WORE MOURNING

ZACHARY GOLDMAN MYSTERIES #1

To those who are broken, and yet go on

1

Zachary Goldman stared down the telephoto lens at the subjects before him. It was one of those days that left tourists gaping over the gorgeous scenery. Dark trees against crisp white snow, with the mountains as a backdrop. Like the picture on a Christmas card.

The thought made Zachary feel sick.

But he wasn't looking at the scenery. He was looking at the man and the woman in a passionate embrace. The pretty young woman's cheeks were flushed pink, more likely with her excitement than the cold, since she had barely stepped out of her car to greet the man. He had a swarthier complexion and a thin black beard, and was currently turned away from Zachary's camera.

Zachary wasn't much to look at himself. Average height, black hair cut too short, his own three-day growth of beard not hiding how pinched and pale his face was. He'd never considered himself a good catch.

He waited patiently for them to move, to look around at their surroundings so that he could get a good picture of their faces.

They thought they were alone; that no one could see them without being seen. They hadn't counted on the fact that Zachary had been surveilling them for a couple of weeks and had known where they would go. They gave him lots of warning so that he could park his car out of sight, camouflage himself in the trees, and settle in to wait for their appearance.

He was no amateur; he'd been a private investigator since she had been choosing wedding dresses for her Barbie dolls.

He held down the shutter button to take a series of shots as they came up for air and looked around at the magnificent surroundings, smiling at each other, eyes shining.

All the while, he was trying to keep the negative thoughts at bay. Why had he fallen into private detection? It was one of the few ways he could make a living using his skill with a camera. He could have chosen another profession. He didn't need to spend his whole life following other people, taking pictures of their most private moments. What was the real point of his job? He destroyed lives, something he'd had his fill of long ago. When was the last time he'd brought a smile to a client's face? A real, genuine smile? He had wanted to make a difference in people's lives; to exonerate the innocent.

Zachary's phone started to buzz in his pocket. He lowered the camera and turned around, walking farther into the grove of trees. He had the pictures he needed. Anything else would be overkill.

He pulled out his phone and looked at it. Not recognizing the number, he swiped the screen to answer the call.

"Goldman Investigations."

"Uh… yes… Is this Mr. Goldman?" a voice inquired. Older, female, with a tentative quaver.

"Yes, this is Zachary," he confirmed, subtly nudging her away from the 'mister.'

"Mr. Goldman, my name is Molly Hildebrandt."

He hoped she wasn't calling her about her sixty-something-year-old husband and his renewed interest in sex. If it was another infidelity case, he was going to have to turn it down for his own sanity. He would even take a lost dog or wedding ring. As long as the ring wasn't on someone else's finger now.

"Mrs. Hildebrandt. How can Goldman Investigations help you?"

Of course, she had probably already guessed that Goldman Investigations consisted of only one employee. Most people seemed to sense that from the size of his advertisements. From the fact that he listed a post office box number instead of a business suite downtown or in one of the newer commercial areas. It wasn't really a secret.

"I don't know whether you have been following the news at all about Declan Bond, the little boy who drowned...?"

Zachary frowned. He trudged back toward his car.

"I'm familiar with the basics," he hedged. A four- or five-year-old boy whose round face and feathery dark hair had been pasted all over the news after a search for a missing child had ended tragically.

"They announced a few weeks ago that it was determined to be an accident."

Zachary ground his teeth. "Yes...?"

"Mr. Goldman, I was Declan's grandma." Her voice cracked. Zachary waited, listening to her sniffles and sobs as she tried to get herself under control. "I'm sorry. This has been very difficult for me. For everyone."

"Yes."

"Mr. Goldman, I don't believe that it was an accident. I'm looking for someone who would investigate the matter privately."

Zachary breathed out. A homicide investigation? Of a child? He'd told himself that he would take anything that wasn't infidelity, but if there was one thing that was more depressing than couples cheating on each other, it was the death of a child.

"I'm sure there are private investigators that would be more qualified for a homicide case than I am, Mrs. Hildebrandt. My schedule is pretty full right now."

Which, of course, was a lie. He had the usual infidelities, insurance investigations, liabilities, and odd requests. The dregs of the private investigation business. Nothing substantial like a homicide. It was a high-profile case. A lot of volunteers had shown up to help, expecting to find a child who had wandered out of his own yard, expecting to find him dirty and crying, not floating face down in a pond. A lot of people had mourned the death of a child they hadn't even known existed before his disappearance.

"I need your help, Mr. Goldman. Zachary. I can't afford a big name, but you've got good references. You've investigated deaths before. Can't you help me?"

He wondered who she had talked to. It wasn't like there were a lot of people who would give him a bad reference. He was competent and usually got the job done, but he wasn't a big name.

"I could meet with you," he finally conceded. "The first consultation is free. We'll see what kind of a case you have and whether I want to take it.

I'm not making any promises at this point. Like I said, my schedule is pretty full already."

She gave a little half-sob. "Thank you. When are you able to come?"

After he had hung up, Zachary climbed into his car, putting his camera down on the floor in front of the passenger seat where it couldn't fall, and started the car. For a while, he sat there, staring out the front windshield at the magical, sparkling, Christmas-card scene. Every year, he told himself it would be better. He would get over it and be able to move on and to enjoy the holiday season like everyone else. Who cared about his crappy childhood experiences? People moved on.

And when he had married Bridget, he had thought he was going to achieve it. They would have a fairy-tale Christmas. They would have hot chocolate after skating at the public rink. They would wander down Main Street looking at the lights and the crèche in front of the church. They would open special, meaningful presents from each other.

But they'd fought over Christmas. Maybe it was Zachary's fault. Maybe he had sabotaged it with his gloom. The season brought with it so much baggage. There had been no skating rink. No hot chocolate, only hot tempers. No walks looking at the lights or the nativity. They had practically thrown their gifts at each other, flouncing off to their respective corners to lick their wounds and pout away the holiday.

He'd still cherished the thought that perhaps the next year there would be a baby. What could be more perfect than Christmas with a baby? It would unite them. Make them a real family. Just like Zachary had longed for since he'd lost his own family. He and Bridget and a baby. Maybe even twins. Their own little family in their own little happy bubble.

But despite a positive pregnancy test, things had gone horribly wrong.

Zachary stared at the bright white scenery and blinked hard, trying to shake off the shadows of the past. The past was past. Over and done. This year he was back to baching it for Christmas. Just him and a beer and *It's a Wonderful Life* on TV.

He put the car in reverse and didn't look into the rear-view mirror as he backed up, even knowing about the precipice behind him. He'd deliberately parked where he'd have to back up toward the cliff when he was done. There was a guardrail, but if he backed up too quickly, the car would go right through it, and who could say whether it had been accidental or deliberate? He had been cold-stone sober and had been out on a job. Mrs. Hildebrandt could testify that he had been calm and sober during their call. It would be ruled an accident.

But his bumper didn't even touch the guardrail before he shifted into drive and pulled forward onto the road.

He'd meet with the grandmother. Then, assuming he did not take the case, there would always be another opportunity.

Life was full of opportunities.

2

Molly Hildebrandt was much as Zachary expected her to be. A woman in her sixties who looked ten or twenty years older with the stress of the high-profile death of her grandchild. Gray, curling hair. Pale, wrinkled skin. She wasn't hunched over, though. She sat up straight and tall as if she'd gone to a finishing school where she'd been forced to walk and sit with an encyclopedia on her head. Did they still do that? Had they ever done it?

"Mr. Goldman, thank you for seeing me so quickly," she greeted formally, holding her hand out for him to shake when he arrived at her door.

"Please, call me Zachary, ma'am. I'm not really comfortable with Mr. Goldman."

Telling her that he wasn't comfortable with it meant that she would be a bad hostess if she continued to address him that way, instead of her seeing it as a way of showing him respect. He hadn't done anything to deserve respect and was much happier if she would talk to him like the gardener or her next-door neighbor.

Not that there was any gardener. Molly lived in a small apartment in an old, dark brick building that was sturdy enough, but had been around longer than Zachary had been alive. The interior, when she invited him in, was bright and cozy. She had made coffee, and he breathed in the aroma in the air appreciatively. It wasn't hot chocolate after skating, but he could use a cup or two of coffee to warm him up after his surveillance. Standing around in the snow for a couple of hours had chilled him, even though he'd dressed for the weather.

Molly escorted him to the tiny living room.

"And you must call me Molly," she insisted.

She eyed the big camera case as he put it down. Zachary gave a grimace.

"Sorry. I didn't come to take your picture; I just don't like to leave expensive equipment in the car."

"Oh," she nodded politely. She didn't ask him who he had been taking pictures of. That wouldn't be gracious. She would have to imagine instead, and she would probably be correct in her guess.

They fussed for a few minutes with their coffees. Zachary wrapped his fingers around his mug, waiting for the coffee to cool and his fingers to warm. It felt good. Comforting. He waited for Molly to begin her story.

"You probably think that I'm just being a fussy old lady," she said. "Imagining something sinister when it was just an accident."

"Not at all. Why don't you tell me why you don't think it was an accident?"

"I'm not *sure* at all," she clarified. "Maybe they're right. Maybe it was an accident. It isn't that I doubt their findings..." she trailed off. "Not really. I know they had to do an autopsy and all that. We waited for months for them to come back with the manner of death. I thought that once they ruled, everyone would feel better."

"But you still have doubts?"

"I'm worried for my daughter."

Zachary blinked at her and waited for more.

"She's not well. I had hoped that once they released the body... and after the memorial... and after the manner of death was announced... each milestone, I thought, it would get better. It would be easier for her, but..." Molly shook her head. "She's getting worse and worse. Time isn't helping."

"Your daughter was Declan's mother."

"Yes. Of course."

"What's her name?"

"Isabella Hildebrandt," Molly said, her brows drawn down like he should have known that. "You know. *The Happy Artist.*"

Zachary had heard of *The Happy Artist.* She was on TV and was popular among the locals. Zachary didn't know whether she was syndicated nationally or just on one of the local stations. She had a painting instruction show every Sunday morning, and people awaited her next show like a popular soap. Most of the people Zachary knew who watched the show didn't paint and never intended to take it up. She was an institution.

"Oh, yes," Zachary agreed. "Of course, I know *The Happy Artist*. I didn't put the names together."

"When it was in the news, they said who she was. They said it was *The Happy Artist's* child."

"Sure. Of course," Zachary agreed. He rubbed the dark stubble along his jaw. He should have gone home to shave and clean up before meeting with Molly. He looked like he'd been on a three-day stakeout. He *had* been on a three-day stakeout. "I'm sorry. I didn't follow the story very closely. That's good for you; it means I don't have a lot of preconceived ideas about the case."

She looked at him for a minute, frowning. Reconsidering whether she really wanted to hire him? That wouldn't hurt his feelings.

"You were going to tell me about your daughter?" Zachary prompted. "I can understand how devastated she must be by her son's death."

"No. I don't think you can," Molly said flatly.

Zachary was taken aback. He shrugged and nodded, and waited for her to go on.

"Isabella has a history of... mental health issues. She was the one supervising Declan when he disappeared, and the guilt has been overwhelming for her."

That made perfect sense. Zachary sipped at his coffee, which had cooled enough not to scald him.

Molly went on. "I think... as horrible as it may sound... that it would be a relief for her if it turned out that Declan was taken from the yard, instead of just having wandered away."

"That may be, but how likely is that? Surely the police must have considered the possibility, and I can't manufacture evidence for your daughter, even if it would ease her mind."

"No... I realize that. I'm not expecting you to do anything dishonest. Just to investigate it. Read over the police reports. Interview witnesses again. Just see... if there's any possibility that there was... foul play. A third-party interfering, even if it was nothing malicious."

"I assume you know most of the details surrounding the case."

"Yes, of course."

"How likely do you think it is that the police missed something? Did they seem sloppy or like they didn't care? Did you think there were signs of foul play that they brushed off?"

"No." Molly gave a little shrug. "They seemed perfectly competent."

Zachary was silent. It wouldn't be difficult to read over the police reports and talk to the family. Was there any point?

"The only thing is…" Molly trailed off.

As impatient as Zachary was to get out of there, he knew it was no good pushing Molly to give it up any faster. She already knew she sounded crazy for asking him to reinvestigate a case where he wasn't going to be able to turn up anything new. For no reason, other than that it might help her daughter to come to terms with the child's death. He looked around the room. There were no pictures of Molly's husband, even old ones. There was no sign she had raised Isabella or any other children there. There were several pictures of a couple with a little child. Declan and Isabella and whatever the father's name was. There was one picture of Declan himself, occupying its own space, a little memorial to her lost grandson. There were no pictures of anyone else, so Zachary could only assume Isabella was an only child and Declan the only grandchild.

"Declan was afraid of water."

Zachary turned his eyes back to her. He considered. It wasn't totally inconceivable that a child afraid of the water would drown. He wouldn't know how to swim. If he fell in, he would panic, flail, and swallow water, rather than staying calm enough to float. Molly wiped at a tear.

"How afraid of the water was he?" Zachary asked.

"He wouldn't go near the water. He was terrified. He wouldn't have gone to the pond by himself."

"How tall was he?"

Molly gave a little shrug. "He was almost five years old. Three feet?"

"How steep were the banks of the pond and what was the terrain and foliage like?" He knew he would have to look at it for himself.

"I don't know what you want to know… there wasn't any shore to speak of. Just the pond. There were bulrushes. Cattails. Some trees. The ground is… uneven, but not hilly."

Zachary tried to visualize it. A child wouldn't be able to see the pond as far away as an adult would because of his short stature. If his view were further screened by the plant life, the banks steep and crumbly, he might not be able to see it until he was right on top of it. Or in it.

"It's not a lot to go on," he said. "The fact that he was afraid of water."

"I know." Molly used both hands to wipe her eyes. "I know that." She looked around the apartment, swallowing hard to get control of her emotions. "I just want the best for my baby. A parent always wants what's best. Growing up... I wasn't able to give her that. She didn't have an easy life. I wonder if..." She didn't have to finish the sentence this time. Zachary already knew what she was going to say. She wondered if that rough upbringing had caused Isabella's mental fragility. Whether things would have turned out differently if she'd been able to provide a stable environment. Molly sniffled. "Do you have children, Mr.—Zachary?"

Zachary felt that familiar pain in his chest. Like she'd plunged a knife into it. He cleared his throat and shook his head. "No. My marriage just recently ended. We didn't have any children."

"Oh." Her eyes searched his for the truth. Zachary looked away. "I'm sorry. I guess we all have our losses."

Although hers, the death of her grandson, was clearly more permanent than any relationship issues Zachary might have.

In the end, he agreed to do the preliminaries. Get the police reports. Walk the area around the house and pond. Talk to the parents. He gave her his lowest hourly fee. She clearly couldn't afford more. He wasn't even sure she'd be able to pay on receipt of his invoice. He might have to allow her a payment plan, something he normally didn't do, but something about the frail woman had gotten to him.

He put in an appearance at the police station, requesting a copy of the information available to the public, and handing over Molly Hildebrandt's request that he be provided as much information as possible for an independent evaluation.

"You got a new case?" Bowman grunted as he tapped through a few computer screens, getting a feel for how many files there were on the Declan Bond accident investigation file and how much of it he would be able to provide to Zachary.

"Yes," Zachary agreed. Obviously. He didn't encourage small talk; he really didn't want Bowman to start asking personal questions. They weren't friends, but they were friendly. Bowman had helped Zachary track down missing documents before. He knew the right people to ask for permission and the best way to ask.

Bowman dug into his pocket and pulled out a pack of gum. He unwrapped a piece and popped it into his mouth, then offered one to Zachary as an afterthought.

"No, I'm good."

Bowman chewed vigorously as he studied each screen. He was a middle-aged man, with a middle-age spread, his belly sagging over his belt. His hairline had started receding, and occasionally he put on a pair of glasses for a moment and then took them off again, jamming them into his breast pocket.

"How's Bridget?" he asked.

Zachary swallowed. He took a deep breath and steeled himself for the conversation. Bowman looked away from his screen and at Zachary's face, eyebrows up.

"She's good. In remission."

"Good to hear." Bowman looked back at his computer again. "Good to hear. It's been a tough time for the two of you." His eyes flicked back to Zachary, and he backtracked. "I mean it's been tough for her. And for you."

"Yeah," Zachary agreed. He waved away any further fumbling explanation from Bowman. "So, what have we got? On the Bond case?"

"Right!" Bowman looked back at his screen. "I've got press releases and public statements for you. medical examiner's report. The cop in charge of the file was Eugene. He likes red."

Zachary blinked at Bowman, more baffled than usual by his abbreviated language. "What?"

"Eugene Taft. I know, it's a preposterous name, but he's never had a nickname that stuck. Eugene Taft."

"And he likes red."

"Wine," Bowman said as if Zachary was dense. "He likes red wine. You know, if you want to help things along, have a better chance of getting a look at the rest of that file, the officers' notes and all the background and interviews. If you have to apply some leverage."

"And for Eugene Taft, it's red wine."

"Has to be red," Bowman confirmed.

"Okay." Zachary looked at his watch. "Can you start that stuff printing for me? Is there anyone downstairs?" He knew he would have to run down to the basement to order a copy of the medical examiner's report. Just one of those bureaucratic things.

"Sure. Kenzie should be down there still."

Zachary paused. "Kenzie. Not Bradley?"

"Kenzie," Bowman confirmed. "She's new."

"How new?"

"I don't know." Bowman gave a heavy shrug. "How long since you were down there last? Less than that."

Zachary snorted and went down the hall to the elevator.

As he waited for it, Joshua Campbell, an officer he'd worked with on an insurance fraud case several months previous, approached and hit the up button. He did a double-take, looking at Zachary.

"Zach Goldman! How are you, man? Haven't seen you around here lately."

"Good." Zachary shook hands with him. Joshua's hands were hard and rough like he'd grown up working on a farm instead of in the city. Zachary wondered what he did in his spare time that left them so rough and scarred. He wasn't boxing after work; Zachary would have been able to tell that by his knuckles. "Hey, how's Bridget doing? Did everything turn out okay...?" He trailed off and shifted uncomfortably.

"Yeah, great. She's in remission."

"Oh, good. That's great, Zach. Good to hear."

Zachary nodded politely. His elevator arrived with a ding and a flashing down indicator. Zachary sketched a quick goodbye to Joshua and jumped on. He was starting to regret agreeing to look into the Bond case.

The girl at the desk had dark, curly hair, red-lipsticked lips, and a tight, slim form. She was working through some forms, those red lips pursed in concentration, and she didn't look up at him.

"Hang on," she said. "Just let me finish this part up, before I lose my train of thought."

Zachary stood there as patiently as possible, which wasn't too hard with a pretty girl to look at. She finally filled in the last space and looked up at him. She raised an eyebrow.

"You must be Kenzie," Zachary said.

"I don't know if I must be, but I am. Kenzie Kirsch. And you are?"

"Zachary Goldman. From Goldman Investigations."

"A private investigator?"

"Yes."

He didn't usually introduce himself that way because it gave people funny ideas about the kind of life he lived and how he spent his time. Most people did not think about mounds of paperwork or painstaking accident scene reconstructions when they thought about private investigation. They thought about Dick Tracy and Phillip Marlowe and all the old hardboiled detectives. When really most of a private investigator's life was mind-numbingly boring, and he didn't need to carry a gun.

"And what can I do for you today, Mr. Private Investigator?"

"Zachary."

"Zachary," she repeated, losing the teasing tone and giving him a warm smile. "What can I do for you?"

"I need to order a copy of a medical examiner's report. Declan Bond."

"Bond. That's the boy? The drowning victim?"

"That's the one."

She looked at him, shaking her head slightly. "Why do you need that one? It's closed. A determination was made that it was an accident."

"I know. The family would like someone else to look at it. Just to set their minds at ease."

"You're not going to find anything. It's an open-and-shut case."

"That's fine. They just want someone to take a look. It's not a reflection on the medical examiner. You know how families are. They need to be able to move on. They're not quite ready to let it go yet. One last attempt to understand…"

Kenzie gave a little shrug. "Okay, then… there's a form…" She bent over and searched through a drawer full of files to find the right one. Zachary had filled them out before. Usually, he could manage to do an end-run and Bradley would just pull the file for him. Officially, he was supposed to fill one out. He didn't want to end up in hot water with the new administrator, so he leaned on the counter and filled the form out carefully.

She went on with her own forms and filing, not trying to fill the silence with small talk. Which Zachary thought was nice. When he was finished, he put the pen back in its holder and handed the form to Kenzie. To the side of the work she was doing. Not right in front of her face. She again ignored him while she finished the section she was on, then picked it up to look it over.

"You have nice printing," she observed, her voice going up slightly. She laughed at herself. "No reason why you shouldn't," she said quickly. "It's just that the majority of the forms that get submitted here are... well, to say they were chicken scratch would be insulting to chickens."

Zachary chuckled. "That's the difference between a cop and a private investigator."

"Neat handwriting?"

"Yeah. Cops have to fill out so many forms, they don't care. You can just call them if you need something clarified. Me... I know if I don't fill it out right, it's just going to go in the circular file." He nodded in the direction of the garbage can.

"I wouldn't throw it out," she protested.

"If you couldn't read it? What else would you do?"

"I would at least try to call you."

Zachary indicated the form. "That's why I printed my phone number so neatly."

Kenzie smiled and nodded. "It's very clear," she approved.

"You'll call me?"

"I'll let you know when it's ready to be picked up."

Zachary hovered there for an extra few seconds. He was enjoying the give-and-take of his conversation with her but didn't want her to accuse him of being creepy. He wasn't the type who asked a girl out the first time he saw her.

He gave her another smile and walked away from the desk. Maybe next time.

3

Zachary had expected that he would need to meet with Spencer Bond, Declan's father, at his office. Men tended to want to act from a position of power, so he would want Zachary to see that he was well-respected and had some kind of influence. Spencer had surprised him by inviting him to the house. In the middle of the day. Surely, so long after Declan's death, he would be working again. Men tended to throw themselves back into their jobs.

Zachary decided Spencer must have taken the day off, or at least the afternoon, in order to meet with Zachary and answer all his questions.

The man who came to the door was similar to Zachary in age. Somewhere in his mid-to-late thirties. He had a young face. Dark hair. Clean shaven. He wore a suit and tie, so maybe he hadn't taken the day off work. Maybe he worked close by and had just taken an hour off to meet with Zachary. That was a little disappointing since Zachary figured he'd need more time than that to go over all the pertinent details.

"Mr. Bond?" Zachary asked politely.

"Yes. You must be Mr. Goldman of Goldman Investigations."

"That's me. Just Zachary, please."

"Zachary." Spencer looked at him for a moment and didn't offer to shake hands. He nodded and opened the door farther, motioning for Zachary to enter.

It wasn't a huge house, but it was simple and spacious. Bigger than anywhere Zachary had ever lived. Well, any *house* he had lived in, anyway. A few coats hung on pegs at the door. A blue man's coat. A couple of short women's jackets. There were a couple of umbrellas in an umbrella stand.

Looking around as Spencer led him through a living room with deep greens and pink pastels, Zachary couldn't see any sign that a child had lived there. No toy boxes or shelves. No fingerprints or crayon pictures on the coffee table. Declan Bond had drowned months before, at the end of the summer. They wouldn't have just left everything out. Maybe for a few days, but not for months.

Spencer led him into an office. Large windows, the afternoon sun streaming in. The room was warm, so either the windows had high-efficiency ratings, or they had a good furnace.

"Have a seat," Spencer muttered, going around the desk to sit.

Zachary selected a chair. Spencer reached over to a bottle of antibacterial gel cleaner and pumped a squirt into his hand. He rubbed his hands together, distributing it. All of this was done in an automatic gesture as if he wasn't even aware of it.

"Do you work from home?" Zachary asked, looking around.

"Yes." Spencer's dark eyes met Zachary's. "Didn't you already read our police interviews?"

"No. I'm still waiting to get everything. The police haven't allowed me access to their investigation notes yet, just the public releases. I'll talk to you and any other witnesses first, and then I'll go back over the police documentation, looking for any inconsistencies or new information. Okay?"

Spencer nodded, seeming satisfied with that.

"At this point, all I have to go by is your mother-in-law's initial statement to me, and a bare outline of what was in the news. Yours is the first detailed interview."

"I'll help you all I can."

Zachary looked over the neat desk and filing cabinets. "I didn't find any mention of what type of work you do."

"I am a reviewer."

Zachary wrote a note in his notepad, considering the answer. "What kind of things are we talking about? What do you review?"

"Product reviews. Anything. Food, cleaning products, toiletries, car accessories, books… anything and everything."

"Really. That must be interesting. Companies just send you products, and you test them…"

"I test them and post product reviews," Spencer completed, nodding.

"That lets you work from home. You don't have another office?"

"No. I work from here."

"And your wife is *The Happy Artist*. Does she spend a lot of time out of the home, or are both of you generally around?"

"Normally she's gone in the mornings. Then we're both around in the afternoon. It depends. She doesn't like to lock herself into a schedule." Spencer's eyes went to the big calendar on his wall, with carefully marked starting and ending times and columns of tasks. Zachary glanced over it.

"What were your child care arrangements? Whoever was home took care of Declan?"

"I was his primary caregiver. Isabella had to be away from the home more than I did. Taping, touring, doing interviews. She had her own artwork aside from the show. Painting, attending showings and schmoozing with the right people…"

"What happened the day Declan died? Can you walk me through the events of that day?"

Spencer swiveled his chair and gazed out the window. His office looked into the back yard.

"Deck was playing out back. Isabella was watching him. In the afternoon. She looked away, and when she looked back, he was gone. She thought he was just out of sight… waited a few minutes… looked out again… called him… I'm not sure how long he was gone before she started to worry. She came and got me. We both searched the house inside and out. Then we called the police. They started a search of the neighborhood."

Spencer stopped speaking. His voice had a flat tone to it, not what Zachary expected from a father talking about his only son's last hours on earth.

"The police organized a search. At what time?"

"I'm sure their records will be more accurate than my memory. I wasn't looking at a clock at the time. Four-thirty. Five o'clock. Something like that."

"And how long did it take to… find his remains?"

"Seven-fifteen. I think it was seven-fifteen."

"So only a couple of hours. You didn't have to deal with days of searching. That's a blessing, anyway."

Spencer stared out the window. "I suppose."

"Did they attempt to revive him?"

"At that point... they think he'd already been dead a couple of hours. There was nothing they could do."

"They put time of death at five o'clock?"

"Or thereabouts."

"By the time you started looking, it was already too late."

"Yes. So they said."

"I'm waiting for the medical examiner's report, but I assume they found water in his lungs. Were there any signs of... assault of any kind?"

"No. Nothing."

"How deep is the pond he was found in?"

Spencer turned his gaze to Zachary. "I've never waded in to find out."

"Natural or man-made?"

"Natural. Why does that matter?"

"If it was man-made, it probably has a gentle slope and fairly stable sides. If it's natural, it could be more treacherous. Deeper. Eroding banks. Maybe... sinkholes. I don't know."

"Oh." Spencer shrugged. "I see."

"Did Declan like to go to the pond? Is that somewhere you went regularly? To feed the ducks, maybe?"

"No." Spencer gave a definite shake of his head, looking almost angry at the thought. "We never went there."

"Molly said Declan was afraid of the water."

"It's a normal fear."

"I didn't say it wasn't a normal fear, but it was a fear he had?"

"I suppose, yes. Molly makes it out to be a lot worse than it was."

"She's brought it up with you as well?"

"Of course."

"What is your opinion? Do you think that he would have been too afraid to get close enough to the pond to drown?"

"No. Kids are unpredictable. He might have seen something that interested him... a dog or a rock... I don't know."

Zachary watched Spencer's Adam's apple moving up and down. The man's face was blank. The newspaper articles had said that he had shown no emotion either on Declan's disappearance or on the discovery of his body. That didn't mean that he wasn't feeling anything. Looking around the office, Zachary could see a framed picture of Declan placed prominently on the desk. On the back of the printer sat a stuffed toy dog.

"Declan liked dogs?"

"He loved them."

"Tell me about your wife."

Spencer reached out to his hand sanitizer, pumped a portion onto his hand, and again rubbed his hands together.

"Isabella was a very loving mother. This has been hard on her."

"Yes, I would expect it to be. Molly is very worried about her daughter's emotional state."

Spencer nodded.

"Do you think she's right to be concerned?"

"She knows her daughter better than I do. I know Isabella is unhappy... but that's how I would expect her to feel..."

"Like you."

Spencer gave a brief nod.

"Where did the two of you meet?"

"When I moved here, I was looking for a support group. Isabella had been put into a program by her therapist. We met. We really hit it off. It's hard for people to understand what it's like..." he trailed off uncomfortably.

"What it's like to have OCD," Zachary guessed.

Spencer didn't look surprised that Zachary had figured it out. It wasn't like he had tried to hide his compulsions.

"Yes."

"You and Isabella both have OCD?" Molly hadn't mentioned what kind of mental illness Isabella suffered from. "What's that like? It must be nice having someone who understands what it's like." Zachary made a motion to encompass the room. "It's a very tidy household," he observed with a smile.

"What you have seen so far. I thought it would be easier, living with someone like me; someone who understood; but we are very different. I think probably more different than it would have been to marry someone without compulsions."

Zachary shook his head, not understanding. Spencer tipped his chair back a little. He let out a sigh.

"Combining our households was a challenge. Isabella had accumulated so much stuff. They didn't live at Molly's current place, which you already saw. They lived in a little bungalow, and it was full to the brim with things. Isabella obviously couldn't bring everything here. She did her best to only bring a reasonable amount, and we tried to make a home."

Zachary nodded, following the story, though he wasn't sure where it was going to lead.

"The dishes were a combination of what I already had and what she brought. I went through them, getting rid of duplicate items or anything that was cracked or damaged. There was a plate that didn't match anything. A chipped blue dish. I got rid of it. This was all done while she was on a business trip, so she would be out of the way and wouldn't know what all I had gotten rid of. So, it wouldn't upset her."

With a little smile, Zachary could see what was coming. "But she noticed the loss of the blue plate."

A longer sigh from Spencer this time. Almost a groan. "That blue plate was the only one she would eat off."

"Oops."

Spencer swiveled to look at him. "That isn't an exaggeration, Mr. Goldman. She really would not eat off any other plate in the house. In the eight years we have been married, she has never eaten off another plate within these walls."

"Never? Then, what…?"

"If she's out at a restaurant, she can eat off their plates. At home, she can't. She can drink out of a cup. She can eat out of a bowl or straight out of the package." Spencer wrinkled his nose at this. "But she cannot bring herself to eat off a plate other than the chipped blue plate I threw out."

"Couldn't you get another one to replace it?"

"No. Even if I got one that was identical, she would know it wasn't the same plate, and she still wouldn't be able to use it."

"Oh." Zachary knew he should be making notes about the experience, but he was too baffled to write anything down.

"Compulsions can be very disruptive," Spencer said. "They can take over your life, out of nowhere. It isn't just a comfortable ritual." As if to demonstrate, Spencer leaned forward to squirt another stream of antibacterial gel onto his hands and scrub it away. For the first time, Zachary was aware of the sharp tang in the air, and noticed how red and chapped Spencer's hands were. "It isn't just a habit; it is something you *must* do. You can't move forward until you do. Do you want to know why I moved to Vermont?"

Zachary leaned forward. "Yes, of course."

"The sign law."

"The no-billboards law?"

Spencer nodded. "Before I came here, I had a compulsion to count billboards. I knew exactly how many there were on every route I traveled. If I was distracted and missed one of them, I had to go back to the beginning of the route and start over again. I was spending hours on the highway, just counting signs. If the advertisement on one of them changed, I had to drive by it twenty times. It had taken over my life."

"And you can't do anything about that?"

"There are therapies. Some people can get over their compulsions without replacing them with something new." His chair creaked. "I came to Vermont."

"Because you knew there weren't any billboards to count."

"Does that sound crazy to you?"

Zachary scratched his head, considering it. It certainly seemed extreme. As did refusing to eat off any other plate for eight years; but Spencer wasn't claiming to be normal. He was describing a pathology. A deviation from the norm.

"I can understand how it must have disrupted your life," he said slowly. "Moving to Vermont and starting over here seems like a disruption too, though. It can't have been easy."

Spencer drummed his fingers on the desk and gave a little shrug. "Yes, it was hard to leave Ohio to come here. Sometimes, even if it's painful, you just need to find a way to get away from your triggers. If I were still living in Ohio, I wouldn't have any kind of life now. I'd be driving up and down the highway endlessly. I never would have met Isabella. Deck would never have been a part of my life."

Zachary was uncomfortably aware of his own circumstances. All that had been taken away from him that everybody else seemed to take for granted.

"Do you ever wish that Declan hadn't been a part of your life? That he'd never been born? The pain of losing him…?"

"No." Spencer's eyes strayed to the stuffed dog. "I think he was meant to be a part of my life, even if it was only for a short time. I wouldn't want to have to give that experience up, even if it was painful."

His face was still blank of any emotion, but Zachary knew that was just a mask that Spencer showed the world. Or maybe it wasn't something he hid behind, but that he was unable to express the emotion he felt. Zachary could feel it there between them. The grief. The anger. The despair.

"Yeah." Zachary sighed and turned the page on his notepad to a clean sheet. "I will have more questions for you later. I guess I should meet your wife now."

"Of course. We'll help in any way we can."

They both stood, and Zachary waited for Spencer to take him to wherever his wife was waiting. Spencer's mouth twitched, and he didn't come out from behind his desk.

"Has Molly told you about Isabella? What to expect?"

"No, not really, just that she's going through a difficult time. That Molly is concerned for her mental or emotional state."

Spencer didn't offer up any further explanation.

"Anything you could tell me that might help this go more smoothly?" Zachary suggested.

"You will find her… eccentric. Or maybe you won't. She wears her heart on her sleeve. She doesn't have cleanliness compulsions. She may act happy and cheerful, but…" Spencer shifted his feet. "That's her TV persona. She'll put it on if she's not comfortable with you."

Zachary nodded, understanding. "Okay. Thanks."

They made the walk to Isabella's office in silence. Zachary kept his eyes open, looking around the rest of the house as much as he could. It was almost clinically tidy.

Then they walked into Isabella's studio. That was where the neatness ended.

Spencer took him up to the doorway and didn't enter. Zachary could understand why. For someone with compulsions for cleaning and straightening, even having such a room in his house must have been painful. Certainly, he wouldn't want to spend any time there.

Zachary knocked on the open door, not wanting to just barge in on

Isabella. She stood in the middle of the chaos, in front of an easel with some abstract daubing, her back to the door. She turned around, and Zachary saw the face that was so familiar from *The Happy Artist* commercials and advertisements. There was one brief, unguarded moment when she looked at him, her face hollow and lined before she realized she was facing a stranger and put on the mask Spencer had warned him about. She smiled brightly, and a fan of laugh lines replaced all the deep frown lines.

"Hello," she greeted, "come in, come in."

She looked around her and found a chair stacked with canvases. She moved the paintings to the side, leaning them against the wall.

"There you go. Make yourself at home."

Zachary sat down but wasn't exactly comfortable. There were canvases and art materials covering every surface, including most of the floor. All manner of brushes, paints, and bottles filled a couple of bookcases. There were tables with a space cleared in the middle for charcoal and pastel sketches. He had the uncomfortable sensation that everything stacked around him was going to fall down in a landslide and bury him.

Isabella herself was not untidy. She had on black pants and a flowing tunic-shirt with several layers of jewelry. Her long, dark hair had been gathered into a ponytail to keep it out of her face. When she appeared on TV, it was often done up in intricate braiding or decorated buns, a nod to the fact that her back was often to the cameras as she worked. Giving the audience something to look at besides her paint work.

"My name is Zachary. From Goldman Investigations."

"I know who you are," she said dismissively, flipping a hand at him as she studied her canvas. "And I know why my mother hired you."

"You know I'm here about Declan's accident."

"Of course." She looked away from her painting and gazed at him briefly, brows raised.

"I don't want to waste your time with small talk. I know this must be very difficult for you."

"Do you want to know why my mother is so worried about me?"

"Sure."

There was a stool nearby for her to sit on while she painted. She dragged it closer to Zachary and sat down. It was higher than Zachary's chair, so he was forced to look up at her.

"The network says I have to wear long sleeves on the air now," Isabella said, pulling up the right-hand sleeve of her tunic.

Molly's concern and the words prefacing the gesture made Zachary expect to see fresh cut marks. There was no sign of self-mutilation or a suicide attempt. Instead, he was looking at the tattoo of a boy's face, with the name Declan under it.

"Do you really think my viewers would find that so offensive?" Isabella demanded. "Why is it a bad thing that I tattooed my son into my skin?"

"Uh, no..." Zachary was caught by surprise and had no idea what to say to this. "No, I think... it's sweet."

"He came from my body, and now he's returned to it," she went on, her voice loud and forceful. "The tattoo artist mixed a small amount of his ashes into the tattoo ink. His body has returned to me and will always be with me."

Zachary did find that surprising, and maybe a little morbid. He didn't know regular people did that kind of thing. In prison, all kinds of materials were burned to make DIY tattoo ink, but he didn't know anyone would mix cremains in with the ink. Was it common, and he'd just never paid attention before?

"My son is always with me," Isabella had continued, while Zachary was lost in his own thoughts. "I don't ever want him to leave me again."

She plucked up one of the pendants that hung around her neck and held it out toward Zachary. He saw, with a mounting feeling of discomfort, that what he had taken to be a vial with rough pearls inside actually contained teeth.

"These are his. Not the teeth from his body, those were cremated with him, but baby teeth I helped him to pull out while he was still alive, and I could touch him and hold them in my hand."

Zachary stared at her. This was why Molly was so concerned. Not just because Isabella was sad, mourning her lost child, but because her mourning had taken her into territory that was... morbid and unsettling.

"Maybe we could talk about what happened that day," he suggested.

"This ring contains some of his ashes," Isabella offered as if she hadn't heard him. She held out her hand toward him, showing off a large purple stone like an amethyst. "You can get jewelry where you can put the ashes into a little chamber yourself, but this one, the ashes are actually suspended in the glass. You see the sparkle inside?"

"Yes."

"This one," she tapped the ring, "the producers will let me wear on air, but the tattoo and the teeth, those are *inappropriate*." Her tone mocked their words. "Somehow those might drive the viewers away. They wouldn't be able to handle my grief." She dropped her hand to her lap. "My viewers know that I lost my child. Do they think I wouldn't mourn him? Do they think after I've taken a few weeks off work, I'm all better? Everything is fine?"

"No. I don't think they expect that. Probably your producers don't either. They're just being... cautious..." Zachary tried to pitch his voice so that it was low and soothing. Isabella was agitated, almost manic, and he didn't know whether that was her normal state, or whether he had triggered her behavior by being there, asking about her son, trying to find some different answers from those she had already received. Did she go off like that on everyone?

Isabella ignored his assurance and went on, itemizing the other bits of hair and ash that were woven or contained within her various accessories. After a while, Zachary grew numb to it. It was no longer shocking or even surprising. He'd never known there were so many ways to carry a memento of your deceased loved one around with you. Obviously, the jewelry companies were ready and eager to provide the products.

Isabella seemed to be winding down. "I sent the rest of his ashes away to a company that makes diamonds. They actually take the ashes—carbon—and add heat and pressure to form them into a real diamond. It's not just ashes suspended in a gem, like this," she indicated the amethyst ring, "or inside a micro urn, like these... but the ashes are transformed into a diamond."

"That's amazing," Zachary obliged. "But you don't have it back yet?"

"It takes a few months to make. I'm hoping to have it before Christmas."

"That would... be a nice present."

"I want Declan to be with me. Always. I don't ever want to be separated from him again."

"Yes. I can see that." Zachary took another breath, looking for his opening. "You must have been very scared when he disappeared."

"I was! It was horrible. You don't know the kind of terror... You don't have any children, do you?"

"No." Again, the lead ball in his stomach. "I don't."

"You could never understand how terrifying it is. He was *right there*. I only looked away for two minutes!"

"I don't think anyone blames you. Children can wander away from even the most diligent caregiver."

She shook her head, not believing it. She knew that it was her fault he had wandered away. It had been her responsibility. She was the one who had fallen down on the job, and the responsibility for his death fell on her. She wore that guilt just like all the leftover bits of Declan's body.

"Can you tell me about how it happened? I know this is a terrible thing to ask of you. You've already had to repeat it so many times. Can you manage just one more…?"

Isabella looked at him, her hands wringing in her lap. Her eyes were once again hollow, the laugh lines gone.

"You don't know what it's like to lose a child," she told him again.

Zachary gritted his teeth and didn't disagree.

"He was playing outside in the back yard." She made a gesture toward it. The yard was not visible from Isabella's studio as it was from Spencer's office.

"And you were supervising him? You were outside with him?"

"I wasn't outside."

"Oh. Where were you, then?"

"I was in the bedroom. It has patio doors that look into the yard. I could see him from there."

Zachary nodded his encouragement. "I see. Do you mind if I… see the bedroom for a minute?"

Her lips tightened, and he knew she was going to say no. She thought that he was going to judge her as a negligent mother, watching her child from a distance instead of being out there with him, playing with him, talking and laughing with him. Had either of the parents really connected with Declan? Did either of them see him as a person rather than a responsibility?

"I'd like to see where the blind spots are," Zachary explained. "Areas where an intruder might have approached and seen and talked to Declan without you being able to see them."

"Oh." Her expression softened, and she nodded. "Yes, I guess that makes sense."

"Just think of it as a security sweep. I need to understand where the weaknesses in the defenses were. I'm not here to accuse you of anything."

"Some people have been very cruel."

Zachary hoped that didn't include Isabella's own husband and mother. She couldn't have been an easy person to live with, wallowing in her grief, wearing her heart on her sleeve, as Spencer had said. Or her child's face on her arm.

Isabella got off the stool and motioned briskly for Zachary to follow her. He fell into step with her. It didn't look like she was the type to hang around waiting. She led him to the bedroom.

"Here."

It was a combination of their styles. Mostly Spencer's minimalist, fussily tidy look. There were elements of Isabella as well. Her paintings were on the walls. A row of frivolous throw pillows across the head of the bed. The closet was clearly divided into his and hers.

Spencer's shirts and suits marched in neat rows across the rod, all carefully ordered, facing the same direction, looking crisp and starched. Isabella's side of the closet was a chaos like her studio. There was no apparent order to the clothing, skirts and pants mixed in with shirts and jackets and sweaters. Fancy dresses with sequins squashed in with hoodies with silly sayings. Hangers were hooked haphazardly from the front and the back. The shoes were in a jumble, not in pairs. Scarves and belts and jewelry hung on a handmade pegboard in no apparent order.

Zachary looked around. The room had big windows, like Spencer's office, and had a good view of the back yard. It was a broad expanse of unbroken white snow. No one building snowmen or forts.

"You were watching from…?" Zachary made a wide motion to indicate the room.

"Right here," Isabella positioned herself in front of the window, a couple of feet away.

"Tell me about that. You were standing there watching him? Putting laundry away?" He felt his face flush as it occurred to him that Spencer probably did the laundry and put it away. His own, anyway. "Reading a book, maybe?"

"No, painting."

He tried to envision the set-up. It didn't fit his idea of a good place for painting. The room was carpeted. There were no painting materials out. Maybe she didn't paint there anymore because of what had happened.

"Your easel would have been here...?" Zachary blocked out the area in front of the window with his hands. "That might have obscured your view."

"No, here." Isabella swiveled to indicate the area behind her. "To make the most of the natural light coming in through the window. If I had been facing into it while painting, I would have been dazzled."

"Right here. So, the light was behind you."

"Angled a little, so my shadow wouldn't fall on the canvas. Yes. Like that."

"Your back was to the window?"

"No." Isabella looked at the imaginary easel and then at the window, frowning. "Well, yes, some of the time. I would look out at him and watch him, and then paint. Then look again."

"You were checking on him occasionally. Not strictly supervising him. He was five and in his own yard. Perfectly safe."

She nodded, her face relaxing. She had been expecting him to criticize her for not watching Declan the whole time. Was that what Spencer had said? What about her mother? It had been in the news, so there were probably all kinds of people, friends and strangers, who had opinions about what had happened and her parenting skills or lack of them.

"Yes, he was perfectly safe," she agreed. "You can see. It's fenced. Gated. He couldn't get out on his own."

"Then how did he get out that day?"

"We found the back gate open," Isabella said, staring across the yard at it. "I don't know who opened it. Deck couldn't have opened it on his own. A neighbor? A stranger? Spencer when he took out the garbage?" Isabella shook her head. "It couldn't have been Spencer. He's so careful about everything. He would never have left it unlatched."

"But it isn't locked in any way. Anyone walking by could have unlatched it."

She nodded. "It never occurred to me to put a lock on it. Do people lock their gates? It doesn't seem... it doesn't seem like something people living in houses like this would do, does it? I can understand someone who lives in a rough neighborhood. Or someone who lives in a mansion with a swimming pool. But our little house?" She shook her head, eyes shiny with tears. "I don't think people here lock their gates."

"I don't know." Zachary shook his head. "I don't know what your neighbors do or don't do. I'm just trying to get a good picture of what happened that day."

Isabella sat on the end of the bed and sighed. "He loved to play outside. He'd play for hours. Take his toys out with him. Ask if he could sleep outside at night. Neither Spencer nor I are into camping; I bet he would have loved it if we were."

"How long was he outside? What was he playing with that day?"

"He was outside for a couple of hours. I don't know what he was playing. He was an only child. A bit lonely. He made games up to entertain himself."

"Are you and Spencer both only children? Or did you have siblings?"

"Spencer has a couple of brothers. I... don't have anyone. Just Mom. I know how lonely it can be, not having any brothers or sisters. I was alone a lot too."

For a moment, Zachary was awash with memories. He too had been alone. Being taken away from his brothers and sisters had been such a shock for him. It was one thing growing up as an only child, not knowing any difference, but Zachary knew the difference. He had been part of a family, and then he didn't have anyone. He was old enough that much of the time he wasn't with a foster family. It would be a group home or residential care. Surrounded by other kids, but all by himself.

He had been lonely for so long. Did that loneliness stretch out as far ahead of him as it did behind? He couldn't face that.

Zachary shook off the memories and faced the problem at hand.

"Tell me about... when you realized Declan wasn't in the yard anymore."

Isabella put her face in her hands. Zachary waited for her to brace up and tell him the story. She probably wanted to. People avoided asking about tragedy, asking about exactly what had happened and how it felt. They pretended that nothing had happened and all was well, leaving people like Isabella to grieve alone, unable to let it all out.

"I was painting. Deck was outside. I was turning to look at him, to make sure he wasn't getting overheated or tired. Or bored. All those things you're supposed to watch out for. But he wasn't. He was happy. Then I looked once, and I couldn't see him. I thought maybe he was somewhere I couldn't see him. Beside the house," she gestured, "or up against it," she indicated the angles. "I waited for him to come back to where I could see him. He didn't. I opened the window and called him." Isabella paused as if waiting for him to answer, but they both knew he would never answer. "I went outside. He wasn't there. I panicked. I was so scared. I looked everywhere in the yard. In the front. In the house. I looked everywhere, top to bottom, and he wasn't here. I went and got Spencer, and we looked together."

She started to sob. Zachary thought he should show her sympathy, but he froze in place with no idea what to do about her tears. In his experience, trying to calm a crying woman just made her cry more, or made her angry. He didn't want to do either one. So, he waited.

"Then we called the police. They got here pretty quickly. They took our statements. They started a search. They made announcements and called for volunteers to help canvass the streets around the house before it got dark."

"Do you think one of your neighbors had something to do with this?"

That was one of the problems with bringing volunteers in too soon. The police had contaminated the crime scene. Too many people had gone tramping through the neighborhood looking for him. Had someone drowned him in the pond, or had it been an accident?

Isabella was shaking her head. "No one would do that to us. Who would do that? It doesn't make any sense."

"People who harm little children rarely make sense. To anyone but themselves. Children aren't killed out of jealousy or greed, like adults. It's completely different."

"I don't see how anyone we knew could have had anything to do with it. I don't think it was one of our neighbors."

"You believe it was an accident?"

Isabella wiped away tears and sat there on the end of the bed, her eyes red and puffy, staring into the desolate back yard.

"Yes. It was an accident. Just... one of those things."

Zachary nodded. "Okay. All right. Is there anything else you think I should know?"

"I can't think of anything."

"Can I see Declan's room before I go? Or have you redecorated it?"

Her eyes widened. "Redecorated? Why would we do that? I don't think it could ever be anything but Declan's room. Ever."

"May I...?"

"It's just next door." She motioned. "So, when he was a baby, I could hear him if he cried."

Zachary took this as his invitation to see for himself. He went down the hall to Declan's bedroom.

It wasn't much smaller than the master bedroom. The walls were painted several shades of blue. He had a kid's laptop computer or gaming system. Toy boxes and shelves. Clothing neatly arranged in the closet. Zachary could see Spencer's influence more than Isabella's. He had expected at least a wall mural for her only child. Zachary walked around the room slowly, looking for anything suspicious or out of place. He wasn't really expecting to find anything. If it had been a stranger abduction as Molly had suggested, there certainly wouldn't be any sign of it in Declan's room. He never knew when he might see something that would become important later in the case.

"Until we meet again, may God hold you in the palm of His hand."

Zachary startled and turned to see Isabella standing in the doorway. She wasn't looking at him and hadn't been speaking to him. She was just looking at the room, feeling her loss. She ran her fingers over her jewelry as if accounting for each piece. She stared down at the tattoo on her arm.

"Until we meet again, may God hold you in the palm of His hand," she repeated.

Zachary walked over to her. He touched her shoulder gently as he stepped back out of the room.

"I think it's time for me to get on my way."

Isabella nodded. She looked down at her watch. "Just let me feed the cat, and then I'll walk you out."

"Okay."

He walked with her into the kitchen. Bright and airy. Zachary watched Isabella as she mechanically picked up a bowl of cat food, dumped it into the garbage, refilled it from a big bin in the closet, and put it back down where it had been. He looked around the house but didn't see any other sign of a pet. They didn't seem like the kind of people who would keep a pet.

"Do you... have a cat?" he asked Isabella, as they walked back to the front door. The food in the dish didn't appear to have been touched. No cat came running when she filled it. The cats that he had known had always come running and yowled for their food as soon as they heard a food can, box, or bag being rattled.

Isabella stopped with her hand on the front doorknob.

"Yes. Mittens." She didn't open the door. "It's been a long time. He wandered off one day and didn't come back… just like Declan."

Zachary suppressed a shudder at her tone. Was there a connection between the two disappearances?

"When did your cat disappear?" he asked. A long time ago could be months back, when Declan had disappeared. Had the boy followed the cat? Had the cat followed him? Was there some other connection between the two?

"When we first got married."

"Eight years ago?" Zachary demanded, remembering the story of the plate.

"Yes… that sounds about right. Eight years ago."

She turned the doorknob and opened the door for him.

"Until we meet again, may God hold you in the palm of His hand."

Eight years, and she was still feeding the cat.

Molly thought that if Zachary re-investigated Declan's death, it would bring Isabella some peace.

But the woman was still feeding her missing cat eight years later.

4

It was a couple of days before the copy of the medical examiner's report was ready for him. Zachary kept himself busy in the interim with his other cases. Surveillance on Pastor Hellerman's wife. A long, tedious review of the accident reconstruction he had done on the Mae Gordon accident. Running background on the interns who had applied to work with Senator Brown. There was plenty to keep him busy.

Martin Ash was running the security check-in at the police station and gave Zachary a big smile as he approached. He had always been friendly with Zachary, even when Zachary was running an investigation that was not popular with the police force, which happened more often than he liked. It had been a while since he had seen the big, black man. Martin pushed a bin toward Zachary for the contents of his pockets. Zachary put his briefcase down on the conveyor belt behind it and walked through the metal detector.

"How are you, my friend?" Martin boomed. "And how is Bridget?"

"I'm good." Zachary picked up his keys and wallet from the bin after it went through the x-ray. "Bridget is in remission."

A look of confusion passed over Martin's face. His brows drew down. "In remission?" he repeated. "She was sick?"

Zachary's heart sank. He had assumed that Martin was part of the grapevine and knew all the details or that they had talked about it at some point already. He was unprepared for Martin's ignorance. For a moment he was frozen, unable to speak. He swallowed and licked his dry lips.

"Uh—yes—sorry, I thought you knew. She had ovarian cancer."

"Oh." Martin shook his head, looking shocked. His smile was gone. He tried to meet Zachary's eyes, though Zachary did his best to avoid connecting. "I'm so sorry, Zachary! I didn't know." He patted Zachary on the back.

"It's fine. I'm sorry to spring it on you like that. It seems like everyone knows all of the details, whether I have told them or not, so I just assumed that you knew, and were asking about the cancer treatments..."

"But she's in remission. So that's good. That means she's clean and they caught it in time."

"Yes, exactly." Zachary tried to force a smile of reassurance. "She's good. She's recovering from the chemo and starting to feel back to her old self."

"Good, good. So, the two of you..." Martin tried to approach it delicately, but he had no tact to speak of, "...does that mean you won't be able to have children? Because of the cancer and the radiation?"

Zachary swore. He should have headed off that inquiry at the same time as he informed Martin that Bridget had had cancer. He should have broken it all at once instead of leaving it open-ended.

"We aren't together anymore," Zachary told Martin gently. "I'm sorry..."

"You broke up?" Martin shook his head. "How could that happen?"

There were other people waiting for security clearance, and Zachary made a little motion toward them. "I shouldn't keep you. You have a job to do."

"I can't believe you guys aren't together anymore." Martin moved like a robot to clear the next person in line, not smiling at him or greeting him. "I thought you two were happy together."

"For a while." But even as Zachary said it, he wondered if it was true. Had they really been happy? He had loved her. He'd hoped for a long life together, but the way things had turned out... things had never been perfect. It had always been rocky. "I think the cancer was just too much for us. Too much stress."

Martin nodded, the corners of his mouth drawn down in a pronounced frown. Zachary didn't think he'd ever seen Martin unhappy before.

"Sorry," Zachary apologized again, getting on his way and leaving Martin to clear the next visitor.

After the run-in with Martin, Zachary was anxious and on edge. Not the best side to show to the new girl in the medical examiner's office. He tried to be pleasant and cordial, but he knew he wasn't pulling it off. Kenzie kept attempting to make small talk as Zachary looked down at the photocopied report in his hand, but he couldn't seem to find the proper responses to keep the conversation going and put her at ease.

"Is everything okay?" Kenzie asked finally.

"Yes… it's fine… I just…" Zachary shook his head, looking for a way to explain. "I just had some news, that's all."

"Oh. I'm sorry to hear that." Her dark eyes searched his face, and she decided not to ask him for details. She took one of her business cards out of the holder on her desk, scribbled on it, and slid it across to him. "Call me, okay? If there's anything in that report that you want to run through. Or if you want to talk."

Zachary gave her a smile that felt stretched and nodded his head. "Thanks; and I'm sorry for being out of sorts. We'll talk."

Kenzie nodded and smiled. He could feel her eyes on him all the way to the end of the hallway before he turned and was out of her sight.

Zachary watched the blond woman get out of her yellow VW. She locked it with her remote key lock as she walked away. It gave a little chirp, and she never looked back.

He knew her routine. Coffee at The Jumping Bean. Not on the terrace because it was too cold and snowy to be open, but inside where it was warm, sitting pleasantly close to the tiny fireplace. Then she would start her errands. The parking zone she was in gave her three hours. She would likely use all of that and then restart the meter.

Zachary sidled up to the car, looking casual like it was his own car. He looked around carefully before sliding the key into the lock and climbing in. He pulled the door shut and was effectively invisible to the crowds walking by.

He went directly to the glovebox for her log file. A ledger where she tracked all her mileage for tax purposes, with client codes and odometer readings noted in her precise printing. Kenzie would have approved. He scanned it for any unusual trips, any unaccounted jumps in the odometer. There was also a plastic sleeve containing all her latest expense receipts, and he thumbed through them carefully, his eyes quick. He looked up once to make sure that she wasn't anywhere in sight. Returning to her car because she'd forgotten something inside. Unexpectedly finding The Jumping Bean closed because a plumbing line had flooded the cafe overnight. Anything could happen.

He checked the visor flaps for anything else of interest, ran his fingers along the cracks of the seats to see if anything had been dropped and lodged there. Poked through the garbage, but didn't find anything other than a stray Twinkie wrapper. Her secret vice.

His search of the car complete, he climbed out, locked the doors again, and walked away.

Zachary sat in his recliner, the medical examiner's report in his lap, a half-eaten lunch on the side table by his elbow. He had only done a page-flip of the medical examiner's report, seeing how detailed it was and if anything jumped out at him. It was relatively short, a cursory review of what the police had said from the beginning was an accident, not a violent death or the mysterious death of a vital person struck down in their prime. The tests and notes all seemed to be routine.

Was there any point in doing more than that? He knew that Molly didn't have much money to put into the investigation. A detailed review of the medical examiner's report, all the police notes he could get his hands on, and re-interviewing everyone he would want to talk to in order to fully satisfy himself that it had been an accident would take a lot of hours and run up the bill unnecessarily.

His discussions with Spencer and Isabella hadn't rung any alarm bells. They both seemed to be just what they were, parents grieving the unexpected loss of their only child, getting through it the best they could manage. There wasn't any sign that it hadn't been an accident.

Other than Molly's assertion that the boy was afraid of water.

Spencer had shrugged the statement off, agreeing that Declan had a fear of water, but that it wouldn't have prevented him from going near the water.

Zachary didn't think that either of them was lying; they were just interpreting him differently.

Zachary ran Kenzie's business card through his fingers, feeling the smooth, sharp edge. Kenzie Kirsch. She had written another number on it; he assumed it was her home or cell number. It was kind of her to give it to him when she saw he was feeling bad. Did she want him to call, or was it just a gesture? He hadn't asked her for her number. Women didn't offer their numbers to men if they didn't want them to call, did they?

Looking down at the medical examiner's report, Zachary reached for his phone. He dialed her number quickly, already rehearsing what he was going to say. Starting conversations with women was not one of his strengths. Give him a suspect interview any day.

"Hello?"

"Um—Kenzie? It's Zachary. Goldman Investigations."

"Zachary! I'm glad you called." He didn't hear any deception in her voice. She sounded genuinely warm. "How are you?"

He listened for background noise that might indicate she was out with friends or a date or doing something she didn't want interrupted.

"I'm okay. I'm sorry for how I was earlier. I... had something on my mind."

"No, it's okay. I understand. Everybody has a bad day now and then. I'm glad you're feeling better." There was a pause. He imagined her sitting by a roaring fire, having a sip of wine before bed. It was a nice image. "Did you have a chance to look at the medical examiner's report yet?"

"Only a high-level review. Nothing that jumps out at me on a browse through. I'll have to spend a few hours going through all the details... if I'm going to pursue the case."

"I thought you had already taken the case?"

"I did. I mean... if I decide to take it any further. The grandmother, the one who hired me, I don't think she has any means of support. Maybe her daughter is helping out with the bills."

"She's that artist on TV, right? *The Happy Artist.*"

"That's the one."

"She's really popular. I bet she makes a ton of money."

"They appear to be well-off, but the grandmother isn't. If there's nothing here to find... I'd just be stealing from her."

"Dr. Wiltshire is very conscientious. I'm sure he wouldn't have returned a finding of accidental drowning if he had any doubt."

"No. I don't want to imply he's done anything wrong. The family just wants someone to go over everything one more time."

"Do you want someone to go over the report with you? That would save you some time and help you decide if there was anything else to do."

Zachary's heart gave a couple of extra beats that almost hurt. "Would that somebody be you?" he suggested.

"It might be." Kenzie's voice was light and playful.

"Could this review be over dinner, maybe?"

"That would be nice."

"Are you free tomorrow night?"

"Sure. Where do you want to meet?"

Hardly believing that such a thing was happening to him, Zachary came up with an acceptable restaurant and time, and they agreed to get together. After he had hung up the phone, Zachary closed his eyes and again pictured Kenzie all cozied up, sipping her glass of red wine.

5

Zachary slept well for once, dreaming of Kenzie, so even though he awoke long before he wanted to be up, he felt lighter and more energetic than he had for a long time. Since he was going to be reviewing the medical examiner's report with Kenzie, he didn't spend any more time on it, but reviewed his notes of his interviews with Spencer and Isabella and typed up a summary of each. He glanced over the news articles and releases he had collected.

The phone rang, and the woman on the other end identified herself as Eugene Taft's assistant and thanked him for his recent gift. Zachary almost laughed.

It had not been easy to pin down Eugene Taft to get access to the police file, and in the end, Zachary had resorted to simply sending him the bottle of red wine Bowman had recommended, with a card congratulating him on his anniversary. Zachary had no idea if Taft was married, or if he had any other anniversary in the recent past or near future, but everyone had significant dates that they celebrated, and Zachary had thought that an anniversary gift would go over better than Christmas wishes. Besides which, he didn't want anything to do with Christmas.

"Yes, Officer Fitzgerald. I'm glad to hear he got it."

There was a hesitation on the other end as Fitzgerald tried to couch her inquiry regarding the bribe appropriately. "You had called the other day to see if Eugene had some time to see you, hadn't you?"

"Oh, I don't need to take up any of his valuable time. He should have received a request through Mario Bowman about allowing me access to a file. It was pretty routine; I'm sure it's just on his desk awaiting his signature."

"Which file was this?"

"Declan Bond."

"Declan Bond," she repeated vaguely. "Oh, the little boy who drowned...?"

"That's the one."

"Are you a reporter?"

"No, ma'am. I'm a private investigator. The family hired me to take another look at the case. Just to ease their minds that he covered everything. I'm not expecting to find anything unusual in the file."

"I see."

"If the request is not there, you could ask Bowman about it. He knows me from other cases I've helped out with."

"I think I will follow up with him," she agreed. "I'll be in touch."

"Tell Eugene 'happy anniversary' for me."

"I will."

She hung up. Smiling, Zachary put his travel mug under the coffee maker and brewed up a coffee to take with him for the site survey.

The scene was bleak during the winter. The skeletons of trees and grasses were stark against the snow. There were no children playing, no dogs running, no ducks swimming. A few black birds flew overhead, the flapping of their wings loud in the silence.

The pond was iced over and had not been cleared, so Zachary could only see the ominous shape of it beneath the snow, like an animal trap waiting to be sprung.

Hopefully, there would be pictures on the police file, as it was surely a far different place during the summer. Zachary paced around the pond, breaking a trail in the snow. A couple of times he stepped farther down than he expected, into an unseen dip or hole. He scanned the yards that backed onto the property, looking for anything suspicious or out of place. Even putting on his most paranoid goggles, he couldn't see anything that indicated danger.

The last thing he did was to walk to the Bonds' back yard. He looked at it from the back, eyes alert for any hiding places, any breaks in the fence, anyone watching out their windows. He examined the gate, which could easily be opened from the back alley and still bore no lock. Anyone could have walked up to the yard and opened the gate. Would Declan have left with them? Would he have gone quietly with a stranger, or put up a fight? Had it been a stranger?

He examined the back of the house. He could identify Spencer's office, the master bedroom, and Declan's bedroom. They all had good views of the yard. A stranger would have had to be pretty bold or sure of himself to walk right into the yard in view of those big windows.

But during the summer, would there have been blinds drawn across the windows? Isabella claimed to have had a good view of Declan, but was she looking through the slats of blinds? Or was she standing in the full afternoon sun? Just because there were no blinds drawn during the winter, that didn't mean they didn't use them to keep out the full heat of the summer.

Zachary looked at his watch and started the stopwatch function. Then he walked back to the pond.

Zachary got to the restaurant before Kenzie, which was intentional. He didn't want to be the guy who showed up late for a date, especially when she was also helping him out. He wanted to show her that she could trust him to be responsible and treat her with respect. After checking to make sure she hadn't shown up there ahead of him, he went back outside and paced around a little, watching for her. Despite the weather having been only mildly cold when he had been at the pond, there was a biting wind. After a few minutes of toughing it out, he gave in and went back into the restaurant.

Old Joe's Steakhouse was a landmark. Casual, but with great service and even better food, everybody knew about it, and it was a wonder that anyone could ever get in without booking reservations three months ahead. Somehow, people knew which hours were the busiest and scheduled their dinners for quieter times, so Old Joe was able to serve a thriving population without becoming elite.

"Are you ready to be seated, sir?" the college-aged boy leaned closer to Zachary to address him over the hum of the crowd. "I have your table ready."

Zachary looked at the door. "I don't know; I was going to wait…"

"We'll bring your guest to you. You may as well sit and have a drink while you wait."

Zachary gave a shrug and followed the boy into the dining area. The tables were close together, and the room was noisy, but it didn't feel overly crowded, just busy. Zachary followed the young man to his assigned table.

"Uh… why don't you get me a beer? I'm not sure what the lady will want."

"Sure. Any preference?"

"No. Whatever's on tap."

He kept an eye on his watch, but it was still too early for Kenzie to show up. When she eventually arrived, a quick glance showed Zachary that she was ten minutes early.

"You're here already," Kenzie observed with a smile. "Neat printing *and* prompt. Have I finally found the perfect man?"

"Not perfect by a long shot," Zachary said with a sigh. "But the longer I can keep you fooled, the better."

"Ha." She sat down across from him. "Then you shouldn't be telling me!"

The waiter came over to take Kenzie's order. She eyed Zachary's beer for a moment, but then ordered a glass of wine.

Small talk wasn't the easiest for him, so after perusing the menu and ordering, it wasn't long before Zachary was digging the medical examiner's report out of his case. They pushed their chairs together so that they could look at it at the same time instead of being across from each other.

"You sure you want to discuss a medical examiner's report over dinner?" Kenzie challenged. "Do you have a strong stomach?"

"I've already been through it. There's nothing too disturbing. It's not bloody."

"Bodies in water bloat up pretty quickly…"

"I've seen the pictures already," Zachary said firmly. "I'm okay with this. Really."

It wasn't until after he said it that he wondered whether she was trying to bow out. He had assumed that she would be perfectly okay with discussing the report over dinner. It had been her idea, after all. She was around the stuff all day, so he wouldn't expect her to be squeamish. But it seemed too late to take his words back.

"That is… unless…"

Kenzie laughed. "No, I'm fine with it. Thanks for asking. Let's go through it, then."

She took the medical examiner's report from his hand and laid it flat on the table, starting in on a lecture on drowning victims, what a medical examiner would expect to find, and what might look different between an accidental drowning and foul play.

"There was no bruising," she pointed out, turning to a page with a series of photos of the body, both front and back. "If you're going to hold someone under the water, then even if it's a little child, there's going to be a struggle, and there's going to be bruising."

Zachary nodded. "Okay. No bruising."

"I'm sure you've seen this one on your favorite forensic show on TV. Someone is drowned in their bathroom, and then their body is disposed of in the river. How do you tell they were drowned somewhere else?"

"Analyze the water in the lungs."

"Right. This is the analysis of the lungs. Their weight, showing they were waterlogged. Then an analysis of the pH, the salinity, the diatoms, any particulates…"

"Diatoms?"

"They take a sample of the water in the pond, and a sample of the water in his lungs, and look for diatoms. It's a unique profile. Like fingerprinting."

"Oh." Zachary nodded. He looked at the text of the report. "And they determined that Declan drowned in the pond."

"Right. He couldn't have drowned anywhere else, or the profile of the water in his lungs would have been different."

"Particulates?" Zachary asked, trying to keep track of all that she was saying.

Kenzie pointed to the section in the report. "When someone inhales water, they also inhale whatever else is in the water. Silt, bugs, plant life…"

"Okay. Right. So that goes back to the pond as well, demonstrating that he drowned there."

"Yes."

"But why so much time spent on tying him to the pond? He was found floating face down in it. Isn't all that already established?"

"We have to double-check everything. Assume nothing."

"Right."

"The next few pages are blood tests..." Kenzie leaned closer to show Zachary. He could feel the heat of her body, and focused for the first time on the black knit dress she was wearing, which clung to her in all the right places. He could smell her scent and his own deodorant as he started to sweat.

Their waiter returned with their steaks, carrying them over on sizzling hot plates.

"Whoops, make some room, folks. Hot plates coming through."

Zachary grabbed the medical examiner's report and case off the table so that the waiter could put the plates down.

"Looks great," Kenzie told the waiter. He checked on whether they needed refills, then left them to their dinner.

"The blood tests were all normal?" Zachary asked. "I don't need to check what each measurement means?"

"Everything falls within normal parameters. Nothing suspicious."

Zachary nodded, and they both dug in. For a while, they ate in silence.

"So how far do I go?" Zachary asked. "We review the medical examiner's report. There's nothing suspicious. Everything I do is chargeable. I could interview a million people, and it wouldn't have any effect other than to run up the bill."

"Well..." Kenzie chewed, considering. "Why did the grandmother hire you?"

"Peace of mind."

"She wants to be sure it was an accident."

"Well... no. She'd rather I found evidence of foul play."

Kenzie's cutlery clattered. She stopped eating and stared at him. "What?"

"She thinks it would ease the mother's guilt if I found evidence that there was a third party involved. She wouldn't have to blame herself for letting Declan wander off under her watch."

"Hmm."

Kenzie ate. Zachary paid attention to his own meal.

"I think, either way, they get some peace of mind," Kenzie said after a while. She was still chewing on her steak and potatoes. "They either get reassurance that there wasn't any foul play, little Declan didn't suffer at anyone's hands, he just slipped away in a few moments. Or they get to let go of a little of the guilt. If there was a mysterious third party involved, then they weren't negligent. There was nothing more they could have done to protect him."

"You think they're going to be happy with the results either way?"

"I can't say anything for sure. What do I know? I think that it was such a shock to them, they're having a hard time accepting it. When something happens out of the blue like that... a healthy kid one minute, and then the next he's gone... they want to believe it's not true. Somebody made a mistake. You see it on TV all the time, cold cases, reversal, someone on death row who was completely innocent... It's part of our culture. So, they're looking for that 'oh, we were wrong.'"

"Could be." Zachary cut pieces from his steak and chewed the tender beef slowly. "I think you're right about the shock. They're all a little... removed from reality. Stuck in disbelief."

She nodded her understanding. "You can understand where they're coming from. It's pretty tough to lose a kid like that. You want to blame someone. Whether it's a stranger, or the police investigation, or the medical examiner. Someone to blame."

"Yeah. Maybe so. As long as they don't blame me."

"As long as they pay you, who cares? Maybe you can offer it as a service. Scapegoat for hire."

Zachary chuckled. Kenzie had some twisted sense of humor.

"Since we can't read the report while we're eating, why don't you tell me about yourself? Have you been a private investigator for long? What made you go into it?"

"My interest in photography, for one. And TV. I grew up on detective shows."

"And is it like you thought it would be?"

Zachary snorted. "I don't carry a gun. I don't break into people's houses. I don't chase down murderers every week. A lot of it is tedious desk work, but yeah, I still enjoy it. I like teasing out all the evidence and solving the puzzle. Although most of what I do isn't that puzzling... husbands and wives cheating on each other, routine background checks, that kind of thing. I don't always get something that I can dig my teeth into."

"Do you come from a big family? Lots of brothers and sisters?"

Zachary was taken aback and immediately on guard. "What does that have to do with anything?"

Kenzie's eyes flashed up from her steak to his face in surprise. "I'm wondering about your background. What makes you tick. It was just a question."

"I don't..." He had been about to say that he didn't want to talk about his past, but that would just send up flares that there was something to talk about. "I don't have any siblings."

"Only child?"

"Well, yes."

"Were you spoiled?" Her eyes were dancing. "I'll bet you were spoiled."

"No. My parents... I lost them when I was young."

"Oh." She blinked and recomposed her face. "I'm so sorry. That was a tactless thing to say."

"You didn't know."

She ate in silence, her cheeks noticeably pink even in the dimness of the room.

"How about you?" Zachary asked. "You have to tell me about yourself. How did you get into the medical examiner's office? I hear people are dying to get in there."

"Oh," Kenzie groaned and kicked him under the table. "You did not just say that!"

"What? It was an accident. I didn't mean that..."

She laughed and shook her head. "You are an enigma, Zachary Goldberg! I always loved science in school. I was fascinated when we did dissections. Couldn't get enough of it. While the boys were horsing around, throwing frog intestines at each other, and the girls were pretending to throw up or faint, I was enthralled. I mean, there I was, for the first time, actually seeing an animal's organs. I'd always understood they were there, and what they did, but I was actually seeing them and holding them in my hands. It wasn't abstract anymore."

"And that's when you decided you wanted to be a death doctor when you grew up"

"It was either that or a serial killer. I thought I'd make more as a doctor."

Zachary laughed. As long as the spotlight wasn't on him, he could have a lot of fun with Kenzie. She was fun and pleasant to be with. "So, are you on your way to becoming a full-fledged medical examiner? I mean… I'm not sure what your training is or what your duties are now."

"I've still got a little way to go yet. It's like… an apprenticeship. I get to work with a brilliant doctor, get some practical experience while I'm doing my schooling. It works for me."

"And do you have family around here?" He was careful to phrase it as a casual question about her family and let her fill in the details, rather than putting her on the spot as she had done with him.

"My parents are about a three-hour drive away. Close enough to get there if they need me, or I need something from them. Far enough away to be independent. So that they don't call me about every little thing, and vice versa."

"Sounds good."

"I *am* an only child." She offered it up, knowing that he wasn't going to ask.

"Spoiled?"

"Not as much as you'd think."

Zachary's steak was gone. He sat back, having a sip of beer and thinking about his case.

"Parents don't always spoil their children, even if they only have one child."

"No, of course not."

"I don't think Declan was spoiled."

Kenzie nodded gravely. "Do you think they were strict with him?"

"Not strict…" Zachary made a face, trying to think of how to phrase it. "Well, maybe strict, but not big disciplinarians. They both have OCD, so there were probably a lot of rules. Things that they wouldn't let slide that a *normal* parent—"

"Neurotypical," Kenzie corrected.

"I think they were probably different than neurotypical parents. And I don't think they were that… *close* to him."

"Well…" She scraped at the gravy and mushrooms left on her plate. "Not all parents are as closely bonded to their children as you would expect. Though sometimes, it's just that they don't show it well. Not all parents are demonstrative."

"Maybe that's it. They act like they cared for him, but it feels funny. More removed."

"That's something you should probably consider."

He raised his eyes to hers. "You think…"

"I don't think anything, but if you're getting a funny feeling about it, you should follow your instincts. See if it leads anywhere."

"Yeah. Okay."

While Zachary was considering whether they should have coffee, or whether he should ask Kenzie if she wanted dessert—maybe they should share one—a group of men and women in fancy dress went to the front of the restaurant and gathered around a microphone. Zachary's heart sank.

"We should go," he suggested. "We're not going to be able to talk over that—"

"No, no," Kenzie protested as they started singing. "I love carolers! They always put me into such a Christmas spirit."

Zachary tried to signal to the waiter for the bill. He needed to get out of there. Kenzie watched the carolers, enthralled. She barely noticed Zachary getting the bill and paying it. Zachary tapped on her arm. "We can go now, Kenzie…"

She looked at him, startled. She took in the fact that he had paid the bill and was rising to his feet, eager to get out of there.

"What's your hurry, Zach? Relax for a few minutes and listen to the Christmas songs."

"I really… I really need to go, Kenzie."

"What's wrong? You didn't seem like you were in any hurry before. Where do you need to go?"

"Out of here." He knew his voice was angry, the words bitten off, but he couldn't explain it to her. He couldn't put it into words.

"The music isn't that bad," she laughed. Then she studied him more closely. "*Is* it the music? Is it some sensory thing?"

He made a gesture toward the door. Kenzie got up, and without any further protest, led the way to the coat check where they retrieved their winter gear.

Zachary breathed a sigh of relief. The door closed behind them, blocking out any residual sounds of the music. Kenzie took his hand, watching his face.

"Better?"

Zachary took a few more deep breaths and nodded.

"What was that? Sensory overload? Flashback? Can you explain it to me?"

"No… I just… don't like Christmas."

"You don't like Christmas."

"No."

"So, Christmas songs, decorations, movies, cookies, you avoid all of that?"

"Pretty much, yeah," Zachary gave a little grimace. "Sorry, I didn't know they did that here, or we could have gone somewhere else."

"Somewhere else where you might not accidentally hear Christmas music."

"Uh-huh." His face was hot, and he was sure it was bright red, but maybe she couldn't tell in the darkness.

"And where does this pathological fear of Christmas come from?"

"I'm not afraid of it. I just…"

"That was more than just not liking Christmas songs. I saw your face."

Zachary looked away from her, trying to put some distance between himself and the emotions. "Can I take you home? Or do you want to go somewhere for a coffee?"

Kenzie was staring at him, not ready to let it go.

"It's just a bad time of year for me," Zachary said. "I'm sorry. It doesn't have to ruin our night, does it? Let me take you for ice cream."

"Ice cream?"

He could see their breaths as they talked. The cold wind was cutting through his jacket and biting his cheeks.

"Uh—hot chocolate?" he amended.

Kenzie laughed, and after a moment of consideration took him by the arm.

D ave Halloran was the producer of *The Happy Artist*. He was a large man, balding, with a florid complexion, who always seemed to be panting and trying to keep up with some unseen race. Zachary had talked to him on the phone, and while Halloran seemed reluctant to meet with him, he eventually agreed when Zachary repeated that he had been hired by *The Happy Artist*'s family, and she wanted him to interview everyone.

In reality, he wasn't sure how Isabella would feel about him interviewing her coworkers. Zachary's employer was Isabella's mother, not Isabella, and the scope of his job was to investigate all avenues to help put Isabella's mind at ease and help her to avoid a breakdown.

He could justify it to Isabella. If any of her coworkers were jealous of her, they might want to harm her through her son. Therefore, he had to talk to them. But he didn't think that was really the case. She was their bread and butter, and if she had a breakdown, the show would be canceled. What he wanted was their take on Isabella herself. How she had behaved since her son's disappearance and death compared with how she had behaved before.

Zachary looked around the room as he sat down. A small office, considering that the producer was the top man on the network's most popular show. It looked more like the size of an accounting student's office than a big-shot TV producer's. There was paper everywhere, reminding him vaguely of Isabella's studio. Binders lined up on top of filing cabinets, stacks of paper and scripts in piles on his desk, a colorful wall calendar so filled with symbols, arrows, and squiggles that it might as well have been written in Greek. There were framed pictures, certificates, and awards plastering the walls.

"We're all very sorry for what happened to Isabella," Halloran said tentatively.

"It's tragic," Zachary agreed. "And from what I understand from Isabella's mother, she has changed since her son's death."

Halloran's eyes were hooded. "I suppose."

"Is that not accurate?"

"I really don't feel comfortable talking about Isabella behind her back."

"This investigation is for her benefit."

"Still..."

"Isabella's mother is very concerned for her welfare. If something was to happen to her..."

Something changed in Halloran's face. "You don't think she would do anything... to harm herself... do you?"

"I've met Isabella once. You're the one who has known her for several years, who sees her almost on a daily basis. You tell me. What would happen to your viewership if you lost *The Happy Artist*?"

Halloran's ruddy complexion drained of color. When he spoke, his tone was flat, but that didn't fool Zachary, who was more interested in the nonverbal indicators. "Of course, that would be bad for the network, but we do have insurance in such cases, which would give us some protection while we changed our line-up..."

Zachary stared at the pictures and awards on Halloran's wall, considering his approach.

"Well then, I suppose there's no point in staying around here arguing. I'll let Molly and Isabella know that you were not comfortable in helping us. They'll have to look elsewhere for assistance." He printed in his notebook slowly and deliberately: *Halloran did it.*

Zachary was sure that Halloran was in no position to see what it was that Zachary was writing. It was the implication that Zachary had gained insight from the fact that Halloran wouldn't help him that was important. It was the pantomime that was meant to have an effect. He might just as well have written *The Cat in the Hat*, but there was a one in a million chance that Halloran's subconscious could tell what Zachary was writing from the movements of his pen or the sound of the scratches on the paper. Or there might be a reflection or surveillance camera of which Zachary was unaware. If there was any chance that Halloran could guess at what he had written, consciously or unconsciously, Zachary didn't want it to be nonsense. He wanted it to be an accusation.

"No, no, I didn't say I wouldn't help," Halloran protested quickly, taking the bait. "I'm just... having difficulty reconciling how any of this is going to help our Isabella."

"You leave that part to me. I've done my best to explain it to you, but I can't tell you everything I know."

Halloran vigorously scratched the top of his bald head, scowling.

"Isabella has always been a little... flighty. She has an artist's disposition. They're not always the easiest of people to work with. She takes offense or gets put off. Or something is wrong, and she gets preoccupied with it. Not because she's a prima donna, she just... gets stuck when things aren't right. The wrong kind of water. Someone gets the wrong shade of paint or the wrong shape of brush. She gets all bent out of shape over it. That's just the way it is when you're dealing with artistic temperaments. Actors are just as bad, or worse."

"Sure," Zachary nodded. "Just because she's brilliant and comes off as happy and friendly on the screen, that doesn't mean that's how she is in private."

"That damn title," Halloran snapped. "Why did we have to call it *The Happy Artist*? Practically doomed it to failure."

"Because you can't exactly have your happy artist in mourning on screen."

He nodded. "And let me tell you, happy she is not."

"She just lost her only child. Who could expect her to be?"

"She didn't *just* lose him. It was months ago."

"And you expected her to be over it by now?"

"Not exactly... but she wasn't the motherly type. She didn't talk about him all the time and post his crayon drawings in her dressing room. She barely mentioned her family." At Zachary's look, he shook his head. "Maybe she was just the private type. Maybe she was all kisses and cuddles at home. I have no way of knowing, but we do have a contract. She's required to be here and to fulfill the terms of her contract. Even before this happened, I wouldn't say she was happy. Off screen. There was always some problem."

"Did she rub anyone the wrong way? Was there anyone in particular who was bothered by her moodiness?"

"*Was* there?" Halloran repeated. "You mean before her son died? You're asking if anyone had a motive to kill her child because they didn't like the way she behaved on set?"

"I'm just exploring the possibilities."

"You can put that one right out of your mind. She was annoying, but no one wanted to destroy her. No one would kill her child just to stop her from showing up for work."

Zachary nodded. He hadn't expected the line of questioning to lead anywhere. "Still, was there anyone who was particularly irritated by her? Or jealous of her success? What would you have done if she had been unable to continue her show?"

"We would have had to change the lineup. I can't be sure who we would have put in her place. We would have needed something new; we didn't have anything that would have the same success in that time slot as *The Happy Artist.*"

"Is there anyone who might have thought that they would get it?"

"I'm sure that all the other shows thought they were as good as she was or had the same draw, but one over another... no. Sorry."

"Do you have a list of the other shows...?"

"You can pull that online. There's nothing confidential about the line-up."

But that didn't stop him from being obstructive. Zachary leaned back in his chair, trying to give Halloran the impression that he was calm and relaxed, finished with the serious questioning.

"How has she been since her son's death? Any... unusual or concerning behavior?"

"She was always eccentric, but since then, things have gotten a little out of hand. That tattoo, all her memorial jewelry... I had a hell of a time talking her into taking off the jewelry when she is on screen. She can wear the ring and one of the necklaces. Not the one with the teeth!"

Zachary suppressed a snort of laughter. He could just see Isabella wearing that one during the show.

"She does not appreciate being told that she has to cover up her tattoo during the show. Can you imagine how distracting that would be? We have to show close-ups of her hands to show technique. Lots of zooming in, and that great big tattoo on her arm! The viewers wouldn't see anything else. Why couldn't she just do something small and tasteful in a part of her body that wouldn't be on the screen? Her ankle. We never show her ankles."

"Was there anything in her contract that said she couldn't get a tattoo?"

"No, but we have the right to make wardrobe and makeup choices, and covering up the tattoo falls into wardrobe, so she has to suck it up."

"And has she?"

"There was trouble over it the first few days, but she's gotten used to it now."

"I gather she can be pretty stubborn."

"Stubborn doesn't even begin to describe it. We've had to have her therapist on site a few times to figure out how to get past her emotional issues."

Zachary raised an eyebrow. "Before or after the accident?"

"Both. More often when we first started the show. Then things settled into a routine, and she does well if everything is routine. It's when something has to change that there's a problem."

"Right. That makes sense."

"Is that everything, then?" Halloran demanded. "I really do have to get back to work here." He made a gesture to take in all the piles of paperwork on his desk.

Zachary nodded. "I'll be in touch." He started to rise from his chair.

"She can't paint blue," Halloran said suddenly.

Zachary froze halfway out of his chair, then sat back down. "What?"

"Since her son died, she can't paint blue anymore. We've had her therapist in, and we're working on it, but it's damn inconvenient. What do you do with an artist who can't paint the color blue?"

"What *do* you do?"

"We can't put blue on her palette, but we can put purple or green. Each time we film, we put a little less red and yellow in those blends, trying to work back to pure blue. But the woman can't paint blue skies or water. When you've got an artist, who is famous for painting landscapes, and she can no longer paint blue skies or water..."

"But you can't fire her for that."

"No. Of course not. That would be discrimination against the mentally ill. We have to find landscapes that don't include blue. Sunrise and sunset.

Trees inside a forest, with no view of the sky. We've started throwing in some portraits and still lifes, even though that's not her thing."

"Nobody with blue eyes."

Halloran nodded. "Nobody with blue eyes. Combine that with trying to edit out her verbal tics…"

Zachary raised his brows. "Her tics…?"

"You've talked to her?"

"Yes."

"She didn't repeat a prayer when she was talking to you? For her son?"

"Oh." Zachary nodded. "May he hold you in the hollow of his hand."

"That's the one. We can't have her saying that every two minutes in the show. It has to be edited out. Every single time. She isn't even religious. I think she's an atheist!"

Zachary wrote a few notes in his notepad. "You would say that her behavior has changed since her son died and that you have concerns about her mental stability."

"That better not get out to the press."

"No, I'm not talking to anybody about it, just making an observation. I wondered whether you shared any of Molly's concerns, and it would appear that you do."

Halloran wrung his hands together briefly. "I hadn't realized how much we have been accommodating her the last few months. Yes, we're all concerned. If this show was to tank because of her mental instability…" He shook his head. "It would be very bad for the network."

Zachary pondered the information he had gleaned from Halloran and the few network employees he had managed to talk to as he scrolled through lengthy Facebook feeds and other social network sites, compiling background on his latest targets of interest.

Isabella's inability to paint the color blue was intriguing. The first thing that came to mind was that blue was the color to signify the birth of a baby boy. Even as they grew up, pink was for girls and blue was for boys. Neither color was exclusive, of course, and gender norms were changing too rapidly to keep track of it all, but in his mind, and in the minds of his generation and older, blue was for boys. Declan's room was decorated in shades of blue and Isabella had said that she would never redecorate or repurpose his room. She intended to keep it just as it was. She must have associated her son with the color blue, and that was what prevented her from painting with it.

He had observed the verbal tic without realizing what it was. While annoying, the repetition of the little prayer was appropriate. For someone who was religious, but for someone who was an atheist, or close to it, it was just one more indicator of how deeply she was suffering from the over-whelming pain and guilt at the death of her son.

Zachary's mind went to his own family, and suddenly he was no longer able to see the screen. He stopped scrolling. For a few seconds, or perhaps longer, all he could do was sit there, with old memories and impressions washing over him, holding him paralyzed. His heart thudded dully in his chest, each beat painful. Why, after all that had happened, was *he* still alive, still carrying on as if he were a normal person?

He remembered the word that Kenzie had suggested. Not normal, but neurotypical. He liked the flavor of the word. It pathologized people with normal brain patterns, the same way that people with normal brain patterns had been pathologizing the atypicals for hundreds of years.

Thinking this through helped to take him away from the memories. He was able to break out of the clutches of the past and look at his screen once more.

After checking through the feeds of his current subjects of investigation, he searched for Spencer's and Isabella's accounts. Unsurprisingly, Spencer's was sparse. Maybe Isabella had set it up for him, as he didn't seem the type who would normally use it himself. Facebook was too messy for someone as tidy and orderly as Spencer.

Isabella had a couple of accounts. She had a personal account. He could see Molly and Spencer on her friends list, but mostly, names and faces of people he didn't know, who had nothing to do with the case. She also had a fan page for *The Happy Artist*. He didn't know whether she had set it up and answered fan queries herself. Chances were, it had been set up by the network, and they were the ones managing it. There were fans sending their condolences, but mostly it was excitement and discussion over her latest shows. The accident had taken place months ago; it was no longer in the public's awareness.

Isabella's personal account, however, was another story. She tended to post Madonna-like woman and child pictures and memes about grief and loss. Zachary saw that Spencer had posted a number of these somber posts onto Isabella's timeline. No jokes and cute kittens for the couple. They were obviously still deep in the grieving process.

The phone rang, and Zachary picked it up without looking at the caller ID.

"Goldman Investigations."

"Mr. Goldman, this is Eugene Taft's assistant? We talked before? I told you I would call you?"

"Yes," Zachary agreed.

"If you would like to come down to the police station, you will be given access to the Bond accident investigation file. You won't be able to make any copies or take anything with you, but you can make notes for your case."

"Great. Will that be available today, or do I need to wait for it to be pulled from storage somewhere?"

"We've already pulled it for you. You can come down anytime."

"Perfect. I'll be down to see it soon."

"You'll need to sign a confidentiality agreement. The information on the files is only to be used in your own investigation, to verify the results of the accident investigation to the family. You are not, under any circumstances, to speak to the media or release any information to them. The police force always has to be sure to keep the details of a death out of the public eye, so that they can be sure of who has legitimate information and who might just be repeating information the police already have and trying to pass themselves off as knowing them first-hand."

Zachary turned this over in his mind. He took a sip of his cold, bitter coffee. "Does that mean the police force had doubts in this case? That there were details held back from the public that would only be known to someone who was there on the scene when it happened?"

"I don't know anything about the specifics of this case. I am speaking in general terms."

"You don't know if they had any suspicions about a third party being involved."

"No, I don't know anything about it," she repeated.

Zachary hung up the phone, still wondering whether she was telling the truth or trying to give him a heads-up.

Spencer looked surprised when he answered the door and found Zachary on his doorstep once again. He stood there looking at Zachary.

"I didn't know you were coming by again, Mr. Goldman."

"Zachary."

"Zachary. Did you find something out? Something of significance?"

Zachary thought back to poring over the police records. All the hand-written notes, pictures, and bits of scribbles. He wished that he could put his finger on one piece of evidence and say, 'here it is, this is what the police missed.' But so far, he was just seeing the same routine information pointing to an accident. No evidence of foul play. No one who wanted to hurt either Isabella or Spencer by hurting their child. There were lists of the registered sex offenders in the area with notations or brief interviews beside each name. Alibis. No one had seen any of them around the Bond home or near Declan. None of them had done any work there.

"No, I haven't found anything out. I just wanted to speak with you and Isabella again, now that I have a bit more information. Just a few additional questions."

Spencer didn't answer immediately, then gave a sigh and stepped back to allow Zachary in. They went back to Spencer's office as before and took their seats.

"I don't know what else I can tell you," Spencer warned. "I wasn't the one supervising Declan when he disappeared. I don't know anything except that he was in our yard, and then he drowned in the pond."

"I understand. How has Isabella been doing?"

Spencer shook his head. "You were here. You saw her."

"I did, but I don't think I'm getting the full picture. I think there is a lot more going on than I can see. Than anyone who doesn't live here would see."

"Of course… that's true of anyone."

"I talked to Isabella's producer and some of her coworkers."

"Yes…?"

"Were you aware that she can't or won't paint the color blue?"

"No. I don't have anything to do with her painting. Why, what does that have to do with anything?"

Zachary found it hard to believe that he wouldn't know even that little bit of information about his wife's painting. Wouldn't it have come up in conversation? "Does the color blue have any significance for Isabella that you are aware of?"

"Blue." Spencer looked at him blankly. "No. Why?"

"I'm just wondering if it has something to do with the case. Maybe she associates it with something. It could be a clue to what happened to Declan."

"No. Compulsions don't really work that way. They aren't logical or symbolic."

"Sometimes they can be traced back to a particular trigger," Zachary pointed out.

Spencer cocked his head, and his eyes narrowed at Zachary. "What would you know about that?"

"It's true, isn't it?"

"Sometimes... but not always; and as far as Isabella not being able to paint the color blue... no, I don't think it has any significance at all. It's just one of those bizarre things."

"What is it that concerns you the most about Isabella right now? Is there anything that worries you?"

"The praying gets on my nerves more than anything. I've gotten used to her... messiness... the way that she collects things... but that same prayer over and over again, it grates on my nerves."

Zachary nodded. "I can see how it would. She's doing it a lot, then?"

"Compulsions are something that you can suppress for a little while by exercising self-control. I can sit here and not clean my hands again, probably for the whole time you are here. Or if I have to go to an outside meeting; but eventually, the urge becomes overwhelming, and I have to act."

Zachary nodded. "And her praying?"

"She can stop while you are here. For a while. As soon as you are gone, she'll start up again."

"Her boss said that they were working with her therapist. Has he come here too? Does he make suggestions of things that you and she can do to address her issues?"

"He's never been here. That's the first I've heard of him going to her work. We are private people, Mr. Goldman. We don't like putting ourselves on display."

Spencer didn't, perhaps, but Isabella did. Every week.

"Is there anything that would help Isabella? Her mother hoped that if I found something, it would alleviate her guilt and help her to recover. What do you think?"

"I don't think this is doing her any good." Spencer shook his head. "I think she needs quiet. Not to be disturbed by people like you and by the network. Just give her some time by herself to sort it all through."

"I see."

"We have a couple of friends who are moving back to town. The Raymonds. I'm hoping that seeing them again, having a girlfriend she can talk to... maybe that will help. They moved to New York seven or eight years ago, and we haven't really seen them since. Maybe they can bring back memories of what it was like before we had Declan. We—she—was happier then."

"She doesn't have many friends that she can talk to?"

"No. It's not easy for someone like Isabella to make friends. She's so emotional, and she lets herself get caught up in her compulsions. People want you to be normal."

"Neurotypical," Zachary suggested.

"Normal," Spencer repeated.

"Okay. Is there anything else? Have you thought any more about what happened the day your son disappeared? Anything at all."

"I've told you all I know."

"Maybe you could outline what a typical day was like around here. For Declan."

Spencer made an irritated noise in the back of his throat and shook his head.

"He would get up in the morning on his own without being wakened. If Isabella was working, he would come find me, and we would have break-fast together. I would play with him, maybe read with him. Then he would play quietly until lunch. I would make sandwiches for us both. Turn on one of his cartoons, and he would fall asleep. When Isabella got home, she would wake him up and do something with him."

He stopped and looked at Zachary.

"And after that?"

"That's when he disappeared," Spencer said. "His day didn't go any further than that."

"But on a regular day, what would happen after Isabella played with him?"

"Our supper hour was pretty early. Then I would take Deck for his bath and get him ready for bed. We would read stories. Maybe watch a TV show. Then he would fall asleep around eight."

"That all sounds pretty... quiet. He didn't get rowdy and noisy? Get into things when he was supposed to be entertaining himself? Argue or cry?"

Spencer scowled, scratching the back of his neck. "Of course. Those are all normal child things. You asked what a typical schedule was. That's what I gave you. But he wasn't a trained dog; he had a mind of his own."

"So, he would disobey."

"Yes."

"Did he ever leave the yard before when he knew he wasn't supposed to?"

"No, never."

"I want you to think about it," Zachary insisted. "He never tried to reach the latch? Never climbed the fence to get a ball that he threw out of the yard?"

Spencer considered these scenarios, actually thinking instead of just answering defensively. "He was a pretty quiet child. Not like some of the little demons you see around here. He usually tried to do what he was told."

Zachary waited for him to work through his answer.

"There was one day when I couldn't see him in the yard. When I went out to look and see what he was doing, he was talking to a woman over the gate. Not the back gate, the one to the front." Spencer made a motion to the side of the house where it could be found, out of sight of his windows.

"Ah. So how did you react to that? What did you tell him?"

"First, I told the woman off for talking to him. Kids may not know better than to talk to strangers, but adults should know better than to approach children who don't know them."

"How did she react?"

"She was angry and defensive. She said he talked to her, and she just stopped to answer him because he was so cute."

"And then you told Declan...?"

"I told him he had to stay in the back where I could see him. Not out of sight of the windows. And that he wasn't supposed to talk to adults who came up to the house. If someone came up to him, he should come inside and get one of us."

"How long was that before his disappearance?"

Spencer rubbed the center of his forehead, thinking about it. "It's hard to say. I don't remember that clearly. Maybe it was a few weeks or a couple of months."

"Did you ever see the woman again?"

"No. Not someone I ever saw again."

"Did you tell Isabella about it?"

"Hm… Yes, I think I did. Just so she would be aware that part of the yard was out of view of the windows, and she should make sure Deck didn't go over there… if he was out of sight, she should check there and make sure someone wasn't trying to talk to him."

"And did she do that the day he disappeared? Did she go outside and check that part of the yard?"

"Yes, of course. So did I. We both checked every inch of the back yard. It was obvious he wasn't there."

"The police didn't find any helpful footprints."

"No. They didn't find much of anything," Spencer agreed.

"Did it surprise you that there wasn't a clear trail to follow?"

"No. Conditions that day… it was pretty dry. It had been for a while. The ground was hard and dusty. Declan wasn't heavy enough to leave a trail to follow."

"And there were no footprints from a third party. No one who shouldn't have been there."

"No." Spencer shook his head. "He just wandered off, Mr.—Zachary. Maybe somebody had been in the yard and left the gate open. Somebody looking for bottles or something worth stealing. Or the woman who talked to him that day, to get back at us for being such rotten parents, in her eyes. Or maybe it didn't latch securely when I took the garbage out because the wind caught it and kept it open. But he just wandered out. He wandered out, and he drowned, just like a hundred other kids."

"Is that what you hope happened?"

"Yes. I'd rather not think there was someone out there who took him to hurt us. Or intending to hurt him. The police didn't think there was anyone else involved. I just want to let him rest."

Zachary thought about Isabella's jewelry, all the parts of Declan that she wore on her body and her skin. She hadn't been able to lay her child to rest.

Zachary couldn't think of anything less restful than dangling in Isabella's constantly moving layers of jewelry.

"Okay." Zachary nodded. "Thank you for your time. I'll let you know if I have any other questions. Feel free to call me if anything occurs to you."

"I'd rather you called before showing up here."

Zachary didn't apologize for the surprise visit. Sometimes, it was helpful to catch people off-balance. He stood.

"And, Zachary…"

He raised an eyebrow at Spencer and waited.

"I do worry about my wife. Quite a bit. I'm hopeful that having the Raymonds back in town will have a positive effect… distract her from her grief and give her someone to talk to. Because…" His lips pressed together. "I don't know how much longer she can go on like this."

7

Zachary recognized the phone number that popped up on his call display and smiled.

"Hi, Kenzie."

"Hey, just thought I'd call and check in on my new PI buddy."

"I'm glad you called. I wouldn't mind having someone to discuss this case with…"

Zachary didn't need someone to talk it over with, but it was the first thing that came to mind. And he wasn't lying; he wouldn't mind discussing it with her.

"Oh, yeah?" Kenzie asked brightly. "How about I treat you to a sandwich at *It's a Wrap*. I love their artisan breads."

He hesitated. It wasn't that he didn't like them too, but it was Bridget's favorite sandwich shop, and he didn't want to risk running into any of her friends there. What were the odds that any of them would approach him? They would all be on her side and wouldn't have anything to say to him.

"Yeah, sure. That sounds great," he agreed. "We could get a booth for a little privacy…"

"Perfect. We should probably hit it early, before the lunch crowd. Do you mind meeting at eleven?"

"Works for me. You're not working today?"

"No, I have a doctor's appointment today and just took the full day off. I'm free until two-thirty."

"Doctor's appointment? Anything wrong?"

"No, it's nothing. I'll see you there? At eleven?"

"I'll be there."

Zachary hung up his phone and decided he'd better shower and shave to make himself presentable. No point in showing up looking like some homeless guy. The look might help him blend in with a crowd while on a job since people didn't want to look at the less fortunate, but it wouldn't work for a date.

He again made sure he was at the restaurant before Kenzie, cornering a booth for them. She wasn't far behind him. They gave the server their orders and exchanged some pleasantries.

"Did you really have some questions about the case?" Kenzie asked, raising one brow mischievously.

"Well... not so much that I had questions, I just thought it would be nice to talk through some of the details."

She nodded. "Sure."

"You said that one of the signs of drowning is bruising. From holding the victim down."

"Right."

"The boy did have bruises."

She shook her head. "Not that were typical of drowning. Did you bring it with you?"

Zachary dug the report out of his bag and slid it across to her. She turned quickly to the appropriate page. "Shins and knees, elbows. All typical of little boys—and girls—in their regular play. He had several bruises, and they were different ages. Fell down one day. Walked into a coffee table another. Skinned elbows on a trampoline a couple of days later. All kids have those kinds of bruises. If he had been drowned, we would expect to see bruises on his neck or back. Those are the kind of bruises a drowning victim gets."

"Ah." Zachary nodded. He hadn't been too concerned about the bruises. He had thought that they looked pretty innocuous, but he wouldn't know without asking. There could have been something atypical there that he simply hadn't been able to see.

"Now what about the nail scrapings?" he asked. "We didn't get time to talk about those before. Why did they do nail scrapings? Are they looking for DNA? Seeing if he tried to fight back against an attacker?"

"Sure. That's part of it. Skin under the nails is always a big red flag. Sometimes you can find other evidence as well. It's like a mini archeological dig." She flipped through the pages and worked her way down the list of what they found under Declan's nails. "The victim had soil under his nails, consistent with what was in his yard, not around the pond. He had no foreign DNA under his nails, so, no, he didn't fight off an attacker. He had a mixture of oil and mineral pigments... oh!" She laughed. "Paint, of course. An oil-based paint. Mostly green."

"Paint." Zachary mulled it over, wondering if it was significant. "I guess as the child of a painter, that shouldn't come as any great shock. He must have been around his mother's work. Probably instructed by her and encouraged to produce his own paintings as well."

"I would think so."

Kenzie continued to flip aimlessly through the medical examiner's report, looking for anything else of interest. "Was he autistic?"

"No. Not that anyone has said. Why? What's in there that would make you think—"

"Don't get excited. It's not anything I saw. I just wondered because a lot of the children who are attracted to water and drown have autism. I don't know any real stats. Just that it seems like a high percentage."

"No, he wasn't autistic. From what the family tells me, he didn't even like the water. He'd avoid it when he could. I wondered whether there were steep or crumbling banks, and he fell in by accident before he even saw it, but I saw the police photos yesterday, and it had pretty shallow banks. To drown in it, he would have had to walk right into it."

Kenzie frowned. "Pretty unlikely if he was afraid of water."

"It's the only argument against it being an accident that I've come across yet. I know that kids can drown in a very small amount of water... but to drown in the pond, he had to actually be in it. A kid doesn't just lie down on the shore and stick his face into two inches of water. And his body was found floating in the pond. He had to walk out into it."

He hadn't put the thought into words before. Kenzie frowned, and Zachary felt a chill. Was Molly right? *Had* a third party drowned the child?

The server brought them their sandwiches, and for a few minutes, they both just ate, enjoying the fresh, crusty bread and thinking over the problem.

"Maybe there was a dog or something else that attracted his attention," Zachary said. "His father said he loves dogs. If he saw one swimming in the pond and thought it was in trouble, or just wanted to see it or pat it... who knows? He could have been trying to retrieve a ball or a Frisbee."

"None were found at the crime scene. Could have been an animal, even a fish near the surface and he thought he could grab it. If he was afraid of water, then presumably he couldn't swim."

"I would guess not."

Zachary's eyes caught on a man walking toward him. A big, broad man with the physique of a halfback. His face broke into a smile when he recognized Zachary.

"Look who's here! Zach, my man! It's been too long! How the hell are you?" He reached out his hand to take Zachary's, but Zachary's attention was caught by the thin blonde woman behind him. He froze, not taking Joseph Reichler's hand, not saying anything, his brain seizing up in his panic at seeing her there.

His own reaction was mirrored by Bridget. She swore when she saw him.

"What are you doing here?" she demanded. As if it was obviously her place and Zachary had no right to be there.

Joseph was turning to look at Bridget with dawning comprehension, realizing belatedly that she and Zachary had a history and might not want to run into each other in such a public place. "Oh, ah, Bridge..."

Kenzie stared from one of them to the other, waiting for someone to explain to her what was going on. A server came over, and blithely blind to their expressions and body language, asked whether they would like to be seated together.

"Maybe we should go somewhere else," Joseph said weakly. "I didn't mean to..."

"I'm not going anywhere else," Bridget insisted as if she owned the place. Like she got her favorite sandwich shop in the divorce. Like she had the right to demand that he vacate immediately. Zachary looked down at his half-eaten sandwich, no longer hungry. The first half sat in his stomach like a bowling ball. He looked at Kenzie, wanting to suggest that they leave.

Instead, Kenzie stuck out her hand toward Bridget and introduced herself. "Kenzie Kirsch. You must be…"

Bridget looked down at Kenzie, her face flushing pink. She was practically quivering with indignation. "Don't you be taken in by him," she warned. "Don't be taken in by the whole hurt-puppy, tragic past act. He's impossible to live with, and not fixable. Move on and find one that's whole, instead of wasting your time on this loser. Do you hear me? Do you understand what I'm saying?"

"I hear you." Kenzie's voice was low and clear, unflustered. "And I think maybe you'd better move on."

"*I* should move on?" Bridget was outraged. "Why the hell should I move on? This is…" It seemed to occur to her for the first time that she didn't have an excuse for her behavior. She didn't own the place or have a restraining order on Zachary. He had the right to eat wherever he wanted, with whomever he wanted. "You're a nice-looking girl," she said to Kenzie in a quieter voice. "He always did have a good eye for beauty. Believe me; you do not want to be roped into a relationship with this man. You will do nothing but suffer."

"Thank you for your advice," Kenzie said coolly, as if it happened every day.

Joseph was making apologetic gestures to Zachary, trying to get Bridget to move on and leave him alone. Just to keep walking. They could find another restaurant. There was no reason it had to be the same one as Zachary.

"My old friend," he said to Zachary apologetically. "I'm so sorry. I never meant…"

Zachary jerked his head at Joseph to just go. No apology necessary. If he left, hopefully, Bridget would follow. Joseph backed away, and after a moment of mulishness, Bridget followed him, whispering imprecations the whole way.

Zachary closed his eyes and let out a long sigh. He was afraid to look back at Kenzie, his ears burning. He felt like rushing out the door, but he couldn't end a second date like that or she'd wonder what the heck was wrong with him.

"Your ex, I assume," Kenzie said in amusement.

Zachary gave a hollow laugh and opened his eyes to look at her. "That was only slightly awkward, right?"

"That was classic. I don't think we could have designed a better scene if it had been planned and directed. Congratulations."

"On creating the perfect scene?"

"On getting out of that relationship. Are you telling me you would still want to be together with her?"

Zachary shook his head, but more in confusion than denial. He still loved Bridget, no matter how badly she had treated him. He would have gone back to her if he had thought there were any hope of reconciliation, but there simply wasn't. She was lost to him forever.

"Were you actually married? Or just dating or living together?"

"We were married," he admitted.

"I thought so. That kind of anger doesn't come from just dating. It had to be marriage."

"I don't know what you must think of me. If you want, I can just pay for this now, and we can get out of here…"

"No need for that. I'm perfectly fine where I am. She's gone away, so you can relax. I don't think she'll be coming back. In fact, I don't know if she'll ever be coming back here again. It's always going to remind her of you and how she made a fool of herself now."

"That won't stop her." It wasn't their first scene. It wouldn't be their last. Sooner or later, one of them was going to have to leave town. The only way Zachary was leaving town permanently was in a coffin.

"Relax. Honestly, I'm fine. It was all very entertaining. Tell me all about her and what a witch she is."

"She was the love of my life," Zachary said hopelessly. "We were once so happy. I don't even know where to start. We lived and breathed for each other, but over time… things happened. Feelings were hurt. We had to weather some storms that… most marriages just don't survive. Ours didn't."

"I'm sorry." She lowered the eyes that had been dancing with amusement just a moment before. "Here I am making light of something that was really tragic to you. I didn't mean to make you feel bad."

"You didn't. There's not much that could make me feel worse than that. When I think about how much in love we used to be, and how it could turn into *that*…"

"She's jealous."

"What? She's not jealous. She's angry. She thinks that I… we disagreed on a very important subject… and I think she blames me for what

73

happened to her. She's not jealous of me. She doesn't want anything to do with me."

"I beg to differ." Kenzie reached across the table and put her warm, smooth fingers over his. "I saw her face. She was shocked to see you here, but she didn't get *really* angry until she saw me."

"She can't be jealous. She hates me."

"No, she doesn't. She's angry with you, but she doesn't hate you."

Zachary shook his head. "You only saw her for a few seconds. I've lived with her. I'm the one who has had to live through this disastrous divorce. I know."

"Okay. You know. Let me just say that she has no right to treat you that way, and I'm sorry you had to put up with that crap. You deserve better."

Zachary shook his head. If Kenzie knew all about everything, he was sure she wouldn't say that.

"Don't let her get to you," Kenzie advised.

"Yeah."

"Let's go across the street for dessert. They have these fantastic, chocolate-mousse-filled croissants. They are just to die for. I don't think I can eat a whole one myself, so even if you're not in the mood to eat the rest of your sandwich, you still have to help me with dessert."

Zachary couldn't help but smile at this. Chocolate-mousse-filled croissants sounded like a pretty good solution to his troubles.

Zachary's next step was to develop a map of the area surrounding Isabella's house. The police had done plenty of sketches of the crime scene and the route from the back yard to the pond, but Zachary had something different in mind.

He started with the list of sex offenders that the police had identified and spoken to and pinned each address on a digital map. Then he went to a few other sites to track down houses that had been reported as marijuana growing operations, where violent crimes had been committed, or which had been condemned by the Board of Health. The pins on the map became thicker. Zachary knew that any other neighborhood would look the same. No one could escape all the sickos.

Once he had his map finished, he would take a drive around the neighborhood, checking out each of the houses in question. Chances were, everything would be quiet, and nothing would seem off. But maybe... maybe someone would object to his surveillance, or a face would be familiar, or someone would act in a way that identified them as a suspect. The police should already have visited most of the houses, just as they had the sex offenders, but there were no notes on the file he had reviewed saying that they had. It was always possible that he would turn up something more.

Checking out all the pinned locations on his map had turned out to be an all-day affair. Zachary had only expected it to take a couple of hours, but he had obviously made his canvassing area too big. He had gone according to the area the police had used for the sex offender canvass, but they had plenty of cops to run them down, and Zachary had only his two feet. At least he didn't need to interview everyone, just to snoop around.

He did end up talking to a few people when he was confronted by homeowners or neighbors who didn't like him sneaking around, but mostly his reconnaissance was ignored. People who wanted to know what he was doing backed off pretty quickly when he explained he was investigating Declan Bond's death. Most of them.

He was footsore and spirit-weary when he got back to his apartment at the end of the day. Second-guessing why he was still investigating the case. Everything pointed toward an accident. There was no malevolent force behind young Declan's death. Just a child who had wandered out of an enclosed yard while his mother's back was turned. Tragic, but there was no one to blame.

Zachary could see from the end of the hall that there was something taped to his door. His stomach tightened. A notice from the landlord that his rent was going up or they'd had to access his apartment because of a burst pipe? A neighbor who had some complaint about him? He drew up to the door and looked at it.

Drop the investigation.

He stared at the note.

It wasn't the first time he'd been told to back out of a case, but it was usually face-to-face with a lover who had caught on to his surveillance and was furious about it. A couple of times by the police, who felt like he was interfering with one of their cases with an accident reconstruction or interviews with the victims. A note on his door; that was a first.

Zachary tried the handle and found, to his relief, that it was still locked. He had envisioned the scene from a bad TV drama; finding the door unlocked and walking into his apartment to find that it had been tossed, maybe a dead body left in the bathtub or something equally sinister.

He unlocked the door and opened it slowly. It was dark. He turned on the light and scanned the room. He realized he had still been expecting it to be a mess. He was still expecting threats and a body or frame. But the room appeared just as he had left it. A little messy, but nothing seemed to have been touched.

Still, Zachary was nervous as he checked each of the other rooms. Including the bathtub. No body. No planted cocaine. No lipsticked threats on the mirror. No dead rat or horse's head in the bed. His heart thudded. He knew he was letting his imagination get the better of him. It was just a note. There were no threats, no profanity; no letters clipped out of a magazine to form the words.

He went back to lock and bolt the apartment door before searching the fridge for something to eat.

8

Zachary slept restlessly. He woke up several times during the night, listening to the noises of his apartment and the surrounding apartments, worried there was someone there.

But even if the person who had left the note were someone who would consider harming him, they would at least have to wait until the next day to see whether he had dropped the case; whichever case it was. He was irritated that they hadn't said which case he was supposed to drop. Did they think that he only had one case at a time? At least the previous threats had been made in person, so he knew which case they were talking about. It was incredibly annoying to be warned off without knowing what he was being warned off of.

Of course, there had been no threat. Only an instruction. That in itself left him feeling unsettled. Drop the investigation—or what? A threat to his life? To his welfare? Perhaps to the case itself? Or maybe nothing would happen. Maybe the most that the note writer could bring himself to do was to leave the note, and that would be it.

The next morning, Zachary downed two cups of coffee before leaving the apartment. Not something that he would usually do before going on surveillance. He would end up having to make a rest stop by midmorning. He didn't know how long he was going to have to wait before he got his opportunity. Maybe it would be quick.

The familiar yellow VW was parked outside the coffee shop, where he expected it to be, but he didn't dare get out and approach it yet. She would spend only a few minutes inside, depending on how long the line-up was. Then she'd be back out with her to-go mug, heading to work or wherever else she had to go. He found a parking space down the block and watched for her.

It was ten minutes before he saw her blond head bob out of the door, and disappear as she got into the car. He shifted into drive and waited for her to pull out. He envisioned her taking a small sip of her hot coffee and then settling it into the cup holder. Maybe changing the station on the radio before she headed out. Buckling her seatbelt. Turning the key in the ignition. Finally, she was pulling out into traffic.

Zachary let a couple of cars pass him before pulling out, putting a cushion between them so she wouldn't spot him.

She didn't go to work, but made an unexpected turn on Main. Zachary followed, lagging behind as much as possible. He didn't know where she was going until she pulled up to the big, square, brick building. The doctor's office.

It was perfect. She would be gone for a long time. There would be no danger of her walking back out and catching him in the act. Even after she went in, he waited another ten minutes to make sure she hadn't forgotten anything in the car.

As he worked, he thought about Kenzie. She had said that she had a medical appointment. That was why she had taken the day off and met with him for lunch. Was she sick? Of course, it could just be an annual physical. Or an eye check-up or dental visit. It could be a hundred innocuous little things.

After looking around the parking lot for surveillance cameras or anyone watching, Zachary felt under the bumper of the car, looking for a good place.

He hated the thought that Kenzie could be sick. She looked well enough. Pretty and in the peak of health. But then, so had Bridget. Neither of them would have guessed that there was anything wrong. She'd had no symptoms. No weight loss or pallor. She hadn't been tired or nauseated. It was disconcerting to find that someone could be so sick without even realizing it.

There was a smooth, clean ledge under the bumper. Perfect for Zachary's purposes. He used a rag to wipe it down blindly, making sure that there was no layer of dirt and debris that would prevent a good mount.

Kenzie had said that the doctor's appointment was nothing. He was going to have to believe her on that count. There was no way to tell what was going on in her life unless he put her under surveillance too.

Zachary pulled out the small black box. He switched it on and made sure that the green LED lit. Then, resting it on his fingertips, he put his hand under the bumper again and bent his fingers to attached the tracking unit to the ledge. It clinked softly. He nudged it with his fingers, seeing if it would slide or shift. It stayed solidly in place.

He stood up and wiped his hands on the rag. He looked around again to make sure that no one had shown up who might be watching him, wondering what the hell he was up to. There was a mother with a child walking from her car into the building, but she didn't look in his direction. He wondered vaguely if she were sick. Surely there were other kinds of doctors in the professional building as well. A gynecologist or pediatrician. He hoped that neither she nor the child was seriously ill. He hoped that she simply had a routine appointment or checkup.

He went back to his car and sat down before checking the tracking app on his phone to make sure that the GPS tracker was transmitting properly. Now he would have a reliable log of every place she went.

Having taken care of the various surveillance and routine background work that had been languishing on his list, Zachary returned to the medical examiner's report. He had just about decided he was ready to close the case and give Molly his final report. He would confirm that it had, in fact, been an accident and there was no indication of any outside involvement. He hoped that, as Kenzie had suggested, Molly and the family would feel better knowing that there had been no holes in the police investigation and that everything had been properly handled and could be put to bed. Then they could lay Declan to rest. Figuratively speaking, since his remains were still dangling and swaying restlessly in Isabella's numerous necklaces and injected into her skin.

Kenzie had said everything in the blood tests had been within normal parameters, but as Zachary read every line of fine print, he could feel his brows coming down. How could anyone who had read the blood test results have come to that conclusion?

Without looking up from the report, Zachary felt for his phone. It went sliding across the table away from his fingers, and he looked up to corral it and to call Kenzie Kirsch.

There was no answer. The call went to voicemail. Zachary ground his teeth. She was probably just helping someone to fill out a form. Or maybe she was in a conference with the medical examiner. Or she had another doctor's appointment.

Thinking about doctor's appointments, he switched quickly to the GPS tracker app and found the latest tracker broadcasting its coordinates. A street map and satellite picture were layered over the latitude and longitude grid, and a quick squint at the street showed that she was back home. Zachary wondered briefly if everything was okay, or if she had gone home to cry or compose herself.

As Zachary was looking at the map, a call rang through to his phone, making him jump at the sudden vibration and the call information flashing up on the screen. He answered the call. "Kenzie, hi."

"Sorry, I was on another call. What's up?"

"Just looking at the blood test results on Declan Bond's report."

"Yes?"

"You said that everything was within normal parameters."

"That's right. No red flags."

"Then why do I see numbers beside alcohol and amphetamines? Surely there's no 'normal range' for alcohol and amphetamines in a child?"

Kenzie laughed. "If you look at the further testing done after that, you'll see that the amphetamine is actually pseudoephedrine."

"And what is pseudoephedrine?"

"It is a decongestant. You probably have it in your medicine cabinet."

"I do?"

"It's in most popular brands of cough medicine."

"Oh… he was given cough medicine?"

"Yes."

Zachary thought about this. "They put alcohol in children's cough medicines?"

"Some of them. They used to contain cocaine! Or they might have given him a smaller dose of an adult cough medicine. People don't want to run out to the drugstore in the middle of the night, so they adjust an adult dose for a child. Not recommended."

"But it wasn't the middle of the night. It was the afternoon. Can you tell how much he was given?"

"I don't think they would have worked back to an exact dosage. No need to do that. Probably just checked to make sure it was within normal parameters. There are lookup tables for that sort of thing."

Cough medicine.

Zachary thought back to the interviews with Spencer and Isabella. Neither one had mentioned Declan being sick. When Zachary had run them through the events of that final day, neither of them had mentioned Declan having a cold or a cough.

"What are you thinking?" Kenzie asked.

"I'm thinking that people give their children cough medicine to make them sleep."

"If they have a cold, yes. It's hard for a child to sleep while they're coughing their heads off or can't breathe properly. It's important for them to be able to get enough rest to get over the virus."

Zachary shook his head, even though she had no way of seeing it. "Not just when they have colds. Some parents do it every night. Or any time they want to go out on the town. Give the kids a dose of cough medicine, and they sleep right through. No danger of them waking up and making trouble while the parents are out."

"People don't do that!" Kenzie sounded shocked.

"More people than you think."

"Really?"

"Really."

"You don't have kids, though, do you?" Kenzie asked.

"No. Why?"

"I'm just wondering how you know that. Has it come up in one of your cases before?"

"No, but I was a kid once."

"And your parents gave you cough medicine to make you sleep?"

He had to smile at the outrage in her voice. "I lost my parents when I was young," he reminded her. "I was that kid who was always getting up at odd hours and getting into trouble. Or staying up all night unable to get to sleep. If I wasn't on sleep meds, more than one home gave me cough medicine."

"That's unconscionable! You don't give children cough medicine to make them sleep. That's completely wrong."

"What would a doctor have prescribed?"

There was a hesitation on the line. "Well, probably an antihistamine or Ambien."

"Have they been studied for use as sleep agents in children?"

"No," she admitted. "It's off-label, but that doesn't make it right to give kids cough medicine to make them sleep."

Zachary shrugged. "I'm not recommending it, just saying it happens. What if that's what happened to Declan?"

"He was drugged?" Kenzie asked, suddenly getting it. "He was drugged and then drowned?"

"That would take care of the bruises, wouldn't it? No need to hold him down."

"His body would still fight back, struggle, even unconscious."

"But it wouldn't be the same. He wouldn't be trying to push himself up and escape, he'd just be flailing, right?"

"I… don't know."

"And all the person drowning him would have to do was make sure his mouth and nose stayed below the surface of the water."

Kenzie swore, not answering.

"How much cough medicine would it take to knock a kid out? Would it be outside the 'normal parameters' table?"

"I don't know. I imagine it would be different for different children. Depending on age, body weight, metabolism, and the way they reacted to the ingredients. Some kids get hyper. Some fall asleep. Some don't show any particular reaction."

Zachary realized he wasn't going to be able to close the case.

Not yet.

Despite Spencer's previous request, Zachary didn't call to set up another interview. He timed his visit for when Isabella would hopefully be home from work, and he'd be able to talk to both of them. Separately, not together.

It was Spencer who answered the door again. He looked Zachary over with distaste.

"Mr. Goldman. Again?"

"I have some important questions to ask you and your wife. I found something the medical examiner's report."

Spencer blinked, his complexion turning ashen. "What do you mean, you found something? The medical examiner determined it was accidental drowning."

"It may be nothing. On the other hand, it might show *modus operandi.*"

"*Modus operandi?*" Spencer repeated. "What are you, a British detective novel? This isn't murder; this is an accident."

"We'll see," Zachary said flatly. "I'd like to talk to Isabella first. Is she in her studio?"

"Of course." Spencer didn't move out of the doorway, blocking Zachary's way.

"I'd like to go talk to her, please."

Spencer stood there for a few more seconds, considering his options. He eventually decided there was no point in slamming the door in Zachary's face, and stepped back to let him in.

"Thank you."

Of course, if Spencer had shut him out, he could have just called Isabella to get her to let him in. Or Molly. She probably had a key too.

He hadn't asked who had keys to the house or if the doors were left unlocked during the day. How many people would have had access to Declan while he was inside the house? Not that it mattered, when there was no key needed to access him while he was out playing in the yard.

If that was really what he had been doing before he disappeared. Zachary was no longer sure that was even what had happened.

What if Declan had been rendered unconscious by a dose of cough medicine, his breathing and heartbeat so depressed that they couldn't be detected? What if they took him out to the pond and left him floating face down, thinking that he was already dead?

Spencer stood there for a moment, then walked away briskly, back to his office, not offering to walk Zachary to Isabella's studio. That was not a problem; he knew the way on his own.

He stood in the doorway watching Isabella for a few minutes unobserved. She was painting, engrossed in her work. There was no blue on her canvas. Her palette was resting on a high table instead of in her hand, and her free hand ran up and down the necklaces, touching and fiddling with the pendants. She released the necklaces and brushed her fingers over the tattoo on her right forearm.

"Until we meet again, may God hold you in the palm of His hand."

Even with no one in the room with her, she was still repeating it. Spencer had suggested she could suppress the tic with an effort of will, but that it would return once she let go. And he was right.

Was it grief or was it guilt? He knew the stats. Most child homicide victims were murdered by their parents. Had her mental decline started before Declan's death, and his drowning 'accident' was only another symptom of how sick she had become? Or had he gotten in her way too often, disrupting the life that she had tried to build for herself, and she had simply had too much? Motherhood wasn't for everyone, Zachary had learned that lesson the hard way. More than once.

Or maybe it had just been a tragic accident that they—or she—had clumsily tried to cover up after the fact.

Zachary tapped on the door before he entered, alerting her to his presence. "Isabella?"

Isabella looked in his direction with a vague expression. It was a moment before she focused on him and realized who he was.

"Oh... Mr. Goldman. I didn't know we were expecting you."

"I have some new questions for you."

She shook her head, looking back at her painting again. She stroked her tattoo, and then her left hand dropped to the necklaces again as she continued to paint. "I've already answered all of your questions. I don't know what else you could possibly have to ask."

Zachary moved farther into the room. He made space on a chair and sat so that he wouldn't be looking down at her or be perceived as being confrontational. Nice and low-key. See if he could get the information out of her without her becoming defensive.

"Tell me again about the day that Declan disappeared."

"I've already told you everything. I've told the police. I've told you. It's still the same. Nothing has changed."

"There is nothing that stands out about his behavior that day before he disappeared?"

"No, nothing at all. It was just a normal day. He was playing outside; I was watching him through the window while I was painting. And then... he was just gone. He wasn't there anymore."

"How as Declan feeling that day?"

"Feeling?"

"Was he well? Happy?"

"Yes, just like normal."

"He wasn't sick?"

"No."

"He didn't have a cold?"

"No."

"Was he a pretty active child? Did he get into things a lot?"

Isabella looked away from the painting to Zachary. "No... he was a normal boy, perfectly normal. He got into things sometimes, but kids do. That's just the way they are."

"He wasn't diagnosed with ADHD? Anything like that?"

"No!" Her mouth formed a thin, straight line. There were a couple of angry lines like exclamation marks between her eyebrows. "He wasn't diagnosed with anything. He was perfectly normal. Perfectly healthy."

She acted as if Zachary had accused Declan of being a serial killer. With her own mental illness issues, was it that awful to suggest that Declan might have a diagnosis as well? ADHD diagnoses were so common; there wasn't *that* much of a stigma attached anymore. Isabella clearly did not like this line of questioning.

Perfectly normal. Perfectly healthy.

"Then why was he given cough medicine?"

"Cough medicine." Isabella stared at him. "He wasn't given cough medicine. What are you talking about?"

"When Declan died, he had cough medicine in his body. In his bloodstream. So why was he given cough medicine, if he was perfectly healthy?"

"He wasn't. I would never give him that poison. It's very bad for children."

"Do you have cough medicine in the house?"

"Of course." She fluttered a hand in the direction of the master bedroom and bath. "Everyone has cough medicine."

"But you didn't have anything for Declan? What would you do if he got sick? Surely you'd give him a decongestant if he was having trouble sleeping."

"No." Her voice was firm. "I wouldn't. There's no proof that any of those medicines are good for children. They've only been tested on adults, and then the results extrapolated. Children's bodies don't work the same way as adults' bodies. You can never be sure what effect they will have."

"You've never given cough medicine to Declan?"

She shook her head. "When he was younger... I don't know, two or three, he had a bad cold, and I gave him some baby cold medicine. Not the liquid, one of those instant dissolve tablets. I didn't know how bad they could be for children, but the way he reacted to it... he was practically comatose for the next few hours. I never gave him cold medicine again."

Zachary's heart sped. "Do you know what kind of medicine it was? What was in it?"

"No... I don't remember. I don't know what brand it was or what the active ingredients were. I've never used one again."

"Would you still have the package around somewhere? It was only a year or two ago; people keep medications around for much longer than that."

"You can check. It would be in the medicine cabinet, down the hall."

Zachary sped out of the room and looked both ways down the hallway, paranoid that Spencer might have been listening at the door and might reach the bathroom to destroy the evidence ahead of him. But there was no sign of Spencer. Zachary found the bathroom and opened the medicine cabinet. He had known before he had a chance to itemize the contents that the children's medicine would not be there. The bathroom, including the cabinet, was pristine. Nothing leaking or out of date. The bottles and sundries in the cabinet stood in rigid rows, equidistant apart. He checked each label anyway. There was, as Isabella had indicated, adult cough medicine. None of the children's cold tablets that she had referred to. She had probably said that she was never going to use them again, and Spencer had taken her at her word and thrown them out.

Zachary took out the cough medicine, wondering even as he took it out if he should have put on gloves first. Surely the police had looked at it already when they determined Declan had cough medicine in his system.

Zachary tried to keep his fingers to the edges where they wouldn't smear any other fingerprints anyway and checked the ingredients.

Pseudoephedrine was listed under the active ingredients and alcohol in the inactive ingredients.

Had Declan been given cough medicine from that bottle? Or had someone else, a third party, given him cough medicine to keep him quiet and compliant? Maybe panicking when he became 'almost comatose.' Certainly, using cough medicine to sedate a child was a widely-known practice, as Zachary himself could attest.

He set the bottle down on the sink and took pictures of the brand name on the front and the ingredients on the back. He put it back in the medicine cabinet where he had gotten it and took another picture. Just in case it happened to disappear before he could get the police to look at it.

If the police looked at it.

Zachary returned to the studio, where Isabella was still painting, running her fingers over the memorial objects, and whispering her never-ending prayer.

"You're right," he told her. "There is a bottle of cough medicine in the cabinet, but not the medicine you gave to Declan when he was younger."

She gave a little shrug of unconcern. "I don't know what would make you think we would give him that. There's no way I would let anyone give Deck cough medicine."

"Maybe he wasn't feeling well, and Spencer gave him cough medicine," Zachary suggested.

"He wasn't sick. I told you that. Spencer knows I wouldn't let him give Declan cough medicine. He would never have done that."

"Maybe he thought he'd just give it a try. Just to see if it would help. He never expressed any concerns to you?"

"No. He didn't say anything was wrong or that he had given Deck medicine. Declan was happy and playing. If he'd had that stuff, he would have been asleep. He wouldn't have been able to walk around. He wouldn't have been playing." When Zachary opened his mouth, she rushed to fill the space. "I was watching him. I would have known if he had been drugged."

"But you weren't watching him the whole time. You were only checking occasionally to make sure he was okay."

"I was watching. I never looked away for long."

"How long? Five minutes?"

She shook her head in irritation. "No, I don't think it was that long. Two or three. I was keeping track of him."

"But then you couldn't see him anymore."

"I know that."

"And you didn't go out the first time you looked and couldn't see him. You waited to see if he came back into view again."

"Only for a few minutes."

Zachary knew how that was. If she said she hadn't seen him for five minutes, it was probably at least ten. From what he'd seen, she got pretty wrapped up in her work, and she could have gone half an hour without thinking any time had passed. It was only five minutes at the most to get from the back yard to the pond. It only took two or three minutes for a child to drown. In fifteen minutes, either of them could have done the deed, without the other realizing they'd been out of the house.

"Could Spencer have left the house without you realizing it?"

Isabella looked away from her painting and studied him, looking confused. "Of course not, he was here the whole afternoon. I don't understand why you're asking that."

"He could have left for five minutes without you noticing, just like Declan could wander off for five minutes. You weren't watching Spencer."

"No... but I was watching his coat."

"What do you mean, you were watching his coat?"

Isabella laughed at Zachary's consternation. "I wasn't painting in here. I was in the bedroom."

"Right. We established that."

"And I was standing in front of the closet. Just a few feet away from Spencer's coat. It was right there in front of my eyes. He wouldn't leave the house without it."

"He could have."

"No! It was a cool day. Spencer would never have left the house without it. He's *very* rigid about it."

OCD as an alibi?

"Do you know what Spencer was doing during that time? Is there any way we can check his alibi?"

"His computer," Isabella said vaguely. "I imagine he left a digital trail somewhere."

"And what about you? Is there any way we can verify that you were in the bedroom like you say you were?"

"Where would I go? I was painting. Watching Deck. I couldn't go anywhere."

"Would Spencer have known if you left the house?"

"You will have to ask him," Isabella snapped. "He has a view of the back yard too. We both had a view of the back yard, and neither of us saw anything."

"You alibi each other."

"Unless you think that we both colluded to murder our son, that's going to have to be good enough for you."

Could they have conspired to kill their son? Zachary couldn't see it, no matter how he tried to mold the picture in his mind. While they were not demonstrative, he believed they loved Declan. One of them could have hurt him in a moment of anger or frustration, or by accident, but he didn't see how either of them could have hurt him intentionally.

And that meant he was back at the beginning again. To a mysterious stranger coming into the yard, or up to the gate, luring Declan out, drugging him with cough syrup, and then abandoning his body in the pond. If the time of death was five o'clock, they would only have had, at most, an hour with the boy. It didn't make any sense.

There was a knock at the studio door. Zachary and Isabella looked up. Spencer hovered in the doorway. He held a cordless phone toward Isabella.

"It's Melissa Raymond," he explained. "I thought you would like to talk to her... set something up, maybe?"

Isabella looked at him for a moment, not excited by the suggestion. Eventually, she laid aside her paintbrush and walked to the door of the studio to take the phone from him.

"You're done here?" Spencer asked, looking at Zachary. "Give them some privacy to talk."

Zachary conceded, leaving the studio so that Isabella could talk privately with her friend. Spencer led him back toward the front door.

"Melissa will be good for her," he said. "She always used to be able to draw Isabella out before. She needs someone to talk with. Someone who isn't a cop or a therapist or a private investigator." He considered. "Or her husband."

Zachary glanced sideways at him. "Marriage isn't for cowards."

"You're right about that," Spencer agreed fervently. "You're married?"

"Divorced."

"Sorry."

Zachary nodded. "Yours has lasted longer than mine did. I hope things improve."

"Neither of us is good with change; we'll avoid it as long as we can."

At the door, Zachary offered his hand. "Thanks for your help. One thing before I leave. Did you give Declan cough medicine? That last day?"

Spencer raised his brows. He pursed his lips and shook his head. "No. He wasn't sick, and I know how Isabella would feel about that."

"When Declan was playing in the back yard, did Isabella leave the house?"

Spencer scowled as he shook his head. "No, I can't imagine she would."

"I'm not asking if she *would*. I'm asking if she *did*. Was there any time that you might have heard or seen her leave? Or when you were away from the windows and wouldn't have seen her leave?"

"But why would she do that?"

"Could she have?"

"No... maybe when I was in the kitchen, but then she would have had to sneak out the front door instead of the back. Or when I was in the bathroom; but I'm sure she was here the whole time. Neither of us left the house. Just Declan."

"How long was Declan playing outside before Isabella said he was missing?"

"An hour... maybe an hour and twenty...?"

"And in your experience... how closely did she supervise him? How often would she have looked out at him?"

"I've never sat down and timed the intervals. I don't know how you could expect me to know. I suppose it depends on how involved she is with her painting."

"And does she tend to get distracted and lost in her work?"

Spencer's hand was on the door, eager for Zachary to be gone. Wanting just to shut the door and be done with him.

"I don't know."

"You don't know if she gets distracted by what she's doing? So involved that she isn't paying attention to what's going on around her?"

"I suppose she does. Anyone does."

"Has there been any time when Declan has gotten hurt or upset while he was in the back yard and Isabella was supposed to be supervising him? Or another time when he was her responsibility, and you got angry at her for not watching him closely enough?"

Spencer's face got red. "I don't appreciate your implications. Declan's death is not Isabella's fault."

"I didn't say it was. I'm trying to establish how long it was between the last time Isabella checked on him and the time that he died. What is the longest possible length of time he could have been missing from your yard?"

"It's impossible to know that."

"Unless you know what time it was that Isabella checked on him last, or have a pretty good guess. Did she look in on him every five minutes? Every ten? Every half hour? Maybe she only checked when he came near the window, or she heard him crying."

Zachary stared at Spencer, waiting for his answer. Spencer was a man who liked an ordered, predictable experience. He must have had certain expectations of his wife, and must have known when she broke what he considered to be the house rules. If she didn't do a good job supervising Declan or she left the house unexpectedly, he would have had some idea.

Spencer wiped his hand down his face in a tired gesture.

"I can't tell you how often she checked on him or how long he was missing from the yard. I know she was in the house and I know that she was supervising Declan playing outside. That's all I can tell you."

Zachary stared into Spencer's face, looking for any sign of deception. He nodded. "Okay. Thanks for your help. Good luck."

He had started to turn away to leave when Spencer's voice recalled him.

"Zachary…?"

"Yes?"

"Your investigation… it will be done soon? It's causing a lot of stress on the family."

"I'll do my best."

9

Looking down at his phone, Zachary realized that he had a voicemail message. Swiping over to the screen, he saw a message had been left by 'unknown caller.' Probably a telemarketer, but some of his legitimate contacts had blocked caller IDs as well. The police department, for one. He tapped the message and held the phone to his ear.

You've been warned to drop the case. This is your last warning.

He pulled the phone back away from his ear and stared at it. A voice changer had been used, which made the voice of the caller impossible to recognize. Which, of course, meant that if he were to hear the caller's voice unaltered, he would have recognized it. Zachary closed his eyes, drumming his fingers on his steering wheel and considering.

The Antonelli insurance fraud case was rumored to involve the mob, but he suspected that any threat that came to him from organized crime would have more finesse, and they would leave no doubt as to which case it was they wanted him to drop. He had a couple of infidelity cases that he hadn't reported on yet, but he had most of the information he needed to finish them off, so there wasn't any point in dropping those cases. The Senator's background checks weren't likely to cause him any trouble. They were all routine, and none of the subjects had any reason to threaten him.

It bothered him that there was no real threat. His 'last warning' was not even a legitimate warning. There was a possibility that the warnings were about the Declan Bond case. It was the kind of case that made people emotional. The police or medical examiner might not like him reinvestigating the case. Isabella and Spencer were tired of his questions, and maybe one of them just wanted him off the case. Or Halloran, worried that word would leak out that his star was being investigated. Even Molly, afraid that the expenses were adding up, but too timid to call him off.

Zachary's address and phone number weren't that hard to find. Everyone had his phone number. His home address was more difficult to find, but only slightly. He wasn't a big name. He wasn't like the private detectives on TV, solving a murder a week. He was a nobody, and there was no need to hide from the public or discontented clients or police. He received threats from time to time. The one on his door had been a little disturbing. He tried to tell himself it was nothing, but whoever had left it wanted him to know that they could reach him. They knew where he lived. That was the message.

He didn't delete the voicemail. If the caller did escalate from half-threats to action, Zachary might need something that the police could trace.

Kenzie had come to Zachary's apartment when he called her, but she seemed cautious and reserved. She didn't have her usual bright eyes and quick smile. They sat in the living room, and he told her about the latest developments in the Bond case, the responses from Isabella and Spencer to his questions on whether either of them had given him cough medicine, and exactly how long he might have been missing from the yard before his death. Kenzie didn't seem to be as interested in the case as she had previously. She stared away from him, her brows down slightly.

"Maybe it's time to let it go," she said finally. "You're not getting anywhere with it. There's no indication that there was foul play involved. So why not let it go? Tell them you've looked into everything you can, and everything seems to be kosher. No need to pursue it any further."

"Not now, when I finally have some actual evidence that there might have been foul play!"

"You haven't found anything new. Nothing that the police haven't already investigated."

"It might not be enough to make any arrests, but I think it's enough for them to investigate it further. The boy was afraid of water. He wouldn't have walked into the pond to drown. He had cough medicine in his system when his parents deny having given him any. He has a previous history of being knocked out by a single dose of cold medicine. Don't you think those things add up to suspicion of foul play?"

"It's nothing *new*. The police knew all that and closed their file. They believe that he did walk or fall into the pond. They already know there was cough medicine in his system. It's in the medical examiner's report."

"You don't think I should bring my suspicions to anybody. I should just tell the family that I agree it was an accident and let it go."

She looked at him steadily. "Yes, because that's what happened. Look, Zachary... you're going to have unanswered questions in any case, right? There are always going to be a few things that just don't fit. That's what happens when we try to reconstruct every detail of a person's life. People are variable creatures, and we can never predict everything. If you look at any death, trying to pull apart every single detail, you can convince yourself that there was foul play, or a conspiracy, or something malevolent. Just because you're looking for it. There will always be clues that don't fit anywhere because they're not really clues. They're just random bits of information. It's never going to fit like a lock and key. Real life isn't *Murder She Wrote*."

Zachary listened to her as he poured some munchie mix out of a box into a bowl and placed it on the coffee table between them. They each had a cold can of beer, but Kenzie hadn't yet touched hers. He shook his head.

"Why don't you want me to continue with the case?"

"Me? I don't care. You can waste your time if that's what you want to do. I thought you wanted my advice as to what to do next." She sat back, moving a couple of inches farther from him and keeping her back straight instead of relaxing into the couch. "And that's my advice. Wrap it up and tell them you're done."

"Is Dr. Wiltshire upset that I'm reviewing the case? Is that what this is about?"

"Dr. Wiltshire couldn't care less if you're looking over his report. It's not like he has anything to hide. He's always very conscientious in his investigations and reports."

"And you just think I should give up and let it go."

She gave a little shrug. "Yes."

He wasn't sure she was telling him the full truth, but he wasn't going to get it out of her with direct questioning. Maybe they'd get around to it from another direction. Zachary picked a pretzel out of the mix and popped it into his mouth.

"So how was your doctor appointment the other day?"

Her eyes widened a little bit. "My doctor...? How did you know about that?"

"You mentioned it to me when we set up lunch. You said you had a medical appointment to get to in the afternoon. I just wondered how it went."

"It isn't any of your business, is it?" She bristled at his intrusion. "That's private."

"Okay..." Zachary held up his hands defensively. "I didn't mean to overstep my bounds. I'm sorry. It's just that with my wife's history—my ex-wife's history—I get worried. Things can come out of the blue... serious things."

Kenzie popped the top of her beer and took a little sip, looking at him. "What happened between the two of you?"

He shifted uncomfortably, not so happy with having personal questions thrown back his way. He tried to avoid it.

"You know how it is between married couples."

"I know something happened that left the two of you pretty bitter."

Zachary nodded.

"Mario Bowman, he said that the two of you were lovebirds, very close, like you had the best relationship in the world. Then everything fell apart. He wouldn't give me any details. Or maybe he didn't know them. Either way, he protected your privacy. I just can't help wondering... what it was that left the two of you both so hurt and bitter."

Zachary swallowed. "It's private," he said. "It's not just my privacy... it's more about Bridget's. She's the one... with the most to lose."

As if on cue, Zachary's phone started to ring. They both looked down at the display on the coffee table between them and saw her name. Bridget.

"How did she know we were talking about her?" Kenzie said in a stage whisper. She covered her mouth, giggling, while Zachary picked up the phone. He didn't laugh. If Bridget was calling him, it was serious. Despite his efforts to move on, he wanted to be there for Bridget if she needed him. He answered the call.

"Bridget? What is it?"

"You just shut up," she snapped. "I didn't call to hear your excuses."

Zachary closed his mouth. He looked over at Kenzie, who could obviously hear Bridget's strident voice, in spite of his attempt to turn down the volume of the call.

"You've been following me!" Bridget accused. "What a low-down, creepy thing to do!" He tried to respond, but she cut him off mercilessly. "I told you not to talk. You stop stalking me, or I'm going to take out a restraining order! I'll get your butt thrown in jail! This is the most despicable thing—if I see your car near me again, I don't care what your excuse is, I am going to have you slammed in jail so fast you won't know what happened. Understand?"

Zachary didn't say anything.

Bridget's voice had risen to a screech. "I said, do you understand?"

"Am I allowed to talk now?"

"Don't get smart with me, you jerk! You stay the hell away from me, you understand? I don't want to see your car in my rear-view mirror! I don't want to see you at any of the restaurants we went to together. I don't want to see or hear about you anywhere I go! You got it?"

Zachary tried to answer, but she hung up. He pulled the phone away from his ear and looked at the screen to confirm that she had terminated the call.

Zachary looked back at Kenzie, his face hot. "You still don't think she hates me?"

She shifted uncomfortably. "No, I don't, but... what's up with that? *Have* you been following her?"

"You're the one who suggested *It's a Wrap*," Zachary reminded her.

"And you're the one who didn't object and say that you didn't want to run into your ex there. You didn't answer my question. *Are* you following her?"

"It's a small world. We still have friends in common. We both still live in town. We're going to run into each other."

She stared at him, waiting for a straight answer. Zachary struggled to come up with something she would understand.

"That's not how it is."

She used silence as a weapon. Zachary shifted and picked a few M&Ms out of the snack mix. He chewed on his lip.

"I might have... driven past her house a time or two, making sure she was okay. Or I might have seen her car downtown. I miss her." He shook his head and blinked to prevent tears from forming in his hot, prickling eyes. "I loved her very much. The break-up was such a shock. It was so traumatic."

"What happened?"

He tried to think of how to tell it without getting cut up over it all over again. The silence gathered around them.

"She was pregnant," he said finally.

Kenzie nodded slowly. "And you weren't ready for a baby?"

"I *was*. I was over the moon about it, but she didn't want it. We were using birth control. She didn't want a baby. I wanted a family of my own, but she... she wouldn't budge."

"That's tough," Kenzie sympathized.

"Yeah. That was the beginning. She said I didn't have any right to dictate... that I had no rights over the pregnancy... over her... It was her body, her choice..."

"And legally, she's right."

"But we were in a relationship. That kind of thing... it's supposed to be something you decide together. You talk about it. You come to some kind of decision together. It was my baby too."

Kenzie just nodded. Her dark eyes were intense, drinking him in. Zachary's heart pounded painfully in his chest as if it were happening all over again.

"She decided it didn't matter what I wanted. She was going to get an abortion. As soon as possible."

Kenzie continued to watch him. Zachary popped another pretzel in his mouth, but it was as dry as chalk. He couldn't even taste it, and it turned to glue in his mouth. With difficulty, he washed it down with a large amount of beer.

"The doctor said that the good news was, she wasn't pregnant. It was one of those point-one percent of cases where the pregnancy test was wrong. A false positive."

Kenzie gave a little intake of breath that Zachary knew meant that with her medical background, she had an idea what was coming next.

"The bad news was that she had cancer. An HCG-producing tumor in her ovary. That was what triggered the false positive on the pregnancy test."

They both sat in silence.

"So that's it," Zachary said finally. "There was no pregnancy. No baby.

No need for an abortion. Instead, she had to have the ovary removed, and chemotherapy."

"And a big elephant in the room."

"Oh, we talked about it," Zachary said. "We talked about it constantly. How I wasn't ready to be a father but thought I was. How she was the responsible one, the one who had to make the hard choices. How she would kill a baby to avoid responsibility. How I was trying to make her feel guilty while she was going through chemotherapy and should only be having positive thoughts. I tried to help her through her treatments, but she didn't even want me in the room. She didn't want anything to do with me."

He sat there in silence.

"What a mess," Kenzie said finally. "I understand what you mean about it being a traumatic break-up."

Zachary nodded. Sweat dribbled down his back. He tried to wash away the lump in his throat with a few more swallows of beer.

"But you have to move on," Kenzie said. "You can't be hanging around her house or following her around. She's right; that is creepy. You could end up in jail if you keep it up."

"I know."

"Then stop it."

He didn't tell her that it wasn't that easy. Not for him. It was so hard for him to maintain a relationship in the first place; letting go of what had been a successful one was more than he could handle.

10

The evening with Kenzie had ended unsatisfactorily. As much as they had tried to move on to more natural topics, neither one could seem to maintain a conversation that didn't lead either to the Bond case or Zachary's relationship with Bridget. They turned on a movie on the TV and cuddled on the couch, but in the end, neither could focus on the show, and they didn't even finish it. Kenzie looked at her watch and announced the need to go home, and Zachary didn't have the energy to argue with her about it. She tried to brush him off at the door, but he walked her down to her car like a gentleman, patting the top of her trunk.

"Sweet ride."

She patted the little red sports car. "It's my one indulgence," she said with a laugh. She bent closer to give him a quick peck on the cheek, but was turned around and sliding into the vehicle before he could reciprocate.

Without making any plans to get together again, or even so much as a 'see you later,' she shut the door and pulled away. Zachary watched the car until it drove out of sight, then made his way up to his apartment.

One of the good things about being a private detective was that on nights he knew he wouldn't be able to sleep, he could work. There was always some surveillance that he could do, following a straying spouse, or else he could stay in and run backgrounds and do other computer work.

He was too restless to sit at the computer, so he donned dark clothing, grabbed his cameras, and headed out. He had a new case, an executive who believed that his wife, a high school principal, was out fooling around when she claimed to be out with her girl friends or working late.

Zachary had her cell phone number, to which he'd previously texted a video file. The video file had a GPS app embedded in it, and provided she was curious enough to see what video an anonymous sender had texted her; he would be able to pinpoint her exact location. He opened the tracker app on his phone and noted the locations of his most recent targets. He noted with satisfaction that the principal now showed up as a virtual pin on the satellite map. A zoom-in suggested she was probably in Rancheros, a rowdy cowboy bar, rather than stuck at her desk grading papers or doing whatever it was principals did.

Once at the bar, he scanned the faces of the patrons, looking for her. He had a good head for faces and didn't need to pull up her picture on his phone to refresh his memory. The bar was busy, the lighting dim with strobing dance lights, and had some private booths that it wasn't easy to see into unless a person were right beside them. He worked his way around the dining area and eventually spotted her at a booth, sitting across from a younger woman, a heavily made-up brunette.

The principal was a blond. Not with bright, shining locks like Bridget's pre-chemo hair, but a dirty blond with short, messy curls. She was comfortably overweight, with the middle-age spread of many fifty-year-old women. Zachary looked for somewhere he could sit to observe them unobtrusively. He found a booth that hadn't yet been cleared of its dirty dishes and sat down, pushing them aside and pretending to be intently interested in something on his phone. He didn't look at the two women. If they glanced at him, they would see nothing but a man occupied with his phone, like any other man who was waiting for his date, or whose wife had abandoned him to go to the bathroom.

"Uh..." a skimpily-clad cowboy waitress hovered over Zachary. "I'm sorry, this table isn't ready yet, maybe I could..."

"It's fine," Zachary said, "just clear it. I'm waiting for a friend, and she wanted somewhere... private. This is perfect. Thanks."

"But..." She stood there for a minute, then shrugged. "All right. If that's what you want."

She cleared away the dishes. "I'll be back to wipe the table down in two shakes."

"Thank you. Much appreciated."

She gave him a nod and a strained smile and took the dishes back toward the kitchen.

Zachary snuck a glance at the ladies at the other table. The younger one was looking his way, and he tried a friendly smile and raised eyebrow. She looked quickly away from him and back at her friend, Principal Montgomery.

Zachary again pretended to be busy with his phone, watching them covertly. He tried to pick up on their vibes. Two coworkers out for an after-work drink? An assignation? Parent-teacher conference?

The dim lights made it difficult to make out more than general features, but a couple of times, dance lights flashed over the ladies' faces. Zachary frowned, studying the second woman's features.

She was young. Younger than he had first thought. Certainly, not the parent of a student. Maybe a student teacher or office aide. Or a therapist who came in to work with the students. He had seen baby-faced professionals before.

Teachers who could almost be mistaken for their students.

The girl's makeup was heavy and had contributed to the impression that she was older. Which was, he assumed, the reason she was wearing it. She was trying to hide the fact that she wasn't old enough to be in the bar, even if it was just soda in her tall glass.

Rather that pull out his full-size camera, Zachary brought up the low-light photography app on his phone. He braced his elbows on the table to minimize any camera shake, and aimed his camera lens at the two ladies, with their heads close together. He looked around casually, keeping his body language relaxed, so it only looked like he was reading or looking something up on his phone instead of taking a picture. He snapped several stills, and then a short video of the two women. While he had the video running, the younger woman reached across the table and held the principal's hand.

Bingo!

The waitress returned, wiped down the table, and pulled out her order pad. "What can I getcha? Or are you waiting for your friend?"

"How about two coffees, to start?" he suggested.

Her face relaxed a bit, and she nodded. "Sure. Nothing else? Desserts? Drinks?"

"We might have to get one of those hot fudge brownie deals. I'll wait and make sure the lady approves first, because I don't want to eat it alone."

She flashed him a genuine smile. "That may or may not be a good idea. No self-respecting woman would order such a high-calorie treat. You know, everyone's on a diet, but if someone happened to order one before she had a chance to say no..."

"Ah," Zachary nodded agreeably, "then why don't you bring me one, and we'll see if I can get her to share it?"

She wrote it down on her order form. "Anything else?"

Zachary leaned forward. "This is a sort of unusual question. I don't usually do things like this..."

"What?" Her eyes narrowed, but she continued to smile pleasantly.

"Don't turn around too fast, but the two ladies at the table behind you. Are you sure they're both legal?"

Her smile dimmed. She obeyed his advice and didn't whirl around to stare. She looked over her shoulder toward the dance floor, scoping the two women out peripherally without being obvious about it.

She swore and looked back at Zachary. "The brunette, right? Doesn't look a day over seventeen." She sighed and shook her head. "I don't know how they let her in without carding her. I'll have the manager come over and check them out. Thanks for letting me know."

He nodded. She walked back away. Zachary continued to watch the couple, a knot of anger growing in his stomach. The waitress returned with his coffees and a brownie with two forks and placed them down without a word. It was some time before the manager came over to talk to the two ladies. Zachary had taken several pictures in the interim, as the two became decidedly more cozy.

The manager, dressed in worn blue jeans and a big cowboy hat, leaned over the table to talk to them, his voice too low for Zachary to catch his words. There were exaggerated movements from the two women, feigning shock and amusement at his questions. He was firm, insisting on proof that the younger woman was legal drinking age. Eventually, they both rose, expressing their outrage, and stormed out of the bar. Zachary watched them go, wondering if he should follow them and pursue the matter further. The manager watched to make sure that they left. He noticed that Zachary was watching them too.

"You're the one who pointed them out to the wait staff?" he asked Zachary.

"Yes. I don't normally go out of my way to ruin someone's date, but…"

The other man scratched his two-day-old whiskers and shook his head. "Can't be allowing underage drinkers in here or we'll get shut down. I appreciate you pointing them out." His eyes went over Zachary's coffee mugs, one full and one empty, and the half-eaten brownie. "Please don't worry about the bill, we'll pick it up."

"Oh, you don't need to do that." Zachary would bill it to the client anyway. "They left without paying theirs, didn't they?"

"Yep."

"Then let me pay mine and tip the waitress."

The cowboy shrugged at him. "If you insist. Again, thanks for helping us out."

After the manager had again withdrawn, the waitress came back to see if Zachary needed anything. "I guess they couldn't prove she was of age," she observed.

"No, I guess not. She didn't bother trying to show a fake ID, at least."

"Can I get you anything else?"

"Just the bill, if you could."

"Sure." Her eyes went to the remains of his dessert. "Your friend never showed up?"

"She had an emergency." Zachary gave an exaggerated shrug. "What can you do?"

"Sorry about that."

"It's fine. Next time."

"Okay. I'll bring you your bill."

After he had settled up, Zachary went out to his car. He sat there with his guts in a knot, trying to decide what to do. He pulled up his tracker to see where Principal Montgomery had gone after leaving the bar. Her phone showed her at a shopping center, which eased his anxiety. Maybe they were going to look at clothes. Try on shoes.

Still, he went to the police station and approached the duty officer. He was pleasantly surprised to see that it was Joshua Campbell, who was normally too high-ranking to do desk duty, but must have had to fill in for a sick officer until they could find someone else to do the job. That meant that Zachary at least didn't have to introduce himself and explain why he would be following someone around and taking pictures.

Joshua finished dealing with the gray-haired lady in front of Zachary. It was a quiet night. Still early, the crazies not yet out. Joshua motioned Zachary forward, giving him a big grin.

"Zach, my friend! What brings you by today? Somebody key your car? Run you off the road?"

He hadn't been run off the road before, but he'd certainly been keyed or had a window smashed. People tended not to like it when he pried into their private lives.

"No, not this time," he said. He hesitated about how to approach the issue.

Joshua raised an eyebrow and waited.

"Normally when misbehavior comes across my radar, it just gets reported to the client, and then it's up to them whether they are going to report a crime or not."

"Yeah. Normally."

"But in cases that involve minors…"

Joshua's smile quickly disappeared. "You got an abuse or neglect case to report?"

"Something like that." Zachary placed his phone on the counter between them and opened his photo app. He swiped through a few pictures and found the one that showed the minor's face most clearly. "This girl. They were at Rancheros. I had management card them, and she wouldn't show any ID. The two of them took off in a huff."

"Could be something. Do you know the identity of either one?"

"The older woman is Principal Dana Montgomery."

Joshua's eyes snapped up to Zachary's face. "Principal?"

"She's a high school principal."

Joshua swore. "Tell me they just like the food at Rancheros."

Zachary flipped to further photos. Joshua looked ready to leap over the desk and go after the woman on foot all by himself.

"You didn't follow them when they left the bar? Any way of knowing where they went?"

"They did go over to the shopping center." Zachary picked up his phone and held it so that Joshua could no longer see the screen. "You won't ask how I know, right?"

"No. You tell me where they are and I'll send someone over there to have a word."

Zachary looked down at the map to make sure they were still at the shopping center, looking at shoes or lip gloss. But the pin had moved in the time that it had taken him to get to the police station and to make his report. He swore and looked at Joshua, feeling sick.

"Motel."

Joshua echoed his sentiment. He clicked on a handheld radio and started giving directions. When he paused for the name and address of the motel, Zachary turned the phone around for him to see.

"I'll get a picture of the two of them to your phone," Joshua told the officer who had answered his call.

He looked at Zachary after clicking off. "Email all the pictures to me," he instructed. He gave the duty officer email address, and Zachary got to work on it.

"I'll have to batch them; it won't send that many at once. And there are two videos."

"Great. Get me the best facial pictures first so that I can distribute them, and then send me the rest."

Zachary nodded.

Joshua was going through the forms under his counter, rattling papers. "I'll need to get your signed statement on what went on over at the bar. Did you get any other names? The manager's?"

"No... some guy dressed as a cowboy."

"Don't they all dress as cowboys over there?"

"I imagine so."

Joshua rolled his eyes. "Then that's not exactly helpful, is it? I'll send some officers over there to find out what they can before anyone finishes their shifts."

He shoved a stack of forms at Zachary. "If you want to move down the counter here while you fill those out, I'd better deal with some of these people waiting behind you. Okay?"

Zachary did as he was told, filling the forms out in his neatest printing, trying to make sure that he got all the pertinent details. It took a good length of time to go through all of them. He sidled closer to Joshua as he finished up with another citizen.

"Done?"

"Here you go."

"Everything signed?" Joshua thumbed through them to make sure that Zachary had signed in all of the appropriate places. He picked up his radio again and made an inquiry. Zachary couldn't make out the staticky response and code talk and waited for Joshua to fill him in.

"They got her," Joshua said with a satisfied nod. "The two of them together in the hotel room, just getting friendly."

Zachary sighed. Things didn't usually move so quickly. He felt like he had run a race when all he'd done was stand at the counter.

"And she is one of the students at Montgomery's school," Joshua informed him.

"I can't believe it. How did she think she was going to get away with it?"

"In my experience, we never catch them the first time. They've always gotten away with it before. Sometimes dozens of times. Predators don't just hunt once."

"Well... thank you for getting right on it. I feel like I did something good today."

Joshua offered a handshake, and they clasped tightly. "You *did* do something good today. That girl's parents are going to be indebted to you." He released Zachary's hand. "Who was your client? Montgomery's husband?"

"I can't discuss private client matters with you... but that would be a good guess."

"Take care, my friend. You should sleep well tonight. The sleep of the just."

Zachary could only wish.

His eyes were puffy and bloodshot in the morning, and it wasn't because of a couple of beers with Kenzie. Far from being able to sleep soundly because he had done something good, Zachary hadn't even been able to lie down to try to sleep. He was too wired. His head whirled with anxiety over how many other students Montgomery had preyed upon, what he was going to tell Mr. Montgomery about his wife's activities, and how he was going to explain going to the police with the information.

But he'd had to. He couldn't stand by while a minor was in danger. He might not be a mandatory reporter, but he couldn't ignore it and leave it up to the client, who might be too embarrassed to do anything.

In the small hours of the morning, he had gone through as much of his busy work as he could, preparing final reports and invoices, finalizing the Senatorial background checks, and for a while just browsing through the various Facebook accounts he was keeping track of. Socially acceptable cyberstalking.

He was just trying to rev his engine with a second cup of coffee when the phone rang. Looking at the screen, Zachary saw that it was Isabella. The idea that she would have any reason to call him made him feel unaccountably worried. She hadn't exactly approved of Molly hiring him in the first place. She had answered questions but hadn't been particularly cooperative. Had something happened? Maybe to Molly or Spencer? He was pretty sure she wouldn't be calling him to tell him she had remembered something new from Declan's last day. Or maybe that she'd found the box of cold pills so he could see what their active ingredients were.

Zachary swallowed hard and answered the call. "Goldman Investigations."

"Is this Zachary?"

"Yes. Isabella. Hi. What can I help you with?"

"It's nothing, really. Nothing that will be of any help to your case. I just thought… I wanted someone to share it with."

Zachary breathed slowly and evenly, wishing it would calm the wild pounding of his heart.

"Sure. What is it?"

"Mittens. He came back."

"What?" Zachary couldn't find the words.

"Mittens. My cat. Remember I told you about him? Well, the cat came back."

"Your cat… that disappeared eight years ago."

"Yes, that's right."

"He came back."

"Yes." She sounded pleased; happy and relaxed like she hadn't ever sounded before. "The cat came back."

"Are you sure it's the same cat?" Zachary demanded, unable to wrap his mind around it. A cat disappears for eight years and then comes back? Was she imagining that a stray she saw was her old cat, Mittens? Maybe she'd even tempted one into the house with a bowl of kibble?

"Of course, do you think I wouldn't know my own cat? He came to the door. He was yowling and scratching to get in. When I let him in, he went straight for his bowl." For eight years, she had emptied and refilled that bowl, and she sounded triumphant. Nobody had believed the cat would ever return, but she had continued to feed it, and she had been right.

"That's pretty amazing. What did... what did your husband have to say about it? He *saw* the cat?"

"What, do you think it's my imagination? Am I that deranged?"

She could be. Zachary didn't know. Maybe she had finally snapped and gone over the edge. Having lost too much, she had decided to resurrect her old pet. She did sound manic.

"Of course, Spencer saw it. He was surprised. But it's Mittens. He knows it's Mittens." Isabella's voice dropped to a conspiratorial tone. "Spencer doesn't exactly like cats. They shed, you know, and their litter tracks. It's just so amazing. I'm so happy. And I think... it must be a good omen for the case. I think that since Mittens came back, that must mean... that you are going to find something in Declan's case. You're going to figure it all out."

"Yes," Zachary agreed. "Maybe I will."

Zachary had called Kenzie several times, but she wasn't returning his calls. He took a quick look at her social networks to confirm that she was not sick or out of town, but she was posting the same type of stuff as usual. He gave her a couple of days. If she had been put off by Bridget's call, she would need a couple of days to cool off. She'd found out a lot about him all at once, and she was apparently the type who needed to think about it for a while before she felt comfortable talking to him again.

It was a painful couple of days. He also called Molly and told her that he would be preparing his final report shortly, wishing that he could have uncovered something new like Isabella had suggested.

"What did you find?" Molly demanded.

"That will all be in my report."

"But you can tell me what you found. Tell me whether you found anything to indicate that it wasn't just an accident. I'll wait for your report, but you can tell me that, can't you?"

"I... I really can't. My investigation was... inconclusive. I didn't uncover anything that the police didn't already know, but there were a few facts that... I think could lead in other directions."

"So, there was someone else involved? Someone took him?"

Zachary didn't like being forced into a corner, especially before he had a chance to write his report. Once he laid it all out in a report, he could just reference the appropriate paragraphs and say, 'it's all there.' He didn't ad lib well.

"It's possible, but I didn't find anything that could be used to persuade the police to look into it further. I don't know what help that is."

"But at least... we would know. Maybe something would come up later on down the line that would let us pursue it. For now... at least we'd know that it wasn't just... negligence."

The way that she said the word made Zachary flash back to his own childhood. Missed meals, ratty clothes that didn't fit, absent caregivers, institutions with thin, hard mattresses and exploitative staff. He held tightly to his phone, and breathed in the smell of stale coffee, trying to ground himself in the present. Declan hadn't been neglected. He'd had two parents who loved and cared for him. He'd been well-fed and clothed. They might not have been perfect, but they were there for him.

The way Molly said it made him wonder what had happened in her past. Had she been the neglected child? Or was she the negligent parent? Or both? Did she hire Zachary because she wanted to assuage her own guilt rather than Isabella's? Maybe she needed to believe that she had raised Isabella to be a good, caring mother, not an emotional wreck who couldn't care for herself, let alone a child. Or a cat.

"I'll write up my report," Zachary promised. He looked at the calendar. "I'll try to get it to you by Friday."

"That's Christmas Eve."

It was, but Zachary didn't understand why that made it a bad day for him to finish his report. Wasn't it good to have it settled before Christmas so that they could be at peace during the season of peace and goodwill blah, blah, blah?

"Right. Christmas Eve," he agreed. "I'll have it to you by then."

But Zachary hadn't written it yet. He had scribbled down some notes.

He had made an outline. He had tried to summarize his thoughts, but he couldn't do it without putting down the words of the report first, to get everything laid out and itemized.

He found himself avoiding his computer, knowing that the work was waiting for him there.

Instead, he decided to go to the medical examiner's office to see if Kenzie were around. If she weren't busy, they could chat for a few minutes. Hopefully, things would be pretty quiet with the Christmas season approaching. People would be going on vacation. Just a skeleton staff at the police station.

Down in the basement, a few red garlands had been strung along the top of the wall, but it didn't make it look festive. It just made it look like a bare, clinical hallway with a tattered red garland running along the top. Like when Zachary had pulled discarded garlands from his neighbor's garbage and tied them to his tricycle. In his mind, he was going to make it into something fabulous, like Santa's sleigh; but it had just been a beat-up old tricycle with streamers tied to the handlebars. He'd gotten in big trouble for stealing from the neighbor's garbage.

Kenzie was at her desk. She hadn't gone on vacation. She had reports stacked up, but it didn't look like she was so busy she couldn't even return a phone call. She looked up at him with an expectant smile, and then some of it dribbled away, leaving her looking serious and questioning. Like he wasn't supposed to be there.

"Happy holidays," Zachary told her. He hadn't brought her a gift. It hadn't occurred to him until then that he might need a little something to break the ice. She was looking awfully cold.

"Merry Christmas, Zachary," she returned, face like stone.

"You decorated. It's very pretty."

"It wasn't me. I think it looks pathetic."

"Yeah… it does."

"Then why did you tell me it was pretty? I don't want you telling me stuff that's not true, just because you think it sounds good or is what I want to hear. I can't stand you lying to me."

Zachary licked his lips. "I'm not lying." His voice was barely above a whisper.

"I don't think you're very good at telling the truth, are you?"

"What do you mean?"

"Just what I said. You haven't had much practice with it. You'd rather tell stories than actually figure out the truth and say that."

"I don't know what you're talking about. I didn't lie to you."

"I don't think you even know what the truth is."

Zachary shifted his feet anxiously. "Who told you I lied? I can't think of anyone who would tell you that, except Bridget. Why would you talk to Bridget?"

She just looked at him, and Zachary knew he'd hit the nail on the head. She *had* been talking to Bridget. Why, he didn't know. Had she approached Bridget? Had Bridget approached Kenzie? He couldn't understand why either one of them would want to talk to the other.

"She said she told you right from the beginning that she didn't want kids. It shouldn't have been any great shock that she wanted to terminate an unplanned, unexpected pregnancy."

"I… didn't say it was a surprise… but I was still hurt. Do you know how it hurts, to have someone tell you they don't want your baby? A part of you? A child would have really made us into a family."

"She says that you were always pushing having children, right from the start, even though she said she wasn't ready. When she felt like you were forcing a pregnancy on her…"

Zachary winced. It was a slap in the face. She made it sound like he had assaulted Bridget. That he had impregnated her against her will. They had always used birth control. He had been willing to wait until she was ready.

"I never forced anything on her. She might 'feel like' I did, but we're talking facts here, not feelings. I never forced her to do anything. Sure, I wanted kids. I still want kids. I want a family of my own." He shook his head, unable to find strong enough words.

"I'm not ready for kids either," Kenzie said. "I want you to know that. I thought you were a guy I'd like to get to know, have a little fun with, but I'm not looking for a serious relationship. Everything about you is serious."

Zachary couldn't think of what to say. He thought he should crack a joke. Make her see that there was more to him, that he did have a fun side. But down there by the morgue, with the sad Christmas garlands, and Kenzie spouting the Gospel According to Bridget, there was nothing he could say that would come out funny or lighthearted.

He swallowed and shook his head. "We're not serious enough to be discussing kids," he said tersely. "That's not why I wanted to see you."

Kenzie stared at him for a minute; then she gave a little laugh. Not laughing at him, just a little cough to break the tension.

"I guess I got ahead of myself, then, didn't I?"

"It's going to be a while before I can talk to anyone about having kids again."

As much as he longed for that missing family, he knew it was the truth. The talk of abortion, the phantom pregnancy, the traumatic breakup with Bridget; it was all too much. Too fresh.

"Yeah." Kenzie looked sorry that she had brought it all up. At least she wasn't calling him a liar anymore. "What was it, then? Why did you come down here? You're done with the Bond case, aren't you?"

"Yes... just trying to put together the final report. It's hard... because I don't really believe it."

"You have to put what you believe in the report. Otherwise, it's just another lie, isn't it?"

"But just like you said... I didn't find anything the police didn't already know. There are no grounds to reinvestigate it. It was... just an accident. A tragic accident."

"So that's what you put down."

"But I don't believe that. I think someone drugged him and drowned him."

"You don't know that."

"How could I *know* it, unless I was there? There's evidence to back it up."

"There isn't."

"He had cough medicine. Both parents said they didn't give him cough medicine."

"Maybe they forgot. Did it absentmindedly. Or they thought they'd be in trouble for it. Maybe they figure he drowned because he wandered into the pond while under the influence of the cough medicine, so they're afraid to admit it. Maybe somebody else had taken cough medicine, and he decided to take a drink out of the little dosing cup without anyone knowing about it. There are a hundred different scenarios, Zachary. There's no evidence of a third party. Just put *that* in your report."

"I suppose."

He knew he was going to have to, but he hated to do it. He didn't want to stir things up between the family and the police. He didn't want it getting into the news again. He didn't want people getting hurt because of him.

"So..." Kenzie gave a forced smile. "What other cases have you been working on? Tell me something interesting about another case. One that doesn't involve a death."

Zachary considered, and told her about the other case that was top of mind. There had been some press coverage, even though the school had tried to keep it quiet. They had tried to distance themselves from the charges against Principal Montgomery, which wasn't possible, when she was dating one of her students.

"I heard about that! That was one of your cases? How did you end up investigating child sex crimes?"

"It didn't start out that way. Just surveillance on a party to see what she was up to. Like dozens of others I've done. This is the first time I've turned up a teacher-student relationship."

"The principal's husband hired you?"

"I can't say who hired me. I'm not at liberty to say."

"But that's who it was."

Zachary shrugged and didn't say one way or another.

"Wow. I'm really impressed. That was a really big bust."

"It was unexpected, but once I knew what was going on, I had to protect the minor."

"You did the right thing. Boy, did you ever. That's amazing."

Zachary was finally able to smile at Kenzie, and she smiled back.

11

It was the day before Christmas, and Zachary knew he was supposed to have the final report ready for Molly. But maybe it was bad timing. She wouldn't want to get that news right before Christmas. He still hadn't managed to work out the language to his satisfaction. He wanted to be able to clearly state that Declan had been given cough medicine, but that nothing had been overlooked in the police investigation. He couldn't say both of those things. Not when the cough medicine seemed so significant to him.

But more than the writing of the final report, the season weighed heavily on him. The last few years he had gotten through Christmas only because of Bridget. His hope for a new life with her. With that whole life shattered, he didn't know how he was going to struggle through one more. It was a crushing weight.

He ignored the calls. He could see by the caller ID that the caller was Molly, and he knew what she was looking for. She wanted his report. She wanted to put the case to bed once and for all and to have a Christmas without guilt for Declan's death hanging over their heads.

As the evening drew on, there was one call from Mr. Peterson, one of

Zachary's former foster fathers. The only one that he had kept in touch with over the years. Mr. Peterson had given him his first camera and had been the only one to encourage Zachary in his photography. Mr. Peterson left a stilted voicemail, his tone concerned.

"Zach… just calling to see how you are. To… wish you a Merry Christmas and make sure you're okay. Okay? Call me back and let me know you're all right… Okay? Pat says 'hi'… Talk to you soon."

There were no other calls. No friends, no family, no special person in his life. When people had asked him what he was doing for Christmas, he'd brushed them off, saying he had plans but remaining vague about what they were. He didn't want pity invitations. He didn't need people trying to fit him in at their Christmas tables just because of how miserable he was.

He found himself in the bathroom, with the medicine cabinet hanging open. Spencer would have been horrified by the mess. Zachary started pulling medications from the shelf. A cough medicine with codeine. Painkillers. Sleeping pills, some of them over-the-counter and some of them prescription. Pills for anxiety. For ADHD. Risperdal. Cold tablets in various daytime and nighttime formulations.

Overdoses were a risky business. Not as certain as a gun or slashed wrists. Not that those were guaranteed either. But with pills, a person might throw them up again. Or wake up three days later with a headache. Or do permanent liver or kidney damage without that last, final sleep they were seeking.

The phone was ringing again. Zachary wearily dragged himself out of the bathroom to the bedroom, where his phone sat on the bedside table, vibrating noisily. He looked down at the screen.

Molly.

Again.

The least he could do was tell her he wasn't going to be able to get the final report to her until after Christmas. Sometimes, things just didn't work out as planned.

He picked up the phone and answered the call.

———

When he reached the hospital, Zachary looked around the emergency room for Molly. He saw Spencer first, pacing back and forth near the windows.

He probably couldn't sit down for fear of catching a hospital infection.

Molly was sitting in one of the uncomfortable, slippery plastic chairs, her elbows on her knees and hands over her face. Zachary sat beside her.

"Molly?" He put his hand lightly on her back. While he wasn't one for touching strangers, she needed some comfort, and it was all he could manage.

Molly raised her face to look at him, and then put it back down in her hands again.

"I called you and called you," she said in a flat, stony voice. "I've been trying to get you for hours."

"Yes. I'm sorry. It hasn't been a good day for me."

It was a stupid thing to say. Once the words were out of his mouth and he heard them, he knew. *He* was having a bad day? Isabella had just attempted suicide and Molly didn't know if her daughter was going to make it.

"I'm sorry," he said quickly. "I didn't mean that. At least, I didn't mean it to sound like that. I'm sorry I didn't answer your earlier calls."

"I know." She sniffled. "It's not like any of this is your responsibility. I just didn't know who else to call."

"You hired me in the first place because you wanted to avoid this. I'm sorry. I failed you."

"You didn't fail me. It was going to happen with or without you. I knew it was. We all saw it coming, but we couldn't watch her twenty-four hours a day. Even if we tried to put her in an institution for her own safety, they'd only do a seventy-two-hour evaluation. If she didn't want to stay and they didn't think she was a danger to herself, they would let her right back out."

"They wouldn't have let her out, would they?"

"They would," Molly said with certainty. "I know they would. We've been here before."

"I'm sorry. I didn't know that. I guess I should have done a little more background on the case."

Molly wrung her hands.

Spencer hovered nearby, pausing from his pacing.

"Like she said, it wouldn't have made any difference. You couldn't have done anything to change it. We were doing our best to keep an eye on her, but... it was bound to happen anyway."

Zachary studied Spencer, shaking his head. "It wasn't inevitable. You can't know that."

"She was getting more and more depressed, slipping further and further into unreality."

Zachary remembered Isabella's bizarre call. "She phoned me. She said that her lost cat Mittens came back. I thought it sounded strange; I wondered if it was a psychotic break... was it?"

Molly raised her head, and she and Spencer looked at each other.

"The cat did come back," Molly said, her voice distant. "I swear, I never thought there was a snowball's chance in hell. Did you, Spencer?"

"No. Of course not."

"I thought it was just crazy talk. I thought it was just Isabella...being Isabella. She would get stuck on things. For years at a time. I don't know how many bags of that damn cat food she went through. Putting food out for it every single day it was gone. It was crazy."

"But now, the cat is back," Spencer said.

He started pacing again.

Zachary sat with Molly. There wasn't much to say to her. She told him about Isabella and Declan, little stories about them. The things that become legends in families. *Remember when...*

Zachary couldn't help thinking about his own history while she talked about her child and grandchild. What would it have been like for him if he had still been part of a family? Would he still have been teetering on the edge like he was? It didn't seem to have helped Isabella to have a loving, interested parent. She had still attempted suicide.

Or maybe Zachary was looking at it all wrong. Maybe he wasn't paying any attention to the dysfunction in the family, and that was the key to Isabella's instability. Maybe the mother who was outwardly loving and kind actually wasn't. Maybe the fact that she was still trying to control her adult daughter's life and to manipulate her mental state was part of the problem. Maybe she was too involved. Too ready to take the reins and control a family that was no longer hers.

Molly had told Zachary on the phone that Isabella had taken pills. The very method Zachary had been considering when he finally decided to answer the phone. Was it a coincidence? Or were they both influenced by some outside factor? Maybe it was the fact that Declan had cough medicine in his system when he died. Zachary's focus on it had directed both of their thoughts to the medicine cabinet.

Was it his fault that Isabella had been impelled to attempt suicide?

"Why do you think she did it?" Zachary asked Molly, in the midst of a retelling of one of her cute stories. "Was it because of my investigation?"

Molly stopped and looked at him, mouth open. "What?"

"Something made her decide to take action. Was it me? Because I was asking her questions?"

"No." Molly shook her head. Her face was chalk white. "No, I really think your investigation was helping. Giving her something positive to focus on. That maybe you would be able to find out the truth."

Unless the truth were that Isabella had given Declan the cough medicine, knowing the reaction he would have to it.

"Then why?" Zachary demanded. "Why now, without even waiting to see what my report said? Was she afraid of what it was going to say?"

"I told her that you were going to give it to us before Christmas. That maybe it would help her to see that it wasn't her fault."

Zachary shook his head.

It was past midnight. Christmas Day. He'd missed his deadline. It was Christmas Day, and he was sitting in the hospital waiting room, trying to comfort the mother of the woman he might have pushed toward suicide.

"It's a bad time of year for suicides," Molly said.

Zachary raised his head to look at her. Unaware that he had been covering his face, in much the same position Molly had been when he first came into the waiting room.

"Christmas is a bad time of year for people who are depressed," Molly said. "There are lots of suicides around this season. It's not your fault."

"I wish I could believe that."

"I don't know why Christmas," Molly went on. "Maybe because people expect to be happy for Christmas, and then when they're not… the expectations make it worse… seeing other people who appear to be happy."

"Isabella bought presents for Declan," Spencer said, his pacing bringing him closer to them again. "I couldn't understand why she would do that. She knew he was dead. She knew he wouldn't be opening presents and spending Christmas with us."

Just like she had fed the missing cat. How many years would she continue to buy her dead child Christmas presents?

Molly looked at Spencer, nodding sadly. "Isabella always loved Christmas. I was hoping maybe she'd perk up a bit for it. That it would be good for her."

"What could be good about Christmas without your child?" Zachary demanded, his throat aching. "How could she look forward to that? How could she celebrate when her arms were so empty?"

Molly and Spencer both stared at Zachary. His reaction was over the top. It was too much. They were wondering what was wrong with him, how he could be so emotional over someone he barely knew. What did he know or care what she felt?

Zachary dropped his head into his hands again. "I hate Christmas."

There was silence. Spencer started to pace again.

"When Isabella was a little girl..." Molly started in on another Isabella story. Then she faded out and gave a sigh. "You must have somewhere to be today. I shouldn't have called you down here when there's nothing for any of us to do. What did you have planned for today?"

If Zachary had used a day planner, there would have been a big, black hole for Christmas Day. He couldn't see anything past it. Just like so many years in the past, he'd been unable to see how his life would continue after Christmas Eve. It was the black beast that swallowed everything else up.

"Nothing. Just taking a break. Staying at home."

"It's different when you're on your own, isn't it? Sitting around in your pajamas watching Christmas specials on TV, because there's nowhere else to go? You don't have any family around here?"

Zachary sat back the best he could in the slippery plastic chair. He massaged his forehead, immensely tired. "I don't have any family."

"You don't? I'm sorry."

He shrugged. "I haven't had for a long time. Not since I was ten. The last couple of years, I had my wife. This year..."

"You're not together anymore?"

"We had a pretty ugly break-up. Yeah."

"You could come over and spend it with us," Molly suggested. Then she seemed to realize what she had just said. "I mean... I guess this is it, isn't it? This is how we're spending our Christmas. Here. Waiting for word."

Zachary nodded. "Might just as well be here as anywhere else."

In fact, it was probably the safest place for him to be on Christmas Day.

Y ou are recently divorced?" Spencer asked, drifting closer to Zachary when Molly took a break to find a bathroom and more coffee. He'd obviously overheard at least part of the conversation with Molly.

"Yes," Zachary admitted. "Just this year."

"What was that like? The whole process?"

"It was... devastating," Zachary admitted. His face grew warm, and he looked far off into the distance, away from Spencer.

Spencer eased back and forth on his legs, looking tired. If he'd been pacing ever since they discovered Isabella, he had to be exhausted.

"Things haven't been good between Isabella and me," he said in a low voice. Even though Zachary had already sensed that, it was difficult for Spencer to get it out in the open. "We've never really been compatible. We thought we were, but we didn't know anything. I told you about the plate."

"The one you threw out," Zachary confirmed.

"Yeah. That's just one example out of many. We've tried to make it work. Set up boundaries, so that she can be comfortable in her studio and know that I won't touch anything, and I know her things will be confined to certain areas. We've set up our timetables and parenting duties..." Spencer paused for a moment, getting past the fact that he no longer had any parenting duties. He swallowed hard, his Adam's apple straining. "So that really, it's just like we're two single people sharing a house, and up until this summer, sharing custody of a child. It's not any kind of partnership."

"And you want to know if you should get divorced."

"I know we should. I've known that for a long time. Since Deck died…"

Zachary waited for a moment to see if he would pick up his broken thought. Zachary and Bridget had only the idea of a child standing between them. A phantom pregnancy that would never be. For Spencer and Isabella, it wasn't academic. It wasn't just an idea. They had shared a child for almost five years. It had, perhaps, been the only thing left holding them together. Having Declan torn from their lives had ravaged both of them. It had damaged them, and maybe their relationship was beyond repair.

"You have to do what's best for you," Zachary said finally, aware of how inadequate the advice was. He didn't know what was best for himself; how was he supposed to give marriage advice to someone else? "For you and Isabella."

"But what if the same thing isn't best for both of us?"

Zachary scratched at a spot on his pants and found that it was a snag. He tried to smooth the pulled fibers back down. Bridget had insisted on the separation and divorce. Zachary had been more than prepared to fight for the marriage. To find a way to make it work again. He had known that if they just worked together, they could heal the rift.

Spencer was on the other side. It was Spencer who had decided his marriage was unsalvageable and that he couldn't move on until he was free. Zachary was supposed to tell him to leave, while his wife was fighting for her life a few rooms away.

Zachary was silent.

"Am I supposed to stay because Isabella needs me?"

Zachary took a deep breath. "For now," he said, telling Spencer what he already knew. "I don't know for how long… but you need to wait and make sure she's going to be okay. Then you two need to have a long talk, and decide how to make the split as pain-free as possible."

Spencer nodded, staring off into the distance. Molly was returning with a tray of coffees for all of them.

"Is that what you did?" Spencer asked.

Zachary shook his head. "No. It's not."

It was almost noon before a doctor came to talk to Molly and Spencer about Isabella's condition and prognosis. He looked at Zachary but wasn't rude enough to ask who he was and why he was there.

"We lost her a couple of times," he said. "But she's finally stable. We've done everything we could to clean her blood and minimize the damage to her liver and kidneys. We won't know what level of functioning they have for a while. There will be a lot of testing to do over the next few days."

"What about brain damage?" Spencer asked.

"We are hopeful that there will be no perceptible brain damage. Only time will tell. For now, she's sleeping, and we want to keep her asleep for the next day or two."

Molly was nodding along. "Can we see her?"

"Yes." He glanced over the three of them. "Family only."

Molly looked like she was going to object to this, but Zachary shook his head. "That's fine. You don't need me in there."

She clutched at his arm. "Are you going to be here when we come back out?"

"No. I think I'll head home now. I haven't had much sleep the last few days. It will be good if I can get some rest."

She held his arm tighter. "We need to know what happened to Declan," she pleaded. "You can see that, can't you?"

He nodded, defeated, unable to answer aloud. Molly let his arm go.

Zachary put his key in the lock and turned it. Nothing happened. There was no resistance or snick as the bolt slid back. He turned the key the opposite way and heard and felt the bolt slide. Then he unlocked it again.

Was it possible that he had been in such a hurry when he rushed from the apartment to the hospital that he had forgotten to lock the door behind him? He stood there for a moment, frozen, listening for any movement. He tried to replay his departure in his mind, but locking the door behind him was so routine he couldn't remember it.

There was no note on his door this time, nothing that hinted at the presence of an intruder.

He slowly turned the handle and pushed the door open, ears pricked for any sound.

There was a noise. He couldn't identify it at first. Someone rifling through the contents of his bedroom drawers?

He didn't have a gun. It had never seemed like a good idea to have a lethal weapon that convenient. Zachary pulled the door shut again, as quietly as possible, and took out his phone.

The police were there in five minutes. No one had left the apartment by the door, and there was no fire escape or way to leave by the window.

"He's still in there," Zachary said in a low voice, which he hoped would not carry as easily as a whisper.

"You know who it is?"

"No. I've had a few threats lately, but I don't know who from. I didn't see."

"I'd like you to go down the hall." The policeman gestured the way they had come. "Don't want you right outside the door. Just wait over there."

"Okay."

He retreated and watched the operation as the policemen pushed the door quietly open and looked around before entering.

If Zachary were a TV detective, he would have had two guns, at least, and would have rushed the apartment all by himself, guns blazing. It wouldn't have mattered whether the apartment was filled with a dozen ninjas with sharp blades, he would somehow be able to overcome them all. Or maybe he'd be the ninja himself and go up against a dozen armed men with his bare hands.

But it wasn't TV.

He heard the shouts of the police as they confronted the intruder. There were no shots fired. In a few minutes, one of the other policemen came sauntering out of the apartment and down the hall. He had a grin on his face.

"You got him?" Zachary asked. "He wasn't armed?"

"We got *her*," the officer said, smiling wider. "And no, she wasn't armed."

Zachary's stomach flipped. Her? She? It didn't make any sense.

If Principal Montgomery had been granted bail, then maybe she had gone to his apartment to try to find any evidence he had of her affair and destroy it. But the lock hadn't been tampered with. He couldn't think of any other woman who would invade his apartment. Kenzie? Even if she had come by to wish him a Merry Christmas, she couldn't have let herself in.

There was only one person who might still have a key.

In his bedroom, Bridget was on her feet. If the police had taken her to the ground and handcuffed her, they had released her again after a short discussion.

"Your intruder was in the bathroom," the policeman said. "Apparently inventorying your medications."

Zachary looked around the room. His drawers had obviously been opened, no longer all closed flush. A tie was sticking out of one of them. He looked over at the bathroom and saw a garbage bag on the floor. There were still some items on the counter where he had left them the day before, but most had been put back in the cabinet or tossed in the garbage bag. Zachary finally looked back at Bridget, baffled.

"What's going on? What are you doing here?"

Her face was bright pink. She tried to look cool and casual but was obviously embarrassed by the scene she had caused. "I couldn't get ahold of you," she explained. "Your phone was going straight to voicemail like it was turned off." She shifted uncomfortably, arms crossed in front of her, ears turning a deep scarlet. "I was worried about you."

Zachary looked at her, at the bathroom, and at his drawers.

"I know it's a bad time of year for you." Bridget's voice faltered. "I called to make sure you were okay. I came over because… I had to make sure you hadn't done something." She glanced toward the bathroom. "When I saw everything out on the counter… I was getting rid of it. Before you could…"

He was so stunned by her actions he didn't know what to do or say. In spite of the way she had screamed at him every time she had seen him, she had reached out to him on Christmas Day, worried about his state of mind. She had abandoned whatever other plans she had for the day to go to his apartment and check on him. To dispose of the pills that might be too much of a temptation for him.

"Do you want to press charges?" one of the cops asked, humor in his tone.

"No. No, I'm sorry I got you all out here... I just heard someone... I wasn't expecting visitors..."

"Better than getting shot or cracked over the head by a burglar. We discourage people from rushing in if they think there's someone in the house."

They prepared to leave, finishing their various notes and calls and whatever else had to be done to document the incident before leaving. They all wished Zachary and Bridget a Merry Christmas and headed out.

And then it was just Zachary and Bridget. Standing there looking at each other, not sure what to say or do.

"I'm sorry," Bridget apologized. "I didn't mean to scare you. I was really worried."

"It's okay. I was at the hospital." He held up a hand before she could rush in, demanding to know if he was okay. "I had a client attempt suicide last night."

She gave a laugh of disbelief. "I'll bet *that* was a shock."

"It was, and it wasn't. The timing was... fortuitous... if a suicide attempt can be fortuitous."

She looked back toward the bathroom. "Because you were considering it yourself." She said it baldly. There was no beating around the bush with Bridget.

"More than considering," Zachary admitted.

"I'll finish going through this stuff." Bridget went back into the bathroom and continued to examine the pill bottles. "Do you want me to stay with you today?"

"No. You go on back, have dinner with Gordon and his family."

She turned and looked at him through the doorway, her eyebrows shooting up. "What? How do you know my plans?"

"I just assumed..."

"You just assumed what? I've never even told you who I'm seeing!"

"It's a small world. I still hear from friends."

She threw a couple of pill bottles away with a scowl and quick, angry movements.

"I told you before; you stay out of my business. Just quit it!"

Zachary leaned against his bureau, watching her. "You're the one breaking into my house," he reminded her.

"I didn't break in. I have a key."

"And you called Kenzie to warn her off?"

Bridget paused, and he saw her biting the inside of her cheek as she thought up a response.

"I felt like it was my duty to let her know... how things are."

"Why didn't you call her when you couldn't find me? I might have been having Christmas with her."

"I did," she admitted.

"But *I'm* the one interfering in *your* life."

"I'm sorry if you think I'm sticking my nose where it doesn't belong, Zachary, but it's for your own safety. Just because things didn't work out between us, that doesn't mean that I don't still care about you. I don't want you to... I don't want you to be unhappy."

Zachary sighed, watching her clear away the last few bottles of pills. Her instincts had been absolutely correct. She knew from experience how difficult the season was for him.

She lifted the garbage bag and tied the top.

"Did you leave me with anything?" he asked.

"A few Tylenol. A few Ambien and Xanax." She shrugged. "If you need something... call me."

What he needed was the life that they had had together.

But she had ripped that away from him, and she wouldn't be giving it back.

13

A few days after Christmas, while Zachary knew that Isabella was still in the hospital, he made arrangements to see Spencer. He called ahead like Spencer had asked him to, as if he were making an appointment with a lawyer or dentist. As far as he knew, Spencer's days were filled with testing and reviewing products on the computer. He didn't have meetings or a school or studio schedule to coordinate. Just sitting in his home office, doing his work there. Zachary wanted Spencer to be in a cooperative mood, not in a hurry to kick him out of the house because he hadn't been prepared to receive a visitor.

He arrived on time, and Spencer opened the door for him before he even had a chance to knock.

Spencer looked as though he had aged ten years. His face was creased and pale. His Christmas obviously hadn't been any better than Zachary's. Maybe even worse. He nodded a polite greeting and took Zachary back to his office and had him sit in the chair. Zachary sat staring at the stuffed dog still perched on top of the printer.

"I want to have a serious discussion with you about Isabella."

Spencer rubbed the bridge of his nose. "What about Isabella? You know everything there is to know."

"Why do you think she tried to kill herself?"

Spencer looked surprised. "Because she is depressed. Grieving."

"But why would she want to kill herself? Lots of people are depressed or grieving. They go to the doctor. They get antidepressants. Therapy. Why wouldn't Isabella do any of that?"

"She did. She went to her therapist. Support group. She didn't want any medications, because of the side effects. She called Molly and had her stay over sometimes. She painted."

"Why wouldn't she take meds?"

"Because they can cause worsening of symptoms. An increase in suicidal thoughts. She didn't want to risk it. She's had meds before. They never seemed to work out well for her."

"It takes some fiddling around sometimes," Zachary said. "Trying different medications and different dosages."

"She didn't have the patience for it. If the first prescription didn't work… she didn't want to try anything else. That was it; she'd had enough."

Zachary doodled in his notepad. He had sympathy for Isabella. He'd been there himself. He knew what it was like to be broken, and none of the things that were supposed to help would.

"Are you sure it wasn't guilt that drove Isabella to suicide?"

"Guilt? I suppose." Spencer gave a shrug. "She felt guilty about Declan getting out of the yard without her realizing it. That she was too late. We all feel guilty for being too late."

"I wonder if it went deeper than that. What if she was the one who gave him the cough medicine?"

Spencer grimaced and shook his head. "She wouldn't do that. She wouldn't give him cold medicine because it might knock him out. It scared her."

"Maybe she *wanted* to knock him out."

"Why?"

Zachary couldn't bring himself to say, 'so that she could drown him.' Not to her husband. Not to Declan's father. "Maybe he was getting underfoot too much, and she wanted him to be quiet and leave her alone. Maybe she wanted to paint in peace."

"Isabella wouldn't do that."

"I know plenty of women who would. Who have done exactly that."

"You do *not* know Isabella!" Spencer snapped. He slammed his palm down on the desk. "Isabella wouldn't dream of doing that!"

He was breathing hard. He coughed, clutching his side. Pain lightninged across his face. Zachary watched him closely, frowning. Spencer swore and felt his ribcage tenderly. Sweat was gathering around his temples.

"Are you okay?" Zachary asked.

"Yeah. I'm fine. Picked up a bug at the hospital, and all of the coughing and sneezing… you know how sore it can make you."

Zachary didn't believe it. "Take a deep breath," he suggested.

Spencer obeyed, and instead of coughing, winced heavily and protected his side. Zachary got up and went around the desk to him.

"Hold still." Without asking or giving Spencer a chance to object, he tugged Spencer's shirt out of his pants and pulled it up. Spencer was too busy guarding his side to stop him.

Spencer's hand covered much of the area, but Zachary could still see black and blue bruises. He tried to nudge Spencer's hand away and caught a glimpse of the dark bruises under his hand.

"You've got broken ribs."

Spencer shook his head. "It's just like I said. From coughing."

"You don't get broken ribs from coughing."

"You can," Spencer argued. "I've done it before." He stopped talking and just breathed for a few minutes, pain etched on his face. "Isabella got rid of all of the cough medicine in the house after you asked if we gave it to Declan. She will freak out if I bring any more into the house. What am I supposed to do? How am I supposed to stop coughing? Maybe honey and lemon. Honey and lemon don't work for a cough so bad it breaks your ribs!" Anger and pain made his voice thin and strained.

"Who's hitting you? Isabella? Or is it someone else you've gotten on the wrong side of."

"No. No one is hitting me. It's just the coughing."

He started coughing as if to demonstrate, and for a few minutes was so racked with choking coughs that Zachary could feel the pain of it himself.

"You should go to the doctor. Maybe you've got pneumonia or bronchitis."

Spencer nodded. He didn't attempt to answer. Sweat and tears streamed down his face. Zachary sat on the edge of the desk, watching him.

"Do you want me to drive you to the doctor?"

Spencer shook his head. He held up one finger, and after a moment managed to get enough breath to answer, without bursting into another fit of coughs. "At the hospital. When I go to see Isabella."

"You'll see a doctor? In the ER?"

Spencer nodded his agreement.

Zachary just watched him for a few minutes, trying to think of what else to say to him, how he could help the man.

"A lot of men are abused," he said. "It isn't just women who are abused by their spouses, but men are afraid to speak up. Afraid that they'll be made fun of. That it makes them less manly and people will look down on them."

Spencer shook his head. "I don't care about machismo, Zachary. Look at me. I'm as geeky as they come. I don't have a reputation to protect." He rubbed his chest and side. "It's not Isabella. It's just from coughing."

It was a crisp, cold day, and Zachary had to keep moving to keep his toes from freezing. Moving around constantly wasn't a very good way of keeping surveillance. People tended to notice a grown man bobbing and pacing as if he badly needed to pee.

He held his camera up and took some random tree shots. He zoomed the telephoto in on a squirrel and tracked it is it busily gathered nuts or pinecones and went up and down the tree. He looked back toward his subject to make sure he hadn't gone anywhere or met anyone and went back to taking pictures of the squirrel.

Maybe if he ever retired, he'd take up wildlife photography. At least he wouldn't have to write up surveillance reports. Retirement was a long way away. If he lived that long.

Glancing back, he saw the subject was on the move again, and swung his telephoto lens the other direction, pretending he was focusing on the waterfowl near the pond that hadn't completely iced over.

As he watched, the subject handed a thick catalog envelope to a man in a long, black overcoat. Mae Gordon's insurance agent. He was given a smaller envelope in return. An envelope that, while thinner, could still contain a pretty nice wad of cash. Zachary clicked away, recording all the details he could.

Kenzie answered the phone after four rings. Zachary had almost decided it was going to go to voicemail, and then there she was.

"I wasn't sure I'd find you at work," he told her. Though, of course, he knew that was exactly where she would be. "I thought maybe you would take off a few extra days for Christmas."

"No, it's a pretty busy time of year down here. Christmas is hard for some people."

"Yeah." Zachary kept his voice carefully unemotional.

"Your ex called me Christmas Day looking for you. She sounded pretty upset. I gather she found you?"

"Yes. Eventually."

"What did she want?"

"Just to wish me a Happy Christmas. Make sure I was okay."

"See, I told you she doesn't hate you." There was reserve in Kenzie's voice. A tinge of jealousy? "That was nice of her."

"You don't have anything to worry about. We didn't get together. She just wanted to make sure I got through Christmas okay."

"I'm not worried," she said breezily. "So… when are you going to tell me about it?"

"About Bridget?" Zachary asked blankly.

"No, not about Bridget! What your deal is with Christmas. It must be one helluva story."

"Oh… well, it's not a fun story. Nothing you want to hear."

"I do, though. You've got me curious."

Zachary hummed. "Not yet," he said. "It's not a story I tell casual acquaintances. Maybe later… when we know each other a bit better."

"You're very secretive."

"I'm just… a private person. There are a lot of things in my past that I'd rather forget. If I have to keep telling the story, I can't leave it behind."

"I don't like secrets."

"It's not a secret. Just private," Zachary repeated.

"Huh. Does it apply to New Year's too? Do you have bad feelings about New Year's?"

"Not specifically."

"Good. Why don't we do something, then?"

Zachary's spirits perked. "I'd like that," he said. "What did you have in mind?"

"I haven't decided yet. Maybe you can help me with that. I don't want a big party. Maybe a smaller gathering, or maybe just watching TV with a big bowl of popcorn."

Either way, the last strike of midnight signaled not only the playing of Auld Lang Syne, but also a kiss. So far, his dates with Kenzie had not been very intimate, and he looked forward to the possibility of that changing.

"I like the popcorn idea," he said. "But I'm open to whatever you want to do."

"Great! I'll put together some options and run them by you, but I'd better be getting back to work here."

"I did have one more thing," Zachary inserted before she could cut him off. She didn't hang up the call.

"Oh. Sorry! What was it you called about?"

"I didn't call just to ask you, but I did want to know…"

"Fire away."

"I wanted to know if it's possible to break a rib coughing."

"Well!" She giggled at that. "That's a funny question. The answer is yes, it is possible. Not real common, but possible. You can break a rib coughing or sneezing. Or blow a blood vessel in your face or eye and end up looking like someone battered you. Or you could have an accident because of coughing or sneezing, banging your head on something in front of you with the force, or tripping, or breaking a tooth or a filling. Or crashing your car. You could do an internet search. There are lots of bizarre injuries that can be attributed to coughing or sneezing."

"Huh."

"Is this a case, or just random trivia?"

"It is a case, actually. A case involving spousal battery… or maybe just a cold."

"That's a tough one. She could be telling the truth. Or it could just be a more creative version of 'I walked into a door.'

"Any way to tell?"

"No. Not really. Just watch for patterns. A broken rib from coughing isn't something that should reoccur with any regularity. Especially in the absence of a cold or pneumonia. Keep an eye on her."

Kenzie had suggested they begin with a nice dinner at the local inn, which was renowned for the on-site chef and his expensive creations. Zachary's pocketbook would certainly take a hit, but he imagined that the dress Kenzie would pick out for such a fancy restaurant on New Year's Eve would be well worth it.

"Are you sure it's okay?" Kenzie had checked. "We're not going to run into your ex there?"

"No. Bridget has other plans for New Year's."

"You know her plans?"

"She told me over Christmas," Zachary assured her. "Besides, I know the kind of things she likes to do New Year's Eve, and quiet little restaurants in out-of-the-way places are not on the list."

"Okay. I just want to make sure. I feel like we always end up running into her or getting a call from her, and I want this one to be just you and me."

"No one else," Zachary promised. "She's going to be with her new boyfriend. They aren't going to be anywhere near the inn."

After dinner at the inn, they would return to Zachary's apartment and have popcorn in front of the TV, if they still had enough room for it. Zach knew that fancy gourmet meals tended to be smaller than the typical burger or prime rib dinner, so he figured he'd still have room for popcorn. He'd been craving it ever since Kenzie suggested it.

He would have the perfect evening with Kenzie, with no interference by Bridget or anyone else.

14

The inn's reputation was well-deserved. Zachary had been a little nervous about trying anything gourmet, which made him think of caviar and escargot and other kinds of raw fish and meats. He wasn't sure he'd be able to stomach anything too unusual. He usually returned to meat and potatoes as his comfort food.

But the restaurant's New Year's menu had been excellent. A whole series of small courses, with tastes from all around the world. Even if a diner didn't like one item, there were so many to choose from that skipping over one or two courses along the way was not a problem. Zachary left the inn with Kenzie, feeling satisfied but not overstuffed. He'd still be able to eat some popcorn while they watched old movies on TV, or whatever Kenzie felt like watching. He didn't care what it was, as long as he got to cuddle up with her on the couch. She had on a daring red dress, and he was looking forward to the chime of midnight, if not earlier.

He helped Kenzie with her coat as they stepped outside and were assaulted by a biting cold wind. At least she'd had the presence of mind to bring more than just a filmy wrap to cover her up while she was outside. A smart woman dressed for the weather in spite of fashion, prepared for any car trouble rather than relying on the car heater for the evening.

"What's that?" Kenzie asked, pointing.

Zachary held the car door for her, then went around to the driver's side to pick up the flyer pinned under the windshield wiper. He got into the car and started it up, making sure everything was set to warm before dropping his eyes to the flyer.

You were told to drop the case. I warned you.

"What is it?" Kenzie repeated.

Zachary's first instinct was to crumple it into a ball and insist that it was nothing, but she was a grown woman and had made it clear she didn't want to be lied to and protected. He handed it to her.

Kenzie's eyes went over the page. A crease appeared between her eyes. She turned it over, examining the blank back as well.

"That's kind of disturbing," she said. "How often do you get these?"

"Third one from this idiot." Zachary checked the controls for the heater again, not wanting to look at her. "Trouble is, they're all as half-baked as that one."

"What do you mean?"

"I mean, he doesn't say which case it is!"

She looked back down at the note and gave a little laugh.

"Oh! Well, that's an ego problem, I guess. He—or she—thinks his case is the biggest and most important, and you should know right away which one it is."

"Exactly. He also never actually makes a threat. Or what? Drop the case, or he'll do what?" Zachary shook his head.

"And you don't know which case it is?"

"I can narrow it down, just because of the timeframe. There are only three or four cases that started before I got the first note that I'm still working on now."

"And which of them would fit the profile of this note?" She squinted at it, considering. "Something personal, I would think, where someone's reputation is at stake. With a... less-than-brilliant target."

"I'm not sure about that. He's smart enough to find my house and my car. It might just be ego, like you said, not lack of intelligence."

"I suppose that's a little more difficult... especially the car, when you're out and about like tonight. How did he know you'd be here? Who did you tell your dinner plans to?"

"No one." He didn't tell her that he didn't really have any friends close enough to care where he was going or what he was doing New Year's Eve. That just sounded pathetic. "It's possible he just happened to see my car in the lot and thought he'd use the opportunity." Zachary shook his head. That didn't sit right. He didn't think it was a viable theory. "You stay here for a minute."

Leaving Kenzie to enjoy the warmth of the heater, he climbed back out into the biting wind. He took a walk around the car, turning on his phone flashlight app to look for markings in the packed-down snow around the car. He couldn't find anything suspicious. He crouched down by the bumper first at the front of the car, then the back, and took off his glove to feel under the bumper. That's where he would have put a tracker. But it could be anywhere on the underside of the car, and he wouldn't be able to do a thorough search until he could get underneath and examine every inch with a good light.

Zachary got back into the car.

"Anything?"

"No. Not that I could find. I'll have to get it up on a lift later to see."

He clenched and unclenched his fingers a few times to get the blood flowing again, and used numb fingers to turn on his GPS tracking app. The chances were not great, but it was worth a try. He searched to see if there were any transmitters nearby that he could pair with. No luck. He skimmed over the map, checking whether any of the subjects he was tracking were close by.

"What's that?"

Kenzie was looking at his phone screen. Zachary shut it off and slid it into his pocket.

"Just a GPS app."

"You don't know how to get home from here?"

"I'm just checking who might live or work nearby, who might happen to drive by and see my car here."

Kenzie put on her seatbelt. "Your car isn't that distinctive," she observed. "It looks like a hundred other cars in the city. Who is going to drive by and know that it's yours?"

She was right about that. They would have to know his license plate or be following or tracking him. It wasn't just serendipity that they had seen Zachary's car parked at the inn.

He sighed and put the car into gear to back out, and then pulled onto the highway.

"Is it just like the other notes?"

"I... don't know. It's pretty generic. Why?"

"I'm just wondering if maybe it isn't about a case. Maybe it's your ex, and she's trying to disrupt our date."

"No." Zachary was certain Bridget was nowhere close to the inn. "It's not Bridget."

"How can you be sure? Like you said, the note doesn't say which case. It doesn't actually specify any threat. Maybe that's because she's trying to disrupt your date, not get you off of any particular investigation. When did you start getting them? Or maybe this one is a copycat. Does Bridget know about the other two?"

"Uh... no. She doesn't know anything about them. I'm the only one who does. Me and the person sending them."

"And you're one hundred percent sure that's not Bridget."

"One hundred percent," Zachary agreed. His skin prickled with goosebumps at the suggestion. Zachary readjusted the direction of the heating vents, trying to get warmed up. "It's not Bridget. You can be sure of that."

"Okay... because you know she's jealous about you seeing me, right?"

Zachary blew his breath out his nose. "I don't know whether it's because she's jealous, or just because she's mad at me."

"She's jealous."

"Why? She's been dating other men almost since the day we broke up. Why would she care if I start seeing someone?"

"People are rarely logical."

There was a period of missing time.

Zachary was aware of a haze of pain. Of someone crying and shouting beside him. He couldn't move. There were lights and voices, the chaos around him making it too difficult to focus on one thing, to figure out what was happening.

"It will be okay," a voice told him. "Help is on its way."

He felt as if everything were upside down. He couldn't make heads or tails of the shapes around him.

"Zachary? Are you okay?" A woman's voice. Not Bridget's. He couldn't figure out whose voice it was.

"What happened?" he asked. But the words didn't come out properly, and all he could hear was moaning.

He drifted in and out, sometimes trying to pinpoint the source of his pain and sometimes trying to turn the world back the right way around again. People kept fading in and out, telling him not to worry. Telling him everything was going to be okay.

Lights strobed in his eyes, so bright he had to screw his eyes shut to avoid their assault. He wanted to put his hand over his eyes because it was still too bright, even through his eyelids.

"Sir! Sir, can you hear me?"

The new voice was loud and insistent. Zachary tried to block it out. His body was cold, and he had an overwhelming feeling of sleepiness. He decided that he must be home in bed. Maybe someone had left the window open. That was why he was having such strange dreams. He was cold, and his body was trying to wake him up. If he just snuggled under the blanket and waited, the furnace would kick in, and he'd be able to go back to sleep.

"Sir! I need you to stay awake. Can you talk to me? Can you tell me where you're hurt?"

Zachary tried to shake his head, but it felt wobbly and weak. The world did a couple of somersaults.

"Sir, can you tell me your name?"

Zachary tried to form the words. Only a moan came out.

"Zachary," a woman's voice said. "His name is Zachary."

"Zachary?" The loud, insistent voice burrowed into his head. "Are you in pain? Can you squeeze my hand?"

The world spun. The loud voice stopped for a while. Zachary tried to process some of the words that whirled around him.

Jaws of life.

Backboard.

Inside his belly, he started to shake. Where was his blanket? Why wasn't he warm enough?

He wished he could get out of the dream he was trapped inside. Maybe he needed to go to the bathroom. Sometimes he had bad dreams when his body was trying to wake him up to go relieve himself. Zachary tried to focus on his body's signals. Did he have a full bladder? Was that why he needed to wake up?

He was just floating in mid-air and couldn't read his body's signals.

Maybe he had left his body in the dream. Maybe he was experiencing an astral projection. He was really somewhere else. Maybe in his bed, maybe sitting in a hypnotist's chair somewhere. He'd had out-of-body experiences before. He'd never told anybody about them, but he'd experienced that removed feeling before.

"We're going to lose him. Zachary. Zachary!"

He tried to rouse himself. The voice was just so damn loud! Why couldn't they just leave him alone? He wanted to fall deeper into the dream. Into the part where he could do things he couldn't do in his physical body. Fly. Breathe under water. Project himself into another plane of existence.

"Zachary! Stay with me, buddy. Focus on my voice. Can you count? Backward from one hundred. Ninety-nine, ninety-eight..."

Zachary wanted to wake up enough to tell the idiot that that was what you did to go to sleep, not to stay awake, but he couldn't rouse himself. His lips moved like he was counting too, but there were still no words, just animal moans.

"Finally here."

Zachary didn't know what was finally there. Maybe he was ready to wake up. He thought maybe he'd fallen asleep riding the bus, and he had reached his destination.

"Cold as a witch's backside," someone complained.

There was laughter and some joking around, but the mood was mostly somber. Zachary wasn't cold anymore. He had finally warmed up. Maybe he had pulled the blanket on, or maybe the furnace had kicked in.

There were more lights in his eyes, so bright that they cut into his brain even through his closed eyelids. He tried to tell Bridget to turn off the light. Just because she couldn't sleep, that didn't mean she had to keep him awake too. He wanted to sink deeper into sleep, to find that peaceful, restful place.

The noise was even worse. Like the building was going to fall on top of him. Zachary tried to reach out to steady himself, to keep the world from falling down around him or to keep himself from falling into the world. More moans came out of his mouth.

"It's okay. Just a few more minutes."

Zachary's head spun. He waited for it to all settle down. How much had he had to drink at supper? He couldn't remember what he had eaten. Or what day it was. He thought it might be Christmas. He'd had too much to drink and he needed to throw up, but he had to wake up and get to the bathroom. He didn't want to barf in his shoes. Doing that once was enough.

There were tearing, rending noises around him. More light. More noise. It was overwhelming. Zachary felt his jaw clench. There was an explosion in his brain. All the sights and sounds were gone, and he was stuck inside his brain, in blackness, with no way to get out.

He didn't know how long it lasted. A second or an eternity. With no external stimuli, there was no way to gauge it.

A moan woke him.

"He's coming back."

The world tipped this way and that, trying to reestablish a horizon. Zachary realized his eyes were open again and he couldn't command them to shut.

There were hands on him. Moving him, then strapping him down. His head felt like a watermelon. He tried to speak to one of the figures moving around him, dark silhouettes against the bright lights.

It's going to be okay. Everything will be all right.

We need warming blankets.

Shock and hypothermia.

Zachary thought the world was right-side-up again. He tried to look around, but he was still in the grip of the nightmare and couldn't move.

"You've been in an accident," a new voice told him.

There were blankets around him, but he didn't feel warm. His body started to shake again. He tried to speak but still couldn't form the words.

"Try to relax. We're going to take care of you. Everything is going to be okay."

Then he was driving again. Or maybe he wasn't driving, but he was in a moving vehicle. He didn't seem to be able to control it or to anticipate the curves and the forces that pulled him to one side or the other. There were unfamiliar noises around him. Beeping and pumping and the whooshing of air. People spoke to him from time to time, but he seemed to be losing his ability to understand them.

Zachary woke from the nightmare with a start. He was in bed. He was warm and not shivering.

But there was still beeping, and other unfamiliar sounds, and the light around him was a flat, uninspiring white. Zachary tried to move. They had him strapped down. He couldn't move a muscle.

Had he attempted suicide? So they had put him in restraints to prevent him from harming himself?

"Wha—what happened?"

"You were in an accident." The voice was soft, female. Reassuring but unfamiliar.

"Drinking and driving," someone farther away said.

Zachary tried to counter this. He would never drink and drive. He might be a screw-up, but he would never put someone else's life in danger.

Or maybe the driver of the other vehicle had been drinking and driving. Maybe that was what the other voice meant.

He was there. Or somewhere else. There was one long shadow across the ceiling he couldn't remember being there before. That must mean that he was somewhere else. He tried to move but again was unable. His previous awakening, or one of them, at least, came back to him.

"An accident," he murmured.

"Yes, you were in an accident," a voice confirmed. Familiar this time.

"Bridget?"

"No. Bridget's not here."

Zachary's head was still spinning. He felt nauseated. But he couldn't move if he needed to throw up. If he threw up when he was flat on his back, unable to turn his head, he'd drown in his own vomit. Zachary tried to keep this thought in his head to convince himself that he couldn't throw up and to push it out of his mind because it was so disgusting and frightening.

"Colder than a witch's behind."

Who had said that earlier?

"Are you cold? I'll get you another blanket."

Zachary wasn't cold, but he didn't object as she unfurled another blanket over him and tugged it this way and that to cover him.

There was a hand on his arm, shaking him. "Mr. Goldman. Mr. Goldman, can you wake up for me?"

Zachary tried to pry his eyes open. It took some work. He finally opened them and blinked a few times, trying to focus and to clear the stickiness from them. He wanted to rub his eyes but he still couldn't move. If it was an accident, why had they strapped him down?

It was a man. A doctor or nurse. He nodded encouragingly. "That's right. How are you feeling today, Mr. Goldman?"

Zachary tried to lick his dry lips with a sore tongue. "An accident."

"Yes. You were in an accident." The doctor waited for him to say more. "Do you remember it?"

"No."

"How do you feel this morning?"

Zachary blinked some more. He tried to turn his head to look around, but that didn't work.

"Are you in pain?"

Zachary considered the question, trying to evaluate his body's signals. "Some."

"That's not surprising. It's actually a good sign." The doctor shone his light in Zachary's eyes. He took Zachary's hand. "Can you squeeze my fingers?"

Zachary wasn't sure whether he succeeded or not. The doctor continued to move around his body, testing reflexes and giving him instructions. He ended up at the head of Zachary's bed, opposite to the side he had started on.

"It was a pretty serious accident. I understand your vehicle is a total write-off. They needed the jaws of life to get you out. There is some spinal cord trauma, but it looks like it is just bruising. We believe that as the swelling goes down, you'll regain full mobility."

Zachary tried to comprehend this. "There was an accident."

"Yes. You don't remember it?"

"No."

"You feeling warmed up now? Your body temperature is back up to normal, but you keep complaining about being cold."

"Cold," Zachary repeated.

The doctor used a thermometer that beeped in Zachary's ear. He took his pulse. He smiled down at Zachary.

"Okay. I'll let you go back to sleep. That's probably what your body needs the most."

Zachary closed his eyes and opened them again, listening.

"Bridget?" he asked.

"The young lady has gone for something to eat. I'm sure she'll be back before long."

Zachary closed his eyes again.

"Hey. How are you doing?"

Zachary opened his eyes and tried to turn his head.

"Bridget?"

"Bridget has been in to see you, but you were asleep."

"She was in an accident."

"No. *We* were in an accident. Not Bridget."

"She was hurt."

"No, Zachary. I was in the car with you, not Bridget. You're mixed up."

143

"Are you sure?"

"Yes. I'm pretty sure." There was a laugh in her voice. "All I have to do is look in the mirror."

"Oh."

She leaned over him so he could see her. Kenzie. Not Bridget. He had taken Kenzie to the inn for New Year's dinner. She had two black eyes and a number of cuts on her face.

"Kenzie."

"That's right."

"You're hurt."

"Superficial."

"Oh."

"You were hurt worse than me, but the doctor says you'll be fine."

Zachary drifted for a while, on the edge of sleep, but not quite able to fall asleep again.

"It was cold."

"Yes," Kenzie leaned closer to him. "It was really cold. They couldn't cover you up because you were upside down."

"I was?"

"Yes."

Zachary's brain worked in slow motion, making it difficult to work through each thought.

"Why?"

"Because the car was upside down. I got out, but we couldn't get you out."

"Colder than a witch's behind."

She laughed. "That's what the fire chief said."

"Oh." He closed his eyes. They were aching from the light. He was close to sleep. "Do you remember what happened?"

The room was darker, or maybe it was a different room. He could still hear the machines, and the PA system, and the people walking around and talking to each other. It was night. Zachary strained to turn his head and look around, but it wouldn't move.

He was still awake when a nurse came in. A black, overweight, middle-aged woman. She smiled down at his face. "Well, look who's awake. How are you feeling, sugar?"

"Okay."

"Good. I just need to check all your vitals and the machine. Can I get you anything? Are you comfortable?"

Zachary licked his lips. "Water?"

She retrieved a cup and held the straw to his lips. The water was tepid but felt good in his mouth and throat.

"Tongue hurts," he noted.

"Yes, it's a little cut up. You had a seizure at the accident scene before they brought you in. I guess you bit your tongue then."

"I did?"

"Or maybe you bit it during the accident. That can certainly happen when the car is rolling over and crashing into a ditch."

Zachary couldn't remember the accident happening, but when she described it so matter-of-factly, panic took over. He could suddenly feel the car rolling, the suspended feeling of not knowing which way was up. Debris was flying around the car, the windows shattering, Kenzie was screaming beside him.

"Whoa, there," the nurse said, laying a hand on his arm. "Calm down. Deep breaths." The beeps and noises of the machines had sped up, complaining loudly. "You're okay, sugar. You're safe here."

She put two fingers over his carotid pulse, even though she could surely hear his racing heartbeat on the machine next to her. Her touch was soothing.

"There, hon'. It's okay. Deep breaths. Blow it all out. Deep breath in... blow it all out... no gasping, you're fine. Just breathe it all out again. It's okay."

She stroked his hair, speaking soothingly, and the panic attack gradually passed. She waited for a while.

"Okay now?"

"Yeah. Okay."

"You've got nothing to worry about. You're safe, and your girlfriend is safe, and we're going to make sure you're all fixed up. Okay?"

"Okay."

"That's a boy. You want another sip of water?"

"Yes."

She gave him the straw again, and Zachary drank a few sips.

"I'm going to go on and do my rounds now, but I'll check back on you again. Don't worry. Even though you can't reach the call button, the machines will let me know if you're in trouble. You can just rest."

Zachary blew out a breath. "Okay."

16

He slept and woke restlessly, never sure how long he had been unconscious or what time of day it would be when he awoke again. Kenzie was often there. Sometimes a doctor or nurse talked to him and tested his reflexes and other signs.

Then there were a couple of policemen beside his bed. Not ones he knew. A department or precinct he hadn't worked with before.

"How are you feeling today, Mr. Goldman?" asked the big, hearty one. His name tag said Farrell.

"Been better," Zachary said, trying weakly for a smile.

"Yes, I imagine you have been. You're pretty bruised up today. You'd make a good addition to a zombie walk."

Zachary tried to think of a clever comeback, but his brain still wasn't operating at full speed.

"I wonder if you can tell me what you remember of the accident?"

"Not much. Just after… them cutting me out of the car."

"What do you remember of that evening? Do you remember going out to eat?"

Zachary tried to replay it in his mind. "Yes… Kenzie. At the inn."

"That's right. You have a nice meal?"

"Yeah. Really good. But I wasn't drunk. I wouldn't drive drunk."

"No. Your blood tests are back, and we know you weren't drunk."

"I wouldn't do that."

"Do you remember going back out to your car?"

"Yes. Was there…" Zachary focused, trying to pin down the ephemeral images. "Was there a flyer on the car?"

"Was there?" Farrell prompted.

"There was… a paper."

"An advertisement for a local bar or band?" Farrell suggested.

"No… no, it was another note." It formed in Zachary's mind. "A threat… because I hadn't quit a case."

"What case?"

"I… don't know which one. They never said."

"They?"

"Whoever was leaving the notes. They didn't say which case I was supposed to stop investigating."

"Do you have any idea?"

"A few… but I don't know for sure."

"You had received other notes?"

"One other note taped to my apartment door; and… a voicemail. It's still on my phone, but they used a voice changer."

"We'll requisition it from your phone company. Since your phone was… not recoverable."

Zachary hadn't thought about his phone until that point. He hadn't thought about whether any of his possessions had survived the accident. He got out of there with his life, and that was as much as he could hope.

"You have an idea of who might be sending the notes?" Farrell pressed.

"Maybe. I'll have to think about it."

"We'll need to question anyone who might be a suspect."

Zachary tried to process this. "Why?"

The other policeman moved. Farrell scribbled something down in his notepad, saying nothing, but keeping an eye on his partner.

"Rick Savois," he told Zachary, who couldn't shake his hand. Savois leaned in close to him, dropping his voice. It wasn't like there was anyone there to overhear him. Who did he think was going to hear? One of the nurses out in the hallway? His partner? "It would appear that your car was tampered with."

"Tampered..." Zachary echoed. He knew he should be angry or frightened, but he was just blank. The idea of someone tampering with his car was unthinkable. "I... I checked the bumpers. For a tracking device."

"A tracking device wouldn't cause an accident," Farrell pointed out.

"Oh... but... if there was an explosive... it wasn't under the bumper."

"No," Savois agreed. "It wasn't a bomb. It was your brake lines."

"The brakes were cut?"

"Looks like it. That fits Miss Kirshe's recollection of the accident. She said that you tried to hit the brake rounding a curve, but nothing happened. It was going too fast to make the curve, went off the side of the road, started to roll..."

The heart monitor started beating faster. Zachary drew in his breath and couldn't get enough oxygen. He gasped harder, trying to drag it in. The two officers looked at him with wide eyes. Farrell grabbed the call button for the nurse, clicking it repeatedly.

"Mr. Goldman, are you okay?" Savois asked, leaning right over Zachary's face, competing for his oxygen. Zachary tried to object, but couldn't speak while he was trying to breathe.

"What's going on here?" A nurse came in. Skinny. With an accent that Zachary would have associated with blacks. Caribbean. Rastafarian. Something like that. But she was white, with big blue eyes and blond hair. "You said you wouldn't be upsettin' my patient. Go on, back up, get out of my way."

The two officers quickly backed away from the small woman. The nurse looked over the equipment and laid a hand on Zachary's arm.

"There," she soothed. "None of that. Your machines are just telling me you're a bit upset. Nothing serious. You just take a few breaths. Nice and slow and easy."

"Can't breathe," Zachary gasped.

"You are breathing. Doin' a fine job of it. In fact, if you don't slow down, you're going to make yourself pass out. Long breaths. Slow down."

She picked up the chart hung on the wall, her eyes scanning it.

"You had a panic attack last night. Is this something you do a lot of? Are you on medication?"

"No—I can usually—control—it." Zachary gasped between the words. His chest was hurting. Maybe it had been damaged in the accident. Maybe his heart had been damaged during the crash, and they didn't know it. He was having a heart attack, and they thought it was nothing to worry about because he had a history of panic attacks. "I'm going—to—die!"

"You're not gonna die, sweetie. Not on my shift."

She went to the doorway and called for one of the other nurses to fetch her something.

"Just calm yourself, Mr. Goldman. It will all be all right. Keep breathing. Out with all the bad air. The problem is carbon dioxide, not oxygen."

Tears started to track down Zachary's face, but he was in too much of a panic to be embarrassed by his childish display.

Another nurse hurried into the room and handed the first a needle and a vial. The Caribbean nurse stood beside Zachary's bed. It seemed like she was moving at glacial speed, waiting for him to pass out, before she stabbed the needle into the access hole on the vial and drew out a dose.

"I can give you a sedative, or you can relax and calm yourself down," she advised him. "Do you really want the needle?"

Zachary breathed heavily, each intake burning all the way down his throat, chest, and side. Did he have broken ribs from the car accident too? Was that what Spencer felt like when he tried to breathe?

The nurse injected the contents of the needle into the IV tube that already fed into Zachary's arm. He hadn't been aware of it up until then. A coldness started to work its way up Zachary's arm, and then it spread to the rest of his body. He could feel his muscles start to relax. The soreness in his lungs faded. The machines slowed their beeping. Zachary started to drift.

"You can't talk to him any more tonight," the nurse told the cops firmly. "You will have to come by tomorrow and try again." She put her hands on her narrow hips. "And next time, try not to upset him."

"Happy New Year."

Kenzie looked surprised at Zachary's greeting. She stopped and looked at him for a moment, looking confused. Then she smiled.

"Happy New Year," she told him back. Her bruises were starting to fade. Or maybe she was masking them with makeup. Either way, he suspected she looked a lot better than he did.

"I guess I missed out on that kiss," Zachary joked.

"What kiss?"

"New Year's. The countdown. The kiss."

"Oh." Kenzie leaned over him and kissed him softly on the lips. Short, fleeting, and gentle. She didn't linger, but gave him a silly sort of smile, then sat down in the visitor chair, where he couldn't see her.

Zachary tried to turn his head to look at her and thought that maybe he made a small movement. The doctor had said that as the swelling went down, he'd be able to do more. Maybe it was starting to heal.

"You're in a good mood today," Kenzie suggested.

"I'm feeling pretty good. I'd like to get out of here soon…"

"I don't think you're going to be waltzing out of here for a while yet. Let's wait until you're mobile."

"Soon," Zachary insisted. "I'm getting better."

"Okay, buddy boy. If you say so."

Zachary sighed, staring up at the ceiling. "Do you remember the crash?"

"Vividly. Still a blank for you?"

"Yeah, mostly. I vaguely remember you being there, talking to me. Being upside down. Cold."

"Yeah."

"But not the actual crash."

"It was freaking scary, so be glad you don't have to. I don't think I've ever been so terrified in my life. I was sure we were both going to die."

"I'm sorry."

"It's not your fault."

"I know… but I feel responsible. If someone cut the brakes because they wanted me off a case… that comes back to me."

"Someone cut your brakes?" Kenzie repeated in disbelief.

"Didn't the police tell you?"

"No! I knew they didn't work… that you hit the brakes and they didn't slow us down. I thought… it was a malfunction."

"Apparently not."

"The letter! Do they think that whoever left the note on the windshield cut your brake lines? Tried to kill us? Or to kill you, at least?"

"Yeah."

She swore softly and was quiet. Zachary couldn't see her expression.

151

Couldn't reach his hand out to touch her and comfort her. "Are you okay?" he asked after a few minutes had passed.

"Sure. I'm fine. No worries." She swore again, in a hard, flinty tone. "I guess New Year's can now take the place of Christmas as your least favorite holiday."

Zachary closed his eyes. She had no idea. Nothing would ever take the place of Christmas as his least favorite holiday. His least favorite season. His least favorite day every year. He had once thought that he could replace those memories. Supplant the bad ones with new, positive, happy family memories. But that was never going to happen. Even if he did someday get married again and have a family, he was never going to be able to root out the memories of the past.

"Zachary?" Kenzie persisted. "Maybe Christmas isn't so bad after all?"

"No. Christmas is still worse."

Kenzie was quiet, considering this. He could see her furled brows in his mind's eye. Trying to imagine what could be worse than being almost killed and paralyzed, at least temporarily, and spending the special day in the emergency room and ICU.

"You're going to have to tell me," she said. "What exactly happened to make Christmas so awful?"

Zachary took long, slow breaths. His heart rate didn't pick up, and the machines stayed quiet and calm beside him.

"It was a long time ago. When I was ten."

"Ten? What happened, you didn't get the toy or the puppy you wanted?"

"No. I was ten... my folks were fighting. It was Christmas Eve, and we all had to go to bed early because of a big fight. They wanted us out of the way while they screamed at each other. Like we couldn't hear them in our bedrooms."

"That sucks."

"I waited until they went to bed, which wasn't until hours later. They fought... not just arguing, but physical. I remember hiding under my covers, scared to death and trying to keep my little brother calm, pretending it was really nothing. I just huddled there, holding him, while they screamed up and down the house, hitting and slapping and throwing things. Then... they finally went to bed."

"Zachary... I'm so sorry." Her voice was much more tender than it had been. He wished he could see her. That she would hold his hand and look at him while he told the story, so he didn't have to see it all in his mind, to feel that terror and anxiety again. But his heart stayed calm. Whatever meds they had started running into his IV were obviously doing their job, keeping him from feeling the worst of the emotions of that day.

"I got up when they finally went to bed. I waited until I was sure they were down and asleep and weren't going to get up again."

"Why? To call for help?"

"No. I cleaned up... picked up everything they had thrown. Straightened all the furniture. I got out the ornaments for the tree. They had gotten a tree, but kept fighting whenever we were supposed to decorate it, so it was just standing there in the corner of the living room, all bare branches. I spent hours decorating it. I needed a chair to get the upper branches, had to keep moving it around the tree to put the garlands on. I untangled and tested the lights, picked out all the best ornaments. The ones with happy memories and special occasions associated with them. Baby's first Christmas. I Saw Mommy Kissing Santa Claus. All the silly ornaments that we made for school projects. Everything. I spent all night getting it all perfect."

"What a sweet thing to do. I'm sure they appreciated it, even if it didn't make things better."

"I got out the special Christmas candles. Beeswax ones that my grandma had brought back from Germany. Set them out. Lit them. Laid down on the couch to stare at all the beautiful Christmas decorations and imagine how everyone would feel when they came out in the morning, and Christmas had arrived. It would be magical. It would bring them all back together. We'd have Christmas together without any fighting."

"But that didn't happen," Kenzie guessed.

"I woke up to a room full of smoke. I couldn't see. Couldn't breathe. Couldn't get out of the room. We didn't have any smoke alarms. Not any that were working, anyway. I was screaming, trying to wake everyone up and get them out of the house, but I couldn't even walk across the living room to find the bedrooms, I was so disoriented."

Despite whatever they were putting in his IV, Zachary choked up. He couldn't help reliving it. The acrid smoke burned his lungs. The terror. Knowing that everybody in the house was going to die and it would be his fault.

"A neighbor's son who had come home for Christmas in the early morning saw the smoke and called 9-1-1. They got my parents and my brothers and sisters out of their bedrooms through the windows. The firemen had to break down the door and search the house for me. Room by room, because no one knew where I was."

"Thank goodness they saved you."

Zachary swore. "No. I wish I'd died. I wish they saved everyone else, and let the house burn down around me. That would have been better."

"You can't say that. No. It's not true."

"You don't know! You have no idea!"

"You must feel terribly guilty," Kenzie said. "But you were only a little boy, trying to do something nice for your family. It wasn't your fault."

"It *was* my fault."

"You can't say that."

"They split the family up."

Kenzie's voice was hesitant. "What...?"

"My parents separated. They put all the kids into foster care. They said we could never be a family again. We didn't deserve to be a family."

"Who said that?" Kenzie was horrified. She stood and leaned over the bed, grasping for Zachary's hand. "What a horrible thing to say! You can't believe it."

"My mother. My parents. They said I was incorrigible. A criminal. They didn't want Social Services to put me into foster care; they wanted to put me in prison. I spent a lot of my teenage years in institutions. All kinds of 'secure' facilities for kids with behavioral problems. Prisons for kids who had never been convicted of anything."

Kenzie stroked Zachary's hair, tears in her eyes. "No. How could they do that? You weren't being bad."

"I did awful things. Not as bad as some of the kids. Some of those kids... they *should* have been in prisons. Or insane asylums. Sadistic, psychotic kids. The kind of adults they could get to work places like that... most of them just as eager to torture you as any of the psychotic little—"

"Shh," Kenzie tried to stem the flow of Zachary's rising rage. He normally did better at controlling himself. The medications must have lowered his inhibitions. Made it easier for him to flap his gums about things he should just keep quiet about. A girl didn't want to hear that kind of thing. Nobody wanted to hear that kind of thing. They would rather deny such places even existed.

"You had to be really bad to be put in a place like that," Zachary asserted feeling hollow and empty.

"You weren't bad," Kenzie whispered, still trying to calm and quiet him. "You were hurt and traumatized. What a horrible thing to do to a child."

H i there."

Zachary turned his eyes toward the door and saw Bridget hovering there. Her glance darted around the room, and then back to him. Kenzie was still at work, Bridget didn't need to worry that they would run into each other at Zachary's bedside.

"Come on in," Zachary invited.

She entered the room, walking up to him, but staying just out of arm's reach of the bed. Like he might reach out and shake her hand or something equally as threatening.

"You're looking better," she observed.

He was finally able to sit up instead of lying flat on his back. Able to turn his head and make use of his arms. In a day or two, they would start him on physio for his legs, getting him up onto his feet for the first time since the accident.

"Yeah, glad to be able to move again," Zachary agreed, rolling his shoulders.

Bridget looked over at the visitor chair, considering. What was there to think about? Did she plan to just stand there beside him, exchange a few words, and then leave again?

"Sit, relax," Zachary encouraged.

She lowered herself to the seat. She held her purse in her lap, clutching it like she might have to leave suddenly and had to have it in her grasp.

"Did you have a nice Christmas?" Zachary inquired politely. "New Year's?"

"Better than yours, apparently."

"You visit what's-his-name's family?"

She narrowed her eyes at him. "You knew Gordon's name at Christmas, so there's no point in playing games with me now."

Zachary shrugged.

"Yes, we went to see his family for Christmas. They live on a little farm that's been in their family for generations. White board house. Red barn. Very picturesque in the snow."

"That sounds nice."

"It was very nice. Get away from the rat race. From all the stresses. Just enjoy a Christmas dinner with the family..."

"I hope I didn't make you too late for it."

Bridget's mouth quirked. "We did have to rearrange things a little, but it all worked out in the end."

"Thanks for... looking out for me."

She got a little bit pink. Zachary didn't like things being awkward between them, but it was better than being yelled at. At least there was some sign that they might be able to have a normal, amicable relationship someday. She still had bitter feelings, he knew. Feelings that she had never shared with him, but had shared with Kenzie about how he had tried to force the pregnancy upon her. The word *force* still made him furious at the implications. That somehow, he had done something violent or dishonest, when all he had done was express an opinion.

"I still care about what happens to you, Zachary," Bridget said carefully. "Even though we're not together anymore, I don't want you to..." she chickened out and didn't say, 'commit suicide' or any euphemism, but, "be unhappy."

She yelled at him for being at a restaurant and called his date to warn her off, but she didn't want him to be unhappy? Her words and her actions didn't correlate.

She *had* called him at Christmas and gone to his apartment to make sure he hadn't done himself harm.

"I care about you too. I never wanted you to be unhappy," Zachary told her. "I just wanted us to be happy together."

"Don't go over that old ground. We were never compatible."

Never. Getting married had been a mistake. It wasn't that they had been compatible and then he had screwed everything up. They had never been compatible in the first place.

She meant it as a consolation, but if anything, it made him feel worse. How would he ever know if someone was compatible? He'd thought they had fit together well. He'd thought she was someone he could spend the rest of his life with. Start a family with. But she'd never been compatible.

Was anyone? Was there some secret combination? Some code that he had to recognize when he dated? This one fits, but this one doesn't...

He had a feeling that nobody would fit Bridget's definition of compatibility. No one would ever be compatible with Zachary. He didn't know of anyone else who shared the kind of background he had come from.

"How are you feeling," Zachary asked Bridget, moving away from the dangerous ground, "now that you are finished your chemo?"

"So much better. Still tired, but I'm gradually getting my energy back. Knowing I have more than a few months to live... that's a comfort."

"I'm glad too."

She touched her wig self-consciously. She didn't need to be embarrassed about it. It looked perfectly natural. Just as soft and shining as her own hair. "And I'll be able to grow my hair back."

"You look amazing."

"All things considered," she temporized for him.

"No. You just look amazing. For anything."

"Oh." She played with the fringe of her hair with the very tips of her fingers. "Well, thank you, Zachary." She looked him over. "When do you think you'll be back out of here?"

"It depends on how long it takes to get back on my feet. How long it takes for the inflammation to go down. I hope... not too long."

"You gave us all quite a scare."

"It wasn't intentional, trust me." Zachary attempted a smile.

"You need to be more careful. Had you been drinking?"

Zachary opened his mouth, and at first, no words came out. He just stared at her. She should have known better. Even if no one had told her it was attempted murder, she should know that he didn't drink and drive. He didn't drink irresponsibly. In all the time she had known him, he had never once been drunk.

He found his voice. "No. I wasn't drunk. Somebody cut my brake lines."

"Cut your brake lines?" her voice was derisive. "What makes you think that? *Somebody's* been watching too many Phillip Marlowe movies."

"I'm not imagining things. I'm not being paranoid—"

"You're always paranoid. Your distrust is what drove us apart."

Not the way he remembered it. Yes, he had sometimes had occasion to question her about her activities, but what did she expect from someone who spent half his time trailing unfaithful spouses?

"The police told me my brake lines were cut," he informed her, instead of attacking her faulty memory. "They wanted to know who would have motive to kill me."

She stared back at him. "That obviously wouldn't be me, since I was trying to save your life just days earlier!"

Zachary felt an uncomfortable chill. He hadn't accused her of being the one trying to kill him. Was her defensiveness evidence that her anger toward him ran much deeper than he wanted to admit? She claimed she still had friendly feelings toward him but had she already regretted reaching out to him at Christmas? Or had her presence in his bathroom, messing around with his meds, been more sinister than it appeared? It was easy to cover it up with the explanation that she was just trying to keep him from killing himself. But maybe she had been looking for a way to conveniently get rid of him, knowing how he handled the Christmas season.

He shook off the thought. Bridget was right; he did have a deep-seated paranoia surrounding his relationships. A paranoia engendered by repeated abandonment and his inability to form a long-term relationship. What else did she expect from him, given his past?

"I know it wasn't you," he said. "It was something to do with work. With one of the cases I'm working on."

"Oh." She nodded. Her face softened. "Which one?"

"I don't know." Zachary rolled his eyes and forced out a breath, frustrated. "It would be nice if people who left threatening notes would be more specific."

Unless it wasn't anything to do with a case. If someone had a personal grudge against him, they wouldn't have any idea what his current cases were. The threats pointing toward his investigations might just be misdirection.

An effort to keep Zachary and the police looking at his current cases instead of his personal connections. That opened up the possibilities to a lot more people.

What about Gordon, Bridget's new boyfriend? He probably didn't appreciate having his carefully-arranged Christmas plans disrupted by Bridget running off to her ex's house to make sure he hadn't offed himself. Zachary knew little about the man. He had done only very basic background on Gordon; little more than his vital statistics and resume. If Zachary dug deeper, what would he find? A history of violence? Connections with organized crime? A propensity to start fistfights in bars? An auto mechanics course?

"Maybe you should consider a change in career," Bridget suggested. Not for the first time. It had been a recurring theme during their doomed marriage. Private investigations work was too dangerous. It reflected poorly on her. She was always full of suggestions of things he could do instead, things that held absolutely no interest to him.

Zachary wasn't looking for a desk job. He liked the ability to leave his computer and head out to the field. He liked the flexibility of working for himself. Having something legitimate to do when he couldn't sleep. If he were really to be honest, he even liked skirting the law. The minor, not-so-legal things he did to dig out the truth and get justice for his clients. Even that was alluring.

"You need to remove me as your emergency contact."

Zachary looked at Bridget.

"You can't have them calling me whenever you get into an accident," she expanded. "We're not together anymore, Zachary. I'm not the person they should be calling."

"Oh."

He considered this. On the surface, it made sense, of course. But who would he put in her place? He didn't have any family. No close friends. He couldn't make every new girlfriend an emergency contact. Someone he barely knew. Besides, what if, like Kenzie, they were in the same car with him when something happened?

"Yeah. Okay."

Zachary couldn't drive and hadn't replaced his car yet, so he took the bus to Molly's house. He was conscious of his legs and feet as he walked from the bus stop to her door. Walking was not yet automatic. He felt like he did when someone was watching him critically. Awkward, like he didn't know where to put his feet. He had to think out every step and was sure he must look jerky and robotic to anyone watching him. He had rejected the idea of a cane for stability but was starting to regret it. If nothing else, it would at least signal to anyone watching him that he had a condition, that he wasn't drunk or impaired but had a good reason for wobbling and hesitating like he did.

Molly answered the door. She looked Zachary over, her eyes bright and curious.

"Come in, come in," she invited, and opened the door the rest of the way, directing him in.

Zachary's toe caught on the edge of the carpet at its transition from the floor, and he skittered a bit but managed to avoid flailing or landing on his face. Molly walked to his right and slightly behind him, holding her hands out a bit like she wanted to catch him or guide him to his seat. He got into the chair and shifted, settling himself in.

"How are you feeling?" Molly asked. "It looks like you're healing."

Zachary nodded a little jerkily. "Yes. I'm doing well. Everything will be back to normal soon. My doctors are happy with the rate of my progress."

"I couldn't believe it when I heard about your accident. They said it was very bad. That you had a spinal cord injury and were paralyzed." She shook her head solemnly. "I certainly didn't expect to see you walking around so soon."

The police must have interviewed her, as one of his clients, to find out her alibis for the times he had received the threats or when the brake lines had been cut. He knew they had been making the rounds, trying to narrow down the suspect list. They didn't have any forensic evidence. No fingerprints or DNA. There must have been tool marks on the brake lines, but maybe nothing could be matched to the tool used. Or maybe matched to a common tool that they all had access to.

"There was just swelling around my spinal cord," he explained. "Inflammation. It's mostly gone, now. I just… have to be careful. Think about what I'm doing for a while until it all becomes natural again."

"No permanent damage?"

"No. I was very lucky."

"And your girlfriend? Her injuries were not severe?"

Had she heard that from the police? Or had she checked up on him through other channels? It wouldn't be hard. A call to the hospital. To one of the reporters who had covered the crash. Not a lot of information had made it into the news articles, but the reporters knew that there had been a second person in the car. They had those details.

"She's... not exactly my girlfriend. We've been out together a few times, but... it's not that serious yet. We're taking things slow." He didn't know why he was telling her so much. What did it matter whether she thought Kenzie was a serious girlfriend or not?

But Zachary didn't like the thought of anyone thinking Kenzie was a serious girlfriend. If someone was out to hurt him, out to coerce him into closing a case, he didn't want them threatening her. Someone who was serious enough to cut Zachary's brake lines might be serious enough to take a hostage.

Surely that wasn't Molly Hildebrandt. She was a little old lady. He couldn't see her crawling underneath his car to cut his brake lines. He couldn't picture her grabbing Kenzie and holding a knife to her throat or a gun to her head. Sometimes it was the least likely suspect, but he still couldn't fit Molly into that role.

"Oh... well, I'm very glad that neither of you was killed or permanently injured. I think we've all had enough of hospitals this winter."

Zachary nodded his agreement. "How is Isabella?"

"She was released December thirtieth. We're still trying to keep a pretty close eye on her. Neither of us believes she's recovered... she's stable as far as the doctors are concerned, but she still won't take the anti-depressants they want her to. She's convinced that they will make her worse."

Zachary scratched his knee intently, considering his approach. "I have several concerns about Isabella."

"Yes. We all do," Molly agreed. She avoided his eyes and didn't ask him what his concerns were. Maybe she figured his concerns were the same as hers, or that she had enough on her plate already and couldn't handle anything more.

"I think... that Isabella was the one who gave Declan cough medicine the day he died. Whether she was scared by his reaction, or she had been expecting it... I suspect she was the one who took him to the pond that day."

Molly's eyes went wide and two bright spots appeared in her cheeks. Her voice when she addressed him was not weak or wavering. There was no uncertainty.

"That is the most ridiculous thing I have ever heard. Isabella wouldn't let anyone give Declan cough medicine. She would never give it to him herself. She would certainly not plan his death or do anything that led to it. You are wrong, Mr. Goldman. Your brain must have been addled by your accident. There is no way my daughter had anything to do with Declan's death."

"You weren't there. You weren't with her. The possibility is still open."

"No. It's not. That's ridiculous. Why? Explain to me why she would give him cough medicine when she knew he would react negatively to it. Explain why she would take him to the pond and drown him?"

"She gave him the medicine so that he would be unconscious and not fight her."

"Why? Why would she harm her own son?"

"Because she didn't want to be a mother. She hadn't realized how difficult a job it would be, and how much he would interfere with her job and with the order she and Spencer had developed in the house. She didn't realize how his care would interfere with her routines, day after day. Every day it wore on her. She wanted to paint. She wanted to tape her shows. She wanted to live a predictable, ordered existence. Declan screwed that up."

"No, you're wrong." A tear slid down Molly's cheek. Was it a sign that he'd hit the mark? He had hit too close to the truth, and she couldn't help reacting? "My daughter wasn't like that. Isn't like that. She loved Declan dearly."

"That doesn't preclude her doing something to harm him. She could love him and still decide that she just couldn't handle him anymore. It happens. You read about it in the news. People who are overwhelmed with their children's care. Or with the stresses at work or in other areas of their lives. They decide that they can't go on like that anymore, and they decide to take the child or children out of the equation."

"She didn't do that. She would never do that."

"Drowning is a common method of disposing of unwanted children."

"Drowning is a common method of disposing of unwanted kittens. Not children. People don't just drown their children because they are inconvenient. They get help. I could have helped her. I could have spent more time there. If she wanted me to babysit Declan, I would have been happy to do it. All she had to do was ask."

Zachary sighed. He wasn't sure what to do with his hands and wished that she had offered him coffee or a cookie so that he could avoid fidgeting. He held his hands in his lap but wanted to move them around, to use them to illustrate his point.

"You say that you would have been happy to babysit him, but maybe Isabella didn't feel like she could ask you. You were already doing too much for them. Or maybe she didn't approve of your parenting methods. Kids often don't appreciate their own parents. They think they know better."

"I was a good mother to Isabella!"

Zachary didn't answer for a few seconds, considering it. *Had* she been a good mother? Or had she done the wrong things and damaged Isabella? No one had offered any reason why Isabella was the way she was. Had she just won the genetic lottery? Or was it the result of something traumatic that had happened in her childhood? Or throughout all of her childhood? Most parents, if confronted, would admit that they had made mistakes in parenting. Maybe Isabella wouldn't agree that Molly had been a good mother. Maybe she hadn't been. Maybe Isabella was incapable of parenting because she hadn't had a good example herself.

"I'm sure you were a good mother," he reassured Molly, trying to keep her calm. "But Isabella might not think so. All children think they can do a better job than their parents." He gave her a conspiratorial smile. One that invited her to agree with him about the follies of children and admit that Isabella might not always agree with her.

"Isabella never had any complaints about the way that I took care of Declan," Molly said sullenly. For the first time, Zachary could see another side of her. The person who wasn't always upbeat and positive. The one who had doubts and took offense and who wasn't the perfect example of a loving, devoted parent. A human being.

"How is Isabella as a wife?" Zachary spun the conversation in the other direction.

Molly blinked at him, disconcerted. "What do you mean, how is she as a wife?"

"Does she enjoy being married? Does she get along with Spencer? How have they made out together?"

Molly opened and closed her mouth. She tried several times to approach the question, seeing a minefield and trying to figure out how to navigate it.

"Being a wife is… hard for Isabella," she admitted.

"I know marriage was pretty hard for me," Zachary said. "I wasn't a very good husband. I wish I could say that I always thought of my wife and that I did everything I could to keep our marriage going smoothly. I made a lot of mistakes. In the end… I drove her away." That was what Bridget said, anyway. The story worked for Zachary's purposes.

"Isabella didn't have a good example of a successful marriage growing up," Molly said. "She never had a father, and I didn't have any strong, long-lasting relationships when she was a girl. She was a very difficult child, and there wasn't any space in my life for a man. She needed all my attention. A man would just have felt neglected."

"That makes it hard. You can't just take your example from TV." Zachary smiled at her. "The Brady Bunch might seem perfect, but that's not the way families really work. Husbands and wives don't always agree. They're not always compatible."

Molly got up and paced across the room, stopping to retrieve the photo of Isabella, Spencer, and Declan. She sat back down with it, showed it to Zachary for a moment, and then sat staring at it.

"I thought her marrying someone else with a mental illness was a bad idea. Isabella thought it would be perfect. They would be able to understand what the other was going through. Because their tendencies were opposite, they would each… complete the other. Spencer would complete her. Would fill in the gaps."

"But that's not the way it worked out, is it? Spencer told me about the blue plate."

Molly smiled softly. "She had that plate since she was a girl. She ate from it every day. She had to have it. When Spencer threw it out… I think that was the first sign that it wasn't just going to be a bumpy ride. It was going to be a rollercoaster. Or a bungee jump. It wasn't going to work… not the way they thought it was."

"How did Isabella react to the difficulties with Spencer? How did she react when he did something that she didn't like, or that interfered with her space or her routines? How did she feel when he did something like throwing out her plate?"

"It would send her into a tailspin. She'd be impossible to talk to for days. She needed her therapist on the set or needed me there to help direct her. To work things out so that she could tape the show. The network understood that she had emotional problems, but... they weren't very understanding."

"Her job was in jeopardy? Because of the way things were going at home?"

"No, I'm just speaking generally. They had trouble with her. Not constantly. Things went very smoothly most of the time. I just meant, when Isabella and Spencer were fighting, it spilled over into her professional life."

Zachary pounced on the word. "Tell me about their fighting."

"No... not fighting... not like you're talking about. I mean disagreements. Conflicts. Nothing physical."

"Are you sure nothing ever got physical?"

"Isabella would never have abided anyone who laid a hand on her. If Spencer had hit her, she would have called the police. I'm sure of that."

"And what about her hitting him?"

"Her hitting him?" Molly laughed and shook her head. "She didn't hit him. Never. She isn't a violent person."

"Spencer has broken ribs. I've seen the bruises. Can you explain that?"

Molly's brows drew down. She shook her head at him, scowling blackly. "She never did anything to hurt him. How could she? He's bigger than she is."

"That doesn't mean she couldn't hit him. I've known little tiny women who beat the hell out of their big, strong husbands. Size has nothing to do with it. Women can be just as violent and abusive as men."

"Not Isabella. That's ridiculous."

"How did Spencer get the bruises? He works from home. From what I've seen, he rarely goes out. Who is beating up on him? Who caused those bruises?"

"I don't know," Molly said flatly. "I've never seen any sign of either of them hurting the other. Isabella has never said anything to even hint at abuse. You've got it wrong, Zachary. I don't know where you're getting this, but you've got it all wrong."

"Have you ever seen Spencer with injuries? Bruises or cuts on his face? Unexplained injuries?"

"No!" Zachary could see it wasn't the truth. She *had* seen it. He could

166

tell by the shock in her eyes. Maybe she hadn't registered the thought that her daughter was abusive, but she had seen unexplained injuries.

Zachary let the silence build for a couple of minutes. He didn't ask anything further, but let Molly think about it. Watched her grow uncomfortable with the silence and try to justify it to herself.

"You've never seen him with unexplained injuries?" Zachary prompted.

"Everybody has accidents. Spencer is no exception."

"What kind of accidents did he have?"

"I don't know. He never really tried to explain. He just brushed them off and said it was nothing. Or sometimes he said it was Declan. They'd been play-wrestling, and Declan had kicked him in the eye. Or Declan had been playing a game with him where Spencer was blindfolded, and he walked into something. I don't know. Things happen. People get hurt. I often get bruises and don't know where I got them. On my legs and knees. Sometimes my arms. It's just part of life. It doesn't mean I'm being abused. I don't believe Spencer was either."

Zachary traced figure-eights on the arm of the chair with one finger. "Maybe you really don't know what was going on," he said. "Maybe they both had you fooled, and you didn't realize. You know that things were difficult between them."

"Yes, but they had worked things out. They had set up boundaries and rules. Ways that they could get along with each other. Live with each other without driving each other totally crazy."

"Like Spencer not going into Isabella's art studio."

"Right."

"What would happen if he did go in?"

She stared at him. "What do you mean?"

"Just what I said. The studio was off-limits for him. What would happen if he ignored that rule and walked in? Or moved something? Or took something, because he couldn't stand the mess?"

"He wouldn't do that. He wouldn't go into her studio."

"Because of the way she would react if he did?"

"Because they had agreed on rules and boundaries," Molly growled. "And he wouldn't *want* to go in her studio."

Zachary thought back to the chaos and disorder that ruled in Isabella's studio. He pictured Spencer standing in the doorway, as he had a couple of times. He didn't hover in the door, wishing that he could enter. He didn't look longingly at the disorderly shelves and tables, wanting to straighten them. Rather, he had hung back as if he couldn't stand to enter.

"What about Spencer's office? Was Isabella allowed to go in there?"

"It was his space," Molly growled. "Is his space. I don't know if she is *allowed* or not, but it's his space, and she respects that boundary. You can't think that she would want to go in there and interfere with his things."

"No, I don't think that. But *would* she go in there? To talk to him? To leave the mail on his desk? To pick up a toy that Declan had left in there? What are the rules?"

"You'll have to ask them."

"And what were the rules for taking care of Declan? They each had separate responsibilities?"

"Yes. Of course." Molly nodded vigorously. "They were very good about sharing responsibilities. Spencer took Declan in the mornings. He made sure that he had breakfast and lunch and played games with him. Did chores or went on walks. Then in the afternoon, it was Isabella's turn. She'd take over so Spencer could work in peace."

"What did she do with Declan?"

"What do you mean? Looked after him."

"You listed off things that Spencer would do with him. Make him breakfast. Play games with him. Take him out for a walk. What things would Isabella do with him?"

"Well… put him down for his nap. It's very important for young children to get enough sleep, or they get grumpy. Being chronically short on sleep makes a person sick, overweight, more prone to catching everything that goes around."

"Uh-huh. And?"

"And what?"

"What else would she do with him? Put him down for a nap. What else?"

"I don't know. A hundred different things. Do an art or craft with him. Watch him while he played in the backyard."

"She didn't spend as much one-on-one time with him as Spencer did. She found ways to do other things while it was her time to look after him."

"There's nothing wrong with letting him nap or watching him playing in the back yard."

"Of course not. That's not being negligent."

"That's right." Molly nodded her agreement.

"But it does show a pattern. It shows that she wanted to continue to follow her own routine, and only did what she had to in order to accommodate Declan."

"You're wrong. She loved Declan. She loved spending time with him."

"Maybe she didn't always share her feelings with you. Maybe she felt like she couldn't tell you how inadequate she felt, or how she didn't want to be with Declan all the time. Maybe she was afraid that you would judge her for not wanting to spend as much time with her child as she possibly could."

"I would never criticize her for that. Parents are people too. You still have to take care of yourself. I would understand that she couldn't take care of Declan all the time. She needed time to herself. Isabella has always needed alone time. Time to regenerate, to work on her art."

"And she wasn't getting that, not when she had to watch Declan while she painted. She didn't really get alone, undisturbed time, did she?"

"She did. Mr. Goldman, you're talking in circles. I know she needed time for herself. She had a husband. She had me. She didn't need to do anything to get rid of Declan. If she wanted help for a few hours, she only had to ask."

"But it wasn't just a few hours. It was every day. Every single day, she had to look after him, listen to his inane, childish chatter, clean up after him. She had to make sure he didn't touch any of her precious things. She had to feed him and change him and be there for him. Children take a lot of work."

"You think I don't know that? I raised Isabella as a single parent. There were no breaks for me. No husband, no grandparents. She was a very high-needs child, and there was no one to help me. Don't you tell me how hard it is to raise a child." She shook an accusing finger at him. "You don't have children. You told me that. You can't understand what it's like to raise a child on your own, but I do. And Isabella wasn't on her own."

"Maybe not; but maybe she felt alone. You had raised her by yourself, but she couldn't raise a child with the help of her husband. She felt like a failure. That's why she killed Declan, and that's why she tried to kill herself, overwhelmed with the guilt of it all. The guilt of not being able to be the parent she wanted to be and the guilt of killing her own child."

Molly stood up. "I'm going to have to ask you to leave."

Zachary didn't move.

"Leave," Molly repeated. She motioned to the door. "If you don't leave, I'll call the police and have them arrest you for trespassing. I've had enough of this." Her lips twisted into angry shapes before she managed to spit the rest of the words out. "Please submit your final report to me. By mail. Then I don't want you to investigate anymore. You will be done."

Zachary stood slowly. He walked to the door and let himself out.

18

It had been an emotional day, and Zachary knew that he needed to take the time to complete the final report on the Bond case and get it off to Molly. Then he had to decide what he was going to do about the case. The more he looked into it, and the more he discussed the merits of the case, the more certain he was that the only culprit could be Isabella.

No wandering child killer had happened by their yard and spotted Declan. They hadn't snatched the child or persuaded him to leave the safety of his yard, dosed him with cough medicine, and drowned him in the pond. The timeline was too tight. The killer's goal had to be drowning him from the start. They hadn't tried to kidnap him or harm him in other ways and been thwarted. They had to have gone straight from taking him from the yard to killing him within an hour or so. The crime suggested a parent. A frustrated caretaker overwhelmed with the pressures of taking care of a child.

But he couldn't go to the police and say that he was sure that Isabella had murdered her only child. There was no evidence to clinch it. The case had already been closed and Zachary could offer nothing to change their minds.

He plowed through the written report anyway. He had already made his opinion known to Molly, so he didn't mince words. He didn't try to phrase the file diplomatically as he had before. She knew what he thought, and he needed to lay it all out without flinching. She could do with it what she liked. Shred it or burn it so no one else could ever read it.

When he was finished—or at least finished the first draft—he sat back in his chair, making it creak angrily in protest. He called Kenzie on an old flip phone he had just activated.

"Are you free for a late dinner?" he suggested.

"I've actually already had dinner. I was starving."

"How about a nightcap, then?"

"Sure," Kenzie's voice was warm, "that would be nice. Where do you want to go?"

His options were getting more and more limited. Nowhere that Bridget might go. Nowhere any of his subjects might go. Not to the inn. Somewhere in town so he could get there easily by bus. Or he could call a cab when he was ready to go home. Maybe Kenzie would offer to drive him home, which might lead to better things.

"How about... there's a little pub called *The Four-Leaf Clover.* Have you ever been there?"

"No... but I know where it is. It's across from *Old Joe's*, isn't it, where we ate..."

"Yes."

"And we're not going to run into Bridget there, right?"

"No. She never went there."

"Let's hope she doesn't start."

The nightcap went well. They were both relaxed, tired after a long day, but happy to have put their work behind them, not still stressing out over it. Zachary was able to stop being so self-conscious about his movements. To stop worrying that he looked like someone with brain damage, and just relax.

"You're glad to be closing the Declan Bond case?" Kenzie asked.

"Yes. I wish I could do something more about it, but that will be up to someone else. I don't have anything new to give to the police, so all I can do is tell Molly my opinion. And that's that."

"Good. I'm glad you're getting that one out of your hair. And the others…? Are you still working on any of the others that… that the note could have been about?"

"I'll have them all closed off soon. I'll start new cases… not have to worry about those other ones anymore."

"Yeah. Good. Because I don't want any more accidents."

"Me neither," Zachary agreed.

Even so, he was still a little nervous when they finished their drinks and went out to Kenzie's little red sports car. Zachary walked around it, looking for anything suspicious. There was no note on the windshield. Nothing attached under the bumpers. He took a good long look under the car for anything that didn't look like it belonged, or any fluids dripping underneath. When he declared it safe and got into the passenger seat, Kenzie didn't tease him about his paranoia.

And he noticed as she backed out and shifted gears that she kept testing the brakes. Pressing down to make sure she still had pressure. Easing out of the parking space slowly and being even more cautious when she pulled out onto the main road, slowing significantly before curves and being unusually careful at intersections. Zachary kept an eye on the mirrors, trying not to be obvious about it. He caught Kenzie's eyes on him a couple of times and knew that she had noticed.

They both breathed a sigh of relief when they made it to the parking lot of Zachary's building, and Kenzie pulled into Zachary's reserved parking stall, empty because he hadn't yet replaced his car. Zachary got out and walked around the front of the car to meet her as she got out.

He swore.

Kenzie looked at him, eyes alarmed, and turned to see what he was looking at. Bridget was striding across the parking lot toward them, and her eyes were blazing. She looked crazed. Zachary checked her hands to make sure she didn't have a weapon. Kenzie backed away and looked at Zachary worriedly. She slid out her phone, and Zachary knew she was dialing 9-1-1, getting ready to press 'send' and get them on the line.

Bridget started yelling and swearing before she reached them, calling Zachary names up and down, her face bright red.

"What's wrong?" Zachary questioned. "What's going on?"

"You dog! You stupid, inconsiderate lowlife! I knew you were a jerk, Zachary, but this takes the cake!"

"What?" Zachary held up his hands defensively. "Tell me what's wrong."

"I took my car in to the shop for some servicing. What do you think they found?"

Zachary swallowed. He glanced aside at Kenzie, then back at Bridget. "Whatever has upset you, we can deal with it," he soothed. "We'll sort it out."

She slapped him across the face. Zachary was too slow and clumsy from his spinal cord injury to react and pull away in time and took the full force of her assault. Out of the corner of his eye, Zachary saw Kenzie moving to place the emergency call and raised his hand to stop her.

"You don't think he deserves it?" Bridget challenged Kenzie. "I should slap him silly!"

"For what?" Kenzie demanded.

"I took my car to the mechanic, and he found something on the inside of the bumper."

Kenzie shook her head. "What did they find?"

"A tracking device! A device that transmits my location, no matter where I go. So that *he*—" she shot a glare at Zachary, "—can know where I am at all times. Any time, night or day, he can look at his receiver, and see where I am. What do you think of that?"

Kenzie looked at Zachary. "Really? Is that true?"

"Ask to look at his phone and computer," Bridget said. "Which is it on, Zachary? Or is it on both?"

He swallowed, keeping his mouth shut. He'd be in trouble if he denied it, and in trouble if he admitted it. There was no right answer. He was glad that all he had on him was his old flip phone, which didn't even have any games on it, let alone the GPS tracker app. The computer back in his apartment was another story.

"Why would you be tracking your ex-wife?" Kenzie asked slowly.

Zachary brought his hand up to his face to rub his forehead. He felt like his hand was disembodied, not actually part of him. He rubbed the furrows between his brow slowly, trying to figure out what to do or say next.

"Bridget. I was just…"

"Just what?" she demanded furiously. "I'm curious. Just what excuse do you think would justify stalking me? What would the police say if I took this to them? You want to go to jail?"

"You were so upset when you ran into me and Kenzie at the restaurant.

You made it clear you didn't want to run into me anywhere. If I could check your location, I could make sure I didn't..."

Rather than looking reassured at this, Kenzie looked appalled. "So those times when I asked you if we were safe to go to a restaurant, to the inn, or somewhere else, the reason you knew Bridget wouldn't be there was you were tracking her?"

Zachary could tell by her voice that she did not want an affirmative answer. He looked at Bridget, a quick sideways glance to see just how angry she was, checking her position to make sure she wasn't going to hit him again, even though he knew he wouldn't be able to avoid it if she did.

"I'm taking out a restraining order," Bridget said. "This is going too far. You stay away from me, and you stay out of my life!"

"Wait a minute here," Kenzie spoke up, addressing Bridget. "You're the one who just hit him. You're the one who freaks out if you see him out in public. Who keeps calling me about him. You came to see him at the hospital, acting like you're all concerned. From everything I've seen, there's pretty good reason for him to want to keep track of your location."

"I *had* to go to the hospital. He still has me down as his emergency contact."

"There's no requirement for you to go to the hospital. You just tell them no."

"And you're the one who broke into my apartment," Zachary said tentatively. "There's a police record of that. Are you going to tell the judge that?"

"I didn't break in!" Bridget shouted, taking a step toward him.

Zachary took a step back. Kenzie moved in closer; her hands clenched into fists. "If you hit him again, I'm calling the cops," she warned. "What's all this about breaking in?"

"Christmas Day," Zachary said. "When I was at the hospital with Isabella's family. She came by here. Used her key to get in. I called the police because I thought she was a burglar."

"You are sick; you know that?" Kenzie addressed Bridget. "Maybe you should get some help. Some therapy. Because you're the one who won't leave him alone. For all I know, you're the one that cut the brake lines on his car."

Zachary watched Bridget carefully for her reaction. He knew that her car hadn't been anywhere near the inn that night. What about Gordon? Had he done her bidding? Or had she borrowed his car, knowing that Zachary might recognize hers if he saw it in the parking lot or following him on the street? He had never asked the police if they'd looked into the possibility that she was involved in the sabotage.

"I didn't do that," Bridget hissed. Her face contorted with rage. "I wouldn't do anything to hurt him. If I need therapy, that's his fault too. Do you have any idea what it's like putting up with his crap day in and day out? With his suspicion and paranoia and having to check and recheck everything? He's never had a healthy relationship in his life. I warned you. You don't want to lose years of your life to this creep. He's like a soul-sucking vampire. It's no wonder I ended up getting cancer. The stress of having to deal with his obsessive behavior every day wrecked my health. I got sick because of him!"

Zachary couldn't have been more staggered if she'd punched him. His gut and his chest tightened, and suddenly he couldn't breathe anymore. His legs were like jelly, and the world turned all wavy in front of his eyes. He knew it had finally happened. He was having a heart attack. She had broken his heart. He had suspected she blamed him for her cancer, but it was the first time she had put it into words.

"Zachary!" Kenzie grabbed at Zachary as his knees hit the ground, then his body. He curled up in agony, clutching his chest and unable to draw breath. "Zachary!"

"Look at him!" Bridget jeered. "Look how far he'll go to get your sympathy. You imagine living with a man who has a panic attack any time you have an argument! I stayed with him because I thought he would die if I didn't. I seriously thought he was going to keel over and die if I left."

"Zachary!" Kenzie was clutching at him. "Should I call 9-1-1? Do you need a pill? An inhaler? What can I do?"

He couldn't draw breath enough to answer her. The world was going dark around him. By the time an ambulance got there, he'd be dead.

"He'll have pills in his apartment," Bridget said grudgingly. "I don't know why he doesn't carry them with him. Or have something he can take every day to prevent it from happening in the first place. If we can get him up there..."

Kenzie put her hand under Zachary's arm, trying to coax him to his feet. "I don't think we're going to be able to get him anywhere. Maybe I should get an ambulance."

"If you just wait, it will pass. An ambulance and admitting him to the hospital will just rack up the bills."

"He's turning blue."

"It will pass," Bridget repeated. "It's self-limiting. He'll either pass out or it will start abating on its own."

It helped Zachary to hear Bridget's calm voice repeating what the doctors had always said. She'd seen him have panic attacks before. She didn't see anything to be concerned about.

"What if it's not a panic attack?" Kenzie asked. "What if it's a heart attack? Or a stroke?"

"It's not."

They both watched Zachary. Gradually, his gasping started to slow, and the world began to come back into focus. Kenzie attended to him, rubbing his shoulder comfortingly and repeating soothing words and phrases.

"Better?" Kenzie asked. "Are you okay?"

Zachary cleared his throat. His chest was still hurting, and his throat felt raw from breathing so hard. He still felt dizzy and a little nauseated. "Yeah. I'm okay."

"You should see a doctor," Bridget snapped. "You know you have a problem, so why don't you do something about it?"

"They can't always control it."

"You haven't even tried."

Zachary started to sit up, taking his time. He stopped and put his head in his hands, closing his eyes.

"I have tried."

"Can you get up?" Kenzie asked.

Zachary let her help him to his feet. He leaned on her, trying not to put too much of his weight on her.

"I think it's time for you to go," Kenzie told Bridget.

"I'll help you get him up to his apartment."

"I don't think so! You've done enough damage."

Bridget stood there for a moment, her mouth partway open, looking for something to say. Finally, she raised her hands in a melodramatic shrug. "Fine. He's all yours. I don't want him in my life."

"Good. Then go."

Bridget turned halfway around. "He has a few Xanax in his medicine cabinet. He'll probably want one of them. Then he'll sleep."

"We'll sort it out."

"Fine." Bridget looked at Zachary. "No more trackers on my car. No following or surveilling me. Not personally, not with electronics, and not by hiring someone else. Got it? Just stay away from me."

"Take your own advice," Kenzie snapped.

"If I were you, I'd have your car checked for trackers too," Bridget told her.

Kenzie looked at Zachary. He tried not to give anything away with his expression. He shifted, easing his weight off of her, trying to get his legs working.

"Okay," Kenzie said. "Let's get you upstairs."

They moved together, awkward and slow. Zachary's heart was still beating too fast, and he was reeling with Bridget's words. It was his fault that she got cancer because he was too needy, too much of a strain on the relationship. No wonder she hated him.

At the door, he couldn't get his key out and fitted into the lock properly, so Kenzie took it from him, unlocked the door, and ushered him in.

"Do you want a pill?"

Zachary looked around the apartment, not sure what to do. Entertain her? Sit down in front of the TV? Head to bed? What was Kenzie expecting? What was the protocol when a date ended with the appearance of a raging ex-wife and emotional collapse?

"Zachary? Do you want me to get you a pill?"

Zachary settled on the couch in the living room. There he could sleep, watch TV, or talk with Kenzie. He dug his flip phone and his wallet out of his pockets and put them on the side table.

"No... I don't think I can."

"You can't?" Kenzie frowned and shook her head.

"Because I had a couple of drinks. The doctor said I couldn't mix them."

She went into his bathroom and opened the medicine cabinet. It was nearly bare after Bridget's Christmas Day visit. She picked up the Xanax prescription, with a few white pills kicking around the bottom. She looked at the bright orange warning stickers affixed to it.

"Yeah, you're right," she agreed. "Is there something else? Anything else that would help?" She looked at a couple of other bottles. Zachary shifted uncomfortably in his seat. He didn't like her snooping through his prescriptions.

"No. I'll be fine," he told her. "Don't worry about it."

After pawing through the cabinet for another minute, she closed it and returned to the living room, sitting down on the couch next to him.

"That was scary," she said. "I thought it was a heart attack. I can't believe Bridget could stay so calm about it."

"She's seen a few anxiety attacks... maybe not that bad, but..."

"It must be scary for you, too."

"Yeah. Sort of."

She took his hand and sat with him for a few minutes in silence. "Do you think Bridget had something to do with the car brakes?"

"No," Zachary answered immediately. "She couldn't ever do something like that. Besides, I checked the tracker. She wasn't anywhere near the inn. She had no way of knowing that's where I was."

"What if someone had a tracker on your car? I don't see how anyone could have known you were there, otherwise. Did you tell anyone?"

Zachary's brain was still in a soup of stress neurotransmitters; he couldn't sort through the question calmly and logically, and wouldn't be able to until he had crashed and recovered. "I don't know."

"You wouldn't have told any of your clients. Any of those cases that you've been working on. Would you?"

"No... I don't think so. I don't remember."

"Someone would have had to have recognized it. Or followed you. Or tracked you."

"Yeah."

"Zachary."

His brain was going fuzzy.

"Zachary."

"Yeah?"

"I'll leave you to go to sleep, should I?"

"Yeah."

"Okay." She got up off the couch and stooped to kiss him on the forehead like a mother might kiss her child. "I'll talk to you tomorrow."

19

His dreams were always disrupted after a panic attack. Like his brain couldn't stop repeating the attack over and over. That was one of the reasons he would normally have taken a Xanax even though the attack had already subsided. He wanted to forget it and sleep, to stop the endless loop of crazy images in his head.

Bridget was a prominent feature in his dreams. So were the images from his distant past. His parents, the fire, some of the subsequent homes that he preferred to forget when he was lucid. Because Kenzie had been present, she was in his dreams too, iterating and reiterating all night.

"He said he'd drop it," Kenzie said, talking on an old-style desk phone with a rotary dial and tightly twisting handset cord. "You don't need to do anything else. He said he's done now."

Zachary couldn't tell who was on the other end of the call. Perhaps his mother, if the twang in the voice was any clue. He couldn't make out the words, just the angry, insistent tone, like Bridget's voice.

"It's over," Kenzie repeated. "I told you that. Just leave him alone now."

Who was she talking to? And why? Who was she reporting back to while he slept?

"He's not going to figure it out. I've told you everything. He doesn't suspect a thing."

Zachary puzzled over her words, trying to unwind the clues. In all the time he'd been investigating the Bond case, he'd never suspected Kenzie of being complicit. She didn't have any connection with Isabella. He'd discussed the case with her openly. All the evidence and his ideas. She'd told him the blood levels were all normal, making no mention of the cough medicine until pressed for an explanation. She had repeatedly suggested he drop the case and not make any waves.

What did she know that he didn't suspect?

"I'll give him something to make him sleep," Kenzie said on the phone. "He won't know anything."

Zachary tried to raise his voice to tell her again that he couldn't take anything. Not after being out drinking. Like in many dreams, especially those anxiety-triggered ones, he had no voice. He was as helpless as a child. Completely at her mercy.

The voice on the other end of the phone continued to squawk. Zachary saw his mother in his mind's eye. It had been so long since he'd seen her that it was only a vague, shadowy memory. He saw long, dark hair like Isabella's. But she was not *The Happy Artist*. Had he ever seen her smile? Their home had not been a happy one. He knew from the time he was small that they were unwanted. All the children. They were vermin, like rats, always in the way, eating the meager supplies of food. They kept her from true happiness and fulfillment.

He tried to compose a speech to his mother in his addled head. To explain to her that he didn't mean to be a drain on her. He was trying to be helpful. Trying to make her love him. Parents were supposed to love their children. That was what everyone said. A mother's love. Like it was the most precious thing in the world.

"He'll sleep right through it," Kenzie promised. "He won't feel a thing."

Zachary started to choke as the smell of acrid smoke curled into his nostrils. He coughed. After that Christmas Eve so many years ago, he was terrified of fire. Just the faintest wisp of smoke would bring it all back. The room was growing warm and then hot around him. He could hear the screams of his family. The blaring sirens and horns, and the shouts of the firefighters. His throat constricted as he tried to breathe, the combination of smoke and heated air scorching his throat.

He tried to scream, but he couldn't.

He couldn't wake up from the dream.

A bright light pierced the thick smoke. Zachary remembered that light from before. The relief of the firefighters finding their way through all the smoke and fire to find him. The relief of rescue from the burning hell he was in.

"Over here!"

Another figure joined the first, spraying down the area around Zachary. The first hefted him up, lifting him out of his seat and carrying him through the thick, burning clouds of smoke. Down a couple of flights of stairs. Out into clear air that was so cold that it caught in his chest and throat making him cough again. There were red, strobing lights everywhere, dark figures hurrying back and forth, shouted orders and discussions and radio chatter.

The fireman put him down on a gurney.

"This one was in the affected apartment. Get a mask on him right away. Keep checking his airway."

An oxygen mask was pressed over Zachary's face before he could say anything. He tried to talk through it but couldn't get out anything coherent.

"Just relax, sir. Lay back, and we'll take care of you."

A blanket was thrown over him. His skin was already cold from the night air.

"Just breathe the oxygen and don't try to talk right now. We'll talk in a little while."

Zachary lay there for a long time, breathing the oxygen and gradually coming to understand that it wasn't a dream. There really had been a fire, not just a memory from the past. He was at his apartment. Outside, in the cold, just like when he was ten. It wasn't Christmas Day this time, but a few weeks later.

"How are you doing there, sir?" A paramedic bent over him, ruffling his hair like he was a little boy. Like they had ruffled his hair all those years ago. "You had a close call. How's your throat?"

Zachary pulled the oxygen mask away from his face experimentally. He was again assaulted by the frigid outside air but managed to avoid coughing.

"It's sore," he admitted, voice strained.

"You might have some inflammation from the smoke and fire. How about the rest of your body? Are you burned anywhere?"

Zachary tried to tune in to his body. He'd been so caught up in his nightmare that he had no idea what else his body was feeling. He had been burned in the first fire, but he didn't know if he'd been burned again. The paramedic was checking him over, not waiting for a response, examining his arms and legs, pulling up his shirt, looking for any burns.

"You're red like you got a sunburn," the man said. "But I don't see anything serious. They'll check you out at the hospital. Unless there's something you're aware of…?"

Zachary shook his head. "No. What happened?"

"You'll have to talk to the firefighters. I don't know. A few people got smoke inhalation, but you're the only one who was in the apartment that caught fire first."

He was glad that no one else had been hurt, but he was confused by the fire. It had started in his apartment? He felt like his dreams had engendered it. That somehow, by dreaming about fire, he had brought it into being. He knew it didn't make any sense, but he didn't understand what had happened.

Eventually, a firefighter came over to talk to him, taking off a blackened helmet and leaning over Zachary's gurney to talk to him.

"Are you able to talk, sir?"

"Yes." Zachary's voice was rough, and his throat hurt, but he wanted to know what had happened. "What happened?"

"You're the one who was in 3C?"

"Yes. I'm 3C."

"Looks like maybe you had been burning some candles earlier this evening and fell asleep. One of the candles burned down, and some papers caught on fire."

Zachary shook his head. "I wasn't burning anything."

"Some candles. Christmas candles."

"No."

The man raised an eyebrow at Zachary, like he was a stubborn child and just needed to admit what he had done. "We understand that it was unintentional. Sometimes things happen. Fires are tricky things. People don't realize how dangerous candles can be. You can never go to sleep while they're burning."

Zachary tried to sit up. "I wasn't burning candles. I would never do that."

"It's nothing to be embarrassed about. People start fires cooking Christmas dinner, smoking in bed, throwing a scarf over a lamp for a romantic atmosphere. Burning candles is just one of those things. It happens."

"I was in a fire as a child," Zachary said, catching the fireman by the front of his uniform and holding on to him tightly, afraid he was going to leave before Zachary could explain. "I *can't* light a candle. They're terrifying."

The firefighter stared at him, his head wrinkling in puzzlement.

"You're 3C."

"Yes."

"That's where the fire started. It started with candles."

"That's impossible. I don't have candles. If I did, they would just be for decoration. I would *never* light them."

"Well, there were, and somebody did. There were apparently no batteries in the smoke detectors."

Zachary's jaw dropped. "There were! I replace them every two months." He could see that the fireman didn't believe him. "I was in a fire," he repeated desperately. "I am very careful. I make sure! I replace the batteries every two months and test the smoke detectors every Sunday."

"Let me talk to my chief. You just stay here." The man sought out a paramedic close by. "You won't take him to the hospital yet, will you? We need to talk to him for a few more minutes."

"Okay."

"Keep an eye on him. Don't let him go anywhere or talk to anyone else."

Zachary was again left alone, sitting on the gurney with his head whirling, trying to understand what had happened. How could a fire start in his apartment? With candles he'd never owned? And no batteries in the smoke detectors?

Another fireman came over to him, this one not drenched in smoke like the first. There was a policeman with him.

"Can I get your name, sir?"

"Zachary Goldman."

The policeman looked startled but didn't say anything, letting the fire chief proceed with his questions.

"And do you want to tell me what happened tonight? What did you do today, before going to bed?"

Zachary tried to sit up straighter. He wanted to look calm and self-possessed. He needed them to believe him and what he had to say.

"I went out for drinks with a friend in the evening."

"You've been drinking?"

"I had a few drinks. Yes."

"And you came back here. Alone?"

"She drove me home and walked me up to my apartment. She didn't stay."

"How long was she here? I'm going to need her name."

Zachary filled in the details the best he could.

"And you didn't light candles for a romantic atmosphere with your girlfriend?"

"No. I was telling the other fireman. I was in a fire when I was a boy. I don't have any candles. I can't stand having them around, and I'd never light one."

"This fire was obviously started with candles. There is plenty of evidence of them in the apartment."

"But I didn't *have* any candles. He said there were no batteries in the smoke detectors. I always have fresh batteries in my smoke detectors, and I test them every week."

"How much did you have to drink tonight?"

"Two, three drinks. Over a couple of hours. I wasn't drunk."

"Did you take anything before bed?"

"No. I couldn't. Because I'd been drinking."

The police chief looked at Zachary and looked at the policeman. "Does that mean that you normally would have taken something?"

"Sometimes I do… a sleeping pill to help me get to sleep. Or a Xanax… because I'd had a panic attack. I didn't take either one because I'd had alcohol and I knew you're not supposed to mix them."

"But even so, you didn't wake up when your apartment started to fill with smoke."

"I… I don't know when I was awake and when I was asleep. I was dreaming about a fire, having a nightmare. I don't know when I woke up. I don't know how much of it was a dream and how much was real."

"How long was your girlfriend there?"

"Just a few minutes. I was tired… she didn't stay."

"Did she want to?"

"I don't know."

"Did you walk her out? Lock the door behind her?"

"No. I was already falling asleep… she saw herself out."

"Are you sure?"

"Yes. I didn't walk her out. I was too tired."

"Are you sure she *left?*"

Zachary felt the cold through his blanket. He was starting to shiver. Another night out in the cold, nearly killed under suspicious circumstances. He thought of Kenzie in his dream. How she knew something. She knew who it was that was trying to kill him. She was helping them. Had he heard her leave the apartment? Or had she merely walked out of the room and waited until she was sure he was asleep? She was the one he told everything to. She was the one who knew about the fire when he was ten. She could have put something in his drink at the Four-Leaf Clover to make him sleep more soundly.

He won't wake up. He'll never know.

"I… I'm sure she did," he protested, but he knew they could hear the doubt in his voice. That they knew very well he wasn't sure. He could never be sure. He'd fallen asleep. He hadn't walked her out. Locked the bolt behind her.

"Mr. Goldman," the policeman said.

"Yes?"

"Are you the same Mr. Goldman who was in an accident a few weeks ago? In a car? Brake lines cut?"

Zachary swallowed. He took in a deep breath. Too sudden; he started coughing and had a hard time getting back under control again.

"Yes. That was me."

"Who is trying to kill you?"

"I don't know."

"This girlfriend. Was she with you before the car accident?"

"She was in the accident with me," Zachary said, sure it proved Kenzie's innocence. "She couldn't have been the one who did it. We both could have died."

"Maybe that was the plan. For the two of you to die together."

"No… I don't even know her that well. We've only gone out a few times."

"Uh-huh. Is there someone else who has motive to kill you?"

"I… the other officers who questioned me after the car accident… they have the details about the cases I was working on… I'm a private detective. I've been getting threatening notes."

"I'd say this goes well beyond threatening notes."

Zachary nodded. He put the oxygen mask over his mouth, both to breathe the warmer air that didn't tear at his throat, and to hide behind it, so he didn't have to speak while he was sorting out his thoughts.

"Anyone else we should be aware of?"

He breathed the warm air, not wanting to answer the question.

"Mr. Goldman?"

"My ex-wife was here tonight too."

"You have an ex-wife? Any reason she might be upset with you? Other than being jealous that you were seeing someone else?"

"She wasn't jealous of Kenzie… but she was pretty mad. She hit me," Zachary touched the cheek that she had slapped. "And she said… that it was my fault that she got cancer."

The policeman's brows furrowed. "And how was it your fault that she got cancer? It's not usually something contagious."

"Because… dealing with me made her stressed. She got cancer because her body's defenses were down… or something. I don't know. Does it have to make sense?"

"When do they?" the fire chief intoned, rolling his eyes. "I've got three exes, and there's no point in trying to reason with them. I'm probably lucky none of them have tried to kill me."

Zachary rubbed at one of the scorch marks on his pants, seeing whether it would come off, or whether the fabric itself was burned.

"She knows… that I would normally take a Xanax and go to sleep after a panic attack. She told Kenzie so."

"So, she had good reason to think you would sleep through just about anything," the cop observed.

"Yeah." Zachary rubbed some more. He was going to have to get new clothes. Not just to replace the ones that he was wearing, but everything. None of the clothes that were in his apartment were going to be salvageable. If they hadn't burned, they would be smoke damaged. "But I don't think it was Bridget. I really… I don't think she would do that. I know she wasn't there when the brakes were cut. She was on the other side of the city."

"Or so she told you."

"No..." He bit his lip and looked at the policeman. "I had a tracker on her car. I know she was on the other side of town."

The cop gave no indication he intended to arrest Zachary for stalking or any other crime.

"With an ex like that, I'd track her too."

20

Zachary was again back at the hospital. After being checked out, he wasn't admitted. He went to the waiting room to sleep in one of the uncomfortable plastic chairs. He didn't have anywhere to go, or any way to get there. At least the waiting room was warm. He was around people, so, hopefully, he was safe from whatever psycho was determined to kill him.

He slept fitfully off and on. More off than on. Eventually, he figured it was late enough in the morning he could call Kenzie. He begged the use of one of the nursing station phones to do so. He was again without a phone of his own, or a wallet, or any other possessions. All he had were the clothes on his back, smelling strongly of smoke and not enough to protect him from the elements.

There was no answer on Kenzie's cell phone, or on her line at the medical examiner's office. He continued to call throughout the morning, growing hungry and crabby and at a complete loss as to what to do next.

Finally, almost at noon, she answered her cellphone.

"Kenzie! I've been trying to get ahold of you."

"So I see. I don't recognize the number you're calling from, though." Her voice was cool. Almost frigid. Zachary's heart sank.

"I'm calling from the hospital."

"Oh. What is it *this* time?"

He didn't understand her attitude. Wasn't she even the least bit concerned? "Well… it looks like whoever cut my brake lines isn't done. Someone started a fire in my apartment last night."

"Oh, did they? Why would anyone do that?"

He tried to figure out whether she was putting on a show for someone who might be listening in on the conversation. Did she not care about the second attempt on his life?

"Kenzie? They tried to kill me. Again!"

"I heard you."

Zachary waited for a few beats, trying to analyze her tone. He tried to picture her in front of him to figure out why she was behaving the way she was.

"What's wrong?" he asked. "Did I do something?"

He didn't need to wait for her answer for it to click in. He should have expected it. He should have known that she, too, would abandon him.

"I took Bridget's advice and took my car to the shop."

He swallowed. "Oh."

"You've been tracking me, too."

"It's not like that…"

"I can understand why you would track Bridget. It makes sense in theory. If you wanted to avoid her, you had to know where she was. But why would you be tracking me? Explain that one."

Zachary concentrated on breathing. He sat down in the chair beside the nursing station, unable to keep his feet. He breathed through his mouth.

"I'm waiting," Kenzie prompted. "Or are you out of excuses now? I'm starting to think maybe there's something to what Bridget's been trying to say. You're not a well person, Zachary. There's something very wrong with you."

"I… I wasn't *stalking* you. I wasn't doing anything sinister or creepy. I just…"

"You just what?" she snapped.

"I have… anxiety. You found that out. There's more to it than just panic attacks. I get… worried about people I have relationships with. I want to know… that you're okay. I know it's sick. You're right. I get scared, and I want to check on you. Just to make sure…"

"To make sure that I'm not seeing anyone else? That I'm not sneaking around behind your back? You don't own me, Zachary. We haven't even talked about dating exclusively. We've just had a few casual dinners together. That doesn't make me your girlfriend, and it doesn't give you the right to follow me around and monitor what I'm doing."

"No. I know that. That's not what I was doing. It didn't have anything to do with whether you were seeing anyone else."

"The hell it didn't!"

He was taken aback by her vehemence. He sat there in shocked silence. The nurse's eyes slid over to him, trying to analyze how much longer he would be. Trying to understand his conversation from the one side that she could hear.

"I'm sorry, Kenzie."

"You think that makes everything okay?"

"No. It's wrong. It was an invasion of your privacy. I was just being... a jerk. A stupid, dysfunctional jerk. I couldn't help—" He stopped and corrected himself. "I could help it. I shouldn't have done it. I should have just put up with the anxiety. Not like it would kill me."

She sniffled, and he realized she was crying.

He had made Kenzie cry.

"I'm sorry. I'm so sorry. I didn't—I did, but—I shouldn't have. I shouldn't have done it."

"You're a really sweet guy, Zachary. I can't understand how you could do something like this. You act like this great guy, all put together, a great catch, but inside, you're like... a little boy... like that little, lost boy who tried to do something nice and accidentally burned the house down."

There was a lump in Zachary's throat. "I don't tell that story to anyone. Especially not someone I'm just dating. I don't think I told any of it to Bridget until we'd been married for a year. Even then... no more than I had to."

He thought of the would-be killer lighting candles to start the fire. Was it someone who hadn't known his horror for candles and fire? Who thought that Zachary having a few Christmas candles lit would be perfectly natural? Or was it someone who knew him, who knew his story and wanted not just to kill him, but to do it in the most terrifying way?

"I'm glad you told me. Because if you hadn't, I don't think I could even begin to understand how you could do something so stupid as to track me electronically."

Zachary just waited.

"That doesn't make it okay, Zachary. It just makes it a bit easier for me to understand why you're so scared of losing the people you love."

Zachary swallowed and nodded, trying to make a noise of agreement.

"You really should be in therapy."

"I have been... but it doesn't make these feelings go away."

"But maybe if you understood them a bit better. Maybe if they gave you some strategies to manage your anxiety..."

"Maybe I need to find someone new. A new therapist. Maybe if I was seeing someone every couple of weeks..."

"Yeah. I think you should try."

Zachary sighed. "I'm monopolizing this nurse's phone. I should probably go."

"Oh. You're at the hospital." She had thawed and now sounded a little concerned about him.

"Yeah."

"Do you have a way to get home?"

"No... but I don't have a home to go to, so that doesn't matter."

She was silent at first, not immediately jumping in to offer him a ride. "What are you going to do?"

"I don't know. I haven't figured anything out. I guess I need to get back to my building, see if I can get in or if anything is salvageable. But then... I haven't got a clue. Maybe a homeless shelter."

"Why don't you get a cab and a hotel room? You'll maybe have to live out of a suitcase for a while, but..."

"I don't have any money. No credit cards, no ID. It was all in my apartment. The only thing I've got is the clothes I'm wearing, and those are pretty ripe."

She sighed. "I've got to work. I've already missed a couple of hours getting my car looked at. I hadn't arranged for anyone to cover my shift. You're going to have to figure things out on your own for now. Call me tonight when I'm off... let me know how you're doing. What you managed to get set up. Okay?"

Zachary swallowed. "Okay."

He had told himself that he didn't expect her to drop everything to pick him up. But it turned out he had. He'd been lying to himself. He needed someone to help him; then he could figure out what to do about getting his identification reissued and finding a place to live. Someone's couch to sleep on for a few nights. When he hung up after the discussion with Kenzie, he put his head in his hands, trying to sort out what to do next.

"What can I get you?" the nurse asked. "Coffee?"

He rubbed his palms into his eyes, trying to soothe the deep ache behind them. "That would be really good," he admitted.

"You just stay there for a minute, I'll get you one from the staff room."

He did as she said. Not that he had the energy to do anything else. He gazed out the wall of windows behind the emergency room chairs. Snow was starting to fall in big, white flakes.

Christmas snow. Magical snow.

Just another reminder that he was again homeless. He didn't even have a coat to keep him warm on the street. What had changed in the decades since he was ten years old, trying to do something to bring his parents and his family back together? He had ended up in hospital then too. More burns on his body than he had this time. A throat swollen and burned by the smoke and the burning air. It was the same thing all over again.

"Here you go," the nurse said compassionately, setting a ceramic coffee cup down beside Zachary. She also set down a napkin with a chocolate glazed donut on it. "You're in luck; there was a meeting this morning with leftover food."

Zachary took a sip of the hot coffee and picked up the sticky confection. "You're a lifesaver, Nurse Nancy," he told her, looking at her name tag. "You don't know what this means to me."

"I gather," she nodded to the phone, admitting to the fact that she had eavesdropped on his call. As if she could avoid it, sitting right there two feet away from him. "Sounds like you're in pretty dire straits. You get something in your stomach, and then we'll see what else we can do for you."

Nurse Nancy and the coworkers she roped into helping Zachary had found a coat that fit him in the lost and found. "People leave them draped over the chairs and get into their cars without realizing they've left them behind," Nancy said. "And when they try to figure it out, they probably don't even think about the hospital. You should see the amount of stuff we get through here."

Zachary nodded politely. It was strange to pull on someone else's clothes, something that didn't quite fit to his skin and that carried someone else's scent. He was grateful for it. He couldn't even go outside without that little kindness. Several people had donated a few dollars so that he wasn't totally destitute and could at least call a cab or buy a sandwich if he were desperate.

Zachary thanked them profusely. They were lifesavers.

Though the hospital was not close to his apartment, he determined to walk back to it. It was something to occupy him while he waited for Kenzie to get off of work and wouldn't cost him any of his meager cash supply.

While the coat was warm enough that he was sweating after a few blocks' brisk walk, he didn't have any gloves, and his fingers turned numb not long into his journey. He swung his hands and clapped them together and pulled them into his sleeves. Eventually, he settled on pulling one at a time in under his coat and clamping it under his armpit until it thawed out. Then he would put it back out his sleeve and pull the other one in, repeating the process on the other side.

It took several hours to walk back to his apartment, as he had expected. When he got there, he found yellow caution tape blocking off all except for the front door to the building, with a police guard there to talk to anyone who wanted access to the building. He stepped forward and looked Zachary up and down, blocking the way.

"Sorry sir, the building is closed."

"I need to see how bad the damage is. If anything of mine can be recovered."

The cop opened his mouth to argue and repeat the stricture that the building was closed.

"I don't have my phone or my wallet. I can't get a hotel without a credit card. I have nowhere to go. I need access to my apartment to see if anything is salvageable."

"Which apartment?"

"Number 3C."

The cop shook his head again. "That's where the fire broke out. You can't have any access to it."

"Please. I need to at least see it. I need to know how bad it is. Should I start on getting my ID reissued, or will I be able to get it back? Can you tell me that?"

"No, I don't know."

"Could you go up there with me? That way you can make sure I don't touch anything, but I can see if I'll be able to save anything, or whether it's all gone."

"I don't have clearance to do that."

"Maybe you could get permission. Is there someone you could call? Explain the situation?"

The cop just looked at him. Zachary spread his arms wide.

"I don't have anywhere to go. I don't have any identification, phone, or money. I don't have anywhere to sleep. I don't have a car. Can you explain that to someone? Help me out, here."

"I can't let you have access to anything in the apartment."

"I understand that. I won't touch or take anything. Just look to see it there's anything that didn't burn."

The man gave an exasperated sigh. "Fine. Let me see if I can get ahold of someone."

Zachary withdrew to give him privacy. He sat on the bench outside the building where people sat to smoke when it was warm out. He cleared a spot of snow and sat with both of his hands under his armpits. A few times he looked back at the cop, who was still on his phone. Sometimes they made eye contact, as the cop looked to see if he were still there. It was a long time, and Zachary sensed that the cop had needed to make a long series of phone calls rather than just one to make any progress. He finally called out to Zachary, motioning him over.

"Mr. Goldman."

He hadn't given his name, so obviously, the cop had managed to get ahold of the officers on the case and to talk to someone who knew the details.

"I have permission to walk you into your apartment. You mustn't touch anything. The arson investigator would like to talk to you when he gets here."

"I'd be happy to talk to him. I'm going to need… somewhere warm to hang out. I'm freezing."

The cop grunted. He motioned Zachary into the building and then locked the door that he had been guarding, barring anyone else from entering while he was showing Zachary to his apartment.

The electricity had been shut off, so they were forced to take the stairs. Zachary's throat and lungs were sore from the fire. His ribs were still healing after the car accident. His ability to climb the stairs and know what to do with his feet following his spinal cord injury was impaired. All of which meant that he acted like a crippled old asthmatic going up the stairs, making the cop wait for him every few steps. Eventually, they made it up the stairs and to Zachary's apartment.

The door hung open, the catch broken through the doorframe. At first glance, the interior was completely black, but as Zachary moved in and looked around, he saw that there were varying shades of black. Some things were completely burned, some were scorched, and some were only blackened by smoke. He walked around, the cop right with him, watching with eagle eyes to be sure he didn't lay so much as a finger on anything.

It was such a foreign landscape. Nothing was familiar. Nothing looked like it was his.

Zachary pointed to the remnants of his phone and wallet on the side table by the couch.

"I guess that answers my question about the identification," he said. The phone was mostly melted, and the wallet extra-crispy. He doubted any of the flimsy plastic credit cards had survived the heat. Nor any cash. He didn't try to touch it and neither did the policeman.

Zachary wandered around the apartment. The computer sat under his desk. Like the phone, much of the plastic was melted and scorched. He was sure it wouldn't start up. Perhaps the hard drive would be recoverable, but he doubted even that. It wasn't the black box of an airplane, carefully shielded from the elements and any expected adverse events.

He looked over the rest of the rubble that remained on his desk. "I had a stack of papers here," he pointed.

The cop looked at the table and shrugged. "They wouldn't have survived. Papers burn the fastest, before anything else."

"But… there's no ash. There should be a whole bunch of ash from the burned papers, and there isn't."

"I'm no specialist in arson. I'm just here to keep the building secure. Talk to the arson investigator if you have any questions. I'm sure he'll want to hear anything you might have to say. Anything you notice."

Between the fire, the smoke, and water damage from putting out the fire, there was going to be very little that was recoverable, if anything. Zachary sighed. He looked at the small kitchen as he walked by.

"Oh... something in the freezer might have survived, right? They say to put valuable papers in the freezer, so they'll survive fire...?"

"Maybe," the cop agreed. "Did you put anything in there?"

"A few papers, yeah. I don't remember what all I put in there. At the time, I got together everything I thought I might need if everything else was destroyed..."

The cop looked at the closed fridge. "I hope you put them in plastic bags, because everything in there is melting and going to stink to high heaven by the time they retrieve anything."

"Yeah. I did. Hopefully..."

"With any luck."

"I don't suppose you could open the freezer, just take a peek inside?"

"Nope. My instructions are not to touch anything. You'll have to talk to Darryl Reimer. He's the arson investigator. He'll be able to give you a time-line if anyone can."

The cop, Lawson, conceded to Zachary waiting inside the building, just inside the doors where Lawson could still keep an eye on him to make sure that he wasn't getting into anything. It was still cold, right in the doorway and all the utilities in the building being cut off, but it was significantly more comfortable than sitting on the cold stone bench outside in the snow. What should have been lunch time had come and gone, and the sun was low in the sky by the time Darryl Reimer showed up. He looked down at Zachary, sprawled on the floor inside the door, tired and bored, trapped with nothing but his thoughts in the little alcove.

"Mr. Goldman?" he inquired.

He was a stocky man. He wore a suit, not a uniform, and it appeared that he had been wearing the same shirt for a day or two. His face was red. He had a small black mustache.

"Yeah," Zachary scrambled to his feet. "You must be Reimer?"

"That's me." Rather than shaking hands, Reimer pulled out a shield, held it up for only an instant, and then put it back away again. "Thank you for sticking around to see me."

He headed toward the stairs, and Zachary followed him.

"I've read both your statement to the police last night, and your statement following the car accident on New Year's Eve. I'm as much up-to-date as I can be without talking to you."

"Uh-huh." Zachary focused on breathing. The stairs were just as difficult to climb the second time as they had been earlier. Luckily, though, Reimer didn't seem to be in great physical shape and was happy to take it much more slowly than Lawson.

"First off, do you have any questions or concerns for me? Anything you'd like to bring to my attention?"

"I looked around the apartment... I didn't see a lot of ash from burned papers on my desk."

"How many papers?"

Zachary went slowly through what he could remember of what was in the piles. The sizes and approximate number of pages of each stack. That took the rest of the way to the apartment. They were both silent as Reimer looked around. He had brought a powerful flashlight with him, so the setting of the sun didn't bother him. He played the light over the desk and nodded thoughtfully.

"It does seem like there should be more," he agreed. He played the light on the floor surrounding the desk, humming tunelessly.

"You had been getting threatening notes about one of your cases?"

"Yes."

"And were there documents from that case on the desk."

"Yeah. Sure. From all of my cases."

"There was some question of whether your wife could have been involved?"

"Ex-wife," Zachary corrected quickly. "Well, yes. I don't think she was, but there's a possibility. I know she wasn't anywhere nearby when my brake lines were cut, so it doesn't seem very likely."

"Right. And there is a current girlfriend?"

"A girl I am seeing, yes."

"And she was nearby when both attempts were made on your life."

"Yes. She doesn't have a motive, though."

"If there's both a girlfriend and an ex-wife, there's motive. Believe me."

Zachary stood in the middle of the room, watching Reimer move around, examining clues that didn't mean anything to Zachary. It was all just blackened fragments of his broken life. None of it told him anything.

"I was dreaming before I woke up to the fire," Zachary said. "And in my dream, it was Kenzie, the girl I'm seeing." He paused, letting the words sink in. "That doesn't mean it has anything to do with her. It was just a nonsensical dream."

"Our dreams often derive from the environment," Reimer observed. "Did you dream about a fire before you woke up?"

"Yes. I was in a house fire when I was a kid. I dreamt I was back there."

"Makes perfect sense, doesn't it? And dreaming about the girlfriend *could* mean that she was here while you were sleeping. It's not a forgone conclusion. Our brains aren't just input and output."

"She was here before I went to sleep, but then she left."

"Did you lock up behind her? Walk her out?"

"No."

"You are only assuming she left. Maybe you dreamed about her because she was here before you went to sleep. Maybe while you were asleep. No way to know."

Zachary was glad that Reimer hadn't taken it too literally. Zachary had been honest, and Reimer hadn't overreacted, taking it as an accusation.

Reimer continued to look around.

"I have some papers in the freezer."

Reimer didn't look up. "Next time, invest in a fire-proof safe."

"Okay... do you think we could see whether they survived?"

"When I get there."

Reimer wasn't in any particular hurry. His doggedness probably made him a good arson investigator. Single-minded, not easily shaken from the trail. Zachary was starting to get cold. The building kept out the chilly wind, but he needed somewhere with a furnace or heater to get warmed back up again. He'd been gradually losing heat all afternoon.

After a long time in the living room, the epicenter of the damage, Reimer finally moved on. He looked into the bedroom, where the damage was not as bad.

"Where were you sleeping? In here?"

"No. In the living room."

Reimer stared off into space. Zachary tried to read his expression and figure out what he was thinking. Eventually, Reimer spoke. "That's one audacious arsonist. Lighting a fire with you in the room? Arsonists normally stay far away from people. They light buildings on fire. Not people. Normally unoccupied buildings, but occasionally they will be bold enough to set a building they know is occupied on fire. When they do, they light the far end, furthest from the occupants. Not in the same room."

He stared off into space some more.

"What does that mean?" Zachary asked finally. "What does that tell you?"

"Most arsonists are firebugs first and murderers second. I think this arsonist is the opposite. I think he was a murderer who took the opportunity to light a fire to achieve his ends. I don't think we're going to find a serial arsonist involved here. This may be his first arson, which means that he's more likely to have made mistakes and left evidence."

Zachary nodded. "That makes sense, since he didn't put a bomb or incendiary device in the car. He cut the brake lines."

"Right," Reimer agreed curtly.

Zachary waited while Reimer made his way around the bedroom. When he was done, he looked up. "You wanted to look in the freezer."

"Yes."

Reimer went to the kitchen, and again surveyed the area as a whole rather than going directly to the fridge. He played the light on the floor and the counters, moving slowly and deliberately. Finally, he made his way to the fridge and opened the freezer door with a gloved finger.

As Lawson had suggested, everything was melted and starting to go bad. A foul, sour smell crept out into the apartment, and murky water dripped down the front of the fridge. Reimer shone his flashlight around the interior of the freezer.

"Where were these papers?"

"They might be under something. They were in a plastic zip-bag." Zachary craned his neck to see over Reimer's shoulders and around his head. "Check… under that pizza box."

The box was, of course, sopping wet and tore when Reimer attempted to move it out of the way. He moved the few items in Zachary's freezer around, and both of them could see that there was no plastic bag in the freezer.

"You're sure you left them in here?" Reimer asked. "You didn't change your mind and put them in a safe deposit box? Or give them to a friend to hold? Those are far safer methods than keeping important documents in your freezer."

Zachary felt the sting of criticism. "Yes, I'm sure. I don't have a safe deposit box or a fireproof safe, or anyone that I could have left the papers with. I put them in a zip bag in the freezer."

Reimer shook his head. "Not there now. What papers?"

"My birth certificate. Copies of my credit cards. Important phone numbers if my wallet was stolen. Or burnt to a crisp."

"They're not here."

"Can I look?"

Reimer stepped back and allowed Zachary to step in. He didn't have any gloves on, and the frigid water immediately made his fingers numb. He pushed the thawed goods around the freezer, sure that the bag must just have gotten wedged between them, or crumpled up in the back of the freezer, but the whole time he was looking, his heart sank. They weren't there. Whoever had come into his apartment had not only stolen or burned all the papers on his desk, but they had also taken the documents from the freezer.

"Why would anyone take those? They aren't of any use to anyone except me!"

"Identity theft?" Reimer suggested.

"But what would be the point of that? You don't go into someone's apartment while they're sleeping and steal their identity and set their apartment on fire! If all you wanted to do was steal their identity, you wouldn't want to alert them to that fact by setting the apartment on fire. If it wasn't for the fire, it might have been months before I realized that those papers weren't in the freezer anymore."

Reimer grunted. "Maybe it has been months. Maybe they were taken out of there a long time ago. You don't have any evidence that it was during the fire."

"No... it hasn't been that long... I've seen them the last couple of weeks. They were stolen during the fire!"

"You want motives, talk to a psychologist. I can help with basic arsonist psychological profiles, but this guy wasn't a firebug. This was something else. He wanted..." Reimer considered, shaking his head, brows drawn down. "This guy wanted to erase you. I don't know. Talk to a psychologist. You're sure there wasn't anything in those papers that was connected with one of the cases you were on? The case that the perp keeps telling you to drop?"

Zachary thought about the contents of the bag and shook his head. It wouldn't be of any use to anyone, except to assume his identity. His identity didn't have anything to do with any of the cases he was investigating. He wasn't an important feature in any of the cases. They were all about other people. It was professional. Not personal.

⁎

Zachary called Kenzie from Reimer's phone. She was getting off work and agreed to pick him up at the apartment building. He still didn't know what he was going to do for the night, where he was going to stay, but he could only move one small step at a time. He had confirmed that he was going to need to get all of his wallet cards reissued, and that was going to take some doing. He didn't have anything to prove his identity. No birth certificate, no driver's license, not even a piece of mail with his name on it. Everything had burned up or been stolen. He wasn't sure how he was going to go about getting it all reissued.

But that was a problem for another day.

Kenzie said she would pick him up. She also, at Zachary's request, agreed to bring with her another copy of the medical examiner's report, though she seemed reluctant to do so.

Why did she care so much about him investigating the case? Was it really because she thought everything had been handled the right way and that he would be burning his bridges if he contradicted the medical examiner or any of the officers who had been involved in the investigation? Or was there something else going on?

Zachary shook the questions off. Kenzie didn't have any connection with the case. The only thing that connected her to the case was the fact that she was an administrator in the medical examiner's office.

He waited in the doorway of the apartment building. Lawson was no longer on shift, but his replacement seemed to have no problem with Zachary remaining there while he watched for Kenzie's car to pull up. It was a relief when he finally saw the familiar red sports car pull into the loading zone.

"Thanks so much for helping me out," he told her, as he settled into the passenger seat.

"Yeah. We'll have to discuss the parameters, though. I talked with Mario Bowman, and he said you could stay with him for a night or two. You're not staying at my apartment."

Zachary was both disappointed and relieved. At least he would have a place to sleep. A warm place. He didn't have to rely on a homeless shelter. "Okay. Thanks. I really appreciate it. I'm just in a tough place now… everything is a little crazy."

"I can sympathize, but I can't let myself be pulled into your problems. We are not a couple, and you are not staying with me, not even on the couch."

Zachary nodded. "Understood." He massaged his hands in the air from the heater, trying to thaw out. He was cold to his core, just like the night of the accident. He was looking forward to spending the next few hours in central heating, no matter where it was.

Kenzie's eyes were on his purple-tipped fingers. She looked back at the road. "You hungry?"

"Starving."

"What are you in the mood for?"

"Whatever you feel like. I can't pay, but I'll pay you back when I get access to my bank account and credit cards."

"No need. I'll treat tonight. Pizza? Italian? There's that buffet place on Hillcrest that has a bit of everything."

"Yeah, let's go for the buffet," Zachary agreed. "Then we can each have whatever suits us." And he'd have no worries about getting enough to eat, making up for a day of nothing but a cup of coffee and a chocolate glazed donut given to him out of pity.

Kenzie nodded her consent.

The ride to the restaurant was mostly silent. Even though Kenzie had agreed to help him out, it was obvious that she was still upset about the tracker on her car. He couldn't blame her; he knew it was not something that he should have done.

They walked into the restaurant, were seated, and went through the buffet. Zachary loaded up his plate and Kenzie very carefully picked and chose small amounts of a few favorite foods. Zachary was a little embarrassed at how his plate compared to hers. It probably wasn't her first meal of the day, though.

After they had sat down at the table, Kenzie slid the familiar medical examiner's report across to him.

"I'm not sure why you need that," she said. "I thought you were closing the case."

"I was. I am. I have to rewrite the final report. All of my materials are gone in the fire."

"You should have saved it in the cloud."

"Where someone else could access it? I never save case files to the cloud."

"Then how are you going to recover all the stuff you lost in the fire?"

"I don't know." Zachary sighed. "I'll have to reconstruct what I can. Request new copies." He groaned as he thought of all his photography equipment and negatives. He had been saying for years that he needed to store stuff off-site. That he needed to find a way to back up his data somewhere safe. He never had. The backups he had made of his computer were in the apartment, just like the computer. A lot of good that did.

Kenzie put a forkful of salad in her mouth and chewed it slowly. "What are your other active cases about?" she asked.

Zachary shrugged. "Adultery. Insurance fraud. Accident reconstruction. Stuff like that."

"The Declan Bond case is the only one about a death."

"Yes."

"Then doesn't it have to be the one that they're trying to stop you from investigating? Who's going to set your apartment on fire over adultery? The only one that makes any sense is the Bond case."

"Only it doesn't," Zachary disagreed. He took a minute to nibble the meat from a buffalo wing before expanding. "I know the principals involved in the case. If it was the mother, which is what I think, it doesn't make any sense that she would try to get me to shut down the investigation. She already got away with it, and no one from the police department is going to reopen the investigation. She wouldn't kill me because I state in my report that she's the only one who had motive and opportunity. Her mother and husband are just going to brush it off. It isn't going to get to her employers or viewers. There's no reason to kill me."

"Why do you think it's the mother and not just an accident?"

Zachary sighed and shook his head. He was starting to get warm inside at last. He wrapped his fingers around his coffee mug while he tried to explain it to Kenzie.

"First, because of the cough medicine."

"So he had cough medicine in his system. That's not suspicious."

"It's suspicious when they all say they wouldn't give him cough medicine. If one of them volunteered and said, 'yes, he was developing a cough, so I gave him some medicine,' then I would be happy with that. No big deal. When the mother says that they absolutely would not give him cough medicine because it knocks him out... that's a different story."

"Tell me more about why she wouldn't give it to him."

"She gave him a children's cold tablet once a couple of years ago. It knocked him out and scared her so much that she's never given him any cold medicine since."

"That's sort of an extreme reaction, isn't it?" Kenzie suggested. She flaked a little fish into her fork and took a dainty bite. "Why wouldn't she just go with a half dose the next time?"

"Because Isabella is all about extreme reactions. She gets stuck and does things that don't make logical sense. Like putting out fresh food for the missing cat every day for eight years. Like refusing to eat off a plate in her own home, because Spencer threw out her favorite. Like not painting the color blue since Declan's death. That's what she's like."

"A little like someone I know who can't listen to Christmas songs and insists on GPS tracking anyone he gets close to."

Zachary scowled, staring down at his plate. He started on a small slice of pepperoni pizza.

"Regardless. Declan reacted to cold medicine, so she was afraid of ever giving it to him again."

"So maybe Spencer gave it to him."

"Spencer obeys his wife's rules. They both have rules to keep the house running. He's learned from the past what happens when he's up against one of her compulsions."

"So, he does it secretly. He doesn't tell her."

Zachary thought about it and shook his head. "He knew how Declan reacted the last time. He wouldn't risk doing it again."

"Like I say, he gives Declan a half dose. The kid is much older now. A half dose would probably be just enough to keep the cold symptoms at bay without knocking him out."

"But then why deny it? Why not just say that he was the one who gave Declan the medicine when I asked him?"

"Because it would get back to his wife. He's keeping it a secret from her at all costs. Because... he doesn't want her to blame him for Declan's death."

"It had to be Isabella," Zachary said stubbornly. It was the only answer that made sense.

"I'm not convinced," Kenzie said. "I think the father could have given it to him, but kept it a secret so they wouldn't get blamed. Or Declan might have drunk out of the dosing cup after someone else took some without anyone realizing."

"At least you're not saying it was a stranger who took him from the yard and gave it to him." Zachary was aware that his tone was sullen. He grimaced at his own reaction. Kenzie was helping him out; he shouldn't do anything to alienate her.

"It's still another possibility," Kenzie said. "You said yourself lots of parents do it to put their children to sleep or make them more compliant. It's a well-known strategy. There's nothing to say a stranger didn't lure him out of the yard with a popsicle laced with cough medicine."

"The *most likely* suspect is still the mother."

"Maybe. That's only speculation. You have no evidence."

"I don't need evidence. They're not going to reopen the case. All I'm doing is making a final report of my findings to the family in a case that is never going to be re-investigated."

"You said she has motive."

"Yes."

"What's her motive?"

"Declan was a pain in the neck. Motherhood is difficult, and she didn't want to do it anymore. She wanted him out of the way."

"That's pretty harsh."

"Not all women are cut out to be mothers." He thought of his mother, of her decision to break up their family and not be a mother anymore. "It didn't fit with her lifestyle. With her mental illness. She just wanted to paint. Not to have to take care of a mewling brat while she was trying to work from home."

"Did she tell you that?"

"No. It was pretty obvious that she didn't give Declan much attention. Even if you believe her story, she lost track of him for an hour or more. Not just two minutes. She wasn't painting facing the window so that she could watch him. She was painting with her back to the window so that she would have to turn all the way around to see him."

"That still qualifies as an accident, not murder."

"If you believe her story. And I don't."

"Did she tell you that she didn't want to be a mother? That she didn't like watching him? That she was glad he was out of the way? Exactly what did she say?"

"Spencer did things with Declan. Read to him, made his meals, played with him. Everything he said indicates he was engaged with Declan. Isabella is the opposite. She put him down for a nap. She sent him out to play while she painted. She was detached. Disengaged."

"They had different approaches to parenting. If she didn't say he was a bother or a distraction…"

"Isabella is OCD. She likes everything done a certain way. A child would just mess everything up."

"Didn't you tell me she's the hoarder? She's the one with the messy studio, and it's the dad who's the neat freak?"

"Yes."

"Then why would she be upset by a child messing things up? She's the one who likes a mess."

Zachary frowned. He switched mid-meal to chocolate pudding. One of the things he loved about buffets was it was not necessary to eat things in order. He could have dessert first. He could have it halfway through. Whenever he wanted.

Spencer would have to eat everything in order. Isabella, on the other hand… she was the one who would be able to mix everything up.

"How does Isabella deal with her OCD?" Kenzie asked. "Is she on medication? In therapy? How does she manage thoughts that intrude in her life?"

"She's in therapy. No meds, as far as I know."

"And Spencer?"

"I don't know which one he's doing right now, if either. He has a sort of unique approach to things that disrupt his life."

"Oh?"

Zachary told her about how he had moved to Vermont because of the billboard sign ban. So that his life wouldn't be overrun by having to count signs all day every day.

Kenzie stared at Zachary. He thought at first that she was done eating and was waiting for him to finish, but she still had food on her plate, forgotten. He looked down at his food, then up at her face.

"What?"

"Spencer deals with his OCD by removing the triggers."

Zachary nodded. "Right."

"He *removes his triggers.*"

21

Getting information from Molly about the OCD support group where Spencer and Isabella had met had taken some persuasion. She had been reluctant to even talk to him again, let alone part with any information.

"Isn't it supposed to be anonymous?" she asked. "It's one of those doctor-patient privilege things. Or like AA. Everybody only goes by their first names, and they're not supposed to talk about what goes on in the support group outside the meeting. People don't want everybody knowing that they have OCD."

"Molly, I really need to talk to somebody who knows a little bit more about Isabella's OCD if I'm going to help," Zachary coaxed. "I'm not asking for the name of her therapist. I just want to know what meeting she goes to. The one where she and Spencer met. Do they still meet every week?"

"I don't know." Molly went into her little galley kitchen and fussed around, making some tea. "Isabella only goes now and then, and I don't think Spencer has been in a couple of years. If you want to know more about Isabella's OCD, you can just ask me. Or ask Isabella herself. We'll tell you whatever it is you want to know."

"I really need an unbiased third party."

"You're not even supposed to be investigating anymore. I told you to mail me your final report. I'm not paying any more."

"I'm not charging you any more. I just want to be sure I have all the details right..."

"Isabella didn't drown Declan. It was an accident. She didn't have anything to do with it, other than that she was watching Deck when he wandered off."

Or she hadn't been watching him. Zachary refrained from reminding Molly that if Isabella had actually been watching him, he wouldn't have wandered off.

"Maybe it wasn't Isabella's fault. I'm willing to consider that."

Molly looked unconvinced.

"I just want to talk to someone who knows the two of them. Outside the family. Someone with more experience in OCD."

Molly's eyes went sideways to Kenzie. Zachary and Kenzie had hoped that having a woman along might soften Molly up a little. He hoped she'd open up and be more cooperative with a woman. That had backfired, with Molly immediately distrustful of the stranger. She had hired Zachary. Not Zachary and Kenzie. Even though they introduced Kenzie as Zachary's assistant, she obviously didn't like it.

"Molly," Zachary tried again. "I don't think it's breaking any confidences to tell us where and when they met with their support group. Surely a lot of people must know those details."

"It isn't exactly a secret," Molly admitted.

"Then if you can just give me the information, I'll get out of your hair."

She still dithered, pretending she had to look it up in her notebook. Kenzie looked at Zachary, and he knew she was thinking the same thing. Molly was just stalling. A couple of times she looked at the phone, an older-model landline, and Zachary wondered whether she was going to call Isabella to ask permission or wait until after they were gone and then call to give her a warning.

Finally, Molly pulled out a scratch pad and wrote out the address and the time of the meeting. She glanced in Kenzie's direction but handed the note to Zachary.

"I don't like this," she warned, just in case they hadn't understood that from her previous objections. "I don't think this is right."

"The reason you hired me was to find out the truth," Zachary said. "And I think I might have found something."

Of course, the OCD group wasn't that day, and they had to wait until the group met again, because a ledger wasn't kept of the individual members with their contact information. Members could exchange information among themselves, but there was no central register kept. It wasn't quite anonymous, but they did their best to respect their members' right to privacy.

The next couple of days were excruciating. While Zachary had plenty to do, trying to start the process of getting his identification reissued when he didn't have any identification to prove who he was, it mostly involved phone calls with long hold times. Bowman was a gracious host, but Zachary knew having a house guest was stressful, and he didn't want Bowman to think that he had to provide entertainment. He just needed a place to sleep and to pick up a few meals until he was able to get back on his feet.

The night of the OCD support group finally came, and Zachary headed over to the meeting place, the basement of a church. There were signs up stating that the group was nondenominational and not associated with the church that provided the space. Zachary stuck his head into the room, reluctant to go in without an invitation.

"Don't be shy," a voice boomed out behind him. "Go on in. Everyone is welcome."

Zachary turned his head to find that the big voice had come from a diminutive, scraggly-blond, thin man who didn't look a day over twenty.

"Uh, thanks," Zachary said. "I don't know…"

"Come on," the young man encouraged. He reached as if to put his arm around Zachary's shoulders to sweep him into the room, and then jerked back before touching him. "Sorry. Sorry. Come on in. There are cookies!"

Zachary stepped in through the door and moved toward the snack table to give himself some space.

"Looks good," he agreed, looking at the sad little coffee station and plates of store-bought cookies.

"My name is Winston," the young man said.

"Uh, Zachary. Good to meet you."

"It doesn't have to be your own name. Just something that people can call you. There's a sign-in sheet over there." He pointed to a clipboard attached to a pen with a string.

"Thanks."

In a few minutes, all the members of the support group had assembled, and they made their way over to the chairs, where introductions were made, and a group leader ran through the usual order of business for the group.

Zachary introduced himself by his first name only, and glanced around the group, trying to analyze all the faces. Who would have known Spencer? Who would have associated with Isabella? Had they made other friends before they had gotten involved with each other? Or had they immediately been drawn to each other to the exclusion of anyone else? Isabella still went to the group sporadically, though she obviously hadn't wanted to show up while Zachary was there.

"I have a friend who used to go to this group. Do any of you know *The Happy Artist*? He's married to her. He told me about this group, said I should come."

They looked at each other for a few seconds, no one saying anything.

"Spencer?" a man with a bushy mustache asked finally. He had introduced himself as Dave. "Long time since I saw him."

Zachary nodded eagerly and looked around at the rest of the group to see a couple of other nods as people remembered Spencer. "Yes, Spencer. He thought the group would help me."

Dave's mouth pursed sourly. "Really. I don't know how much it ever helped him."

"He came here, didn't he?"

"Yeah, he came, but I don't think he ever really invested in the group. He thought he was better than the rest of us."

"That's not fair," the redheaded woman called Angie spoke up, shifting uncomfortably and darting quick glances at Zachary. "He never said he thought he was any better."

"He didn't have to. It was obvious from his attitude."

"He didn't share with the group?" Zachary asked.

Angie sipped her coffee not from one of the foam cups provided at the coffee station, but from a chipped ceramic mug, reminding Zachary of the story of the plate Spencer had disposed of.

Dave shrugged. "He shared... inconsequential stuff. Fluff. The things that didn't matter. The work that we're trying to do here... it can be pretty painful. Gut wrenching. People dig down deep and bare their souls. Then someone like Spencer comes along, pretending that he's got it all together."

Zachary nodded, trying to work through this. "He did seem like he had it all. Married, good job, taking care of his little boy…"

"Appearances can be deceiving," contributed the woman in a blazer and skirt. Zachary couldn't remember her name. Something that started with an M? She looked professional and perfectly coifed. Was she referring to herself or to Spencer when she said that? Maybe both.

"Did you know him?" he asked her.

"I remember him. He did act like everything was going pretty well for him, but I think he had problems he didn't want to talk about."

"Everybody has things they don't want to talk about," Dave said. "But we have to share them if we want to overcome them. This *inner work*; it's not for cowards."

"What did he talk about?"

There were looks exchanged around the circle.

"Maybe you should talk to him," Angie said. "We're not supposed to be sharing information about other people."

"I just wondered," Zachary said. "With the trouble he's been having since his son died… I wondered if he ever talked about Declan when he was coming here."

"I heard about that," Angie said with a nod. "Poor Spencer and Isabella. I can't imagine what they must have been going through. They both loved that little boy."

Zachary didn't want to press the question, worried that the harder he pushed, the more they would push back about not wanting to talk about someone else.

"I lost my parents when I was a kid," he offered. "My whole family. I'm just starting to realize how much it affected me…" He paused, and no one said anything. "Not just grief," he explained, "but… psychologically… the fear I carry into other relationships."

There were nods and noises of agreement from around the room.

"It must have been hard for Isabella and Spencer to parent, with both of them being OCD… and so different from each other."

"Spencer didn't talk much about Declan," Dave said. "He was more likely to talk about business stuff than anything personal. Isabella was more likely to talk about the difficulty of being a parent, responsible for someone else. Spencer just stopped coming. Like he didn't need the group anymore."

"He was complaining about intrusive thoughts," M said. "I thought maybe he'd open up, but then he faded out. He hadn't ever been one to come every week, but it got less and less often…"

"It's only been Isabella the last couple of years," Dave agreed.

"What does that mean, intrusive thoughts? Is that like his counting compulsion, before he came to Vermont?" Zachary intentionally dropped another hint that he knew all about Spencer and his history.

Winston was frowning at Zachary. "You have OCD and you don't know what intrusive thoughts are?"

Zachary snorted. "Well, I know what *my* intrusive thoughts are, but I thought that was more… PTSD. Flashbacks. I can't imagine Spencer getting as emotional over his own thoughts as I do. He's so… ordered."

"He was, though," Angie said. "There was one day when he broke down about it. I think he was too embarrassed to come back after that."

Zachary leaned forward. "What did he say?"

She shook her head slowly. "I don't remember what it was… I don't think he told us anything specific. Just that… he had to do something to get them out of his head. He didn't know how long he could keep fighting them."

Apparently, he had kept fighting them for two more years, alone.

And then what had happened?

Finding the name of Spencer's therapist turned out to be easier than talking Molly into giving up the OCD Anonymous group. He told the group that Spencer had suggested he go to a doctor that he had seen for a while. A Dr. Bloom…? Or was it Chen? He had gotten so many different recommendations; he couldn't remember which had been Spencer's.

"Dr. Snowdon," Dave supplied. "I went to him for a couple of years too. He specializes in anxiety disorders."

"Snowdon…" Zachary mused. "I don't think that was it… are you sure?"

"Yes. He works out of the health center in Vermont Plaza. An old guy, but he knows his stuff."

"Is he still around? Maybe Spencer is seeing someone new now. Didn't Snowdon retire?"

Dave grew more vehement. "No. No, I saw him just a couple of weeks ago. He's still practicing. That's where Spencer went. I don't know if he is still seeing him or not, but he was using Snowdon. I'm one hundred percent sure."

So, Zachary had the name of Spencer's therapist. Other members of the group had given him other suggestions as well in case Snowdon wasn't taking any new cases or wasn't a good fit for Zachary.

Zachary went home, back to Bowman's couch, feeling good about himself. He was making progress. The case was going to go somewhere; he would soon be able to lay everything out for Molly and the police. He'd had a couple of cookies at the support group, a treat he didn't allow himself very often.

When morning rolled around, he looked up Dr. Snowdon's address and credentials. He anticipated that getting in to see Dr. Snowdon and getting any information out of him was going to be very difficult. Who else was going to have better insight into Spencer's psyche than his therapist?

He camped out in the waiting room after introducing himself to the receptionist. She said that he would not be able to see Dr. Snowdon, who was completely booked with sessions for the day. When Zachary sat down to wait, she shook her head and ignored him for the first hour. After that, Zachary watched her get more and more fidgety, looking at him when she didn't think he was looking and whispering to other office staff behind her hand. Zachary continued to leaf through magazines, covertly studying the patients who came in for their sessions.

They all looked remarkably normal. At the support group, there had been a few people who were dressed strangely or had an odd personal appearance, and some who were obviously bacteriophobes, constantly rubbing their hands with sanitizer, or wiping down their chairs. At the doctor's office, everyone gave the appearance of perfect normality. Zachary examined himself. He supposed he had some obsessive-compulsive tendencies himself, but he took care to look normal to other people. He had it down pretty well. No one gave him a second look. Most of the time.

The receptionist was talking to a white-haired, heavyset man in a t-shirt and khakis, making frequent glances in Zachary's direction. Zachary turned his head and made eye contact with the man he assumed was the doctor. He walked over to Zachary, his creased face showing his puzzlement.

"Mr. Goldman, is it?"

"Are you Dr. Snowdon?" Zachary stood up and offered his hand.

Snowdon shook it. "Yes. I must confess, I'm not sure why you're here..."

"Could we talk privately?" Zachary glanced around at the other people in the waiting room, who although they didn't look at him, were all ears.

Snowdon sighed and shook his head. "Follow me."

He led Zachary to an office. It was pretty much like Zachary expected. A computer and desk. A couple of chairs and a couch. More magazines, fake plants, a few bookcases lined with books, certificates on the walls, a picture of his family on his desk.

Zachary sat in one of the chairs and made himself comfortable. "This is very nice."

"Now, if you would explain to me what you're doing here...?"

"I'm a private investigator. One of your clients has come up in one of my investigations, and I wanted to talk to you about him."

"You must know I can't do that. Doctor-patient confidentiality applies."

"I didn't say I was going to ask you questions about him. I said I was going to talk *to* you about him."

Snowdon scowled. "Really, I don't see how I can help you."

"One of your patients is Spencer Bond. He has OCD."

"I can't give you any information on any patients."

"Spencer is married to Isabella Hildebrandt, *The Happy Artist*, who also has OCD."

"That may be." Snowdon shook his head. "I am sorry I can't help you."

"They have a son named Declan, or they did until he died last summer."

Snowdon's gaze sharpened and he didn't make any objection.

"I know that one of the exceptions to doctor-patient privilege is when you think that someone might harm themselves or others."

"Yes, of course."

"If you knew that Spencer was going to harm his child, you would have had to speak up. You would have gone to the authorities and had him committed."

"That never happened."

"No. So, I guess you didn't know ahead of time that he was going to harm Declan."

"Do you have proof that he had something to do with his son's death?"

"You didn't say, 'Spencer would never do that.'"

"Is that a question?"

"No. I just think that if I was a psychologist, I would have some idea as to whether a patient was capable of something like that."

"I don't think anyone could claim to know what their patients were capable of. Not one hundred percent."

"No. You didn't think Spencer would hurt Declan, did you?"

Snowdon just looked at him.

"I know some things about Spencer's past behavior," Zachary said.

"Oh, do you?"

"He came to Vermont because of the billboard signs law. He had a compulsion to count billboards, and it was disrupting his life, so he moved to Vermont where there were no billboards to count."

Snowdon cocked his head to the side a little, considering this. Then he sat down at his desk.

"That's what Spencer told you?" he asked.

Zachary nodded. "And I know that he got rid of Isabella's mismatched stuff so that he wouldn't have to look at it, even though she would only eat from one plate. He didn't say that he didn't know it was the only plate she would eat from, but I think that's what he wanted me to believe."

"You don't sound like you believe it," Snowdon suggested.

"No. I don't think he could have helped noticing that his wife only ever ate off one plate. One that was chipped and didn't match anything. It would have been like a big, red, flashing light for him, wouldn't it? Of course he knew it was the only plate she would use."

Snowdon shrugged, not sharing his opinion or his knowledge one way or the other.

"I also think..." Zachary ventured into guesswork, "that he got rid of her cat because he didn't want it shedding and tracking dirt around the house."

"Really?" Snowdon seemed surprised at this revelation. "Did he tell you that?"

"No. I have a suspicion that if we called their friends, the Raymonds, we would find out that he gave them the cat. I assume they swore never to tell Isabella about it. They ended up moving out of town; maybe that's why he picked them. The cat was missing for eight years. Then when they moved back into town, the cat suddenly showed up again. I don't think that was a coincidence."

Snowdon nodded, sucking in his cheeks. He didn't give his opinion one way or the other. Zachary took a deep breath.

"So we come to Declan," Zachary said. "A kid takes a lot more time and energy to keep up with than a cat."

"That's true," Snowdon agreed. "But parents develop a stronger bond. A different kind of bond, with their children. As much as the cat ladies would like us to think it, loving a cat isn't the same as loving your offspring."

"And you can't just give a child to your friends and ask them to keep quiet about it."

"No," Snowdon offered a little smile at this. "I would agree with that."

Zachary couldn't sit still in his chair any longer. He got up and started to pace back and forth across the room. A beep sounded from Snowdon's desk phone. He hit a button in reply. 'I know I'm running late. I should only be a few more minutes.'

He raised his eyes to Zachary. "We do need to move things along, here."

Zachary paced back across the office. "What would make someone with issues like Spencer, with the same kind of coping mechanisms as him, decide that murdering his child was the only thing to do? That's the part I don't understand. If he needed more help, he could have asked for more help. A housekeeper. For his wife to do more. A nanny. They had the money."

"You've taken quite a leap. I'm not aware of any evidence that Spencer did anything to hurt Declan. The child wandered out of his yard and drowned. It's tragic, but there's no reason to suspect foul play. Is there?"

"He had cough medicine in his bloodstream. His mother refused to give him cough medicine. Or to let anyone else give it to him. He didn't take it himself. He didn't find it when he wandered from the yard. He wasn't given it by a stranger who took him from his yard. The only explanation I can find is that Spencer gave it to him. Spencer decided to do what he always did. Get rid of a compulsion by getting rid of the trigger."

Snowdon tilted his chair back. He rubbed his chin, thinking about it. He didn't look at Zachary as he let out a long breath of air.

"There are many different kinds of obsessions and compulsions. Some people have hand-washing compulsions. Or an obsession with everything being straight and square. Or in groups of four. For other people, it's collecting things. Hoarding china figurines, or cats, or pop can tabs. That's another kind of obsession."

"Right," Zachary agreed. "Spencer and Isabella were both OCD, but they had different kinds of obsessions. Spencer was neat and tidy, and Isabella was a collector. It was hard for them to live together, butting up against each other's obsessions."

"But there are also obsessions that are rarely discussed. It's one thing to go to your doctor or support group and say that you washed your hands forty times yesterday, that you're stuck in a rut, and that you need some kind of intervention. Our society is pretty understanding about that kind of compulsion. They may even see it as a virtue. I've heard people say that they wish they were OCD so that their houses would be clean."

"Uh-huh...?"

"No one ever wants to be the crazy cat lady. We still recognize and talk about hoarding. It's still something that you can get help for if you decide it's time."

"Both Spencer and Isabella were going to a support group for a while. Spencer was coming to therapy with you."

"But there is a whole world of obsessions that our society is not as understanding or accepting of."

Zachary cast his mind over what he had learned in the case, and what he had observed about Spencer, trying to find something that didn't fit. Zachary's own compulsions were less acceptable. People didn't think of stalking when they thought of OCD. They didn't think about his constant agonies over relationships as part of a mental illness. That didn't seem to fit into the puzzle. Not Spencer's puzzle.

Dr. Snowdon got up and went over to his bookshelves. He pulled a thick volume down and returned to his desk with it. He opened it and flipped through the pages for a couple of minutes. Then he stopped, marking the place with his finger.

"Obsessions with Sexual Content and Obsessions with Violent Content," he announced. "Intrusive thoughts can cause the sufferer great distress. Patients are often reluctant to seek support for fear of being labeled pedophiles, homosexuals, or wife-beaters."

"*What?*" Zachary was stunned. He stared at Dr. Snowdon, trying to find the words to express his thoughts. "What are you saying? That Spencer

—that OCD patients—can be pedophiles? That's one of the obsessions that people don't talk about?"

"No, no, don't misunderstand." Dr. Snowdon held up a finger on his other hand as if lecturing a class. "They have intrusive thoughts. Unwarranted fears that they could hurt a child or another loved one. They are not sexual deviants, but they fear that they could be. Imagine how you would feel if you had thoughts about causing harm to your wife or your girlfriend. Or your child. Imagine how you would feel if you had these thoughts constantly, whenever you were around them. You loved them and would never do anything to harm them, yet you constantly imagined doing them violence."

Zachary tried to understand the concept. "So, it's not that they want to hurt their child, but hold themselves back…"

"No. They have no desire at all to hurt the child, but they keep seeing themselves doing it."

"They don't have a compulsion to hurt them…"

"No. They have intrusive thoughts. Imagine that you don't want to walk to the edge of a cliff, not because you're afraid you'll fall, but because you're afraid that you will jump."

Zachary sat back down. He stared at the big book on Snowdon's desk. "Did Spencer ever tell you he had this kind of intrusive thoughts?"

"People with thoughts like these will rarely go to a doctor for help. It's a taboo topic. Usually, they will go to great lengths to avoid the triggers, or to avoid getting into a situation where they could act out the intrusive thoughts. Statistically, a patient who is having these kinds of thoughts is *less* likely to actually do harm to their loved one, not more."

"Then if Spencer had intrusive thoughts about hurting or killing Declan, he would be highly unlikely to be the one who drowned him. Which makes Isabella the lead suspect again."

Snowdon didn't smile or confirm Zachary's interpretation. Zachary pressed his lips together and tried to figure out what he had missed.

"Putting aside the statistics," Snowdon said, "your earlier question was what would make someone decide to murder their child? Someone who had, in the past, resorted to drastic measures to *completely eliminate* the triggers of other obsessive behaviors or intrusive thoughts."

Zachary made the connection. "So maybe it wasn't because Declan was messy or disturbed Spencer's order. It wasn't that Spencer didn't want to be distracted or interrupted from his routines. It was because the only way to stop having these violent or sexual intrusive thoughts about his own son was to eliminate the trigger."

Dr. Snowdon slowly closed the book. "Most people never mention these things to their doctors," he reiterated. "A doctor would probably have no idea if his patient was having these kinds of thoughts."

22

When Zachary got out of his meeting with Dr. Snowdon, he tried to call Isabella. There was no answer. He looked at his watch. It was late enough in the day that she shouldn't still have been taping. She should have been back at home unless she had shopping or other errands outside the house to be done. He tried several times, and she didn't answer. Finally, he tried Molly's phone.

"I need to talk to Isabella," he said. "She isn't with you, is she?"

"No. She should be home. Maybe she is just painting and doesn't want to be disturbed."

"It's important that I talk to her. Can you call her and see if she'll answer you? She wouldn't ignore your call, would she?"

"Don't count on it," Molly laughed. "When she gets into a work, she could be on another planet. She wouldn't know if a tornado blasted through the house."

"Can you try?"

"Sure, I guess. What's this about?"

"I need to talk to her about Spencer. About whether he's ever had a particular set of symptoms."

"Why don't you just ask him?"

"I don't think this is something that Spencer would want to discuss with me, but he may have mentioned it to Isabella."

"I've spent a lot of time in that house. I could probably tell you anything you're wondering about."

Zachary didn't think Spencer would have told his mother-in-law about having thoughts that were so repugnant to him. It was a long shot that he would even have shared them with Isabella.

"I just wondered about intrusive thoughts," he said lightly. "If you would please call Isabella and see if she'll answer... I really need to meet with her to get her thoughts."

Molly sighed. "I'll do what I can, but if she's lost in a painting, one of us will probably have to go over to the house to get any response out of her."

But Molly couldn't get a response from Isabella. She wasn't too worried but did want to check it out and make sure Isabella was okay. "I think she's been getting better, since the hospital. They finally got her to take some meds that seem to be helping. If she'll keep taking them. Sometimes... suicidal behaviors can be hard to spot."

Zachary made an effort not to laugh aloud at that. In his experience, very few people even knew what to look for. Depression didn't always look like depression.

He called Kenzie to see if she could pick him up to take him to the house. Kenzie yawned in his ear. "Yeah, I was already thinking of clocking out early today," she said. "I don't know why I've been so tired the last few days. Fighting a bug, I guess." There was a pause. "It's three-thirty now. Let me finish up, and I'll pick you up at four."

"Thanks," Zachary tried to put all the appreciation he could into his voice. "I know it's a pain in the neck. Hopefully, I'll have a new car and be able to drive soon. Once everything goes through."

"Yeah. Then hopefully you can avoid getting yourself killed."

She said it flippantly, but he hoped she was right. He'd had enough of threats and near-death experiences. If Kenzie were right, and the case that he was supposed to drop was the Bond case, then he needed to take care in his approach. Walking up to Spencer's door might not be the best approach.

Kenzie picked him up in good time, and they met Molly outside the house.

"Do you have a key?" Zachary asked. "I'm not sure ringing the doorbell is particularly safe."

She frowned at him, shaking her head. "How is ringing the doorbell not safe?" she challenged. "You think you're going to get electrocuted?"

"No," Zachary said lamely, as they walked up the sidewalk. He dropped his voice so that Molly wouldn't hear as she marched up the sidewalk ahead of them. "More likely stabbed in the eye."

Kenzie glared at him. "That's not funny."

"No."

Molly rang the doorbell. When there was no answer after a few tries, she called both Isabella's and Spencer's cell phones, but couldn't get ahold of either one of them. She looked at Zachary.

"I don't know where they could be. They didn't say that they were going on vacation or running any errands. They both like their routines, and this is where they always are in the afternoon."

"You don't have a key?"

Molly finally produced one. "I never use it. One of them is always here…"

"She gave it to you in case of emergencies, right? And I think this is an emergency."

"Just because they're not answering the door, that doesn't mean that it's an emergency," Molly disagreed. She fit the key into the lock and turned it. "You don't think that she's done something, do you?"

"You said she'd been doing better."

"She has. I'm… just not sure…" Molly picked up the pace and hurried as quickly as she could without losing her poise. They reached the studio right behind her. It was empty.

"Where is she?"

"Maybe she's sick. In bed. Or in the shower." Kenzie rattled off a few possibilities.

Molly looked suddenly drawn and gray, sick with worry. "She would have told me if she was sick…"

Zachary led the way toward the master bedroom, and Molly and Kenzie followed. It was obvious that she wasn't in the bedroom either. The bed was neatly made. It hadn't been touched since Spencer had stretched the sheets taut that morning.

But there was something different. There was an easel set up in front of the window on a carpet of newspapers, the sunlight streaming from outside. Zachary walked around it to see what painting Isabella had been working on. The canvas was untouched.

The three of them stood there, looking around at the rest of the room. Looking for anything that was out of place or might give an indication of where Isabella might have gone.

It all looked as it had last time Zachary had been there, other than the easel. Spencer's side of the closet neat and orderly. Isabella's side looking like a bomb had gone off. Just as it had the day of Declan's disappearance, Spencer's light summer jacket hung in a prominent position.

Spencer wouldn't go out without his jacket. That was what Isabella had said. Of course, it was winter, and he would be wearing a heavier coat at those temperatures.

His blue jacket.

The one that had hung in his closet to give him an alibi the day of the murder.

When Zachary had visited the house the first time, that blue jacket had been hanging on a peg at the front door. It didn't belong in the bedroom closet. That was why it stood out in Isabella's memory.

She hadn't been able to paint the color blue since Declan drowned.

"The blue coat," Zachary said, pointing to it. "He's copying the day that Declan drowned. He had put the coat there so that Isabella would think he was home, but he wasn't. He is the one who took Declan from the back yard." Zachary looked at his watch. "Declan disappeared from the house around four o'clock and died at about five."

"What do you mean he's copying the day of the crime?" Molly demanded. "Why would he do that?"

"Because it worked the first time, and because he's obsessive. If it worked the first time, then he has to copy every detail for it to work again."

"To work again? Declan is dead. Are you saying he's having some kind of breakdown?"

Zachary stared at her. How could she not understand what was going on?

But Kenzie had figured it out. She grabbed Zachary by the arm.

"We'd better find them," she said urgently.

Zachary nodded. He and Kenzie led the way back out of the house. Out the back door. They followed the fresh prints in the snow. Molly followed behind, murmuring in confusion that she still didn't understand what was going on.

23

The snow made it difficult to move quickly to the pond. The sun was already dipping below the horizon. Zachary's heart raced as they followed the trail in the snow to the little pond. It was frozen over. Spencer was in the middle, working at breaking a hole in the ice with a hatchet. Isabella lay beside him, half-sitting and half-reclined.

"Izzy!" Molly shouted out, finally getting an inkling of the danger her daughter was in.

Kenzie prevented her from dashing out onto the ice. "It's not safe," she warned. "We don't know how thin the ice is. You could all go into the freezing water."

Molly froze, her eyes wide, wanting to rescue her daughter, but unable to do anything.

"Stay back!" Spencer ordered, looking up from his work.

"How's it going, Spencer?" Zachary asked casually, as if they had just run into each other by coincidence on the street.

"Just stay back and leave me alone. I have to do this."

"I talked to Dr. Snowdon."

"So what?"

"I learned some things from him that I didn't know before. About how some people with OCD have intrusive thoughts. They are afraid to go to anyone for help."

Spencer continued to hack away at the ice, enlarging the hole he had started.

"I didn't know that before. About how some people have thoughts about harming their loved ones. When they wouldn't ever do anything like that."

"I can't deal with it anymore," Spencer said. "I can't shut them off. The only way to get rid of the thoughts is to get rid of the triggers." He shook his head, his voice breaking. "I love my family. I can't... I can't keep seeing them like that."

"There are other ways they can help you. There are medications. Therapies. You never talked to Dr. Snowdon about your thoughts, did you? You never gave him the opportunity to tell you that it was treatable. That there were things that he could do to help you. You don't have to fight this alone, Spencer. There are people who will help."

"They can't do anything," Spencer disagreed. "I've already tried everything else. I know the way my brain works. This is the only way to get rid of the thoughts."

Zachary could see Kenzie out the corner of his eye, working away on her phone, using her own body and Molly's to shelter the glow of the screen from Spencer as she called or texted for help.

"You're a pretty smart guy, Spencer," Zachary said in an upbeat tone. "You really thought things through and planned this out, didn't you? You knew that Isabella would be distracted from watching Declan. You knew that the cough medicine would knock Declan out. Keep him from fighting back or waking up while you... took care of him. You fooled Isabella. You did leave the house without your summer jacket. You left it hanging there for her to see. In the bedroom, not at the front door where it belonged. You wanted her to believe that you were still in the house. She knew that you couldn't leave without the coat."

"I *can* leave without the jacket," Spencer offered. "I just don't like to. It's comfortable. I know what temperatures it is good for. I always wear it... but I don't *have* to. Even when I have a compulsion, I still have willpower. I can resist for a while... until it becomes too uncomfortable."

"But her unconscious mind picked up on what her conscious mind didn't. The color blue. It was wrong. It shouldn't have been in the bedroom; it should have been at the front door. Did you know that was why she couldn't paint the color blue anymore?"

"I didn't know for sure."

Zachary could hear the ice creaking as Spencer moved closer to Isabella. He grabbed her arms and dragged her toward the hole. Zachary was holding his breath, waiting for it all to collapse. In his mind, he was playing out what they would do. They would save Isabella first. He would lie down on the ice to spread his body weight across as wide an area as possible. They would need rope. Maybe his coat. He could take off his coat to stretch out to Isabella. If she were able to grab it.

She was murmuring to herself and didn't seem to have any desire to move away from Spencer. He must have drugged her just like he had drugged Declan. Zachary watched Isabella, trying to hear what it was she was saying. Did she have any idea what danger she was in? What was going on?

"Until we meet again, may God hold you in the palm of His hand."

Zachary breathed out, his chest hurting. "Of course, you were the one sending me threats," he observed, still trying to keep Spencer talking. Trying to keep him engaged and occupied. "But you never said which case it was I was supposed to drop."

Spencer looked up at him for a minute, frowning. "I thought you would know."

"Not if you don't tell me, amigo."

"Oh."

"Is this your first attempt on Isabella's life?" Zachary asked. "Or had you tried that before too?"

"She tried to commit suicide before."

"But was it really suicide? Or did you have a hand in that as well?"

"She was depressed. She felt guilty about Declan." Spencer shook his head. "I don't know why when she wasn't the one who did it. I had to live with the reality of what I had done to turn off those awful thoughts."

"You didn't encourage those feelings in Isabella? Maybe give her a couple of nudges toward suicide? You were posting mother and child pictures on her Facebook."

Spencer looked away. "Encouraging someone to commit suicide is against the law," he said. "I never did that, but I might have... manipulated her environment."

He wouldn't encourage his wife to commit suicide because that was against the law, but he would kill her himself. It made no sense to Zachary.

But in Spencer's mind, it did. With his disordered thinking, it was the best he could do.

"You had me fooled. I thought it was Isabella who had killed Declan."

"Isabella? I told you she would never do that."

"You can't always tell what someone is capable of doing."

Spencer looked at Isabella lying on the ice. "I know. There's no way she could have done anything to hurt Declan. She loved him… like a mother. It was different for her. She didn't have those thoughts. Those visions."

"You would have gotten away with it. The police didn't find anything suspicious."

"And then *you* had to come along. Why couldn't you just leave us alone?"

"I was just doing my job."

"They said that you were paralyzed after the car accident, and I thought I was safe. But they were wrong. That car accident should have killed you. The fire should have killed you. None of that worked. The only thing that worked was this." Spencer gestured to the pond and his wife. "I hit on the magic combination the first time, and I didn't even know how lucky I was. Isabella didn't die. You didn't die. Only Declan."

Zachary glanced at Kenzie, trying to get some idea from her as to when help would arrive. She made a wry face and gave a slight shrug with one shoulder. *Who knows?*

"I get it," Zachary said. "I know you think no one else can understand, but I get it."

"How could you?"

"I have… thoughts… too. I have had since I was ten years old." Zachary swallowed hard. "I've never told anyone."

Spencer stopped chopping the ice and looked across the pond at him. "What thoughts do you have?" he asked. In the failing light, his eyes were just hollows. He looked skeletal.

"I think that people are going to leave me. My wife. Anyone I'm dating. My wife did leave me… and I still think about her all the time. I want to know who she's seeing, what she's doing. I put a tracking device on her car so that I could know where she was all the time."

Spencer was standing there looking at him. He had stopped digging the hole and moving around, for the moment.

"I put trackers on other people too," Zachary said, glancing at Kenzie and grimacing. "Sometimes… people I hardly even know. It started with work, with people I was surveilling, but I couldn't stop with that. I had to know where everyone was. Everyone in my life. I stalk them by GPS. I check social media to see what they're doing all day long. I profile anyone they might be dating or spending too much time with…"

"That makes sense," Spencer said. "But the thoughts I have…" He looked at his wife and shook his head. "You can't imagine how horrible they are."

"You need to get help. There are things they can do to help. There are other ways."

"No… the only way to stop the thoughts is to remove the trigger. That's the only thing that has ever worked for me." Spencer looked down at Isabella with a groan. He grabbed her leg and tugged her toward the hole in the ice.

"Until we meet again, may God hold you in the palm of His hand," Isabella repeated.

Zachary stepped out onto the ice.

"Zachary, no," Kenzie protested in a whisper.

"I have to do something."

As he started to slide his feet across the ice, gingerly feeling his way along and listening for the sounds of cracking, he saw red flashing lights coming through the trees. The police were finally there, but Spencer was tugging Isabella those last few inches toward the hole, and the ice he was standing on could break and dump them both into the water at any time.

"Did you ever go ice skating as a kid?" Zachary asked, trying to distract Spencer and fill the silence. "I never had skates, but we used to go out on the pond, like this, sliding across it in our shoes." He was almost within reach of Isabella, which was both bad and good. He was now adding his own weight to the sheet of ice. "I used to love winter then. Sliding on the ice, building snowmen, Christmas…"

He'd almost forgotten that. Almost forgotten that he had ever loved Christmas. Like any other child. It had been a magical time of year. Not because of presents, because they rarely got anything worth mentioning. Not like some of his friends who got new toys, the latest games, the most popular movies, even new clothes, but because it was the season of peace and love. He could remember sitting in the living room with his mother, drowsy, staring up into the fully-decorated, lit-up Christmas tree. She told him stories and sang parts of Christmas hymns, and he felt the magic of the season.

"Come on, Spencer. Let's get you help."

Isabella started to slide into the hole in the ice feet-first. Peacefully, without a sound, just like Spencer had planned. Zachary threw himself down on the ice, sliding the rest of the way on his belly. He grabbed her coat and her arm and kept her from sliding the rest of the way in. The ice crackled under his body.

"Until we meet again, may God hold you in the palm of His hand." Her voice was drowsy and far away.

"Not yet, Isabella," Zachary growled. While she might be ready to meet her maker, he was not ready to let her go.

"Let go!" Spencer protested, his voice rising from despair to anger for the first time. "You're ruining it! Let her go in! It's the only way the thoughts are going to stop!"

"You can't get rid of thoughts of doing something terrible by doing something equally bad or worse." Zachary clenched his teeth with the effort of holding Isabella up. He could hear the police arriving, yelling to one another, coordinating their actions, but he was locked into the moment with Spencer, unable to move his eyes to the right or the left.

"You have no idea. You have no idea of how horrible the thoughts are. You wouldn't believe that I could think things that are so... so depraved. This is a mercy. For her to go peacefully and be with Declan again. It's what she wants."

"They'll help you, Spencer. They're going to get you help."

Spencer seemed to become aware of the police for the first time. He looked around in horror, his eyes getting bigger. He looked once more at Isabella, then finally abandoned his mission, making a run for it.

He didn't get far.

Zachary was relieved to have Spencer's extra weight off the shelf of ice. He breathed out slowly, tightening his grip on Isabella.

"Now it's time to get you out of here to where you're safe."

Hands grabbed Zachary's ankles. Two strong hands on each leg.

"You got a good grip on her?" a voice demanded.

"Yes."

"Hold tight. We're going to pull you back from the hole."

He tightened his grip. "I'm ready."

The voice gave a three-count, and then they pulled. Zachary kept ahold of Isabella.

They both slid easily across the ice, her body completely out of the water.

"That's it," Zachary breathed. "You're safe. You're okay."

Zachary and Kenzie stood watching as Isabella was covered with blankets and loaded into the ambulance.

"Glad it's not you this time?" Kenzie asked.

"Very glad," Zachary agreed. He rubbed his arms even though he was dressed warmly enough for the weather. "I'll bet she's colder than a witch's behind."

Kenzie laughed, nodding. "You did good," she said. "You saved her."

"This is not how most of my investigations end. I'm glad she's okay." He shook his head. "I didn't want it to be him."

"No one did."

"Any idea what she was given?" one of the paramedics asked them.

"My first guess would be cough medicine," Zachary said. "But I'm not sure if he could have gotten her to take it. He could have slipped her a prescription for anxiety. Valium, maybe."

"We'll have to get them to run her blood when we get her to the hospital."

"We might be able to find out from Spencer," Kenzie suggested.

Zachary looked at the police car they had put Spencer in. Hands over his face, Spencer was crying uncontrollably. "I wouldn't count on it. It's probably going to be a while before he can talk."

"You're both all right?" The paramedic looked from one to the other. "How are you feeling?" he asked Zachary.

Zachary brushed at the snow coating the front of his jacket from sliding across the ice. "Yes, I'm fine."

"You didn't get wet?"

"No. Just Isabella."

They watched as the ambulance pulled out a few minutes later. Molly would follow it to the hospital and give them the information they needed to admit her daughter.

"What are you going to do for excitement now?" Kenzie teased.

"I'm looking forward to going back to a non-exciting life. A nice insurance fraud, that's what I'm feeling like right now. Following someone around for three weeks to see if they really do have a whiplash injury."

Kenzie smiled. "Sounds incredibly boring and tedious."

"Exactly."

"And what about... your health?" She stared at the police car Spencer sat in rather than looking at Spencer. "Sounds like you've still got some issues to work through."

"I guess I'm like Spencer," Zachary said. "I always figured I could just keep it to myself and muscle through it on my own, but maybe... the cookies at the support group weren't so bad."

Kenzie gave a smile of approval.

"Cookies are good," she agreed. "That would be a good place to start."

EPILOGUE

Zachary settled into his easy chair with his morning cup of coffee and turned on the TV. He didn't often watch morning TV, but there was a show on that he wanted to check out.

The theme song for *The Happy Artist* started to play, and the opening credits played while showing different angles of Isabella painting in past episodes. It was the first new episode of *The Happy Artist* since Spencer's arrest, and she'd been sorely missed in the intervening months. Then there was a view of Isabella sitting on a stool facing the camera, talking about the painting she would be undertaking for that episode. She seemed calm and relaxed, much more in her element than she had been when she and Zachary had both appeared on a talk show interview the previous day.

Then she had looked small and vulnerable. She seemed uncomfortable in her own skin and looked like she was wearing the wrong clothes or colors. Unlike the producers of *The Happy Artist*, which insisted that she keep her tattoo covered up and her memorial jewelry to a minimum, the talk show wanted to show her off in all of her mourning regalia. She had short sleeves that she kept tugging at, and the numerous chains and pendants made noise whenever she moved. Her mic had to be repositioned several times to find a placement that didn't pick up the clinking.

They had run Zachary through the details of the investigation, more focused on his two near-death experiences and Isabella's suicide attempt and her close call at the pond than they were in how he had developed the case. Then the cameras were focused back on Isabella, stroking the tattoo on her arm, gazing off into space, her lips mouthing the familiar words.

Until we meet again, may God hold you in the palm of His hand.

"And how are you feeling now, Isabella? Have you been able to move on, knowing the truth of what happened to Declan?"

"Yes… I'm doing a lot better now. It's horrible, knowing what Spencer did. At least I know… it wasn't my fault, and that Declan didn't suffer. He just went peacefully to sleep and never woke up."

"Are you getting the help and support that you need?"

"What I didn't know is that for the few months before the arrest, Spencer had been manipulating my environment. He had messed with my social media feeds, blocking out friends and changing my interests to dark and depressing things, so that whenever I went online, I just felt worse and worse. He blocked numbers on my phone and email as well, so that people couldn't reach me. They didn't know he had blocked them." She turned her head to smile at Zachary. "Zachary has been so good in helping me sort it all out since then, so that I have the support of my friends and colleagues again, instead of feeling so isolated and alone."

"That must have lifted a big weight off your shoulders."

"It did. I guess Spencer thought that if he could make me depressed enough, he wouldn't have to do anything directly. I would just kill myself. He almost succeeded."

"And are you getting professional help?"

"Yes. Yes, of course. Things are much better now."

"What would you say to Spencer now, if you were face-to-face with him?"

Isabella bit her lip, her brows drawing down. "I guess… I'd tell him I was sorry."

There was a noise of exclamation from the host, but Isabella went on, ignoring it.

"I wasn't a very good mother. I should have paid more attention to Declan and taken care of him more. I shouldn't have left him for Spencer to take care of all the time. I should have noticed that something was wrong… I should have asked Spencer about what was going on, but I was just focused on myself. On my comfort and my profession."

She sighed and stared pensively off. Her fingers brushed over the tattoo again, and she looked down at it as if she hadn't been aware she was touching it.

"He's here with me all the time, now," she said. "He can't ever wander away now."

Isabella stopped speaking, but he could still see her lips mouthing the words.

Until we meet again, may God hold you in the palm of His hand.

Isabella gave a brave smile and brushed a few stray cat hairs from her dress.

She was much better on her own show. She sat on the stool she was comfortable and familiar with and chattered to the camera about colors and tones and shades. She was wearing the clothes that suited her, even if she did have to wear long sleeves to cover up her tattoo. And just one necklace and ring. Nothing that would be too distracting as she painted.

Zachary sipped his coffee while he watched her begin to daub the canvas. A beautiful seascape started to appear. Cerulean blue waves and fluffy white clouds scudding across a sky of celestial blue.

HIS HANDS WERE QUIET

ZACHARY GOLDMAN MYSTERIES #2

*To shock those who didn't know
and acknowledge those who have been shocked*

1

Mira Kelly put the pictures of her son down on her kitchen table, one at a time, like they were precious treasures she thought Zachary might try to run off with.

Photographs were Zachary's passion. Ever since Mr. Peterson, his foster father at the time, had given him a used camera for his eleventh birthday, he'd been taking pictures. It was that passion that had eventually led him to his profession. Not a department store photographer or a wedding photographer, but a private investigator. It gave him the flexibility to set his own hours, even if many of them were spent sitting in a car or standing casually around, waiting for the opportunity to catch a cheating spouse or insurance claim scammer in the act.

Zachary ignored the lighting and framing issues in Mira's pictures and just looked at the boy's face. He was a teenager, maybe thirteen or fourteen. Still baby-faced, with no sign of facial hair. Dark hair and pale skin, like Zachary's. Quentin's hair was a little too long, getting into his eyes in uneven points. Zachary couldn't stand hair getting in his face and ears and kept his short. Not buzzed like foster parents and institutions had always preferred, but still easy to care for. The first few pictures of Quentin didn't give a clear view of his eyes. His eyes were closed, hidden by his shaggy hair, or his face was turned away from the camera. Then Mira put one down on the table that had caught his eyes full-on, looking straight through the camera. Blue-gray. Clear. Distant.

Mira kept her fingers on the photo, reluctant to release it to him. "Quentin was a beautiful baby," she said. "Everyone always said how beautiful he was. Not cute or handsome, *beautiful*. He could have been a model. But he didn't smile and laugh when you smiled or tickled him, like other babies. He laughed at other things; the sunlight filtering through the leaves of a tree, music... I didn't realize, in the beginning..." She wiped at the corner of her eye. She'd been resisting tears since she had first greeted Zachary.

Isabella Hildebrandt had said that Quentin had been autistic when she asked Zachary if he would meet with Mira. The boy had been living at the Summit Living Center, some sort of care facility, when he had died suddenly. 'Died suddenly' was a euphemism that Zachary particularly hated.

Mira was convinced that Quentin's death couldn't have been suicide. "He wouldn't have done that," she insisted again, looking at the picture that showed Quentin's eyes.

"Why not?" Zachary asked baldly.

He could see that his bluntness surprised her. She was used to people talking about her son's death in veiled terms. Coming at it sideways and trying to comfort her. But that wasn't Zachary's job. Zachary's job, if he took the case, would be to find out the truth about Quentin's death. And if he was going to do that, he needed Mira to speak plainly instead of soft-pedaling euphemisms.

"He... he couldn't." She stumbled over the words, looking for a way to explain it. "That just... wasn't something that he would have been capable of."

"Physically, you mean?"

"No, he was healthy physically, mostly, but... he had autism. He didn't have the ability... mentally... to decide to do something like that, and plan it out, and follow through." She shook her head. "The idea is ridiculous."

"Because he was mentally handicapped."

"No... not handicapped. I just don't think... I don't think he could have understood what it meant, to kill himself. And I don't think he could have planned it out. There is other stuff that can go along with autism... His executive planning skills..."

Zachary wasn't sure what that meant. He looked at the other angles of the case. "Was he depressed?"

"He was happy at Summit. It was a good place for him. The only place that had been able to manage his behavioral issues."

Zachary looked at the haunting eyes that looked up from the photograph. "This is a recent photo?"

"Yes." Mira looked down at him. "I know he's not smiling for the picture. But he never smiled for pictures. He *was* happy at Summit. They were able to get him off of all of the meds that the other places had put him on. So that he could be himself and not a drugged-out zombie."

"Sometimes depression isn't obvious. People are often taken by surprise by suicides." Zachary looked away from her uncomfortably. Other times, depression was obvious, and friends or family members did everything they could to head it off. Like with Isabella Hildebrandt, when her mother had hired Zachary to look into her son Declan's untimely death, hoping to bring Isabella some peace. They'd been unable to prevent her suicide attempt. Only luck and quick-acting professionals had been able to bring her back. As they had done for Zachary in the past. "When you say they took him off of his meds... did that include antidepressants?"

"No, he was never on antidepressants. He was on other medications to keep him quiet. I couldn't have him at home anymore, because he was too much of a danger to my younger sons. And me."

There was a snapshot on the fridge of Mira with two younger boys, maybe eight and ten. Mira was a slight, small woman. The ten-year-old was almost her height. There were no pictures of her with Quentin, but Zachary suspected he was taller than she was by a few inches. Even though Quentin had a slim build, a child in the midst of a meltdown could be very strong. Looking down at the pictures of Quentin on the table, Zachary saw another child in his mind's eye.

Annie Sellers had also been autistic, and well-known for her rages. He had watched, through the narrow observation window of his detention cell, as several members of the Bonnie Brown security staff had tried to bring her under control. She was slim and small, but even three guards together could barely hold on to her to get her into a cell.

Zachary blinked, trying to focus on the case at hand. Annie was in the distant past. He couldn't do anything for her. No one could.

"How long had Quentin been at Summit?"

"Two years. They turned him around completely. He was not the same child."

"And you hadn't noticed any changes in behavior recently. Anything at all."

Mira bit her lip. She was a strawberry-blonde with a pixie cut. She kind of reminded Zachary of a forty-year-old Julie Andrews. The same shape to her face. But there were fine lines that told the tale of a hard life. There was no sign of a man in the house. Raising three boys as a single mother was not an easy job, especially when one of them had behavioral issues. Summit was a good two hours' drive from Mira's house, which meant that she wasn't visiting him daily.

"He'd been agitated the last few times I went to see him," Mira said finally. "They said it was probably just hormones, and they were increasing his therapy sessions to address it."

Zachary scratched a note to himself in his notepad. "What do you mean by agitated?"

"More... anxious... more... behaviors..."

"Describe to me what that looked like. What exactly was he doing?"

"Picking at his skin... flapping... He was voicing and didn't want to sit down to visit with me. He wanted to walk around to visit, but they said... his therapist said he needed to work on sitting quietly to visit. When they forced him to sit down, he started banging his head or got angry, and they had to take him out and cut our visit short."

Zachary wrote down each of the behaviors. "He didn't usually do those things?"

"No, he'd been pretty good at Summit, they could usually suppress them."

"Is there something that triggers them? When he lived at home, did he do them all the time, or just sometimes?"

Mira ran her fingers through her hair. There were bags under her eyes, camouflaged with makeup. She looked exhausted. She probably wasn't sleeping.

"Yes, when he was frustrated about something... Before he died, I felt like he wanted to tell me something. But it's difficult for him. If I'd been able to walk around with him, talk with him some more, I might have been able to figure out what it was. But they said he had to go back to his room."

"So he *could* talk...?"

"He was mostly nonverbal. He had a few words. He would take my hand to show me something or ask me to do something for him. But Summit said I needed to force him to use speech." Mira sighed heavily. "They said that if I ignored his nonverbal communication... he would use words more..."

"Oh." Zachary nodded. "Then he could, if he had to?"

Mira frowned and tugged at a lock of hair. "Well... it was hard for him. They said that if he could speak some of the time, then he could speak all of the time, if he just worked at it. When he was at home, we would use pictures, gestures, whatever we could." She wrapped the lock around her finger. "It wasn't like he was just being willful or lazy when he wouldn't speak. That's what Dr. Abato says, but I always thought... Quentin was doing the best he could, and that we should let him use PECS or signs or whatever he needed to communicate..."

"That makes sense," Zachary agreed, giving her a nod of encouragement.

"They said that I was just babying him. Keeping him from progressing. They said if he was ever going to get out of Summit, maybe on a work program or something, he would have to be able to speak. To get along in the real world and be treated like everyone else, he needed to be able to speak."

"And it was working? You said that his behavior had improved at Summit. Did that include his speech?"

Mira picked up one of the photos from the table and stared at it, her eyes shiny with tears.

"Scripted speech," she offered finally. "They were very proud of how well he was doing with scripted speech."

"What's that?"

"I would come to visit him, and he would say, 'Hi, Mom.' And I would say hi to him. He would ask me how I was doing, and I would tell him and ask him how he was. He would say, 'fine' or 'happy' or 'well.' But that was it... if I asked him what he had been doing, or who his friends were, or anything like that, he would fall apart. He would cry and mope and shake his head at everything I said. Then when it was time go, and I would say goodbye and hug him, he would pick up the script again. He'd say, 'Bye, Mom. Love you. See you next time.' They'd taught him how to say hello and goodbye..." Mira's voice cracked. "But they had just trained him to say the words. He still couldn't have a conversation. He still didn't have a script for what came between hello and goodbye."

"Maybe that would have come."

"Maybe... but conversations are complicated. I don't know how many different scripts he could have learned. There are so many different pathways a conversation could have followed."

Zachary looked at the yellow envelope at Mira's elbow that she had not yet opened. She was assiduously ignoring it.

"Do you want to take a break?"

Mira looked relieved. She let out her breath. "Yes. How about some tea? Can I get you a drink?"

"Tea would be great," Zachary agreed. He was not a tea drinker, but it was a soothing ritual for those who were. It would help Mira to calm down and move forward again.

She got up from the table and moved around the kitchen, putting the kettle on and rattling the cups and saucers and other bits. She opened the kitchen window a crack, letting in a breath of fresh, cool air.

"How long have you known Isabella?" Zachary asked her.

Isabella, *The Happy Artist*, beloved local TV personality, had connected the two of them. Zachary had been the one to investigate her son Declan's death and, in spite of the hell she'd been through as a result, she seemed to be grateful to Zachary.

"I've known Isabella a long time. Since we were both in school. We weren't really close friends. But I watched her when she started painting on TV. Quentin loved to watch her show. I knew Isabella had used a private investigator, so I called her..."

Zachary nodded.

Mira set their cups on the table and filled them. Zachary stirred his, not really interested in drinking it.

"I can look at those when I get home," he said, nodding to the unopened envelope. "There's no reason you have to look at them again."

Mira hesitated, considering his offer, then shook her head. "No. I can do this."

She took a couple of determined gulps of piping hot tea and picked it up.

2

O
h, that poor boy," Kenzie sympathized.

It wasn't the first time Zachary and the attractive brunette had looked at photos of dead bodies together over dinner. Being attached to the local medical examiner's office, Kenzie had a strong stomach, so things that would have made a normal woman queasy didn't bother her one bit.

Not that Quentin Thatcher's photos were gruesome. Strangulation was bloodless, and his body wasn't bloated and swollen like Declan Hildebrandt's had been. But they were still stark and depressing.

"His mother saw these?" Kenzie asked. "She's a stronger woman than I would be. I could never look at photos of my dead child like this."

"She had a pretty hard time with it," Zachary said. "But yes... she's strong."

"The poor woman."

Zachary had a sip of his soft drink and nodded. "I feel bad for any mother who has lost a child."

Saying it brought back painful memories of his break-up with Bridget. The loss of the child he had expected to raise with her.

Kenzie looked at him, her brows drawing down. "I hear a 'but' in there somewhere..."

"No, no, not at all. I do feel sorry for her."

"Okay."

They were silent for a couple of minutes until the waiter brought their meals. Kenzie poked at her phone, not speaking to him, and he got the feeling she was waiting him out, trying to force him, by not asking questions, to say what was on his mind. Just like Mira had been told to ignore Quentin's nonverbal communication so he would be forced to use speech.

Zachary cut into his steak, pretending that he was checking to make sure it had been cooked to his specifications. It had been, of course, and he really wasn't that picky as long as it wasn't bleeding. He just wanted to look at something other than Kenzie, patiently waiting for him to spill his guts. Outside, it was raining, the intermittent traffic passing the restaurant with that familiar swish of wet roads.

"I guess she just irked me a little," he admitted. "She did what the institution said to, even though she didn't think it was the best thing for her son."

"But they are the professionals."

"Sure… but I've dealt with a lot of doctors. They're not always right. In fact… they are frequently wrong when they're dealing with messy stuff like mental illness. Or autism and the other conditions that go with it. They have so many patients to treat. They only have a few minutes to spend on each case. But Quentin's mother only had to deal with him. She raised him for the first twelve years. She knows him and what he needs better than they do."

Kenzie twirled her fork through spaghetti marinara, her movements smooth and dexterous. "But she doesn't have the training. The doctors and therapists have studied the best way to treat kids like this. All of the latest research. All of the different methods. The mother doesn't have that."

"Maybe not… or maybe she does. Parents have a lot of resources available now. Internet, support groups, millions of books. They can spend hundreds of hours researching what's best for their particular child." He paused, chewing a couple more bites of steak. "But… I don't get the feeling she ever did any of that. She just let the institution dictate what she should do."

"Do you think the doctors were doing something wrong, or do you just not like his mother toeing the line?"

"I don't know yet. I'm trying to go into it with an open mind." Zachary looked down at the pictures of Quentin still on the table, the dark bruises around his throat. "If nothing else... they didn't stop him from killing himself."

Kenzie nodded. "He should have been closely supervised. They should have known if he was suicidal and have had him on a watch."

Zachary took another sip of his cola, wishing that he had something stronger. When he started to get anxious, like the case was already making him, he liked something to take the edge off. Kenzie watched him put the glass down. He wondered whether she could tell what he was thinking, whether she knew that he was craving a real drink. He breathed out, long and slow, trying to release the knot in his belly.

"She feels guilty for institutionalizing him," he told Kenzie.

"Of course. I'm sure every parent who has a child like that does. But she did what she had to do."

Zachary laid down his fork, unable to pretend that he was interested in his steak anymore. "She also said that when she took him there, when she had to go home and leave him behind... she felt relieved."

Kenzie looked at Zachary, her eyes traveling over his face like she was reading a book. "That sounds pretty normal too. He was probably exhausting to take care of. Getting bigger and harder to control. Maybe even violent."

"Yes. He was. She said she feared for her other children."

"And herself, even if she didn't say so. Even a child can hurt you when they're in a rage. More so when it's a teenager who doesn't understand how much damage they could do."

"Yeah." Zachary looked down at his plate. He picked up his napkin and dabbed at his mouth, covering up the grimace he couldn't check.

"What is it?" Kenzie asked, when a few minutes passed in silence.

"Nothing. It's nothing."

"I think I know you well enough by now to tell you're upset about something. Why don't you tell me about it before it builds up into something worse?"

He tried to swallow a lump in his throat. Kenzie let him sit and stew for a while longer. Her eyes went to the photos and she picked through them with two fingers, moving them around. She didn't point out anything suspicious.

"My mother," Zachary said finally. "I told you that she didn't want me. She had me put... into a place like that."

Kenzie put her hand over his. "Oh, Zachary…" She shook her head. "I still don't understand how she could have done that. I really don't. I don't think that any child deserves to be locked up for making a mistake. And that's what it was. A mistake."

"I did things I knew were wrong. I knew, and I went ahead and did them anyway. I wore her ragged. She couldn't manage all of us. It wasn't just her. I never lasted long in any foster family; no one could manage me. No matter how many meds they put me on, no matter how much therapy I did, I always ended up back at places like that."

"But you made it. You're okay now. You turned out alright. You might have had the childhood from hell, but you're not a child anymore. Everything turned out okay."

He wondered if she really thought that he was okay. Whether he could pass as normal to her. His past always plagued him, floating in his peripheral vision, clouds of darkness that threatened to overcome him the moment he let his guard down. People could tell, even if they didn't understand what it was about him. They could always tell that he was different.

He swallowed hard. "I just couldn't help wondering, when Mira said that, how my mother felt when she told the social worker to put me away. I always wondered if she regretted it. If she ever felt the least bit sorry about breaking us up. Abandoning us like that. But what Mira said she felt…" Zachary struggled mightily to keep his cool and not allow his voice to crack, "…was relief."

Kenzie's hand squeezed his more tightly. "I'm sure she felt all of the other things that Quentin's mom felt too. Guilt. Regret. Sadness. No parent wants to institutionalize their child."

"*She* did."

"She said she did. But I'll bet she cried."

Zachary thought about this. She thought about all of the times she had screamed at Zachary or his siblings. Hit them. Punished them unfairly. She hadn't been exaggerating when she told the social worker she was at the end of her rope and couldn't do it anymore. He had done that to her. Had she regretted it? Had she cried, once she was out of sight? Once it was all over and she could let down her guard? He honestly couldn't picture it. The last thing he had seen of her was her unrelenting anger.

"I don't think she cried," he said finally.

But Mira had.

3

After parting ways with Kenzie with a friendly peck on his cheek and nothing more, Zachary headed back to Mario Bowman's apartment. All was quiet; Bowman had left the light on for Zachary in the living room and had already gone to bed.

Bed.

Zachary's mind was a storm of thoughts and questions about the case, impressions from the evening, and the intrusive flashes of memory from his own past. There was no way he would be able to go to sleep without help. In the bathroom, Zachary took out his prescription bottles one at a time and set the pills in a neat row. Two sleeping pills. One anti-anxiety. One antidepressant. His hand hovered over the non-prescription bottles as well. An over-the-counter antihistamine? Stress vitamins? Valerian?

The reason he hadn't had anything to drink at the restaurant was because he had known what was coming. He had known that he wasn't going to be able to settle down for bed. That his emotions and the memories had all been stirred up and there was no way he was going to be able to sleep without an aid. Several aids.

He left the rest of the bottles. He would go with the pills he had already selected. He knew that he could take all of them together. He had before. And the combined punch would, he hoped, let him forget Quentin's haunting face and get a few precious hours of sleep before he was again pacing the room.

He swallowed the pills dry and checked the time on his phone. He would give his body half an hour to start to absorb the pills before lying down. Then he would be able to sleep, or get some semblance of sleep. He went back to the living room and turned the TV on, volume low, and tried to lose himself in a sitcom. But he didn't even know what he was watching, much less follow the jokes. He just stared at the screen filled with silly, joking people, and tried to let it all expand to fill his brain and push out all of the other pictures and impressions that crowded in vying for his attention.

At the half hour mark, he did as he had planned and lay down on the couch, pulling the blanket up over himself and closing his eyes.

For a long time, he lay staring at the back of his eyelids, amebic red and black, searching for peace. He could feel the sleeping pills working, slowing his heart rate and breathing, dulling the thoughts but not silencing them. The knot of anxiety loosened, and he tried to push himself the last few inches toward sleep.

Then he was dreaming. He saw himself in a cell at the institution Mira had put Quentin into. The Summit Living Center. He had never been there, but he had been enough places like Summit that his brain filled in the details. A bunk attached to the wall, immovable. A stainless steel toilet affixed to the wall, equally immovable. No sink. No desk or counter. No lamp, just the bright fluorescent overhead lights. No windows. Only the narrow rectangular window set into the heavy steel door that kept him locked in the cell. Zachary went to the window. Except he wasn't Zachary. He was Quentin. Zachary wasn't sure how he knew the difference, but he knew he was not in his own skin. He was in Quentin's body, at Summit, looking out into the hallway.

At first, he closed his eyes. He didn't want to look through the narrow window. He knew what he was going to see. But the dream went inexorably on and he was looking out the window, into the hallway, watching as they brought another resident to the cell next to his. It was a girl. A young girl, blond and pretty. Or she would have been pretty if she hadn't been a kicking, screaming, spitting ball of arms and legs thrashing to get away from the guards.

Her screams went on and on. He didn't know how she could keep screaming her throat raw like that. The noise hurt his ears and he covered them up, trying to block it out, groaning himself with the pain of the noise drilling into his head. And then the noise stopped abruptly. He rose to his feet. He hadn't realized that he had been crouching low to the floor, waiting for the assault of the noise to pass over him. But then it was gone, and he was drawn back up to look out the window of the door, as if he were a puppet on a string.

The girl was on the floor. She lay face down, unmoving. One of the guards was hitting her with a balled-up fist, and the other was sitting on her. Her hands were cuffed behind her back, but they still continued to assault her as if she were fighting back. He reached for the door, wanting to hammer his fists against it and shout at them to stop. But the door was too far away. He couldn't find it with his fists. And when he tried to shout, he was voiceless. Nothing came out. He had to tell them to stop it. To leave her alone. Didn't they see that she wasn't moving anymore? Even the rise and fall of her breath had stopped. He raised his head and howled wordlessly, soundlessly, impotently.

The voiceless scream was so violent that it woke Zachary up. He clutched at the cushions of the couch underneath him, trying desperately to feel them. To ground himself there in the apartment, on the couch, instead of far away in the institution, helpless in a detention cell, powerless to help himself or anyone else.

He knew the girl's name. Knew because he had seen her before, almost thirty years previous. He had watched the police take her down. Seen them beat her into submission, manacle her wrists, kneel on her until she was silenced and no longer fought against them. She had been no older than he was. Ten or eleven. No threat to the security and police.

In real life, they had realized something was wrong. They had gotten up, rolled her over, and made sure that she had started breathing again before taking her away to the police station to be booked for assault after biting one of the guards.

Annie.

Like Quentin, she had been autistic. That had been how she was differentiated from any other Annie. Not as Annie Sellers. Not as blond Annie or little Annie. But as autistic Annie. It had been her title and her identity at the home. And everyone knew about her tantrums and behavioral problems. They knew how difficult she was for the staff to control. Maybe she didn't belong there. Maybe she should have been in some specialized treatment facility instead of a home for unwanted children. Bonnie Brown was a stopping place between foster care and juvenile detention. They didn't need a judge or a conviction to lock the children up. Zachary, Annie, and dozens of other kids whose crimes ranged from ADHD to autism to psychosis and sadism.

"Annie." Zachary said it out loud. It had been a long time since he had dreamed about her.

He'd never forgotten her, but he had been able to banish her from his dreams for a number of years.

But she was back, and he was vibrating, shaking with anger and impotence over the way she had been treated. He *had* pounded on the door all of those years ago. Pounded on the door and screamed and gotten himself a beating for misbehaving.

She had started breathing again.

That time.

When Bowman came out in the morning, Zachary was pacing up and down the living room rug.

Mario Bowman, balding and potbellied, not yet in his police uniform, leveled a look at Zachary. "You're going to wear a path in my carpet."

"Yeah, sorry… I just couldn't sleep."

"Do you ever sleep? You're up when I go to bed. You're up when I get up. That's if you're here and not out on surveillance. You've heard how important sleep is to your health, haven't you?"

Zachary sighed. "You know I would if I could."

"I know, bro. That's why I worry about you."

"I got in a few hours last night."

"A few being…?"

"I don't know. Three hours, maybe."

"Not enough."

"So, I'll sleep better tonight. That's the way it works, isn't it? You're short on sleep one night, so you are tired and get a better rest the next."

"I'd agree if I hadn't actually seen your sleep habits over the past few weeks."

Zachary entered the kitchen ahead of his friend and pressed the button on the coffee maker. They both stood watching it while it pottered and bubbled away, a thin stream of coffee eventually starting to fill the pot.

"You were out with Kenzie last night?" Bowman asked, smothering a wide yawn with the back of his hand.

"Yeah. Had dinner at Old Joe's. It was good."

"The two of you sharing anything more than photographs and medical examiner's reports?" Bowman suggested, giving him a sly, sideways look.

Zachary shrugged uncomfortably, watching the coffee pot as if it were the most important thing in the world. "We're going slow. She's... well, Bridget kind of spooked her. And we've had... a few other rocky places. I don't think she's ready for a serious relationship, and I'm not really the hit-and-run type." His face heated up. Zachary scratched the back of his neck, turning away from Bowman slightly to hide his flush. "So right now... it's mostly business. Friendly, but professional."

"I think she'd go for you, if you were willing to work at it a bit."

The coffee maker was finally dripping its last and Zachary moved in with his mug. He filled both his and Bowman's, while a few stray drips hit the hot plate and sizzled. Bowman was the guy who knew everyone's likes and dislikes and how to get things done by sending a little sugar—or caffeine, or alcohol—the right direction. If he thought Kenzie might be swayed in Zachary's direction, there was every possibility he was right.

"I'm willing to work," Zachary said cautiously. "If it's actually going to go somewhere."

"Did you at least get through dinner without being interrupted by Bridget?"

Zachary nodded. He took a sip of his coffee, still too hot for him to drink. "Yes. Thankfully."

Bowman grinned. "A date always goes better if the ex doesn't show up raging. Even if it is just a business date."

Zachary blew on the surface of the coffee. "You have no idea."

4

The morning was clear and refreshing and Zachary had enjoyed the highway driving. He was sorry to arrive at his destination and have to get down to work. Sitting in the parking lot, he studied the building before entering. It looked like a hundred other facilities. Like a school or a small hospital or Bonnie Brown or one of the other places that he had gone for school or therapy or to live for a few months. A squat red brick building, sprawling as different wings and phases had been added on. Dr. Abato's assistant had given him driving directions and instructions as to how to find the visitor parking and the right door to enter so that he wouldn't be wandering around clueless for an hour. It was a good thing, because he suspected he could quickly be lost in the twists and turns of the building. That would not help his investigation.

There was a tap on his window, and Zachary turned to see a security guard standing there looking in at him. His heart immediately started pounding like he'd been caught doing something he wasn't supposed to. He'd had experience with security guards at places like Summit. They hadn't been pleasant. Zachary rolled down his window.

"Sorry, am I in the wrong place?" he asked. "Dr. Abato's secretary gave me directions, but if I ended up in the wrong parking lot…?"

"No." The guard shook his head like Zachary was an idiot. "But you've been sitting here in your car for a long time. Thought something might be wrong. Do you need assistance?"

"No. Sorry. Just thinking and getting myself prepared." He pulled out his key, opened his door, then realized he needed to roll his window back up. He reinserted the key into the ignition, feeling a warm flush on his cheeks. He rolled the window up.

The guard stood over him as if he might be trying to get away with something.

"Sorry." Zachary wasn't sure what he was apologizing for. He wasn't doing anything wrong by sitting in his car.

"We get some real kooks around here," the guard said, one hand still resting comfortably on the butt of his taser. "People who don't think there should be facilities like this, that people with disabilities should all just be at home somewhere." He *tsked* and shook his head. "Not like these kids have anywhere else to go."

Zachary tried to swallow the lump swelling in his throat. "No," he agreed.

The guard hitched up his heavy utility belt and watched Zachary lock the car. He walked beside Zachary toward the double doors Dr. Abato's secretary had directed him to.

"You a reporter?" the guard asked.

"No." Zachary mentally assessed himself. What would make the guard assume that he was a reporter? "No, I'm just here for a tour."

The man grunted. "Most of the strangers I see back here are reporters. You're obviously not a parent." He chuckled.

Again, Zachary considered himself as if he were standing in front of a mirror. What about him said, 'not a parent?' He was certainly old enough. At forty, he could have a child of any age up to twenty. He was still wearing his wedding ring; the guard had no way of knowing that he was divorced. What was there about him that said he wasn't a father?

"No," he admitted, "no kids."

The guard stopped at the doors and nodded to Zachary. "Well, enjoy your tour, then."

Zachary went in. He couldn't restrain a backward glance once he was through the doors, and saw that the guard was still standing there watching him. Making sure he got where he was supposed to be going. Zachary walked up to the reception desk and introduced himself to the sour-faced, middle-aged woman in a nurse's smock that was sitting at the computer.

"He's expecting you," the woman acknowledged. She picked up her phone and pressed a button. After a short pause, she announced Zachary's name, then hung up. "He'll be right out."

Dr. Abato was a younger man than Zachary had expected. He had dark, well-groomed hair and wore a dress shirt and tie under his white lab coat. As Zachary got close enough to shake the doctor's hand, he saw that the man's lean face was faintly lined; older than he looked at first glance.

"Mr. Goldman, a pleasure to meet you," he said pleasantly. "I'm always happy to accommodate anyone who wants to learn more about the facility. We're quite proud of the work we do here."

Zachary nodded and pulled back from the handshake. Dr. Abato was just a little too jovial and held on a little too long. It felt false. Like a camouflage. He wasn't sure if Dr. Abato remembered the reason that Zachary was there to tour the facility. That he wasn't a reporter or the parent of a prospective resident, but a private investigator looking into a death that had occurred there. Could Abato have forgotten something like that?

"This way," Abato invited, touching Zachary's arm for a moment to direct him out of the lobby into one of the adjoining hallways. Zachary noted the security locks on the door they passed through. Abato wasn't punching a number into the PIN pad or swiping a security pass, but Zachary had a feeling that if he had turned around to test any of the doors that they walked through, they would all be securely locked.

The walls were painted in bright colors and were liberally sprinkled with framed posters of cartoon and movie characters. The initial corridors that they walked through were well-maintained. No dented, scuffed, chipped walls. But Zachary supposed they were still in the administrative area, which would be easier to maintain with no access by residents. Abato was looking sideways at Zachary, watching him for his reaction.

"It's very bright and cheerful," Zachary obliged.

"We take great pride in making this a happy place, a place children can enjoy being."

Zachary nodded. Some of the hospitals he had been in had made an effort to decorate with cheerful themes, but it didn't fool anyone into thinking the patients would choose to be there instead of home. It had never made Zachary feel any better about being in some psych unit instead of being well enough to function on the outside.

Rather than making him smile, the glossy, colorful posters at Summit made him feel anxious and trapped. He focused on breathing deep and slow. Pushing his breath out completely before taking in another lungful of air to ensure he didn't start hyperventilating. The oxygen would make him feel less anxious. Breathing slowly would keep his heart rate down. It would keep his autonomic nervous system calm, so he didn't dissolve into a panic attack.

In theory.

Dr. Abato was talking about the facility, motioning in random directions as he talked about their various features and programs. Zachary tried to focus on what he was saying to process the words, but he couldn't. The words were English, but Zachary couldn't string together the thoughts. He just kept smiling and nodding so Abato wouldn't notice his reaction.

"Residents come to us from all over the country," Abato said. "Summit's programs are unique, it's one of the only facilities of its kind."

Zachary nodded again. Abato opened a door and motioned for Zachary to go through ahead of him. Zachary walked through the door, transported from the silent, peaceful hallway into a chaotic, noisy carnival of flashing lights and arcade games. He froze, senses overwhelmed by the change in the environment.

Abato's hand was on the small of Zachary's back, walking him the rest of the way through the door so that he could shut the security door behind them. He laughed at Zachary's reaction.

"It's quite something, isn't it?" he said proudly.

Zachary looked around. There were children of various ages playing electronic games. There was a ball pit, a climbing wall, and what looked like hamster-tubes to crawl through. The theme of bright colors and cartoon posters continued.

"What is it?" Zachary asked.

"This is a reward room. When a student is able to reach the goals that his team has set to moderate his behavior, he is allowed a 'big reward.' They get smaller rewards for every good behavior, of course, that's how we are able to teach them. But we have found that they are far more motivated, especially the higher-functioning kids, when they have that big 'Disneyland' reward to work toward."

Abato motioned Zachary forward. Zachary tried to focus on the details and shut out the assault of the noise and lights and bright colors. It was not as busy as he had thought at first. Not theme-park-busy. The residents were quiet and well-behaved, mostly playing separately rather than in clusters. Abato's 'kids' ranged in age from around nine years old to teenagers and young adults, with a couple who were obviously in their forties or fifties. Each resident had a staffer standing nearby or helping them with what they were doing. Most of them had on school backpacks. Zachary noticed that the aides had small boxes hanging from their belts with pictures of the residents they were responsible for. Maybe for meds, schedules, or emergency protocols.

"This is our store." Abato pointed out a glass-fronted retail store where Zachary saw girls' frilly dresses, handbags, snacks, magazines, and other sundries that a commissary or gift shop might have. "Those who want to can earn tokens that can be redeemed for items in the store. So they can save up for things that they want, learn how to budget, and other important life skills."

Zachary nodded. "That's cool."

He had been places that used token economies to allow kids to make purchases, and had always found it humiliating and dehumanizing. You made your bed? You got a token. Eat with your fingers at dinner? You don't earn your meal token. Participate in class? Token. Ask too many questions and irritate the teacher? No token. And after weeks or months of bowing and scraping and being forced to do every little demeaning task the staff asked him to, he would be able to buy a chocolate bar, or writing paper, or a key chain with a cartoon character on it.

There were a couple of girls looking at purses in the rewards store, shaking their heads at each other, whispering, and looking frequently over their shoulders at the supervisors.

A boy was walking toward Zachary and Dr. Abato. He had pink cheeks and a sunny expression. He was probably eleven or twelve, but had the open, guileless expression of a much younger child. He was walking directly toward Zachary, eyes on him.

"Walk on by," the male aide with him instructed. "Don't bother the doctor. He has a guest."

But the boy gave no indication that he heard. He continued to move directly toward Zachary and the doctor. The aide reached out and nudged the boy's shoulder, steering him off to the side. The boy opened up his arms as if to envelop them both in a hug. The aide grasped one arm and jerked him away, pulling him forcefully away from them. Zachary slowed, opening his mouth and turning to look. But Abato pressed him forward.

"Don't stop and give him attention. That would be rewarding bad behavior. He needs to learn how to behave appropriately and to listen to his aide when he is told something. Just keep going and don't even show that you saw him."

There was a yelp from behind them, and despite Dr. Abato's stricture, Zachary looked back at the boy, who was starting to cry, his arms bent and hands close to his face, shaking.

"He's fine," Abato said. "Just part of the learning process."

He directed Zachary around a corner. "The games can be overstimulating for some of the kids. Some of them are uncomfortable with the noises and flashing lights, or just with being around so many other students. So there are quieter reward rooms as well."

Zachary peeked into the rooms that they walked by. A pool table in a room with dim lighting. A shelf of books and a couple of beanbag chairs. Computers in study carrels so that the user was not distracted by the others sitting close to them.

"We have an incredible success rate," Abato bragged. "We have succeeded in improving the behavior of some of the country's most intractable students. They can learn! Even those who refuse to talk. Who refuse to toilet or take care of themselves. We can teach them at Summit. And you can see how they love it here."

All around, Zachary saw quiet, cooperative children who, despite being taken away from their families and institutionalized, appeared to be happy and thriving. There was little physical intervention, with staff members hovering nearby or giving verbal instructions and rarely having to physically redirect the residents. Maybe it wasn't the kind of place where Zachary had lived, where he'd had to be vigilant all the time to avoid being victimized. Maybe a child like Annie could live happily at Summit.

Dr. Abato gave an expansive smile. "You're looking at the best place in the world to send your special needs child. The very best of the best."

Zachary gave a brief nod, not sure what to say to this. They walked into a bright, sunlit room. An arboretum of some kind. Big skylights, tall trees, bushes, flowers, the sound of trickling water. There were a few children there, standing quietly or walking around looking at the ground. One of them, a boy of about seventeen, looked up through the branches of the trees at the blue sky, moving his fingers rapidly back and forth in front of his eyes. The staffer standing close to him said something to him. The boy made no response. He just continued to shake his fingers in front of his eyes, letting out a delighted laugh. Dr. Abato looked at Zachary and checked his watch. "I'm sure you'd like to linger here, but I have other appointments, so we need to move on. There are other things I would like you to see before our time here is up."

Zachary nodded, turning away. He heard the aide prompt the boy again. He turned his head to look back. Suddenly the boy let out a shrill yell. He clenched his hands, his face an ugly grimace, his back arched. He shrieked something incomprehensible. The other children in the arboretum were looking his way, their faces white and anxious, eyes wide. One of them started hitting his forehead with his fist. The teenage boy's aide moved in and took him by the arm, speaking in a low, firm voice, and escorted him toward a door the opposite direction from where Zachary and Dr. Abato were going.

Zachary was shaken. The boy had seemed to be perfectly happy and then had suddenly started yelling. Was he angry or upset about something? Was the mood shift simply part of autism? Zachary knew that Annie had been prone to tantrums and meltdowns. Mira had said that Quentin had been violent. So he assumed it was just part of the behavior that one expected with autism.

"Nothing to be concerned about," Dr. Abato said, reading Zachary's face. "If the students cannot control their behavior in the reward rooms, they will be taken back to their units. You can't expect perfection. They are still learning."

Zachary nodded. "I just wondered... if there was something specific that triggered his outburst. If he was upset or... something happened...?"

"Sometimes we can identify the antecedent, and sometimes we can't. The more we can identify about what triggers outbursts or bad behaviors, the better we can do at eliminating inappropriate behaviors."

"Sure. That makes sense."

The talk of eliminating inappropriate behaviors made him uncomfortable. He couldn't count the times in the past that someone else had been passing judgment on his behaviors without understanding why he acted the way he did. Sometimes Zachary himself hadn't been sure why he acted the way he did. But sometimes… he just felt like the adults in his life were being unfair. They stood at the periphery, uninvolved in his life except to decide when he was behaving and when he was not behaving, punishing him according to their arbitrary decisions.

"Does he talk?" Zachary asked, motioning to the boy who had been taken away.

"Justin? No. He's completely nonverbal, despite our best efforts to find his voice." He made a gesture toward where the boy had been standing. "Other than yelling, that is. We've tried to help him to find his words, but he's very resistant. Very stubborn."

"So you can't ask him what it is that sets him off."

Abato looked at Zachary for a moment. "No, he can't tell us what it is that bothers him. But even if we could ask him to explain it to us… I doubt it would be of any help. These children tend not to be very self-aware. Even the higher-functioning and non-autistic kids that we get… asking them to explain what's going on in their minds doesn't make much difference to the therapy. They lie, they don't know, they are manipulative. Sometimes it is actually the lower-functioning kids who are easier to treat. They can't argue with you." Dr. Abato gave a little laugh and shake of his head at the irony.

Zachary just looked at him.

"We want our students to be happy," Dr. Abato said. "But it's up to us to figure out what is going to make the child happy. Not the child himself."

5

They headed down a long corridor and took a turn. "We are leaving the reward rooms, and entering the treatment wing," Abato explained. "You've seen what it is that the children are working toward, what their goal is as they work with our therapists. Now we get down to the nitty-gritty, and you see what exactly it is that we do here."

"Great."

The new corridor they entered was lined with rooms with viewing windows. So they could look into the various therapy rooms to observe what was going on without being seen by the child being treated. Zachary bit his lip. His stomach turned. He felt like a voyeur. The thought of someone else watching and listening to him during any kind of therapy session was repellent. He'd been through many different treatments and therapies as a child and as an adult, and he had always been told that what went on between him and his doctor or therapist was private. No one else would ever see or hear what he said or did. But at Summit, the residents were on display. Not just to other doctors or therapists, but to anyone who happened to be touring the facility during their session.

Zachary thought at first that they would just walk quickly past, catching a glimpse of the kind of work they did. But Dr. Abato looked down at the clipboard he was carrying with him and picked a room out. They didn't stand at the hallway observation window, but went into an anteroom to the therapy room, where there was another window and they could sit down, turn on the speaker to hear what was going on, and watch the session as if it were the latest in reality TV.

Abato motioned to a chair and sat down himself. There was nothing Zachary could do but sit beside him, looking for a way to voice his discomfort.

"This is Raymond Maslen," Abato introduced. "Age five. He has been coming here for about a year. He is not a full-time resident, but comes here for our day program. He is in therapy for forty hours a week and goes home to his mother and his family in the evening."

"What kind of therapy?"

"What we do here is almost entirely ABA. That's Applied Behavioral Analysis. It's a system of reinforcing positive behavior and ignoring or imposing a consequence for negative behavior."

Abato threw the switch to turn on the speaker so they could hear what was going on in the therapy room. Raymond had wavy hair, reddish brown, a bit on the long side, and the face of an angel. The woman who was working with him had masses of blond hair. She wore a purple smock and was just a bit on the heavy side. Raymond was laughing as she played a game with him, blowing his face with a red toy she held in her hand. Every time she blew his face and hair with it, he squealed with delight. She put the toy down on the table and looked at Raymond with a very hard, intense stare.

"You're doing really good, Ray-Ray," she said in an encouraging voice. "You're having a good therapy day today, aren't you?"

He looked at her as if he weren't sure what she was talking about, then gave a nod of his head, sort of a diagonal lowering of his head that could be taken as a nod, but might equally have been a shake.

"You're having a good day today," the blond woman repeated. "You are, right? You nod your head." She nodded her own head emphatically.

The little boy gave a more certain nod, but it was still somewhat sideways, as if he really weren't sure and wanted some way out of it if challenged.

"Nod for Sophie," the woman instructed. She straightened Raymond's head so that it was perpendicular, and pressed his chin, encouraging him to nod. When that didn't work, she put one hand under his chin and the other on the top of his head and put him through the motion of nodding straight up and down. "Good, Ray-Ray! That's right!" she praised. She patted him on the cheek and tickled him under the chin. "Good boy, Ray-Ray."

He clapped his hands excitedly. Sophie caught his hands and pressed them down to the table gently, stilling them. Raymond tried to clap again, and she pressed them more insistently to the table, held together. "No. Quiet hands," she insisted. "No clapping. You can clap if we play a clapping song. Otherwise, keep them still."

She held them for a moment longer, then lifted her hands off of his. He kept them still.

"Good boy, Ray. Good quiet hands." She kept her voice soft. Raising her voice would, Zachary figured, just get him excited and clapping again, which, for some reason, was forbidden.

"Now, listen to what Sophie says, okay? I want you to follow me and do what I say. Can you... touch your nose?"

Raymond raised one hand off of the table and looked at it, then looked at her, evaluating whether this was something he was allowed to do.

"Touch your nose," Sophie repeated. She did not model the behavior, but waited for him to follow her verbal instruction.

Ray-Ray curled his other fingers in, leaving his index finger in a pointing position. He looked at her to see if he was doing okay so far. She didn't give any indication whether he was doing well or not. The little boy raised his finger and very slowly moved it toward his face, eventually touching the very tip of his nose.

"Good job!" Sophie praised. "That's right! You can have one lick of your candy." She picked up a lollipop from a bowl next to her and held it out to him, allowing him to touch his tongue to it. Then she pulled it away and put it back down.

"Now touch your ear. Touch your ear, Ray-Ray."

He moved more confidently this time, raising his index finger to touch the tip of his nose.

"No!" Sophie said so sharply that not only did little Raymond jump, but Zachary did too. She pulled his finger away from his nose and leaned closer to him, clearly into his personal space. "No, Raymond! I didn't say nose, I said ear!"

His smiley face was gone, crumpling up like he was going to start bawling.

"No," Sophie warned. "No crying. I want you to touch your ear. Do it now."

His face froze. He looked at her for a moment, hovering on the edge of tears.

"Touch your ear," Sophie repeated.

He again made a pointer finger with great concentration. But he didn't touch his ear or his nose.

"Your ear," Sophie said. She reached out and pinched Raymond's earlobe. "Touch your ear."

Ray-Ray still hovered, hesitant.

"Touch your ear." Sophie grasped Raymond's little clenched fist and raised it up beside his face, touching his fingertip to his earlobe. "Good!" she praised immediately. "Touching your ear. Good listening, Ray-Ray. Have a lick." She picked up the sucker from beside her and held it out to Raymond, allowing him one lick.

The stricken expression had disappeared from his face, and he was cheering up. Sophie put the sucker back down in the bowl.

"Now, touch your ear."

The little boy ran his fingers through his hair, tousling it and winding a lock around his finger. Sophie waited.

Ray-Ray raised his finger and touched his earlobe a second time.

"Good boy, Ray-Ray!" Sophie praised. "Good job." She tickled his neck and offered him a lick of the lollipop. "One more time, and you can play with the toy. Okay?"

He started to clap, and Sophie pressed his hands back down to the table again.

"Ready? Touch your nose, Ray-Ray."

He made a pointer finger and touched his ear.

"No!" Sophie slapped her hand down on the table.

Ray-Ray burst into tears.

Zachary realized he was gripping the sides of his chair, his knuckles white. He looked over at Abato.

"It's okay," Dr. Abato assured him. "He's fine. He'll calm down in a minute."

"Isn't she being pretty harsh with him? He's just a little guy and he hasn't done anything wrong."

"We need to be very clear when he is giving the right response and when he is not. There can't be any confusion. He needs immediate, clear feedback."

When Zachary didn't respond, he explained further.

"It's like training a dog," he said logically. "When the dog sits, you give him a treat, right? And when he jumps up, you tell him 'no' and push him down. He learns to do the things that earn him a treat, and to avoid the things that cause an unpleasant response."

Zachary was uncomfortable with Ray-Ray being compared to a dog. It might sound like a logical course of action, but he was a child, not an animal.

"But teaching a child, especially one as disabled as the kids we treat here, isn't as simple as training a dog," Abato said. "He doesn't just need to sit and stay. He needs to learn complex language, behavior, social skills, life skills. If that little boy is ever going to be independent and contribute to society instead of being a drag on it, he has a lot to learn."

Zachary looked at the little boy, already starting to settle down and wipe his tears away. "He doesn't seem that... different," he said. "He seems like any other... neurotypical kid."

"Does he?" Abato considered Raymond through the glass. "That just shows you how well we are doing with him. How far he has come since he started with us. When Raymond was first evaluated by our staff, he couldn't sit in a chair. He flapped and clapped his hands all the time. He couldn't follow a single instruction. He chattered constantly about his favorite show. Top Gear."

Zachary couldn't help but smile at that. Maybe Ray-Ray would grow up to become a mechanic. It was a useful skill. If he'd already started learning about car engines at age five, he'd be an expert by the time he was an adult. Fixing his mother's car. Maybe all of the cars on the block.

"You may think that's cute behavior," Dr. Abato said. "But it is dysfunctional. And when he's seventeen and aggressive and won't be dissuaded from his pet topic, it stops being cute. He won't be able to make friends, get a job, or have any productive interaction with his community. If we don't break him of it. How functional is it for him to be able to tell you how to put an engine together if he can't tell the difference between his nose and his ear?"

"Well... okay," Zachary admitted. "He needs to learn those things. Or whatever he can."

"Kids like Raymond have to be explicitly taught how to function in society. They don't pick it up by just watching other people. We have the ability to make him indistinguishable from his peers, if we have enough time with him. That's the goal here. Not just learning to touch his ear or his nose. But to break down every skill he needs to know as a functioning human being, and teach them to him, one step at a time. We'll repeat the same exercise a hundred times. A thousand times. Ten thousand times. Whatever it takes for him to learn it."

"Wow. Okay."

They turned their attention back to Sophie and Ray-Ray. Ray-Ray was no longer crying, but still looked miserable. His hair was more untidy than ever. He motioned to the toy on the table. "Play time?"

"No, Ray-Ray. It's not play time. No toys if you can't do what you're told."

He looked around the room. His gaze lingered on a cupboard mounted on the wall. It was out of the boy's reach, and a padlock hung through the eyelet of the latch, keeping it shut. The padlock wasn't locked, but perhaps if Raymond had been older and taller, it would have been, to keep him away from whatever was in there. Zachary's heart went out to the little guy. He remembered having nothing as a foster child. Having only his clothes and toothbrush in a plastic shopping bag and having that taken away from him by a foster parent. Having them act as if it were their own property, to do with as they pleased. As if Zachary himself were another piece of their property, to acquire, use, and dispose of as they pleased. Sophie and Dr. Abato thought they had every right to treat Raymond as they pleased. To take away his possessions and lock them up. To train him to do what they wanted him to. Because he was just a child. A broken child who needed to be fixed.

"Go home?" Ray-Ray asked.

"No. It's school time. You need to work hard. If you do what I tell you to, you can play with a toy. And you'll go home when we're all done."

He flapped his hands beside his face. Sophie pressed them to the table. "Quiet hands."

Ray-Ray held his hands together on the table, his expression pained. Sophie went on with the session.

"I want you to come give me a hug, Ray-Ray."

Zachary was taken aback. He looked over at Dr. Abato to see if he would put a stop to this, but he didn't. Sophie waited.

"Stand up," she instructed eventually.

Ray-Ray sat there, looking at the toy on the table and at his hands held quietly on the table in front of him. When he didn't respond, Sophie stood up herself. She reached around the little table and pulled Ray-Ray to his feet.

"Give me a hug," she told him again.

The boy stood there like a statue for a moment, then started to shuffle toward her, inching his feet forward, until he was close enough to press his body against hers. He didn't reach up and put his arms around her.

"Give a hug," Sophie prompted again. She reached down to grab Ray-Ray's arms and wrapped them around her body. She held them there for a moment, then let them go, praising him. "Good hug, Ray-Ray. Hugging is nice, isn't it? Hugging makes people feel good." She grabbed the lollipop to give him a lick.

Zachary ventured another look at Abato, still waiting for him to step in and intervene. Abato gave him a supercilious smile. "Hugs are a necessary a part of our social construct as shaking hands," he informed Zachary. "We hug our friends and family as a greeting, to comfort each other, to initiate a romantic relationship… we can't get along in life without human touch, no matter what sensory defensiveness we might have. Don't you think Raymond's mother wants to be able to hug him when she says hello or puts him to bed at night? Wants him to be able to hug his grandmother when she comes to visit? Wants him to grow up and meet a nice girl and have a relationship? Of course she does. All parents want those things for their children. And that's our job here. To teach kids all of those little things, so that they can be comfortable and make friends and function normally."

Zachary looked back at the therapist and her charge. Sophie continued to put Raymond through the paces, requesting hugs, making him hold her tighter or longer, until he was responding on command each time.

6

L et's see how he is able to generalize this skill," Dr. Abato suggested.
Zachary frowned, not sure what the doctor meant. Dr. Abato
stood up and Zachary followed his lead. The doctor smoothed
back his hair and went to the door of the therapy room. He checked to
make sure that Zachary was following him and let himself in.

Sophie looked up to see who was interrupting her session and gave Dr.
Abato a plastic smile. "Doctor."

"Raymond." Dr. Abato waited for the boy to look at him. "Come give
me a hug." He opened his arms in invitation.

Ray-Ray looked at Dr. Abato, then back at Sophie, waiting for her
instruction. She remained silent, not giving him any indication one way or
the other what he should do. A few seconds of silence ticked by. Then the
boy moved slowly to approach Abato and give him a hug. He barely
touched Dr. Abato, then withdrew again quickly. Abato reached around him
and gave him a squeeze, holding on to him firmly. Ray-Ray squirmed to get
loose.

"Good job," Sophie praised when Dr. Abato released him. "Doesn't it
feel good to get a hug?" She tousled Raymond's already-messy hair and
offered him another lick of the lollipop.

"Now give Mr. Goldman a hug," Dr. Abato instructed, waving a hand
in Zachary's direction.

"Oh, that's okay," Zachary protested. "He doesn't know me. I'm just here to observe…"

"He needs to generalize instructions," Abato said firmly. "And he needs to learn that a hug is normal, non-threatening contact so that he doesn't overreact defensively to them in the future. We know what we're doing here, Mr. Goldman." He looked at Raymond again. "Give Mr. Goldman a hug."

Ray-Ray turned toward Zachary. To his surprise, the boy didn't shuffle and approach him reluctantly as he had done with Sophie and Dr. Abato. He threw himself at Zachary, wrapped his arms around him, and clung to him tightly. Zachary looked down at him, not sure how to react, then put his arms gently around the little boy and rubbed his back gently. "There," he said gently. "There, that's okay."

Dr. Abato chuckled. "Okay, let him go now, Raymond."

Raymond continued to hold on to Zachary, his grip not loosening. Zachary wasn't sure what to do about it, continuing to rub Ray-Ray's back soothingly. But Sophie wasn't waiting for anyone else to act. She strode across the small room and grabbed hold of Raymond, peeling his hands away from Zachary.

"You need to listen," she chided.

The boy struggled, striking out blindly with fists and feet, letting out a howl of protest. Sophie took him back to his chair and dropped him back into it.

"Proper sitting," she told him, holding him in place. "You know what to do. Show me proper sitting."

He gradually stopped struggling and sat still. Sophie went back around the table to her seat and looked across the table at him.

"Look at me, Ray-Ray."

He sat there with his face blank and his eyes distant, not acknowledging that there was even anyone else in the room.

"Raymond. Look at me. Eye contact."

He didn't budge.

"This kind of defiant behavior is not acceptable," Sophie snapped. She reached across the table, holding Raymond's head between her hands, and centered his face directly in front of her own. She leaned forward, just inches away from his face, eye-to-eye.

Raymond started to howl as if she were hurting him. He clawed at her hands and spat at her, trying to pull away.

"No," Sophie said firmly. "Stop. I'm not letting you go until you listen. You make your body quiet and show me good eye contact, then I'll let you go. I can't talk to you until you show me eye contact."

He continued to struggle for what seemed like an eternity. Zachary stood there, his whole body rigid, wanting to rescue the little boy. But Sophie and Dr. Abato were silently insistent. With no other options, Raymond finally stopped trying to get Sophie to let him go and looked into her eyes with his tear-filled brown eyes. He whimpered and sniffled, but didn't struggle. Sophie let him go. Ray-Ray's body immediately slumped.

"No," Sophie warned. "Proper sitting."

He was coaxed into an attentive sitting posture, shoulders back, feet flat on the floor.

"Hands on the table," Sophie instructed. "Show me quiet hands."

With a great effort, as if he were holding bowling balls in them, Raymond arranged his hands on the table, both of them cupped slightly, one hand resting in the other. Sophie nodded.

"Good hands," she approved, and stroked his messy hair. "That's a good boy."

Zachary was exhausted as Dr. Abato led him out of the therapy room. All he had been doing was observing, yet he'd been so tense and rigid, his heart pounding so hard, he felt like he'd just had a huge fight.

Dr. Abato smiled at him cheerfully, as if he'd been energized rather than drained.

"He's come such a long way," he told Zachary. "If you'd seen Raymond when he first came to us, you would not believe he was the same child." He looked at his watch, frowning. "It did take a long time, though. I have time to take you to Quentin's room, and that will have to be it. I have other things I need to do today, I just can't spend the whole day talking to you."

"Okay. Lead the way." Zachary was relieved that there was only one more thing to do; then he could go home and veg for a while and get his energy and his perspective back again. Even with all of the brightly-painted, well-lit rooms, the institution felt oppressive. It reminded him too much of all of his hospital and institutional stays. He couldn't help feeling like if he stayed there too long, they would lock him up again. They would see through his thin veneer of civilization and realize that he too needed to be properly trained before he could function on his own in the real world.

The doctor continued to patter away as he led Zachary down the halls, out of the therapy wing and into living quarters. Zachary barely heard a word he said. It was probably in all of the online information on the institution's website anyway. Zachary could review it later, when he was at home and could concentrate on the words without being distracted by his own demons.

Abato stopped at a door and opened it for Zachary. "This was Quentin's room."

Zachary looked around. He wasn't sure what he had expected. A pool of blood? Quentin's sheets still on the floor? An untouched crime scene?

It was just a small, square room. A bunk attached to the wall. A small, drab, institutional dresser with four drawers. A little closet with no doors and no hangers on the rod. Painted semigloss institutional white, scuff marks and chips here and there. They would repaint it and put another boy there.

Zachary rubbed the back of his neck. "Were you here when they found him?"

"It was early morning, I wasn't on yet. We do have medical personnel on staff. Of course, we have to, dealing with residents who are violent or self-injure. Nonverbal residents can't always communicate that they're sick or hurt and can be seriously ill before we find out something is wrong. Even if we're just dealing with day-to-day colds and flus, we need someone on staff. Epidemics can run rampant in places where so many people are in such close contact."

"So someone on site was called? Who was it that found him?"

"One of the unit supervisors, when he didn't come out for breakfast."

Zachary could visualize it. The reveille or breakfast bell rang, and everyone lined up for their food. Someone noticed Quentin's absence. A supervisor went to find him, discovering he had died in the night.

"The photographs show that he was on the floor instead of on the bed," Zachary said, sketching out the location of the body in the cell with his hands and evaluating the view angle from the observation window set in the door.

"Yes. That's right."

"Is anyone checking on the residents at night? Are the doors locked or unlocked?"

Dr. Abato pursed his lips. "Most of the doors are unlocked. If a resident is prone to wandering or is a danger to others, they are locked. But most of them, no, not locked."

"And was Quentin's?"

"Quentin could be violent. If he'd had any episodes during the day, his door would probably be locked. But I'd have to get someone to check the records. See if it was logged."

"There's not a rule that it has to be recorded? It might not have been?"

"No, there's not a specific rule about recording locks. But everything out of the ordinary is supposed to be logged. We keep detailed records on therapies, behaviors, how many times a child has to be prompted... all of that. If his door was locked, I expect someone would have made a note of it."

"Wouldn't the supervisor who opened his door be able to tell you? Whether she had to unlock it or not?"

"No." Abato smiled. "We all have proximity keys." He showed Zachary a plain bracelet around his wrist. "When you reach out to open a door, it unlocks. She wouldn't notice whether it was locked or unlocked, because she would be able to open it either way."

"Oh." Zachary nodded. "That's cool." He thought about it. "They're all individually programmed? So different staff would have access to different areas."

"Yes, of course."

"So who would have had access to Quentin's room?" Zachary made a gesture to indicate his surroundings.

"Anyone with an administrative or high-security rating. The unit supervisors and security staff. His therapists."

"Why would his therapists have access to his room?"

Abato raised his brows. "So they could come and get him when it was time for a session."

"A supervisor or guard wouldn't just open it for them?"

"Why, when we've got this system that allows personalized access? No need to bother anyone else, they just collect the kids they need."

Zachary felt a sudden wave of cold. He rubbed his arms. "Are all of the unlocks logged? So you know who has been in and out?"

"I don't know. I suppose they're probably recorded in the system somewhere."

"What if a child disappeared? You would need to know who had gotten them out."

"We don't have children disappearing," Abato said slowly, his brows drawing down. "We've never had an issue like that."

"All it takes is one."

"Well... I'll certainly take a look into that. I'm sure the unlocks must be logged somewhere."

"Can you find out who accessed Quentin's room in the twenty-four hours before he died? Didn't the police ask you for that?"

"No. They just asked about how he was discovered. When anyone last saw him alive. How he had been."

"What did you tell them?"

Abato shrugged. He looked around the little room. "Let's walk and talk. I need to get you back to your parking lot and get to my meeting."

Zachary was reluctant to leave the room so soon, but it was obvious there was nothing hidden there. The police forensics unit wouldn't have missed anything. If they'd even been there. The room was completely bare.

He followed Abato out to the hall. "Can I take a quick turn around the unit? Just to get a feel for it...?"

Abato took an impatient look at his watch and nodded. They walked briskly around the unit loop. Bedrooms like Quentin's and a few small gathering rooms along the outside. An administrative desk or nursing station, storage and utility rooms, and restrooms on the inside. Typical for any hospital or institution. Abato nodded to the staff members as he escorted Zachary through the unit but didn't stop to make introductions. He had already made it clear that he was out of time. It felt like he had been there for at least half the day.

Abato jerked his head to the left as they exited the unit and led Zachary down a blue corridor.

"We'll take a shortcut here."

"You never said what your answers were to the police's questions."

"What?" Abato looked at Zachary vaguely, seemingly distracted by something else. "Oh. No one had noticed anything unusual about Quentin's behavior, no. Of course, we asked everyone. And even with hindsight, we couldn't identify any behavior that might have been concerning. Nothing to indicate that he was depressed. But then… he didn't have a lot of words. He wouldn't have been able to tell us much, even if he had been inclined to."

"He didn't try to communicate with the staff?"

"No. Do you know the derivation of the word 'autism,' Mr. Goldman?"

"Uh…" Zachary shook his head. "No. I thought it was just a diagnosis…"

"It was a word used by both Kanner and Asperger to describe one of the key facets of the disorder they were observing in the children they were treating. Auto, from the Greek word for 'self.' Children who were withdrawn into themselves, who kept separate from other people, who lived in their own realities. It was a word that had been used to describe people with schizophrenia, but they noticed a qualitative difference from schizophrenia. These were not children who lived in a fantasy world, but they lived in the world of themselves, didn't naturally reach out to others. So, no. Quentin did not try to communicate whatever emotional issues he was having with the staff. Like most autistic children, Quentin did not seek out contact with other people. He just wanted to be by himself. That was his normal."

"Okay. What about their other questions? When he was last seen alive? There were no bed checks?"

"He was last seen alive when he went into his room to go to sleep. No one… no one noticed anything unusual or of concern during bed checks." Abato frowned to himself, walking faster so that Zachary almost had to run to keep up. Anything other than a normal-paced walk still felt awkward to Zachary since his car accident, and he was worried about tripping and falling flat on his face. Abato looked around, noticed Zachary lagging, and slowed a little to continue the conversation. "They didn't go into his room to check on him. Just looked through the window."

"But he was on the floor, not on his bed."

"Kids like Quentin can be unpredictable. It's not unusual to find one curled up asleep under his bunk or hiding under a table."

"So they *did* see him on the floor?"

"Yes, of course. It is my understanding that the guard who was doing the bed checks that evening has been let go. We are not asserting any negligence, but for Summit's optics, it was best for him to find other employment." Abato took a deep breath. "Quentin died by his own hand, Mr. Goldman. It's tragic and we all feel horrible that we weren't able to prevent it. But in the end… maybe it's for the better."

Abato stopped walking and turned to Zachary, speaking in a low, confidential tone.

"Quentin was never going to be able to leave here. He was never going to be able to be independent and live a life outside of an institution. Maybe if his mother had gotten him into our program when he was young, like Raymond, instead of waiting until he was twelve, violent, and intractable, we could have done more for him. But once a child passes ten or twelve... we can't always turn them around. All we're doing is trying to make things tolerable for their families. They want their kids off of meds, being taken care of by someone else, somewhere they can go and visit once a week or once a month and pretend they're living a happy, meaningful life."

"So you knew Quentin wasn't happy."

"We do our best to make our residents happy. And he was probably happier here than he was anywhere else. But it was obvious that we were not going to succeed with him. He was never going to be able to pass as normal. He was going to be here for the rest of his life. We just didn't realize how short that would be."

They started to walk again, at a slower, more thoughtful pace.

"I saw some residents who were older in the reward rooms," Zachary said. "But I haven't seen a lot of them around. You have mostly teenagers and young adults?"

"The older adults tend to be in self-contained units. They unfortunately tend to have shorter lifespans than non-autistic adults. Much higher incidence of cancer and other diseases. They don't have the self-awareness and communication skills to seek treatment early on. And in most cases, the family members choose not to prolong their suffering."

His words made Zachary feel physically sick. Abato was eager to show off the successful children and teens in his program, the ones who might someday be able to 'pass as normal,' but he seemed like he was just dressing up the fact that they were just warehousing the older adults, waiting for nature to take its course.

Quentin was *not* better off dead.

He didn't need to die so that someone else could take his place in the program; someone who was more likely to 'succeed.'

His mother, at least, hadn't wanted him to die.

7

D r. Abato walked Zachary back out to the reception area where he had first arrived. He held up a hand to indicate that Zachary should wait for a moment, while he talked to the receptionist in a lowered voice. He nodded his thanks and then joined Zachary again.

"We've got some protesters outside the grounds today," he informed Zachary. "Your best route out of here is to turn a left out of the parking lot and circle around to the freeway entrance. The protesters know that they're supposed to stay off of the grounds and are not allowed to block traffic, but they have been known to do it in the past. Just keep your car crawling forward and don't make eye contact, and you should be able to get out of here alright. If you do get stuck, stay in your car with the doors locked. Our security will do their best to get them out of your way, but your best bet at that point is to dial 9-1-1. The police will be far more likely to respond to your call that you feel threatened by the protesters blocking your way than they would to a call from us. Just a matter of police officers identifying better with an individual citizen than to a big corporate entity."

Zachary felt overwhelmed by it all, but he nodded his understanding. "Okay. Thanks."

"You will be more of a target if a guard escorts you out, or I would have someone walk you to your car. You'll be alright?" Abato leveled a piercing look at him. Zachary felt like Ray-Ray being forced to look Sophie in the eye.

"Sure. Thanks so much for your hospitality. I'll call you with any follow-up questions? And you'll get back to me on the security lock logs?"

"Of course."

Dr. Abato shook Zachary's hand, his grip too tight for comfort, and Zachary was happy to be able to get away from him, to get away from everyone in the oppressive place and get back to his car. Sitting in the driver's seat of his new Civic, Zachary just breathed for a few minutes, trying to calm the shakiness in his thighs and his abdominal muscles and to re-center himself. He had known it would be a rough day. Not just because he was investigating a child's death, but also because of the institution itself and his own past. Because of Annie and his other memories of places like Summit.

But now that part was done. He'd seen what he needed to there. He would finish reading the medical examiner and police reports and deal with any further questions over the phone or email. Unless there were further details that required him to return to Summit, he was finished there.

Taking one last deep breath, Zachary pulled the car out of the parking space and at the exit of the parking lot, turned left. There was a small cluster of protesters. He remembered Dr. Abato's advice not to make eye contact, and avoided looking at their faces. He focused on the road ahead of him and tried to pretend they weren't even there.

He got past them, and it wasn't until then that he looked at their signs in his mirror and saw Quentin's face.

Bowman was off of his shift when Zachary got home, exhausted from the drive to and from Summit, from the tour and the anxiety that plagued him there, from thinking about it, and from trying not to think about it.

"You look like death warmed over," Bowman observed. "What exactly did they do to you in that place? Put *you* in the rubber room for a few hours?"

"It was just... a tiring day," Zachary said, trying to brush it off and not allow any images of detention cells to bubble up from the past. "All of the driving and everything."

"Have you had anything to eat?"

Zachary was trying not to put Bowman out by expecting him to supply all of the meals while Zachary was living there but, once again, he had forgotten to provide for himself and had gone home empty-handed, without groceries, fast food, or even a thought about meals.

"Uh... it's fine. I'm not hungry," he said truthfully. "You don't need to make anything."

"When I say anything, I mean anything. Did you have breakfast? Lunch?"

"Uh... no. Just... coffee this morning."

"You said you were going to grab something on the road. On the way there."

"Yeah... I guess I got distracted. I forgot."

"It's no wonder you're so skinny! Did Bridget ever get you eating three meals a day when you were living with her?" Mario readjusted his belt, lifting his belly and patting it ruefully. "I could never forget to eat."

"Well... some of the meds I take kill my appetite. I don't really get hungry." Zachary tried not to think of Bridget and the life with her that he had lost. The heartache was more than he could handle.

"I'm having dinner, so what do you want?"

He swallowed. "Whatever you're making is fine."

"Burgers and fries?" Bowman suggested.

"Yeah, sure."

"Alright. I'll throw them on."

8

Ray-Ray held the cold, hard metal of his piston to his face, trying to be still. Mommy said he had to stay in bed, and he was trying, but he was uneasy. He turned onto his side, and the weighted blanket shifted and settled back over him, soothing. Like the man's hands when he had hugged Ray-Ray.

Ray-Ray's brain was a motor that ran all the time. It didn't stop when it was bedtime, and it didn't stop while he was asleep. Mommy said he slept like a windmill, when he finally slept. A windmill was a big fan, like in an engine, and she meant that his arms and legs were always moving, not that they went in circles. When Mommy slept, she was still, like a car that had been parked in the garage at night.

But Ray-Ray's motor kept running. When he didn't have something else to occupy his attention, like watching Top Gear, his brain replayed the events of the day over and over again. Examining them from all angles. Analyzing his mistakes and everyone's scripts. Top Gear was a TV show, and that meant it followed a script, Sophie said. One that was written ahead of time so that everyone knew exactly what to say and do next. Real life had scripts too, but they weren't all written out ahead of time, you had to pay attention to figure out which one to use. Ray-Ray wasn't very good at figuring out which one to use. The word that came most easily to his tongue was 'no,' and that just made Sophie angry.

It made everyone angry. He was not supposed to say 'no.'

Usually.

Ray-Ray hadn't seen the man before. He didn't usually see new actors at Summit. He saw Sophie, Mrs. Beale at the reception desk, the doctors, and a scattering of smaller parts; other kids who went there for school, their teachers, other aides and staff whose bodies and voices and movements had become more familiar to him. But the man was someone new. Ray-Ray was sure, as his brain reviewed every other day he'd gone to Summit, that he'd never seen the man there before.

Mr. Goldman.

'Hug Mr. Goldman,' Dr. Abato had said. So the man's name was Mr. Goldman.

He looked different from the other people at Summit. He came from somewhere else. He smelled like another place. Coffee, sweat, a chemical smell that new kids at Summit sometimes had. Mr. Goldman didn't smell like home and he didn't smell like Summit.

And it was like he had a light inside him, shining out through his windows and headlights. A light that shone on Ray-Ray and made him feel safer, like he'd felt when the man put his arms around Ray-Ray and told him, 'There, that's okay.'

He'd felt okay for a few seconds. Safe and warm and protected. Like he felt with Quentin. And then Sophie had pulled him away and made him do proper sitting and quiet hands and eye contact, until he felt so small and far away that he didn't know who he was.

Ray-Ray pressed the piston against his cheek again, feeling the cool, smooth metal and inhaling the smell of machine oil.

9

Zachary fell asleep sometime after supper. He and Bowman ate in front of the TV and, with his blood sugar stable, his mental exhaustion from the day at Summit, and physical exhaustion from not sleeping, it wasn't long before Zachary's eyes closed, and he fell into a restless sleep. He knew he shouldn't go to sleep early, or he wouldn't be able to sleep at night, but his brain and body were too overwhelmed to get up and do something else. He kept prying his eyes open for a few seconds, only to be overcome and drift back off to sleep.

At some point, Bowman got up and went to bed, leaving Zachary in the living room with the TV droning on. Bowman knew from experience that if he turned the TV off, Zachary would be instantly awake and unlikely able to get back to sleep again all night, so he just left it playing.

Zachary's tour of Summit had stirred up a lot of memories of Bonnie Brown and other institutions, hospitals, and group homes he had been in. The memories were fluid, time and place shifting and flowing from one to another.

There were hands on him, gripping his shoulders tightly. A male voice. "You were asked to go to the common room, Zachary."

"I don't want to," he protested, trying to pull away.

"I didn't ask if you wanted to. That's where you're supposed to be."

"Only if I want to. I don't want to watch some stupid movie."

"It's not optional."

Zachary tried again to pull away. Usually, he was allowed to stay in his bunk if he didn't want to join in on the planned activities. The man dug his thumb into the nerve in Zachary's shoulder, making his legs buckle with the sudden pain.

"You're coming."

Zachary didn't have it in him to argue any further. It was all he could do to keep from crying. He wasn't going to be seen in tears in front of the other residents. He didn't resist as the staffer steered him toward the door. He couldn't even raise his voice to ask why he had to go.

He wasn't going fast enough for his escort, which meant he was manhandled further, a strong hand on his arm hustling him forward, making him stumble over his own feet. When he got to the common room, he pulled away and looked around to decide where to sit.

"There," the man told him, pointing to an empty seat.

Zachary shook his head. That would put him next to Roddy Rodriguez, and he had no desire to be within arm's reach of Roddy Rodriguez.

"Sit there." The instruction was accompanied by a rough nudge toward the seat.

"No! I can sit where I want."

"You can sit where I tell you to," the man growled. "There."

Zachary angled toward an empty seat along the wall. The man grabbed him, moved him closer to the seat beside Roddy, and when Zachary didn't comply by sitting down, brought a hard forearm down into the hollow of Zachary's neck and shoulder, forcing him down into the seat.

Fury blossomed in Zachary's chest, but he was helpless to defend himself. A slight preteen, he had no chance of winning against the big, burly staffer. He saw Roddy laughing at him. Roddy was a ruthless bully and Zachary had even less defense against him. He erupted from his chair, swinging at the guard. Let them put him in a detention cell. Let them knock him around and leave him in handcuffs. At least he'd be safe from Roddy and he wouldn't have to sit through whatever teachable moment the staff was trying to coordinate.

Zachary saw red, and then black, and then he was awake, on the couch, staring at the TV screen like it was the enemy.

Zachary swore and tried to catch his breath and relax. He closed his eyes, still on the edge of sleep. If he didn't wake himself up any further, he'd be able to find sleep again. Maybe more restful this time.

He flowed into another dream. Innocuous. Relaxed. *Not in a facility this time. He was in a department store. Bored. Walking with a woman who had to be a foster mother.* There had been too many to remember so many years later. Her name was something musical. Lyra? Viola?

"Quit dawdling," she told him, looking back over her shoulder.

Lyra. Definitely. Zachary sped up a little, not really making much of an effort. When she stopped looking at him, he dawdled again, looking around at the merchandise.

They stopped in the boyswear department. Zachary started looking through t-shirts with licensed cartoon characters on them. He never got to buy new clothes. It was always hand-me-downs from other foster children, or uniforms, or something from the thrift store that looked like it had been left on the side of the road.

"Oh, cool," he paused at a Spider-Man shirt. "Can I have one of these?"

"No," Lyra said flatly. Non-musical. No inflection.

Zachary looked at her, trying to discern what her objection was. Price? Something the school wouldn't allow? There were no swear words, no blood and gore. He let go of the shoulder of the Spider-Man shirt.

"What can I have?"

"I'll decide what you can have."

He waited for further direction. But she didn't offer any enlightenment. She went to a wall of drab, dressy shirts. Zachary wandered through the racks, looking at other clothes. Daydreaming and imagining what he would buy if he could have anything he wanted.

"Zachary!" Her voice had a snap in it. "Get over here."

Zachary located Lyra and moved back through the racks to where she stood.

"You are not to wander off. You're supposed to be right here at my side. Understood?"

"I was just looking over there—"

"Is that right by my side?"

"No."

"Then that's not where I said you need to be, is it?"

"No," Zachary muttered, low, angry.

"What?"

He raised his voice, eliminating all traces of emotion. "No, ma'am."

"I need you to stay right here by me."

He grunted and stayed put. She grabbed him by the shoulder and turned him around to hold a shirt up to his shoulders in the back. When she draped it over her arm, he turned back around.

"Could I have a blue one?"

"No."

He looked at the wall of shirts, and looked sideways at her. "Can I have another color?"

"No." She nodded to the olive drab shirt she had draped over her arm. "This is fine."

"Won't I need more than one?"

"I'll get another one if that fits you. After you try it on."

"In another color?"

"No."

Zachary ground his teeth. "Why not? Is there a school uniform?"

"No. This is what you're getting, and I don't want to hear anything else about it."

He'd never been able to choose his own clothes before, so Zachary wasn't sure why it should bother him so much that he didn't get to choose the color he liked. But he was there, standing in the department store, able to express his opinion. And there was more than one color. They were all the same price. It wasn't a uniform. So why couldn't he choose a different color?

"Are we getting pants?"

She looked at him. "Yes, we're getting pants too."

"Which ones can I look at?"

"You can stand here with me. I'll pick out what we are buying."

"Can't I look?"

She didn't answer, which Zachary supposed was as good as a 'no.' He bit the cuticle of his thumb. It hurt, but it distracted and calmed him. He didn't care about clothes. Why worry about it? He should be happy that he was getting new clothes. He didn't know when the last time was that he'd had new clothes. Maybe when he was a baby. Or maybe even then his family had been too poor to buy new and had picked up what they could find at the thrift stores. It would be a new experience to put clothes on his body that had never been on anyone else's.

"Stop fidgeting."

Zachary dropped his thumb from his mouth and tried to stand still. Lyra held a pair of black pants up to his hips, frowning.

"You're so thin," she complained. "And I suppose you'll hit a growth spurt as soon as I buy you anything."

And, of course, he had. They changed around his meds, she was a good cook, and in a couple of months he'd put on twenty pounds and shot up three inches. Then it was back to thrift-store clothes and hand-me-downs, with his barely-worn new clothes being stored away in closets and boxes for the next skinny boy who happened to need them.

Zachary rolled over. The light from the TV was bothering him, but he was too tired to get up and turn it off. If he did that, he would wake himself up and he wouldn't be able to get back to sleep again.

The low murmur covered up the noises of the building and made him feel like he wasn't alone.

So he pulled his blanket up over his face to block out the light from the TV screen, and closed his eyes, seeking sleep again.

He should have known that trying to go back to sleep a third time would undo everything. He wanted to go to a more peaceful place. Like when he had gone from the dream about Roddy Rodriguez at Bonnie Brown to the dream about shopping with Lyra. But instead of finding a happier memory, he found himself in the detention cell at Bonnie Brown, his face pressed to the window, watching Annie die while he screamed and banged impotently on the door.

Zachary waited until mid-afternoon to call Kenzie. She sounded happy to hear from him and ready to take a break from her work.

"Zachary! I've been wondering how your case is going. Did you get in at Summit? Or are they blocking you?"

"I went there yesterday. Spent a few hours there, touring the facility, seeing what it is they do. Saw Quentin's room where it happened."

"Well, what did you think? What did they seem like?"

"It's a lot to go over," Zachary said slowly. "Do you want to get together for supper again? I don't want to take you away from your work for too long."

She made a little groan that communicated she would like to get out of there sooner. But Zachary knew she was diligent about her hours and wasn't going to sneak off just because there was something more interesting to do.

"Yeah, let's do that," she agreed. "Where do you want to go? We haven't done the buffet for a while."

"Sure, that's good for me. Just give me a call when you're off, and we'll head over."

That way, whether she left early or had to work late, they wouldn't be waiting on each other. Kenzie agreed and, after muttering a bit more about her work, told him goodbye and got back to it. Zachary hung up the phone and sat there looking at it for a few minutes, wishing she would call him back and say that she was just going to take off, and she would make up her hours later. Or maybe someone else would call him, just to chat and cheer him up. But there weren't a lot of people who would call him just to chew the fat. New clients, current clients asking for progress updates, insurance agents, but not friends.

He sighed and got back to work, signing on to his new laptop and waiting while it connected with the cloud, where all of his documents were now stored so they couldn't be destroyed in a house fire. Or an office fire. Or a hard drive breakdown. He'd learned the hard way and he wasn't leaving his data at risk again.

The time passed slowly, but eventually Kenzie called to say she was done and on her way to the restaurant. Zachary packed his laptop and notebook into a slim portfolio and headed out to meet her. He thought briefly about Bowman's comment that Kenzie would be interested in a relationship if Zachary would work on it. But he wasn't sure what the next step would look like.

So the meal followed their established pattern. A bit of small talk about the weather and how things were going at the medical examiner's office, a few jokes about the stiffs she worked with. Dishing up their meals from the buffet and sitting down to discuss the nitty-gritties of Zachary's case. Kenzie was ready the minute she sat down and stabbed a baby corn-cob with her fork.

"You look about bursting to tell me all about it," she said, "so go for it. What did you find out?"

Zachary tried to keep his narrative chronological, to explain what he had seen, in the order he had seen it, but he was easily distracted and quickly segued completely to the therapy session with Ray-Ray. Kenzie listened carefully, nodding in understanding.

"That all sounds about right," she said. "I mean, it all goes back to Pavlov, doesn't it? Conditioning them to give a certain response to a certain stimulus? Getting more complex, of course, but when you break it all down, that's what they're doing."

Zachary nodded. He rubbed the bridge of his nose, up to his forehead. Trying to smooth out the frown lines he could feel there. He ate a few bites of the random foods piled on his plate, trying to come up with a response.

"I just... I guess I'm having problems with treating people like animals," he said. "Like you say about Pavlov... training them like dogs. Like they aren't thinking, feeling human beings."

"It may not look like they care, Zachary, but I'm sure they do. All of the therapists that I've ever dealt with have had loads of empathy for their patients. But you can't necessarily let that dictate how you deal with them. Right?"

"If you had seen... it felt abusive. Not giving him any breaks, shouting and making loud noises and threatening him when he made a mistake. Grabbing him and forcing him to do what she wanted him to..."

"If she had been doing something wrong, the doctor wouldn't have let it go on. He would have interrupted the session to make sure that Raymond was safe and pulled the therapist out or corrected her in how she was administering the treatment. But he didn't, right?"

"No. He sat there watching... said that Raymond was okay... kept bragging about their program, how many people wanted to get into it. From all over the country... I can't imagine how parents would actually want their kids to go through that, if they knew what was going on."

"I'm sure they do know," Kenzie said. She speared a length of asparagus and cut it neatly into several pieces. "They would have gone through an orientation. Watched videos. Gone through training of their own. Because the kids that go home are going to need consistency when they're not at Summit. They need to be getting the same responses no matter which environment they are in."

Zachary thought about Ray-Ray's face crumpling when he was corrected after giving the wrong response. The idea of Ray-Ray's mother treating him the same way as Sophie had, taking away the things he loved, yelling at him, forcing his hands and his body to obey, made Zachary's stomach tighten. He took a deep breath and let it back out again. He wasn't investigating Summit's therapy methods. Not unless those methods had led to Quentin's death. He was there to determine if the police were right and Quentin had committed suicide. He wasn't there to stop them from making Ray-Ray cry.

"They physically restrain him," Zachary said, jumping right back into it. "What if that was what happened to Quentin? What if someone put him in a choke hold because he wouldn't do what they wanted him to, and accidentally killed him?"

"It's a big jump from restraining a five-year-old's hands to choking out a fourteen-year-old. You didn't see them physically harm the little boy, did you? They didn't do anything to hurt him?"

"No… they were rough, though. A lot rougher than I think you need to be with a child who is so small and defenseless."

Kenzie gave him a warm smile. Zachary wasn't the stereotypical hard-boiled detective of pulp fiction. He wasn't the rough-and-tough, beat-the-hell-out-of-suspects type that got all of the pretty girls on TV and in paperback novels. But Kenzie seemed to like that about him. She didn't act like she was disappointed that he had a soft heart instead of a hard fist. That he didn't carry a gun. That most of his work was tedious computer research rather than sweating suspects. That all seemed to be okay with her, and even won him a soft smile and hand-holding when he got all sentimental about someone.

"Sometimes therapy can be uncomfortable," she said. "You've had physiotherapy, right?"

Zachary nodded. Most recently, he'd had physio to get him back on his feet after the accident, to retrain him to walk after the spinal cord injury that had left him temporarily paralyzed. And long before that… he could remember the therapy he'd had when he was ten, after the fire. He was glad that she'd referred to physical therapy rather than to the years of visiting all manner of counselors, psychologists, and psychiatrists. He could look more dispassionately at physio and talk about it. "Yeah. A few times," he agreed.

"Did it hurt?"

Zachary raised his brows, surprised by the question. "Well… yeah, it did." If she thought that physiotherapy was all roses, she should think again.

"In fact, it can be pretty brutal, can't it?" she prodded.

"Yes."

"I've had friends who have done physio. Friends who have done boot camp and said that physio is worse."

Zachary nodded.

"But that's not abuse, is it?" Kenzie went on. "Even though they push you really hard, and it hurts, even makes you cry, that's not abuse."

Zachary could see where this was going, so he didn't answer immediately. Kenzie had a sip of her drink, and looked at him, eyebrows raised.

"It *can* be abusive," Zachary stonewalled.

She cocked her head, considering. "I suppose so. They could take it too far. Reinjure you. Push you to do something painful just because they wanted to see you sweat. But that's not the norm. I think usually they're pretty good at knowing where to stop. Exactly how far they can push each patient."

"Yes. Usually."

"Well, that's my point. That just because it's painful, that doesn't mean it's abuse. It's like… debriding a burn. In order for the burn to heal properly, you need to scrape all of the dead skin away. They say it's very painful. But it has to be done."

Zachary caught his breath and held it. All of a sudden, he was ten years old and back in the hospital. After the fire that had burned his house down and ruined his family forever. It was more than just remembering what it had been like, he could feel the burns all over again. Most of the burns had been on his arms and legs, and inside his throat from breathing in the superheated air. He'd been lucky not to have more of his body burned. At the hospital, they had put him on heavy painkillers, but even with opiates in his IV drip, debriding the wounds had been excruciating. It had taken several nurses to complete the process, some of them holding him down while the others took turns scraping the wounds clean. Zachary screamed, cried, and threw up, but they still had to do it.

"Zachary."

Kenzie was far away from him. He could hear her, but he wasn't in the present anymore. He was far in the past, trying to fight off the nurses who tortured him. Lashing out like an animal, screaming with pain.

"Zachary." Her fingers moved from his hand to his wrist, gently resting over his pulse. "Come back to me, Zachary. You're okay."

There was another murmured voice, but Zachary couldn't make it out.

He was barely holding on to Kenzie's voice; he couldn't see or hear anyone else.

"No. We're fine. Just give us some space." She touched Zachary's shoulder. His cheek. "I'm sorry, Zach. Are you okay? Come on. Just talk to me. Tell me about it."

Her hand went back to his wrist again, first taking his pulse and then stroking the white scars across it.

"Have a drink. A nice cold drink." She guided his hand to his glass, and Zachary automatically closed his fingers around it. Brought it up to his mouth. Took a few sips of the ice-cold soft drink. The restaurant started to resolve around him.

He wasn't in hospital. He wasn't having his burns treated anymore.

That had been years before. Decades.

"Better?"

He could see Kenzie, her dark curls and bright-red lipstick. He could see the fine lines around her eyes as she studied him, worried. Zachary took another sip of the cold, sweet drink. He held it in his mouth while the bubbles fizzed on his tongue, then swallowed it down.

His throat was fine. Not sore. Not burned.

"Sorry," he croaked out.

She wrapped her fingers around his and gave them a little squeeze. "Tell me about it. What happened?"

She knew so much of his sordid past. The really bad stuff. Yet he was still embarrassed to show this weakness in front of her. To have to explain it.

It could have been worse. She'd seen him collapse in a panic attack before. Helpless as a baby lying in a heap on the frozen sidewalk. And she still chose to go to dinner with him. Having a flashback wasn't as bad as *that*. And he didn't have to tell her the whole thing. She already knew most of the story.

How he had been the one to light the fire. How he had ended up destroying everything.

"A flashback," he said softly, breathing out and in and out again. It seemed like it had been a long time since he had breathed last.

Years.

Decades.

"Yeah, I thought so." She rubbed his shoulder soothingly. "What about?"

"The fire… but afterward. The… debriding."

"Oh!" Her mouth was small, her eyes wide. She swore. "Oh, I didn't think. I didn't know… I didn't realize you were burned that badly. You never said…"

"I don't like to talk about it. It's not your fault."

Zachary unbuttoned the cuff of his right shirtsleeve and pushed it up. He showed her the scars on his arm. Old, pink, stretched scars.

"Oh, Zachary." She touched it. Like she didn't really believe what she was seeing. "Oh, I'm sorry. You never said it was that bad. I wouldn't have used debriding as an example if I'd realized."

"You're right, though," Zachary tried to get the focus off of himself and back onto Summit and Raymond and the therapy program. "Therapy can be painful. Physically. Mentally. And I'm not a professional, so what do I know? How can I judge whether they're doing it right, and how soft or hard she should be with him? They're the experts. Dr. Abato kept telling me how advanced their program is, better than anyone else's. He kept telling me how they succeed where everyone else fails. What do I know, walking in there for the first time?"

Kenzie nodded. She let go of him and went back to eating her supper as if nothing had happened. He appreciated the gesture. She didn't spend the whole night treating him like a baby. She didn't ask him why he wasn't on a medication that would stop the flashbacks and anxiety. She just went back to what they had been doing and acted like nothing unusual had happened.

Zachary was getting looks from the diners at nearby tables and some of the wait staff. Had he been that obvious? Caused a scene? He didn't think he had shouted or cried, but he couldn't be sure. He thought that he had just withdrawn, gone back in time in his mind, but that shouldn't have been noticeable to people sitting at the other tables. Zachary poked at his meal, looking for something appetizing. He didn't feel like eating anything more, but he knew he needed to. He'd learned that he had to eat whether he was hungry or not. He needed to take care of himself. He didn't want Kenzie seeing him as a sick, broken person.

"What did you find out about Quentin?" Kenzie asked. "Nothing out of place in his room?"

"No. Well, yes and no. I'm still looking for some more answers. Who saw him last. If they did bed checks. If anyone went into his room."

"Do you think they were negligent?"

"When they found him, he was on the floor. Not on his bunk. The medical examiner's report said he'd been dead for four to six hours. If he was on his floor for six hours, shouldn't someone have noticed?"

Kenzie considered, nodding slowly. "Unless that was normal behavior for him."

"Abato said some kids hide under their beds. Sleep on the floor. That it wouldn't have been out of the ordinary."

"But was it out of the ordinary for Quentin? Did he usually sleep on his floor or on his bed?"

Zachary pulled his notepad out of his case and added the question to a list of other similar ones. "I wish I'd been able to spend more time talking to the people who were in charge of his unit and less time on the tour. Dr. Abato didn't know much about Quentin's habits or what had happened the night before they found him. He didn't even know if they had computer logs of when Quentin's door had been opened. They're all electronic locks. So there must be a record of when they went in there."

"Only if it was locked."

Zachary stared at her, realizing that she was right. Dr. Abato had said that the door would only have been locked if Quentin had been involved in an incident earlier in the day. And if his door had been left unlocked, there would be no security log of who had opened the door.

"If it was locked," he agreed. "And Dr. Abato couldn't tell me whether it had been. One of those questions that I'm supposed to be getting answers to later."

"They must have had to answer them for the police too."

"I'm not sure. I get the feeling that the police investigation was pretty... cursory."

"They're required by law to investigate any homicide, including suicides. But if everything looked like suicide, I'm not sure anyone would be wasting their time digging down deeper."

Zachary nodded. He took a bite of red Jell-O gelatin. There was a bit of ranch dressing on it, but just on the edge. He sucked it around his mouth, liquefying it like he used to when he was a kid. Jell-O had always been a favorite. As long as they didn't put anything weird in it. Peaches were okay. But not carrots or cottage cheese.

"I would talk to his therapist," Kenzie said. "Not a behavioral therapist, but a psychotherapist or counselor. Someone who would know whether he was depressed."

"His mother didn't think he was depressed. But she said he was…" Zachary strained to remember her exact words. "Agitated. They were increasing his therapy sessions."

"So find out who he talked to. Find out what they thought was wrong."

Zachary nodded. "I will… but I don't know if they will be able to tell me anything. He didn't really talk, so how would they know?"

"They're trained professionals. They would notice changes in his behavior. His demeanor. Even if he couldn't speak, he must have had other ways to communicate."

"His mom said that they wouldn't let him communicate any other way. They wanted him to speak, so they wouldn't pay attention if he tried to communicate another way."

"His therapy or counseling would have been different," Kenzie assured him. "If something was bothering him, they would have worked with whatever communications method he had."

"Okay. I'll find out, then."

"A lot of people with autism deal with depression or self-harm. I'm sure they'll have protocols in place to evaluate their residents, even if they're nonverbal."

"But if he was depressed, you don't think it was because of anything they were doing at Summit."

Kenzie cocked an eyebrow. She shook her head. "No, not at all. Like I said, it's very common. And Summit has a sterling reputation."

"The police report said that they've had other deaths. I haven't looked into the details yet, but doesn't that make you suspicious?"

"People are going to die there. At any institution. But not violent deaths…?"

"I haven't looked them up yet," Zachary repeated. "The police didn't seem to think they were anything to be concerned about."

"But it's your job to look at it all again," Kenzie said, giving a melodramatic sigh. "It's your job to be suspicious. I get that. But how many deaths are we talking about? If it was anything out of the ordinary, it would have been in the news, and I don't remember hearing anything like that."

"I don't know. Half a dozen, I think."

"Half a dozen? In how long? This year? Five years?"

"Since it opened."

Kenzie laughed. It wasn't a mocking laugh, but genuine amusement. Zachary shifted uncomfortably, staring down at his plate.

"Since it opened, Zachary?" Kenzie repeated. "They've been operating thirty, forty years. Six deaths in thirty years is nothing. Probably just natural causes."

"No, I think those are deaths that were investigated. Suspicious deaths."

"Even so, one death like Quentin's every five or six years? You'll see more than that in any municipal jail."

"You think so?"

"Absolutely. I'm sure it's a shock to the parents when something like this happens, but kids commit suicide at home, too. The institution can't prevent every death. It's just not possible."

The following day, Zachary spent some time re-reading the police reports in the small hours of the morning, until he was sure he had taken in every word and sorted out all of his questions. He still didn't have all of the answers he wanted from the staff at Summit, and a couple of polite emails and voicemail follow-ups had not produced any results. By the time Bowman got up, Zachary had decided to go back to the institution. He needed to talk to the psychologist who had been treating Quentin. To the supervisor of his unit and the person who had discovered the body. The night staff who hadn't noticed anything was amiss. And if he were there in person, Dr. Abato couldn't put off his questions in the hopes that he'd just stop asking.

"Where are you off to so early?" Bowman asked after a few gulps of scalding-hot coffee. Zachary had put his into a travel mug and was waiting for it to cool.

"Back to Summit Living Center."

"More questions to be answered?"

"Yes… I've gone over everything I can, but there are still holes in what the doctor over there told me and what was in the police reports. It doesn't seem…" Zachary tried to word it tactfully, "like it was… investigated very deeply."

Bowman shrugged. "No skin off my nose. It's not our police department. And suicides… they're not investigated the same way as other homicides. If there's nothing on the surface that's suspicious, the police don't spend months sifting through the details. Why would they? Ninety-nine percent of the time, if you walk into the room and it looks like a suicide… it was. It's only on TV that murderers try to cover up a killing by making it look like suicide. Or Victorian murder mysteries. In real life, if someone takes a bottle of pills, or slits their wrists, or hangs themselves… you walk in, you do your scene survey, talk to the family, forensics does their bit, and you wait until the lab comes back with all of the details confirmed. The medical examiner makes his ruling, you write your summary, and the case is closed."

Zachary nodded. That pretty much confirmed what he'd read on the file. Very high-level, superficial. "If it looks like a duck…"

"Exactly," Bowman agreed. "Even in cases where the family didn't know the person was depressed… it's not usually that big of a surprise. After the initial shock wears off… they admit that they knew there was a problem. Addiction, depression, a series of traumas… when someone commits suicide, there's usually been a long lead-up."

Zachary pretended to take a sip of his coffee, even though it was still too hot for him, just so he could hide any changes in his expression. Bowman didn't know much about Zachary's own history. He didn't know he was talking to a self-qualified expert on suicide. Zachary cleared his throat.

"You're probably right," he said. "It probably was. But his mother is paying me to investigate, so if anything doesn't fit… I'll find it."

Bowman grinned. "You're a good investigator. That's why she hired you. I wish you all the luck."

He looked down at his watch. Without looking at his, Zachary took the hint. "I'd better be heading out. Got some driving and thinking to do."

Bowman gave him a little salute. Zachary grabbed his soft-sided briefcase and headed down to his car.

Unlike the previous day, it wasn't clear and fresh, but pouring rain and dark due to the thick clouds. A miserable day to be caught outside, but he was warm and dry in his car. Once he was settled and on his way in the Civic, Zachary called Mira and gave her a brief non-report.

It was a lengthy commute to Summit, but Zachary found it easier to think in a moving vehicle. He didn't know the psychology of it, whether his ADHD restlessness was satisfied by a constantly changing horizon, that he had something to occupy his hands, or whether it was the soothing swish of the tires on pavement. It didn't really matter why. He just knew that distance driving was one of the few times he could really sit still and think without distraction. Maybe he should have chosen the profession of a long-distance trucker instead of a private detective.

He mentally ordered and prioritized the questions he had. Who he wanted to talk to. Bowman was probably right; once Mira started to accept her son's death, she would realize that there had been signs. That Quentin hadn't been happy with himself or with his living situation. That he suffered from depression, even though he couldn't express it to her. It didn't necessarily have anything to do with having him institutionalized at Summit. Depression was rarely simple cause-and-effect. Not everybody who thought their lives sucked was suicidal, and people who appeared to have everything could be deeply depressed.

By the time he reached Summit, the rain had cleared, and the sun was peeking out from behind the clouds. Zachary hadn't set up an appointment, so he decided he should go to the front entrance instead of the private entrance he had been directed to the last time. See the front face of the institution. Ask for the people he needed to talk to before confronting Dr. Abato.

But he hadn't counted on the protesters. He didn't know if there were actually more than there had been on his previous visit, or if he just hadn't known how many people were actually there because he'd been at the private entrance. But there were a lot of them. They waved their signs at him angrily, shouting words he couldn't understand through the closed windows of the car. Zachary continued to inch forward, forcing his way into the parking lot, where he sat for a moment and considered whether to call for assistance. Abato said that security staff presence just tended to inflame the protesters. And he really didn't want to call the police when the fact was that he didn't have an appointment or anyone waiting for him and could just as easily have conducted interviews over the phone.

After sitting for a few minutes, he took a deep breath in, unlocked his door, and forced himself to pick up his bag and step out of the vehicle.

The protesters immediately homed in on him when they saw him walking from his car toward the front door. As soon as he reached the side-walk, they were closing in, shouting at him and thrusting their signs toward him. Zachary frowned, looking at the signs and trying to take them all in. The ones about Quentin made the most sense to him. Of course people were upset that one of the children at the institution had died. They wanted someone to be held responsible, even if it was suicide or an accident. They wanted accountability. For someone to agree that it should never have happened and that they wouldn't let it happen again.

But other signs didn't make immediate sense.

Zachary shook his head at a woman who pushed her way in front of him. "What is all this?" he demanded. "I don't know who you think I am, but I don't work here."

"Do you know what goes on in there?" the woman demanded. She had ash blond hair and deep wrinkles around her mouth and throat, making it look like she'd recently lost a lot of weight and her face was collapsing in on itself. There was a harsh, M-shaped frown line between her eyebrows. She wore blue jeans and a shapeless t-shirt. Maybe the mother of one of the residents there. Or a former resident.

"Yes," Zachary said. "I was here a couple of days ago. Got a tour. Watched a therapy session. I've seen what goes on."

"Really? Did they show you the aversives? Did they let you see how they treat residents they consider stubborn or violent? The hard cases?"

Zachary let the words sink in. The woman gave him a little shove back on his shoulder. Nothing that hurt Zachary, but he was shocked that she would touch him. Organized protesters were normally trained in what qualified as a peaceful process and what they could not do. Of course, pushing around someone who was trying to get past the protest was way out of line. Something that could get her arrested and jailed for assault. If there had been any police officers around.

"Tell me about that," he suggested.

She looked surprised at his response. She looked around, then back at Zachary. Not straight on, but sideways, wary, as if she were no longer sure what to think of him. He could be a threat. He could just be teasing her, stringing her on like he was interested in what she wanted to say when really, he just wanted to get past her to the big brick building.

"What?"

"Tell me what you mean. What are aversives?"

She again looked around, then leaned in toward him, too close into his personal space. But he was surrounded by jostling protesters, so he wasn't sure why he even noticed how close she stood to him.

"An aversive is something you do to cause the subject pain whenever he performs a bad behavior."

Zachary thought back to Ray-Ray's therapy session. "Do you mean like yelling at him or forcing him to do something he doesn't want to? Physically?"

"I'm not talking about yelling. I'm talking about causing pain." She pointed to one of the signs with a lightning-bolt symbol on it. "Like skin shocks."

"Skin shocks?" Zachary shook his head. "Really? I thought shock treatment was out in the seventies."

"Shock treatment is passing an electrical charge through the brain. ECT. Not the same thing as skin shocks."

A male protester jostled Zachary. "Like cattle prods."

Zachary looked at the lightning bolt sign and then at the woman. "They don't use cattle prods. That wouldn't be legal."

"I said 'like cattle prods,'" the man repeated. "Cattle prods. Stun guns. Skin shocks."

"I didn't see anything like that."

"Of course not," the woman scoffed. "Do you think they would let you see that on a VIP tour? They're going to try to show the institution in its best light. All the good stuff. Show you kids playing happily and appearing to have a good time in their therapy sessions. Just like the pictures and videos on their website. Do you think they would show you what it is really like?"

"No." There had been tours through Bonnie Brown and other facilities Zachary had been housed at too. He remembered the way they had been lectured on giving the VIPs a good experience so that the facility could get more money. How they had sanitized everything, making sure that the kids were all in clean, fresh clothes, and that anyone who they knew would give the tourists a bad impression was hustled off to detention or another unit. They were ordered to smile and play nicely and answer questions positively if they wanted to earn a treat and avoid retribution. The VIPs never got to see what the institution was really like in day-to-day operations. Real life was messy and raw. Kids who had been locked up because they were too difficult for foster families to deal with were not cute, polite, respectful automatons.

The protesters were quieting a little. The fact that Zachary was listening to them instead of just shoving his way through was having an effect.

"I'm Margaret Beacher," the blond woman said, thrusting her hand toward Zachary.

He had a hard time catching her hand squarely and ended up squeezing her fingers instead of getting a good grip. She pulled away and stood there looking at him, her eyes boring into him.

"And what's your name?" she demanded, as if he'd missed an important cue.

"Zachary. My name is Zachary Goldman."

"What are you doing here? If you're not working here and you don't know enough about the program to know what an aversive is, why are you here?"

Zachary bent to put down his briefcase, which was starting to get a little heavy. "Can I get a little space? I'm feeling a bit claustrophobic."

The protesters looked at Margaret like she was the one in charge, but she didn't give them any sign. The majority stepped back, giving Zachary a bit more room. Some looked elsewhere, eyes sharp for anyone else they should talk to. Missionaries looking for a convert.

"So?" Margaret demanded. "Who are you and what are you doing here, Zachary Goldman?"

"I'm a private investigator. I'm here looking into Quentin's death." Zachary nodded toward one of the signs with Quentin's picture on it.

Margaret's eyes got big. "A private investigator?" she squawked.

"Yes. Don't go getting all excited. It's not like on TV. I'm just here to ask some questions, follow up on some reports." Zachary indicated his briefcase. "It's lots of paperwork and talking to people. Not all romantic..."

"But you're looking into Quentin's death."

"Yes."

"So you don't think it was suicide."

"I haven't come to a conclusion yet. There's no reason yet to think that it wasn't just what it looked like. But I'm trying to find out."

"His mother doesn't think it's suicide." She said it like it was something he didn't already know.

Zachary nodded. "I know. She hired me."

"Quentin Thatcher didn't have to die," Margaret said loudly, her inflection like a chant. Everyone raised their signs in agreement. "Quentin Thatcher didn't have to die!"

Zachary studied Margaret. "What do you think happened?" he asked. His brain was buzzing through the possibilities. Her chant wasn't that he was abused, neglected, or murdered. Their statement wasn't that it wasn't suicide, but that he didn't have to die.

"Autistic people all around the world are being hurt and traumatized by ABA therapy. It has to stop! They have to stop treating neurodiverse people like they are animals."

Zachary looked for somewhere they could sit down. There was a low landscaping wall between the grass and the sidewalk, and Zachary motioned to it. "Let's sit."

She joined him, sitting just an inch too close. Zachary slid down a little and took a breath.

"How are they being hurt? By skin shocks?"

"By skin shocks. Other aversives like pinching, hitting, kicking, holding, strong smells, loud noises, hot pepper sauce, whatever their tormentors can think of to punish them for behaving the wrong way. For being autistic instead of neurotypical. Do you have any idea what it feels like to be punished for who you are? For the way your brain was formed? Something you have absolutely no control over?"

Zachary watched an ant carrying a crumb along the sidewalk block in front of him. He'd spent his entire childhood being punished for something he had no control over. Not autism, but other diagnoses. For being incorrigible. A troublemaker. When all that he'd ever wanted was to be good.

"You don't believe me?" Margaret demanded, her tone aggressive.

"Yes. I believe you."

"Oh." She gave him another look and lowered her voice to a more reasonable tone. "When ABA was first devised, Lovaas recommended slapping or pinching. He said to practice on your friends, so you knew how hard to hit so that it would hurt, but not do permanent damage. Cause the autistic child pain every time they responded the wrong way, and they would learn not to do it. Reward them every time they responded the right way, and they would learn to do the right thing instead. Or, you could always torture them until they gave the right response, and then stop."

Zachary looked at her. "This is an approved therapy?"

"It's mainstream. Almost all of the autism therapies are based on it. They all make their own adjustments, of course, but even if you take the aversives out of the loop, it's still torture."

They hadn't been hitting or shocking Ray-Ray, but Zachary had still felt like they were going too far. Like they were doing something dirty and callous instead of teaching him. But Kenzie had pooh-poohed the idea. Sometimes therapy was painful. Like physiotherapy or debriding a wound. Zachary gave a little shudder just thinking of it again. Trying not to let himself get swept away by the memories. He needed to think clearly about Ray-Ray's therapy. Good or bad?

"And how did shocks come into it?" he asked Margaret, who was looking impatient for him to get it all through his head.

"Shocks were a wonderful new development. You can't standardize a pinch or a slap. I might slap one way, and you might slap another. Yours might not be hard enough to be effective, and mine might be too hard and cause damage. We can practice on each other like Lovaas says, but we'll still end up with everyone in Summit punishing differently. But with shocking, you can set all devices to one level, and everybody can administer exactly the same punishment for wrong behaviors. Hurt them enough to deter them, but not enough to harm them permanently. Unless, of course, they have a heart condition or something, and you kill them."

"Has that happened?"

"Children have died."

Zachary thought of the reported deaths at Summit and wondered whether he would be able to get any details on the deaths other than Quentin's.

"Or," Margaret says, "they might just be injured. Burns and blisters. Or with other aversives, maybe atrophied muscles from being strapped to a restraint board for weeks, months, even years." She gave a shrug as if that were nothing. "Or maybe no physical injuries. Maybe just PTSD for the rest of their lives from the hell Summit puts them through. Or whatever ABA program they are in."

"But you said that not all programs use aversives."

"Even without aversives, therapy can still cause PTSD or other anxiety or emotional problems."

Zachary scratched the back of his neck. "Do you have proof of that?"

"I *am* proof of that."

He looked at her, studying her face and her body language. "You did ABA?"

"Yes. I did."

"What for? You aren't autistic, are you?"

"Yes, I am."

"You... must be very high-functioning. I wouldn't have guessed it..."

"Do you think that's a compliment?" she snapped.

Zachary fumbled for an answer. He had clearly said the wrong thing. He'd somehow insulted her. And he didn't know what he'd done or how to undo it.

"You think I want to be like *you*?" Margaret persisted, her eyes flaming.

"Like me?" Zachary let out one bitter bark of laughter before he caught himself. "No, I don't think you would want to be like me."

Neither of them said anything for a few minutes. Margaret looked like she had a lot more to say on the subject, but she closed her mouth and just looked at him.

"Why do you say I wouldn't want to be like you?" she asked finally, in a normal, non-confrontational tone. "What's wrong with you?"

"What *isn't* wrong with me?" Zachary rolled his eyes. "I wouldn't even know where to start."

The other protesters were milling around, holding up their signs, occasionally yelling at the passing motorists. As parents arrived for therapy, they were harassed, and in some cases simply got back into their vehicles and drove away. Others came out of the facility and made their way back to their cars, sheltering children from the yells and sneers of the crowd.

Zachary watched one such mother and child make their way in tandem toward their vehicle.

"Don't you think it's ironic that you're scaring the same children you're claiming need to be protected?"

Margaret turned slightly to look at them. "Wouldn't you steal Jewish children away from the Nazis if you could? Even if you scared them in the process?"

"I'm not sure you can make that comparison."

"They are torturing children," Margaret said with a loud voice. "They need to be stopped."

"They need to be stopped!" echoed one of the other protesters in a yell. The chant was picked up for the next few minutes.

"You don't think so?" Margaret asked. "You don't think it's wrong for them to imprison these children because they are different? To shock them, or withhold food, or restrain them for weeks on end?"

"I don't know what to think. This is all new to me."

"Well... that's honest. I guess I should be glad you're not telling me that I'm a liar. I get that a lot. Or that I'm trying to ruin the lives of all of the families of the children here. People don't like it when you threaten to take their comfort away."

"Do you mind if I get my notepad out?" Zachary gestured to his briefcase.

"I'm not holding a gun on you. You can do whatever you like."

Zachary got out pen and paper. "What about the kids who are violent?" he asked. "It's not a matter of their families' comfort, but their safety. Quentin was here because he was violent. His mother feared for herself and her other children. What would happen to families like that if you shut down all of the ABA programs? Or even just Summit?"

"ABA isn't the only way to deal with violence. There are other methods out there. What about the thousands of autistic people who aren't at Summit? I don't see them creating havoc. Their families have found other ways to manage difficult behaviors."

"Other than medicating them?"

"Sometimes medications are appropriate. Sometimes they're not."

"What else can they do?"

Margaret looked at the brick building for a minute. "How about taking them out of therapies that traumatize them? Making accommodations? Improving communication? Whatever form of communication they prefer, instead of pushing speech. Reducing stressors instead of escalating problems?" She shook her head. "I was violent as a teenager. I didn't know how else to react to people I felt were attacking me. And trust me, there were plenty of things my parents and therapists could have done other than terrorizing and torturing me with ABA and other aggressive therapies."

But those therapies had apparently worked, since Margaret was no longer solving her problems with violence. How could anyone know what the outcome would have been if Margaret's issues had been solved through other means?

He wondered if he should go into the building, now that the conversation seemed to be winding down. He had listened to the protesters' side. He would be remiss if he didn't ask the staff at Summit for their response. He couldn't make any kind of judgment without hearing both sides of the story.

"So what's wrong with you?"

Margaret wasn't looking at Zachary, and at first, he thought she was asking someone else. But her silence and waiting attitude convinced him that she was asking him.

"I have PTSD too," he told her eventually. It was easier without her looking at him. He didn't feel so much like a bug under a magnifying glass. "I was in a fire when I was young. I haven't done a lot of psychotherapy. I was forced into it when I was younger, and I don't like other people digging around in my brain. But the guy I've started seeing says my PTSD probably originated way before the fire. With the way our—my—parents were."

"How were they?"

"They fought a lot. A lot. Constantly. Not just arguing. It was like a war zone. And I guess that means we—I—developed PTSD just like someone in a war zone."

"You have flashbacks to the fire? To them fighting?"

"Yes." Zachary turned his head to look at Margaret. She looked off into the distance. Her jaw was rigid. Teeth clenched. "And you have flashbacks to therapy?"

"Yes."

It seemed like a bizarre idea at first. But he thought about watching Ray-Ray being bullied by Sophie and Dr. Abato, and how it had stirred up so many unpleasant memories for Zachary. And he thought about how Kenzie had compared therapy to debriding. And he'd instantly flashed back to debriding. If debriding his burns—something that had to be done for him to heal properly—had caused him that much trauma, then why not the behavioral therapy that Ray-Ray and Margaret had gone through?

"Were you in a program like this, where they shocked you?" he asked Margaret.

"No. No physical aversives. But plenty that was uncomfortable and painful *in here*," she tapped her head. "Mental and emotional abuse is still abuse."

"Of course." Zachary made a few more notes for himself. "I should go in there now. I have more investigating to do."

"Yes, you do. Will you call me later? Let me know what you find out?" Margaret pulled out a business card wallet and put one into Zachary's hand.

"I really can't do that," Zachary said. "You're not my client. There is confidentiality. I can't share my findings with you just because you're interested."

She gave a grimace. When Zachary tried to hand the card back, she pushed his hand away sharply. "Keep it. Call me if you have questions." She looked over at the looming brick building. "You *will* have questions."

Zachary felt like he had moved into a parallel reality. Even though he had not been through the front doors of the building before, the themes and architecture were the same as they were throughout the rest of the building. The receptionist had a soupy smile pasted across her face. The potted plants and furniture were the same. But everything felt different. When he had walked into Summit before, he had been open to it being positive. To being impressed by what they were doing and to give them the benefit of the doubt. He'd done his best to compartmentalize the emotions and memories that the institution had stirred up in him and to focus on what Abato was showing him, no matter how uncomfortable it made him. But after talking to Margaret, he was no longer able to separate his own feelings about institutions from Summit. Were all institutions corrupt? Was it inevitable that there would be abusers? Bullying? Predation? There had been everywhere he had gone, and it sounded like Summit and the other facilities like it were not exempt.

So in spite of the bright colors and cartoon themes, Zachary felt a pall of darkness over the whole place. The knot that had been in his stomach on his first visit there had at least doubled in size.

"How can I help you?" the receptionist asked, the smile forced over her tired, cynical features.

"There are a few people I need to talk to," Zachary explained. "I've cleared all of this through Dr. Abato. He took me on a tour of the facility earlier in the week."

She frowned at him. "I didn't get any memos from Dr. Abato. No emails or messages that you would be making inquires, Mr....?"

"Zachary Goldman," Zachary enunciated clearly. He looked at her expectantly, spelling it out slowly so that she got the message and wrote it down on the pad on her desk. "And I need to talk to Quentin Thatcher's psychotherapist, his residential unit supervisor, the person who discovered his body, any night guards who were on shift in his unit the night he died, and... his behavioral therapist and any aides he may have had."

He waited between each person's role, waiting for her to write them down. She looked at the list. "That's a lot of people. They won't all be on shift today, and of those who are, most of them will be busy. If you don't have an appointment, people won't have the time for you. We all keep very busy here."

"I'm sure you do," Zachary said, in as understanding a tone as he could manage, trying to give the impression of being calm and professional while the back part of his brain was flipping out. "To start with, you can get me their names. Then I can contact them and see how many can meet with me today, and how many I can schedule for another day. I'm from out of town, so I'm sure you can understand how I need to see as many as I can in one day. I can't be back and forth for ten different appointments."

She squinted at him, either trying to figure out the best way to thwart him or trying to decide if she should make an effort to help him.

"I'll see if I can get the names for you," she said finally. "It's going to take a while."

"I'll just be waiting over here." Zachary motioned to the couch in the reception area.

Zachary's list of witnesses was quickly whittled down to one. The night staff were not on. The aide who had been with Quentin most recently was booked up and he would have to set up an appointment later.

"He doesn't have a psychotherapist," the receptionist said. "He has a BCBA, but she's got back-to-back appointments all day."

Zachary frowned. "He doesn't have a psychotherapist?"

"Our program here is focused on ABA. We are proactive in avoiding problems, rather than waiting until they become issues."

"You must have someone on staff to deal with depression, learning disabilities, things like that."

"We're not treating mental illness and learning disabilities. We're treating developmental and behavioral issues."

"But other conditions can go along with autism."

She just stared at him blankly.

"So no one was treating Quentin for depression."

"No."

"Who prescribes medications if they are needed?"

"Dr. Abato or one of the other senior staff. But no medications that are behavioral crutches. We demedicalize as soon as they get here."

Zachary had been on med holidays several times in order to 'establish a baseline' with a new doctor. A hellish process of getting all of the chemicals out of his system and then trying desperately to hold it all together until they started adding prescriptions back in one at a time. It was better as an adult, when he could use just what he needed under whatever circumstances he was in and could tell a doctor to take a hike if he wanted to reduce the number of prescriptions Zachary was using. A med holiday was never a holiday for him.

He closed his eyes briefly, his heart going out to Quentin and all of the rest of the kids who were going through the same thing. Off of the medications that would help balance out their brains, instead being controlled by punishing electric shocks. What was it Margaret had just been saying?

Do you have any idea what it feels like to be punished for who you are? For the way your brain was formed? Something you have absolutely no control over?

He knew; he'd spent his whole childhood living it, but at least the punishments he had faced for his incorrigible behavior hadn't included electrical shocks. Prescriptions weren't the full solution, but the right ones made things a little easier to handle.

Zachary looked down at the list the receptionist had made.

"So who is left? There's someone I can talk to?"

"The unit supervisor for Quentin's unit. Her name is Nancy Whitmore. She can come out and see you. I'm afraid the rest... you'll have to make appointments with them." She slid the paper across the desk to him. She had filled in the names and numbers where appropriate.

"So where do I find Nancy Whitmore?"

"She will be out to get you when she's free. She said it wouldn't be too long."

Zachary wondered whether, like Dr. Abato, Nancy Whitmore was making a point to him. She had more important things to do than talk to an interfering private detective. She was a busy person. But at least she had agreed to talk to him. He was sure she could have told the receptionist the same thing the others had, that they were too busy and couldn't meet with Zachary, no matter how far he had come.

So he smiled and nodded politely, and went and sat down on the modern, flat, uncomfortable couch where he had spent the last forty-five minutes. Sooner or later, she would be out to see him, and he could get some of his questions answered.

11

Eventually, Nancy Whitmore came to fetch Zachary. She was a redhead, her hair short and frizzy, her clothing a size too large so that it was sloppy and didn't fit to her form properly.

"Zachary Goldman?"

Since he was the only one sitting there, it was a good bet. Zachary pushed himself to his feet. "Hi. I guess you're Ms. Whitmore."

"Just Nancy, love. Why don't you come with me, then? You were here just a few days ago, weren't you? With Dr. Abato."

"Yes. But I didn't manage to talk to you. I appreciate you taking the time today, with no appointment. You must be busy."

She made a sweeping-away motion with one hand. She led the way to the other side of the reception area to an unimpressive unmarked door.

"Things are pretty quiet for most of the day. Until the kids start getting finished with their sessions. Then we have a few hours of barely-controlled chaos before bed."

Zachary nodded, smiling. He appreciated her good humor. The supper hour through bedtime was always difficult in institutional settings. Tired, cooped-up, and frustrated kids in a less-controlled environment. Kids coming off their meds and rebounding. Dealing with low blood sugar, meals, and trying to keep things peaceful until night meds and lights out.

"The arsenic hour," he'd heard one of them refer to it as. Except that it was more than just an hour.

"So you're the head supervisor for the unit Quentin was in."

"That's right. Here most of their waking hours. Someone takes over at night, but of course things are pretty quiet then."

"How was Quentin that last day before he died?"

She ran her fingers through her already-frizzed-up hair. "Quentin was Quentin. He wasn't one of the easiest children."

"What does that mean? In terms of his usual behavior?"

"Parents often wait until their children are completely out of control and they can no longer manage them before putting them into a program like Summit. That puts a lot of pressure on us, trying to get a child from intractable to manageable. If they get them in early on, it's much easier to train them."

"That makes sense."

"When Quentin started out at Summit, he was on strong antipsychotics and still couldn't be controlled. He was violent and there were other children in the home, which made it an emergency situation. He would be held in the municipal jail until a placement could be found for him. And the municipal jail doesn't have the training or resources to deal with a violent teen with autism."

Zachary had seen the inside of a couple himself. Sitting by himself in a barred cell, while the adults in the other cells, the real criminals, catcalled and mocked him, uttering threats and sordid remarks when the guards were out of hearing. Feeling like he'd been dumped there like a bag of trash. No one to turn to. No one who wanted to deal with one more minute of his crap.

"Mr. Goldman?"

"Zachary," he corrected automatically. "Sorry. Just thinking."

She motioned him through the big door, which turned out to be the security door for Quentin's unit.

"So he came here," Nancy said simply. "Home sweet home." She made a twirling motion to include everything in the unit.

"Can we sit down and talk somewhere? Do you have logs of what happened that day and night that we could look at?"

"We log everything." Nancy considered for an instant. "I suppose the response room would be the best. Just let me grab some books."

Zachary waited while she got together what she thought she would need. The unit was quiet, just a few supervisors around, no residents in sight. They were in therapy for long hours every day. They probably wouldn't be found in the unit during the day unless they were sick.

"Had Quentin been sick recently?"

"Sick? No, who told you that?"

"Just wondering. Sometimes an illness can lead to depression…"

"No. He hadn't been sick."

Zachary sat down and glanced over the books that Nancy had collected. "So what do we have?"

"This is Quentin's personal file." She nudged a black binder toward him. "That should contain everything you need. His therapy logs, any observations made during the morning and evening, outside of his therapy. Any… negative behaviors and consequences. Anything that is applicable to him should be in there."

Zachary opened it up. "By consequences, do you mean punishments? Aversives like electric shocks?"

She studied him for a minute, uncertainty written on her face. "That is part of the program here," she agreed. "That's one of the keys that helps us to reach kids like Quentin. Just saying 'no' isn't effective at all on a child like that. There are some children where that's all you need to do. But kids like Quentin need a stronger aversive."

Zachary slowly turned the pages of the binder. It appeared to all be in chronological order. Logs from various sources. Mostly from therapy and the daily log of the unit, checking off the steps to his daily routine. A few narrative lines here and there.

"Okay. And what have you got there?"

"These are the unit logs. Everything that is written in the unit logs should have been transcribed to the personal files. But if you want to double-check…"

Zachary nodded. He looked at the last couple of therapy logs. A brief entry as to what behavior was being taught, followed by long rows and columns of checkmarks and X's. Mostly X's.

"So the checkmarks mean that he showed the right behavior, and the X's mean he showed the wrong behavior," he suppositioned.

Nancy nodded. "Right."

"And when he got a checkmark, he got a reward?"

317

She smiled at him. "You know the way the program works. Very small rewards, so that we can stretch them out over the length of the therapy. Obviously, you can't give a child a candy for every right behavior, when you're going to have them repeated hundreds of times throughout the day."

"One lick of a lollipop."

"The favorite reward for many of our children. Children with autism can be very motivated by food. You wouldn't believe the number of lollipops and gummy bears we go through here. I go home, and I can't stand anything that smells like a gummy bear!"

"And when he got an X, he didn't get a lick or a gummy bear."

"Right again." She nodded.

"Did he get an aversive?"

"Yes. More than likely."

"So can I interpret this log to mean that every X represents an electrical shock?"

"No, no. You'd have to talk to the therapist or his aide. He might have gotten any aversive. A stern word. Planned ignoring. Taking something away from him. There was a court ruling..." she trailed off, looking hopeful that he already knew about it and would jump in with the details.

But Zachary shook his head, indicating he didn't know about it.

"There were threats that they were going to shut the program down. Some video that got out there on the internet and was being shown out of context. What did people ever do before they could upload to the internet? But our parents are very strong supporters of the program. So they argued in the court to keep the program going. Eventually, the judge agreed, but with some specific guidelines. One of them was that skin shocks were only to be used if a child was being violent or could not physically be controlled without it. So they wouldn't have used shocks for the aversive during therapy. Unless he was being violent."

"Can you tell from the log?"

She turned the binder around so she could look at it right-side-up. Her eyes went over the various headings and comments on the page.

"Well... yes, his therapist does note that he wouldn't cooperate without physical intervention. And Quentin... I know the boy. If he didn't like something, he would hit, bite, spit..."

"So they would have used shocks as the aversive."

"Yes."

"For every one of these X's."

"Maybe not all of them… but probably."

Zachary ran his eye down the column, tallying up the X's. He turned the page and kept going.

"So the day before he died, he had around sixty shocks during therapy."

Nancy swallowed. "If you say so. I wasn't there. You'll have to talk to one of the people who was."

Zachary looked down the evening and night log. It was strange not to see a section for night meds to be checked off. The logs that he'd seen kept at other institutions had always included morning and night meds.

"It looks like there was an incident before lights out." He rested his finger under the brief words in the log. "What is 'Loss of Privilege Food'?"

"Well, as I said, a lot of the residents are very motivated by food."

"Yes."

"One of the negative reinforcers that is used is the Contingent Food Program."

"What does that mean?"

"It means that food is withheld until the desired behavior is demonstrated."

"During his therapy."

"For as long as necessary to reliably demonstrate the desired behavior."

"You starve him until he does what he's told."

"They don't starve. That's why Loss of Privilege Food is provided. At the end of the day, if their nutritional intake has not been adequate during the Contingent Food Program, they receive Loss of Privilege Food."

Zachary breathed out long and slow. He knew what was coming. Prisons sometimes provided meal replacement foods. Foods that were designed to be unpalatable, but to meet dietary requirements. They had the appropriate levels of calories and macronutrients that were needed, and they were given a vitamin supplement, but the bricks of food replacer were like eating sawdust held together with beef fat. Not pleasant. Not something the prisoners eventually acquired a taste for.

"What was the Loss of Privilege Food?"

"I told you, the food that they received at the end of the day if—"

"No, what is it made of? What form is it in?"

She sucked in her cheeks, looking at the stack of binders. There wasn't any point in avoiding the question. If Nancy refused to answer, he would get it from someone else.

"It's like a meatloaf," she explained. "Ground meat mixed with potato flakes. Spinach and liver powder for additional nutrients. It meets all of the RDAs."

"Would you eat it? Have you tasted it?"

"Uh… it's not meant to be appetizing. They're supposed to be motivated to earn their regular food."

"I don't suppose it's served with gravy and biscuits."

"No… just served cold."

Zachary's stomach turned over. "How long was Quentin on the Contingent Food Program?"

"I'm not sure. It had been a while."

Zachary flipped backward through the daily logs, looking for the notation on each day's chart. It had been more than a while. He returned to the evening before Quentin's death.

"What does this say?"

Nancy leaned closer to the page.

"Uh…" She was reluctant to read what Zachary had already clearly understood. "It says that he refused his Loss of Privilege Food."

"So he went to bed hungry? He didn't get his RDA that day?"

"We can't starve them," Nancy protested. "He could go one day refusing the Loss of Privilege Food, but after that we had to take positive action."

"And…?"

"Force feed it to ensure that he'd had adequate nutrition."

"How?"

"What do you mean?"

"I mean, was he tubed? Fed by mouth? How was he force fed?"

"Uh…" She shifted uncomfortably. "By mouth."

Zachary shook his head in disgust. They wouldn't give him regular food because he liked it and they wanted to use it as a reinforcer. But he still had to get calories and he refused the crap food they tried to give him, so they had held him down and forced it down his throat.

Nancy cleared her throat a few times. He looked at her face and saw that she was struggling with emotion, holding back tears.

"It's not right," she whispered. "I've never agreed with the Contingent

Food Program. It's cruel. Food is the only pleasure some of these kids get. To use it against them is… inhumane."

And there was more on the log sheet. They both knew it.

"Were you here or had you gone home?"

"I was still here. I go home right after supper."

"So you saw them doing it. Forcing him to eat the alternative food."

"Yes." She dabbed at the corners of her eyes. "I was here… I saw. It was my job to make sure he got the food he was supposed to."

"Were you the one who did it?"

"No. I couldn't. The security staff and a couple of aides…"

"And he gagged."

"Yes. Some kids are very sensitive to certain textures. Quentin often gagged on the Loss of Privilege Food. It's sort of a lumpy paste…"

"So what happened?" Zachary was looking at the log sheet. He didn't need her to tell him what happened, because it was right there on the log sheet in front of him. But he wanted to hear it from her. To understand just how far the institution was willing to go to break the children they had charge of.

"He threw up. That made them angry. But it wasn't like he did it on purpose! He wasn't just being willful. They shocked him for throwing up. Kept shocking him for struggling. Eventually… they got it down. And it stayed down."

"And what happened after that?"

"By then, it was lights out. I stayed until they had gotten it all down him, a couple of hours past my usual shift change. And then I went home. They were getting him ready for bed."

"What had to be done to get him ready for bed?"

"Changing his clothes. They were soiled. Showering him off. Giving him night clothes and returning him to his room."

Zachary felt like he needed a shower himself. He had done nothing to Quentin; he hadn't participated in his torture. But he felt like he had, just by living his life in ignorance that such barbarism was being practiced right there in his own country. He went on eating what he wanted and sleeping when he could, oblivious to the practices that Margaret Beacher was protesting.

"I expect that after all that, his door was locked."

"No." Nancy shook her head. "Not while I was there. Quentin didn't wander at night. He preferred to stay in his room. We didn't need to lock his door."

"Dr. Abato said that if there had been an incident during the day, his door would be locked at night."

She rolled her eyes. "Dr. Abato isn't here at night and there are no policies that say Quentin's door should be locked if he refuses food. If he'd been violent with one of the staff or the other kids, that would be different. But he hadn't been. He'd just had trouble with therapy."

"He came here because he was violent, didn't he? You didn't have trouble with him with other residents? Or just not that day?"

"Kids are violent in different ways for different reasons. Quentin was pretty typical. He would get angry and violent when he was frustrated. If someone was in his space or took a toy away from him. He couldn't communicate what he wanted. But he didn't wander at night and he didn't attack people at random."

She was silent then, but the tilt of her head and the way that she was leaning toward him suggested that she wasn't finished talking, so he waited.

"If he did get upset or threatening, seeing this is usually all it took to back him off." She tapped one of the little boxes on her belt. The ones with pictures of the children.

"What's that?" Zachary asked. "I thought they were pill boxes, but if you don't give them meds…"

She pulled one of them straight and flipped it over, so that Zachary could see the red button recessed in the back. An inkling of what Nancy was telling him crept into Zachary's consciousness. All of the guards and aides with boxes on their belts. Boxes with pictures of the residents stuck to them. Not pill boxes. Not schedules. Not keys. A single button that did only one thing.

"That's how you give them shocks?"

"Yes."

Zachary just stared at it. He had thought it was sweet, each of the staff members carrying with them the pictures of the kids they helped care for. He couldn't have been farther off base.

He went back over what Nancy had said last in his mind, rewinding the track and replaying her words. "And Quentin understood what it did. If you showed him your remote, he knew you were going to shock him."

She nodded.

"And that kept him from attacking anyone."

"If he got upset and started to show threatening behavior, seeing the remote would stop him in his tracks. Usually."

"So… him being violent like he was when he was at home… that wasn't a concern."

"Not usually. Though he'd had *some* issues lately. We were usually working on more complex issues."

"Like…" Zachary thought back to his interview with Mira, "speech."

"Speech is one of the most important social skills. If he could have become more adept at communicating with others… it would have been a huge step for him."

"Was that something he could learn to do?"

"He was definitely showing progress. He was able to engage in short conversations."

"His mother said something about them being scripted."

"That's how we start. Getting them to repeat phrases. Learning that one response generally follows another in conversation. It's very complex and takes a long time to teach, but broken down into the smallest building blocks…"

Zachary nodded slowly.

"His mother said that he'd been agitated on her last few visits. Had you noticed any difference in his behavior?"

Nancy ran her fingers through her hair again. "I would say… he'd been having some issues. Maybe hormones. Teen moodiness. More aggression with a boost in testosterone."

Zachary flipped back several pages in his notebook. "She said that when he got agitated, he picked his skin and flapped. He made noises and didn't want to sit down. And banged his head."

Nancy gave a little shrug. "Those are all pretty common behaviors for kids with autism. We try to break them of stims."

"Stims?"

"Self-stimulating behavior. Repetitive, self-soothing behaviors that children with autism often have. Lovaas dictated that all behaviors that make them appear different need to be eliminated, so that nothing will set them apart from their peers and they can become full members of society."

"But… is that really possible?"

"Some of our kids have gone on to become very successful. You really can't tell, looking at a young child, which ones will be successful and which ones will limit themselves. A child that you would have thought was low-functioning leaps over hurdles, and one that you thought was high-functioning and really didn't have that far to go just can't seem to get any movement at all. We tell parents that the younger they can get their kids into the program, the better their chances are. That's just emphasized when you get a child like Quentin, who's basically been allowed to do whatever he wants to for the first twelve years of life and is being asked to work at something for the first time."

"His mom made a mistake not getting him into a program sooner?"

"Yes. He hadn't had any discipline, any consequences. She had babied him. So the program was quite a shock for him."

Zachary grimaced at her choice of words and bit his lip to avoid saying 'literally.'

"You said that he liked to stay in his room and didn't wander at night, so his sleep was pretty good?"

"Most of our kids have some sleep issues. Especially if they've been taking sleep aids for years before they come here. We find that a strict schedule, with no variations in lights-out and wake-up time on weekends and holidays is the best remedy."

"They didn't get negative consequences—aversives—if they had sleep problems?" The institutions Zachary had lived in had been pretty strict about any nighttime activities that varied from the prescribed sleep and wake time. No getting out of bed. No wandering. No trips to the bathroom. No complaining about having nightmares. Even having nightmares was considered bad behavior. So was sleepwalking.

"We tried to keep things calm and relaxed after lights-out," Nancy hedged. "You don't want to be upsetting the residents at bedtime, when they're supposed to be settling down."

"No shocks after lights-out?" Zachary ventured.

"Well… not usually."

Zachary scratched his head and wrote a couple of lines in his notepad. It was obvious Nancy didn't want to make things sound any worse. Zachary decided to back off a little. If he wanted her to answer any more questions, he was going to have to take it easy and not back her into a corner. She was currently his only cooperative information source.

"Tell me what happens after lights-out. Bed checks? What's the night-time supervision like?"

"The security staff make sure that everyone is in their rooms and accounted for. Some of the kids pace or stim for a long time before going to sleep, so there's no rule that they have to be in bed, just in their rooms. There is someone on the unit all the time, making sure there are no problems. Security does rounds a few times each night." She pulled one of the binders out of the stack and flipped pages to find the night that Quentin had died.

Zachary studied the initialed spaces. The initials were not readable, but the same squiggly mess was on each of the lines. Two hours apart. Which meant that Quentin's death should have been noticed on three separate checks.

"And the guard who signed off on these checks is no longer with Summit?"

"Dr. Abato said he should have noticed Quentin's death some time before it was discovered. So… he was asked to resign his position."

"To take the fall. So that it would look like Summit was taking this seriously."

"He *should* have noticed something was wrong," Nancy said.

Zachary nodded. He tried to visualize everything in his mind. He had seen the bedroom. He had seen the pictures of Quentin's body in the bedroom before it was removed. He had spent many hours locked in rooms like that, peering through windows like the one in Quentin's door. The viewing angles were limited. A child lying on the floor might be difficult to see clearly.

"The person who found him in the morning. Was that… you?"

Nancy nodded. She looked tired. Like she had seen too much, and she just didn't want to see any more. Too much sadness. Too many kids in pain. Too much loss.

"Yes. I went to see why he hadn't come out for breakfast. He'd been on Contingent for so long, he was always one of the first ones out, looking for something to eat."

Zachary refrained from pointing out that they would then refuse to give him breakfast because he wasn't able to demonstrate all of the proper behaviors. He waited for Nancy to gather her thoughts and tell him what had happened.

Nancy stared off into space, looking past Zachary.

"I thought maybe he was sick. Or maybe he'd just given up after the night before. I opened his door and I saw him on the floor."

"Did you know right away…?"

"I didn't want to accept it. I imagined he was still sleeping or not feeling well, or that it was some kind of prank or joke, and someone was watching to see what my reaction would be."

Zachary had been in that type of situation before. There was always the initial moment of disbelief. The moment when his brain refused to believe what he was seeing and sought any other explanation.

"He was on the floor with his blankets around him, but he didn't look like he was asleep." Nancy swallowed, and went on, voice strained. "He had wrapped his blanket around his neck and then twisted it tighter and tighter…"

The pictures from the police hadn't shown that. The blanket had been removed from his throat in order to check his pulse or administer first aid.

"How was it positioned? Did it look like he could have done it himself? The twisted ends… were they in the front…? Not the back?"

Nancy nodded. Her hands moved of their own accord, as if she were untwisting the blanket. Fingers gentle.

"I couldn't believe it. I kept thinking that it was all a mistake. A nightmare. But there he was, stiff and cold. Like he was made of wax."

"I'm sorry. That must have been very hard on you."

She nodded, blinking tears.

"I have another question for you, and I know it's very difficult. But… did he have the ability to form the intent to commit suicide?"

"I'm not sure what you mean."

"Just… this is a child who couldn't carry on a real conversation. Who lashed out when he was upset. Who banged his head. Did he… did he have the ability to decide he wanted to kill himself and then devise a plan like this to strangle himself, and then to follow through with it? I would think… those are some sophisticated thought processes. Could he do more than just react to a stimulus? Did he have the ability to think all of that out?"

Nancy looked at him. She stroked the smooth cover of one of the binders.

"I don't think I'm qualified to judge," she said finally. "So often, I would think that a child wasn't paying any attention to me. That they hadn't even been aware of the fact that I was talking to them, much less actually paying attention and able to understand what I had said. Just to have them do something that proved me wrong. I think that difficulty with speech is the most disabling thing for our kids... No feedback into what's really going on in their brains. Quentin might have been brilliant; I have no way of knowing. He was definitely adept at resisting a stimulus. He proved *that* to us time and time again. But was it evidence of higher reasoning abilities? Or just stubbornness? Or maybe he had no idea what we wanted him to do. Maybe it was an accident. Maybe he was just soothing himself with deep pressure, and then it was too tight, and he couldn't get it off."

"Who was here that night and had access to his room? If his door wasn't locked, then that includes anyone with access to the unit."

"That would include practically everyone at Summit. We can all go from wing to wing and unit to unit with very few restrictions. I can give you a list of the people I know were here that night. But everyone who *might* have been here? Like I said. Anyone."

"Was there anyone who had a problem with Quentin? Someone he got into fights with? Or who resented him? Someone he had hurt or made to look bad in one of his violent outbursts?"

"No," Nancy shook her head. "It's not like that. We're just here to do a job. Sure, it's stressful and some of the residents can be miserable to deal with. But at the end of the day... we go home, and they stay here." She shrugged. "As far as any of the other residents doing something to hurt him... no, no one in the unit would do that. We have other kids at Summit too, kids who have mental illness or are delinquent rather than developmentally disabled and they're different... I'm sure some of them would be able to do something intentionally violent or evil. But our kids with autism, no. All of the children in this unit are the same. They are all developmentally delayed, not mentally ill or delinquent. They don't make enemies with each other. Mostly, they'd rather just be left alone."

Zachary nodded and made a couple more notes. "Did he have any particular friends?" he asked. "Do any of them develop friendships...?"

"Of course, yes. Even those who are the most socially awkward still seem to be able to transcend language and social convention and hit it off sometimes. It can be quite sweet. I know that Quentin had one little fellow who was quite attached to him. They went to therapy one after the other, so they would pass in the hallway or waiting area. Started noticing each other and waving. This little guy gave Quentin a hug one day. And another day, Quentin spontaneously tries his 'hello, how are you?' script on him. So cute."

Zachary nodded. "Who was his friend?"

"Raymond. Ray-Ray, they call him."

"I met him. So does that mean Sophie was Quentin's therapist too?"

"Yes."

Would Sophie have seemed like a big, scary woman to Quentin as much as she did to Ray-Ray? Remembering how dogged she had been about getting Ray-Ray's compliance, Zachary had to wonder how she got the compliance of the bigger, stronger, more violent boy.

But he knew how.

With sixty shocks in one session, as recorded in Quentin's log book.

Zachary had planned on getting a good night's sleep. It had been a long, emotionally taxing day, and it would have been best if he could have gotten in a full night's sleep for once and woken up refreshed in the morning, ready to take on the day.

But he'd emailed Margaret Beacher when he got back to Bowman's apartment, asking for some more information and she had emailed back some reference material. He didn't want to go to bed until he'd had a chance to look over what she'd sent.

He skimmed over articles by adults with autism who echoed what Margaret had said about ABA and similar therapies causing long-lasting problems such as PTSD and other issues that the ABA practitioners had never anticipated. Margaret's was not a lone voice.

One of the files she sent him was a book by Ivar Lovaas, whose name Zachary had heard several times in connection with ABA. He opened it up, expecting that it would be filled with a lot of clinical studies and dense medical language, but it was written as a guide for parents and was quite readable. Zachary started to skim over the introduction, then stopped and went back to the beginning to read it carefully. He checked the copyright page. The copyright was 1981, not the Victorian Era. He used his cursor to highlight a few of the lines in the introduction.

No one has the right to be taken care of, no matter how retarded he is. So, put your child to work; his work is to learn.

They have no right to act bizarrely.

No right? Zachary's mind immediately went to Margaret Beacher talking about being punished for who she was. According to Lovaas, she had to be trained to act like everyone else. Lovaas gave instructions to parents on managing their child's weight, clothing, hair, and appearance to make sure they couldn't be differentiated from their peers.

Zachary went on to read the next chapter, outlining the basics of the program. He read about the reward system he had already seen in action, using small treats and praise to encourage the desired behaviors. Then the references to punishments started to pop up. Zachary read on.

By becoming firm with your child, and perhaps making him a little upset or scared by yelling at him or hitting his bottom, your social rewards (saying "Good" and your kisses and hugs) become almost immediately more important and effective for him. It is as if he appreciates you more, once you have shown him that you also can be angry with him.

Zachary put his hands over the words and looked away from the page. He closed his eyes, breathing evenly.

Zachary was intimately familiar with the phenomenon Lovaas referred to.

'Traumatic bonding' resulted when the victim was alternately abused and rewarded by the perpetrator and was most effective when the perpetrator controlled the necessaries of life, such as food and freedom of movement. It was the abuse/remorse cycle that made battered wives and abused children cling to and defend their abusers. In kidnap situations it was referred to as Stockholm Syndrome. It was the method cults used to brainwash their victims and gangs used during initiation to gain the loyalty of their members.

Of course, Lovaas hadn't intended the parent to traumatize the child. He apparently didn't anticipate that his training methods would cause PTSD. Spankings were not commonly considered abuse in the eighties. But what looked 'a little upset' to an adult could actually be an expression of trauma in a child. A few pages later, in recommending that adults practice hitting friends to see how hard was hard enough, Lovaas reported, "We have heard about children who have been hit or pinched so hard that their skin is dramatically discolored. It seems quite unnecessary to use such strong physical aversives." Well, bully for him.

Zachary left the document on his screen and got up to pace across the room. Lovaas's words made him physically ill. He was nauseated. He tried to focus on the movement of his body and not slide into flashbacks. He wasn't sure how many more times he could read words like "Use as much physical force as is necessary to make him complete the task" before he succumbed.

He returned to his computer and went on to the next page, hoping it would be less offensive, and found:

You may have to exert considerable physical force to help him comply. You may at such times run the risk of bruising or physically hurting the child, or the child you are working with may be physically so big that you can't budge him. This is a serious drawback.

Zachary clicked ahead to the next chapter. It was, unfortunately, titled "Physical Punishment," so he had a pretty good idea it wasn't going to be any less upsetting. He went into the kitchen and made a pot of coffee. He would have preferred alcohol, but he couldn't combine that with his meds.

With caffeine and Xanax on board, Zachary paced for a few more minutes, then went back to the book. Lovaas made a good argument for putting a stop to life-threatening behaviors like self-injury, extreme aggression, chewing on electrical cords, and running in front of traffic. Any parent could see the importance of eliminating the activities that could get their child killed. Zachary could almost see the justification for using aversives in those cases. But then Lovaas threw the baby out with the bathwater in advising:

For other sets of behaviors, the decision of whether or not to use physical punishment may seem less clear-cut, although these behaviors may be just as damaging to the child. For example, there is a group of behaviors, such as endless rocking, spinning, eye rolling, arm flapping, gazing, etc., that seem quite "addictive" to many children ... You may attempt to suppress such behaviors by using punishment.

Of course, he recommended using non-physical punishment before resorting to causing pain, but if nothing else worked, "painful electric shock" was offered as an option.

It was almost morning when Zachary finished working his way through the book and closed his computer. His eyes were itchy and aching. After an emotionally challenging day, he'd spent the night working through the text, fighting to stay focused and to push his way through the anger and nausea it engendered. Even with chemical aids, it was a hard-fought battle, and he fell into his blankets on the couch thoroughly exhausted.

For once, sleep came easily. His brain had been trying to shut down for hours, assaulted by the images brought on by the book and Zachary's past. When he finally let go, he spun quickly into darkness.

The images that came to his dreams this time were not of Annie at Bonnie Brown. Instead, Quentin's face stuck in his mind. And Ray-Ray's. And those of others he had seen at Summit just in passing. He saw a menacing Dr. Abato with a cattle prod. Children who were crying or afraid.

Zachary himself had been silenced. He couldn't speak to Dr. Abato. Couldn't protest the treatment of the children the institute was supposed to be helping and protecting. Abato and Sophie and the other staff he'd been introduced to talked as if he weren't there, yelled at him, pushed him from place to place and forced him to perform menial tasks; gluing pages, washing floors, putting toys into a bin, just to have them dumped out again and to repeat the job again. They gave him terse commands, like an animal. Like Lovaas instructed in his book.

Sit! Good sitting.

Quiet hands!

Touch your nose.

Touch your ear.

Give me a hug.

Any time he hesitated, someone grabbed his hands and forced him to perform the task. He felt demeaned. Humiliated. When he did well, and they tried to put a gummy bear in his mouth, he spat it out, disgusted.

And then he was watching as Quentin fought and fought against their commands. He tried to escape Sophie's strong hands as Dr. Abato stood by, brandishing the cattle prod, getting closer and threatening to shock him.

Ray-Ray was there, in the other direction, crying about something. He was alone, his face pressed against the observation window, babbling something incomprehensible to Quentin. Dr. Abato was there and grabbed Ray-Ray by the arm to pull him into the room. Quentin and Ray-Ray gravitated toward each other. Quentin held the smaller boy against himself protectively, sheltering him from Abato and Sophie. Quentin's eyes were hidden by his fringe of hair.

"Leave them alone!" Zachary tried to shout. He couldn't get the words out. Nothing would come out of his mouth. He tried to move between the boys and Abato. Dr. Abato just laughed and shoved the cattle prod toward Zachary, hitting him in the shoulder with it.

Zachary let out a shout, trying to pull away from the jolt of pain.

And he was on the couch. Or half-on, half-off the couch, hands raised defensively against Bowman, his shoulder still buzzing with the charge he had only dreamed.

"Chill out," Bowman said. "It's okay. Relax. You were just dreaming. Hell, I thought we were under attack the way you were screaming."

Zachary tried to catch his breath.

"Are you okay?" Bowman asked.

"Yeah." Zachary blew out a stream of air and looked up at the ceiling, trying to banish the dream. "Yeah. I'm sorry. I just... I guess it was all just a dream." He shook his head and shuddered. It had felt real. He felt like he had been there. Like he had been one of them. It made perfect sense that he would identify with the residents at Summit, after all the times he had been institutionalized, all of the times that he had been silenced and prevented from making his own choices. From being his own person.

"That must have been some nightmare."

Zachary pushed himself into a sitting position on the couch, rather than sprawling like a spider across it. He rubbed his eyes and looked around, trying to get reoriented.

It was getting light out. Bowman sighed and sat down on the couch next to Zachary. He had on pajama bottoms and a robe, not done up, so that Zachary could see his hairy belly and drooping physique. Bowman's hair was mussed and he smelled sweaty and garlicky.

"Look, Zach," he said slowly. "You know it's time for you to move on. You've got your check for the fire from the insurance company. That means you have the money to put down a deposit on a place of your own. You need a place where you have the room to move around as much as you like, your own bed, to keep whatever hours you want. You need all those things. You can't just stay here forever."

Zachary rubbed his forehead, his face hot and uncomfortable. He hadn't even been the one who had asked Bowman if he could stay there. That had been Kenzie. And it had been for 'a few days' while Zachary sorted out his problems and got back on his feet again. Zachary had long since outstayed his 'few days.' Bowman had been remarkably patient about having someone around the place. He even seemed to like it sometimes. But it had to be wearing for him to have someone underfoot all the time. For him not to be able to use the living room whenever he wanted to, or to come and go without worrying about disturbing Zachary, or to bring a lady friend home.

"Yeah, you're right," he agreed sheepishly. "I should have been out of here ages ago. I'll find something and get out of your way. I'm sorry."

"No, no need to be sorry. I'm happy to help out someone down on his luck. What were you supposed to do with no home, or car, or even a wallet? I was glad when Kenzie said you needed something. It's just time now."

No one has the right to be taken care of.

The phrase echoed in Zachary's head. He was a grown man. Not a teenager. Not like the residents at Summit. He had the ability to take care of himself, and he needed to do it instead of relying on Bowman or someone else. It didn't matter how anxious it made him to think about living on his own again. About how he had already burned two homes to the ground. That wasn't going to happen again. He had lived on his own for twenty years. It was wrong to go on taking advantage of his friend. Before he had moved in with Bowman, they had barely been nodding acquaintances. They certainly hadn't known all of the intimate details of each other's lives. Bowman had known about Bridget and the disastrous end of their relationship, but he didn't know the details, only the broad strokes.

"You don't have to be gone tomorrow," Bowman said, putting his hand on Zachary's knee. "But it's time to start finding alternative arrangements."

"Yeah. For sure. I'm sorry to have put you out for so long."

Bowman nodded. He pushed himself back up from the couch. He stood looking down at Zachary.

"You're going to be okay?"

"Yeah. I'm okay. Just a dream."

"You're still seeing that new therapist...? And going to your group...?"

"Yeah. Of course." Though Zachary had skipped both that week, deeming the homicide case to be more important than sessions where they would just tell him the same things they had been telling him the past few weeks. He knew that they were supposed to be helping him, but he couldn't help but feel like they just stirred things up that were better left alone.

"Good. Try to get back to sleep."

Bowman returned to his bedroom. Zachary wondered whether Bowman would be able to go back to sleep again. The faint light of the rising sun meant that it wasn't long before Bowman would have to be up and getting ready for his Saturday morning shift.

Zachary knew that if he tried to go back to sleep again, he would only keep on dreaming. And Bowman would not be able to get any more sleep if Zachary kept waking him up with nightmares.

Zachary opened up his computer and started searching for a new apartment.

As much as he was learning to hate Summit Living Center, Zachary knew that he had to go back again. He had spent the weekend focused on finding a new living arrangement, pretending that he didn't have anything else pressing to do. But when Monday rolled around, he knew he had to leave the house-hunting alone and head back to Summit. He hadn't learned everything he could from the witnesses. He hadn't fully investigated the circumstances surrounding Quentin's death. Before he could decide whether Quentin had killed himself or had had a little help in that direction, Zachary needed to better understand what Quentin had been going through.

"We don't have a lot of people who want to know all of the details of Electric Shock Devices and how they fit into a therapeutic program," Dr. Abato told him, after having Zachary sit down in one of the big cushioned chairs of his spacious office. "A few reporters. Every now and then, someone else from the outside who wants to see how it works."

Zachary nodded. So far, he had been surprised that Abato was willing to talk about the shocks and hadn't told him to stay away and just drop the case. He kept waiting for Dr. Abato to say no, he couldn't see anything else. But Abato had instead said that Zachary could observe shocks being administered and be shown how ABA worked using shocks as an aversive.

"I understand that it all sounds rather barbaric," Dr. Abato said with a reassuring smile. "But it really isn't any different than what regular parents do with regular kids in need of discipline every day. A spank or a slapped hand or arm to deter a child from reaching for a hot stove or to put an end to a tantrum. We're doing the same thing, just on a larger scale. And by using the skin shocks, we can ensure that the discipline is always consistently applied and there is no risk of injury."

Zachary was reserving judgment on that one.

"I've arranged for you to observe a training session with one of our residents and his parents. Parents need to be trained in how to control their children properly so that when they are able to return home, they don't lose the progress that they have made in the program. The parents can keep applying the program consistently so that the child can continue to learn and grow and become more normal and independent."

"But you can't really make them normal," Zachary said. "I mean, there's no cure for autism, right? What you're doing here is trying to make them act more normal, to develop better skills and functioning... not to cure them."

"If we can make them indistinguishable from their peers, then what do you call that? Do you call that a cure? Autism is a developmental delay, so even if they develop to their full potential, it is going to take longer for them to get there. But having taken longer to get there, are they then cured? It's all a matter of semantics, Mr. Goldman, and I'm not sure it matters. Our goal here is to push them as far as we possibly can, to become as normal as they possibly can be."

"Okay," Zachary agreed uncomfortably, not sure what to make of Dr. Abato's answer.

"Come with me."

Dr. Abato once again escorted Zachary to his destination. But this time, their destination wasn't the reward rooms or even the therapy rooms. It wasn't the living quarters that Quentin had been housed in. Instead, Abato took him to another unit. Though it had the same layout as Quentin's unit, it was obvious as soon as they arrived that it was different. Zachary could hear yelling and banging going on behind the doors. He caught glimpses of residents who looked wild or furious. Young children, older adults, but mostly teens, and mostly boys. Zachary believed without being told that the cell doors were all locked.

Dr. Abato was watching Zachary for his reaction. "A little different, isn't it?" he asked indulgently, seeming to enjoy Zachary's discomfort. "It's one thing to philosophize about what is best for children with autism; it's quite another to see the sort of war zone they can cause."

"Yes," Zachary agreed.

They went past the individual bedrooms to a larger room that Zachary was reluctant to call a meeting room, even though that was what the plaque beside the door said. Meeting Room B.

It was a large, empty room. No table and chairs. No rug or bean bag chairs. It was completely bare. But it wasn't unoccupied. There was a boy who appeared to be fifteen or so, a stocky boy with brown hair curling down over his ears and into his eyes, a round, cheeky face that had probably made him a cute baby and little boy. But cute wasn't what he was anymore. A woman and a man were focused on him. The woman had blond and gray hair pulled back into a half bun, and the man was husky, with shaved-short hair and stubble on his face. They both looked irritated and angry. There was also a therapist standing nearby, with smooth red hair and a white smock, and a slim, blond female aide with a heavy utility belt hung with shock remotes. One of which was bound to have the stocky boy's picture on it.

Dr. Abato took Zachary to an observation window, where they sat down to watch like it was a movie being played for their own entertainment.

"This is Angel Salk," Dr. Abato told Zachary. "And his parents, of course. We won't go in, as it looks like the room is quite crowded enough already. We'll just observe for a while."

Zachary nodded, his stomach tight with anticipation.

"Angel is violent, a danger to both himself and others. We are having some success in teaching him, but his parents need to learn how to control him. They are here to see how it all works."

They seemed to have caught Angel and his parents mid-confrontation. Angel had his back up against the wall, both parents in his face. The man grabbed Angel's wrists in one hand and his shoulder in the other and shoved him violently into the wall.

"You need to listen!" he said to Angel in a furious tone.

Zachary was ready to jump right through the window to save the boy from the assault. But neither of the professionals seemed to find it the least bit disturbing.

"Mom, you need to get in there too," the therapist directed. "You need to show him that you are both united. He can't play one of you against the others like he might have done in the past."

The mother moved in closer, but was clearly reluctant to touch her son.

"Put your hand on his chin," the therapist said. "Open his mouth. Tell him he needs to use his words."

When she reached her hand out, Angel tried to pull away, thrashing his head back and forth. But the father had a tight grip on him and kept pressing him against the wall. The mother eventually managed to grasp Angel's chin, and she pulled it down, squeezing her fingers into his cheeks between his teeth to separate his jaws farther.

"Use words," she said, her voice quiet, catching in her throat.

"Louder, Mom," the therapist instructed. "He needs to hear your directions clearly, or this doesn't work."

"Use words!" the woman said in a near-shout.

Angel was wincing and trying to pull away. Then he suddenly went rigid and cried out. Both parents looked at the therapist in surprise. It was the aide who had pressed the shock button, but the therapist nodded that this was the correct action.

"Tell him again," she said. "Don't let go. Give him the same instruction again."

"Use words." The woman's voice was quieter this time, but still clear.

Angel yelled something incomprehensible around his mother's fingers.

Again, the same reaction as Angel suddenly went rigid again, his arms splayed out.

Zachary looked at Abato, who apparently saw nothing to be concerned about. Zachary studied Angel, seeing the cuffs around his arms and legs, wires leading under his clothes, and then out of his clothes and into the black backpack he had on. The same black backpack that Zachary had seen so many of the other residents wearing. He had thought they were school-bags, but they were apparently part of the shock device.

"Tell him again," the therapist said.

"Use words," the mother said. Her voice dropped slightly. "Come on, Angel. Be a good boy. You can use your words."

"Don't coddle him. Don't use more words than are necessary for him to understand what you expect of him."

"Use words," she said again.

"No!" The sound burst from Angel's throat in protest.

"Good talking," the mother said immediately, looking over at the therapist for approval. "That's good talking, Angel." She stuffed something into his partially-open mouth.

Angel gagged and struggled, breaking free of his father. He bounced to the other side of the room, hands up defensively like an animal ready to claw someone's eyes out. He was closer to the observation window, so Zachary could see him better.

Angel's arms were pitted with scars and scabs. He had a bruise on his forehead, mostly hidden by his messy brown locks. His parents had apparently not read Lovaas's instructions on keeping their son's hair properly cut so that he wouldn't look different from his peers.

Angel went rigid again and let out an animal-like cry. He reached for one of the armbands and slid his fingers underneath the shocking device. There was another shock from the aide.

"Leave the electrodes," the aide snapped. "Don't touch the electrodes."

Angel tried again, then flailed his arms and tried to shake off the pain of the shock.

"You need to control him again," the therapist instructed. "Hold him in one place and give him the instruction again."

"But he did it," Angel's mother protested. "He spoke."

"Once. He needs to do it every time. Without fighting."

The father circled, trying to get ahold of him again. Angel evaded capture and was shocked again. His father managed to get ahold of him during the couple of seconds he was being shocked and shoved him into the wall again.

"Use words," the mother instructed, her voice high and tight, not holding on to his jaw this time.

Angel's father grabbed his jaw and squeezed until Angel was forced to open his mouth. "Use words," he growled.

Angel garbled out a sound, but if it was speech it was incomprehensible. He was shocked again. The mother started sniffling and protesting.

"You need to be strong with him," the therapist ordered. "You can't be crying and letting him control the session. You are in charge. Whatever he does to manipulate you, you have to be strong and resist it. Give him a different instruction. Tell him to give you a hug."

Angel's father let go of him so that Angel would be able to obey the instruction if he were so inclined. Angel backed away from them, scratching his arms and then his face. He started to flap his hands beside his face.

"No stimming," the aide said, immediately shocking him.

Angel went rigid, but as soon as the shock was finished, he was flapping again, faster and more frantic this time. He opened his mouth and started to make a noise, a guttural hooting.

"He's trying to communicate," Zachary said to Dr. Abato.

"He's merely voicing."

Another shock, which stopped Angel in his tracks for a moment, and then he started flapping again. Another shock within seconds of the last, and he fell to the floor, screaming in pain and scrabbling at another electrode that must have been on his torso under his shirt.

Angel's mother cried out and she took a step forward to go to him. But Mr. Salk reached out and stopped her. "He's just trying to get attention," he warned.

"He's hurt! My baby."

"He's not hurt," the therapist said. "He's just fine. He's dramatizing to get your sympathy. You need to ignore this behavior. Insist that he get up. Tell him to give you a hug."

Angel's mother was unable to follow the instructions. His father made a noise of disgust and reached down to grab Angel by the arm. He was a big boy; he had to be at least a hundred and eighty pounds, but Mr. Salk had no trouble pulling him to his feet.

"Hug your mother," he instructed. His expression was blank. If he felt any sympathy for his son, he had shut it down and locked it away in order to continue with the training session.

Angel held his arms wide. He didn't look in his mother's direction or walk over to her, but the invitation was there. His mother crooned and got closer to him. "Good boy. Good boy, Angel," she praised, putting her arms around him. His arms went tightly around her body in a squeeze that was clearly not meant to be a gentle hug of affection, and Mrs. Salk yelped in pain.

Angel's arms flew open as he was shocked, and his mother freed herself, her face pale and frightened. Angel flapped his hands. "Ma!"

"He didn't mean to," Angel's mother excused him. "He didn't mean to hurt me." She put her arms out for him again. "Gentle this time, Angel. Give me a nice hug. Gentle."

Angel continued to flap his hands, not approaching his mother, trying to watch all of the people in the room at once.

"No stimming," the therapist commanded. If anything, Angel flapped harder. He moaned, pacing the room. He jolted with another shock.

"Give me a hug," Angel's mother repeated.

"No..." The word was a long moan. Angel's head snapped back with another shock.

"He's trying to talk," Zachary said to Dr. Abato. "Isn't that what you want?"

"He is refusing to speak when he's asked to speak, and speaking when he's asked to hug," Dr. Abato said. "Does that sound like he's being obedient or manipulative?"

"I don't think he's being intentionally disobedient," Zachary protested. "He's upset. Confused."

"And you're drawing upon what expertise?" Dr. Abato asked, his lip curling slightly.

"I don't have any expertise. I'm just observing..."

"Well, we have decades of expertise and training between us. And we have dealt with Angel before. This is typical, and he's suckered better than you. He'll do whatever he can to resist doing what he's told. We need to break him of that behavior if we're going to get anywhere with him."

Zachary shook his head. "This isn't right. He's got to have some basic human rights."

Quentin had undergone sixty shocks the day he had died. Zachary now had a much clearer picture of what that entailed. And they had withheld food. *How was what they were doing any better than the torture in a POW camp?*

"I understand this is hard to watch. You asked to see how the skin shock therapy works. I'm not sanitizing it. Angel is just the type of child that we need the shocks for. He has been in dozens of other programs that have not been able to help him and curb his violence. This is the only program that has any chance of rehabilitating his behavior, and his parents know it. Do you think they would go through this if they thought there was any other way?"

Zachary swallowed and shook his head. Obviously not. Especially not his mother. But his father too had been driven past his limits, disengaging from his own emotions in order to continue the therapy.

"Let's do some sensory work," the therapist suggested. "Angel is obviously sensory-seeking at this point. Flapping. Hugging too hard. Behaving in a way that demands we hold him still. Acting-out behaviors that he knows will get him shocks. He's actually seeking out the negative attention."

His parents both nodded as if this made sense. Zachary shook his head. The suggestion that Angel wanted to be shocked was ridiculous. It was obvious that it caused him pain and distress.

"We know Angel," Dr. Abato reminded Zachary. "You haven't seen the lengths he goes through to get attention."

"Sit with him on the floor," the therapist directed. "Make sure he's sitting properly, and we'll work on desensitization."

"Sit down," Mr. Salk ordered in a loud voice.

Angel didn't comply. He jolted with a shock and brushed at his arm as if trying to flick away a fly or stinging insect.

"Sit down."

He still ranged about the room as if he couldn't stop moving. Zachary could see him trying to watch everyone at once, an impossibility even in the small space.

"Angel, please sit down," his mother contributed, her voice pleading.

When he didn't obey, he received another shock. His father caught him, grappled with him for a minute, and tried to throw him to the floor.

"Stand clear of him," the aide instructed. Zachary switched his attention to her, and he watched her finger depress the button on Angel's remote once, then again, and again, without giving him any time to recover or comply in between. Angel howled and fell to the floor writhing and trying to pull the electrodes away from his skin. "He's got his arm band loose," the therapist told the aide. "You'd better secure it."

In spite of the fact that Angel was a large boy and known to be violent, the aide didn't appear to have any fear of approaching him. She picked up Angel's right arm, and Zachary could see that the electrode band had slipped from its previous position. There was a large red welt where it had been attached. The aide moved it to just below the welt and tightened the band again to secure it in place.

"He has a mark," Zachary told Dr. Abato. "There must be something wrong with the electrode. It's not supposed to cause any damage, is it?"

"Repeated shocks can cause some redness. It's superficial and will fade. The aide has reattached the cuff away from the irritated skin. That's appropriate."

"But what about the other electrodes? If that one has caused damage, aren't the others doing the same thing? Shouldn't they all be moved? Maybe he's had enough today."

"Just watch, Mr. Goldman. Let's give them a few more minutes."

Zachary pressed his lips together and watched the mother and father sit down on the floor with their son. The aide moved Angel into a sitting position, prompting him with 'Good sitting, Angel. Show us good sitting,' and guiding his limbs into place until he was sitting cross-legged in a triangle with his parents.

"Good job," his mother praised softly.

"Let's work on light touch. You are going to work on giving Angel light touch and encouraging him to give you light touch in return," the therapist explained.

Both parents nodded, looking at him.

"Mom, I want you to rest your hand on Angel's arm, and to stroke it gently downward."

"He doesn't like—" she started to protest.

"I'm aware he doesn't like it. That's why we're trying to desensitize him."

Angel's mother put her hand tentatively on Angel's forearm and brushed it down the length. Angel jerked back, grimacing as if she had hurt him.

Zachary leaned forward, trying to get a better look at Angel's arm. As he had noted, the surface of Angel's arm was pitted and dimpled with scar tissue and small red scabs. It must have been painful for him.

"That's gentle touch, Angel. Can you give your mother gentle touch?" The therapist moved closer to the little group, making Angel cock his head sharply to keep an eye on her.

Angel's mother lifted his hand and placed it on her arm to encourage the desired action. Angel jerked back, his shoulders hunching protectively. He scratched his arm and started picking at one of the scabs.

"No picking. Show your mother gentle touch. Give gentle touch."

When he continued to pick the scabs, Angel received a jolt. He turned his head to watch the aide, completely aware who it was causing him pain.

Angel's mother again picked up his hand and placed it on her arm, then gently drew it down. "See, Angel? Gentle touch. Good job!"

She put her hand into her pocket and produced a small candy, but when she tried to put it in his mouth, Angel batted her hand away, sending the candy flying across the room. He went rigid with the resulting punishment shock and tried to reach the electrode positioned behind his back. Zachary frowned. *Was* Angel preferring the shocks over the positive reinforcer?

"Dad, your turn. Give Angel a gentle touch and then encourage him to reciprocate."

Mr. Salk gave Angel's arm a cursory pat.

"That's not enough," the therapist scolded. "Give his arm a slower, gentle stroke."

Angel's father scowled at her. He put his hand again on Angel's scarred, pock-marked arm and stroked down gently.

Angel again reacted as if the touch were painful, flinging his father's hand off and making a mad-bull sound of protest. His shoulders went back at a shock and he dug at his belly, trying to get at an electrode under his shirt.

"Give your father a gentle touch," the therapist ordered, her voice hard. The contrast between the words and the woman's tone was surreal.

Angel reached his hand out and placed it on his father's meaty arm.

"Good," the therapist praised. "Good gentle touch. Give him a reward, Dad."

Angel's father pulled away from his son's touch and checked his pockets. Mrs. Salk handed him a candy. He held it out toward Angel. Angel pincered it between his fingers and held it up to his nose.

"In your mouth," the therapist told him. She looked at Angel's father. "Put it straight in his mouth, don't give him the opportunity to play with it."

"Last time I did that, he bit me."

"In your mouth," she said again, as Angel touched the candy to his tongue. The therapist sent a look at the aide, who again pressed the shock button.

Angel flung the candy away. He struck out at his father, howling in pain or anger. Mr. Salk turned aside to avoid a blow to his face, getting hit in the shoulder instead. Angel writhed on the floor. Zachary again saw the aide hitting the button repeatedly, overriding the built-in two-second shock, cycling through all of the electrodes.

So much for delivering a consistent punishment every time.

"Stop them!" Zachary told Dr. Abato, grabbing him by the arm. "They can't do that! She's not following the protocol. She can't keep shocking him like that! Stop them!"

Abato looked at Zachary for a moment, his dark eyes glittering. Then he reached out and rapped his knuckles twice on the observation window.

The adults in the room all looked at each other. Angel paid no attention to the noise, moaning and making loud, incoherent noises of protest, his body doubled up on the floor. The therapist nodded at the aide, who went to the door, opened it, and looked out at the observation chairs to see what was wrong.

Her eyes widened when she saw Dr. Abato sitting there.

"This session is over," Dr. Abato said calmly. "Return Angel to his room."

"His parents came for a full day of training," she protested. "They had to drive all that way and we've just barely started…"

"Explain to them there is a problem with the equipment. We'll have to reschedule."

She stood looking at him for a long moment, then nodded and returned to the meeting room.

The therapist's face grew red as the aide explained the cancellation of the session to the Salks. The aide coaxed Angel to his feet and took him from the room. His hands were flapping as he was escorted past Zachary and Dr. Abato. The therapist apologized to Angel's parents and she stalked out into the hallway to find out what was going on. Dr. Abato rose from his seat to talk to her. Zachary was happy to get to his feet. His whole body was clenched in a tight knot. He turned his head back and forth to try to loosen up his muscles.

"It would appear there is a problem with the ESD," Abato told the angry therapist. "Miss Kelly was having to press the remote several times to get a proper shock. We may need to re-evaluate alternatives."

"He was getting a shock, that was obvious!"

Dr. Abato glanced over at Zachary. "Mr. Goldman noticed that Miss Kelly was having to press the remote several times. Whether that is an equipment malfunction or whether it is becoming less effective, I don't know. We will have to investigate further."

The therapist glared at Zachary, then apparently decided she'd better listen to Dr. Abato. She nodded. "Fine."

"Please have his parents reschedule for another day."

She nodded again and walked back into the meeting room to discuss it in a low voice with Mr. and Mrs. Salk.

"We will look into this matter," Dr. Abato told Zachary. "I appreciate your help."

"You would have let her just keep shocking him continuously."

"Sometimes the equipment malfunctions. I'm glad you noticed there was an issue. I'm sure I would have seen it before long, or Miss Kelly would have brought it to our attention, but your quick eye was a great benefit."

Zachary wondered if Dr. Abato ever quit putting on a show.

"Do you count that as one shock or several in the therapy log? Was Quentin shocked sixty times in his last therapy session? Or several hundred?"

Dr. Abato raised his hands in a calming gesture.

"Where *was* the log sheet just now?" Zachary looked back into the meeting room. There was no paperwork in evidence. Neither the therapist nor the aide had been marking the prompts and the shocks on a session log.

"Miss Stewart will be filling it out as soon as she sees the Salks off, I'm sure."

"It's supposed to be filled out in real time. Every prompt and response. Every time he is shocked. You can't just remember that and fill it in later!"

"You're right, of course. Real-time record keeping is a very important part of the program. I will talk to Miss Stewart about it."

"This is ridiculous." Zachary's anger was rising, his voice getting louder. "What you're doing here is abuse—"

"What we are doing here, Mr. Goldman, is saving children and saving their families. Do you know how many people are trying to get their children into this program? Families who are at the ends of their ropes and have nowhere else to go. No other hope. We can only fit so many Quentins and Angels into our program. There are limits as to how many people this facility that accommodate. And that means that for every child you see being helped here, there are a thousand others across the country who are just as bad off. Who need our help just as desperately."

"You can't just keep shocking them and hoping that something works. You could be causing them injury. Maybe Quentin had a weak heart and the shocks were just too much for him. You don't know, do you?"

"Quentin Thatcher had a full physical, including an EKG, just like every other child who enters our program. He didn't have any heart problems. Nor do any of the children who enter the program. You led me to understand you had seen the police report and photos. If you did, you know Quentin died of strangulation, not from skin shocks."

13

Zachary was speechless. He stood there shaking with anger, trying to put his thoughts into words that would somehow reach Dr. Abato and make him see what he was doing to children like Quentin and Angel, and even ones like Ray-Ray who were not being shocked, but who were still being traumatized by the punishment/reward cycle that Lovaas so unashamedly promoted to gain psychological control over them.

"Would you please wait here while I deal with a few points?" Dr. Abato requested.

"What are you doing? I want to hear."

"This is not part of the tour. I have administrative matters that need to be dealt with, and that is not any of your business. If you will please just wait here for me, I won't be long."

There wasn't anything Zachary could do but agree. He didn't have the right to be wandering through the institution on his own. If he tried it, he was just going to end up stopped by one of the security staff. Dr. Abato strode out of Zachary's sight.

Angel was confused by the abrupt end to his therapy session. He flapped his hands anxiously beside his face, unsure what to expect next. Being released from a therapy session early in the day was something unknown to him. Kelly led him by the hand to his room.

His skin was still buzzing. Angel scratched at it, trying to calm the itching of a hundred fire ants under his skin.

"Angel. Here. Come here," Kelly encouraged, taking him to the desk in his room. She picked up a pump-bottle of lotion. "Here, cream. Let me put some on for you."

He held both arms extended out from his body, and she pumped cream, cold to the touch, onto each one.

"You rub it in now. I know you don't want me touching you, so you do it. Rub it in, Angel. Come on."

She pretended to be rubbing lotion onto her own arms. Angel mirrored her movements, matching the timing of every movement to hers.

He couldn't rub the cream where the bands went around his arms, which was where it burned the most. He moaned as he tried to slide his fingers under the arm bands.

"Since you're done your session," Kelly was looking at the printed schedule. "That means you have computer lab."

Angel tried again to get his fingertips under the armbands, but Kelly caught his fingers and gave them a tug.

"Computers. You like the computers, don't you, Angel?"

He barely heard her. He did like computers, but he was distracted by the change in schedule and the man who had been in the hallway when he got out. He knew Dr. Abato, but not the man with him. The other man had been angry. His fists were clenched and shaking. His demeanor was a welcome change to Angel, because Angel was also angry. Usually the people who were angry were the ones with the shockers, but the man in the hallway had not had a shocker.

Angel let Kelly pull him out into the hallway. The man was still there, his eyes wide and his fists still clenched. His face turned toward Angel.

"Where is he going now?" he asked Kelly.

"Computer lab."

"Mind if I tag along?"

Kelly's body shifted and her grip on Angel's hand tightened. "Who are you, again?"

"Zachary Goldman."

Angel liked the name Goldman. He envisioned a tall statue of a man made of solid gold. That would really be something. He mouthed the name Angel Goldman to himself. The two names went together well. Kelly started to move down the hall again without telling Zachary Goldman that it was okay for him to go along, but he followed along with them anyway. As they went by the unit administration desk, Zachary Goldman spoke to a woman whose name tag said Agnes Peal. "If Dr. Abato is looking for me, I'll be in the computer lab."

Mrs. Peal made a motion with her hand like she wanted to stop him, but he didn't pay any attention. Angel kept his head turned so that he could watch Zachary Goldman out of the corner of his eye as he walked with them. Goldman didn't try to touch him or ask him questions.

Zachary could see Angel keeping an eye on him, but Angel seemed calmer than he had during the therapy session and didn't make any threatening movements.

Kelly too kept looking at Zachary, but she was more circumspect about it. Looking at him when she thought he was distracted by something else. She didn't know that Zachary had learned in places just like Summit to have eyes in the back of his head; to always be aware of everyone's movements around him. She'd have to be a lot more careful to keep him from seeing her nervousness over his going to the lab with her.

Zachary had given her his name, but not who he was or why he was there, so she had to be wondering whether he had the right to go with her or if she should be stopping him.

"Here we go, Angel," Kelly announced, steering Angel into the computer lab. Angel looked around and headed for an empty chair. It appeared to be somewhere he knew the expected behavior and was willing to comply. He hadn't, Zachary noted, had his ESD equipment swapped out. His arm cuffs were still at different heights, exactly where they had been after Angel had pulled one of them loose and had it reattached below the inflamed skin. Dr. Abato hadn't been concerned enough about the possibility that Angel's equipment was faulty to ensure that it was fixed or replaced. Zachary was sure that, like him, Abato knew very well that Kelly hadn't been pressing the button repeatedly because she wasn't getting a good shock. She had been attempting to escalate the punishment.

It was a strange feeling, seeing the pretty young blond and knowing that she had essentially been torturing Angel. As much as Zachary knew it wasn't true, it was hard not to associate beauty with goodness. He simply didn't expect someone as pretty as she was to be someone who could intentionally hurt a young boy. Angel had been thrashing and crying on the floor and she just kept pressing that button.

Even so, Angel hadn't avoided her after leaving the meeting room. He hadn't protested about her being the one to escort him down to the computer lab or pulled away from her touch as she directed him there. It would appear that the alternating cycle of pain and rewards had securely bonded Angel to his aide, as Lovaas had predicted.

Kelly didn't follow Angel to his computer to stand behind him, as a few of the other staff members were doing. Instead, she stood a short distance away, watching not just Angel, but the other students in the lab as well. Zachary studied the boxes hanging from her belt. Angel's wasn't the only student whose remote she carried. How many of the other children in the lab did she have the ability to punish?

Most of the other students in the lab were wearing backpacks, and if Zachary looked closely, he could see the wires leading out of them that connected to the electrodes. How naive had he been to think they were simply bags of schoolbooks, not even seeing the wires?

A couple of the aides watching over the busy students were talking to each other in low voices, laughing occasionally. Zachary couldn't hear what they were saying, and moved a little closer, trying to catch the gist of it. As he got closer, he saw one of the kids near him make a deliberate motion toward him. He turned his eyes to her, careful not to move too fast and appear confrontational.

The girl angled a paper toward him, keeping her face toward her computer screen. Zachary looked down at the page.

HELP ME

It shouldn't have surprised him that some of the residents had the ability to write a communication. He had met Margaret, who appeared to him to have all of the abilities of a neurotypical woman. If there were women who could pass as non-autistic, there had to be younger people who also appeared to be neurotypical. Teenagers, children, all age groups. Nancy had said they had some residents who were not developmentally disabled, too. Kids who were mentally ill or delinquent.

Zachary looked at the back of the girl's head. She didn't look at him. But he could tell by the angle she had her head cocked at that she was still paying attention to him. She didn't have an aide hovering right behind her, so Zachary sat down in a vacant computer chair the next station down from hers and turned it toward her slightly.

"Are you okay?" he asked, barely above a whisper.

She tapped away at her keyboard. She appeared to be playing a game or manipulating a three-dimensional object for a math question. "I want to get out of here," she whispered back, not looking at him.

"I'm sorry... I can't do anything about that."

"You gotta. You gotta do something."

"I'm just a visitor. I don't have any power around here."

"Power." The girl snorted. "We're all wired for power around here."

"What's wrong? You look... like you're okay."

"Oh, yeah. I'm great."

"What's wrong?"

"You know what day it is today?"

"Uh... Monday...?"

"Yeah. And Monday is when the staff review all of the weekend security footage to see what happened over the weekend."

"I still don't see...?"

She didn't answer at first, looking intently at her computer screen as if working out a complicated puzzle. A shadow passed over Zachary, and he realized that someone had been standing close behind them.

"It's catch-up day," the girl said, barely opening her mouth. "They watch to see what everyone did over the weekend and if you did anything that should have been punished, they give it to you Monday afternoon."

"No!" Such a policy went directly against Lovaas's program, which dictated that a reward or punishment should be given within one second of a good or bad behavior. To wait several days and punish retroactively was completely wrong.

She nodded infinitesimally. "Just sittin' here... waiting... waiting to see who gets shocked and who gets away."

"That's not fair!"

He could see her smile. Unamused. In agreement with his assessment. Zachary massaged his temples, trying to figure out if there was something he could do. It seemed like a hopeless cause. How was he supposed to do anything to change the institution's policies? Newspaper articles had been written, trials had been held, protests had been made, and inspections had been done. And no one had been able to fight the administration of Summit and the devoted parents who insisted their children needed to be there and needed ABA therapy to keep them safe.

The two aides who Zachary had been trying to hear drifted closer to him. He kept his head down, trying not to look as if he'd been talking to the girl or had any interest in the conversation.

"It works best if you catch them off guard," the older man said. "An unexpected aversive is more powerful than one that the kid is expecting and already braced for. They build up a resistance over time. That's why the doctor is trying to get these new ESDs passed. The ones we've got now," the guard tapped one of the remotes on his belt, "they're stronger than the ones we started out with. Work a lot better. But even with how strong these ones are, some kids are barely affected by them. They can sit there and just look at you while you press the button. Just daring you to do it again."

The younger of the two aides, a boyish-faced redhead, nodded earnestly.

"I guess that makes sense."

"So what works best is if you can stand across the room. Even around a corner. Where they can't see you and won't be expecting anything." The aide glanced around at the students working industriously away on the computers. All heads down. All fingers on the keyboard. A boy at the end of the room laughed and started to flap his hands excitedly. Zachary watched the aide reach for one of his remotes, take a quick glance at it to make sure it was the right one, and punch the button.

The excited little boy gave a shriek and nearly fell out of his chair. The two aides laughed. Zachary saw red. It was all he could do to clamp his fingers around the table and hold himself back from jumping up and punching the aide who had pressed the button. The other students in the room were looking around, eyes wide and anxious. An aide who was closer to the boy who had been shocked settled him back in his chair, warning him not to disturb others with his noises and flapping.

Zachary could see that Angel was no longer engaged with his computer program. He would look at the computer for a moment, and then turn around and look warily at the aides. Was he vigilant because of the other boy who had been shocked? Or like the girl, did he know that it was Monday and there might be retroactive shocks in store for him? A teenage girl seated a few chairs down from Zachary started to rock back and forth and to cry quietly. The atmosphere in the room thickened, everyone hyper-aware of her behavior. Zachary watched the older aide who had been showing the young redhead the ropes to see if he would be the one to respond, shocking her unexpectedly from a distance. But he didn't seem to be concerned about it. Maybe he knew that hers wasn't one of the remotes hanging from his belt. A female aide moved toward the girl instead and coaxed her to stand up and leave the room.

Zachary could see Angel starting to rock, could see his anxious looks around the room increasing. Would Kelly catch his anxiety escalating and remove him from the lab, as the girl's aide had? Or would she try to shock him into quiet, compliant behavior?

The girl who had written 'help me' pounded on her keys, glancing at Angel and at Zachary. "Just chill, Angel," she murmured, very quiet so that one of the aides wouldn't hear her or wouldn't know the sound had come from her. She was too far away for Angel to have heard her. She just wanted to avoid what was coming next.

And so did Zachary. He didn't know what to do. Approach Angel and tell him it was okay and to calm down? Talk to Kelly and see what she could do to settle Angel down without shocking him?

Zachary had the feeling that Kelly's go-to solution would be to shock Angel. That's what Dr. Abato kept saying worked, even if he did think that the effectiveness might be wearing off somewhat for the boy.

Angel was probably one of the kids that Abato was hoping to get his new, upgraded device approved for.

353

14

"It doesn't work, Angel," the girl beside Zachary said, her voice a little louder than it had been. "It doesn't work. Nothing does. Even if they send you home. They still send you home with these." She tapped one of her armbands. "They train your folks to shock you, so even if you can get away from this place for a few days, even if you can get a weekend pass, you can't get away from them. You can't get away from this crew and their shocks!" The girl's voice had gradually risen and was slightly sing-songy. She was definitely starting to attract the attention of the staff, and that wasn't good for her. It was distracting some of the attention from Angel, but Zachary was afraid that she was just setting herself up for trouble.

"Shh. Better stay quiet," he urged.

"They're going to do it anyway. You can't stop it. None of us can stop it. They're going to do it anyway, no matter what!"

The older aide had noticed Zachary and was frowning at him, trying to figure out who he was and what he was doing there.

"Shh," Zachary tried again to soothe the girl and keep her from escalating further. It felt impossible. He saw himself again facing Annie, on the other side of a steel security door, unable to do anything to help her or to stop them from hurting her. "Come on. What's your name?"

"They don't care about your name. Your name doesn't matter, only whether they have your picture."

Zachary supposed that was true.

"It's Monday!" the girl said suddenly, in a loud voice. She turned her head and looked directly at the older aide. "It's Monday, so why don't you just go ahead and do it?"

The aide reached for his belt. Zachary saw what was going to happen an instant before it took place.

"No, wait, you've got—"

The man pressed the button on the box, meeting the girl's eyes. She didn't move. But a few seats down, Angel shouted and splayed out his arms. He made a gurgling, choking noise. The aide looked down at the box in his hand, realizing that he'd just hit the wrong button. He swore and moved his hand over one to grab the box with the girl's picture on it. Double-checking that he had the right one this time, he pressed the button on the second remote. The girl immediately reacted, throwing her head back and laughing. The hair rose on the back of Zachary's neck at her paradoxical reaction. The girl slammed both palms down on the table with a crack like the lash of a whip. Her eyes were bugging out and she looked like she was on a fairground ride, her whole body vibrating.

The seconds seemed like hours. All of the shocks that Zachary had seen had been the prescribed two-second shocks, other than when Kelly had been pressing Angel's button repeatedly to stack them up. Zachary turned his head to look at the aide to see if he was still holding down the button or pressing it again, but the older man's hand was no longer on the remote. But the girl still juddered and made guttural noises of protest beside Zachary, starting to slide out of her chair.

"It must be malfunctioning!" Zachary shouted. He grabbed one of the armbands and tried to pull it away from her skin and undo the Velcro closure at the same time. It was difficult to work with when the girl kept bucking and vibrating, unable to help herself. The smell of singed hair wafted up to Zachary's nose, making him nauseated, triggering flashbacks. Zachary struggled to keep from slipping back into the past. He got one armband off, but the girl still had three other electrodes that he could see, plus whatever was on her torso under her clothing. "Help me!"

The experienced aide was finally at Zachary's side, pushing him away. Rather than starting to work on the second armband, he went for the back-pack, doubling one of the girl's rigid limbs up to get her out of it. He yanked the backpack away, tearing at the wires to disconnect them. The girl collapsed, sobbing.

The aide dropped the backpack to the floor.

"The battery pack's in the backpack," he informed Zachary. He wiped sweat from his forehead with the back of his arm. "No battery, no juice. She'll be okay. We'll get this unit to the shop for repairs."

Zachary was still gasping for breath. He could smell burnt flesh, could feel his own skin shriveling and searing in the fire. The girl was injured, and the aide was more worried about getting the ESD fixed than getting her help. Zachary knelt back over the girl, fumbling to remove the second armband to assess the damage.

The aide swore, staring at the blisters already forming where the electrode had been. "Just get out of the way. We'll get her to the infirmary."

He reached down, grabbing the girl's arm where it wasn't burnt, jerking her to her feet.

"Get the other electrodes off," Zachary said. "Get them off so they're not rubbing against the injuries."

"Don't worry about it," the man growled. "These kids don't feel pain like you do. Didn't you see Trina laugh when I shocked her? She wanted me to do it. She asked for it!"

"She's injured, and she does feel pain! We need to get the electrodes off and get them to bring a gurney—"

"She can walk." The aide gave the girl a pull that made her stumble. "No need for a damn stretcher. It's not that bad."

He headed for the door, with the girl in tow, moaning in pain.

Zachary Goldman was still kneeling on the floor beside Trina's backpack. He had helped Trina; maybe he would help Angel too. Angel turned his head back and forth, looking around the room. Kelly was across the lab, talking with one of the other aides, not paying Angel any attention. He got out of his seat and moved as quickly as he could toward Goldman. Goldman was a man who made things happen. He made them stop Angel's therapy session. He made them take off Trina's backpack. Angel wanted his backpack off too.

When he reached Goldman's side, the man was hunched over like he was in pain. The scent of Trina's burned hair and skin still hung in the air. Had Goldman been hurt by the electrodes when he'd tried to remove them from Trina's arms? Angel grabbed Goldman's arms and tried to ask the question, but the words wouldn't come to his mouth. They always fled when something bad happened so that even the few he could normally get out wouldn't come out. The sounds that came out instead were angry, animal-like noises, frustratingly incoherent.

Ants still crawled beneath Angel's skin. He heard Kelly, way on the other side of the room, far and faint, call out to him to stop. He struck out wildly, trying to stop her, trying to head off the shock he knew would be coming. If Goldman would just help him to take off his backpack, the shocks would stop for him too. He could go home and there would be no more shocks. He could put up with the hitting and other pain, if he just didn't have to be shocked anymore.

He yelled in frustration, holding on to Goldman and trying to show him the marks the electrodes left behind. Goldman would let him go to the doctor too, with no electrodes. They could put cream on his skin where he picked and gouged at it to stop the ants, and he could watch the TV mounted up by the ceiling. Angel had been to the hospital many times, and he liked it when there was a TV.

Then the shocks came. It was too late for Goldman to prevent them. Fire raced through Angel's body from one location to another. Kelly was pulsing the button so that the shocks didn't go away, but multiplied like a hundred wasp stings inside his veins.

"Stop!" Goldman shouted. "Just leave him alone. I'm okay!"

The shocks stopped, the wasps gradually subsiding. Goldman was trying to pull off Angel's backpack, growling curses. Then his hands were gone. When Angel opened his eyes, squinting through the red haze to see what was going on, Goldman was being pulled away by a couple of security staff, and more stood by to take Angel back to his unit.

Zachary watched them take Angel away, fighting back waves of fury and frustration. Angel was not fighting the security staff who led him away, but he still voiced and groaned. Kelly trailed after them. Zachary felt impotent, on the very edge of being able to understand what Angel was trying to communicate, but unable to interact with him further.

He didn't understand what had made Angel come after him like that. Maybe he was confused after being shocked. Maybe it was because Zachary was the stranger there and Angel thought he was a threat. Maybe it was simply because he had been the center of attention and Angel had focused in on him.

Once Angel was removed from the lab, the security guards who had pulled Zachary away from Angel let him go. Zachary looked around the room at the pale, frightened faces of the other children.

After seeing three of the children shocked in quick succession, everyone seemed to just be waiting to be attacked or shocked themselves. They didn't go back to working on their computers, they just kept looking around at each other and at the aides and guards, waiting for it to happen again.

Zachary prodded the tender tissue around his eye where Angel had hit him, already swelling up.

"Are you alright, sir?" one of the security guards asked. "I'm not sure who gave you permission to be in here, but you have to be aware that some of the residents can be violent."

"Yes, I was aware of that," Zachary said. Though he had to admit, he hadn't foreseen being attacked himself. It drove home the message that Mira and Dr. Abato and others had been trying to convey to him; that living with a violent, unpredictable teen or adult was an untenable situation. Even in an institution like Summit, equipped with intensive therapy, aversives, one-on-one aides, and security staff couldn't guarantee safety.

No one had suggested Quentin might have been killed by another inmate. But if the majority of the doors in his unit were not kept locked, then any of the other residents in the unit could have sneaked into his room during the night and strangled him.

The one hole in that scenario was lack of motive. But did the residents need the same kind of motive as neurotypicals? Hadn't Angel just attacked Zachary out of the blue for no discernible reason?

Maybe one of them had a beef with Quentin, or maybe they were just acting out of impulse, confusion, or an effort to communicate something.

If the staff knew or suspected that Quentin had been killed by another resident, would they cover it up? Zachary had to think that they would. They were already under scrutiny for their use of aversives and a resident killing another would indicate that their program wasn't quite as effective at quelling violence as Dr. Abato had claimed. It wouldn't be hard to convert a third-party strangulation to a suicide. The staff had removed the blanket that had been wrapped around Quentin's neck, so there was little that could be concluded from the scene. If there had been evidence that it had been another resident, it could have been removed.

"Mr. Goldman!"

Zachary turned around to see Dr. Abato approaching. "I did ask you to stay and wait for me." Abato looked around. "What's been going on here?"

One of the guards filled him in on the attack by Angel. Dr. Abato shook his head, but his expression was smug.

"Let's get you some ice for that," he suggested, and indicated the direction he and Zachary should walk. "I'm afraid you've just had a crash course in what we deal with every day here. I did my best to warn you, to explain the type of problems we are dealing with, but that's not quite the same as when it walks up and hits you in the face." He chuckled at his own turn of phrase. "Quite literally, in some cases. Like our residents, you need to learn to follow instructions. This wouldn't have happened if you stayed put."

"It just would have happened to someone else," Zachary argued. "Angel was upset because he was shocked by mistake. And the girl who they meant to shock, her device malfunctioned, and it kept shocking her. She had electrical burns. I had to help get them off of her…"

"There will always be equipment malfunctions," Abato sighed. "As I'm sure anyone who uses computers knows well. She'll be taken care of, and she'll be just fine. If it helps, you should know that the pain sensation is quite different for people with autism than it is for you or me. You'd be amazed at some of the injuries I have seen where the resident doesn't even seem to know that they are hurt. They don't have the same connection to their body as we do. So even though this was a terrible thing to happen to her, she's probably already forgotten all about it."

"Her skin was burned and blistered!"

"As I say, the severity of the injury really doesn't seem to have an impact. Sometimes a resident goes quiet, and you really don't know what the problem is, because they don't act sick or hurt. Then you do an exam and find that they have a broken bone or ruptured appendix and never tried to tell anyone."

Zachary tried to square this with what he had seen in his few visits to

Summit. The electric shocks certainly seemed to cause pain. The kids that he had seen shocked reacted immediately, crying out, going rigid, even falling to the floor. They didn't look like unfeeling zombies.

But the girl *had* initially laughed when she was shocked. Abato had suggested Angel might be seeking the shocks rather than avoiding them.

And Lovaas… what had Lovaas said? He had said something along the lines of some children being rewarded by negativity and punishment, so that the parent or therapist had to be very angry and hard on them to get the proper results, and that weeks or months of such intense therapy could be taxing on the parent. *Poor parents, having to be so hard on their kids.* Zachary shook his head, thinking about the arrogance of such a statement.

"Angel is one of those that I have concerns about," Dr. Abato said, though Zachary hadn't asked. "You saw how difficult it is to get his compliance, even with multiple shocks. We have a little engineering company that helps us to work out problems with our electronics, and they're working on a device that is more powerful that our little units. More along the lines of the stun belts they use for prisoners when they go to courts or have disciplinary problems. I am trying to get authorization to introduce them into our program for problem students like Angel. But so far," he gave a little shrug, "no luck getting the necessary approvals."

Zachary said nothing. Abato gave a shrug.

"But parents will have their way. Sooner or later, the bureaucrats in their little glass towers will be forced to see the reality of the situation. That these kids need stronger measures. That they're not the same as we are. They are physiologically different. If we're going to achieve any progress with them, we need to be able to do whatever it takes. However unpalatable that might be."

Zachary stared down at his feet as he walked down the hall with the man who had to be the biggest lunatic in the asylum. "It seems like the devices they have on now do enough damage. I can't imagine anyone approving something more powerful."

"But that's just the point, don't you see? The damage occurs when you have to keep shocking repeatedly. Like Trina's ESD malfunctioning. You don't get damage from one shock. If you can give just one shock; one shock that is enough to get their attention and stop them from harmful behavior, then you don't have to shock them again. They learn the first time. Do you know how much faster it is to train a dog with a shock collar? There's no comparison! Why would anyone train any other way? If you can give one shock and get compliance, it changes the child's life. It changes *everyone's* lives."

They arrived in a first aid room, and Abato went to a mini-fridge and retrieved an ice pack for Zachary. "There, that should help."

Zachary put it over his face. The cool pack made his throbbing face feel a hundred times better.

"You said this is one of the only facilities like this in the country," he said.

"Yes." Dr. Abato drew himself up proudly. "That's right."

"Where do all of the other kids go?"

Abato shook his head. "Excuse me... what?"

"All of the other kids with autism. Kids who are violent like Quentin or Angel. Or who are adults now, not teenagers. Where do they all go? They can't all come here."

"Well, no!" Abato laughed. "I think we'd have to expand quite a bit for that. Where do they go...? They go to institutions, ninety-nine percent of the time. Because family members don't want them in their homes. They can't live independently, and they can't live with their families. It's too dangerous. So an institution. Like Summit, but not like Summit. Because they don't have a progressive program like ours, so they can't actually break kids of violence."

Zachary nodded. Abato motioned to a couple of tubular chairs clustered around a break room table and they both sat down.

"Because they are violent, they have to be kept in isolation. There are no classes, no reward rooms, no socialization. A locked cell that they only see the outside of if they need to go see the doctor. Sometimes restraints to keep them from hurting themselves. Or, since the family tend to prefer it, put them on medications that reduce violent behaviors. Antipsychotics, anti-anxiety pills, sedatives. They drug them into a stupor, so they can't do anything. They can't form a thought. They can't carry through an action. They probably can't stand up or sit down without assistance. Kids like Quentin and Angel become zombies. Their parents don't like it. They don't like to lose their kids. So they pull them from those places and try to get them in here."

"There isn't anything in between?"

"Where is the in-between? We use ABA to train them to behave. Others use physical or chemical restraints to keep them from harming themselves or others. There is no middle ground, no other way to overcome the violent behaviors."

"It just seems like… there are so many people with autism or other disorders… they're not all in institutions."

"Ones that are that severe are. You can't keep a child like that home." Abato wiped a hand over his face, frowning. "Though, there is one other option some parents take."

Zachary didn't like the sound of that or Abato's foreboding expression. He knew that Abato, with his flair for the dramatic, was waiting for Zachary to ask what it was. He hated to give him the satisfaction, but Abato was waiting.

"What?" Zachary finally prompted.

"You hear about it in the news more and more," Abato drew out the tension. "I don't know whether it is happening more, or if we are just hearing more of it due to modern communication systems. But more and more, you hear about parents who are killing their children. Especially children disabled by autism."

Zachary had known he would regret asking.

"Maybe it is something that used to be kept under wraps," Abato said. "Socially acceptable euthanasia. A pillow over their face while they sleep. Poison. Carbon monoxide. Throwing them off of a bridge. Parents are very creative. When they get to the end of their ropes, when there are no more services, no one else to help, they are burdened with a child who will drag them down for the rest of their lives…"

"You sound like you sympathize with them," Zachary snapped. Acid burned in his chest. How could anyone think that there was any excuse?

"Of course I do. I see them every day, these parents who have been ground down and crushed by year after year of taking care of a child—or children—who are emotional sinkholes. They pour everything into them and get nothing back. Or maybe their reward is a black eye," Abato nodded at Zachary's face. "Or a broken arm. Or a ruptured kidney. Do I think it's right to kill your child? Of course not! My whole job—my whole life—is about helping these children. And their families. I will do whatever it takes to save every child I can from being drugged into a stupor, restrained twenty-three hours a day, or killed by the people who are supposed to be protecting them."

Zachary wished he could tell himself that Abato was exaggerating. That children like Angel and Quentin were not being consigned to either live in a hellhole or be killed by their caregivers. But he knew it was true. Every time he saw such a story in the news, his first reaction was a sense of relief that his mother had made the choice to break up the family and put the children into foster care rather than killing them. He'd read, with horrified fascination, the stories of mothers who drowned their children one at a time in the bathtub. Or stabbed them in their beds. Or drove them into the lake. Everyone nodded gravely and commented about what a hard row she'd had to hoe. Too many children. Children with handicaps or special needs. Children who were violent and too big to handle any longer.

Zachary's mother had lived it. Six children too close together in age. An abusive marriage. Grinding poverty. No relatives to help. Social programs that had already been tapped out. Then the final straw... the house burning down. Being left with no home and no possessions.

She could have killed them, just like those other mothers who had chosen family annihilation. Many of them had not faced as many challenges as she had. But for some reason, she hadn't. She'd given up on them, rejected them, but she hadn't killed them.

Zachary's first reaction was always relief and a sense of gratitude that she hadn't.

But often, the feeling was followed by a sense of hopelessness. Looking back over his life and all of the trauma and suffering that had followed her choice. Had she been weak to choose to leave them to someone else to take care of instead of dispatching them like a litter of unwanted kittens? His pain and suffering could have ended three decades earlier, instead of being in the position he was in; alone, beaten down, hopeless, and once again homeless.

Dr. Abato nodded gravely. "We have to put a stop to it, Mr. Goldman. I have to save as many of these children as I can, by whatever means I can devise. To hell with rules and regulations. Somebody has to do something for them."

His eyes were dark as burning coals, a lone voice crying out in the wilderness.

15

He was headed back to his car when he saw the woman standing a few feet outside the doors, a cigarette between her fingers. Dark hair pulled into a smooth, sleek ponytail. Young and pretty with perfectly-applied makeup. A common sight. Except for the one detail that Zachary's shutter-quick eyes immediately took in. There was no smoke coming from her cigarette.

He saw the way that her head turned slightly in his direction when he exited the building. He slowed a little, waiting to see whether she was going to confront him, but she didn't. Would she follow him to his car? Had she already planted a bomb or tracking device on his car and stayed to watch the fun?

Zachary measured the distance from the woman not smoking to the protesters. Was she one of them? Camouflaged by her nicotine habit so that she could get right up to the building when security was supposed to be keeping the protesters back fifty feet, at the property line? But she didn't look over at them. Didn't flash them any sign or signal.

Zachary stopped and patted his pockets as if he were looking for smokes of his own. "Do you have another one?" he asked, giving up on finding anything. "I'm trying to give it up by not carrying them with me, but... after this place... I need a hit."

She looked nervous about Zachary talking to her, but she complied, pulling out her own pack of cigarettes and handing one to Zachary.

"You're right," she said cautiously. "It's… quite the place."

She didn't stare at his black eye or ask him what had happened, which suggested she already knew. Zachary held the cigarette she had handed him and didn't light it up or ask her for a light. They both stood there with their unlit cigarettes. Her face started to get pink. She was very attractive. Very young. It was probably her first job out of college.

"Alright!" She blew up, as if he'd been interrogating her. "You caught me. I wasn't out here to smoke, I was out here to get a chance to talk to you."

"Here I am," Zachary said, giving her a weak smile and handing the cigarette back to her. "What did you want to say?"

"Someone said that you're here to investigate Quentin Thatcher's death."

"They would be right."

"You don't believe it was suicide?"

"Suicide is still a possibility," Zachary said. "If you think he could actually form the intent to kill himself. What do you think?"

She put both of the cigarettes back into the pack, which then appeared to be full. He didn't smell stale smoke on her and wondered if she had bought the cigarettes just for the ruse.

"I don't know. I'm no expert in suicide."

"Okay. How well did you know Quentin?"

"I worked with him a few times. Just a few. I didn't know him well."

"And you don't know if he could have killed himself?"

"I suppose he could have. Accidentally or intentionally, I don't know. He was a sensory-seeker."

Zachary rubbed the back of his neck. "What does that mean?"

"A lot of children with autism are thought to feel things differently than… a neurotypical adult. They may be overly sensitive and avoid certain kinds of sensory input. Or they may be less sensitive and seeking more sensory input—banging into walls, stimming, hugging, running, swinging. Just like some normal adults like to bungee-jump and some can't step down from a chair without holding on to it. Most children are a combination of both, seeking some sensations and avoiding others."

"So Quentin was a sensory-seeker. He wanted more input."

"Right. With a blanket wrapped around his throat, twisted up tight so that it strangled him... he could have just been seeking deep pressure. He might not have known that it could harm him until it was too late, and he couldn't get it unwound again."

"It's possible. The blanket had already been removed from the body when the police got here, so there's no way to analyze the way it had been twisted. The police say he could have done it to himself."

She nodded and didn't add anything. She had frown lines between her brows. Lots of stress indicators.

"What's your name?"

"Oh. Clarissa. Clarissa Hill. I'm an aide here. I help with therapy sessions, provide one-on-one support..."

"Right. And sometimes you supported Quentin."

"Yes."

"Shocked him?"

Her lips squeezed tightly shut.

"That's how it's done here, isn't it?" Zachary asked. "I'm not going to pretend I don't know what's going on."

"Yes," she admitted. "That's how it's done here. So yes, I have shocked Quentin. And other kids that I have been in charge of. It's part of the job."

Zachary nodded. Her face was white, and she didn't know how to deal with Zachary just waiting to be told whatever it was she wanted to tell him. She had probably anticipated that he would interrogate her. Ask her a lot of questions. And she would have to hold back and give him just the few bits of information she wanted him to have. But Zachary didn't do that. He just waited. He watched a bird flying overhead, waiting for her to sort out her thoughts.

"How do you feel about your job?"

"I love it. I love helping people. Helping these kids to do things their parents were told they would never be able to do."

But...

Zachary waited for it.

Clarissa's face crumpled. "I hate it. I hate the shocks and other aversives. I hate not being able to communicate with my kids because Dr. Abato says they have to use speech and there are no communications boards or sign language, or any other kind of assisted communication allowed. I hate not being able to get down to their level and figure out what their wants and needs are. To get a real look at their personalities. I hate the damage that we are doing."

"If you're helping them to do things that their doctors said they'd never be able to do, then how are you damaging them? Isn't that good?"

"Have you heard what they have to say?" Clarissa gestured toward the protesters. "Have you heard what actual adults with autism have to say?"

Zachary nodded. "I have."

"If what we are doing is actually traumatizing them and not helping them to become better people, then what are we doing here? Why cause them pain if we're not making them any better?"

"I believe you." The guilt in her eyes seemed genuine. "I wonder, though, if there are some people who get something out of hurting them."

"Sadists?" Clarissa shifted her feet, looking toward the big double-doors of the building that they had exited. She cleared her throat. "I guess there are anywhere, aren't there? Statistically, there are bound to be a few."

Zachary wasn't looking for statistics. He had already seen for himself. He had already seen aides who enjoyed shocking students. If Clarissa had been working there for weeks or months, or even years, she would know beyond a doubt that some of the men—statistically it was more often men —who held the remotes in their hands were enjoying inflicting pain.

"Okay," Clarissa admitted. "Yeah, there are a few of those. It does go on."

"And were any of them working with Quentin?"

She opened her mouth to answer, then thought about it more deeply. "I don't know. I'm just... not sure."

"Could someone on Quentin's unit, either a staff member or another resident, have strangled him?"

"Quentin was strong. Smothering or strangling someone takes a lot of strength. They fight back hard."

That gave Zachary pause. "Yes," he agreed.

"I don't know... I guess someone else could have done it. But there's not any evidence of it, is there? And what motive would anyone have?"

"What motive do you think they could have?" Zachary bounced the question back at her.

She was silent for a moment. "Can we walk to your car or something? I didn't plan on talking here by the doors where anyone could walk by and see us together."

Zachary nodded, and they started a slow wander toward the parking lot.

"A cover-up," Clarissa started to list possible motives. "Sadism. If it was another resident, or Quentin himself, it could be accidental. Even... some twisted kind of mercy killing. To release him from his troubles."

"Did Quentin have a lot of troubles?"

"Sure. Of course. He was violent, unpredictable. He didn't get to see his family much, and when he did, he got more upset. More angry. Maybe someone... just wanted to put an end to the pain."

It was territory that Zachary hadn't explored, but it was possible.

As they made their way past the protesters, Zachary saw Margaret Beacher making her way toward them. He didn't know whether to warn Clarissa there might be trouble, or let it just play out and see what happened. He ended up saying nothing.

"Who's your *friend*, Zachary?" Margaret asked, looking Clarissa over.

Clarissa looked at Zachary anxiously.

"Clarissa is one of the aides here," he told Margaret evenly. "She helped with Quentin. So she had some things she wanted to tell me."

"Do you people know what you're doing in there?" Margaret demanded, wheeling on Clarissa.

Clarissa was not quick to answer. "Yes," she said eventually, "and I know you don't like it."

"*Don't like it.*" Margaret gave a mocking laugh. "That's what you call an understatement." She looked at the other protesters for their reactions. There were a few jeers and catcalls, but nothing too threatening. "What you do in there, your *therapy*, it ruined my life."

"What am I supposed to do? Quit? I'm helping people." Clarissa's voice was sharp, defensive.

"What you do doesn't help. It causes damage. Irreparable damage."

Clarissa took a deep breath, but ended up saying nothing. What could she say? She'd already admitted to Zachary that she knew they were causing harm.

"You should get out of there," Margaret said. "You should get out of there, and get out of ABA, and start treating autistic people with decency and respect."

Clarissa looked close to tears. "I need that job. And those kids need me. I love my kids."

"You love them? If you loved them, you wouldn't hurt them."

"But I do love them. And I want to help them. And I need to do the therapy that they're there for. If I don't do it, someone else will." She glanced at Zachary. "Maybe someone who *does* want to hurt them."

"You'll hurt them so someone else doesn't? What kind of lame excuse is that? Somebody is going to do it, so it might as well be you?"

Clarissa gave a helpless shrug. "Isn't it better if it's someone who loves them? Who wants the best for them?"

"What hurts more, being brutalized by someone who hates you, or someone who loves you?" Margaret shook her head. "Someone who *pretends* to love you."

Tears brimmed over Clarissa's eyes. "You don't know what it's like in there." Her voice was cracked and shaky. "You don't know what it's like to have to be there every day. I'm there because I want to help. I want to make a difference! I haven't slept through the night since Quentin died. A few hours here, a few hours there... but whenever I do, I dream about Quentin. The... the hopelessness in his eyes... he hated it here. He wanted to go home."

"Of course he did," Margaret agreed. "Don't you? At the end of the day, don't you just want to go home, where it's comfortable and safe?"

"After two years, I didn't even think he'd remember home. Any home-sickness he had initially should have disappeared... it had been two years."

"He was autistic, not amnesiac. Why wouldn't he remember home?"

"Dr. Abato said they wouldn't. That they regarded Summit as their home. After a few weeks, they wouldn't remember anywhere else."

"Why wouldn't they?" Margaret challenged. "They were getting skin shocks, not ECT. Not lobotomies."

Clarissa swallowed hard and scrubbed at her eyes, smearing her mascara. "Do you know we're not even allowed to talk to each other?" she asked. "Under our employment agreements, we're not allowed to talk to media or anyone about the institution's protocol. And we're not even allowed to talk to each other. No personal discussions, even on breaks. No discussions of the cases or therapies except in case review meetings. The only conversations we can have are to communicate with each other during therapy or a follow-up report. Anything else is personal discussion and we're not allowed."

Zachary blinked at this. He'd never heard of such a policy before. He could understand that Summit didn't want their employees gossiping or debating the merits of skin shocks or going to the media. But to completely ban all personal discussion seemed cruel and dictatorial, seriously over-reaching.

Of course, Clarissa could be telling a story. Those tears could be fake. They had come on disconcertingly fast. She could be trying to manipulate him.

"You have to talk," Margaret said. "You can't listen to them. You can't let them control you like that. How do you think the Nazis convinced people to commit the atrocities that they did? Do you think all of the soldiers and citizens who helped them were horrible people? They were doing what they were told. They were convinced that what they were doing was right and necessary. They listened to what they were told."

Clarissa looked back over her shoulder at the building. "They can still see me here," she said. "We need to get out of sight."

Margaret waved her concerns away with one hand. "As far as they're concerned, I'm blocking you and you're just trying to get past me. Terrible how the police can't do anything about the protesters setting up camp here day after day."

Clarissa sniffled and gave a weak smile. She rubbed her forehead. If she'd been sleeping that little, she probably had a hell of a headache.

"'The only thing necessary for the triumph of evil is for good men to do nothing,'" Margaret quoted. "If you stand by in silence, because they told you not to talk, and you keep shocking defenseless children and taking away their rights to make choices and be who they are because you're afraid someone else will do worse damage, then you *are* the problem. If you're not fighting against the evil people who are pushing these therapies, you are as guilty as they are."

"They aren't evil," Clarissa protested. "They want to help the children. Their parents want them to be there. They know all about the aversive therapy. They have to sign off on it. And the parents know what is best for their kids—"

"Their parents have been told it's the best thing. They've been given statistics. They've been told horror stories. They've been shown videos of children who have miraculously recovered and look normal. And they want that for their children. They've been told that whatever the cost, it's worth it to have children who are indistinguishable from their peers. Whose brains have been wiped and reprogrammed to always give the right response. All of their uniqueness and individuality stripped away. Because the only way for an autistic person to succeed is by not acting autistic."

Clarissa opened her mouth to argue the point, but she didn't have the oily smoothness of Dr. Abato. She'd been indoctrinated just like those parents had been, but the arguments didn't come naturally to her lips She looked at Zachary, as if he might jump in and tell her why it was okay.

"They're even telling you the same lies as the Nazis," Margaret said. "That autistic people are subhuman. No more than animals that can be trained with a system of pain and rewards."

"I know they're not animals."

"Do you believe that the only way to teach autistic children is with ABA?"

Clarissa's reluctance was almost comical. "I don't know," she said finally. "It's the standard for treating autism, isn't it? I suppose there might be other therapies, but I've only been trained in ABA. That's what *everyone* uses, not just Summit." She rubbed her forehead again. Zachary could see the lines of fatigue not fully disguised by her makeup. "Using ABA without aversives may not be as effective, but lots of people are doing it, so it must have some efficacy."

"What about *no* therapy?" Margaret suggested.

"No therapy?" Clarissa repeated stupidly. "How could you treat children with autism without therapy?"

"Maybe they don't need to be treated at all. Maybe just because our brains are different, that doesn't mean that we are defective. That we need to be reprogrammed somehow."

"But these children aren't like you. They can't communicate. They have no life skills, no social skills. Some like Quentin are violent."

"Why?"

"What?"

"*Why* are they violent?"

"Why?" Clarissa shook her head in confusion. "Because they get frustrated. They can't communicate. They have sensory overload. Sometimes because they are hurt or ill… I don't know."

"And which of those things do electric shocks fix?"

"It… stops them."

"So you don't care about fixing the underlying problems. Just stopping certain behaviors."

"We're trying to teach them to communicate properly. So that they can tell us what's wrong."

Zachary watched the two of them argue back and forth, fascinated to hear the two different viewpoints explored.

"What is 'communicating properly'?" Margaret asked. "You mean communicating the same way that you do."

"Well... yes. The way *everyone* does."

"Not everyone, or there wouldn't be anyone to teach. Why not try to figure out what communication method works for them? If they have trouble learning yours, why don't you learn theirs? Why is speech the ultimate solution?"

Clarissa shook her head, looking at the group of protesters. "I wish we were allowed to use ASL or PECS, but Dr. Abato is right... You speak. That's how you get along in the world. It's just... so much harder if you can't use speech to communicate. People aren't going to take the time to figure out what you are trying to communicate. But if we can teach them to talk like everyone else..."

"Do you see these signs?"

Clarissa looked at the various signs people were holding. There were various words and phrases about getting Summit shut down. There were pictures of Quentin. Lightning bolt symbols. And various other combinations of pictures and words.

"Yes."

"Do you understand them?"

"Yes, of course."

"But they are not speech."

"No... but in a way... I mean, they represent speech. It's just another medium."

Margaret arched her eyebrows. "Oh. I see."

Clarissa turned away from Margaret, her face red and eyes still teary. She grasped Zachary's arm. "I wanted to talk to you," she said. "I wanted to help you. I feel bad about Quentin. I want his mom to know... that we loved him here." She squeezed Zachary's arm more tightly. "Everything we did was to help him. We're devastated by what happened."

Margaret opened her mouth. Zachary shook his head at her sharply. The time for arguing methodologies was past. He needed to find out what Clarissa knew. To tease out details that she didn't realize were important.

"I know you cared about Quentin," Zachary said in a low voice, as soothing as he could manage. "What happened was tragic and unexpected, so of course you're knocked off your feet about it. Do you mind talking to me about it?"

"No, of course not." Clarissa shot another look toward Margaret. "Just... can we just talk somewhere private? Not because I know any secrets or anything important to your investigation. I just... would like to be alone for this."

"Sure. I don't know the area. We could check the GPS to see what's close. Or is there somewhere you and your coworkers go...?"

"No. We're not allowed to... fraternize..."

"Where do you go?" Zachary asked Margaret. "You must know all of the places nearby."

"There's a diner two blocks down," Margaret pointed the direction they should go. "Blue and white striped awning. They have good grilled cheese sandwiches."

"Okay." Zachary looked at Clarissa. "You want to walk or take my car?"

"Let's walk."

He nodded. The started down the sidewalk toward the diner. The road was fairly straight, and they could see the striped awning before they got to the end of the first block.

"You haven't been sleeping?" Zachary asked.

"No. Not for long. Every night I think it will be tonight, that my body is so tired it has to give in. And I end up tossing and turning or sitting up... until my eyes finally close and I start dreaming. But I just keep dreaming about Quentin. And I wake up and I'm so sad for him. I know I shouldn't be, he's gone on to a better place, and all that. And I really do believe that. But I still feel so sad, so guilty."

"Of course. That's a totally natural reaction. I imagine the sleeplessness will wear off... like you say, your body will take over and insist that you sleep."

Though that had never been a workable strategy for Zachary. He needed something to help him sleep. He didn't like having to take meds to sleep, so he would go as long as he could without, but eventually he would break down and take something so that he could shut down his brain and get a few hours of unbroken sleep.

"I don't know," Clarissa said. "It started before Quentin died. It's been going on for some time now…"

"When did it start?"

"I'm not sure exactly… a few weeks… a month or two… things just started falling apart in my life. I stopped being able to sleep. Started having nightmares. Couldn't focus during the day. I feel like… like something bad is going to happen. All the time. But I don't know what."

They walked for a minute in silence. Reaching the diner, they found a seat, and both ordered the grilled cheese sandwich, then looked at each other like an awkward first date.

"What were your nightmares about before Quentin died?"

"Not all that different… the kids at Summit. Sometimes Quentin, sometimes one of the others. Dreams that they were hurt or dying, and no one would help me. Or dreaming that…" She tapped on the Formica table with a long, polished fingernail, "… you're going to think it's stupid."

"No. I won't. I have some doozies myself."

"Sometimes that I am a resident there. That I am the one with autism. Or that I don't have autism or anything wrong with me, and I am still locked up there and can't get out or do anything but sit in my room or in therapy. It was really… terrifying. I know that's silly. It wasn't that there was anything bad happening to me, just that… I didn't have any control over my life. No control over anything."

"Yeah. That would be pretty frightening."

And it was the truth of the situation for every one of those kids. If they did well, they could earn their big rewards. They could go to the fancy reward rooms and play video games, or crawl in the ball pit, or pick one of the quieter rooms. And that was the highlight of their lives. The rest of the time, they had no choice over where they could be, what they could do, no choices at all.

There were residents without autism there too. Youths who were too violent, runaways, who couldn't fit in with families or whatever other living situations they had been in. Kids like Zachary had been. He couldn't imagine being stuck in a more terrifying place than Summit. Things had been bad enough at Bonnie Brown and some of the other institutions or homes he had been in. But at least at Bonnie Brown, they didn't give him electrical shocks. He'd been treated roughly. Had guards who figured it was okay to tune him up if he were misbehaving. But the thought of being wired like the residents at Summit, where anyone who had authority over him could punish him at any time, even from across the room, was daunting.

He'd seen Angel writhing on the floor. Trina, with her skin cooking under the electrodes. All of it court approved. Their parents signed off. The courts signed off. Everybody said it was perfectly okay to punish children and adults who had been judged incapable of controlling their own behavior. How was that fair?

"Mr. Goldman?"

Zachary roused himself and focused in on Clarissa, who was looking at him with questions in her eyes.

"Sorry. Did you ask me something?"

"No... just... I thought you were going to say something else, and then you kind of... drifted off."

Zachary placed both of his palms on the table, trying to feel the cool, flat surface, to ground himself in the present with the sensations around him. It was a bright, friendly place. A sort of a fifties or sixties diner theme. Comfortable home cooking. He could smell their grilled cheese sandwiches on the grill; the waitress would be bringing them to the table soon.

"Do you know if anyone else you work with is having the same kind of symptoms?" he asked. "Sleeplessness, anxiety, depression...?"

"Like I said, we aren't allowed to associate with each other. We're not supposed to talk outside of the therapy sessions, only to sort out logistics, get reports filed, that kind of thing."

Zachary waited. There were rules, and then there was what really happened when there were no snitches around to report the rule-breaking.

"I guess... yes, there are a lot of others who complain about having trouble sleeping. Or who drink too much. Or who take a lot of sick days. It's kind of a running joke, taking all of your sick days in the first three months of the year... turnover is pretty brutal, we're always having to train new staff. Dr. Abato likes to get people right out of school, when they haven't already been trained in other methods. So that therapy sessions don't get 'contaminated' with someone else's program or ideas."

"A lot of people quit? Or are fired?"

"I think more quit than are fired. Even though the rules are strict, there aren't a lot of people breaking them flagrantly enough to be fired. Everybody wants to keep their jobs. Wants to do the best they can to help these kids. They need us."

"Everybody talks about kids," Zachary observed. "But a lot of the residents are adults, aren't they? And not all just eighteen or nineteen."

"Oh, I know. But that's how we think of them. As our kids. Even if they're older than us. Because they're like children. They need us to look after them. To care for them."

"You get pretty attached to them."

"Yes. We're everything they've got. It's like a parent-child relationship. And I guess that's how we see it, even if they are older. A lot of the really old residents aren't doing any therapy. They've advanced as far as they can, and they're just… living out their lives. So I didn't really work much in those units. Now and then to cover when they were understaffed. But there's not a lot to do, other than making sure they are fed and washed."

"What do they do with their time? Do they just sit around all day?"

"It depends on their level of functioning and what their interests are. Some do puzzles or have a hobby. Something that their families keep them supplied with. As long as they don't have anything that can be used as a weapon, Summit is pretty open to whatever pastimes they choose."

"What did you think of Quentin?"

She couldn't hide the fact that she was startled by his sudden change of direction. But the waitress chose that moment to bring them their plates, so Clarissa had time to change gears and think about her answer.

"I don't know… in what way? He wasn't a happy boy. He was homesick, even after two years. Signed for his mom a lot." She tapped her cheek with her forefinger. "And you know that he came to Summit because he was violent."

"But the shocks took care of that."

She gave a little shrug. "They seemed to, mostly," she admitted. "I hate the ESDs, but they do seem to work."

"Lovaas, the guy who wrote about ABA?"

"Yeah…?"

"Did you know that he recanted later? That he said that shocks didn't work in the long term. The children became inured to them over time. And he said what they had learned in ABA didn't generalize over other environments." Zachary paused. "Is that the right word? Generalize?"

"Yes," Clarissa agreed faintly.

"Dr. Abato thinks the solution to getting used to the pain is just to increase the shocks. Increase the pain level to get control over them again."

Clarissa frowned as she took a bite of her sandwich. Zachary nibbled at his own, but had no appetite. It was perfectly done. Just crispy enough. The cheese melty, the butter salty, but he couldn't eat it.

"But he can't do that," Clarissa said. "There's already controversy over whether the phase-two ESD we are using right now is acceptable. It works for most of the kids, and the court won't rule against us using it because the parents say they have nowhere else to go. But another device? A stronger one?"

"The kind they use to control adult prisoners," Zachary informed her. "That's what he said. And I guess if they're already in use in other circumstances, maybe it won't be impossible to get it approved."

"I don't think they could ever get it approved for use with our kids."

"Do you want to leave Summit?" Zachary asked after a lengthy pause in the conversation.

"I do... and I don't... I want to help children, and it's a good job with good pay and benefits. But it's eating me up. I can't sleep. I can't think. It's not making me happy." She pushed around the remaining corner of her first half-sandwich. "It didn't make Quentin happy."

"I think you need help."

"Me? Help with what?"

"Someone to talk to about your symptoms. You should talk to a psychologist. A therapist. Someone."

"It's nothing. It's just stress. Being upset over Quentin's death."

"I don't think so. I think it's more like PTSD. And you said it started before Quentin died."

She picked up the bottle of Heinz ketchup on the table and spilled a pool onto her plate. "This better be real Heinz, and not just a Heinz bottle refilled with generic stuff." She dabbled the second triangle of her sandwich in the ketchup and took a bite. Since she didn't complain about it being generic, Zachary assumed that she found it acceptable. She pretended for a couple of minutes to be completely engrossed in the meal, then finally looked up at him again.

"PTSD?" she repeated. "How could it be? PTSD is for war veterans. People who have been through traumatic events. Not ABA therapists!" She made a wide shrug.

"I don't know. I know about PTSD... but not all of the kinds of events that can cause it. But what you're describing... it sure sounds like PTSD to me."

"I don't get flashbacks," she said, a slightly derisive note in her voice. "What would I flash back to? A therapy session? They can be pretty raw, but I don't think it counts as a war."

Or war crimes.

Zachary wasn't so sure. What he had seen that day had been pretty traumatic to him. And Clarissa was a young girl, seeing that and worse every day for months. After a few hours of seeing the shocks used, Zachary had been ready to curl up in a ball and shut the rest of the world out. He knew that Angel and Trina would both be haunting his restless dreams along with Quentin. And Zachary was tougher and more experienced than Clarissa.

"I still think you should talk to someone," he said. "Get some help. And maybe a prescription to help you sleep."

16

I have a question," Zachary said suddenly. He was still poking at his barely-touched sandwich, while Clarissa was nearly done with hers. The afternoon sun shone through the diner window.

"What is it?" She looked anxious about what he might ask her. And he could ask her a lot of uncomfortable things. But most of them didn't need asking, unless he was trying to make her feel worse than she already did.

"No, it's nothing to be concerned about. Just… some of the logistics of the shock devices they're using at Summit."

"Um… okay. What about them?"

"They're bulky, with the backpacks, and pretty complex with all of the wires and electrodes… how many?"

"Six."

"Six electrodes that have to be attached. The residents just let you put them on every day? Or put them on themselves? How does that work?"

"Kids that are pretty compliant, it's not a problem. Some of the more reactive patients, it can be difficult. With the worst cases… they keep them on at all times. You always have at least one electrode attached, so then you can… shock them… if they are fighting against having the others attached. Each electrode is like a cattle prod or stun gun, with the positive and negative poles close together, so each one operates independently."

"And they keep them on all the time? How? When they are sleeping?"

"Yes. When they're sleeping. I don't imagine it's too comfortable sleeping with the backpack on, but they get used to it."

Zachary couldn't imagine trying to sleep with such a device attached. From what he understood, children with autism often had sleep issues. Those would be magnified a hundred times by having to sleep with ten pounds of batteries in a backpack and six electrodes attached to their bodies.

"What about hygiene? Do they bathe? Shower?"

"Shower," Clarissa confirmed. "They have to keep one arm electrode attached and hold that arm out of the water."

Zachary closed his eyes to picture it. "How do they do that?"

"Sometimes they need help. It is pretty hard to wash with one arm out of the shower. Or for them to understand why they need to. Some of them are dyspraxic—not very well-coordinated."

"And by help, you mean… one person holding on to their arm to keep it out of the water, and maybe another one doing the washing?"

Clarissa stared off into space. Zachary watched her curiously. In spite of the fact that he'd dealt with his own PTSD for thirty years, he'd never watched someone else having a flashback. He waited for her to return to herself.

Clarissa looked back at him, blinking and looking like she was just coming out of a fog.

"What?"

"You don't have flashbacks?" Zachary asked.

"No."

"What was that? Where did you just go?"

"Nowhere. I was just thinking about something else. Daydreaming."

"Who was in the shower? Who were you remembering?"

Clarissa shook her head. "They're so defenseless. And with the electrodes… to never be free of them… it's just so sad."

"Yes." Zachary finally pushed his unfinished sandwich away from himself. "It is."

Kenzie didn't have time to get together for supper. Things had been busy at the medical examiner's office and she had other evening commitments. She didn't tell Zachary what those commitments were and, after dancing around the issue and not being able to get to a satisfactory answer, Zachary forced himself to let it go. If he acted like a jealous boyfriend, demanding to know where she was going and who she was seeing, they would never be able to move their relationship forward. He'd lose the friendship and the resource that she was to him.

But she did agree to a phone call while she was on break, eating a vending-machine dinner at her desk. So he uploaded the information he wanted her to look at and waited for her call.

When the phone rang, Zachary had been trying to calm himself with a game of solitaire, and nearly launched the phone across the room in his surprise. He tapped the green button to answer and put it to his ear.

"Kenzie? Hi."

"Hi, Zachary. I don't have much time, like I said, but I've got a few minutes for you."

"I want to go over the medical examiner's report again."

"I see that. Is something bothering you?"

"No, just... now that I've been there, and seen how they operate, I want to review it again, see if I can pick up anything else."

"Okay. What first?"

"His mother said that one of the things that he did when he was anxious was picking his skin."

Kenzie made a noise of acknowledgment. "Yes... I can see that. Pretty obvious from the photos. We discussed it the first time."

"I know. So I didn't look at his skin very carefully to begin with. I figured all of the scabs and scars were from him picking at his skin."

"Uh-huh."

"But now I'm wondering if any of the damage was done by the electrodes."

"What electrodes?"

"From their skin shock therapy. It's one of the aversives that they use. Their preferred one, so that they can give the same punishment consistently every time."

"Uh... okay. And you think they might have caused some damage to the dermis?"

"I saw a girl today who was burned by a malfunctioning unit. Blisters. Second degree electrical burns. So I wanted to know if any of Quentin's injuries might have been burns, or started as burns and he picked them as they scabbed. Would you be able to tell that?"

"From these photos? Probably not. Where would the electrodes have been located?"

Zachary described the locations of the arm and leg electrodes. "And apparently two on the torso, but I'm not sure of the positioning. I couldn't see those ones."

Kenzie hummed as she looked through the pictures on her screen. They hadn't done any really close shots of the skin on his arms and legs, where he had picked at his skin. But they were good quality digital photos and could maybe be enlarged enough that Kenzie could see the details she needed.

"I really couldn't say one way or the other," Kenzie said. "The best spots to look at are his torso, where he couldn't pick his skin as easily through his clothes. Mostly, he picked at his arms and a little on his legs. There are a couple of places on his stomach and back where I could be looking at burns from the electrodes. But it's pretty hard to tell from the photos."

"So, maybe."

"Sorry I couldn't be more of a help. What else?"

"The cause of death was strangulation."

"Right."

"What could they tell from the bruises on his throat? On TV, they can always tell what caused the bruises. Chain links in a ligature, hand size in a manual strangulation, they can always tell."

Kenzie snorted. "I gather you've already guessed that isn't always the case."

"I was hoping that a closer examination of the bruises might give us some more information."

There was silence while Kenzie examined the report. "There are probably more photos available than are in the medical examiner's report, but from these, and the narrative description, no. Can't tell much. It was not a narrow ligature like a belt or a chain. Something wider that left an indistinct bruise."

"But no pattern or impression that might be helpful?"

"No."

"The institution said that he had the ends of his blanket wrapped around his neck and twisted tight."

"That's consistent."

"But could it have been something else? Maybe a chokehold?"

"Yes, an arm across his throat, especially if it was someone wearing sleeves, wouldn't leave a mark that was significantly different than a blanket. Unless the person giving the chokehold had cufflinks or something else distinctive that left a mark."

Zachary pictured the aides and security guards at the institution. Even Dr. Abato didn't wear cufflinks. The white lab coat of a doctor with no embellishments on the sleeves, over a dress shirt. He hadn't noticed the shirt sleeves extending out of the jacket.

"No, not a lot of cufflinks around at Summit. So, nothing useful? You don't see anything the medical examiner might have missed?"

"The report seems to be complete. I'm sorry, I'm not seeing anything else."

"Nothing that you question even a little? Look twice at?"

"The cause of death is obvious. I can't speak for the police investigation, how thorough they were, but no, there's nothing in here that suggests it might have been a third party. No stray fibers, finger marks on his neck, anything like that."

"He'd never attempted suicide before."

"The suicide rate among people with autism is pretty high. It may have been his first attempt, or it may not have been. It might not have been noticed before, if he'd tried the same method and failed. He might just never have tightened it that much before."

Zachary closed his eyes. He tried to avoid the image of Quentin twisting the ends of the blanket tighter and tighter. He could hardly breathe thinking about it. He would never have thought of that method himself. Had someone else suggested it to Quentin? Had someone killed him? Or was he just seeking the comfort of deep pressure and went too far? Maybe Mira would be happier with that suggestion. That it wasn't intentional, and it wasn't murder, it was just an accident. Quentin hadn't understood what he was doing.

"You still there, Zach?"

"Yeah. I'm here."

"You okay?"

He let the question sit for a few minutes, thinking about it. The case was disturbing on many levels. More triggering for him than Declan's case had been. He wanted to help the other kids at Summit, but what could he do? The public already knew what was going on there. They knew the broad strokes, even if they didn't know the details like Zachary did. And they still wanted Summit to remain in operation. Was the public's fear of people who were different that pathological? They kept saying it was because the residents of Summit were violent, but Zachary found them to be eerily like him, or like he was when he was younger. He had not been violent, but they had locked him up repeatedly because he didn't fit anywhere else.

"Zachary? I asked if you're okay."

"Yeah. I guess. It's been a long day, Kenz. And this case is pretty disturbing. I know you don't have time to talk about it right now, but the things I saw over there today… I think you would change your mind about the kind of place Summit is."

"They're very highly acclaimed," Kenzie said. "I know their methods are controversial, but the parents swear by them."

"Yeah," Zachary agreed. "I know. But I think if you saw what I did, you'd think differently. We'll have to talk about it another time."

"Sure. Will you be okay…? Are you alone?"

Zachary rubbed the bridge of his nose and looked around. Sitting in the living room of Bowman's apartment, he hadn't even looked to see if Bowman was home.

"I think so." He got up and went into the kitchen, where Bowman's shift calendar was posted on the fridge like a kid's drawing. "Yeah. Bowman should be back in another hour. I'll be fine."

Waiting for Bowman to get home, Zachary pulled out Margaret Beacher's business card to look up her number, which he hadn't yet put in his phone as he should have. He tapped it in and listened for it to ring. She answered it after just a couple of rings, which probably meant the first ring on her end.

"Hello?"

"Margaret? It's Zachary Goldman."

"Yeah, I know," she agreed. "What do you want?" She didn't say it in a challenging way, but it still disconcerted Zachary a little for her to completely bypass the usual niceties. He was used to having to go through all of the usual 'how are yous.'

"I have some questions for you," he said. "But... they're not about shocks or Summit specifically."

"Okay. Go ahead."

"When you talk about yourself or the residents at Summit, you say 'autistic person.' I thought... the politically correct thing these days was person with autism."

Margaret laughed. "You spend the afternoon talking with the cute aide from Summit, and that's what you call me about? Person-first language?"

"Well..." Zachary was grateful that she couldn't see him blushing. "I just... well, I noticed that at Summit they say it one way, but you say it the other. I didn't know if it was like... black guys calling themselves the n-word, or what."

She chuckled again. "Political correctness says that you can't put autism first, because I am a person first and autistic second. Autism is not my identity, just something I am afflicted with. I hate to tell you, but... it is absolutely who I am. It is a *pervasive* developmental delay. That means it affects every aspect of my life. Political correctness says that you can't put a negative qualifier at the front of a person's identity. You are allowed to say a brilliant woman, rather than a woman who is brilliant. But you aren't supposed to say autistic woman, because autism is negative. It's like disabled or mentally handicapped. You're not supposed to admit that it is what you identify me by. That it's the first thing you see."

"But you want it to be first, because..."

"Because it *is* my identity, like I said. That's my community, my tribe. It's the language I speak. It's how I approach life. It's how I succeed or fail. It may make people uncomfortable, but that's just too bad."

"So is it only okay for someone who has—for someone who is autistic— to say it that way, or do you want everyone to use it?"

"You can do what you feel like. But I'm quite happy to be called autistic. That's what I am."

"Okay. Got it."

"And while you're at it, you can lose the 'non-verbal' designation as well. A lot of our community prefers 'nonspeaking' over 'non-verbal,' but what difference does it really make how we communicate?"

Zachary considered. "Summit makes a big deal about making their kids speak. I don't really know about other communication methods. Do they work?"

"Have you ever written a note? Typed an email? Nodded your head?"

Zachary again felt a flush of embarrassment. "Of course."

"Then you've used alternative methods of communication. Did it work?"

"Yeah."

"Yeah. Sometimes it works better than others. And sometimes nonspeaking communication works better than speaking. Just be open to other methods of communication and don't assume that speaking is the only option."

"Yeah. Makes sense."

"How did your visit with that aide go?"

"I wish I could say she gave me information that would crack the case... but she didn't really have anything new. It was really just more of the same."

Margaret made a noise in her throat. "Why was she so eager to talk to you, then? She was acting like she held the key."

"I think... she just wanted to talk to someone about what it was like to work there."

"You feel sorry for her?" It was more of a statement than a question.

Zachary considered it. "I do, and I don't," he admitted. "I can see that it's not an easy place to work and I wouldn't wish PTSD on anyone. But... she chooses to stay there. She knows what she is doing is harmful to others, but she stays there. Maybe she's not trained to do anything else, but..." He trailed off, uncertain.

"I wouldn't believe anything she says," Margaret said. "I was tortured by people like her for years. She may put on a nice front for visitors, but behind the scenes, when it is just her and a child, she's not that same person."

"Yeah." Zachary's own experience with institutions and caregivers confirmed this, and maybe that's why he was reluctant to feel too sorry for Clarissa despite her apparent issues.

He'd seen too many women and men who were all sweet smiles for the public, social workers, and school teachers, but behind the scenes, it was a whole different story.

When Bowman walked in the door, he froze. He sniffed the air. He looked around and saw the pizza box on the table.

"Any left?"

"It just got here."

"Nice!" Bowman opened the box to see that it was untouched. Zachary walked in from the living room, and they both got out plates and dished up a slice each. "What's the occasion?"

"Well, I figured you'd be tired at the end of your shift…"

Bowman raised an eyebrow at Zachary. As it was the first time that Zachary had ever surprised him with pizza, Zachary supposed he had the right to be skeptical.

"I wanted to pick your brain," Zachary admitted.

Bowman nodded. "Here, or living room?" As the one guy at the station house who knew how to bribe anyone, he had no problem with Zachary buying his time.

Sitting at the kitchen table seemed too formal, too much like a meeting with an agenda. So Zachary motioned to the living room. "We can relax better in here."

Bowman threw another piece of pizza on top of the first, grabbed a beer from the fridge, and followed Zachary into the living room. They ate for a few minutes without saying anything. Mario with gusto, Zachary just picking at his toppings.

"I know Summit Living Center is out of your jurisdiction," Zachary said.

Bowman nodded, chewing a big bite of the pizza. "Way out of it," he agreed.

"But close enough that you might hear some rumors about what goes on there?"

Bowman considered this, looking serious. "I might have heard a few things over the years," he admitted.

"Do the police have a lot of involvement at Summit? They deal with violent residents, so I would assume that sometimes…?"

"No, not that I've heard. I don't think they call the police to deal with problems with their kids. Not like some of the schools and institutions."

Zachary pulled a section of crust off of his pizza slice and worried it. "Some of the places I was at, they would call the police if someone assaulted the staff."

"Yep. Pretty common. But Summit keeps things quiet. They have some kind of therapy to deal with violent students, so they just deal with it themselves. Internally."

"So the police never get called in to arrest someone for being violent."

"No, not that I heard of. And there'd probably be a lot of questions if they ever did, because the police there would know what kind of people they have at that institution. That they probably aren't competent. Don't have the judgment. It's like when we get called to a school to arrest a six-year-old. If you're smart, you ask a lot of questions before you put the cuffs on a little kid. You know it's going to get reviewed. It's going to get to the papers—the internet. So you make damn sure there's cause for an arrest."

"Yeah. I remember when they arrested a girl with autism at one of the places I was at." Zachary paused to swallow and take a deep breath, keeping himself as calm as possible. "The police were pretty ticked off when they brought her back, because no one had told them about her... disability."

"I would have given them crap if it was me, you can bet on that. They should have known better."

Zachary nodded. He took a bite of the pizza, focusing hard on the sweetness and spiciness in an effort not to let himself slide back into the memories of Annie.

"What about other stuff? They've been investigated before, right? And then they had to be called in with Quentin's death. Have you heard anything else? What they've had to go there for? How they felt about it?"

"I can try to hook you up with someone local... I don't know very much. They get calls sometimes. There was one in the news a few months ago, you've probably already seen it online, where a mother was trying to take her child out, said that they wouldn't release him. She said that he'd been abused. The police went in with her, and there was no trouble getting him out. She just had to sign the right papers. When they investigated, the boy—or was it a girl? —was covered with bruises. But the staff said it was all self-inflicted. You know how some of these kids hit themselves or bang their heads when they're upset about something."

Zachary had read something about the incident. The news articles had kept the story very small, had sided with the institution. Made it sound like the mother was crazy or attention-seeking. But having seen Summit, Zachary was a little more inclined to side with the mother and to believe that there had been something going on there. Even if the child was self-harming, chances were, he would have been shocked for it. And maybe the mother had decided she didn't like the shock therapy as much as the other parents did.

"I get the feeling that the director over there is something of an egomaniac," Bowman said. "He likes the publicity that the place gets, even if it's controversial. They've been investigated enough times that nobody really wants to go take another look."

"Yeah." Zachary picked a piece of pepperoni off of his pizza. "He makes a big show out of how open they are. How transparent. But the therapies they use... I just don't know how the authorities can let them keep it up."

"As long as they've got the parents and the courts behind them, they can do pretty much anything they want."

"Do you know the officers who handled the investigation? Of Quentin's death?"

"Haven't heard through the grapevine. Who was it?"

Zachary put his plate aside, happy to be rid of it, and opened his laptop. "Trainer and Benz."

"No, don't know them personally. You concerned that the investigation was mishandled?"

Zachary drummed his fingers over the keys. "I don't know what to think. I think that if the police were told that it was a suicide, that's what they would investigate. And if there wasn't anything that jumped out and said, 'not a suicide,' they would just put it to bed."

Bowman nodded. "Yes. Sounds about right. If you can't disprove it... why put the family or the institution through all of the anxiety of a murder investigation? You don't investigate a suicide the same way as a murder. It would cause too much extra work."

"And so far, I haven't found anything that says, 'not a suicide.'"

"Do you think it wasn't? What does your gut tell you?"

"My gut tells me... I'm not finished yet."

Zachary felt depressed putting the thought into words. He did not want to go back to Summit again. He'd had enough of the place. Much more, and he'd be a basket case himself. "There are still... unexplored corners."

"Well, be careful. If it is a cover-up, you don't want to go turning over too many stones and making yourself a target. The reason police officers have partners is so that someone can watch their backs. You don't have anyone watching yours."

Zachary nodded. "Thanks. I'll be careful."

It wasn't *really* late when there was a knock on the door, but late enough that Zachary wondered who would be knocking on Bowman's door at that hour. Bowman lived a pretty quiet life and didn't get a lot of visitors, scheduled or not.

Bowman was in a food coma, slumped on the couch after having eaten nearly the entire pizza. He roused a little at the knocking, but didn't get up to answer it, so Zachary did.

He didn't check through the peephole before opening the door, which was a stupid thing to do. He knew better than that. Bowman was a cop and Zachary was a private detective. Both of them could have unsavory visitors. He should have looked through the peephole and kept the chain on until he was sure who it was and that Bowman wanted to let them in. But he too was tired, his brain spent three times over.

Bridget was at the door.

For a moment, Zachary just stood there, stunned by her loveliness. By her unexpected appearance on his doorstep. His shocked brain ran through several different reasons she might be there. Did she want to get back together with him? Was she in trouble? Did she think that he had done something wrong?

He immediately searched his memory for anything he might have done to tick her off in the past few days. The compulsion to chase after her was still so strong, even with medication, group therapy, and his psychologist, that some days he felt like a junkie in withdrawal. In actual physical pain over her absence. He wanted to follow her, to watch her, to know where she was every minute of the day. So far, he'd been able to resist stalking her any further. It helped to have a case that occupied his attention as much as the Quentin Thatcher case did. It kept his brain from falling back into the same ruts again. Helped him to think of things other than Bridget late at night when the loneliness was the worst.

"Aren't you going to invite me in?" Bridget demanded.

She didn't look happy. Zachary again racked his mind for the reason she had come. What she was upset about. An old argument? A break-up with her new boyfriend?

"Zachary."

"Yes, yes," Zachary stepped back from the door, opening it the rest of the way and motioning her in. "Come in. I'm sorry, I'm just surprised to see you, that's all."

Bridget marched in as if she owned the place. She clutched her purse under her arm and looked around, her eyes sharp.

She looked into the living room and spotted Bowman on the couch, snoring. "Well, I guess we can talk out here." She motioned to the table.

Zachary pulled out a chair as she did and sat down.

He had missed her. It was nice to get together with Kenzie, but he didn't know where that relationship was going, if anywhere. He'd made some pretty serious mistakes. He and Bridget had been together for a couple of years, madly in love at the start, and he still hadn't recovered from the events that had blown them apart. Bridget had gone on, was in remission from cancer, and was in another committed relationship, leaving Zachary far behind. She was the one who had gone through cancer, but he was the one who couldn't recover.

"I just wanted to see how you were doing," Bridget said.

Flat, expressionless. Zachary couldn't read her. She put her purse on the table and crossed her legs, waiting for him to tell her how he was. Zachary looked around the kitchen for some inspiration, but it didn't come.

"I'm okay," he said tentatively. "Why?"

Her eyes scanned his face. "You're not looking very well. Are you sleeping?"

"The best I can."

"Maybe you should get something stronger. Or a sleep study. Sleep is very important for good health."

Zachary nodded, avoiding her gaze.

"Kenzie said you are having some trouble with a case you are on," Bridget said finally, with a sigh.

"Kenzie called you?"

"She was concerned about you. Said that she couldn't make it over to check on you, and did I think you would be alright. She didn't ask me to come over, but I offered."

Zachary had no idea how to feel about that. Angry? Violated? Infantilized? Comforted?

"So, how about a drink and you tell me about it?" Bridget suggested.

He searched her face for some indication of her interest level. Or for any affection or tender feelings toward him. Why would she come all the way over just on Kenzie's suggestion? She must have some kind of feelings toward him. The last few times they had seen each other, she had been angry, bursting-at-the-seams furious. Kenzie had said that just proved that Bridget still had feelings toward Zachary. But when she was worried about Zachary, who did Kenzie call? Bridget. Did that mean that Kenzie didn't consider Bridget a threat to their relationship? Or that there was no relationship, no possibility of a relationship past the level of friendship?

He got up and went to the fridge. "Uh… there's not much selection. Beer? Water? Maybe coffee?"

"Too late for coffee, I'll never sleep. And you'd better not either."

"Coffee doesn't keep me up. It helps to calm me down."

"Tea?"

Zachary checked a few cupboards, already knowing the answer. "No. Sorry."

"Well, I guess we'll go with water, then."

Zachary couldn't help but notice she had dictated what his drink should be as well as hers. His natural reaction was to go for the beer just to be oppositional, but that would cause problems when combined with his meds, and he was going to need to take something to sleep. And while coffee really didn't keep him up, he was afraid that just the suggestion might be enough to keep him from falling asleep.

So he ran them each a glass of cold water, with a squirt of lemon juice from a plastic lemon lurking in the back of the fridge, and sat back down with her. Bridget sipped the water delicately.

He studied her as she drank. She was as lovely as she had ever been. Better color since she was off of all the cancer treatments. A little bit more flesh on her face, rounding out her features and making it so that her eyes didn't look quite so large. Her hair was very short, but it was undoubtedly her own rather than a wig, and he knew that she must be over the moon that it hadn't changed color or refused to grow back.

"So, tell me about it," Bridget prompted.

Zachary could dance around the issue and say that he didn't know which case Kenzie was talking about. After all, he was always working several cases at a time. The bread and butter came from insurance claims and adultery, not homicides. Not suicides.

"Did she tell you anything about it?"

"No. She was in a hurry."

"It's a possible suicide... a young boy in an institution. Autistic." Zachary took a big gulp of his water and almost coughed. He'd put way too much lemon juice in it.

"That sounds pretty grim. Who wanted it investigated, his family?"

"Yes. Single mom, two other boys at home. Feels guilty that she put him there. Guilty for being so relieved to get him off of her hands."

"You don't think she had anything to do with it?"

"No. It was overnight, she wouldn't have been there."

"Oh, good. I don't like it when it's the parents. That's always so sad."

Zachary recalled Dr. Abato talking about parents at the end of their ropes, murdering their own children. "Yeah. It is. But that doesn't seem to be possible in this case. Either he did kill himself—on purpose or by accident—or someone there at the institution killed him."

"Why?"

"I don't know. I'm trying to figure it out. The place is... like a funhouse. Things aren't what they seem. Therapies that should be helpful, and instead are harmful. Things that you can't imagine being allowed in modern times, and people are insisting that they are good. Holding them up as saving their children and their families. Staff getting PTSD from the things they are being forced to do to the residents."

Bridget frowned and shook her head. "That doesn't sound likely. What are they doing that is so bad?"

"Giving them electrical shocks," Zachary snapped, and Bridget's eyes widened. "That or hitting or pinching them. Restraining them. Forcing them to perform actions over and over and over again. Essentially torturing them until they comply."

Bridget's head tilted, and Zachary saw her attitude change. Disbelief. Not shocked at what he had said, but doubting that it was true.

"This is happening!" he insisted. "I'm not exaggerating it. Or imagining things. There have been court cases. Do an internet search on the institution. You'll see. It isn't a secret."

"If there have been court cases, then I *know* you're overreacting. No judge is going to let them take actions that are going to be harmful to the children."

"Because the parents and therapists say it is helping. And that they're willing to do anything to help their children to become normal. To have some hope of a happy life. Because if they can't help them to recover, the alternatives are pretty dire."

"You've always had such a tender heart," Bridget said, her tone disdainful. "You always feel so bad for people. Even when they've put themselves in the middle of trouble. You need to toughen up. Or don't take these cases. You can't let them affect you like this."

"If I don't investigate it, who is going to? These kids need me. Quentin needs me, and the other kids that are being abused at Summit. Who else is going to help them?"

"You're not Superman. You can't just fly in there and save the world. You're inflating what your job there is. You're supposed to be investigating one child's death. To see whether it was suicide. You are not there to overthrow the social structure and save everyone else. That is not going to happen. If you think that's what you're going to do... then I think you'd better get in to see your psychiatrist right away. Because it might be the symptom of a manic phase."

Zachary couldn't find the words to argue with her. He took another sip of his too-sour water to try to cover his lack of verbal ability. And in the back of his mind, the doubt that she'd planted started to grow. It was true that an inflated sense of self-importance, of grandiose thinking, was a symptom of bipolar depression. Zachary's depression had always remained unipolar; the only manic episodes he'd ever had were triggered by medications.

Was he inflating his role at Summit? Thinking that he was there to do more than just investigate how Quentin died? He knew that he wanted to save the other children who were in danger, but did he think he could?

He tried to focus on the present and evaluate his own thoughts dispassionately. The trouble with disordered thinking was that the brain didn't know its own thoughts were disordered.

"I don't think I can change everything or change everyone," he said slowly. "I'd like to be able to help them. I'd like to be able to change the kind of therapy they do there, their whole approach to helping people with autism and behavioral problems..." He shook his head. "But I know I can't do that. I just want... to save a few of them. To start something. I don't know. I want to make a change, but it's not going to be something that changes the whole institution. I can maybe change things for one or two people. Maybe."

Bridget's shoulders dipped. "That's good. I want you to get help if you're having trouble recognizing reality."

"I'm not. It's just a very emotional case."

"And you think these *therapists* are getting PTSD from these therapies, not the patients?"

"Oh, the residents are too. I've talked to people who went through these kinds of therapies when they were children, heard how it still affects their lives. But yes, I think the staff members are getting PTSD too. The atmosphere there, the strict control over them, taking too many sick days, not being able to sleep, flashbacks to what they've been doing at the institution... it's PTSD. I recognize it."

"I don't think you can get PTSD from something that you do to someone else," Bridget said. "That just doesn't make any sense."

"Why not? Don't you think you would be traumatized if you were forced to torture someone?"

"No, I don't think that's possible. I think that if someone chooses to do it, it's because it isn't affecting them. Maybe they're psychopaths. But being traumatized by some therapy that is making people squeamish...? It doesn't follow."

Zachary let out his breath. He glanced toward the living room, trying to decide whether to get up and get his computer. He didn't want to wake Bowman up. Bowman had enough sleep interruptions due to Zachary's nightmares and sleep issues.

"I looked it up," he said. "There's a kind of PTSD called PITS. Participation-Induced Traumatic Stress. It is a real thing. Soldiers who have to kill at close range. Executioners. Even animal shelter workers who have to euthanize animals."

Bridget still looked skeptical, but seemed ready to believe that there might possibly be such a thing. Or at least until she had proof one way or the other.

"This really seems like... you've dug yourself into a hole. You were only there to look at one death, and now it's all of the inmates. All of the staff. You're losing focus."

"Maybe."

She waited.

"I'm going to be okay, Bridget. I know Kenzie was worried, and that this all sounds a little bit much... but I'm not here alone. And I'll... I'll dig myself out."

"You're taking your meds?"

"Yes."

He didn't tell her *mostly* or *when he felt like he needed them.* Because he knew that just wouldn't be good enough for black-and-white Bridget. He was taking his medication when he needed it, so the answer was yes.

"And you're not having suicidal thoughts?"

Zachary thought back over the last few days and shook his head. "No. Just... the regular stuff. I'm not suicidal."

"And you're not going to get yourself in trouble?"

"I'll be careful. I'm not going to do anything stupid."

"Okay." Bridget nodded. "I should head for home. And you know... you can call me, if you need something."

It was a very different position from when he was in the hospital and she was raging over still being listed as his emergency contact. He still hadn't changed it, either. If something happened, then Bridget was the one they should call to find out his history and to give the doctors direction. He wasn't putting that on Kenzie, and who else did he have?

Bowman snorted and stirred in the living room. They both turned their heads and looked toward the room to see if he was going to wake up. Zachary heard scratching, and then Bowman pushing himself up from the couch.

"Zachary?"

"In the kitchen."

Bowman cleared his throat, scratched some more, and made his way into the kitchen. When he saw Bridget, his posture became straighter and he grinned widely.

"Bridget! It's been forever since I saw you. How are you?"

"I'm good, Mario. How have you been?"

"Oh, wow. You look fantastic, woman. I thought someone said something about you being sick."

Bridget patted at her short hair self-consciously, her cheeks going a flattering pink. "Oh, really, Mario!"

"No, it's true. Isn't it Zachary? No wonder you didn't tell me she was coming over, you dog. You wanted her all to yourself."

Zachary fought his own flush. "I didn't know she was coming," he squeaked.

"Oh, sure you didn't," Bowman teased.

"I was just getting ready to go," Bridget said, standing up and giving him her fingertips to shake. "I hope Zachary hasn't been too much trouble for you?"

As if he were a child, or a dog Bowman was boarding for her. Zachary knew she was fishing, checking one more time to make sure she didn't need to be concerned about his welfare.

"Aside from the fact that he never sleeps?" Bowman responded. "No, he's a good houseguest. Even bought me pizza today. But he's looking for some place new, aren't you, Zach?"

Zachary nodded. "Yeah. I've called a few places, still need to look at them. Once this case settles down a bit…"

Bridget nodded slowly. "That's great," she said in a tone that was just a little too bright for the circumstances. "I'm glad you're getting on your feet again."

Would she prefer that he stayed at Bowman's indefinitely just so that he had someone to look after him? Did she think that he couldn't manage on his own, in his own place? It hadn't worked out very well after the divorce, but Zachary had lived on his own before and had been okay. He could do it again. As long as he was careful with his health, he would be just fine.

He walked her the short distance to the door. Bridget leaned in close like she was going to kiss Zachary on the cheek. Instead, she whispered in his ear, her warm breath on his skin.

"Maybe you should drop this case. It doesn't sound like you've found anything to indicate it's not suicide, so maybe you should just let it go. Then it can't keep you up nights."

He gave her a peck on the cheek, hugged her with their bodies apart and his hands on her shoulders, and saw her out the door.

17

Zachary's dinner with Mr. Peterson had been arranged a couple weeks earlier, before Zachary had taken the Quentin Thatcher case. It meant a drive in the opposite direction from Summit, so Zachary knew he would have to take a day off from his investigation at the institution. Maybe just let everything settle and percolate for a day, and go into it with a fresh viewpoint on Wednesday.

So he worked on other cases during the morning, cleared up paperwork and checked the logs of a couple of cars he had been tracking to look for patterns of behavior. He made a few phone calls. Did some virtual stalking on social networks. A lot of detecting was tedious research and paperwork, but it had to be done.

Mid-afternoon he was happy to lay his paperwork aside and get into the car. As he drove toward Mr. Peterson's home, leaving Summit farther and farther behind, with the brilliant greens of spring all around him, Zachary felt a weight being lifted from his shoulders.

Mr. Peterson—Lorne—was one of Zachary's former foster parents. The only one that he had kept in touch with over the years. While he'd only lived with the Petersons for a few weeks, it was Mr. Peterson who had given him his first camera, who had helped him to develop his film over the years, and who had suggested Zachary had the skills to be a private detective if he wanted to put his photography skills to some practical use.

Being a foster child, with no supports after he turned eighteen and very few after he was sixteen, Zachary had to find a job as quickly as he could, and certainly didn't have the kind of money that would be needed to become an artist showing his work in galleries. But private eye work was something he could do. He was good at candid shots, at melting into the background, and observing others. He picked up quickly on body language and little things that were out of place. He was good at anticipating what was going to happen before it did. Hypervigilance was a helpful trait for a detective.

Mr. Peterson had moved into a nice little bungalow a few years earlier. Similar to what he had lived in when Zachary had lived with him and his wife. It signaled an end to the series of seedy apartments Mr. Peterson had lived in since his divorce and the beginning of a new era for him and Pat. They had been a couple for twenty years. More than that. Society had finally reached the point where their relationship could be openly acknowledged.

There were pink tulips in the neat front garden. Mr. Peterson opened the door as soon as Zachary pulled in front. His face was wreathed in smiles. He looked older than when Zachary had seen him last. The little hair that he had left was whiter than Zachary remembered. He might have put on a few pounds. How long had it been since Zachary had seen him last?

"Zachary, so good to see you!" Mr. Peterson shook his hand warmly and slapped him on the back in a half-hug. "How are you doing? Come in!"

Zachary was hustled into the house. Pat was in the kitchen, but came out wiping his hands on a towel to greet Zachary.

"Hey, Zach. How was the drive?"

"Good. No traffic. And it feels good to get away. I didn't know how badly I needed this."

Pat smiled. He was still in good shape, but he wasn't a young man any more. His age fell between Zachary's and Mr. Peterson's, but he wore the years well, becoming more mature and distinguished.

"Well, you two sit down and start on getting caught up. I'll have dinner on the table in a few minutes."

Zachary sat down. There weren't very many places where he felt like he belonged in the world. Mr. Peterson's was one of the few. Maybe the only one, until Zachary found a new place for himself and settled in.

Mr. Peterson's eyes traveled over him. Lines on his forehead deepened and the little fan of wrinkles around his eyes disappeared. "Are you okay, Zachary? How is the house-hunting going?"

"I'm actually looking now," Zachary said. "I've got calls in to a few places, so it shouldn't be too long before I find something. Then I guess I'll need furniture and household stuff before I can move in. Just the basics. A couple more weeks, maybe."

"Good. It can't be easy just sleeping on couches."

"Well, I've done it enough before." Zachary shrugged. "But I'm wearing out my welcome. I was only supposed to be there a couple of days."

"You can't be expected to get back on your feet in a couple of days. It takes time to get your identification reissued and get your insurance check. Suddenly being without *anything* is more than just a setback."

Zachary shrugged again and didn't know what to say to that.

"So, what are you working on?"

"I have a new case. A boy who might have committed suicide. His mother hired me to look into it."

"Suicide." The lines on Mr. Peterson's forehead became more pronounced. "Do you really think that's a good idea? Doesn't that... I don't know... trigger feelings for you?"

"The possibility that it might be suicide hasn't really bothered me. I can think about it without having suicidal thoughts... but other things about it have been..." Zachary didn't want to say anything that would worry Mr. Peterson. He already had Kenzie and Bridget fussing over him. "Some of the other aspects have been... bothering me a little."

Mr. Peterson nodded. His eyes got a little wider. "What other aspects?"

"He was in an institution. He was autistic and couldn't live with his family anymore." Zachary tried to swallow the sudden lump in his throat. He wasn't talking about himself; it was Quentin. Zachary's institutional life was long in the past.

"Ah. So that hits a little too close to home?"

Zachary made a little motion with his hands, trying to downplay it. But the words stuck so badly in his throat that Mr. Peterson had to know it was a problem.

"It isn't much like any of the places that I lived. Except maybe the living units, which are pretty much the same as any detention cell." He saw again the room where Quentin had died. Remembered Annie; Zachary trapped on the other side of the security door, unable to do anything for her. Screaming for help.

Mr. Peterson sat beside Zachary on the couch and put a comforting hand on his back. It was warm and firm and grounding. "What happened?" he asked quietly. "I know Bonnie Brown wasn't the greatest place to be, but it was your safe place when you couldn't be with a family."

"Yeah," Zachary agreed. "I chose to go back there. Christmases. When things got really bad. There were times I just couldn't function in a foster family."

"So, what happened? What are you thinking about?"

Zachary swallowed, trying to clear the lump in his throat so he could speak clearly. "I never talked to anyone about it."

"Someone was hurting you? That place was full of traumatized kids. Kids who had been abused and could become perpetrators."

"It's not that..." Zachary didn't deny the fact that there had been predators there. As there surely would be at any similar institution. "It's... when I was there, a girl died, in the room beside mine."

Mr. Peterson shifted, studying Zachary seriously. "You never told me anything about that before."

"I never told anybody."

"What happened?"

Zachary stared at the framed pictures on the mantle across the room. Some of them were photographs he had taken. Portraits of Mr. Peterson and Pat together. A small one of himself as a young man, standing on the street, sideways to the camera, bashful about having his photo taken.

"She was autistic."

"How did she die? Was it suicide?"

"She stopped breathing. In the night. When they went to wake her up in the morning, she was dead."

"So it wasn't suicide or a suspicious death. Just one of those things."

"Yeah." Zachary breathed, staring at the picture of himself. "Maybe."

"Do you think something else happened to her?"

When he thought about it, Zachary's guts cramped up. He remembered the security guards, the police, Annie screaming. Too many images at once, overpowering.

"You're not there, Zachary."

You're not there.

Zachary breathed in a deep lungful of air. He could smell Pat's cooking. He was in Mr. Peterson's living room, not Bonnie Brown. Though Mr. Peterson had calmed him with a hand on his back before, he wasn't touching Zachary anymore, cautious of triggering a worse reaction.

"She had been violent the day before." Zachary forced the words out, hoping they would help him to sort and stabilize the images. "Assaulted a guard. They called the police, had her arrested. She was still upset when they got there. Fought the police. She got like that. Everyone there knew she had meltdowns. Tantrums, they called them. Like she was a toddler."

He breathed a little more easily. Blinked and tried to remain present. Annie was in the past. Zachary wasn't a child anymore. No longer eleven and helpless. It had happened decades earlier.

"You think this tantrum had something to do with her death?"

"I don't know. Maybe. Maybe something happened to her while she was fighting with the police."

"What?"

"I don't know." Zachary shook his head. "I don't remember."

Neither of them said anything. The silence drew out.

"I don't remember," Zachary repeated.

"Okay."

"Everybody ready to eat?"

Zachary looked up and saw Pat standing in the doorway, his stance indicating that he had been there for some time, waiting for the right moment to speak.

"Yeah," Zachary agreed, getting up from the couch. "It smells really good."

Mr. Peterson didn't spring up as quickly as he would have a few years previous. It took a moment of creaking and rebalancing, but then he was smiling and striding toward the table, as if denying the fact that his body was aging.

"Just give me a second to wash up," Zachary told them. He headed to the bathroom, waiting for a few moments in the still, quiet closeness of the space for his body to calm down, for the cramps to ease. He splashed cold water on his face and then toweled it off.

He returned to the dining room table to find Mr. Peterson and Pat talking companionably, not acting like he had put them out or made them wait for a long time. Zachary took a surreptitious glance at his phone before sliding it back away, trying to gauge the passage of time and anchor himself. When he was on his meds, time was more of a constant; it didn't grow and shrink so dramatically.

He forced a smile and seated himself. "Thanks for inviting me," he said. "It's good for me to get away for a bit. Get away from work."

"And then I go and bring up your case," Mr. Peterson said. "Sorry."

"No, it's okay. I didn't mean that."

They passed the dishes around and dished up. Zachary tried to hide the fact that he wasn't taking very much, spreading the food out and commenting on how good it looked. Pat knew by this time that Zachary didn't have much of an appetite when on his ADHD meds, so Zachary really didn't need to cover the fact up, but he still worried about Pat being offended.

"How's the photography going?" Pat inquired, attempting to pick the topic that was least likely to trigger a reaction from Zachary. "What are you working on these days?"

"Nothing right now. Lost all of my equipment in the fire."

"Oh… I didn't even think. I'm sorry."

Zachary shrugged. "The insurance company will cover replacing a lot of it. Can't replace the photographs and negatives, though. I didn't keep duplicates anywhere else, or digital records in the cloud. Now… I know better."

"That's a devastating blow," Mr. Peterson said, real pain in his voice. He was a photographer too. He could understand how hard it would have been to lose all of his artwork. "I'll make you copies of everything I have. And I've got a couple of cameras I don't use. Let's go through equipment after dinner and I'll give you some stuff to take back with you."

"You don't need to do that," Zachary protested. But his spirits lifted at the thought of getting his hands on one of Mr. Peterson's treasured cameras. He'd bought the digital camera he needed for his surveillance work, but he still preferred real film for his art. He smiled his appreciation and had a couple of bites of his dinner.

When Zachary got back from Mr. Peterson's and checked on the voicemails that had been piling up while he'd had his phone turned off, he listened a couple of times to one from a soft-spoken woman.

Mr. Goldman, my name is Ava Kennedy. I'm the mother of a girl at Summit Living Center. I wondered if you could talk to us sometime in the next few days. I'd really appreciate it.

She gave her number, stayed on the line breathing for a moment, and then clicked off. Zachary wrote down her information. Was it possible that she or her daughter knew something about Quentin's death? Some piece of information that was missing from his investigation? It was late in the day to be calling anyone back, so he put it aside to deal with in the morning.

He was feeling nice and calm and relaxed after his visit to Mr. Peterson's, so after checking over his camera stops one more time and making sure his film was loaded and properly advanced, he took some sleeping pills and stretched out on the couch. He lay on his stomach with one arm hanging over the edge of the couch, resting his hand on the camera, the cool metal reassuring. Then he closed his eyes to go to sleep.

Ava Kennedy was a striking black woman, perhaps a few years older than Zachary. While her face was unlined, she looked tired and worn. She shook Zachary's hand briefly, her slim hand small in his.

"This is Tirza," Ava said, indicating the teen girl sitting on the bed, staring steadfastly away from them. She was a gorgeous girl with many of her mother's features and a vague, innocent air. Her hair was done in neat corn-rows.

Ava sat down on the bed beside her daughter.

"Hi, Tirza," Zachary greeted.

Tirza whispered something, turning briefly toward her mother, then away again, tugging on her earlobe.

"It's okay, Tirza," Ava said. "This is Mr. Goldman; he's here to help."

Zachary wasn't sure how he was supposed to be helping Tirza. Ava had been cryptic on the phone, saying that she would fill him in when he got there. He wasn't sure what Ava thought her daughter had to do with Quentin's death, if there was any connection at all. Maybe she wanted to hire Zachary for another case and it was nothing to do with Quentin.

He noted that Tirza did not have on a black backpack and electrodes. That made her one of the minority of students who was being treated without skin shocks.

"What is it you wanted to talk to me about today? Do you have concerns about something here at Summit?"

"I... don't know," Ava said unhelpfully. "I'm hoping you can help to sort that out. I didn't know where to go, and then someone said that you were a private investigator. I thought maybe there was something you could do to help."

"So this isn't anything to do with Quentin Thatcher's death?"

"I don't think so."

"Okay... well, I'm not sure if I'm prepared to take on another case right now, especially one that might have something to do with Summit. My plate is pretty full..."

"Would you listen to our story and then decide? If you say you can't help, I'll understand."

Zachary looked into her earnest, pleading eyes. He nodded.

"Alright. Go ahead."

"Tirza is autistic, like Quentin. She was part of an after-school program here. Living at home, going to the public school in a mainstream program with accommodations for her needs. Working on social skills and whatever else needed a little work here."

Zachary nodded encouragingly. He tried to make eye contact with Tirza, but she looked steadfastly away, acting as if she were unaware of Zachary's presence or what he was doing there.

"About a week before Quentin died, Tirza disappeared. Between when her aide at the school made sure she was ready to go and when the car that was supposed to pick her up and bring her to Summit arrived." Ava shook her head, expressing her confusion over this. "She had the same routine every day. She'd never had any trouble getting from her locker to the car. But half an hour later, I got a call from the car service saying that she had not shown up. Asking if she was sick. I dropped everything and went over to the school, but she wasn't there. I called the police."

Ava looked at her daughter with concern. Zachary could see no sign that the story was distressing for Tirza.

"They treated it like a *runaway* case." Ava's tone was outraged. "I explained to them that she was autistic. That she wasn't a rebellious teen who might have just gone off shopping with a friend or meeting a boyfriend. She wouldn't have gone anywhere other than the car, unless someone took her away. She went to the car every day."

"You managed to find her again, obviously."

"I wouldn't leave them alone. I wouldn't let them just brush it off as a runaway case. Forced them to issue an Amber Alert. Went to the media and made sure it was well-publicized that she was the victim of a kidnapping, not a runaway. Started an investigation into whether there had been any strangers hanging around the school, or whether anyone had been paying an unusual amount of attention to her."

"Doing all of the right things."

"Apparently. Forty-eight hours from when she disappeared from the school, she was found wandering beside the highway."

Zachary looked at Tirza again. She would be an attractive target. A beautiful young woman not equipped to defend herself.

"How was it handled?"

"They questioned her as a runaway. They called me to come pick her up. Case closed."

"They closed the case? What did she say to them?"

"She said she had gone with Damien."

"Who is Damien?"

"I have no idea. They decided Damien was her boyfriend and that she had just decided to spend a couple of days with him, unconcerned about the people who might be worried about her."

"Has Tirza told you anything about what happened?" Zachary looked at Tirza, unsure whether he should be addressing her directly. He had never liked it when social workers or foster parents talked about him as if he weren't standing right there.

Ava nodded. "She gave me a very detailed account about going with Damien and being... passed around to a number of different men. She told me what happened to her. She's not just making up a story."

Zachary swore. "Oh, Tirza. I'm so sorry."

Her eyes flitted over to him and then she put her face against her mother's shoulder, pressing into her.

"What did you do? Did you go back to the police with this?"

"Yes... but I don't know how seriously they are taking it. They are still pretty insistent that this is just rebellious teenage behavior. They said they will investigate, but I don't hear anything back from them. I don't know if they're doing anything."

"What about her therapist? Isn't there someone she can talk to here who will back her up, say that she's not lying?"

"They say she is just repeating what she heard somewhere else. That she's not... high functioning enough to be able to put an experience like that into words."

"No," Tirza protested, banging her fist against Ava's body. "No, no, no!"

"I know, Tirza. I know you're telling me the truth," Ava assured her.

Tirza quieted.

"Are you... is she still taking the after-school program here?" It was obvious to Zachary that they had to be there for another reason. It was morning, so Tirza should have been at school, not due for her after-school program until her day was done.

"She hasn't been able to go back to school. Or to function at home. I don't know what to do with her. She's regressed. Before this happened... she was pretty independent. She was going to school, could do things at home without me supervising her constantly, she had friends and was a happy girl. But now..." Ava put an arm around Tirza and cuddled her close. "When I take her to school, she cries and won't stay there. She doesn't want to talk. She's depressed and self-harming. I can't watch her all of the time to make sure she doesn't hurt herself. Or do what Quentin did..." Ava trailed off, looking at Tirza, obviously not wanting to put ideas into Tirza's brain. She sighed, eyes shiny with tears. "So I've had to put her into residential here. Even though I really don't want to."

"That must be very hard."

"Everything that we worked so hard for is gone, because this man, this Damien, stole her away from us. How could anyone be so depraved? To take such an innocent life and do what he did."

"You're lucky you got her back at all. They could have—" Zachary checked his tongue before blurting in front of Tirza, "—hurt her instead of letting her go. They must not have thought that she could identify them."

"She could describe their clothes and what they did to her. But I don't know if she could ever testify in court and be considered a competent witness. So they were probably right. They don't have to worry about what she could say about them."

"No, Mom." Tirza first tapped Ava on the leg, and then made a chopping motion. "No more. No." Her words cut off and she looked at Zachary pleadingly for a moment before hiding her face against her mother again.

Zachary looked at Ava to get her interpretation of Tirza's words and gestures. But Ava shook her head, not quite sure.

"No one is going to hurt you anymore," she told Tirza. "You're safe here. The bad men can't get to you here."

"No." The chopping motion again, as if she were karate-chopping Ava's thigh. But while she did continue the motion until her hand reached Ava's leg, it was obviously not a violent motion. Not intended to hurt. She jerked her hand in Zachary's direction.

"What, Tirza? Use more words," Ava prompted.

Tirza pulled her face back from Ava. She brought the arm that had been behind Ava's back in front of her body. She made the chopping gesture again, into her flat hand, and motioned at Zachary.

"Stop," Ava said. "Stop... Mr. Goldman?"

"Zachary," he corrected automatically.

"What do you want to stop, Tirza?" Ava asked. "Mr. Goldman— Zachary—is here to help. You want him to stop something?"

"No. *Him*." Tirza motioned to Zachary again, and again made the sign for 'stop.' "Him, him, him, him." Each time she said 'him,' she moved her hand over slightly, as if there were a row of men standing beside or behind Zachary.

And for the two days she had been gone, there had been a row of men, Zachary realized. It made his heart ache to think of what she had been through for those forty-eight hours. How terrified she must have been, not understanding what was going on. Or understanding and not able to stop it.

"Baby." Ava kissed the top of Tirza's head. "It's over. It is stopped, sweetie. They aren't going to hurt you any more."

Tirza looked toward her room's open door. She again buried her face in Ava's shoulder.

"No. No more."

"That's right. No more. No more hurting Tirza. Tirza is safe."

She rubbed Tirza's back and hugged her. Zachary watched a man walk down the hallway, past Tirza's room. He saw Tirza look up briefly at the sound of footsteps, and then she hid her face again quickly.

"Tirza," Zachary addressed her in his gentlest voice. "Tirza, no one here is hurting you, are they?"

Tirza moaned and again made the 'stop' gesture with one hand.

"Is somebody here hurting you? Touching you?"

She murmured and cried into her mother's shoulder.

"Does she understand what I'm saying?" Zachary asked. "Has she told you anything to indicate that she might be... being victimized here? It happens in a lot of institutions. I'm sure they have to pass police checks to work here, but..."

"I just don't know," Ava admitted. "She keeps telling me to stop it. No more. I think it's just anxiety or flashbacks, I don't think she's still being hurt. I don't think that anyone here would... Everybody has to be vetted. I don't think..."

But she couldn't know. None of them could know for sure whether Tirza was still being hurt, except Tirza herself. And she was not giving them the information they needed.

"I think it's just anxiety," Ava repeated, trying to sound more certain.

A woman walked up to the door. She was wearing a lab coat, like most of the therapists. An affectation, since none of them were doctors who were doing anything messy and needed to have their clothing protected. It was just a uniform to identify them as doctors or professionals. Was the lab jacket supposed to make it look like they had had more training than they did? Zachary remembered Clarissa telling him they liked to recruit aides and therapists right out of school, so their methodology wouldn't be contaminated by other practices.

The woman gave the room a big smile. "We have company today, do we, Tirza? That's nice, isn't it?" She focused her gaze on Ava. "Mom, it's time for Tirza to go to therapy. Would you tell her good-bye, and I'll get her on her way?"

Ava pulled gently back from Tirza, trying to extricate herself from the girl's grip. "School time, Tirza. Time to go."

Tirza didn't argue or fight, but she made it obvious from the way she sat slumped on the bed that she didn't want to go.

"Get up," her mother coaxed, pulling on her hands. "Get up off of the bed and on your feet. Therapy time. You need to get your skills back. Work hard again."

Tirza slumped down farther, uncooperative. The therapist put her hands on her hips. "This wouldn't be a problem if you'd let her wear an ESD."

"She's already traumatized enough. She doesn't need to be abused further by being given electrical shocks."

Bravo for her. Finally, someone standing up for her child's rights.

"Okay, then you need to move out of the way and I will get her going. Tirza, come!" The therapist's voice snapped. Tirza darted a glance at her. "Out," the woman repeated to Ava, and looked at Zachary. "And you too. I can get her to move."

Ava sighed. She stroked Tirza's hair. "You need to listen, baby." Then she moved out of the room. Zachary followed her reluctantly.

The therapist wasn't gentle or patient. She gave Tirza commands in a loud, unyielding tone, and when Tirza didn't immediately obey, she pushed, pulled, and prodded her to get her to move. Eventually, Tirza was on her feet and being escorted out the door. She wasn't crying or protesting her treatment. The therapist nodded at Ava, ignored Zachary, and marched Tirza off down the hall.

Ava motioned to Zachary, and they both went back into Tirza's room to talk for another minute.

"So, this doesn't have anything to do with Quentin's death," Zachary said.

"No… It's just… the police said that kids are often victimized by people like this that they meet online or in chat apps. They agree to meet someone without the parents' knowledge, not realizing that they are opening themselves up to a predator."

Zachary nodded. "Yes. I've seen it before."

"But Tirza didn't have a phone. She didn't have internet access. She didn't use a computer, except for a self-contained communications device, not hooked into any network. Nobody contacted her while she was at home. It was either someone at the school, or someone here."

"She couldn't tell you which?"

"She calls them both 'school.' I can't work out how this guy met her. The school and Summit both say there's no way. He doesn't work there. And there haven't been any strangers hanging around. They would have found him on the cameras."

"It's more likely to be someone from the school, since that's where they took her."

"Yes."

"And you said she cries when you take her back there. Not when you bring her here."

"Because that's where she was taken from. She doesn't want them to take her away again. But..." Ava motioned to their surroundings. "You saw she still asks me to stop them when she is here."

Zachary nodded.

Ava gave a wide shrug. "I can't say it's someone from the school. And I can't say it's someone from here. I have to just trust them at both places and let her keep going back somewhere she might have been stalked or victimized before. It's not much of a choice."

"No. So, you're looking for someone to investigate and find out who took her? It would not be easy, and my plate is already full with Quentin Thatcher's death."

"I just... I thought that since you're looking at things with fresh eyes here, getting to know how the place works... you could just tell me if you saw something. If you thought there is something to be concerned about. A security risk, or a person you get a bad feeling from. Just... anything you happen to come across."

"I don't think I'm going to be able to help you."

Ava's face fell. But she didn't argue or reproach him.

"I'll tell you if I hear or see anything," Zachary promised. "But don't get your hopes up. Because I don't think... I don't think I'm going to come across a pedophile while trying to get to the truth in Quentin's case."

"Okay. I understand that. And... thank you."

Zachary nodded. "Do you think I could watch her therapy session for a few minutes?"

"I'm sure we could get permission."

Ava led the way to the nursing station at the middle of the unit and smiled at the woman seated at the computer.

"Mr. Goldman would like to watch my daughter's therapy session. Would that be alright?"

The nurse or supervisor shrugged. "I don't see why not, if you give your permission. Do you know the way?"

Ava shook her head. "I have to go. If someone could take him there...?" At Zachary's look of surprise, she explained. "It's best if I leave while Tirza's occupied with something else. She's very clingy and if I try to separate from her, she cries and makes a fuss. It's better if I'm just not here when she gets back. And I need to run some errands and take care of the rest of my household."

Zachary accepted this. The supervisor waved down a security guard and indicated Zachary. "Can you escort him down to the therapy wing? Tirza Kennedy's session?"

The guard agreed. He escorted Zachary through the hallways, which were becoming a little more familiar and not so much of a rabbit's warren.

"Here she is." The guard stopped at one of the observation windows, and Zachary saw Tirza sitting across the table from the therapist who had bullied her out of her room.

"Thanks." Zachary sat down on one of the chairs. The guard nodded. "Flag someone down when you're done," he instructed. "Don't go wandering around."

Zachary agreed. He watched Tirza through the window. The therapist seemed to be working with her on speech. Prompting words and phrases which Tirza dutifully repeated, staring off distractedly into space. Her mother said that she could describe the men and what they had done. But Zachary hadn't heard her say more than a handful of words voluntarily. And those sporadically, haphazardly, without grammar.

"Eye contact," the therapist prompted, putting her hands on Tirza's cheeks to turn her head until Tirza was looking at her directly. Tirza's hands came up to cover her face.

"No, quiet hands. Keep your hands folded on the table." The therapist grasped Tirza's hands and put them back down on the table, joined together. Tirza kept her hands there, was praised, and the therapist went back to getting Tirza to repeat words back to her.

She used a communications device at the school. If they brought it to her at Summit, would she be able to tell them more about the men she was afraid of? Whether she feared someone who was actually there, or just the idea of men who might hurt her and flashbacks to the men who had hurt her. Zachary couldn't understand why Summit wouldn't allow the use of communications methods other than speech, as Margaret had suggested.

Zachary's mind drifted to Ray-Ray Maslen. He wondered how the little boy was doing. He had known Quentin. Had gotten used to seeing him after their sessions. Did he miss Quentin now that he was gone? Or did Ray-Ray not even remember that he had existed?

Zachary watched Tirza. She obeyed her therapist's commands. Each phrase repeated back perfectly. She was prompted for a few scripts like Quentin had been learning, where she was expected to give the correct reply to prompt words or phrases such as 'how are you?' or 'good-bye.'

Zachary thought about Ray-Ray's session. 'Touch your nose,' 'touch your ear,' 'give me a hug.' He had read through Lovaas's reasons for teaching commands like those in his book. By teaching simple commands and imitation, the therapist then had the tools to move into more complex behaviors and interactions that the child needed to learn. Interactions like hugs and kisses were taught because they were required in everyday life. Giving grandparents a hug when they arrived. Kissing Daddy good-bye on his way to work. Desensitizing the child so that he wouldn't have a meltdown if auntie or cousin wanted a hug when it was time to go.

Tirza continued to obey each prompt.

And Zachary saw both Ray-Ray's and Tirza's sessions meld before his eyes.

Hug me, Tirza. Good girl.

Give me a kiss and you can have a candy.

Touch your lips, Tirza. Touch your stomach. Touch me here. That's right. Good girl.

In his manual, under rewards for good behavior, Lovaas had listed "kissing, hugging, tickling, stroking, fondling."

Take a child who had been trained to follow every command an adult gave them. A child who had been trained to obey immediately, without question, and to expect treats, praise, and physical touch or games in return. Who had learned to expect pain and punishment for any wrong response. That child became the perfect victim. A child with no boundaries, no defenses, and no instinct to fight back.

A beautiful, innocent girl like Tirza would do whatever she was told.

19

Tirza was parroting the lines that the therapist was feeding her, but her mind was far away. In her brain, she was somewhere safe and protected. Not where she had to answer questions and do as she was told. She was curled up somewhere deep inside her brain where no one could reach her. Still trying to process everything that had happened to her.

The new man seemed nice. The Gold Man. But Damien had seemed nice too. Damien had praised her and told her that she was a good girl. Tirza had been happy to please. But then Damien took her away, said that she was supposed to go along. Her mother had said so. And she was always supposed to do what her mother said.

Tirza didn't know what to do. She had tried to answer the questions of the policemen, but they had thought she was a bad girl, a girl who had run off and done bad things to make her mother cry. She tried to use her words, like she'd been taught, but the police officers didn't like what she said and kept feeding her new lines.

At home and able to use her computer again, she'd tried to explain it to her mother. Her mother didn't think she was a bad girl. Her mother didn't believe that she would run away and go do bad things. But typing the things that had happened to her made it too real and too frightening. It was like bleeding into the computer and not being able to stop the flow or the pain inside her. Like being forced to open her eyes when the light burned them. It made her even more afraid. What if Damien or the men came back? What if they took her away again?

A slap on Tirza's hand brought her attention back to the game. She couldn't let her thoughts be distracted to the point that she stopped vomiting back the words to the therapist, or she would be punished. She was tired of being punished. The men had hurt her. Even when she tried to do everything they told her to, they still hurt her.

Her mother had said she shouldn't let men touch her body. She should protect herself. Fight back. But whenever Tirza fought back against the grown-ups, she was punished and told she was a bad girl. Her body wasn't hers. She wasn't allowed to say no or to decide where to go or what to do. If she resisted, they just took hold of her and forced her to perform.

It wasn't her body. It was theirs. Theirs to control and do what they want to.

Maybe the Gold Man could help, like her mother had said. He would stop them from hurting her more.

Damien would come back for her.

Damien could come to her room. Could take her out.

And she had to do what Damien said.

20

Zachary couldn't look at Tirza's shadowed, hollow eyes any longer. He got up from his observation chair and wandered to the other therapy rooms in the cluster. He didn't like that he was becoming accustomed to watching the therapy. It wasn't so shocking, it didn't disturb him as much, even with his dawning realization that by doing what they were, they were making autistic children into the perfect victims. How could so many professionals be wrong? Zachary couldn't claim, as a layman and someone who had not seen more than a handful of autistic children, that he somehow knew and understood more than they did. That would be the height of arrogance.

He stopped, for a moment fighting vertigo. Once again, he saw little Ray-Ray Maslen on the other side of the glass in therapy with Sophie. It gave him a sense of *deja vu*, especially after he had just been thinking about them. Could the therapy help Ray-Ray to grow up to be a strong, independent man? Able to make his own way in the world, like any 'normal' man? Could they make him indistinguishable from someone who did not have autism? Make him function just like one of them?

Ray-Ray was sitting at the table, looking engaged, eager to please his therapist. He beamed when he got an answer right and frowned or cried when he responded in the wrong way and was corrected.

Sophie was making him repeat words when she pointed to the pictures on a board she held in front of him. When Ray-Ray got nervous or excited, he started to flap his hands, and Sophie physically repositioned them, admonishing 'quiet hands' every few answers.

Ray-Ray twisted in his seat, pivoting his little bottom one way and then the other, attempting to keep his upper body calm and still while burning off nervous energy below the level of the table.

"Quiet hands." Sophie again restrained Ray-Ray's flapping and put his hands on the table in front of him. "Quiet hands, Ray-Ray."

He kept them still with obvious effort.

Zachary studied Ray-Ray's hand positions. One hand was cradled in the other, where Sophie had put them. Not clasped or side-by-side, but one supporting the other. Both were curved slightly, but Zachary could see the vague semblance of the sign Tirza had been making. There was no chopping gesture, he just held them in position as he had been told to, but Zachary could still see the subtle sign Ray-Ray was making.

Stop.

Sophie ran him through the exercises relentlessly. As Zachary had been told, Ray-Ray and the other children were in many hours of therapy every day. It was a full-time job for them. Sophie made her demands and Ray-Ray did the best he could to give her the proper responses, to smile, to frown, to repeat words and gestures that were mostly meaningless to him. He could do nothing to protest this treatment. It was where the professionals wanted him to be. Where his mother wanted him to be.

All he could do was hold that one sign in his hands, his therapist oblivious to the silent plea.

Stop.

Zachary asked whether he could speak to Tirza when she got back from her therapy session. The woman at the nursing station in her unit considered the request.

"You can't talk to her in her room without supervision. You can talk to her in one of the meeting rooms, where you can be observed and surveillance cameras record everything."

"Sure, that would be fine," Zachary agreed. He would even accede to direct supervision. If Tirza were his daughter, he wouldn't have wanted any men talking to her alone.

Tirza was obviously anxious when they put her in the meeting room where Zachary waited for her. She looked around, ducking her head in and out of the open door, rocking and fluttering her fingers in front of her eyes.

"Can you tell me what's wrong, Tirza?" Zachary asked. "What are you afraid of?"

Tirza looked out the door again. Despite the fact that he was a stranger to her, a man she hadn't worked with before, presumably like the men she had been victimized by, she didn't seem worried by him, but by the people who were outside the meeting room in her unit. People she should have been familiar and comfortable with.

Tirza paced around the small meeting room. Zachary could relate to her need to keep moving.

"Quentin," Tirza said abruptly.

Zachary looked at her. "Quentin? Did you know Quentin, Tirza?"

They were housed in the same unit. The residents didn't seem to socialize with each other much—it wasn't in their nature, according to Dr. Abato—but that didn't mean that Quentin and Tirza didn't know each other. If Quentin was friends with Ray-Ray because they had therapy sessions one after the other, he might certainly have known Tirza as well.

Tirza made the hooked-together fingers that Zachary recognized as the sign for friend.

"Quentin was your friend?"

Tirza made some huffing noises, nodding her head. She ran light fingers over her cornrows. Zachary did his best to read her body language, every movement that might have meaning.

"Do you know what happened to Quentin?"

Tirza voiced several loud cries. She put her fingers up to her eyes, her mouth open and her features pointing down in an anguished frown. Tears gathered in the corners of her eyes, and she made the *friend* sign again, fingers tightly locked to each other.

"I'm sorry your friend died," Zachary said. "You must be really sad about that, and then everything that has happened to you... that's pretty scary."

Scary was a word that he would use in talking to a six-year-old. Zachary mentally scolded himself for talking to her like a child instead of a young woman who was nearly an adult.

"Do you know why Quentin died, Tirza?"

She moaned and approached Zachary. She took him by the arm and tugged, obviously expecting him to go with her. Zachary followed, though he was not sure about going anywhere with Tirza. She was vulnerable, and he didn't want anyone thinking that he was taking advantage.

Tirza led him past the nursing station, where the woman who had put him into the meeting room watched them stroll down the hallway together, her eyebrow raised. It was, Zachary hoped, obvious to any onlooker that it was Tirza leading him, and not the other way around.

Tirza led him to one of the individual cells. Zachary didn't think it was her room. That had been at the other end of the loop. The one that Tirza had taken him to was empty. No personal effects. Not that any of the rooms had had very much in them by way of personal touches.

But Zachary had an idea that it was Quentin's room. He had approached it from the other direction when he had been there with Dr. Abato. Tirza looked around the room, flapping her hands.

"This was Quentin's room, wasn't it?"

She made a sound Zachary took as acknowledgment.

"Do you know how Quentin died?"

She moaned and flapped. Zachary was frustrated by not being able to communicate with her. So close to having some answers, and so far away. Would she be able to tell him if her mother were there to help interpret her sounds and gestures? Would she be able to give a detailed account if she were allowed her computer at Summit, as she had given her mother following her kidnapping? Had they intentionally deprived her of her voice? Dr. Abato said it was to force residents to use verbal communication, but what if it were the opposite? To deny them any communication at all? By keeping them from using their preferred methods of communication, they kept residents from talking about what went on at Summit. From describing what was happening to them during therapy or after lights out.

But there were still students who had good speech at Summit. Students like Trina, the girl with the malfunctioning ESD. She had been able to tell him about the procedures at Summit, about what she feared. It didn't make any difference; still, nobody listened to her or to Zachary about it. Was there a tipping point? A point at which if there were enough voices, the public and the courts would start to listen? Did Summit keep it below that tipping point by silencing as many voices as they could?

"Quentin was your friend," Zachary said, starting again at the beginning, hoping he could gain some momentum.

Tirza touched Zachary's arm.

"And he died in this room. After Damien took you away from the school."

She flapped hard and stood on tip-toe.

"Did Damien hurt Quentin?"

She looked at him sideways, one hand again resting on his arm. Was that *yes*? Did she even understand he was trying to ask her a question?

"Is Damien here, Tirza?"

Tirza looked at the open doorway.

Was the man who had taken her away out there? Was it someone employed by Summit? Maybe a therapist that worked at both the school and Summit? Or who had followed Tirza to school? Had he gone there to snatch her, since there were too many cameras or witnesses at Summit?

He decided to approach it from the opposite direction. "Was Quentin sad? Did he kill himself?"

Tirza started to scratch herself. Not just the light scratching of itchy or dry skin, but digging her nails in as she raked them down her arms, as if she intended to peel layers of skin right off. Zachary reacted instinctively, grabbing her hands and trying to hold them still.

"No, no Tirza. Don't do that. It's okay. It's alright. Please, calm down."

She struggled to free herself. Zachary was not a big man. Stunted by early malnutrition and meds, never eating enough to put himself into a healthy weight category. He was taller than she was, but only just, and her struggles were frantic and powerful. He'd been warned that the autistic residents could be strong and not deterred by pain in the same way as he was. Tirza was like a writhing snake in his grasp. He was afraid of hurting her, but she didn't protect herself or hold back from hurting him. Zachary let go, worried that trying to control her would only escalate her behavior. He went to the doorway to call for help.

"Can I get someone here? Please?"

One of the supervisors glided down the hall toward him, unhurried. She wasn't an old woman, but older than all of the fresh-faced aides and thera-pists, her face lined with experience. She took in the situation in a glance.

"And this one without an ESD," she muttered.

"Can you do something?"

"Tirza!" The woman moved into the room, crowded with three people in it. "Tirza, you stop!" She clapped her hands, the noise surprisingly loud in the small room, echoing off the walls. She grabbed Tirza's hands and pulled them away from each other. "Stop!" She let go of one and slapped Tirza on the thigh, not as loud as the clap, but still hard enough to make Zachary wince. "Stop. Show me your hands. Show me quiet hands!"

Tirza was bullied into folding her hands together, compliant, her self-injurious scratching stilled. Impressive, but it also made Zachary squirm.

"What is she doing in here?" the woman asked. "This isn't her room. And who are you?"

"Zachary Goldman. I'm investigating Quentin Thatcher's death."

"Oh, yes. So I've heard." Her lips pressed together. "So you know this was Quentin's room. Tirza doesn't belong in here."

"Tirza said she and Quentin were friends."

"Yes, I imagine she did."

"Did they spend a lot of time together? Did they talk to each other?"

"They were closer to each other the last few weeks. Quentin acting possessive about her. Hormones; they can cause strange behavior in these kids."

"They weren't... uh, boyfriend/girlfriend...?"

"Certainly not. He might have been sweet on her, but there was no hanky-panky going on here."

Zachary laughed, embarrassed. Hanky-panky? At least she had answered his question.

"But Tirza... I thought she wasn't in residential until after her kidnap-ping. How did they know each other?"

"She went home most nights. But she has a room here, because some-times her mom couldn't pick her up right after therapy, or she wasn't able to watch her in the evening and needed Tirza to be somewhere supervised for the night. She paid full residential rates, even though Tirza was not here most nights."

Zachary nodded. "Ah. I see. So she saw Quentin when they were both done with therapy, if she came back here to wait for her mother or stayed overnight."

"Yes." The woman cast a glance at Tirza, standing between them, looking down at Zachary's feet. Her hands were still in the proper position. But she had bloody scratches down her arms. "I'd better have someone clean her up. You'll be going, then?"

21

The woman who had helped get Tirza under control took her out to the nursing station to get someone to escort her to the medical offices. Zachary saw Clarissa, the aide who had helped Quentin out, talking to another staffer, getting some child's schedule amended. She saw Zachary and Tirza come out of Quentin's room. At first, she frowned, looking confused. She saw Tirza's injured arms and her face softened into an expression of compassion.

Clarissa finished getting the schedule sorted out and then approached Zachary. She introduced herself as if they had never met before, a charade that Zachary assumed was intended for the woman helping Tirza.

"Is there anything I can help with?" she offered, looking back and forth between them.

"Well, if you don't have anywhere you need to be in the next few minutes, you could take Tirza to medical."

Clarissa looked at Tirza's face, but didn't get any eye contact. "Sure, of course," she agreed pleasantly. "I can help Tirza."

She put her hand under Tirza's elbow to escort her down the hall. Tirza moaned and pulled away from her, taking Zachary's arm in both of her hands.

"Oh, looks like Tirza has a little crush on you," Clarissa laughed. "Why don't you come along so that she'll cooperate? It's so much more complicated dealing with the residents without ESDs."

Zachary suspected that Clarissa wanted to talk to him without the risk of the other staff overhearing, so he agreed readily. Not that he would have refused anyway; he would much rather walk to the medical wing with Tirza than have to watch her being *encouraged* to comply.

"Sure. Lead the way. Come on Tirza, I'll walk with you. You probably know the way all by yourself, don't you?"

Clarissa took a couple of steps. Zachary gave Tirza a little tug on the arm. Tirza resisted at first, but she didn't fight him like she had when he'd tried to stop her from scratching herself. It was just an initial balk, then she matched pace with him.

"Find out anything new?" Clarissa asked in a lowered voice.

"I don't know... not really. A lot of dead ends, mostly. I found out that Tirza and Quentin were friends. But Tirza can't tell me anything about his death."

"No. She wouldn't have been here when it happened. I don't know if she has any idea what happened to him. Just that he stopped coming one day."

Zachary looked at Tirza's face, blank, apparently oblivious to their conversation. But he'd learned from the others that he couldn't assume that the appearance of not attending meant anything. She could be listening to every word.

"I think she knows more than that. She took me to his room. She got upset when I was talking about him... I think she wants to tell me something, but I don't know what it is." He shrugged. "Maybe just that she misses him."

"Probably. I don't think there's anything else she would be able to tell you. It's too bad she's regressed so much after the... runaway incident. She really was doing remarkably well. She could carry on a conversation... a little awkward, maybe, some starts and stops, but she was far more verbal than she is now."

"Runaway?" Zachary repeated. "Do you think she ran away, rather than being kidnapped?"

Clarissa gave a short laugh and shook her head. "I know her mom would like to believe that she was kidnapped by some mysterious person. But that's just wishful thinking. She doesn't want to admit that Tirza ran away, then got in deeper than she anticipated. Got scared and discovered that she didn't have the skills to make it on her own after all. She was back within forty-eight hours. I don't think any kidnapper would have just let her go. With the danger that she could identify them...?" She flashed him a smile.

"Maybe he didn't think she could. Maybe he figured she wasn't any danger to him."

"Kidnappers don't just let kids go."

"They do if there is too much heat. If they think there are too many people looking for them. If they let her go, everything quiets down and goes back to normal. If they... do something more permanent, people are outraged. They don't give up on finding out what happened to her."

Clarissa shook her head doubtfully. "There may be a few cases where that has happened... but I doubt if it happens very often."

"Maybe she escaped from wherever they were holding her."

"Or maybe she wasn't being held anywhere, by anyone, and just wandered aimlessly until someone found her and called the police. Don't read too much into it. The mother... believes what she wants to believe. She gives the police a big song and dance with all of these details she says she got from Tirza. But look at her," Clarissa made a little motion to the girl. "Have you been able to get more than a word or two out of her? She didn't tell her mother all of those details. Her mother is making it up, trying to convince herself that Tirza wasn't a runaway."

Tirza's grip was tightening on Zachary's arm. He looked at her but couldn't see any change in her expression. He patted her hand briefly, hoping to comfort her.

"Here we are," Clarissa said with a smile.

They walked into the medical wing and a doctor or nurse in a lab coat approached. An older man, considerably taller than Zachary, with a good build.

"Tirza has some scratches that require treatment," Clarissa told him.

He looked at Clarissa's arms and nodded. "We'll get those cleaned up. Come over here and sit down, Tirza."

Tirza didn't respond immediately, but Zachary guided her over to a chair and she sat down. Zachary looked around as the doctor treated Tirza, taking the opportunity to see part of the institution that he hadn't had access to previously. He couldn't see a lot; most of the medical wing appeared to be a network of examination or treatment rooms behind the doctor.

"Were you here Monday when a girl was brought in for burns from a malfunctioning ESD?" Zachary asked.

"Trina?" asked the doctor. "Yes, I was here."

"Does that happen very often?"

"There are occasional malfunctions. But no, I wouldn't say often."

"What about other burns from the ESDs being used too much."

The doctor looked up at Zachary and raised his brows. "No, of course not."

"No burns, no marks from the shocks?"

"Skin shocks are entirely safe."

Zachary switched direction. "Were you on duty when Quentin's body was discovered? Were you called to attend at the scene?"

The doctor looked back down at Tirza's scratches, cleaning them with antiseptic wipes. Tirza didn't flinch at the sting. She just sat there, staring up and to the right.

The doctor sighed. "I was on duty when Quentin's body was discovered, but I stayed here while Dr. Weiler went to attend to the scene."

"What did he tell you about it?"

"If you're the private detective I keep hearing about, then you've already seen the police and medical examiner's report. You know more than we do. All Dr. Weiler did was go have a look, confirm that there was nothing that could be done for Quentin, and call the police."

"Was the blanket wrapped around his neck when Dr. Weiler got there? Or did he remove it?"

"He wouldn't have removed it. He wouldn't compromise the scene like that. The unit supervisor had already removed the blanket and altered the scene."

Zachary considered this. "Removed the blanket *and* altered the scene?"

"Altered the scene by removing the blanket," the doctor rephrased. "I'm sure she didn't mean any harm. People without medical training often react the wrong way in an emergency. Or in a thing like this, where it isn't an emergency." He shrugged. "I guess she didn't know any better."

Zachary paced, trying to get all the facts straight in his head. He felt like he was right on the edge of a breakthrough, if he could just line everything up the right way.

Suicide? Accident? Murder? Was it even possible to know the answer? Despite all of the money that was lavishly spent at Summit on reward rooms and developing technology, there were no surveillance cameras in the residents' rooms, or even in the corridors outside the rooms. Only at security points; at entrances, major corridor intersections, and meeting and therapy rooms. They had the night-time security logs, but Zachary already knew they hadn't noticed Quentin's death until the morning, so he didn't put much stock in their being accurate. Quentin's door had not been locked, so there was no record of who had come and gone from his room.

Was there any connection between Tirza's kidnapping and Quentin's death? Was it just a coincidence? Was Quentin's agitation before his death just due to hormones? Maybe to his relationship with Tirza? Did he understand what had happened to her?

What was Zachary missing? Despite what he'd been told, he had a hard time believing that the skin shocks hadn't taken a physical toll on Quentin. All of those shocks couldn't be good for him. Or had he been choked out during a struggle with a security guard or someone else who came into his room and they had covered it up with the twisted blanket? Could Quentin really have successfully killed himself, either on purpose or by accident, with the blanket?

Zachary couldn't count how many times he had slept in a cell like that. While he had known it was possible to hang himself using his blanket or pants, if he could figure out a way to rig them up, it had never occurred to him to use them as a ligature. How had Quentin thought of it? Of course, it was disingenuous to assume that because Quentin was autistic, he couldn't have thought of something that Zachary hadn't. Zachary didn't know how Quentin's brain worked.

"Zachary?"

Zachary stopped pacing and blinked at Bowman. Just getting home from his shift. "Uh... yeah?"

"What's going on?"

"Just thinking. Working on a case."

"Out here?"

Zachary became slowly aware of his surroundings. Not in Bowman's apartment. He'd never even made it in the door of the apartment building, but was pacing up and down the long sidewalk outside the building.

"Oh. Yeah. Thought I'd get a bit of fresh air. Save your carpet the wear and tear."

Bowman gave him a long look. "You're okay? Nothing to worry about?"

"Sure. I'm fine. Just give me a few more minutes and I'll be up…"

"No rush, take your time. I just wanted to make sure…"

Zachary shrugged, trying to look as calm and relaxed as possible. Hopefully, he hadn't been talking aloud to himself while he paced. Doing that in his own apartment was one thing. Doing it while pacing the street could be interpreted the wrong way.

Bowman headed into the building, acting as if it were perfectly normal for Zachary to be pacing outside. But Zachary had a bad feeling he'd crossed the line. Even so, he wasn't quite ready to go up to the apartment. He felt like he was so close to sorting everything out; if he could just stay in the groove for a few more minutes, he was bound to come to some conclusion.

Five minutes later, his train of thought was broken again by his phone ringing. He looked down at it. Kenzie. *At least Bowman hadn't called Bridget.* Zachary answered the phone and held it up to his ear.

"I'm fine," he assured Kenzie. "I'm just walking outside. Clearing my head."

"I was just wondering…"

"Don't try to pretend Bowman didn't call you. He's not that subtle."

"Well… okay, then. Yes, he called me. Thought you were behaving a little… strangely."

The sooner Zachary could get out of there and find a place of his own, the better. He didn't need babysitting.

"Kenzie, since I've got you on the phone; you're sure that Quentin died of strangulation? He couldn't have died of something else and it was just covered up, made to look like strangulation?"

"Well, no. It's pretty clearly a case of strangulation. Bruises on his throat. Petechia. Swelling in his face. Cyanosis."

"It couldn't be anything else?"

"No. Like what?"

"Electrical shock."

"I thought we'd been through this already. The shocks that the institution uses are not enough to kill a person. And even if they were, there are no signs of death by electrocution. Only of strangulation."

"Yes, but couldn't—"

"Zachary." That ever-so-sane voice that women used to bring Zachary down to earth. Teachers, foster mothers, girlfriends; they all seemed to have it. One of those things they knew instinctively.

"No," Zachary anticipated.

"No," she agreed.

"Okay. Fine."

"Anything else?"

"He was dead for hours before he was found."

"Yes."

"He hadn't been moved?"

"No."

"He didn't have any signs of violence on him? Like he'd been in a fight or altercation."

"No. Scabs and scars from self-harm. Nothing that looked like it was from a fight."

"Had he ever tried to commit suicide before? Scars on his wrists or any other sign?"

Kenzie was slower to answer. "No."

"Would you consider that to be unusual? If he caused his own death, it would be normal for there to have been previous attempts, wouldn't it? People work up to it. It takes a few tries to get it right."

"Not all the time. It would be normal to find signs of previous attempts. But not necessary for a finding of suicide."

"Okay."

"You should go up to your apartment," Kenzie advised. "Have some supper. Relax and go to bed."

"Yeah. I will."

"Mario's worried. And he's not the type to panic over nothing. If he's concerned, you need to think about why."

"I'm fine," Zachary insisted.

"Good. Then take care of yourself. Are you about ready to close this case?"

"I'd really like to tie it to institutional abuses. Even if he did commit suicide, it was because of his treatment there."

"But you don't have any way to do that."

"I'd really like to say otherwise. But... no."

"Not every one of your big cases is going to turn out to be homicide. Sometimes an accident is just an accident and a suicide is just a suicide."

2 2

Zachary spent Thursday on other things. Catching up on some of his other cases. Filing paperwork. Visiting the apartments that were still on offer to see if he could settle on a place. It was a beautiful day for being out and about, but none of the apartments suited him. Every time he looked at one, he thought of Bridget, what she would think about it, and how things had been different when they had lived together.

Was it crazy that he missed being bossed around by her? That he missed her rants over floor coverings, paint colors, and blinds versus curtains? It had all meant that he was part of a couple. Bending to her will or making a compromise meant that he was with someone. That he was functioning as part of a unit instead of being alone. Just like he had wanted ever since he was ten and lost his family forever.

He had no idea what Kenzie's views were on floor coverings. Was she a hardwood floor girl, or did she like something soft underfoot? What were her favorite colors? Did she hate orange as much as Bridget?

It was strange to miss something so mundane.

He collected the mail at his mailbox, something that he knew he had to keep up with better than he did. But who sent anything important by mail anymore? Anything important would come to him by email, too urgent to trust to the post office.

There were a couple of car trackers he needed to retrieve. They were not hugely expensive, but it still made sense to get them back when he could. Besides the fact that he didn't want to leave evidence of his activities. Leave a tracker on a car too long, and he risked someone finding it when doing an oil change or other car maintenance. And that wouldn't turn out well if they figured out where it had come from.

Thursday afternoon Zachary started writing his report on Quentin's death. He still wasn't sure what he was going to write, but he started organizing the points and laying everything out, hoping it would coalesce into something more substantial by the time he was done. His conclusion—that Summit was guilty of child abuse, maybe even human rights violations— couldn't actually be tied into the point that Mira had hired him to determine: Whether Quentin's death had really been suicide.

If he were clever, he could tie all of the possibilities back to the abuses by Summit. Quentin committed suicide because he was being abused by his therapists. He had had no hope that he would ever be able to escape the abuse. Or, Quentin was killed by one of the Summit staff members. Maybe during therapy, because he was growing more violent and was not responding to the shocks. Maybe while being restrained in a choke-hold by one of the security staff in anger, or in self-defense when Quentin attacked a staff member. Maybe because there was something darker going on at Summit, and Quentin had been in the way. Or maybe it had been accidental. Negligent security staff hadn't noticed or cared that he was on the floor all night. Weakened by starvation and multiple shocks, he had been trying to self-comfort and had gotten his blanket twisted and knotted up too tightly and quietly passed away into the night.

There were ways to blame Summit no matter what the manner of death. But that didn't matter if he didn't know which one it really was. He needed hard evidence.

Then Thursday night, late in the evening, Clarissa called.

"I wanted to know if you had figured anything out," she said, her voice low, as if someone might overhear her. "Did you figure out what really happened to Quentin?"

"I'm working on my report right now," Zachary said, though he had laid it aside some hours ago. "It's pretty damning against Summit Learning Center. The information that you've given me, together with the information I've gathered from other sources... it's pretty obvious that they're playing fast and loose with the rules. If the police and the parents knew what was really going on out there at Summit... I don't think you'd have a program anymore."

"Really?" She breathed in his ear for a moment. She sounded nervous. Zachary wondered why she had called. Did she have more to tell him? Something she had forgotten or held back before? A connection she had just made? "Mr. Goldman..."

"Zachary."

"Zachary. Can I see you again?"

"Sure, of course," Zachary agreed. "Where did you want to meet?"

"I had... I wondered if you wanted to see how the ESDs work."

"I've already seen how they work."

"Not all three versions. And I thought maybe... you'd like to try it out yourself. See what it really feels like. Instead of just watching or reading what everyone says about them..."

Zachary considered. He had ventured to ask Abato before. But Abato had brushed off his request with some comment about how they had to follow regulations and only deploy them as the court had instructed. They couldn't 'play around' with them, using them in an unauthorized manner. There were strict protocols to be followed.

"You think I could?" he ventured.

"Yeah. I could get you in there. If you meet me at Summit after six tomorrow night, I can use my pass to get us into the engineering lab and you can try them out."

"What do you mean, all three versions?"

"The initial units that were used, the ones approved for use by the FDA. Then the amped-up units Dr. Abato had engineered that are in use now. Like Quentin had. And then... these new ones he's working on. The ones that he wants to switch to."

Zachary's mouth was dry. He took a swig of the lukewarm water sitting on the side table.

"The stun belts? You could access those too?"

"Sure. You won't want to try one of those, but I can at least show them to you."

"Yes. Yes, definitely." If he could see one of the stun belts, to confirm that Abato really was serious about using them for the more violent patients; that would certainly put the story over the top. No one could doubt that

Abato was unbalanced to want to use those on children. No one would approve of the use of such a device in a facility like Summit.

Maybe Abato had already been experimenting with the stun belts. Who was to say that he hadn't tried them out a time or two? On a child like Quentin who was no longer responding well to the phase-two device, who was getting more violent again after an initial period of success. A device like that could have unexpected consequences. Maybe Clarissa could help him tie it to Quentin's death.

"Okay. You can meet me here at six, then? I'll let you in a side door, so no one asks any questions about what you're doing there after hours."

Zachary agreed, and she gave him the details.

Zachary was pumped up about being allowed to see all of the equipment in the engineering lab, including the phase-three devices Abato was hoping to introduce into the program.

Clarissa came to the side door she had directed Zachary to, not in her lab coat and professional clothing, but some kind of casual Friday or after-hours look. She had on a ball cap with a green crest, with her hair in a ponytail hanging out the back. She had on a neat t-shirt and exercise pants made from some sort of high-tech fabric. They made her look slimmer than the boxy lab coat had, the material clinging to her shapely, well-muscled legs.

"Come on," Clarissa invited. She looked around, making sure no one was watching. The protesters apparently went home at the end of the work day and all of the students who went home had been picked up by their parents. The streets and sidewalks around the building were eerily quiet.

Zachary followed her into the building and stuck close to her side, noting the surveillance cameras in the various corridors they walked through. Clarissa obviously hadn't been thinking much about security when she had invited him to look at the equipment. She might be able to get into the lab with her security pass, but that was going to leave a record, and so did every camera they passed on the way there. It would be easy for anyone who looked at the tapes to follow them through the building.

But hopefully, that wouldn't matter. By the time anyone looked for him on the tapes, Zachary would already have broadcast to the world what he found there, and it would be too late for anyone to do anything about it.

Clarissa reached for the security door that led to the engineering lab, and Zachary held his breath, half-worried that it wouldn't open for her, despite her certainty. But the knob moved easily in her grip and she swung the door open.

They both stood there for a moment, making sure there was no movement inside. The lights were still on, but the room echoed with their footsteps. No one else was there. Clarissa nodded in satisfaction and let the door shut behind her. It hissed shut and clicked as the lock engaged. Clarissa moved around the lab with familiarity. Zachary was mildly surprised that she would know her way around there. As an aide, he wouldn't have expected her to be familiar with the engineering work.

"They're over here," Clarissa said in a hushed voice. She made sure that Zachary was following her. As she picked out pieces of equipment from a labeled shelf, Zachary got out his phone and started a video session. She stopped and stared at him. "What are you doing?"

"I want to get this on record. Proof of exactly what they're doing here."

He was afraid she was going to argue. She had that look on her face. Finally, she shook her head and smiled slightly. "Sure, whatever you want," she agreed.

"If you want me to be able to get things changed around here, get the aversives removed from the program, if not shutting them down completely, then I need proof."

"I hadn't really thought about it. I guess that makes sense."

She continued to get the equipment assembled, pulling a battery backpack off the shelf. "Why don't you get that filming and set it on the counter? Then it won't shake or fall down or anything and your hands will be free while you test out the ESDs."

"Makes sense," Zachary agreed. He set it up to record and propped it up on the counter. He looked at the screen, and then walked over to the spot it was pointing at. "Okay. How's this?"

"Perfect," she approved. She showed him the electrodes in her hand. "This is the phase-one unit. You ready to give it a try?"

Zachary tried to suppress a shudder. Was he really going to let her attach that to his body and press the button? He gave what he hoped was a confident smile. "I'm game. Let's do it."

She strapped electrodes to his arms and calves, positioned on bare skin. Then she had Zachary lift his shirt and attached electrodes to his back and stomach. She helped him to put the backpack on, lengthening the straps so that it would fit. Zachary tried not to think about the diminutive frame that it must have been fitted to previously.

"Are you ready?" Clarissa gave him a big smile, enjoying his discomfort.

Zachary blew out a breath. "I guess I'd better be," he said. "Are you going to give me a countdown, or—"

Before he could finish, he was seized with a jolt to his back that made him shout and splay his arms out in surprise.

It was a two-second jolt, just like all the units were programmed with, but two seconds was enough.

"Hey!" He coughed, trying to catch his breath.

"What do you think?" Clarissa asked, laughing.

"I can see why giving an unexpected shock is so effective," Zachary said, trying to keep his voice steady and not give away how much it had hurt.

Dr. Abato and articles Zachary had turned up on the internet had said that it felt like a bee sting. Zachary, never a big outdoorsman, had never actually been stung by a bee. But he couldn't imagine a bee sting would be quite that painful. His skin was still tingling. It had been more like a hundred bee stings, all at once. He had expected, when he was trying to imagine what it was going to be like, that he'd be able to resist the pain. He might flinch, but he'd be able to keep his body still. He wouldn't shout or cry. It would be like an accidental shock when touching both contacts on a battery or doing some home wiring. But the split-second before he dropped a screwdriver was nothing like the full two-second shock.

"Have you ever felt that?" Zachary asked Clarissa.

"Yeah. I tested it out on myself. I wanted to know exactly what I was doing to the kids that I was treating. That it wasn't going to cause them any permanent damage. Nice and quick, and then the pain is gone. But it's a good jolt, isn't it?"

Zachary breathed in and out. It didn't hurt anymore, but he could still feel the effects. Racing heart. Stunned senses. Feeling like the air around him was buzzing. It wasn't an experience that he would want to repeat. He could understand aversion therapy and how it worked. He wouldn't want to do something that would cause that shock a second time. He might forget just how bad it was in a day or two, but an occasional jolt would be enough to keep Zachary on task and toeing the line.

Clarissa moved closer to him and started to remove the electrodes. "Are you okay?" she asked, her voice still shaky with muffled laughter.

Zachary offered his arms and legs to her in turn. "Sure. I'm fine. No permanent damage, isn't that what everyone says? It was just one shock."

"They get accustomed to it over time."

"That's what I hear." Zachary tried not to let Clarissa see how his legs were shaking. He wondered in passing whether she had accidentally given him a phase-two device rather than a phase-one. Could she tell them apart? Had one been put on the wrong shelf?

Clarissa put the equipment away, and then picked up the next one.

"How much stronger is the phase-two than the phase-one?" Zachary asked, leaning on the counter behind him for support.

"Three times," Clarissa said brightly.

Three times.

Zachary again stood still as Clarissa again rigged up electrodes. She positioned them slightly differently so that they weren't right over the same patches of skin as the first time. He wondered if she did it that way on purpose. How many times would it take before the shocks started to leave marks on his skin?

"This is going to be bad, isn't it?" Zachary asked, trying to prepare himself for the next shock.

She didn't answer, making some minor adjustments. She straightened up and grabbed the remote. Zachary's stomach clenched. He could understand why even just seeing the remote could be a deterrent. He'd only been shocked once and just the thought of her pressing that button made his heart start to race, sending another surge of adrenaline through his body.

Clarissa gave a little salute with the remote and pressed the button. Zachary let out an involuntary yell. If the phase-one had felt like a hundred bee stings, the phase-two was like a thousand. Clarissa said it was three times as strong, but there really wasn't a comparison. He found himself thinking of the first shock as if it had been a slap on the wrist. The phase-two made his head spin. If he hadn't already been leaning on the counter, he would have toppled over. As it was, he arched into the countertop, bruising his back.

It took Zachary a few minutes to catch his breath and find his voice again. "Holy crap. That's the shock you've been giving these kids? That's what Quentin had sixty times in a row the therapy session before he died? If anyone even kept a correct count and the log wasn't a complete fiction?" He took a few more deep breaths. "They're getting accustomed to this level?"

Clarissa nodded. "Hard to believe, isn't it?"

"Wow. I don't believe that they don't feel pain. But I can understand why Abato might think so. I can't imagine getting used to that."

Without warning, Clarissa pushed the button again, activating the electrode on his right calf. Completely unprepared, Zachary flailed, tried to catch himself on the counter, and landed in a heap on the floor. He stayed there after the shock stopped, muscles quivering.

"Okay," he said weakly. "So that's how it feels to get shocked a second time. I think I'm done. Help me to get these off." He reached for the Velcro strap of one of the armbands.

A third shock made Zachary slam the back of his head into the floor. Tile over concrete was not a friendly floor-covering. Zachary groaned. For a few minutes, he just lay there, his whole body like jelly.

"Normally, we'd insist that you get back up," Clarissa said in a friendly tone. "No lying around in therapy. We'd get you back on your feet or in your chair, sitting properly, and then continue with the lesson."

"That's cruel," Zachary said. He tried to figure out what he was still doing on the floor, his thoughts as scrambled as eggs.

"You know..." Clarissa's tone was conversational. "I didn't think you were going to be a problem at first. You'd come in, take a look around, see what the police saw, and come to the same conclusion as they did. That Quentin Thatcher committed suicide. Why not, trapped in a place like this? Dr. Abato is so proud of his reward rooms, loves showing off the videos of the kids who progress so well with ABA, all of those happy faces on the website and posters and all of the other promotional material. He just loves showing everyone what a wonderful place Summit is. But would you really want to live here?"

"No."

"No, of course not. The parents say this is what's best for their kids. Really, they're just glad their kids are off of their hands. They are somewhere they are safe and everybody else is safe from them. It isn't an institution, it's their home. And the children are all happy here, aren't they?"

"They're not all happy," Zachary disagreed, trying to get his arms under him to push himself up into a sitting position.

He couldn't see Clarissa very well from his position on the floor, so he didn't see her reaching for the button, but he knew when she had pressed it again, because the bees stung and he went crashing back the floor. He tried to make sense of why she was shocking him. She had offered to help him. She wanted to show him what it felt like to be one of the residents at Summit. Was that it?

"No, they're not happy," Clarissa said. "You can get them to smile. You can get them to laugh and to pretend to be normal, but they're still not really happy. They eventually come to accept this as their home. They stop asking to go home with their parents, and they say they're happy here. But it's not true!" She said it explosively. "They're just saying what they're told to say. What we train them to say."

"Uh-huh." Zachary shifted his arms to prop himself up, then thought better of it. The last time he had tried that, she had shocked him. *See how quickly he could be trained?* "What about Quentin? Was he happy?"

"Of course not. Quentin had given up on being able to go home to his mom and brothers. He had settled into the schedule here and did pretty well with the therapy and routines. But then Tirza happened."

"What? What does that mean?"

"Tirza was staying in Quentin's unit now and then when her mom needed a babysitter. Quentin's hormones must have started kicking in, because he was noticing her. Starting to get friendly with her." Clarissa moved closer to Zachary and nudged him with her toe. "Can you get up?"

Zachary wasn't sure. He shifted and tried to roll over and then push himself up. As soon as he'd levered himself up a few inches, another shock hit him. He collapsed to the floor, landing on his face this time.

"What...? Why...?" he couldn't finish the thoughts, let alone the sentences.

Clarissa bent down and started to remove the electrodes. Zachary was so relieved he couldn't hold back a flood of tears. No more shocks. He could go home and sleep. Write his report. Whatever it was he had planned to do.

He stared at Clarissa's face as she worked over him. She was pretty. She smiled at him frequently, but her smile was like a shark's. Predatory. Like she had enjoyed hurting him.

As she removed the electrodes, his eyes moved from her face to her hat.

A baseball cap with a green crest on it. He had noticed it before, when she had first let him into the building. He tried to focus his eyes on the words. It felt like his eyeballs were twitching back and forth, bouncing around in his head. He forced them to focus in on the words, but they didn't make any sense. Even when he could make out the shapes of the letters, the words themselves didn't make any kind of sense. Then he realized that he was looking at a school crest. He didn't understand the words because they were the school's motto in Latin.

But he could make out the words around the crest, with the name of the school on them.

St. Damien High School.

D amien."

She raised her eyebrows questioningly. Then she glanced upward, toward the bill of the hat, as if she could see the crest on the front.

"My school," she said.

Zachary lay there, wondering what to do next. What was she planning? Just to let him go home? None of it made any sense. If *she* was Damien, why had she asked him there? It hadn't been to give him more ammunition against Summit. She didn't want them closed down. Not if she was running some kind of sex trafficking operation.

His thoughts buzzed around in his head, trying to settle on one thing, one explanation that tied it all together. He should get up. But the aversion training was working. He didn't want to try getting up again. Not while there was still a single electrode left on him. And Clarissa didn't remove the last one, nestled against his back.

Instead, she brought over a black girdle.

"Elegant, wouldn't you say?" Clarissa asked. "So much simpler than the phase-one and -two devices. No messy cords, no backpack. Everything is self-contained and just goes under the shirt. Out of sight, out of mind. People don't get so worked up about what they can't see. Of course, this one gives you more than skin shocks. It passes the electricity through your body."

She pulled up Zachary's shirt and started to wrap it around his torso. Zachary fought back. His motions were sloppy, and his arms felt like spaghetti, but he didn't want the phase-three device on him. He couldn't let her put it into place. Clarissa just reached down and pressed the remote, activating the one electrode still on his skin. Zachary tried to protest, but it just came out as a *Zzzz* sound and he bit the tip of his tongue. While his ears were still ringing, Clarissa wrapped the girdle around him and did it up at the back, where Zachary could feel the hard boxy shape of the built-in battery pack. Once it was in place, Clarissa slid her fingers up under it and removed the last electrode of the phase-two device. She rolled him onto his back.

"Comfy?"

"Don't," Zachary protested.

"You be a good boy and I won't have to."

He waited for her to hit the button anyway. She didn't.

"Why?" Zachary asked, his voice weak.

How was he going to get out of there? He was at her mercy in a locked room and no one knew where he was. He tried to calm his frazzled nerves to come up with a strategy.

TV detectives never got in that kind of trouble. Or if they did, they had some kind of brilliant escape plan. Using the device against her or building one of his own like MacGyver. Talking her down. A backup team in the next room, just waiting for the point at which they could arrest her for everything she had done.

Which was what? Kidnapping Tirza? Killing Quentin? Zachary didn't even have any proof she was involved in Tirza's kidnapping. Just a ball cap with the word Damien on it. Suggestive, but not proof of anything. It might just as easily have been what had given runaway Tirza the inspiration for a fictional kidnapper's name.

"Why what?" Clarissa asked.

"Why are you doing this?" Zachary croaked out.

"Hmm. Good question. Because I want to hurt you? Because you are getting in my way? Because I've been wanting to see how the phase-three works?"

Zachary lifted his hand to rub his forehead and she stiffened, hand on the remote. Zachary decided he didn't need to rub the sore, tense spot on his head, and rested his hand back down.

"But… your PTSD… You don't like shocking…"

"Well, I might have fudged a little on my symptoms. For dramatic effect. You can just look the symptoms up online, you know."

Her face was close to his, close enough to see the puffy bags under her eyes and the fine lines of fatigue around them.

"But you… look tired."

"Yeah," Clarissa agreed. "I tend to stay up too late at night, watching recordings of the therapy sessions." She sighed. "The videos don't give me quite the same thrill as actually shocking them in real life." She glanced over her shoulder at Zachary's phone, the red dot indicating that it was still recording. "Nice of you to provide me with a nice high-def video of *your* therapy session. The pictures from the surveillance cameras can be pretty grainy." With a nod, she indicated one of the cameras mounted in the corner near the ceiling.

"Aren't you afraid of them seeing you here?"

"No. Nobody checks the video until the next day, or if an alarm goes. Night security just keeps an eye on the entrances and does a walk-around a few times a night. By the time they look at it, I'll have it taken care of."

Zachary was baffled. "How?"

"One of the first things they taught me when I started working here was how to edit digital video. Cut out what we don't want a record of. Repeat frames if we need to fill the timeline. Surveillance video is so simple; empty hallways and empty rooms to replace whatever you cut out."

"But… how can you access it?"

"It's all in who you know. Make friends with someone who knows the password. They never change it. Too lazy. So even if your friend has to leave…" She shrugged. "No problem."

She hadn't just acted on impulse when she'd invited him. She knew exactly what she was doing. She'd done it before. Zachary closed his eyes, trying to focus his thoughts. The effects of the shocks were wearing off, but he didn't want her to know that. He stayed still and didn't try to get up. He talked slowly, as if he were still stunned. His brain wasn't quite up to speed, but he was starting to work through the scenarios.

"You kidnapped Tirza. You're Damien."

"Damien doesn't exist. Just like the police said. There's no one by that name working here or at the school. There were no strangers lurking around. Just students and teachers, just like normal."

Clarissa might have done some outreach therapy program at the school. Or she might have pretended she was a student. She was small and slim enough that no one would take a second look at her. Not without a reason. It was the perfect camouflage. One student among hundreds.

"Why didn't Tirza say who you were? Why didn't she name you? Say that you worked here?"

Clarissa laughed lightly. "What do you know about prosopagnosia?"

"What?"

"Many people with autism have some level of prosopagnosia. Face blindness. Tirza might be able to describe my hair and what I'm wearing. Some of my features. But she can't recognize me out of context."

"Context?"

"If I'm supposed to be her aide in the therapy room, she knows who I am. If I show up at the school without my lab jacket in a baseball cap? She doesn't know me from Adam." Clarissa chuckled at this. "Literally."

"Didn't she say… Damien was a man? A man took her?"

"Maybe she did. Or maybe they misunderstood or just assumed. She *did* meet a lot of men." Clarissa smothered a laugh. Was she even aware how depraved she sounded? "Differentiating gender and using the right pronouns is difficult for Tirza. She's used to being corrected. If she said 'she' when talking about Damien and her mother or an advocate corrected her to say 'he,' Tirza would think nothing of it."

"You knew she… couldn't identify you."

"That was never a concern. A hat and a gruff voice, and I was somebody totally different to her. A stranger."

Zachary tried surreptitiously to undo the stun belt behind his back. The more she revealed to him, the more certain he was that she never intended for him to get out of there. She hadn't just brought him there to try out the ESDs. To entertain herself with shocking him a few times. Zachary wasn't Tirza. He could identify Clarissa. The more she explained, the more certain he was that she never intended for him to get out of the engineering lab alive.

"What about… Quentin…?"

"What about him? He's dead. He's not going to identify anyone."

"Is that why…?"

"Is that why I killed him? What do you think this is? Confession time?" There was an irritated edge to her voice. She was happy to talk about shocking, or about victimizing Tirza. But Quentin was another story. "Quentin's death had nothing to do with Tirza's... disappearance."

Her eyes went to the side, avoiding his. Zachary wondered why she was bothering to lie about it. She had essentially admitted to kidnapping and trafficking Tirza. To tampering with video recordings. That she was addicted to causing others pain. Why was she stopping short of admitting what had happened to Quentin?

Obviously, it wasn't just an accident.

Zachary took advantage of Clarissa's gaze being away from him to try to unbuckle the stun belt. His fingers still felt like they were buzzing. They were clumsy and weak. Nothing felt right. How many thousands of times had he unbuckled a belt in his life? Why couldn't he remember how to get the tongue out of the hole just because it was behind his back? He couldn't remember which way to pull the strap to free the tongue enough to push it back out through the hole. In his head, he cursed in frustration. Why couldn't he undo a simple buckle?

Then the blast hit. Zachary's body arched on the floor. Pain tore through his body, deep down inside. He was on fire. Every muscle in his body tensed. He saw nothing but red. And it went on for an eternity.

The stun belt was exponentially more painful than the phase-two device.

When it ended, his voice stopped screaming and dissolved into slobbering wet sobs. Clarissa stood over him, her eyes wide. Zachary tried to make sure he was breathing, not sure he remembered how. The mechanics of it all seemed too complex. Clarissa's nose wrinkled, and she waved her hand in front of her face.

"At least we can make sure our residents using a phase-three are diapered," she mocked.

Zachary was too overwhelmed to even care.

Clarissa looked around, as if she were waiting for someone. An accomplice? Of course there was an accomplice. Someone who had given her the security password. Someone who had helped with kidnapping Tirza; maybe acting as getaway driver, maybe just sampling the goods. But she had suggested that the security guard who had helped her was no longer there. Had she given him access to the building? Or had security been too lazy to change the outside door codes either? She was expecting the ex-guard to come and help Clarissa dispose of Zachary's body.

"Where is he?" Zachary asked, when he could get enough breath to get the words out.

"He's…" Clarissa's head jerked up as she stopped herself. She looked at him, eyes narrowed. "You really are devious, you know that? You have a way of worming yourself in…"

A compliment to the man on the floor, lying in a puddle of his own fluids. So clever, Zachary. So very clever.

She continued to stare at him, her expression gradually changing to a smile again.

"What does it matter?" she asked. "Who cares what you know now? It's too late. You were too slow in putting together the pieces of the puzzle."

"You were very good," Zachary whispered. "Good at covering up."

She preened at that. She was proud of herself. Of being able to operate right under the noses of the administrators at Summit Living Center. Routinely changing videos to cut out anything she didn't want them to see. Getting around any security measures. Trafficking Tirza almost right in front of them, everyone completely blind to her deception. Except for the security guard. Was anyone else in on it? The unit supervisor who had shed tears for Quentin? Ego-driven Dr. Abato? Who else had known?

Clarissa played with the remote for the stun belt. Unlike the sharp-edged boxes that housed the buttons for the phase-two devices, the remote was small and sleek like the one Zachary had on his keychain to unlock his new car. He watched her with wide, worried eyes, afraid she was going to slip and hit the button again. Or do it on purpose. Zachary's own breathing rasped in his ears. Was it supposed to sound like that? Had she damaged his lungs or his heart with the stun belt? Zachary wasn't a big guy. The belt was designed to restrain two or three hundred pound muscle-bound men. Not someone like him. It was like putting too thin a slice of bread in the toaster. It was going to cook him. Burn him to a crisp.

"Quentin was *his* fault," Clarissa sneered. "No one was supposed to be… damaged. No scars or evidence of what was going on."

Zachary swallowed. His mouth was dry as cotton. He nodded, encouraging Clarissa to go on. "Just… business," he suggested.

"Well, not just business." She chuckled. "I mean… to start with, it was just for fun. But we thought… why not expand? Why not make a bit of money out of it?"

She disgusted him.

Clarissa saw him shudder, but just smiled, probably attributing it to the aftereffects of the shock.

"It wasn't just Tirza… and Quentin… was it?"

"Of course not! Tirza wasn't even here most of the time. That's why we had to… get access to her using a different method. She's such a pretty little thing. And very cooperative. There was demand, so we had to find a way to supply her. Usually it was one of the others."

"How?"

"Watch the security checks and shift changes and find the right times to remove them. Security doesn't go into the rooms, so a shape in the bed is all they need to see." She shrugged. "Out for a few hours in the night. Back in bed by morning. No one knew the difference."

"*They* knew."

Clarissa considered this for a long moment. "I don't know if they did," she said, lips pursed. "They're so removed, so disconnected. Did it really make any difference?"

Clearly, she had no intention of stopping, even with her partner no longer working there and the slight wrinkle of disposing of Zachary. Zachary had to find a way to put a stop to it. To save himself and to stop her from continuing to victimize the residents of Summit.

"Then what happened… to Quentin?"

He hesitated to try to take off the shock belt again. But how else was he going to be able to get up off of the floor? Every time she shocked him, he got weaker. Slower. Less able to get himself out of the situation. It was like the shock was killing off brain cells, making him stupider and stupider with every shock.

Clarissa scowled. "Why do you have to keep going back to that? He's better off, you know. He wasn't happy. He wasn't ever going to get out of here. He was getting too used to the aversives, and once Dr. Abato started using the phase-threes…" She ran her fingertip over the red button. Zachary tensed.

"He's never going to get permission to use them," he countered.

"He will. He's very good at getting what he wants. And even if it doesn't get approved… I don't think that will stop him for long."

Zachary felt a chill. Probably just the aftereffects of the shocks. Or lying there wet on the cold floor. Would Dr. Abato really just go ahead and use the stun belts on children like Angel?

"It's not safe... They're not like the phase-twos."

"No?" She waved the remote teasingly in front of him. "You're saying you wouldn't want me to shock you again?"

"They'll cause... permanent damage."

She returned to the previous topic. "What happened to Quentin was a mistake."

"What happened?"

"Stupid Steiner meant to shock Abilene. She was being too noisy, resisting. So he shocked her. But he hit the wrong button. Hit it a few times before he figured out why it wasn't working. The idiot."

Steiner. Zachary filed away the name for when he got out of there, so he could tell the police. Tell them the whole story.

If he got out.

That wasn't looking too promising.

"So after we got her out of there, Steiner checked Quentin's room to make sure he was okay. Saw that he was lying on the floor."

Zachary cleared his throat. "Dead...?"

"No..." Clarissa stared off into space. "On the floor. The blanket wrapped and twisted around his neck. He was tangled up, choking. He had wrapped it around his neck and he got stuck when he was shocked."

Zachary nodded, waiting breathlessly for the details. Or maybe he was breathless from the shocks or from imagining Quentin lying there in his cell, trying to breathe.

"I told him to get the blanket off of Quentin. Do CPR. Get the portable defib..."

"Nothing worked...? Why didn't you call medical? Pretend you were there for something legitimate and get him help?"

Clarissa shook her head. Her expression was dark. She was no longer giggly and laughing about the whole business. How fun it was to shock, molest, or sell defenseless children. The lines around her eyes became more prominent.

"Stupid *pig*," she said angrily. "He didn't even try to help Quentin. He said Quentin was just a troublemaker. Better if he was replaced by someone else." Clarissa turned burning eyes on Zachary. "He twisted the blanket tighter!"

Zachary felt his mouth drop open. "What?"

"Steiner killed him!"

"No."

"Gave it another twist and crouched there over Quentin watching him choke to death! Men!" Clarissa railed. "They never know what's good for them. Always have to push it too far. Everything was fine until then. But he had to get the police there investigating. And then you. The police came and were gone in a couple of hours, but you...! You have to talk to everybody. Look at *everything*. Ask about things that have nothing to do with his death. You couldn't stop at investigating Quentin's death, you have to dig into every nook and cranny, all of Abato's dirty little secrets."

And *her* dirty little secrets. She was ranting on about the injustice of Zachary's investigation instead of Quentin's death. How he had inconvenienced her.

If she had just left him alone, Zachary would have closed his investigation. She could have had her institution back, to play whatever games she devised. But she was too impatient and had to take things into her own hands.

"You need to learn to just mind your own business," Clarissa said, pointing the remote at him accusingly. "Why don't you get a life?"

"Why don't you?" Zachary snapped back, stung.

Impulsivity was one of the hallmarks of Zachary's behavior, a psychologist had once told Zachary's foster mother. The trouble was, there were no drugs that would reliably reduce or eliminate impulsivity. Zachary knew. He'd tried them all. His impulsivity would be the death of him one day. And it looked like that day had come.

Clarissa seemed to suddenly remember what the remote was for. She looked straight at Zachary, her eyes deep pits of blackness, and she pressed the button.

24

Zachary couldn't think and yet he knew he was dying. He couldn't reason or evaluate his body objectively, he just knew that the stun belt wasn't meant to be used multiple times like the ESDs, and the fire racing through his nerves toward his heart was going to kill him when it got there.

He'd read about the stun belt. He knew objectively that the shock lasted eight seconds and delivered 50,000 volts of electricity. But that didn't equate to the agony that stretched out interminably.

And then there was a light.

Zachary blinked.

He couldn't see anything, but there was a light.

And if there was a light, that meant he was alive. Didn't it?

Zachary tried to swim toward consciousness. The pain wasn't the same anymore. It wasn't burning its way through him. There was a dull ache deep down inside his bones and tissues. But that meant he wasn't dying anymore, and if he wasn't dying, he needed to wake up and figure out how to get out of the engineering lab.

He blinked again. There was a light. It was closer than it had been. Not close enough to reach, but getting closer.

It was a long time before he was able to really see anything. A light on the ceiling. Closer than he expected. And the floor was not as hard and cold as it had been. He tried to figure out where Clarissa was. She had to be close by and he had to figure out how to get out of there before she could shock him again. Maybe she had gone to the bathroom. Or to let the ex-guard in. Wherever she was, it gave him a few minutes to figure out how to get free.

He reached behind his back, trying to find the closure on the stun belt. He couldn't feel it. He grew more desperate, his fingertips burning as he searched for it.

Zachary heard approaching footsteps, heels on tile, and panicked. He had to get out. He couldn't get the stun belt off, so he would have to run. His legs were still weak and shaky. He tried to roll over and push himself up.

"Zachary. Hey. Stay put. Don't move."

He fought through a few moments of terror before processing that it wasn't Clarissa's voice. It was someone else. A woman's voice, but not Clarissa. A voice he knew.

Her voice hovered over him, her hand rested gently on his chest.

Kenzie.

What was Kenzie doing in the engineering lab at Summit?

"Hey. How are you feeling?" Kenzie asked.

"What... why're you here...?"

"I'm here to see you. To make sure you're okay."

Zachary frowned, trying to sort it out. He blinked and scanned the part of the room within his vision. It didn't look like the engineering lab.

"Where...?"

"You're in the hospital."

Zachary closed his eyes and opened them again. Tried to make sense of the inputs. She was right. It was a hospital room. The bustle of voices and footsteps. The paging system. The smell. He'd been in enough hospital rooms he should have recognized it.

He wasn't sure why he didn't figure that out right away. Was his brain permanently scrambled?

"What happened? How?"

"You should just relax. Take your time. The doctor said that you need time to recover."

"No, tell me how."

Kenzie boosted herself up to sit on the edge of his bed, her leg warm against his.

"I'll tell you about it if you'll be quiet and stay still."

"Yes. Okay."

"You should have told someone where you were going. If you're going to investigate cases alone, you have to at least let people know where you're going to be."

Zachary nodded a little. "Suppose," he agreed. "But what happened? How did I get out?"

"You set up your phone to record your meeting with Clarissa."

"Yeah."

"Not just to record it," Kenzie said. "To live broadcast it."

"Right. I thought... it would be the fastest way to get the word out... to show people what was happening at Summit."

"I got an alert that you were broadcasting. I didn't check it right away... I feel bad about that; I should have."

"Why?"

"If I'd checked your stream right away, I could have helped you faster... you wouldn't have had to go through all of that."

Zachary closed his eyes. "Did I get all of it? Everything she said?"

"Yes. All of the sickening details."

He breathed out. "Everything. About shocking kids for her own gratification. Kidnapping Tirza. Killing Quentin."

"Yes. Only she didn't kill Quentin. But she did help cover it up, so they can charge her as an accomplice."

"Good."

"It was horrible," Kenzie said. "It was awful to see her torturing you like that. Not to be able to get there to stop it. I called Mario, got him to open up your computer and have a look. He knew where you were and got in contact with the local police. Every second that ticked by... trying to convince them about what was going on, that you were at Summit, waiting for them to get there and get into that engineering lab... it was awful. It didn't take long objectively—seventeen minutes from the time we called them—but every second was an eternity."

"Wasn't so great for me either," Zachary admitted. He gave her a rueful smile.

"I guess not."

"I didn't know if anyone was watching. If anyone would see what was happening before it was too late. It's not like I have a lot of followers. I could have just been broadcasting to empty air or people might think it was some kind of joke."

"You have a few more followers now," Kenzie said. She tucked her hair behind her ear and laughed. "It sort of went viral. A bit late, but it's been shared all over the world now."

"Yeah?" Zachary was both embarrassed and pleased. He'd never had anything go viral before. He was proficient with social networking, but he'd never hit on the secret formula to actually have a post spread like that. He felt for Kenzie's hand and she grasped his in hers. Everything hurt, but he was happy to feel her touch. "If the police had gotten there sooner... they might have been too early. Before she'd had a chance to tell the whole story. At least this way... we have the answers."

"I suppose. But maybe the police could have gotten it out of her, instead of her continuing to use the stun belt. You're lucky to have survived. You're lucky they got there in time to treat you."

"Lucky me," Zachary murmured.

Kenzie snorted.

Zachary took a deeper breath than he had attempted before, trying to analyze his body, to see how badly he was injured.

"Is it bad?" he asked. "Or... is it okay now... is that it? I mean... what about permanent damage?"

"Those belts are not meant to be used more than once. They're much higher voltage than the ESDs at Summit. If they were used as an aversive like the other units, kids would be dying. Dr. Abato wanted to re-engineer them, to come up with something that was somewhere in between. Stronger than the phase-twos, but not as strong as the stun belts."

"So what does that mean? Is there permanent damage...?"

Kenzie hesitated. He squeezed her hand a bit tighter, trying not to wince.

"Only time will tell," she said finally. "Right now, it looks like you could make a full recovery... but your body will need time to heal, and we won't know for a while if there is any permanent damage."

"Like what?"

"She kept shocking you. They're only supposed to be used once. The belts are positioned to send a shock through the kidneys, not just deliver a skin shock. Your kidneys are working, but not at full capacity. The doctor isn't sure whether there will be scar tissue, or whether it will all heal up. It's like a burn, only internal."

Zachary had dealt with enough burns before. He gritted his teeth, focusing on the feeling of Kenzie's hand in his, trying to avoid slipping into the past. "Okay. What else?"

"Well, of course, with electrical shocks, there are concerns about whether there is any damage to your heart. And to your body's own electrical impulse system. Nerves. Movement. Brain."

"I can talk. So that's good."

"Yes. It seems like everything is operating normally, but they'll be wanting to do a lot of tests over the next few days."

Zachary let go of Kenzie's hand and brought his fingers up to his eyes to examine them. They were tender and reddened.

"They're burned."

Kenzie nodded. "The electricity will leave your body however it can. Feet and fingertips... anything in contact with ground... kind of like if you were struck by lightning."

Zachary closed his eyes and for a while was just drifting, dozing a little. Kenzie shifted.

"Don't go," Zachary told her. "Stay here."

"I'm staying. I just thought maybe I'd move to the chair."

"No, stay here. Where I can see you."

She gave him a tolerant smile. "Fine. For a few more minutes."

"Are they closing Summit down?"

"Closing them down?" Kenzie gave him a puzzled frown.

"Now that people have seen what's going on there."

Kenzie shook her head. "People already knew what was going on there. The aversives, I mean. Quentin's death and Tirza's kidnapping, that's different, but that wasn't operating under Summit's auspices. It was a couple of bad apples. And they've been arrested."

"They got... the man? The guard?"

"Steiner. Yeah. They got to him before he'd heard about your broadcast, luckily. Caught him off guard, so to speak. They're both being charged, and they'll go away for a long time. You ensured that by recording Clarissa's confession. But as far as Summit's operations go... nothing is changing."

"But the kids! They can't use the stun belts on children—"

"And they won't. They never were in use. They were only being used as a prototype, to try to develop Summit's phase-three device."

"But they can't just keep ramping up the power. Lovaas said that they would just keep getting acclimatized to the next level of pain, and then they'd have to increase it again. It doesn't end. Not until it's so high that children are being permanently injured or killed."

"They'll never get a higher-voltage device approved. The FDA is already threatening to ban the use of the phase-two device. It's okay; you don't have to worry about them using something that is going to cause permanent harm."

"Tell that to Margaret."

Kenzie raised an eyebrow. "Margaret?"

"All of the autistic adults who have PTSD or other problems because of therapies like ABA. And Tirza and others who are abused because they've been trained so well to do whatever they're told."

"I don't think you can put the blame on ABA. Those things are going to happen no matter what therapy you use. Or even if you didn't do anything at all." She put her hand over his again. "I think that you're seeing what you are... well, because of your own experiences. You've had some experiences with institutional abuse and therapies that you don't feel helped you. So you're naturally more sensitive about it... more sympathetic to others who have gone through it too."

Zachary's vision wavered. He tried not to get stuck in the past. He was in the hospital with Kenzie sitting beside him. Probably thinking what a putz he was for putting himself in harm's way. For being so weak. Women like Kenzie liked a strong man. She wanted someone she could have a good time with. Not someone who was always wrapped up in saving the world and failing miserably. Kenzie wasn't like Bridget, looking for someone to fix. He liked Kenzie for being a strong, independent woman. But could he ever be the kind of man she was looking for?

"You can't put the blame for all of the things people with autism go through on the therapies they've done. Think of how much worse off they'd be if they hadn't had therapy."

"But we should listen to the people who know. The people who have been through it."

"They're really not the best qualified to judge," Kenzie said gently. "They're... well, looking at it through the lens of their own experience. Distorted. I think the ones who are the best qualified to judge are the professionals. And the parents, who have seen how far therapy has brought them. These people can't remember what they were like before therapy, when they were little children. They can't judge where they would be if they hadn't ever had it."

"So the autistic adults are all wrong? What about the ones who have autistic children of their own, who see how much less stressed their children are when they're not being forced into therapy?"

"Of course they're less stressed if they're not being taken out of their comfort zones. But that means they're not being forced to progress, either. It's like we talked about before... sometimes therapy is painful. But that doesn't mean it's bad or unnecessary. Places like Summit offer an important service. Just think of where those people would be without it."

Zachary closed his eyes. He thought about Quentin and the life he'd lived in the two years before he died. Away from his home, his family, and his friends. Shocked into compliance. Zachary could understand why the therapy had worked to begin with. The shocks Zachary had received had kept him on the floor, even when he knew his life depended on getting up and escaping Clarissa. He tried to imagine how 'agitated' Quentin had been those last few weeks, when sixty or more shocks in a therapy session had not been enough to control his behavior.

And Tirza. Not controlled by shocks, but still conditioned to accept whatever abuse Clarissa and her clients inflicted on her.

Angel, his own parents being trained to hurt him, with nowhere safe to escape to.

Trina laughing and writhing on the floor, her skin burning under the electrodes.

And little Ray-Ray, his quiet hands forming a silent plea.

Stop.

Just think of where they would be without Summit Living Center.

EPILOGUE

Zachary saw a movement out of the corner of his eye and turned his head toward the door of the hospital room, startled. He pushed himself up slightly from his slumped position.

"Mr. Peterson!"

"Lorne," Mr. Peterson corrected with a laugh. "I've told you, you're old enough to call me Lorne, Zachary."

"I know… Lorne…" Even having known him for so many years, Zachary was still uncomfortable calling his old foster father by his first name.

Mr. Peterson pulled the visitor's chair closer to Zachary's bed and sat down. He looked Zachary over. "So… how are you, Zachary?"

"I'm fine. Doctors said I probably won't have any permanent damage. Just… one of those things." He shrugged. "You didn't need to come… I'll be out in a few days…"

In fact, the doctor had said that physically, he was well enough to go home any time.

"I just wanted to make sure… I got the feeling when we talked on the phone that things weren't going well."

Zachary let his breath out slowly, staring off into the distance. He knew he didn't have to put on a front for Mr. Peterson. He had seen Zachary through dark times before. "No," Zachary admitted. "This whole thing is getting me down… I thought… when people saw what was going on, there would be an uproar… they'd insist on shutting Summit down. But even after seeing it… they still don't care."

"That must be discouraging. If they were forced to close or change, you could at least feel like it had been worth the pain."

"Don't people care about anything? It's okay if people are being tortured, as long as it's not them? Guys like Dr. Abato say it's okay, autistic people don't feel pain the same way as we do. Like they're a different species. It's not right to treat *anyone* like that." Zachary's voice cracked.

"No." Mr. Peterson shook his head. "When I saw that video… I couldn't even watch it all, Zachary. I had to turn it off. That woman nearly killed you. I can't imagine allowing someone like that around children and other vulnerable people."

"But they said she's just one bad person. It doesn't mean anything. It doesn't make the institution bad."

"There's some truth to that. One bad person doesn't make the institution bad. But the fact that they didn't supervise her closely enough to see what was happening under their own noses… the fact that they put a weapon in her hand and pointed it at a vulnerable population… that they routinely edited videos of therapy sessions… and that their supervision was so lax that residents could be trafficked right under their noses…"

"Then why doesn't anyone care about that?"

"People don't want to have to get out of their comfort zones. To have to make changes. They'll watch the video and be all shocked about it… but that's as far as it goes. Then it's on to watching cats and cucumbers."

Zachary rubbed the space between his eyebrows. He was exhausted. Which made no sense at all, because he was spending most of the day sleeping. After weeks and months of insomnia, he suddenly couldn't stay awake. Though he knew it wasn't just sleepiness.

"What have they got you on?" Mr. Peterson asked, as if reading his mind. "An SSRI? Mood stabilizer?"

"SSRI… but then they gotta take me off of stimulants, so they're experimenting with other combos… waiting to see if they will work…"

"And it may take a few weeks before they know."

"Yeah."

Mr. Peterson was quiet for a few minutes.

"I was wondering something," he said finally.

"Yeah? What?"

"I was wondering about the girl you told us about when you came to visit."

"Annie?" Zachary had meant to pretend not to know what Mr. Peterson was talking about. But her name just popped out of his mouth before he could stop it.

"Annie. That was it. The little girl that died, right?"

"Uh… something like that. Or maybe it was Amy." His cheek muscle ticked, giving away the lie. Mr. Peterson was not fooled.

"Annie," he repeated. "Did you ever talk to anyone about her?"

"What do you mean? I talked to you."

"I mean did you ever talk it over with a therapist? The police? Or maybe get in touch with her family?"

"No. I talked to the therapist at Bonnie Brown… but I didn't tell them anything. Just… pretended I didn't know anything… that… it didn't matter."

"If this business at Summit was bothering you… bringing up memories of what happened to Annie, then maybe you should do something about that."

Zachary gave a short laugh and shook his head. "It's too late. It was almost thirty years ago."

"If it's still affecting you, maybe you need to talk to someone about it."

"No," Zachary said flatly. "There isn't anything to say. I didn't know her. She was just the girl who died in the cell next to me."

"It still upset you. Why don't you talk to her parents? Tell them what happened that night?"

"I don't remember what happened."

"Your body does. It's bothering you. It might have been thirty years ago, but your body still cares that you haven't dealt with it. And her parents, they won't have forgotten her. It would mean something to them to hear that someone still remembers her and cares what happened that night."

"I don't know how to reach them. I don't even know… where they live. Their names. They probably moved away."

"Maybe you could hire a private investigator to find out," Mr. Peterson said wryly.

Zachary rolled his eyes and shook his head. "They won't want to hear from me," he insisted.

But a couple of weeks later, Zachary and Mr. Peterson pulled up in front of the Sellers' house. A dark brick bungalow with neat gardens in the front filled with various kinds of greenery, but no splash of color from spring flowers.

"Is this the right thing?" Zachary asked Mr. Peterson. Not for the first time. "I mean... they put their daughter to rest years ago. Here I am, stirring up memories for no reason. What good is it going to do for them to hear this?"

Mr. Peterson considered the question seriously, even though he'd already answered it, in one form or another, half a dozen times. "If it was my child... I'd want to know. Even if it was years later."

Annie's father answered the door. He had been a tall man. He was still taller than Zachary in spite of how stooped he had become. Zachary was glad he had asked Mr. Peterson to go with him. Lorne seemed to know what to do; he connected with someone in his own generation. Introductions were made, and Mr. Sellers invited them in. They went to the living room, where they met Mrs. Sellers, a tiny woman, and the introductions were repeated. They all sat down. Zachary stared into a hexagonal china cabinet with some Royal Dutton collector's pieces in it as if that were what he had come for.

"Zachary." Mr. Peterson gave him a nudge.

Zachary looked at Mr. and Mrs. Sellers, a knot in his stomach. He shouldn't have bothered them. He should have just left them in peace. They'd dealt with their daughter's death decades before.

"You said... this was something about our daughter, Annie," Mrs. Sellers said. "I really don't understand... what this is all about. How you even know about her."

Zachary looked down at his hands, unable to keep his gaze on her face. On her sad eyes.

"I was at Bonnie Brown years ago. When she... was there."

"You couldn't have been more than a boy," Mr. Sellers said. "You couldn't have worked there when Annie was there."

"No. I didn't. I lived there. A resident. Like your daughter."

"Oh." They both considered that.

Mrs. Sellers inched forward in her chair. "Did you know Annie, then? Were you friends?"

"No... I knew who she was. Heard about her. But she was normally in a different unit than I was."

"Ah." She nodded.

Zachary found it impossible to continue. The silence grew. He couldn't even look at Mr. Peterson, afraid of being pushed into the conversation before he was ready.

"I have pictures of Annie," Mrs. Sellers offered. "Would you like to see them?"

"Yes. Sure."

She got up and retrieved a photo album. It wasn't thick. It started with Annie as a baby, looking like a perfectly normal baby, happy and healthy. Gummy smiles in faded Polaroids. Pictures with her family. But as she got older, her different-ness became more obvious. The distant gaze. Fingers screening her eyes. Limbs skinny and awkward, mottled with bruises and bite marks. Fewer pictures with her family. An occasional candid shot of her playing alone, isolated.

In the last pictures, she looked just how Zachary remembered. The thin, dark-haired girl who didn't want anyone to touch her. It unlocked a flood of memories. He had been suppressing the images for years, trying not to remember, but they were still there, as clear and crisp as if it had been just the day before.

"What happened?" Mrs. Sellers asked, her voice shaky. "Were you there?"

Zachary nodded. There was a lump in his throat and his eyes stung. He relived the outrage he had felt then, combined with the terror that if he didn't stay out of it, he would be next.

"I was in the detention unit," he said. Maybe they already guessed that part. "I kept screwing up. Getting in trouble. When they brought her in, she was screaming, kicking, having a... a tantrum, they called it. A meltdown. I don't know what triggered it."

"She did that," Mr. Sellers said. "That's why she was there. We couldn't handle her anymore."

"She managed to bite one of the guards." Zachary was amazed that the names still came to him easily, so many years later. "Berens. It was really bad. Bleeding. So after they got her into her cell, the one next to mine, they called the police. Had her charged with assault."

Mr. Peterson looked surprised at this, but her parents didn't.

"Why would they do that?" Mr. Peterson asked. "If they knew she had autism… she couldn't help it, could she?"

"They did that. Schools do it now. Call the police on little kids. Kids with disabilities. Like their behavior is criminal."

Mr. and Mrs. Sellers nodded. They must have been acutely aware of it whenever such a story hit the news.

"So the police came," Zachary glanced up at them and then stared back down at his hands. "She was still… mid-meltdown. If they'd just left her alone, she would have calmed down… wouldn't she?"

"Eventually," Mr. Sellers agreed.

"They didn't tell the cops she was autistic, just that she was violent and had assaulted Berens. He showed them the injury. Still bleeding. So when they took her out of her cell…" Zachary swallowed. He tried to just go on. It would get harder before it got easier. "They were hitting her. Punching her with their fists and yelling at her to stop fighting." A glance at their faces showed Mr. and Mrs. Sellers intent, living the story, and Mr. Peterson listening in shocked horror. "They got her down on the ground. Prone. One of them kneeling on her while they handcuffed her hands behind her back."

Zachary put his hands over his face, needing to escape from their gazes. The details of the memories didn't dim. His shoulders shook as he tried to keep his body under control.

"She stopped breathing. The cop, he got off of her and they turned her over. She started… started breathing again. She was mostly conscious and was breathing when they took her away."

Zachary rubbed his aching eyes. He opened them and looked down at her picture again. If he could just finish, maybe he would stop being haunted by what had happened.

"They never told us that," Mr. Sellers said.

Zachary nodded. Of course they hadn't told her parents. They hadn't even filed an incident report. He took a few deep breaths, again trying to calm himself. "Other cops brought her back a couple hours later, gave the staff hell for not telling anyone she was autistic. The guards put her back in her cell…"

Mrs. Sellers was crying softly. Mr. Sellers put his arm around her. "Did they hit her again?"

"No. She was quiet. But they... they put her in there, on her bunk, in handcuffs. When they found her in the morning, they took the handcuffs off before anyone got there to investigate, so they wouldn't know."

Everyone was quiet. Mrs. Sellers continued to cry, looking down at the photo album and stroking one of the pictures with her thumb.

"Sometimes when they arrest someone, and they lay them prone, with handcuffs on... it makes it harder to breathe... it's called positional asphyxia. I've researched it..." Zachary explained, the guilt weighing heavily on him. "She was in that position all night..."

"All of these years," Mr. Sellers said. "We've wanted to know why. If it really was just because she was... frail. Or if something happened. We knew about the arrest, but they said it couldn't have had anything to do with her death. Just a coincidence."

"Why didn't they tell us?" Annie's mother demanded. "Why didn't they just tell us the truth from the start?"

"They were afraid of losing their jobs," Mr. Peterson suggested. He rubbed Zachary's shoulder, watching his face with concern. "Getting sued. The institution getting into the papers and losing their funding... there would have been a lot at stake for them, if it was determined that they caused or contributed to her death. Whoever made the decision to leave her there in restraints could have ended up in prison."

"I never told anyone." Zachary gulped. "I had to talk to one of the cops who came and investigated, but... I didn't tell him she was left in handcuffs."

"You were only a boy," Mr. Peterson reminded him. "You couldn't have known how important it was."

"I *did*, though," Zachary insisted. "I knew they were covering it up. I knew it would get them in bigger trouble if the cops found out." He rubbed his eyes and arched his back, trying to loosen the tension in his shoulders. "But I was afraid to say anything. Berens... he'd beat the hell outta me if I did. I'd already gotten in trouble for making noise when they arrested her. Shouting and banging on the door. He'd already beat on me for that. I was just... I was too small to defend myself."

His face burned. For years, he'd lived with his cowardice in keeping his mouth shut. He'd told himself that it didn't matter. That it didn't make any difference. When all along, he knew her parents deserved to know the truth. He'd balked when Mr. Peterson suggested he get in contact with them to make peace with his past.

But having gotten it out, finally letting the burden of his secret go, he felt the weight lifting from his shoulders. It was easier to breathe. He had thought that the pain in his chest was an aftereffect of the electrical shocks, but maybe there was more to it than that. The more he'd learned about Summit and the life children like Annie led, the worse he'd felt about failing Annie all those years ago.

"Thank you for coming," Mrs. Sellers sniffled. "Thank you for finally giving us the answers."

"I was worried... I would just be stirring things up."

"No. We've never been able to let it rest. Maybe now... now that we finally know..."

Mr. Sellers nodded his agreement.

Mr. Peterson patted Zachary on the back. "You did the right thing, Zachary. Maybe now, you can let the past go too."

"Let's go see who's at the door," Ray-Ray's mother said.

He didn't like to leave his project, but she waited, holding her hand out for him, and eventually Ray-Ray got to his feet and took her hand and went with her to the door. The actors who came to the door didn't ever want Ray-Ray, but his mother wanted him to be in the same room as she was. She said he got into trouble too fast if he was out of her sight.

"Who do you think it is?" she asked him.

"Jeremy Clarkson?" Ray-Ray suggested. Not because Jeremy Clarkson had ever come to his door. But that was who he would have liked it to be.

His mother laughed and shook her head. "What a silly boy."

She opened the door and Ray-Ray saw immediately that it wasn't Jeremy Clarkson. The man was smaller, his hair was darker, and he was not as old as Jeremy Clarkson.

"Hi, come in," his mother said in a pleased voice. She tugged on Ray-Ray's hand. "Aren't you going to say hello to Mr. Goldman?"

The name triggered a memory in Ray-Ray's brain. He blinked rapidly and tried to remember what it was.

The man he had met at Summit in a therapy session.

Give Mr. Goldman a hug.

He remembered the lines. Remembered the scene. Mr. Goldman was the man who had been kind to Ray-Ray. Had hugged him gently and made him feel safe. He had been there, in Ray-Ray's therapy session. A special guest star.

Ray-Ray let go of his mother's hand and moved toward Mr. Goldman. He stopped, facing him, and tentatively put out his arms. Mr. Goldman stepped forward and gently enfolded Ray-Ray, like two gears meshing together. Mr. Goldman patted him on the back, just like Ray-Ray remembered from the first episode. Ray-Ray did the same thing, patting Mr. Goldman on the back.

"Hey, bud. How're you doing?" Mr. Goldman said in a soft voice.

Ray-Ray recognized the script. "I'm fine, how are you?" he responded, taking care not to run his words together.

His mother made a noise of approval and ruffled his hair. "Good job, Ray-Ray. How about showing Mr. Goldman what you're working on?"

The two of them released their hugs and Ray-Ray took Mr. Goldman by the hand to lead him back to the kitchen. Mr. Goldman looked at the items scattered across the table.

"Well, this looks interesting. What are you doing?"

Ray-Ray looked at his mother. Before, he hadn't been allowed to talk about cars. When he was at Summit, if he tried to talk about cars during therapy, Sophie got mad and yelled. But his mother nodded her head, which meant it was okay.

"Taking apart a carburetor," he informed Mr. Goldman. "To clean it. See, this is the float," he pointed. "These are the jets... that's the choke."

"Wow. That's pretty cool!"

Ray-Ray looked back toward his mother. She was still smiling. He climbed up onto his chair and got back to work.

"He looks happy," Mr. Goldman said.

"He is... much happier... and he's still growing and progressing. I was always terrified that if we didn't do all of the therapy we could, everything that was available in every aspect of his life, he'd stop his progress. They always told us the only reason he was learning was because of the therapy."

"He looks like he's learning plenty!" Mr. Goldman said with a chuckle. "I don't know how to take a carburetor apart."

Ray-Ray's mother turned on the teakettle. Ray-Ray stopped and listened to it for a moment. He liked the way it ticked like a radiator when it was heating up.

"He's learning more than just how to take cars apart. He was always good at that! But his speech is improving. Social skills. It used to take hours for him to unwind after getting home from Summit. He would be so stressed out and touchy. He keeps on an even keel better now. Our home life has really improved. Before... we were talking about when he would need to start residential at Summit. He was becoming so unmanageable at home."

She paused for a long moment. Ray-Ray looked at her and saw her looking at Mr. Goldman with very shiny eyes. She touched Mr. Goldman on the arm like she might want a hug too. "Thank you. I never would have dared to pull him out of Summit before your investigation. I'm so sorry for what you had to go through, but without you, I never would have gotten my Ray-Ray back."

Ray-Ray shook his head and picked up his screwdriver, pondering her meaning as he removed the air screw.

Zachary looked around the little diner and spotted the black woman and her daughter in the back, at a table near the kitchen. He could smell French fries and grilled cheese sandwiches. And ketchup. The good stuff.

Zachary led Margaret up to Ava's table.

"Uh... hi."

Ava had been talking to Tirza. She looked up from their conversation. "Oh! Mr. Goldman. I was watching for you, but then I got distracted." She motioned for him to take a seat across from them. Zachary slowly sat down. He gave a nod to his companion.

"Margaret, this is Ava and Tirza."

Margaret thrust her hand toward Ava before sitting down. She didn't offer to shake Tirza's hand, but gave a nod in her direction when Tirza looked up.

A slightly robotic voice came out of Tirza's computer. "Hello Gold Man."

Zachary grinned. "Hey. You got your voice back. How are you doing?"

"Fine," Tirza spoke the word aloud immediately, as if cued, then shook her head and turned her attention to her keyboard, tapping something in. "No, not fine. Hurting," her computer voice announced.

A couple of people sitting nearby turned to look at them, studied the computer and the girl, then eventually went back to their own conversations.

"I'm so sorry," Zachary told Tirza. "How can I help?"

She shook her head. "Can't... Not at Summit now... Done there... Thank you." She raised her gaze from the computer and looked at him out the corner of her eye.

"You're welcome... but I didn't really do anything to help you..."

Ava reached across the table to grasp Zachary's hand. "You did help. When I saw your video... I couldn't leave Tirza there. Not one night. Not one more session. I don't know what to do now..." She looked at Margaret and gave a helpless shrug. "I don't know what else to do."

"We'll talk it over," Margaret assured her. "There are other options. If Summit closed tomorrow, there would be places for all of their residents to go. One way or another. I'd be out a job, but nothing would make me happier." She turned her head to look at Zachary. "Not that I think they're ever going to close their doors. But at least Zachary's experience persuaded a few parents to pull their kids out. Maybe you can't change the whole world... but you've changed the whole world for a few people."

Zachary looked at Tirza, choking up. Physically, Tirza was completely different from Annie, but he could still see something of Annie in her. Maybe Annie's memory would finally leave him in peace.

There were still too many Quentins and Angels trapped in Summit or other places they were being abused.

But maybe he had made a difference for just a few.

SHE WAS DYING ANYWAY

ZACHARY GOLDMAN MYSTERIES #3

To those who have been silenced

1

Z achary Goldman?"

Zachary nodded distractedly at the man with the clipboard. The movers were wrestling his couch through the doorway of the apartment, turning and angling it to get it through. He wasn't sure whether they were inexperienced or whether the door was narrower than a standard door. He hadn't expected them to have any trouble getting his few pieces of new furniture inside.

"Mr. Goldman."

"Yes?" Zachary's eyes were drawn back to the bald, sweating man in a grey jacket, who was thrusting a clipboard toward him.

"I'm here to hook up the TV."

Zachary had guessed as much from the crest on his uniform.

"Yeah, sure."

"You need to sign the work order."

Zachary pulled his eyes away from the movers again to scan the heading and the signature line of the form on the clipboard.

"This says you're done."

"I am."

"But you just got here."

"I don't need to do anything here," the man said impatiently. "All of the wiring is done in the utility closet. I'm all done."

"Oh... then I guess I need to test that it's working."

Their eyes were both drawn back to the movers as there was a crunch of the couch meeting the doorframe yet again and one of the movers swore angrily at the other.

"It is working," the TV man said. "I've tested it all out."

"But in here," Zachary motioned to the apartment. "I should test it in here, make sure it's hooked up to the right apartment."

The bald man rolled his eyes at Zachary's presumption. "Come on, buddy. I've got other jobs to do. This one has already taken longer than it should have."

Since Zachary hadn't even seen him until that moment, he had no way of knowing whether it was true, or whether it had been a two-minute hook-up. He knew he really ought to check to make sure everything was working. If he signed the work order saying that everything was done, and then ended up having to call the company to get it fixed, it would be an extra charge. He looked at the movers in the doorway, wondering how much longer it was going to be before they could get the couch in through the door, so he could get in to test the TV and make sure he was getting all of the channels.

"Uh, if you'll just wait for a few minutes..."

"Do you even have your TV unpacked yet?"

That was going to be another problem, Zachary realized. The TV wasn't even out of the box yet. In fact, it was probably still down on the truck. He couldn't remember it being brought in yet.

"No," he admitted. "Could you maybe come back after your next job? Or take your lunch break now and come back in half an hour? I'll get these guys moving and get it all plugged in..."

The man thrust the clipboard at him again. "Just sign the form, buddy. If there's a problem, you'll have to put in a call."

"But how long would it take to get you back here?" Zachary had dealt with enough utility companies to know that it could be days.

"I've done my job. You're not going to need anyone to come back. Just sign the form."

Zachary sighed and took it from him. The form was dense with fine print, and he knew he should read it all, or at least skim through it before he signed it. There was another volley of swearing from the movers, and a long creak of protest from the couch as they tried to bend it through the doorway. Zachary winced and looked over at them. He scribbled an unreadable signature on the form and handed it back to the TV guy, who took it, ripped off a carbonless copy for Zachary's records, and left without a word of thanks. Zachary went over to talk to the movers about the couch.

"We're going to have to cut it into sections," the older of the movers said, wiping his forehead with the back of his arm. "Otherwise, it's never going through this door."

Zachary looked at the damage they had already done to the doorway and the wall around it. The couch was obviously not going to fit. And he wasn't sure how anyone was going to reassemble it if they cut it up to get it through the door. He imagined the pieces sitting in his new living room forever, unusable.

"It will have to go back to the store. I'll have to get something smaller that will fit through."

The two men looked at each other, rolling their eyes.

"Sorry," Zachary apologized. "I'll call them."

At least his phone was a cell and didn't have to be wired in at the apartment. He was sure that would have gone wrong too.

The movers left the couch in the hallway as they went down to bring the next piece of furniture in off the truck. Hopefully, the bed. He could live without anything else for a few days, but he was really looking forward to sleeping on a bed again, after the months of sleeping on Bowman's couch. Not that the couch wasn't comfortable. But it was a couch. He would have his own space back, out of Bowman's way. A bed of his own. His own TV.

Zachary looked around the small apartment. He had viewed it in the evening a couple of weeks before, when the lighting had been softer, and it hadn't looked quite as dingy as it did in the late morning sun. The landlord had said that he would repaint it, but it was obvious he hadn't.

There was a tentative knock on the open door of the apartment, and Zachary pulled himself from his consideration of the merits and deficits of the apartment to turn around and see who it was. Another utility man, the landlord, the movers…

But it wasn't any of those. It wasn't another form or agreement he was going to have to sign. It was a petite blond woman. Her hair was still much shorter than she preferred it, but at least it was her own hair. It had come back in just the same as before chemo, no change in color or curl, as the doctors had warned it might. Bridget's face was filling back out so that she no longer looked sick or waifish, but like herself.

"Bridget! Come in!"

She lifted the grocery bags by way of explanation. "I brought you some things."

Zachary hurried over to relieve her of her load. He hesitated, always unsure how to greet her appropriately.

"You didn't have to do this." Zachary indicated the bags, settling on just taking them from her without any handshake or friendly kiss on the cheek.

"I figured you would be busy with all of the other arrangements and wouldn't have the time to feed yourself properly."

Zachary put the grocery bags on the counter in the kitchen and started to go through them. The fridge was already plugged in, luckily, so nothing would spoil if he put it all away.

"That was really thoughtful. I hadn't even thought about food," Zachary admitted. He ran a hand over his hair. He kept his dark hair short, so it wasn't messy even if he happened to forget to comb it when he got up, but he couldn't remember if he had bothered to shave when he got up that morning. He hadn't expected to have to be presentable for anyone. He scratched his jaw and found it was covered with stubble. Not just one day's growth but probably a few. Another of the things he didn't put a lot of thought into, especially if he was on surveillance. People didn't pay much attention to a man who was a little unclean or rough-looking. They tended to avoid eye contact, in case he might ask for money or a job.

"No, I didn't think you would," Bridget agreed. She grabbed a carton of milk from one of the bags and put it into the fridge, then proceeded to unpack the other items. Zachary grabbed a few dry goods to put into the cupboard before she could do the whole job herself.

When they were finished, Bridget turned and looked at the rest of the apartment. Most of it was visible from the kitchen.

"This is nice."

Zachary was sure that, to Bridget's critical eye, it didn't qualify as 'nice.' He knew how exacting her standards were. She would never even have considered the place for herself. But Zachary wasn't going to be doing a lot of entertaining. His needs were modest and, despite the little bit of recognition he had garnered on a couple of recent cases, his cash flow was thin and irregular, and he needed to be sure not to get anything that would be too expensive for his usual income.

"Thanks. Um… I'd ask you to sit down, but I don't actually have anywhere yet…"

"It will be nice for you to be back in a place of your own again. I'm sure Mario was a good host, but you both need your own space."

"Mario's been great." Mario Bowman really had been a lifesaver, letting Zachary come to stay with him for a 'few days' when Zachary's own apartment had burned down, and allowing him to continue to recover there until he was able to get back on his own feet again. Zachary hadn't been comfortable intruding on Bowman all the time; he couldn't imagine how uncomfortable it must have been for Bowman to have someone else in his territory, always underfoot, for what had ended up being weeks on end. "But no one will be happier than him that I'm out of there now."

The movers arrived, with kitchen furniture this time, so in minutes, Zachary and Bridget were able to sit down to visit.

"You'll have to take care of yourself," Bridget said. "You won't be able to rely on Mario to keep the fridge stocked or make supper."

"Yeah, you're right." He would have to make sure he was eating properly, something that was too easy for him to forget when he was distracted by a case or other things going on in his life. "I'll be fine. I've done it before."

"Yes… but not well."

It was strange that Bridget was there. It was nice of her to bring him food and help him to get settled, but he wasn't quite sure why she would. They weren't together anymore. She didn't have any responsibility to look after him, as she was always quick to point out. Yet, in spite of the rift between them, she kept showing up, acting like she still cared what happened to him. She had gone on and was together with Gordon Drake now. Zachary was seeing Kenzie occasionally, though they hadn't really settled into a dating relationship yet. Bridget should have just moved on and not had anything to do with Zachary.

"I'll be fine," he assured Bridget. Maybe that was all she needed. Just some reassurance that he wasn't going to end up starving or in the hospital, somehow making her feel guilty for having broken up with him.

But Bridget didn't make any move to get up and leave. She tapped a nail on the tabletop, a nervous gesture that was out of character for her. The ticking of her nail against the table ratcheted up his anxiety.

"Is... there something wrong?" Zachary ventured. "Is everything okay with you?" He had a sudden sick feeling. What if she had relapsed? What if the cancer had come back?

Bridget instantly read Zachary's expression. "No, no. I'm fine," she assured him. But her eyes filled with tears.

Zachary instantly went into full-blown panic. Her anger and criticism he was used to dealing with. Even her blame. But her tears were something he didn't know how to handle. Bridget never cried. Even when she had told him about her diagnosis, it had been with dry eyes and a flat, stoic voice.

"What is it? What's wrong? What can I do?" He reached out to her, and she actually took his hand, squeezing it for comfort. She blinked rapidly and looked up at the ceiling, trying to avoid shedding the tears that had gathered in her eyes. If it wasn't the cancer, what was it?

Bridget breathed deeply to calm herself. When she spoke, her voice was even, but she talked more slowly than usual, and he knew it was a struggle for her to keep from crying.

"I don't know if I've ever mentioned my friend, Robin Salter, to you."

Zachary flipped through his mental catalog. He was good with names. As a private investigator, he needed to be able to make connections between people quickly, and it was amazing how often a previous name came into play on a new case. Seven degrees of separation became a lot less in a smaller community.

"Not that I remember," he said, feeling bad he couldn't make any connection to the name. Someone she worked with? Was in a club or other organization with? Bridget was very social; she and her family had a lot of friends.

Bridget waved away the apology in his voice. "I didn't know her while we were together. We were in treatment together."

"Oh. She had cancer too?" Was it appropriate for him to ask what kind? Or was that impolite? Invasive?

"Yes. Ovarian, like me. Only..." There was a slight waver in her voice. She was doing her best to hold it together, but she was right on the edge. She cleared her throat and took another deep breath. "Hers didn't go into remission. It metastasized."

Zachary's stomach was a tight knot. That could have been Bridget. The doctor had warned them that treatment might not be successful. Only thirty percent went into remission. Zachary had dealt with the specter of death before, but not like that. Not looking at his beautiful, vibrant wife and knowing that she could die in a matter of months.

"And they… there was nothing they could do?"

"They tried. But she knew she was terminal."

"I'm so sorry, Bridge."

Bridget swallowed. "She died on Friday."

He squeezed her hand, wishing there was more he could do to comfort her. "I'm so, so sorry."

Bridget stared off into space. He wondered whether she was imagining her own life if things had gone differently. Her own death. What if that had been her? What had she accomplished in her life? Who would be mourning for her?

"I need your help."

Zachary blinked, surprised. Even when they were together, Bridget had not asked him for help. She had been happy to be in charge of everything. She took on extra responsibility like it was a new suit to add to her extensive collection. Even now, with the divorce well behind them, she was still bringing Zachary groceries and fussing over his health and his ability to take care of himself.

She never asked for help.

2

I don't think she died of natural causes."

That wasn't what Zachary had been expecting to hear. He furrowed his brow, studying Bridget and trying to divine her meaning.

"You said she had cancer. Terminal cancer. It had metastasized."

"Yes."

Zachary sat back in his chair.

"I want you to look into it. I'll pay your fees."

"You don't need to pay me," Zachary objected. "You're my…" He trailed off. She wasn't his wife. They weren't family, not any longer. Categorizing her as his ex didn't make it sound like a close relationship.

Bridget didn't seem to notice his awkwardness. "Nobody else thinks anything of it. Her family, her boyfriend, not anyone. Or at least, if they do, they aren't saying anything. But I know it wasn't natural. It wasn't her time."

"Sometimes people go before they are expected to," Zachary pointed out. "Pneumonia, or an infection, or just because they gave up."

"She hadn't given up. I had just talked to her. She wasn't ready to go. She was still fighting."

"Chemo can be very hard on the body." He remembered the doctor talking to him and Bridget about how difficult the treatment could be. That for some people with very advanced or aggressive cancers, it was better to have a few months with good quality of life than to eke out a few more in complete misery.

"I know that," Bridget's voice was getting harder the more he protested. Losing that vulnerable, teary edge and growing angry. He could deal with her anger better than her tears. "But I saw her, Zachary. She wasn't ready to go. She wasn't!"

Zachary nodded slowly. "Okay. So, what is it you think happened? You think they made a mistake in her treatment? An accident?"

"Maybe."

Zachary scratched his jaw, thinking it through. He didn't have any big cases on the go. Just the routine insurance claims, cheating spouses, background checks; the kind of cases that were his bread and butter. Routine work he could survive on. As long as Bridget's case didn't take up too much of his time, he could afford to take it on as a favor. If it ended up taking up too much time, she was prepared to pay him. More than likely, it would just be a few inquiries to find out what had happened and then he could put Bridget's mind at ease.

"Are you sure you want to do this, Bridget? It could just end up making you feel worse, keeping it fresh. It might hurt Robin's family and friends and cause resentments."

Bridget nodded. Her jaw muscles were tightly clenched, but otherwise she gave no sign of her deep emotions, smiling pleasantly as if they were discussing the weather. "I realize all that, but... I think it's important."

"Is it what Robin would have wanted? I mean... she was dying anyway, would she really have wanted to make a big deal over it?"

A flush started to creep up Bridget's throat.

"You don't think it's important?" she demanded. "You think that those few months aren't worth anything? That they can just be written off? Our time here is important, whether it is years, or months, or days. No one has the right to take them away from us."

"Okay. I just want to make sure it's really what you want. When someone starts poking around in a case like this, people can get pretty worked up. You might not think that anyone would care, you think that everyone else would just want to know the truth, but it can cause... really bad feelings... even threats of violence."

"I'm prepared to deal with that." The rosy flush had risen all the way to Bridget's ears. She was steamed, but she was holding back because she wanted Zachary to take the case. She knew that if she exploded, he could simply say he wouldn't take the case. He wasn't obligated.

But he would take it, even if she did blow up at him. He would always do any favor she asked of him.

"So, will you? Will you look into it for me?"

"Yes. Email me all of the information you have on Robin and the hospital or treatment program and I'll see what I can find out. I just wanted to be sure you knew what you were getting into."

Bridget's shoulders dipped and her jaw relaxed. "Thank you, Zachary. You don't know what this means to me."

He allowed himself only a fleeting vision of her expressing her gratitude to him in other ways. Of her softening toward him and realizing how good they were together, how important they were to each other.

But that wasn't why she was there. That wasn't why she had come.

There was a knock on the open door, and Zachary startled, jerking his head around to see who was there. For a split second, he worried that it would be the landlord, upset about the couch sitting in the hallway and the damage to the doorframe and wall. But it was Mario Bowman, smiling at them. He was balding, overweight, and always looked a little seedy when he wasn't wearing his police uniform. But he was a devoted friend who had gone above and beyond the call of duty to help out a man who was hardly more than an acquaintance at the time. Zachary's respect for the cop had only grown as they had gotten to know each other better. Bowman was one of the good guys. One of the best.

"I thought I'd get a start on these boxes." Bowman was leering as if he'd just caught the two of them in a heated embrace. "If you two don't mind being interrupted."

Bridget was on her feet before Zachary, letting go of his hand and stepping over to greet Bowman with a peck on the cheek. "Mario! What a delight to see you again! I'll bet you're happy to be getting rid of this scoundrel."

Zachary made it belatedly to his feet, feeling off-balance for just a split second before he managed to gain his equilibrium. While it appeared to everyone but his physical therapist that he was fully recovered from his last couple of 'accidents,' Zachary was acutely aware of every movement or reaction that took a microsecond longer than it used to. Those instants frustrated him, and all the more when he was the only one who noticed them and everybody else thought he was overreacting or imagining things.

Bowman looked at Zachary with an expression of affection. "Well, to tell the truth…" he trailed off, letting the phrase hang for a moment, "yes, nothing would make me happier than to see the back of him."

He gave Zachary a rough hug around the shoulders to show that he meant no ill will toward Zachary. And Zachary knew it was true, Bowman would be happy to see Zachary out of Bowman's apartment, but even happier to know that Zachary was safely installed in a place of his own.

"So, shall I start bringing things up?"

"Yes, sure," Zachary agreed. "There really isn't much though."

"Not much." Bowman rolled his eyes at Bridget. "It's amazing how much one person can acquire in the space of a few weeks."

He slapped Zachary on the back and headed back out into the hallway to go get the things he'd brought over in the car.

"It isn't that much," Zachary repeated to Bridget, his face warm. When he had moved in to sleep on Bowman's couch, he'd had nothing but the clothes on his back, which weren't even all his own. He hadn't even had a wallet or any means to pay for anything else. But Bowman and others had chipped in to get him clothes, a suitcase, and what other little necessaries Zachary needed until he was able to access his bank account and credit card account, and then to get the settlement money from the insurer so that he'd be able to get established again. He had a new laptop and some photographic equipment, a few files for the cases that he'd worked on since losing everything, his clothing… but it really wasn't more than would fit in a couple of suitcases.

He followed Bowman down to the car and bent over to pick up a suitcase, looking into the car. "What's all this?"

Bowman picked up a couple of boxes, carefully stacked and balanced. "Just a few little things."

Zachary lugged his suitcases, trying to figure out what else Bowman had packed. There couldn't have been that much more than would fit in his suitcases. Bowman had shooed him out of the apartment early that morning, telling him that he'd better be ready well before the first workers were scheduled to get there, and that Bowman would pack everything up and take it over.

Bridget was still there when they got up to Zachary's apartment. He hadn't been sure whether she would stay around or if she would take the first opportunity to disappear. She took the box that Bowman had stacked on top of the one he was carrying and set it down on the kitchen table to look through the contents. Zachary looked down at an assortment of dishes, sheets, and towels. He looked over at Bowman. A bachelor himself, Bowman didn't exactly have a lot to give away.

"Just a few things I wanted to get rid of," Bowman offered with a shrug. "I mean, you're going to need all those sorts of odds and ends, and my place is getting cluttered."

"You didn't need to do that."

Showing no hint of being self-conscious, Bridget started to remove the dishes and find the appropriate places for them in the kitchen. When Zachary looked at her with his mouth open, looking for a reason to object, she just shook her head.

"Why don't you go unpack your clothes?"

"Uh… okay," Zachary agreed, and took the suitcases into the bedroom to get a start on them.

Zachary was exhausted at the end of the day when everyone was gone, and he was left in his new apartment all alone. He had furniture, other than a couch. The TV and internet were both working, and his various possessions and the donations from Bridget and Bowman were all neatly put away. The apartment felt sparse and empty, but it was a start. After years of being a foster kid barely able to hold on to the one possession that really mattered— the camera given to him by Mr. Peterson—he was used to starting over with nothing. And he knew that he would start to collect new possessions at a rate that would have alarmed Bridget had they still been living together. She never could understand his need to hold on to absolutely everything. Like a grandparent who had lived through the depression, Zachary knew what it was like to want. Parting with anything, no matter how small and insignificant, was difficult.

It was probably a good thing he didn't have a couch, so he couldn't lie down and go to sleep in front of the TV in the living room like he had been doing at Bowman's house. Doctors had always told him that was poor sleep hygiene and that he wouldn't really get the REM sleep he needed to be alert and mentally healthy. It would be his first night sleeping in a bed in months, and he was looking forward to being able to stretch out and not worry about running into the ends of the couch or falling off the side as he had several times.

It was no surprise that when he lay down to go to sleep, he was not the least bit sleepy. His brain whirled around and around, going over everything that had happened during the day, analyzing it, thinking of all of the things he should have said and done instead of what he had. What kept returning to him over and over was the conversation with Bridget about Robin Salter. He probably should have said no. He should have at least been more resistant and given Bridget a day or two to think about it before agreeing to help. The more he looked at the problem, the more obvious it became that it was a minefield, with no safe way across. If he didn't find any evidence that it was not a natural death, Bridget was going to be angry and think that he had not been trying hard enough and had not done a good job. If he did find evidence that the hospital had covered up a mistake or something else, she was going to be angry about Robin's life being cut short before her time was up and she wouldn't have anyone to vent to about it except for Zachary. There was no one else behind her on her mission to find out the truth, so that put Zachary directly in the crosshairs either way.

What if she didn't accept his findings? What if the police or the doctors didn't? What if he had suspicions but couldn't prove anything?

Zachary got out of bed and wandered out to the living room. He turned the TV on and began to pace, trying to silence the arguments going around his head and to get into a rhythm. He checked out the fridge, but he wasn't really hungry, and despite the fact that Bridget had filled it with food, nothing appealed to him. He would have to make a start on it the next day, because otherwise, a few days down the line, things were going to start going bad and he wouldn't be able to keep up with them.

His body was exhausted before he started, so it was no wonder that he quickly tired of the pacing and had to sit down. He had an easy chair, but he wanted to lie on his side rather than recline and was too antsy to stay in the chair.

He ended up lying on the carpet where the couch should be, a throw pillow between his arm and his head, watching inane infomercials on TV until he fell asleep.

3

Bridget had emailed Zachary all of the details she had on Robin Salter and her doctors and treatment. Having been in treatment together, she had some knowledge of when the doctors were likely to be reachable and some other helpful details. She also provided links to Robin's various social media sites, and Zachary spent a few minutes browsing through them to get to know the woman he was trying to get some justice for.

She was a black woman with a narrow face and small features. Attractive in her older pictures, but obviously sick and suffering in the more recent ones. Her hair had been shaved close for a few weeks, and then she only appeared in headscarfs and hats, obviously having lost her hair to her cancer treatments. She had a smile in the older pictures. Grim and determined in the more recent ones.

There was a memorial page set up where her family and friends had posted pictures, memories, and tributes to her. Zachary tried to read them dispassionately, but he couldn't help feeling for the people who had lost her. Her passing had, as Bridget had said, been sudden and unexpected, even though she had been given a terminal diagnosis. Zachary made a list of questions to ask the medical staff, trying to stay focused on the task at hand and not to get distracted by the badges showing that he had announcements to read in his own feed. That would wait; he was working.

Zachary transferred whatever information he would need for the interviews to his phone, grabbed his keys, and headed out. He carefully locked his apartment door behind him and walked to the elevator. The elevator bell dinged, but he didn't get on, instead retreating to his apartment door and double-checking the locks. He looked around for anyone suspicious. He needed to be aware of everyone around him, not allowing himself to be lulled into a sense of false security. There could be no more break-ins, no more fires, no more accidents. He checked the locks one final time and walked down the stairs instead of taking the elevator.

The first person he asked for in the oncology department at the hospital was Dr. Aaron West. The nurse at the nursing station shook her head.

"He's in surgery at the moment. I'm not sure when he'll be available."

"Could I set up an appointment? Or does he do rounds at a certain time? There must be some kind of arrangements I could make."

She looked up at the computer screen, and then down at her paperwork, though she must have had a pretty good idea what Dr. West's regular schedule was if she'd worked there for any length of time. She was an older woman with round glasses and short, limp brown hair. She maintained an air of suspicion listening to him.

"And you want to consult with him on which patient's care?"

Zachary licked his lips. "Robin Salter."

She looked up at him quickly. "Robin Salter? But she died."

"Yes. I still have questions for him with regard to her treatment and prognosis."

"Well, obviously she doesn't have a prognosis at this point."

"No." Zachary's face warmed. "I mean what her prognosis was before she passed. What the expectations were for how she would be treated and… how long she had left."

The nurse still looked at him as if he were crazy. "Why would you want to know that? You're not related to Ms. Salter."

She didn't say it as a question. And he supposed she probably had a pretty good idea that he wasn't blood related to her simply evidenced by his white skin.

"I've been asked to look into any irregularities in Robin's care." He hoped by using her first name, he could humanize Robin Salter and make the nurse more sympathetic to his cause. And to distract her from what he was actually asking.

"Look into...? What are you talking about? Ms. Salter had cancer and she died. There wasn't anything irregular about that."

"There have been some questions..."

She stared at him, not open to the direction of the conversation at all. Zachary tried to give her a warm smile to thaw her cool attitude.

"Were you involved in Robin's treatment? Were you close?"

She scowled. "Patient care is confidential. Do you have some kind of release from the family consenting to this... investigation?"

"No, at the moment I'm just exploring whether there is actually anything to investigate. I take it you don't have any concerns."

"Of course not."

He nodded agreeably. "My wife was treated here. I don't know if you remember... Bridget Downy...?"

Her penciled eyebrows rose. "Your wife is Bridget Downy? I don't remember seeing you before."

"My ex-wife," Zachary amended. He let out a slow breath. "Cancer is very hard on families. She... withdrew from me... our marriage didn't survive."

"But she did. She went into remission, didn't she?"

"Yes." Zachary forced another smile, showing how pleased he was that she had survived her treatment and the horrible disease that had been growing inside her. How pleased he was with the excellent care she had received from the oncology center. People could read things like that in body language and facial expression. Much more clearly than anyone expected. He noticed a slight loosening of the nurse's body muscles. A little more relaxation in her face and shoulders. "Bridget has always been very positive of the care that she received here." That, at least, was true. "Look, I'm sure there is nothing to this business about Robin Salter. But... it is my job to look into it, so that's what I'm doing. Once I've talked to Dr. West and anyone else who might have insight into her care and her death, then I can report to the family that there wasn't anything unusual or unexpected about her death..."

"I suppose."

"Should I make an appointment to see Dr. West? Or do you know when a good time to see him would be?"

The nurse lowered her voice to a more confidential tone. "I don't think it will be too long before he's here for rounds. Unless something goes south with the surgery, it shouldn't take long. He can talk to you then."

"Thank you, that's great. You must have him well-trained."

She gave a little chuckle. "These young doctors. Someone has to take them in hand."

"I can imagine. Were you... closely involved in Robin's care?"

The nurse nodded reluctantly. "Yes, I suppose so. But there wasn't anything unusual about her case. Sometimes... people go before you expect them to. That's just the nature of disease."

"Yes. I'm sure there isn't anything to it." He squinted at her name badge, difficult to make out with black text on a shiny gold background that reflected the light. "Nurse Betty?"

"Betty Hoogner," she agreed, wetting her pink lips and giving a curt nod.

"I think I remember Bridget mentioning you." He paused. "You always remember the good ones. Angels of mercy." He was afraid that might be over the top, but Nurse Betty lapped it up. It didn't matter that Zachary hadn't supplied any details of what she had done to make Bridget so grateful.

"Well, that's so sweet. I remember Bridget being a lot... easier than Robin."

Zachary couldn't imagine Bridget being particularly easy to nurse, given how strong-willed she was. But she was good at managing people and was very gracious when the situation demanded it. In situations that didn't involve Zachary. When they had first met and started to see each other, he had thought she was the sweetest and loveliest women he'd ever met. Everybody had flaws, but finding out Bridget wasn't so perfect after all had been a shock.

"It must be hard being that sick," he said. "I guess you deal with a lot of people who aren't very grateful to be here."

Betty nodded her agreement. "And as nurses, we understand that. We know that nobody chose to get sick and to have to come here. And that we're seeing people at their very worst. Some people... manage it better than others."

"Did you like Robin?"

"Like her?" Betty said blankly. "Well, we do get attached to some of our patients, but mostly we try to maintain a professional distance. Otherwise, it can be very hard working somewhere like this where you lose so many people."

"And Robin wasn't one of the ones you let yourself get attached to."

"No. That isn't because she was a bad person, you know, just…"

"I suppose when you knew she was terminal…"

"It might sound callous," Betty said, "but you have to maintain some emotional distance, or it's just too hard."

"Was there anyone who took care of Robin who was really attached to her? Or who really disliked her?"

"No. I can't think of anyone."

"There isn't anyone who ever said anything about her that worried you?"

Betty shook her head emphatically. "No, certainly not."

Zachary stared off past Betty, committing everything to memory and mentally checking his list of questions to ask. While he would have liked to pull out his phone to write down her answers and consult his notes, he knew if he did, Betty would become self-conscious and stop sharing.

"Can you tell me about the day Robin died?"

Betty patted down her already limp, shapeless hair with one hand. "I don't know what I can tell you."

"You weren't on shift that day?"

"Yes, I was on shift. I'm on every day, really." It was no wonder she seemed so worn. With her obvious years of experience, she should have ranked a little time off. Working every day, especially in an emotionally taxing setting like a cancer treatment center, seemed like a recipe for physical or mental collapse. "I just mean… it wasn't like it was an eventful day. Nothing noteworthy really happened. It was just… the day Robin died."

"Did she have visitors?"

"Yes, a few. She was doing pretty well… up until the end. She had a few people in and out. Her boyfriend, family members…"

"Did she… just die in her sleep? Or did something happen?"

"She was in a lot of pain. We'd increased her painkillers and she slept a lot. Her family was in to see her Thursday evening, and then… Friday morning, she was gone."

"She wasn't on some kind of monitor that would tell you when her heart stopped? Ring an alarm?"

"Despite what you see on TV, very few patients are actually hooked up to a heart monitor at the hospital. Unless they actually have some kind of heart problems that need to be monitored. We aren't notified every time someone's heart stops." Her gaze drifted away from Zachary. "This is a cancer ward. We don't generally take heroic measures. We don't try to bring someone back once their heart stops."

Zachary thought about that. It made sense. And he knew that he himself had rarely been on a heart monitor during his hospitalizations. He *had* been after experiencing a series of electrical shocks, but not during other hospital stays.

"I guess in Robin's case, it was a release? It was good that she didn't suffer longer?" Zachary suggested.

"Yes, that's true… cancer can be a very difficult way to go. We do our very best to fight it back, but often in the end, the monster wins."

"Robin's death was unexpected."

"No."

Zachary focused on Betty's face and raised his brows in query.

"Her death was not unexpected. The timing was," she clarified.

"Ah. Right."

"We knew she was terminal," Betty reiterated. "The cancer had spread through her body. It was only a matter of time."

"But she ended up having less time than you had thought."

"You never really know. Sometimes the doctor gives a person a month, and they live ten years. Sometimes he says they have a few months, and in two or three days, they're gone."

"In cases like that, where they are gone so quickly, is it investigated?"

"No, honey. Why would it be?"

Zachary tried not to bristle at her patronizing manner.

"We know what killed her," Nurse Betty said. "Cancer killed her. We are just grateful she is at rest and no longer suffering. We go on and take care of the living."

Zachary rolled this thought around in his mind for a few moments, examining it. "And you don't think that anyone maybe… decided to help her along? Decided to release her from her pain?"

"Certainly not. You may hear of that kind of thing on TV, but it is very rare. All nurses are not 'angels of death.' Why risk going to prison by interfering with the natural course of things? Patients go when it is their time. Like the coming of the Lord, we don't know the day or the hour. Robin died because she had cancer. That's all. There's nothing else to tell."

The nearby elevator dinged and a group of young doctors and interns got out, chattering away as they entered the unit. Nurse Betty straightened and immediately stared at her screen, typing busily, as if she hadn't been chatting with Zachary.

"There is Dr. West," she said, giving a nod.

Zachary turned and studied the group of young men and women, looking for a gray-haired doctor. But he couldn't sort out which of them was the doctor who had been in charge of Robin's treatment and turned back to Betty for help.

"Dr. West," Betty called out. "There's a gentleman here to see you."

One of the youngsters broke away from the group and approached Zachary. At first glance, he hardly seemed older than twenty, with his geeky glasses and artfully-swept hair. He had to be at least thirty to be in the position he was in, likely much older, but his face was unwrinkled and still boyish. He did hold himself with the upright confidence of an experienced doctor and he didn't have the sleepless eyes of an intern.

"Yes, sir," Dr. West acknowledged. "What can I do for you?"

"I was wondering if I could have a few minutes to talk to you. Privately. I know you have rounds now, and probably a very busy schedule, but if I could get half an hour of your time...?"

Dr. West adjusted his glasses. "I am sure we could find some time, Mr..."

"Goldman. Zachary."

"And what is this about, Zachary?"

"I'm... looking into the death of Robin Salter."

"Looking into... I'm sorry, who are you? Are you with the hospital?"

"No. I'm not—"

"Then I don't understand. There is no reason to 'look into' Ms. Salter's death. Are you a police officer?"

"I'm a private investigator. I've been asked by a friend of Mrs. Salter to look into any... irregularities. Just to put their minds at ease. Her family's and friends'."

"Her family didn't ask me about this. I didn't get the sense anyone had any concerns."

"It will just take a few minutes, and then I can reassure them that everything looks perfectly normal…"

He continued to say 'them' even though there was only Bridget. It sounded better if there were more than just her. Especially since she wasn't even family.

Dr. West didn't look reassured.

"Mr. Goldman's wife was treated here," Nurse Betty told Dr. West. "Bridget Downy. She went into remission."

Dr. West smiled warmly. He was, it seemed, more inclined to humor the spouse of a patient they had managed to save. Maybe he understood that Zachary would be inclined to be positive toward the facility that had helped her.

"Oh, I see. One of our alumni! Then I would guess that you know the quality of the care that our patients get. We are very good at what we do. We have one of the highest-rated cancer treatment programs in the country."

Zachary nodded and continued to look as agreeable as possible as Dr. West extolled the program, the building, the doctors, and even the nurses, finally earning a thin smile and nod from Betty as well. The small herd of young doctors had stopped talking among themselves and were all standing close by, listening in, eyes alight with interest at what was going on.

"I'm sure that's exactly what my report will reflect," Zachary agreed, when Dr. West started to wind down. "We were always very happy with the treatment here. I can see that they continue to hire high-quality staff." He attempted to include both Betty and Dr. West in his smile of approval. There were some people that just couldn't be over-flattered. They would drink up everything he offered and more, without ever suspecting any insincerity. "And I don't want to keep you. You have so much to do here and there are people waiting on you. Are you free after your rounds? Maybe I could buy you lunch?"

"I am engaged for lunch. But maybe this afternoon, three-ish?"

"That would really be great."

"Perfect. You can get the directions to my office from—" Zachary saw Dr. West's eyes slide over to Betty's name badge, but he managed to continue on without a pause, "—Nurse Betty. I won't have a lot of time to meet with you, but we could go over your concerns, provided we are only talking in general terms and not breaking doctor-patient privilege."

Zachary had been worried he was going to run up against claims of confidentiality at some point. He was going to need to get access to confidential patient records, and he wasn't sure how he was going to do that unless he could get the family's consent.

"I'm sure we can work things out," he assured Dr. West. "We could talk about how things were when Bridget was being treated here and discuss hypothetical situations."

Dr. West considered this and then nodded, appearing to accept the suggestion. "Well, I look forward to meeting you, then…"

"Zachary."

"Right. Zachary. I'll see you this afternoon."

He rejoined his group of young cohorts and led them to the first patient room.

Zachary smiled at Betty. "He seems like a very nice fellow."

"He's a good doctor," she agreed. But she looked like she'd eaten something bad. She pulled out a note card and wrote down an address and sketched a small map. She handed it to him slowly. "I didn't say anything to you that was a breach of confidentiality," she asserted.

Zachary shook his head immediately. "Of course not! You're a trained professional. I already knew about Robin's diagnosis and her death. And anything else you said was certainly general knowledge. Her family visited her. She was in pain. There's nothing secret about any of that." He intentionally substituted the word secret for confidential. Whether Nurse Betty had actually revealed anything that might be considered confidential or privileged information or not, he wasn't sure. But she hadn't said anything that had surprised him or that Robin or her family would have objected to.

Betty looked reassured. She patted her flat hair down again and nodded. "We do have to be careful of these things."

4

Zachary was left with several hours of dead time. He hadn't really expected to be able to see Dr. West immediately upon just showing up. He would have to be back at the hospital in the afternoon, and in the meantime, he needed to fill the time productively.

Bridget had given him some of the names of Robin's family members and, with a few quick searches, Zachary was able to find phone numbers for them. The first one he managed to reach was Vera Salter, Robin's mother, and she agreed to meet with him if he wanted to drop by and see her. Zachary found her living in a small brick bungalow in a middle-class neighborhood. Despite the fact that she had told him he could stop by, she answered the door in her housecoat and looked surprised to see him.

Zachary introduced himself again, worried that she might not understand why he was there. Grief could do things to a person. Zachary remembered what it had been like to lose his family. And later, to lose Bridget. They weren't even dead, but he still grieved for each one of them, and if he let himself get caught up in it, hours and days could pass while he walked through life in a fog, not really taking in anything that was going on around him.

"I'm Zachary Goldman, Mrs. Salter. My wife is—was—a friend of Robin's."

She nodded slowly, giving Zachary her hand to shake, but she looked right through him as if he weren't even there. Zachary looked into her broad, dark face, searching her eyes for some connection. Her tightly-curled hair was cut close to her head and had more gray in it than black.

"I don't know your wife," Vera said vaguely.

"You've met her. Bridget Downy. She's petite, blond... well, she was blond, is blond now, but when she was in treatment... I don't know if she would have had hair when she met you."

"Bridget," Vera echoed.

Zachary nodded. Vera motioned for him to enter the house, and Zachary looked around, wondering whether anyone else was there to keep an eye on her, or whether she was normally more together. There was a skateboard at the door and a pair of Nike sneakers, which suggested that Vera wasn't the only one living there. Zachary followed her to the living room and looked at the pictures on the mantel and side tables.

"You have a lovely family. Tell me who everyone is."

Vera brightened. Her features livened up a little and she almost smiled. "Here is one of the whole family," she said, choosing one off of the mantel. A posed studio shot, with everyone standing stiffly in front of a fake background. "This is my husband Clarence. He died years ago. And my girls, Robin and Gloria," she indicated the pretty girls standing on either side of their parents. There was a man standing next to Robin. Tall, head shaved bald, a long face that made him look a little sad, in spite of his camera-ready smile. "That was Stanley," Vera said. "He and Robin were engaged. We thought, when we had this picture taken, that he was going to be a member of the family. But... they broke up. Robin always wanted to cut him out of this picture, but I couldn't bear to ruin it that way."

"That's understandable."

"And this..." Vera laid a finger beside a little boy standing in front of Gloria, his dark eyes sparkling with mischief. "This was Rhys."

She pronounced it 'Reese,' like the peanut butter cups. There was something about the way Vera said his name that made Zachary wonder what had happened to her grandson. He took a quick inventory of the other pictures, looking for Rhys in them. There were a few of Rhys, gradually getting older, with his mother or his grandmother, and a couple of school pictures where he was alone. But the sparkling, smiley boy was gone. In his place was a solemn, distant-looking boy. Zachary's mind went back to the children he had met at Summit. Was he autistic? Neurodiverse? What was it that made him look so far away?

"My poor Rhys," Vera said, shaking her head. "He hasn't been the same since Clarence died."

Zachary thought about that. He looked around the room and at the other pictures for more clues as to what had happened to the family. Was the boy still mourning his grandpa so many years later? Had they tried anti-depressants? Counseling? Was there something more that Vera wasn't telling him?

"Rhys lives here with you?" he suggested, looking at the skateboard and Nikes.

"Yes. This has always been his home, with Grandma and Grandpa. Sometimes Gloria has lived here with us... and sometimes she's been... other places. But Rhys always stays here with us. And sooner or later, Gloria always comes home again."

Zachary nodded. It was good that Rhys had a stable home. He didn't have to live like Zachary had, passed from one foster family to another, never knowing how long he was going to be there or how bad the next one would be. Or when things got too bad, shunted off to an institution until Zachary could stabilize and they were ready to try something else.

"You must love him very much."

"I do. He's a very special boy."

In the back of his mind, Zachary heard the other boys. The ones who would pick up the word *special* and turn it into something sarcastic and cruel. He wondered again just how Rhys was special. Something set him apart and made him unhappy, and Zachary didn't think it was just losing his beloved grandparent. There was more to it than that.

But that wasn't what he was there to investigate.

Zachary took a surreptitious look at his phone to make sure that time hadn't gotten away from him. He still had plenty of time to visit with Vera before he needed to be back at Dr. West's office. He asked her other questions about the family, trying to get a feel for the dynamics and how Robin had fit into everything. She was the older sister, a bit of a perfectionist, a bit bossy, the sister who always had to be right and needed her parents' praise and attention. Zachary could see parallels between the things Vera said about her daughter and Bridget. The two women had been drawn together by more than the fact that they had both been diagnosed with cancer and were in treatment together. They had an affinity with each other that went much deeper than that.

Zachary sat on the couch beside Vera as she went through the photo albums she had pulled out.

"I know these days everybody has their children's pictures on their phones. But I'm old-school. We used to have them printed and then put them into albums, and I never did get into all of that fancy scrapbooking. Just putting pictures in a book, to look back on later and remember."

"I don't see anything wrong with that." Zachary looked over the pictures of Robin and the others. "I'm an amateur photographer myself, so I understand the magic of developing prints and of being able to hold them in your hands. It's not the same as zipping through pictures on an LCD screen."

"That's right," Vera agreed. She touched the pictures as she turned pages. They were in roughly chronological order, so he could see the girls growing up before his eyes. In the early days, they had always been together. About a year or a year and a half apart in age, Vera had often dressed them up the same way, and the girls had obviously been each other's best playmates in the younger years. But then as they progressed through school, there were pictures of each girl alone, pictures of them with other girls, or with boys, going on to develop separate interests and relationships.

Robin was with boyfriends more often than Gloria, but Gloria was the one who'd had a baby. There was no loving spouse or father in any of the pictures, just Gloria by herself or with Rhys. He'd started out as a small, swaddled baby in arms. There were no pictures where Gloria was looking at her baby with that beatific, Madonna-like expression that photographers were always trying to catch. Instead, she was looking at the photographer or off to the side, the child in her arms barely more than a prop, already forgotten. There were plenty of pictures of Rhys with both his grandma and his grandpa, playing at the park or doing woodwork in Clarence's shop, raking leaves or playing a card game. All of those things that grandparents did with their children, at least in the idealized lives Zachary saw on TV.

And then Clarence was gone. Rhys's smile was gone. In pictures of him with his grandma, he was staring off into the distance, never engaged with her or with the camera man. It was like the whole world was marching by him, and he didn't have a clue.

"He was really affected by the loss of his grandpa," Zachary observed.

Vera nodded. She opened her mouth to explain further, then thought better of it. A secret. Something she wasn't ready to divulge.

"Did Robin and Gloria stay close?" Zachary asked. "Or I should say, did they reconnect again when they got older?"

"Not like when they were children. They were both very strong women. And strong women…"

Zachary thought of Bridget. "They don't always get along with each other. Or with others. My wife always said that if a woman is assertive and says what she wants, she gets called… well…" he didn't want to shock Vera with the language Bridget had actually used. "Some not very complimentary things."

"People say they want men and women to be equal, but the truth is, women are still trained to put others before themselves, to be caregivers first, and to care about outward appearances. You don't get a man by being ugly and pushy. And you need a man."

Zachary sighed. "We still have a ways to go in that department. I know that in the families I lived with, it was always the mother who was in charge of the cooking and cleaning and childcare. She could delegate some of it, but she was the one who was responsible for those areas. It was her job to see that things got done, and to take the blame if they didn't."

"We've come a long way. But we're not there yet."

Zachary nodded his agreement. His eyes were caught by the picture of Robin with someone else on the mantel. It was off in the corner, so he hadn't noticed it right away. It wasn't the same man as had been in the family picture with her. Stanley. It was someone else.

Before Zachary could ask Vera for details, the front door opened and a woman walked in. After looking through pictures for an hour, Zachary knew the oval face and long, carefully-styled wavy hair. She had obviously taken great care to apply her makeup, but it didn't hide the bags under Gloria's eyes or the beginning of crow's feet at the corners of her eyes. Her mouth was turned down even before she realized they had company.

Gloria stopped and looked at Zachary as she kicked off her heels. "Who are you?"

"This is Zachary, Gloria," Vera explained, surprising Zachary by remembering his name after all. "His wife was one of the other ladies in Robin's unit. At the treatment center."

"Was?" Gloria repeated cautiously. "I'm sorry, did she…"

"She went into remission," Zachary was quick to fill her in. "She's starting to get her hair back and feel like herself again."

There was pain in Vera's eyes. Maybe in Gloria's too, but she masked it better.

"I'm sorry. That was insensitive." Zachary's chest hurt when he realized he'd made them feel worse. They had lost their family member, and Zachary blithely told them that his was all better. How could he be so stupid? His brain whirled as he looked for a way to take it back and make them feel better. "I didn't mean it to come out like that. I just didn't want you thinking she was—she had passed—I didn't want you thinking you had to feel sorry for me. You have your own troubles, you don't need to worry about mine."

Both women were silent, apparently uncertain how to deal with his verbal diarrhea. Zachary clamped his mouth shut. Talking wasn't making it any better. If there was a way to make it any worse, that was exactly what he was going to do. So he would shut up.

"Well, anyway..." Vera sighed. "Zachary heard about Robin's passing and he came over for a visit."

Gloria was clearly suspicious. And she had a right to be. Men didn't just go around visiting elderly women who had lost their daughters. Not without some kind of motive. Men were predators and women like Vera were prey. Zachary slid a couple of inches away from Vera as discreetly as he could.

"Bridget was worried about you," he told Gloria, encompassing the whole family with his 'you.' "With Robin passing so unexpectedly..."

Gloria walked the rest of the way into the room and put down a large, heavy-looking handbag. It was brown leather, with lots of shiny clasps and decorations, mirroring the chunky jewelry Gloria wore. She was a forceful woman with a big personality. It was only natural her accouterments would say 'look at me.' The exact opposite to Zachary, who strove to make everything about himself less visible and less memorable. He was always trying to fade into the background where he could just watch and listen and find things out without people even remembering he was there.

"If Bridget was worried, then why isn't Bridget here?"

"She... wasn't up to it. She has to be careful and conserve her energy for when she needs it." This was far less true than it had been a few months before. He didn't know how much Bridget was able to do, but she seemed to be pretty much back to her old self. The way she had been before the cancer had struck.

Gloria sat down in one of the armchairs. Her gaze was piercing. Zachary had to look away.

"Robin's death was not *unexpected*," Gloria said. "I'm not sure where you got that idea. Surely if your wife had cancer, you know all about it. When the cancer travels to other parts of the body—liver, bones, lungs—then you know they don't have much time left. We knew Robin was living on borrowed time."

"Oh… from what I heard, I was under the impression—Bridget was under the impression—that it happened earlier than the doctor had said. That they thought she still had time left. Months, even."

"What are a few months?" Gloria's voice was thick with grief. "Before the cancer, everyone thought she had a lifetime ahead of her. Time for… all of those things left undone. But a few months? A few months is nothing!"

Zachary looked for a way to formulate an answer. But Vera was sitting beside him shaking her head.

"I would have wanted more time with her. A few months would have been wonderful. I would have taken a few days. A few hours. It was so quick."

"You were surprised, then?" Zachary turned his head back toward her. "You didn't think she was ready to die yet, did you?"

"No," Vera agreed emphatically.

"It doesn't matter if she was ready to die," Gloria said. "That's not the way it works. We don't get to pick our time. It just comes sneaking up behind us, and then… it strikes."

"I didn't think it was Robin's time," Vera said. She looked at Gloria. "Do you?"

Her strength was of a different sort than Gloria's. Gloria was all challenge and hard edges. Vera was strong too, but in a different way. She didn't bend under her daughter's insistence. She just looked at her, waiting for her answer.

Gloria sagged, losing much of her bravado. "No. You're right… she should have had… more time."

That meant there were three people who didn't think it had been Robin's time to go. Maybe Bridget was on to something. Maybe she wasn't just afraid that it could have been her. Frightened that she might be looking in a mirror.

Zachary let them just sit in silence for a few minutes, thinking about Robin and about how she had been taken from them too quickly.

"Do you think..." Zachary wanted to speak as quietly as their own consciences. He wanted them to think it was their own idea. "Is there any possibility that there was a mistake? That the hospital might have done something...? A wrong treatment, maybe? Things do happen..."

Vera and Gloria both stared at him. Neither one jumped in with the exclamation that he could be right. It wasn't something they had already been thinking. It wasn't something that they immediately discounted, though, either. They looked at each other. Gloria shook her head and eventually, Vera followed suit.

"No," she agreed. "The hospital was always very good. The staff was very friendly and respectful and well-trained. I never felt like they didn't know what they were talking about. They were always willing to take the time to explain everything."

"Robin died because she had cancer," Gloria said flatly. "There wasn't anything anyone could have done. She had cancer, and that's what took her. It was her time, even if we didn't like it." Gloria looked at her mother. "God's timing is never the same as ours, is it? The Lord chooses his own time."

"His ways are higher than our ways," Vera agreed. They both seemed to be happy with this answer.

But Zachary had never been a religious person. He had lived in some foster families who had strong Christian beliefs, but he'd never understood their faith in what couldn't be seen or heard or demonstrated in any way. It seemed like people just wanted to delude themselves. Vera and Gloria might believe that Robin had been taken before her time, but they were willing to lay that on God and accept it as His will.

Zachary wasn't willing to do that.

"You wouldn't mind, would you, if I asked around a little bit?" he suggested. "Bridget asked me to look into it, see if anything was suspicious or out of place. I'm sure it's nothing, but you wouldn't mind me asking a few questions, would you?"

Vera shrugged. "We don't know the answers to any of your questions."

"What do you mean?" Gloria raised her voice. "Ask who a few questions? Is that why you're here? To nose around here and see if one of us had anything to do with Robin's death? I can't believe the nerve!"

"No, no, I wasn't accusing you of anything. I just wondered whether… I've been making some inquiries at the hospital, and I wondered if you would mind if I said that you wanted the answers too. That you wanted to make sure it really was Robin's time to go…"

"Who *are* you?"

"He's Bridget's husband," Vera told her daughter, not understanding what Gloria was upset about.

"Something isn't right here," Gloria said. "He's asking questions at the hospital? He comes here asking about Robin? He wants our permission to… what, investigate?"

Zachary shrugged, hoping she would wind down and decide that was okay if he didn't let it become a confrontation.

"I don't remember ever seeing him visiting the cancer unit," Gloria said to Vera. "Do you? Do you remember ever seeing him before?"

"Well, no…"

"Bridget isn't my wife," Zachary explained. "She's my ex-wife. When she found out she had cancer… she didn't want me around. She wanted to face it by herself, without any… distractions. She didn't want to have to worry about anyone else's needs. Just to focus on her own recovery." He swallowed and took a minute to try to slow his breathing and keep himself from getting too emotional. Bridget had been right. She had been able to put all of her energy into healing and had recovered. Robin had not been able to do the same. "We're still on good terms. She asked me if I would look into Robin's death. And just make sure that everything was… usual. Nothing irregular."

Gloria suddenly swore. Zachary could see by her expression that it wasn't that she didn't believe him. She had just put it together. She knew who he was.

"You're that private investigator. You've been on TV and the internet."

"A private investigator?" Vera repeated in a tiny voice.

"He's conducting a murder investigation." Gloria's voice shook. "He thinks someone killed Robin!"

"I'm just looking into it." Zachary tried to calm her. "There isn't any evidence here of murder. I'm just looking at the circumstances. Making sure that there isn't anything that might indicate that it might not have been…" he trailed off, too tangled up in the words and emotions to continue.

"Well, you can leave us out of it. You don't have our permission to do anything on Robin's behalf or my mother's behalf. You can't use our names. We don't want you to pursue this any further!"

Zachary put his hands on his knees and pushed himself up. It was time to be heading back to the hospital again anyway.

"Can I leave you with my card in case you have any questions or you change your minds?"

"No," Gloria snapped.

Zachary took one out anyway and put it beside Vera before leaving.

5

Meeting with Vera had not gone as well as Zachary had hoped, but neither had it gone as badly as he had feared. He had learned a lot about Robin's family and background. They hadn't found the circumstances of Robin's death to be suspicious. He might not have their blessing to continue with the investigation, but he did have more facts and a clearer picture of the person Robin had been.

He was driving back to the hospital when his phone rang. Glancing at the display, Zachary answered it hands-free.

"Bridget? Is everything okay?"

"Why wouldn't everything be okay?"

Zachary didn't respond, momentarily tongue-tied. Was she looking for a status report already? Had she changed her mind and realized looking for an outside cause in Robin's death was a waste of time? She didn't normally call him unless there was something wrong. Usually, because she was upset about something Zachary was doing.

"I just called to see if you were going to look into Robin Salter's death," Bridget said in a more conciliatory tone. "Nothing is wrong."

"Okay. Good. I'm already on it. I've talked to a few people, one of the nurses, her family; I'm just on my way to talk to Dr. West."

"He's probably pretty busy."

"I have an appointment with him."

"Oh. That's great." Bridget took a deep breath. "Thank you so much, Zachary. I really appreciate you taking this on. I know you're probably busy with all kinds of other cases."

"I can make time for it. So far, everything seems to be fine. Nobody seems to be worried or suspicious of anything that happened. Like you say, it was quicker than anyone expected, but that does happen sometimes."

"I know..." Bridget sounded distant. "It's just that... she was still so strong. And then all of a sudden, it was over. She was sick for a few days, and I thought she was just tired and she would get over it with some rest, and then they said she had passed. It doesn't make any sense."

"She was sick before she died?"

"Just a couple of days. It shouldn't have been the end."

Zachary kept his mouth shut and didn't argue with her about it. If Robin had experienced a worsening of symptoms, then that argued for natural causes, not some accident or medical neglect by the hospital.

"I'll do what I can to find out," he promised.

"Thank you, Zachary. I do appreciate it."

Zachary got goosebumps. He remembered the way that she used to talk to him. The way that she used to make him feel. It made him warm and happy to be appreciated by her. Maybe they were getting past the rift that the cancer had caused. Maybe Bridget was getting to the point where she was willing to accept that they had broken up because she had pushed him away, not because he had done anything wrong. Maybe deep down, she still loved him, and this was her way of trying to reconcile with him.

"I lo—you're welcome, Bridget. You know I'm always here to help." He didn't want to be needy. She had asked for his help. That meant she wanted him to be the strong one and to support her. She had to be the one to set the emotional tone. He'd follow her lead.

"Talk to you later," Bridget's voice was stronger for a moment, and then she was gone, the connection terminated. Zachary's phone decided to start playing his music and he hit the button on the stereo to stop it, not wanting to be distracted by the noise.

For the moment, he just wanted to bask in the knowledge that she needed him. Bridget needed him and appreciated him. Maybe there was a chance for them after all.

Dr. West didn't keep Zachary waiting for too long. Zachary sat in the waiting area tapping randomly through his phone, reviewing the notes he had made and questions he should ask. There weren't a lot of coughing children in Dr. West's waiting room, like there were when he went to the walk-in medical clinic for one ailment or another. Instead, it was mostly older women and couples, sitting quietly with magazines or whispering with each other.

He was escorted into Dr. West's office by a receptionist in a flowered nurse's smock. Zachary had been half-expecting to be led to a typical exam room, but of course Dr. West actually had a real office where he got paperwork done and had meetings or made phone calls. It was similar to doctors' offices Zachary had seen on TV; a wall of bookcases filled with thick volumes, a heavy wooden desk, a couple of chairs for visitors to sit in. There was a thin computer monitor on the corner of the desk, and the surface of the desk was covered with various piles and files of paper. There was more to being a doctor like Dr. West than just seeing patients.

"So, Mr. Goldman." Dr. West looked down at a file open on the desk in front of him. Robin's file? Had he been reviewing it before Zachary arrived or was it just an unrelated file and he found it easier to look at something else than to have to look Zachary in the face?

"Zachary."

"Zachary." Dr. West gave a nod. "What can I help you with? Like I said before, there is the matter of privilege to be considered."

"I'm just curious about Robin's last days here. From what Bridget said, Robin seemed to be doing quite well. Bridget is normally a pretty good judge of other people. She was shocked that Robin went so quickly."

"It isn't unusual, after someone finds out they are terminal, for them to... let go. They make peace with their fate, tie up any loose ends, and let themselves go."

"Bridget didn't feel like Robin had done that. She said Robin was still fighting. She wasn't giving in to the cancer."

Dr. West shrugged. "We can't always see what people are really thinking, can we?"

"What was your feeling? How much time did you think she had left?"

"Doctors are notorious for being wrong about these things. You would

be amazed at how many doctors get sued for not properly predicting someone's death date. In either direction, early or late."

"Really?" Zachary considered the circumstances under which someone
would sue the doctor because they had lived longer than he had predicted.
"Wow. But you didn't expect that Robin would die as early as she did?"

Dr. West rubbed his hands together, then folded them on top of his
desk. "No. I didn't. But as surprised as I was that she went so quickly… I
never suspected any… outside influence. I don't know exactly what you're
looking for, but I never saw any problems with Robin's care or sign of
outside influences. I think you're just looking at a case where the cancer or a
related condition took her sooner than anyone expected."

"That's pretty much what I expected. I know that when Bridget was
here, she always said she was treated well and that the staff were very kind. It
wasn't like some of the horror stories you hear of people getting sepsis sitting
for days in the emergency room. Very clean, very professional." Zachary
wasn't worried about laying it on too thick. Doctors had big egos. And the
more senior the doctor, the bigger his ego.

Dr. West smiled in appreciation. "We work very hard to provide a clean
and homey environment for our patients. We know that no one chose to be
there, and that the more comfortable and happier they are, the better they
are able to fight cancer and tolerate the treatment protocol."

"You're doing a fine job."

"Thank you. It's really good to hear that."

"You haven't had anyone other than Robin who has died quite a bit
earlier than you expected?"

Dr. West frowned and shook his head. "No, there's no pattern that indicates we've got a resistant bacteria on the ward, or some kind of contaminated supplies or medications. Everything has been perfectly normal, no
signs of trouble. And Robin's death itself… as I said, it's not abnormal or
unexpected. She just went before we predicted. That happens."

"Have you had any staffing changes lately? Anyone new, or anyone
you've had to let go?"

"Working in oncology is difficult. People come and go. There's always
turnover. It's very taxing to deal every day with people who are dying."

"I would imagine so," Zachary agreed. "You read in the news sometimes
about staff in hospital wards or care centers who decide to take matters into
their own hands."

"Angels of death," Dr. West said flatly. His smile was gone. He looked toward the door as if he were expecting someone to enter. Or to leave.

"Right. They're not the type of people you expect to be murderers. It's not done out of malice. It's more along the lines of... assisted suicide. Except without consent."

"Just because you've heard it in the news, that doesn't mean it's common. That kind of thing is very rare. Just like nursery nurses stealing infants. It happens a few times, and suddenly it has a name, it's a recognized pattern. People suddenly think it's a common occurrence. But it isn't. There have only been a handful of these 'angels of death' ever identified in the whole country. You're more likely to be hit by lightning than killed by one of these so-called angels."

Zachary nodded. "I've never seen any sign of that kind of thing going on," he agreed. "Certainly, Bridget never had any fear that someone was going to do her in while she was at the treatment center. It's all a little over the top. I'm not even sure what you would look for, if you were administering a department like this. Is there a checklist of things to watch for? Things that should tip you off that you have an 'angel of death' on your staff?" He shook his head in disbelief.

Dr. West fell for it hook, line, and sinker. He leaned forward, dropping his voice like he might be overheard discussing such a thing. "There have actually been studies into this kind of thing. Red flags for medical serial killers. I attended a seminar while on a medical retreat. It's one of those things that comes up during insurance reviews. Are your stats all in line? Are you aware of the red flags for medical serial killers? Do you have a proper vetting program and monitoring in place?"

Zachary nodded, mirroring Dr. West's body language by leaning toward him. "Like what?"

"Carers who have a higher rate of deaths of patients in their care, obviously. Depression, personality disorder, preferring night shifts. People who make their colleagues nervous or have drugs in their possession."

"How would you know that? How would you, as the head of a program like this, be aware of any of that? You'd have access to the death statistics, but do you get a breakdown of what staff members were on duty during each death?"

"It's up to the employees in the department to notice and report any patterns. Obviously, if we had a rash of unexpected deaths or an increase in mortality rate, we would do a deeper review, but these people can be very sneaky. How would you know someone had drugs in their possession without doing a search? You can't just randomly search people's lockers or pockets. How would you know someone had depression or a personality disorder? You're not allowed to ask during an employment interview. We have moms who prefer the night shift because they want to be home with their kids during the day. You can't start accusing them of being serial killers because they've asked for night shift."

Zachary chuckled. "No. Good way to get slapped."

Dr. West laughed, agreeing.

"But you've never had any worries about that?" Zachary asked. "You've never had any scares, or had those doubts cross your mind because a death was unusual or unexpected?"

Dr. West sat back again, hands folded in his lap, staring up at the ceiling. "I'm sure every hospital head of department has at some time or another. Or every head of oncology, anyway. You've been told to be vigilant, so you ask yourself 'could it happen in my unit?' 'Is it happening in my unit?' But no... I've never had any real concerns or suspicions."

"No one you were relieved to let go, because they gave you the creeps? No patients complaining about unscheduled medical treatments or visits...?"

Was there a flicker in Dr. West's eyes before he shook his head? Zachary leaned back as well, thinking it over.

"How does it usually happen? How do these angel-of-death cases go undetected for so long?"

"In a lot of cases, it's insulin overdose. Insulin is naturally found in the body. The person just goes into a coma and dies. When you're dealing with someone who is already on death's door, that's not an unusual event. No one would order an autopsy, and even if one was ordered, the pathologist wouldn't find anything. Insulin breaks down within forty-eight hours, so even if they're looking for it, they're not likely to find it."

And they were already past the forty-eight hour mark since Robin's death.

"You have to get a confession in those cases," Dr. West said. "Or catch them in the act. There's no other way."

"Would you even stock insulin in a cancer ward? Would that be normal?"

"Certainly. Diabetic people get cancer. At a higher rate than non-diabetics, in fact. And anyone with pancreatic cancer is going to get diabetes. Some of the cancer treatments we are using can cause diabetes. It's important to monitor and manage patients' blood glucose levels."

"I didn't know that. I guess that's not something Bridget ever had to deal with, so I wasn't aware of it. What about Robin? Did she have diabetes? Before or after the cancer?"

Dr. West shook his head, but then his eyes drifted down to the file open in front of him. His attention was taken from Zachary as his eyes flicked back and forth over the papers. He turned a couple of sheets over.

"That's confidential information," he said. "I wouldn't be able to tell you if Robin had high blood sugar a day or two before she died that required the administration of insulin."

Zachary stared at him. "She did?" But he understood that Dr. West couldn't confirm or deny the information. He had said only that he couldn't tell Zachary the information. It wasn't something that would ever hold up in court, but it was a direction for him to go.

"I couldn't tell you," Dr. West repeated. "Like I said, a lot of patients get high blood sugar. That's not unusual. It's not cause for concern. It's just something that we keep an eye on."

"Is there any way to tell how much insulin she was given?"

"It's on her chart, if you had permission or a court order. But you don't."

"And can you match your insulin inventory to the charts? Can you tell for sure if she was given the right dose, or do you just assume that she was?"

"My staff know how to administer insulin."

"Yes…" Zachary let Dr. West think about that for a few minutes. Knowing how to administer insulin made the staff potential suspects, it didn't prove their innocence. Robin could have been given the wrong dosage of insulin either by accident or on purpose. If they had an angel of death on the staff, which Dr. West had pointed out was pretty much impossible to tell, then they could have administered the wrong dosage of insulin and gotten away with it.

Dr. West started to flush. "I don't like your implication, Mr. Goldman."

"Zachary."

"Mr. Goldman. I explained to you why we have insulin stocked. I explained to you that Ms. Salter required insulin because of her cancer or her treatments. You can't then jump to the conclusion that she was overdosed on insulin and that's why she died. I told you there was nothing suspicious about her death and I am sticking to that statement. Ms. Salter died of natural causes. Not insulin overdose.

"Except there's no way to know that."

"I'm telling you."

Dr. West's phone rang. He looked at it for a moment, his brows drawing down in a frown. Then he picked it up. "Dr. Aaron West, oncology."

He listened to the caller, the frown disappearing and his eyes instead going up in surprise. His eyes riveted on Zachary instead of getting that unfocused look people usually got when they talked on the phone, imagining the person on the other end of the call instead of seeing what was in front of them. He nodded and listened to the rapid voice on the other end. Eventually, the caller wound down so that Dr. West was able to speak.

"Yes, Miss Salter," he agreed.

Zachary's heart sank.

"Yes, I understand. Yes. I appreciate your call, thank you for letting me know."

He made a few more calming and affirming noises, and was eventually able to hang up the phone. He put it down firmly, eyes still boring into Zachary.

"You led me to believe that you had been hired by Robin's family to look into her case."

"No." Zachary kept his voice flat and empty. "I told you that Bridget was concerned. I didn't claim to be hired by the family."

Dr. West scowled. "Whether you said it or not, you clearly wanted me to believe it."

"What you believed isn't my responsibility," Zachary pointed out. "I didn't tell you that Robin's family hired me."

"I think it's time for you to leave."

Zachary nodded, getting to his feet. He kept a purposefully vague and unemotional exterior, but inside, his heart was racing like he was already on the run. He was aware of every twitch Dr. West made, ready for a full-blown confrontation. But luckily, Dr. West kept his own emotions under control and didn't make any threats of violence. He allowed Zachary to simply retreat the way he had come and didn't pursue him or call security.

Zachary walked back past the reception desk and gave the pretty recep-tionist a smile and a nod, projecting the impression that everything had gone as he had hoped and all was well between him and Dr. West. If he ended up having to call her or ask her for further information, he didn't want to have given away the fact that Dr. West had sent him packing. If she were under the impression that Dr. West had cooperated with him fully, she would be far more accommodating of any further queries.

6

It was late enough in the afternoon that Zachary decided to simply go home. He could have a bite to eat, check his email and voice messages, and plan out his evening. But when he got home and looked in the fridge at the food Bridget had brought him, nothing appealed to him. His appetite was usually suppressed by his meds, and he and Bridget had never really seen eye-to-eye on dietary choices. Bridget was, of course, big on whole foods, salads, vegetables, and juices, all those things that helped her to keep her figure and to have a strong immune system in order to fight the cancer. While she was not a vegetarian, she eschewed red meat and stuck to occasional skinless chicken and fish. Zachary had no desire to eat either one.

Every foster home had been different, but instead of adjusting to a wide variety of cuisines, Zachary had gotten pickier and pickier. If forced, he would eat whatever was put on the table in front of him. He'd never had a showdown with a foster father over food where he'd been physically force-fed. He'd seen it happen to others. But given the choice, his diet was limited to highly processed foods. Peanut butter sandwiches. Pepperoni and sausage pizzas. Cheese burritos. Greasy fast-food hamburgers. Along with plenty of coffee and cola.

Bridget's "clean" diet of fresh fruits, vegetables, and lean meats just didn't cut it.

Zachary checked his email, made some notes about what he had learned on the Robin Salter case, and pondered over calling Kenzie.

Previously, he wouldn't have hesitated to call her to get her insight and suggest that they go out for dinner. But previously, Bridget had been out of the picture. Not only had she divorced Zachary, but she'd been furious with him. She hadn't wanted to see or hear from him. She didn't want anything to do with him unless it was her own idea.

But that had changed. Suddenly she was in his life again. Asking him for favors. Thanking him. Making him feel like he was worthwhile instead of a piece of dung that had stuck to her shoe after the divorce. He thought he might have a chance with her again.

And that made calling Kenzie a difficult decision. Would it upset Bridget? She'd tried to warn Kenzie away from Zachary before. But she'd also called Kenzie when she thought Zachary needed someone to check in on him. Bridget was too unpredictable for Zachary to be sure how she would react to a potential rival now that she was back in Zachary's life.

Not that he and Kenzie were hot and heavy. They were friends, but Zachary still wasn't sure where he stood with her. Bowman assured him that Kenzie was interested in him and he had a chance of snagging her if he approached it the right way. But Zachary had been too uncertain to pursue her. He'd almost scared her off in the beginning, and he wasn't sure she trusted him yet.

Eventually, Zachary picked up his phone and dialed.

———

The phone rang a few times before Kenzie picked it up, and Zachary wondered whether she was in the morgue rather than at her desk. She'd been getting a little more time with hands-on work recently, and that meant when the phone rang, she had to decide whether to let it ring, or to stop what she was doing, take off her gloves and whatever other protective gear she was wearing, and then go to the phone.

Eventually, Kenzie answered the phone. "Is this my favorite private eye?"

Zachary snorted. "Do you know any other private eyes?"

"No."

"Then I guess that's a yes. This is your favorite private eye."

"What's up?"

"I have a new case." He wasn't about to tell her that it was an unpaid case, or that it had come to him through Bridget.

"Something of interest to the medical examiner's office?"

"Well… Probably not something that will ever come across your desk, but I am investigating whether it might *not* have been natural causes."

"What makes you think it is not?"

"The client thinks it might not be. I'm not so sure yet."

"What makes him think it wasn't natural causes?"

"It was unexpected. Well, not unexpected… but before it was expected. She had cancer. It had metastasized. But they thought she still had a few months."

Kenzie made an irritated noise. "That doesn't sound like anything to me. Just because someone dies of cancer a few weeks before you expected them to, that doesn't mean anything."

"I know. That's what I keep hearing. But I'm looking into it, asking some questions… just exploring a little."

"And…?"

"I don't really have anything for you. She had high blood sugar, so she was being given insulin. I just wonder…"

"If someone gave her too much?"

Zachary didn't say anything, waiting to see what Kenzie had to say without his input.

"It's a stretch, Zachary. Yes, she could have been given the wrong dosage of insulin, but chances are, they would figure it out right away and would dose her with glucagon. She'd recover just fine."

"What if it wasn't accidental? What if someone gave it to her on purpose?"

"Like who?"

"I don't know. One of the nurses or other staff. An 'angel of death.'"

"Really? You haven't found any evidence that there's an angel of death there. If you had, it would be all over the place. I would have heard."

"No, there's no evidence. It's just… she went before her time. Everybody thought it was too early. I thought… if it wasn't caused by an accident, an accidental overdose, or drug interaction, or allergic reaction… some kind of treatment that was contraindicated… then what? I know it's rare, but you can't deny the fact that it happens."

"There is no angel of death operating in this town. We would have heard something about it if there was."

"These people can operate for years, cause dozens of deaths before they are caught."

"You're going to have to show me some kind of evidence. Show me the numbers. Show me the number of people who died before they should, and that it's different than the averages. Give me bodies, Zachary."

"I can't."

"Of course not," she agreed. "Because there aren't any. No one was murdered. One woman with cancer died before her family thought she would. That's not a crime. That's not a pattern. That's just one person."

"I know."

Kenzie sighed. "I'm about ready to wrap everything up here tonight. Have you eaten?"

Zachary had been debating whether to ask Kenzie or not, puzzling over the complication Bridget posed. He hadn't expected her to ask him.

"Uh... no... not yet."

There were a few seconds of silence as Kenzie analyzed Zachary's clearly hesitant tone.

"Do you not want to eat? Did you have other plans?"

"I could eat." Zachary winced as he heard the pitch of his voice go up. He sounded too cheery. Too bouncy. Like he was trying to cover something up.

"You could eat. But you haven't already. You sound weird. Is everything okay?"

"Yes. Everything is *fine.*"

"Do you want to hit Old Joe's? I'm not really in the mood for buffet tonight."

"Old Joe's is great." Zachary looked at the time on his phone screen. "Is seven too early? Do you need more time than that?"

"Seven would be fine. I'm already famished."

"I'll see you there, then. You don't need to be picked up?"

"I've got my baby."

Kenzie's little red sports car was her pride and joy. Zachary smiled.

"I'll see you at Old Joe's."

Zachary took his time getting to Old Joe's, knowing that Kenzie had to get cleaned up and had farther to travel than he did. He took his time locking the car, checking the door handle to be sure the electric door locks had worked, and scanning the parking lot for anyone behaving suspiciously. He'd never had any trouble with his car in the parking lot of Old Joe's, but he was still wary.

Zachary checked the locks one more time, then went in.

He was surprised to find Kenzie there ahead of him. She already had a drink and had started in on the basket of rolls on the table.

She *had* said that was famished.

Zachary sat down, smiling. Kenzie nodded to the bread basket to encourage him to take a roll for himself, her dark curls bouncing.

"I hope you don't mind, I already ordered."

"You said you were hungry."

"I got you the prime rib and baked potato. That's what you usually go for, isn't it? We can tell them to change it, if you want something else."

"No, that's perfect."

Kenzie nodded. "There's something to be said for having a 'usual.'"

Zachary agreed. The waitress brought over a Coke, also Zachary's usual, and he accepted it with a nod and a smile.

"How long are you going to spend on this case?" Kenzie inquired. Her red-lipsticked lips were marred by a few white crumbs from her roll.

"Did you skip lunch?"

"Uh…" she considered, thinking back over her day. "Yeah, I think I might have. That would explain it, huh?"

"Yeah. You should keep granola bars in your desk or something. So you don't have to starve if you aren't able to get out to eat."

"That would make too much sense. I should do it. Although, maybe substitute 'chocolate bar' for 'granola bar.' Admit it, you would too."

"Uh-huh." Zachary thought about the fridge full of healthy food he had no desire to eat. At least Kenzie had known better than to order him a salad.

"And the case…?"

Zachary tried to circle his thoughts back to Robin Salter. "What about it?"

"How long are you going to dig around looking for something that isn't there? Sometimes people get sick and die. She was under a doctor's care. They certify that she died from the cancer… and unless you've got proof otherwise, you're going to have a helluva time convincing anyone to take another look."

"You're right. But sometimes… I *have* had success in cases that everybody says aren't murder."

"Lucky breaks?" she offered with a teasing smile.

"Hard work," Zachary insisted. And she knew it was true. He had put a lot of time and effort into those cases. It was just when he thought he was at the end of the investigation and there was nothing left to find that everything fell into place. He knew better than to be put off by the appearance of an accidental or natural death. Sometimes, it wasn't an accident.

Zachary took a sip of his cola thinking about this. Could there be an unseen hand tipping the scale in Robin Salter's death? Someone malicious?

"Zachary?"

He blinked and looked at her. "Just thinking about the case."

"Tell me some more. She had cancer. She was terminal. Was she suffering? In a lot of pain?"

"I don't know. I know near the end, she was in more pain, that's what the nurse said. But Bridget saw her and said she still seemed strong. She was still fighting it, and was still in good shape."

"Bridget?"

"Uh…" Zachary looked at Kenzie, realizing he had let her name slip out. He hadn't intended to tell her that. "Bridget knew her. They both had cancer."

"That's quite a coincidence."

"Not really, they met in treatment."

"No, I mean that Bridget happens to know this woman whose death you're looking into. Just coincidentally."

Zachary swallowed. He smiled and nodded. "She said she didn't think it was Robin's time to go. From what she said, Robin still had good quality of life."

Kenzie stared at him and he waited to see whether she was going to challenge him about the origins of the case or whether she would focus on what he was saying.

"That puts a hole in your angel of death theory."

"What? Why?"

"Because medical serial killers are usually one of two types. Either they see themselves as angels of mercy, releasing people from pain and suffering, or they like to be in the middle of the drama, part of reviving or trying to revive the person again."

Zachary concentrated on what she was saying. "Okay. So you think they wouldn't have done it to put her out of her misery if she wasn't really suffering."

"Right."

"And they wouldn't just let her die in her sleep if they wanted to be part of trying to save her."

"Exactly."

Zachary nodded, considering the possibilities. "The nurse that I talked to said they don't take heroic measures to revive patients. Not when they are just going to die anyway. Maybe this angel of death is a new employee. Maybe they didn't know that, and thought there would be a big drama if Robin died, but they were disappointed."

Kenzie shrugged. "That's a lot of speculation."

A cheerful waitress brought them each their dinner orders. Zachary didn't try to talk to Kenzie while she gave her full attention to her dinner. He picked at his prime rib and potato. He had hardly eaten, so he knew he needed to, and it was more appetizing than the rabbit food. Zachary took another bite of the rib as it finally occurred to him that if he wanted something particular to eat, then he'd better stock his kitchen, rather than expecting Bridget or Bowman or somebody else to provide what he wanted. He'd gotten lazy while he'd been living with Bowman, neglecting the things he needed to do for himself. Not that he'd ever been the best at self-care, but he could at least manage to go grocery shopping so he wouldn't need to go out or order pizza every night.

He looked up to find Kenzie studying him.

"Think of something?" she suggested. "About the case?"

"Uh… no. Things I need for the apartment."

"Oh. I should get you a housewarming gift. What do you need?"

Zachary was flummoxed. He couldn't tell Kenzie he needed groceries. The next thing he thought of was the couch, but he couldn't tell her he needed that either. He needed something in between. Something small she could pick up in the housewares department.

"Oh… uh… I could use… a toaster."

"A toaster? I could handle that. Anything particular? Wide slice, retro look, maybe a toaster oven?"

"No. Nothing fancy. Just… a regular toaster."

"Consider it done."

Zachary let out a sigh of relief.

"If you want to pursue this unnatural death angle, you need to have a suspect," Kenzie said, slowing down on her dinner and considering the matter at hand. "Because it doesn't fit an angel-of-death killing."

"It could have been an accident."

"Yes. But you're going to have to get access to her charts and the hospital's other records to prove that. If it was an accidental overdose of something like insulin, you're going to need all of their inventory logs. You'd have to show that it was an accident before being able to get the evidence that it was."

Zachary had a bite of potato and chewed it slowly. In spite of all of the toppings, it was bland and tasteless.

"You're not going to get an autopsy based on baseless speculations, and even if you did, the medical examiner might not be able to find anything. Any insulin in her system would be gone. It could be another cause, but with the extent of her illness and her treatment, all kinds of things are going to be off."

Zachary frowned, a tight band forming across his forehead. "What do you mean?"

"If she was diabetic because of her cancer or because of her treatment, then you can bet that all kinds of other damage had been done to her body as well. Chemotherapy is an attempt to kill cells without killing the person. Sometimes it is successful, but sometimes it causes too much harm for the person to recover from."

"If that was the case… if chemotherapy killed her, that's not considered a medical error?"

"No. The patient signs off on all of the risks. They are told that it could kill them. They're given all of the stats and figures, and have to decide it's worth trying. It's not a medical error or even an error of judgment. You just don't know how a person's body is going to react and what complicating factors might be present."

"Like diabetes."

"Diabetes, anemia, heart problems. A compromised immune system means a simple virus or bacterial infection could kill you. Allergies to one of the medications. The body turning against itself and attacking its own cells."

"That's a lot that can go wrong."

Kenzie picked at her vegetables, cutting a spear of asparagus into short lengths and impaling a few of them on her fork.

"You didn't… go over any of this when Bridget was in treatment?"

"No." Zachary's cheeks heated and he stared down at the puddle of juices on his plate. "I tried to be there for her, but she didn't really want me involved. She didn't want me to come to her doctor's appointments or to her treatments. It wasn't long before she said she wanted me out of there, period. So… I left."

Kenzie shook her head. "I really don't understand her. I would think she would want the support. I can understand breaking up because your partner won't be there for you or thinks you are overdramatizing your illness… but I don't understand breaking up because you just don't want them around anymore."

"She blamed me for her getting cancer in the first place."

It still hurt to say it. He remembered Bridget's attack, her venom. It was his fault. His fault for being so needy and paranoid and obsessive. The stress of living with him was what had compromised her body's defenses and allowed the cancer to take root.

"You didn't cause Bridget's cancer," Kenzie said firmly.

"But the stress—"

"I've met Bridget, and let me say she has problems that existed long before she met you. I don't know what her childhood or family situation were like, but I have no doubt that this anger she has didn't start when she met you. It goes a lot deeper than that. She's a toxic person. Maybe she's toxic to herself as well as to you."

"No," Zachary protested. "She's very loving. She has a lot of friends and she loves her family. Everyone is drawn to her. When we met, she was so kind and caring. It wasn't until later that she got… angry." He closed his eyes for a minute, trying to focus on the blissful days earlier in their relationship. Before he had screwed everything up. "It was just like my mother… she couldn't deal with my behavior. She tried and tried, but in the end, she couldn't do it anymore. She had to… expunge me from her life."

"What your mother did was incomprehensible. And that's not what Bridget has done. She keeps hanging around, coming back either to rail against you or to take care of you. Or now getting you involved in some nonsense case because she can't stand for you to be out of her life. If you were the problem with the relationship, then why hasn't she gone on?"

"She has." Zachary put a big bite of potato in his mouth to give him a few moments to formulate his objection. "She has a new boyfriend. Gordon. They went home for Christmas, she met his family. They have a normal relationship."

"I highly doubt it."

"They do. She *has* moved on."

Even though he said it, he wanted Kenzie to argue. He wanted her to insist that Bridget wasn't over him and didn't have a good relationship with Gordon.

"Bridget has most definitely not moved on."

Zachary couldn't help the warm, satisfied feeling that flooded through him at Kenzie's words. If Kenzie was right, then Bridget keeping in touch with Zachary even when she insisted she didn't want anything to do with him was a sign that she hadn't let him go. Actions spoke louder than words. She could say all she wanted to that she didn't want Zachary around, didn't want him keeping tabs on her or showing up in any of their old haunts, but her actions said she was still interested in him. Their lives were still intertwined. Even though she was in a relationship with Gordon and claimed she and Zachary were over, there was still a chance at reconciliation.

"You think she still has feelings for me? That she cares about me?"

"I know she does." Kenzie's dark eyes were intense, her gaze so heated that Zachary had to look away from her. "She shows up at your house on Christmas Eve? Asks you to take on an investigation without any merit? I told you before, that level of anger she has against you when you do something she deems to be wrong doesn't mean she hates you. She wouldn't waste time being angry at you if she didn't care for you. She'd just call the police."

Zachary didn't want Kenzie to start thinking about the mistakes he had made in the past. He was doing better at not being so obsessive about his relationships. He was past all of that. He didn't want her starting to worry about it again.

"What about another suspect?" he questioned, changing the topic abruptly back to the investigation. "You think someone other than a doctor or nurse could have been the cause of Robin's death? I met her mother and sister, but I don't see how it could be either of them."

Kenzie's brows squeezed together in a scowl, scrutinizing him and undoubtedly worrying about the reason for his change in direction.

"It could be the same thing as an angel of death. Wanting to end the pain and sickness. Family members can be very sensitive to that kind of thing. Have you considered assisted suicide? Maybe Robin arranged her own death."

"Wouldn't that mean the doctor *was* involved?"

"Maybe, maybe not. Maybe he wouldn't assist her. They might have just looked up methods on the internet."

Zachary sat back, considering it. Neither Vera nor Gloria had given him any reason to suspect them of being involved in Robin's death, but if it was assisted suicide, or euthanasia without her consent, what would he have seen?

"I suppose it's possible. The nurse said that Robin was in more pain before she died. Maybe her sister decided that it was too much…?"

"Only the sister? You've eliminated the mother as a suspect?"

"Well… yes. She didn't strike me as being capable of pulling something like that off. She wouldn't be searching the internet, she's not computer savvy. And she struck me as being… forgetful. Not quite all there."

"Dementia?" Kenzie suggested.

"Not quite… just… old. A little… vague."

"Well, the sister then. Or maybe a boyfriend? Did she have someone?"

Zachary thought back to the pictures at Vera's house. The man Robin had been engaged to, but then broken up with. The other man he had seen a picture of her with that Zachary hadn't had a chance to ask about. He'd been distracted by Gloria's arrival and had forgotten to pursue it.

"Yes… she might have. I'll have to ask the nurse, or maybe Bridget. I did see a picture of her with a man."

"I would suspect him before her sister. I think most women would ask a partner for help before a sibling."

Zachary tried to imagine what Bridget would have done. If she hadn't gone into remission and had been told her case was terminal; if she had been in a lot of pain and knew it wasn't going to get better, would she have asked Zachary for help? Of course, she'd broken up with Zachary, so the situation was different. He couldn't see her ever being desperate enough to ask him for help with something like that. But would she have gone to her family? He couldn't think of a way to ask her.

7

Zachary didn't feel too badly about having to call Bridget up to ask her more questions about Robin and her possible boyfriend. Whether or not there was any chance it had been assisted suicide, he at least had a reason to call Bridget and discuss the case with her more fully. He considered the clock when he got home after dinner and decided she would still be up and it would not be too late for him to call her. They went through the usual 'are you okay?' and reassurances before Zachary was able to introduce his question.

"You didn't say anything in your email about a boyfriend," he said, "but I saw some pictures at her mother's house… it looks like she was in a relationship before she died?"

"Well…" Bridget drew the word out, not committing to an answer immediately, which Zachary thought seemed suspicious. "Yes, she did have a boyfriend. But I didn't want you to jump to conclusions and focus on him, because I'm sure he had nothing at all to do with her death."

But that was what she had asked Zachary to investigate. She should have given him all of the pertinent details if she really wanted him to come to the proper conclusion.

"His name is Lawrence Long," Bridget revealed, uncomfortable with the silence. "He's a really sweet guy. Like I said, I'm sure he had nothing to do with Robin's death, so I don't want you going after him like he's a suspect."

"He has to be a suspect. The boyfriend or partner is always a suspect."

"He didn't have anything to do with it, Zachary. Trust me on this one."

"I still need to talk to him. He might know things that no one else could tell me."

"But he didn't do it," Bridget said firmly. "He didn't have anything to do with Robin's death."

"Do you have any contact information, or do I need to look him up?"

She knew that he could find Lawrence Long and all of his details. Zachary *was* a private investigator. Skip tracing and background searches were his bread and butter. He had access to all of the best tools. If she didn't provide him with the information, it would take him all of ten minutes to search it out himself.

"I don't have his address or his email... but I do have a phone number."

"That will do."

Bridget was still prickly, but she gave it to him with yet another assertion that he hadn't had anything to do with Robin's death.

"Does he know that I'm looking into this? Have you talked to him about your suspicions—your *concerns*," Zachary amended his wording before she could interrupt him to do it herself.

"Yes, on a basic level. He knows that I was surprised by how suddenly she went, and that I have an ex who is a private investigator. I didn't tell him outright that I was going to have you look into it, but he knows enough that he won't be surprised."

"They were just dating?" Zachary asked. "Not married?"

"Uh... yes... just dating."

"Did she give him medical power of attorney?"

"I don't know. Does it matter? He didn't end up having to make any medical decisions on her behalf. She was gone before then."

"If she gave him medical power of attorney, he might be able to get me access to her hospital records. Her family doesn't want me to have anything to do with it, but if Lawrence was her representative..."

"You'd have to ask him." Zachary was about to speak again when she interrupted him. "But Zachary..."

"What?"

"You may not find him any more accommodating than Robin's family. He believes it was just a natural death."

Zachary wasn't about to give up on Lawrence before he even had a chance to talk to him. There was still a chance the man could get Zachary permission to see Robin's records.

"Bridge…"

"Yes?"

"Out of everybody involved with Robin, you're the only one who thinks that it wasn't a natural death."

"So?"

"Are you sure you're not transferring your own feelings onto Robin?"

"This isn't about me."

"It could be. If you hadn't gone into remission, this is something you could have been facing."

"This is something I *did* have to face," Bridget countered. "I already had to make these decisions. I had to decide how long I was willing to fight the cancer. I had to decide which treatments I would accept, just how far I would go."

There was an unexpected lump in Zachary's throat. He should have poured himself a glass of water before calling her. He cleared his throat and swallowed, trying to continue the conversation without letting his voice break.

"And did you discuss that with Robin?"

"No. No, of course not. It's so personal. The answer is going to be different for everyone. Robin and I were friends, but… not that close."

"She never told you how long she wanted to continue treatment, or whether she would want to end her suffering at some point."

"She wouldn't," Bridget's voice was brittle. "She was still fighting. She hadn't given up. She didn't end her own life."

"Are you prepared for the fact that I might find something different?"

"You won't. I know Robin. This might have been a medical error, but it wasn't suicide."

Lawrence Long was the man Zachary had seen with Robin in the picture on Vera's mantle. He looked younger than Robin, a slight black man with short braids all over his head, a thin mustache and thinner soul patch. Zachary recognized the pain and grief in his eyes, still all too fresh in the wake of Robin's death.

Lawrence had been reluctant to meet with Zachary, but he had agreed. They had arranged to meet at a coffee shop rather than at Lawrence's home. Zachary's brain immediately went into overdrive analyzing this fact. Was there something at Lawrence's home that he didn't want Zachary to see? Was there a secret, or just several days' worth of takeout or dishes that he hadn't been able to deal with during his period of mourning? Did he want to meet at the coffee shop so that he wouldn't be reminded of his grief and would have more incentive not to cry in front of Zachary? Or was it somewhere he had gone with Robin and he wanted to be near her memory?

Lawrence nodded a greeting when Zachary introduced himself, and offered his hand to shake. It was thin and narrow, like a woman's hand, and he offered it like a dead, limp fish, not gripping Zachary's hand when he took it. Zachary let go hastily. Was this spiritless, self-effacing man really the dynamic and strong Robin's partner?

They both sat down, and a waitress came over with two cups of coffee Lawrence had already ordered. Zachary took a sip of his and then set it down.

"I'm so sorry for your loss," he offered. "I can't imagine how difficult this must be for you."

He *could* imagine; he'd been through plenty of loss of his own. But it was a lesson he'd learned from social media articles on dealing with other people's grief. Never presume to know how they are feeling. Let them tell you instead.

Lawrence nodded. "It was such a shock. I know that seems like a ridiculous thing to say, because we all knew she had terminal cancer. But it was still a shock, to leave her seemingly stable and strong one day, and to find out the next day she was dead."

Tears brimmed in his eyes, but he stared off into the distance and didn't shed them.

"That's what Bridget said," Zachary agreed. "It was just such a shock. She didn't feel like it was Robin's time to go yet."

"I guess we were wrong about that." Lawrence took a drink of his coffee.

"I suppose so. Bridget thinks that maybe there was an accident or medical neglect involved. Something the hospital did or didn't do…"

Lawrence tapped his fingers on the table. His eyes were far away. "No. I don't think that. We were all surprised, but the Lord giveth and the Lord taketh away. No one knows the mind of God."

It was similar to what Gloria and Vera had said. Zachary knew better than to let the religiosity bother him. They were just words, platitudes like the prayer Isabella had kept repeating after Declan's death. The words didn't really mean anything, but ritual behavior sometimes helped people deal with their grief. It was better than falling into a bottle.

"You think it was just God's timing?" he asked. "Nothing else?"

"Yes. They were very good at the hospital. I never had any concerns about Robin's care. She never complained about them..." Lawrence trailed off, then made a face, wrinkling his nose and giving a little grimace. "I mean, she didn't complain any more about them than she did about anything else."

"She *did* have complaints, then?"

"Robin had high expectations. She was often disappointed when other people didn't rise to meet them. But there wasn't anything she said that I thought meant anything... it was just normal, everyday stuff."

"Like...?"

"I don't know. Bringing dinner late. Fire alarms going off in the night. Nurses not showing up promptly when she pressed the button." Lawrence shrugged. "I don't want to imply that she was a drama queen, but... the littlest things could set her off."

"Yeah, those don't sound like things that were unusual or indicated a problem with the care."

"Exactly."

"Overall, you think she was satisfied with the care?"

"Overall."

"How was she the last few days? I understand she was in more pain, the staff were trying to control her high blood sugar... was there anything else? How did she seem to you?"

"I really don't see the point of any of this," Lawrence said abruptly. "Nobody has said that there was anything irregular about her death. The doctor already signed a death certificate. Her body was released to the funeral home. Why are you asking questions?"

"I'm sure it's nothing," Zachary assured him. "I'm just asking a few questions, but everything seems to be just fine. Perfectly normal. I just want to be able to reassure Bridget that there was nothing unusual about Robin's death. She just died a little earlier than anyone had expected."

"Bridget," Lawrence repeated.

Zachary wasn't sure where Lawrence was going. They had already mentioned Bridget, that Zachary was her ex, that she had some concerns.

"Yes. You met Bridget…"

"Yes, I know," Lawrence said impatiently. "But what does she have to do with any of this? She's not police or FBI or anything. How can she start an investigation?"

"I'm a private investigator, not a police detective or agent. Anyone can hire me. And Bridget asked me to look into Robin's death."

"But you aren't anyone."

Anyone official, he meant. Anyone with a badge.

"Uh… no. I'm not anyone."

"Don't you need my permission to investigate? Or Robin's family's?"

"No. I don't need anyone's permission." Zachary didn't like the direction the conversation was going. He needed to change something before it all broke down. "Were you Robin's medical attorney?"

"What?"

"Did you have the authorization to make medical decisions on Robin's part if she was unable to? If she had a stroke or went into a coma. Had she appointed you to make decisions for her?"

"No." Lawrence frowned at Zachary like he was saying something crazy. "Robin was able to make her own choices."

"But she knew that at some point, she might not be able to. She didn't make any arrangements?"

"No."

Zachary nodded. So Lawrence would not be of any help with Zachary getting his hands on Robin's medical records. He let his breath out slowly. It didn't matter, then, whether Lawrence approved of the investigation or not. But it was still in Zachary's best interests to distract Lawrence from who had authorized anything.

"That's fine. I just wondered. When was the last time you saw Robin? Was she in good spirits? Or was she in pain?"

"I saw her on Thursday, but she was pretty tired and I didn't stay for long. Wednesday was the last day I spent any length of time with her."

"How was she Wednesday?"

"She was good."

"One of the nurses said she was in more pain the last few days. But Wednesday was good?"

"She had a lot of pain, down in her bones… I don't know if that meant the cancer had spread to the bones… they weren't monitoring to see how it was progressing… they knew it had spread and they couldn't stop it. We didn't think she'd have any more pain-free days and I guess we were right." Lawrence wrapped his fingers around the mug, trying to draw in the heat. "We had… our last date."

Zachary blinked away the stinging in his own eyes. He gave a nod of encouragement. "What did you do on this last date?"

He expected something brief. Watching a movie together on her in-room TV or having bowls of ice cream. One poignant moment that they never guessed would be their last bit of happiness together.

"Robin had planned the whole day. She had it all laid out. We went to the park for a horse and buggy ride. She'd always wanted to do that. She bought a hat just for that ride. We had a picnic on a blanket in the grass, wicker basket and real china and all. Laid in the sun for a long time. She said the sun felt good on her bones. She was very tired, but she'd planned it all out, so she didn't want to go back to the hospital…" Lawrence paused for a sip of coffee. He cleared his throat and went on. "We went to the carousel. She couldn't sit on one of the horses, but the ones with a sleigh and a bench… I wrapped the blanket around her, and we just went around and around until I was too woozy to handle it anymore. We ordered popcorn and cotton candy, but she couldn't eat more than a bite or two of each." Another pause while Lawrence wiped his eyes and stared out the coffee shop window for a while. "We sat in the car, listening to the radio, and she fell asleep. When the sun went down and the stars came up, I woke her up, and we watched for a falling star to wish on."

He didn't seem inclined to say anything else. Zachary let him sit in silence for a few minutes before speaking up.

"That sounds like a wonderful day."

"It was our last date. She had it all planned out, exactly what she wanted to happen."

"Maybe she did sense that her time was getting short."

Lawrence's mouth twisted. Zachary looked away, giving him his private grief.

Zachary thought for a long time about his meeting with Lawrence. It left him with an unsettled feeling; too many questions had not been answered. It didn't fit together the way he expected it to, even though Lawrence had provided some of the key pieces that should have laid Bridget's worries to rest.

He wasn't sure what path to pursue. He knew how he wanted to proceed, and that was to bring Bridget into the investigation. He always appreciated Kenzie's suggestions and her medical knowledge, and there was always the tantalizing possibility that they might be able to move on to a more intimate relationship; but his relationship with Kenzie wasn't the same as what he had had with Bridget. Bridget had been his one love, the one bright light in his life, and if there was a chance of getting her back...

"Zachary?" He was startled by Bridget's voice in his ear.

"Oh—Bridget!" He blinked at the phone in his hand, not even aware he had dialed it.

"You *did* call me."

"Sorry, I was distracted. I wondered if you wanted to... get together to talk about the investigation. Discuss what I've found so far and where to go next."

"Oh..." Bridget's voice was hesitant. "Have you found anything?"

"Nothing certain. No real evidence. But some things came up in my discussion with Lawrence..."

"Okay. Well, then, I guess we should get together to talk. Later this afternoon?"

"That would work for me, if you're free." Zachary assumed that Gordon would still be at work, so there would be no chance that Bridget would bring him along or be pressed for time. "Do you want to come here?"

"Better if we meet in a neutral setting, I should think," Bridget decided. Even though she never seemed to have a problem showing up at Zachary's apartment on her own whim.

Zachary accepted her suggestion, and a couple of hours later, they were wandering through the very park Robin and Lawrence had spent their last date in. Bridget selected a bench for them to sit on for their chat. Zachary sat close to her, but his mind was drawn to the romantic ride, picnic, and other special experiences Robin planned before her death.

"So...?" Bridget prompted, attempting to bring Zachary back down to earth. "What did you find out?"

"Do you mind waiting for a minute?" Zachary didn't wait for her to answer. He stood up and fished a tiny digital camera from his pocket. He took a panorama of shots, turning in a circle to get the full 360 degrees. "Could we walk over to the carousel?"

"Zachary…"

"I'm not just being impulsive. Come with me and I'll tell you what happened."

She conceded and walked by his side over to the carousel, while he told her about the last date. Bridget's eyes darted around the park as she envisioned everything that had happened. She was quiet while Zachary took pictures of the carousel and other sights.

"What do you think it means?" she asked finally. "You think she knew she was dying, and it was her final good-bye? A bucket list of all of the things she wanted to do on a date?"

Zachary shrugged. He had been telling himself that all of the pieces fit together, but he knew that they didn't.

"Vermont has legal euthanasia."

She frowned at him, tiny creases appearing between her eyebrows. "End of life choice," she corrected. "Not euthanasia."

"If Robin had wanted to end her life after finding out that her cancer was metastasized and she only had months to live, she could have asked her doctor for assisted suicide."

"Yes."

"But she didn't do that. No one has said that she wanted to choose to end her life on her own terms."

"No. They're all pretty religious. They probably thought it would be a sin."

"If she were going to end her own life, then that last date with Lawrence made sense, right?"

She nodded.

"But Lawrence never said that's why she did it. He said she had the day all planned out, but he didn't say she had planned her death. He was surprised she died when she did, just like everyone else."

"So…?"

"So, if she hadn't planned her death, why have one last date? Why not… a number of special little events that would be easier for her to tolerate? Lawrence said how tired she was. She couldn't manage to get through the day on her own and was wiped out the day after. If she hadn't planned to die, she could have sprinkled each of those date ideas over the next two or three months, or however long she had."

Bridget considered. "I don't know."

"She never told you she'd planned her death. Her doctor didn't say he'd helped her. Her family didn't say she did, and Lawrence didn't say she did. So it wasn't suicide, right?"

"Right."

"Then it doesn't fit."

"Okay…" Bridget's voice was cautious. "Then it doesn't fit. So… what, then?"

"Then is Lawrence lying?"

"Why would he?"

"Nobody else was with them. He took her out for the day… brought her back exhausted… she slept all the next day, and then she died."

"You think he did something to make her sick?" Bridget shook her head adamantly. "No. I don't believe it."

"Something didn't feel right. When he was telling me all of this, I knew something was off. His eyes, his body language, he was trying to hide something."

Bridget watched the carousel. It was a cooler day, so there weren't a lot of families out in the park or a lot of children on the carousel. The cheerful music played and the horses circled endlessly. Zachary pictured Robin and Lawrence there.

"Zachary, Lawrence didn't kill her. He didn't do anything to make her sick. He didn't help her commit suicide. I saw him with her. He worshiped her."

"Maybe he wanted to put her out of her misery. The nurse said that her pain was getting worse, more difficult to manage. Lawrence said the pain was deep down in her bones. He was afraid the cancer had gotten into them. Bone cancer is one of the most painful things a person can go through. Maybe he didn't want her to have to deal with it."

"I don't believe it. No. I was there when he found out that Robin had passed. I was at the hospital. He was devastated by the news."

"Someone can still be devastated when they are the cause of a tragedy." This Zachary knew without a doubt. He had plenty of personal experience in that area.

"No. He was shocked. He couldn't believe it. No one is that good of an actor."

Zachary scowled to himself. Bridget had a knack for reading a situation so that she could respond in just the right way; the perfect hostess, friend, and lover. Could she be that wrong?

"Something is off," Zachary repeated. "It doesn't fit."

8

Zachary went back to the treatment center the next day, hoping to find Nurse Betty on duty again on the same shift. She was, but she was busy away from the reception desk taking care of patient needs and minor emergencies, so it was some time before he could talk to her again.

"You're back again," Betty observed. "Didn't you get everything you needed from Dr. West?"

"Dr. West was very helpful." Zachary searched Betty's face for any sign that Dr. West had told her not to talk to Zachary or informed her that he didn't have the permission of the family to conduct his investigation. Apparently, he had either not gotten around to it, or hadn't thought it necessary to let his staff know. "I just had a few more questions. I'm sorry, I know I'm being a pain."

"You've been very patient. We like patience around here." She laughed at her word play.

Zachary smiled along with her. "You know Robin's fiancé, Lawrence," he said, deciding to promote Lawrence from boyfriend to fiancé for increased sympathy.

Betty nodded immediately. "Yes, of course. Poor fellow. We were the ones who had to inform him that Robin had passed."

"That must have been hard on you too. He took it pretty hard?"

"Of course. Anyone would. It was a shock; we hadn't anticipated her dying that soon."

"But at least he'd had a chance to say goodbye."

Betty's penciled brows drew down. "What?"

"Their last date. On Wednesday. Wasn't that their goodbye date?"

Betty pursed her lips. She started to shake her head, but then stopped, uncertain.

"I just thought..." Zachary let his voice trail off, giving her time to think about it before going on. "They went out and did everything Robin was never going to be able to do again, and then on Friday, she..."

"She didn't commit suicide," Betty said, providing Zachary with the nugget of information he was fishing for. "There was no end of life prescription. We would know. Everyone on the nursing staff knows if there is an end of life prescription."

"Oh." Zachary let his puzzlement show. "Then what happened on Wednesday?"

"She went out on a day pass. They went out together, she and Lawrence. I don't know if it was a date. I thought... maybe they had people to see or arrangements to make..." Betty shifted uncomfortably. She let her gaze wander to her computer while she reviewed the past week's events. "She was very tired when they came back. It was obvious she had done too much. She was in a lot of pain. She said, 'I'm just glad I got that out of the way.'"

"Not exactly something you would say about a big romantic date."

Betty rubbed the space between her eyebrows as if trying to remove the frown lines there. "No."

"They didn't show you pictures of everything they had done? The carriage ride, the picnic, the carousel...?"

"No."

"How did Lawrence seem? He must have been happy after such a big day with her..."

"No. He was very subdued. Concerned about Robin being so weak, but... distant. And he didn't stay with her. He often stayed late, watched her go to sleep."

"But he didn't on Wednesday."

"No."

"And did he come on Thursday?"

"I didn't see him."

"He said he dropped in briefly, but she was sleeping."

Betty shrugged. "He might have. She did spend most of Thursday sleeping."

"Did that surprise you? Were you concerned in any way?"

"She'd obviously had a busy day and been exhausted Wednesday, so... we were concerned that she get enough rest and not catch anything... we were happy she was sleeping. Patients need sleep."

"You didn't think maybe he'd given her something?"

Betty's eyes were wide. "Given her something? What would he give her? He's not a doctor."

"I don't know. Alcohol. Valium. Ambien. Percocet or Oycotin. Or maybe something that conflicted with one of her meds. You must have patients that think they can just take whatever they want without talking to the doctor. Or they know they're not supposed to and sneak something."

"Well... yes. That's true. But I never thought Robin had taken anything. Just that she was worn out."

"You said she'd been in more pain the final few days."

"Yes."

"You didn't think she took anything extra for it? On top of what you were giving her? Lawrence said he was worried the cancer was into her bones."

"We weren't sure why she was in so much pain. But we were managing it, she wouldn't have needed to take anything else."

"And Lawrence couldn't have decided she needed something more and slipped it to her? Even into her IV without anyone noticing?"

"Anything is possible," Betty said, frustration edging into her voice. "I can't prove she didn't take anything and nobody injected anything into her port. But did I think anything had? No. Do I think anyone did anything to cause her death? No. Ask it as many ways as you like, Mr. Goldman, it was just Robin's time. Nothing will convince me otherwise."

"Did Lawrence get along with Robin's mother and sister?"

Betty's eyes widened. She didn't answer immediately, weighing her answer. "They seemed... civil. Not warm. I think there was a little competition as to who was going to sit with her. Not like some patients where when someone new arrives, the previous visitor leaves to make room."

Zachary tried to envision what the dynamic between Lawrence and Gloria would have been like. Gloria, a strong and outgoing woman and

Lawrence, hesitant and uncertain. Would he have stood up to her? Or was the contest between Robin, wanting Lawrence to stay, and Gloria, wanting him out of the way?

"Did you get the feeling there was animosity there? Maybe the family didn't approve of him."

"Well, he was very different than her. But I don't know what they thought of him, they never said anything in front of me."

Zachary decided to do some research on Lawrence before approaching him again. He needed to know for sure who he was facing. Even someone who seemed quiet and self-effacing could be explosive when confronted. Zachary was investigating someone he thought might have committed homicide, even if it was just classified as a mercy killing or an unauthorized assisted suicide.

Lawrence Long had a number of social media accounts. He was, it would appear, an artist. He created sculptures and paintings, the kind that ended up getting installed as public art, drawing the ire of a public who wanted to know what the heck it was supposed to be. Big shapes, bold colors, and cobbled-together junk. Too sophisticated for Zachary's artistic sense. He was a photography man to the bone, dedicated to capturing the real world, raw and unflinching. Lawrence's kind of work gave artists a bad name.

But maybe art was a shared interest he could approach Lawrence with. Rather than just showing up and demanding more answers, essentially calling Lawrence a liar, he could come up with a ruse that would put Lawrence more at ease.

So, with a little thought and another phone call, Zachary soon found himself in Lawrence's studio. In other words, his garage.

Zachary was prepared for another studio like Isabella's. She was one of the messiest people he had met, with towering piles of materials that threatened to topple over and bury them both. Zachary had always emulated Mr. Peterson, the foster father he had learned photography from, whose tiny darkrooms were always meticulously organized, with everything assigned a place. It was the one place Mr. Peterson had kept clean and ordered. It had soothed Zachary's anxiety and had kept him from getting distracted. He was able to focus on developing pictures, achieving a sort of a zen state that he didn't get from anything else in his life. So he kept his own darkroom and filing system the same way and tried to apply the same principles in the rest of his life, finding it easier to put things away and clean up after himself immediately than to let himself get overwhelmed by disorder.

Lawrence's studio was something in between. Messy, but with a semblance of order and not filled to the gills with junk he would never use. He had several large sculptures in the center of the room, with paintings on easels and other supplies on benches and shelves around the edges of the garage. Scraps of metal, what looked like car parts, and other items that Zachary wouldn't have expected to be used in art.

"Come on in. Make yourself comfortable," Lawrence invited without inflection.

Zachary didn't offer to shake his hand this time. He looked around and selected a stool that had originally been red, but was speckled with various colors of paint. Zachary looked at it carefully and ran his hand over the surface to make sure that none of the paint was wet, before sitting down.

"So, what was it you wanted?" Lawrence asked. "You were looking for pictures of Robin?"

"I thought it might help Bridget," Zachary explained. "I think that Robin's death was just such a surprise to her, she's really obsessing over it in a way that isn't healthy. I thought that if I could pull together some pictures, maybe put them together in a slide show or a collage, it would give her something to hold on to. Something to remember Robin by. And then maybe she wouldn't be so... at such loose ends about Robin's death."

Lawrence considered this, his expression veiled. He wasn't so sure about meeting with Zachary a second time, even under the new pretense. Did he have a guilty conscience?

"Doesn't Bridget have any pictures of her? Couldn't you get them off her Facebook memorial page?"

"But I want something special for her. Something from those last few days of Robin's life. I was thinking, when you were telling me about the lovely date you had with Robin the Wednesday before she died... that maybe if Bridget could see those pictures, could see both how frail she was, but also how happy she was, right up until the end... maybe that would calm her down."

"It's quite personal," Lawrence protested. "I mean, Robin and I... that was our last time together. I didn't really anticipate anyone... sharing those moments with anyone."

"I don't need anything that's too private. Just maybe... a picture of her on the carousel... smiling. Enjoying that last day."

Lawrence didn't respond right away. Maybe Zachary was giving off some signal that he wasn't sincere.

"Surely you took some pictures," Zachary cajoled. "And you two were out in public, so they couldn't be *that* racy!"

It didn't bring even the ghost of a smile to Lawrence's face. He sighed, and finally motioned Zachary over to a computer in the corner of the garage. Not a great place for a piece of equipment that could be sensitive to dust or other contaminants in the air from Lawrence's work. But maybe it was just a cheap one that he kept to be able to pull up pictures of models while he painted.

With a few taps and clicks, Lawrence opened up his photo folder and hunted down the pictures from the previous Wednesday. He started to page through them quickly, not giving Zachary a chance to get a good look at any one of them. Robin's thin, wan face. A few smiles, but mostly she was looking away from the camera, pensive or detached. She didn't look like a girl on a bucket-list date. No big smiles. No romance. There were very few pictures that included Lawrence as well. Zachary made a motion for Lawrence to stop.

"Wait, go back. I want to see that one with the two of you together in the carriage."

Lawrence looked unhappy about the request, but backed up until he stopped on it.

"Oh, that's very nice," Zachary said. And on the surface, it was. The happy couple in the fairy-tale carriage, all sweet and happy. But neither of their smiles looked sincere. Though Lawrence had his arm around Robin's shoulders, she sat stiffly, as if he were a stranger instead of her beloved. They held themselves apart, posed for the camera, but exuding no real warmth.

"Could I get a copy of that one?"

Lawrence grudgingly agreed and marked the photo to be copied. He continued to go through the photos that had been taken that day, with Zachary stopping him occasionally to request one of them.

It was all as Lawrence had said. The carriage ride, the picnic, lying in the sun, the carousel, the cotton candy. It was obvious that Robin was exhausted by the end of the batch of photos. She had done way too much. Lawrence had taken one last picture of her at the end of the day, being tucked into her bed at the cancer treatment center, looking directly at the camera with a hard, unfeeling smile.

"Can I—"

"Not that one," Lawrence said. "That's the last picture I have of her. I don't want… I don't want anyone else to have that one."

Zachary wouldn't have wanted anyone else to have that one either. It said too much. Something was wrong. Robin and Lawrence were not happy lovers, back from a tiring day, having done everything Robin had set out to do to make her last day with Lawrence special. Something else was going on.

He waited for Lawrence to copy the pictures to a thumb drive. He didn't want to do or say anything that might antagonize the man until Zachary had the pictures safely in his pocket. He tucked them away and looked at the computer screen, still thinking about that last picture.

"When are you going to tell me the truth, Lawrence?"

"What?" Lawrence was obviously startled by the question.

"It's obvious you're trying to hide what happened that day. It's as clear as the nose on your face. So tell me. Quit trying to string me along."

Lawrence looked back at him, eyes wide and shifting back and forth. He walked over to one of the sculptures in the middle of the garage and looked it over, comparing it to the final product in his mind's eye, touching the cool surface and pretending that Zachary wasn't there to ruin everything for him. Zachary said nothing, letting the silence build. Lawrence knew something and he needed to confess it to Zachary. If he didn't, he would just go on feeling guilty and worrying that one day someone was going to find out his secret.

"It was supposed to be our last date," he said finally. "Robin didn't know she was going to die so soon, but she intended it to be our last date. She wanted to end on a high note, to have a perfect last date, and remember everything that way…"

Zachary frowned, his forehead getting tight as he thought about it. "Are you saying…"

"She broke up with me." Lawrence's voice was rough. "This whole thing was… I don't know whether it was supposed to make me feel good or to make her feel better about dumping me."

Zachary could feel his pain. It cut a little too close to his own heart, being dumped by Bridget when she was going through treatment. There was something terrible about being dumped by someone when they should have needed you more. Something so damaging about being told 'I have to eliminate everything that isn't positive or necessary from my life in order to fight this thing. So you've got to go.' No matter how Bridget or Robin tried to soften that message by surrounding it with special experiences or long-winded explanations, the message was still the same.

I'm dying and I don't want or need you anymore.

Zachary pictured that last photo on Lawrence's computer. Robin going to sleep with a grim smile on her face. Exhausted, but satisfied about having booted a negative force from her life. The Zacharys and the Lawrences took too much time and attention and didn't give enough back, so they had to be jettisoned at the earliest opportunity. Get rid of the drag and the excess weight.

They made up names to make it sound like a positive move. Rid yourself of toxic people. Put on your own oxygen mask first. Self-care. Words that would let them justify their selfishness and forget about the wounded and bleeding they left behind.

Lawrence was looking at Zachary, waiting for his reaction. A long time seemed to have passed since he made his confession. Zachary tried to focus his brain and pull himself out of the past. He'd dealt with worse things than being dumped. He'd dealt with all kinds of pain and abandonment before. Being dumped by Bridget should have been nothing.

"I'm sorry." His voice was weak and gravelly. Zachary cleared his throat and tried to speak with confidence and authority. He wasn't the one who was wounded. Lawrence was. Lawrence was the one who needed reassurance and understanding. "I'm sorry that happened to you. That really sucks."

"Yeah." Lawrence laughed bleakly. "You said it, brother."

He looked back at his sculpture again. Zachary looked at the twisted pieces of metal. It was sharp and raw and dangerous-looking. Zachary wasn't one for abstract art, but he could see the attraction to this one. He could feel the raw emotion and anger when he looked at it. Lawrence was displaying no anger himself. He let it out in his art, but he wasn't opening up that side of himself to Zachary.

Had he shown it to Robin? Had he gone back to see her on Thursday with a plan? Get her to take him back, or else?

"You must have been furious. Her playing with you like that. Acting as if she could make up for the pain with a nice last date. Who does something like that?"

"Robin could be very manipulative," Lawrence admitted. "She did things sometimes... she acted like she was playing by the rules when she wasn't. Not so much manipulating your actions... but trying to manipulate your feelings."

Zachary nodded. "I can see that. You were supposed to be grateful to her for that one last day. You were supposed to remember her as being someone generous and loving, not someone who pulled the rug out from under you."

"Yeah." Lawrence sighed, looking up at the large iron sculpture. "So is that all? You found out my secret. You got everything you need now?"

"I'm sorry. But... I had to know what really happened. I can't complete my investigation if it's all built on lies."

"Well, congratulations."

"I'm not happy about it, Lawrence. But I needed to know."

"I didn't hurt Robin," Lawrence pronounced. "I couldn't do that. I'd never do anything to hurt her. If she died because she did too much on Wednesday... that's not on me. That was all her own plan and her own doing."

9

Zachary had a restless night full of broken sleep and annoying fragments of dreams. He replayed the conversation with Lawrence over and over. He saw the slide show of the photos he had viewed, including the last photo that had ever been taken of Robin while she was alive. Worse than that, he re-experienced being dumped by Bridget, time after time. Feeling again with agonizing clarity the shock and pain of her cutting ties with him. He wanted to be fresh in the morning, so he didn't want to take any pills to help him sleep. That ended up being a mistake. He should have chosen some dopiness and med hangover to looking like a red-eyed zombie in the morning.

He had decided that a visit with Kenzie was in order. Not over the phone or over dinner this time, but in a more official capacity. He put coffee into his travel mug, put an icepack over his eyes for a few minutes to try to reduce the tell-tale redness, and headed off for the police station. The medical examiner's office was in the basement. A lot of the officers knew him and he was no Phillip Marlowe or Magnum P.I., packing heat wherever he went, so getting through security didn't create any great difficulty.

In the basement, Kenzie was at her desk, efficiently dealing with the paperwork and incoming phone calls, tapping away at her computer to look things up or book appointments in. She looked up at Zachary's approach and gave him a little smile.

"Hey. What are you doing here?"

"Just thought I'd come and see how everything was going."

"Right." Kenzie laughed. "This isn't exactly a place that people just drop into for the atmosphere. Not even you, Mr. Zachary Goldman."

"Really? I hear people are dying to get in."

"Shut up."

Zachary couldn't help snickering. "Okay, I know. I've used that one before," he admitted, "but you have to give me a chance to get warmed up. I'm a little stiff."

"Do you want me to find a scalpel and use it on you? Because I will."

Zachary smiled. She studied him, her brows going up. She pressed her lips together as if she had just applied her red lipstick.

"So what's up with you? You look like hell."

"Just one bad night. It's nothing."

"The way you take care of yourself, one bad night could do you in. Have you had anything to eat since I saw you last? You look like the walking dead."

"I've eaten," Zachary protested. And he had. A little of the fruit that Bridget had bought. And he had found the time to go grocery shopping, even though he knew both Kenzie and Bridget would be appalled if they saw what had been in his cart and now resided in his kitchen. Prepackaged snacks and meal replacement bars. Frozen pizza, lasagna, and roast beef with potatoes. Energy drinks to supplement his coffee intake. He needed to clear more of Bridget's food out of the fridge before it went bad. "I told you. I just had a bad night."

"I don't want you ending up in here. No offense, but I don't need the likes of you cluttering up the drawers. And who knows what Dr. Wiltshire would find when he opened you up. Nothing but coffee and pills, I suspect."

Zachary shrugged. "Probably."

Kenzie sat back in her chair, stretching and still watching him. "So? What's up?"

"Robin Salter dumped Lawrence two days before she died."

Kenzie considered this. "How do you know that?"

"He admitted it to me. I told him I knew he was trying to hide something from me about that last day he spent with her, and he admitted that it had all been the build-up to breaking up with him."

"What day? What happened?"

Zachary briefly described the last date. He held up the thumb drive with the pictures on it. "You want to see?"

Kenzie reached for it, her eyes widening. "This feels a little voyeuristic," she confessed, bending down to plug it into her tower. "I don't really need to see them…"

But that didn't stop her from clicking on the drive icon when it popped up on her screen, and scrolling through the pictures. She nodded, her eyes riveted to the display. "Just look at them. They're trying to act like a lovey-dovey couple, but they couldn't be farther away from each other. And their expressions… talk about painful. I can't understand why they would go through this whole charade."

"I don't know when she told him she was dumping him." Zachary watched the pictures scroll over Kenzie's screen. "I think he must have known pretty early on, even if she didn't tell him, that something was wrong. Just look at his face and the way he's holding his head." Zachary felt a stabbing pain through his heart. The pain of breaking up with Bridget was still as fresh and raw as it had been that day. The betrayal. The physical illness of losing her, of her abandoning him as some broken thing, just like his mother had done decades before.

"Zachary!"

The ringing in his ears was too loud for him to hear Kenzie's words. He stared at the couple on the screen with the feeling of a heavy truck gradually sliding down an icy hill, gravity inexorably getting its own way.

"Here, sit down." Kenzie had come around the desk and was shoving a chair behind his knees, forcing Zachary to sit. She put her hand on the back of his neck. "Do you need to put your head between your knees? Do you need to take something?"

"No." He forced out the words. "I'm fine."

"You're fine if gray is your natural color. Take a few deep breaths."

Zachary did as he was told. His vision gradually expanded until he could see Kenzie and her desk and everything around them instead of just the pictures on the monitor.

"Maybe you should turn that off." Zachary motioned to the screen.

Kenzie frowned, but she did as he said. "They're your pictures," she said. "It's not like this is the first time you've seen them."

"I know. I don't know why. Just that I can't look at them right now. I can't... I just keep seeing Bridget."

"Bridget? Why?"

Kenzie knew his story, so he wasn't sure why she couldn't put it together by herself. "Because she broke up with me while she was in treatment too. I just... can't seem to separate the two of them. Maybe that's why Bridget needs to know what happened to Robin. Because they're so much alike, she sees herself in Robin."

"Why would anyone break up while they were going through treatment? I thought that would be when you needed people around you the most."

"Yes. But apparently not *toxic* people."

"Toxic," Kenzie scoffed. "That's what you call someone who won't just go along with everything you say and do. The only way you could be toxic to Bridget is if she ate you, and then only because of your meds. She wanted out, pure and simple. She wanted the freedom to do whatever she wanted."

It was a lot of insight for someone who had said just a second before that she had no idea why Bridget would break up in the middle of chemotherapy.

Kenzie removed the drive and handed it back to Zachary. He shoved it down into his pocket.

"What would it take to get the medical examiner involved?"

"In what? In Robin Salter's death?" Kenzie's tone jumped several notes.

Zachary just nodded. He knew it was going to be an uphill battle. He couldn't just suggest that the medical examiner look at a death that had been deemed to have been a natural, doctor-attended death. He didn't have any standing in the case or in the political structure.

"Good grief, Zachary. You know she had cancer. What proof do you have that it was anything but the cancer?"

Zachary tapped the drive in his pocket. "I have these pictures. Lawrence's confession that she dumped him. His statement and the nurse's, saying that he went back to see Robin on Thursday, after she dumped him. Why would he? If it was you, wouldn't you stay as far away from her as you could?"

"Are you telling me you didn't go back to Bridget and try to convince her to take you back?"

Zachary swallowed. "She said she needed space, so I gave her space. I thought she'd change her mind in a day or two."

"And you never went back to see her to try to talk her into getting back together?"

Zachary suspected she would only think him dishonest if he continued to deny it. "Well... yes. I did."

"And did you poison her?"

"No!"

"Then what makes you think that Lawrence did? If you are so struck by the similarities of your cases, then explain that. You had no intention of killing Bridget, did you?"

"I couldn't. I would never have even thought of it."

"Why would Lawrence?"

"He's... he's suppressing his anger. I can see it in his sculptures. And Bridget didn't die two days after she broke up with me. Robin did."

"What evidence do you have that he had anything to do with her death?"

"Nothing. She was in more pain the last few days. The doctor and nurses were surprised that she died when she did. It would have been easy to put insulin or something else into her IV. You don't think it's enough that she mysteriously died right after they broke up?"

"She didn't die mysteriously. She had cancer."

"But it wasn't the cancer that killed her."

"How do you know that?"

He looked at her. "I guess I don't, without an autopsy."

"You think you have enough to convince Dr. Wiltshire to do an autopsy? When the body has already been transferred to a funeral home? For all we know, she might have been embalmed or cremated already."

"I was hoping that you would talk with Dr. Wiltshire... maybe recommend to him that there was reason to be suspicious."

"It's very irregular. I don't want to get in trouble for getting involved in something that is none of my business."

"Isn't it your business to find out why people died?"

"People who come in here through proper channels. We can't investigate every single death."

"I think there's enough here to at least give it another look."

Kenzie looked at her computer, ignoring Zachary. For a few minutes, they each sat there, Zachary trying to think of what he could say to convince Kenzie to at least present the case to the medical examiner. Kenzie answered several phone calls and processed forms. Eventually, she looked across her desk at Zachary.

"Tell me why you're doing this, Zachary."

"I want to find out what really happened to Robin. If she was murdered…"

"But why? Tell me it isn't because you want to get back together with Bridget."

Zachary felt like she had sucker-punched him. For a minute, he forgot how to breathe. What could he tell her? Of course he had taken the case because of Bridget. Of course he wanted to get back together with the love of his life. But he couldn't tell Kenzie that. He didn't want to risk losing her too. He focused his gaze just below her eyes, so he didn't have to meet her intense gaze.

"I want to find out the truth." His voice sounded strangled in his own ears.

"Because of Bridget."

"Don't you think Robin deserves justice?"

She just looked at him. Could everyone read him so clearly? Zachary looked down, blinking, not wanting her to see his desperation.

"Bridget isn't coming back, Zachary," Kenzie said firmly. "She's playing with your heart. Using your feelings toward her to get you involved in an investigation is really low. Can't you see how she's using you?"

"Robin Salter was murdered," Zachary said firmly. "She shouldn't be buried without anybody even knowing that."

"What's all this?" A man's voice came from behind Zachary. Kenzie looked up, all color draining from her naturally fair complexion. Zachary turned around to see who was there. At first glance, Zachary would have through him just another lab technician. But the name badge on the man's lab coat gave him away as Dr. Wiltshire, the medical examiner. He was a clean-shaven older man, the hair on his temples gray, a pair of rectangular reading glasses sliding down his nose. He had a couple of files in his hands and had obviously come out of the lab to give them to Kenzie.

"It's nothing," Kenzie said evenly, giving Zachary a glare that was obviously meant to keep him quiet. But it was his one chance to present the case to Dr. Wiltshire and he wasn't going to pass it up.

"It isn't nothing," he insisted. "When a woman dies unexpectedly two days after she dumps her boyfriend, don't you think that is suspicious?"

Dr. Wiltshire pushed up his glasses and looked at Kenzie. A red flush at her neckline was spreading upward.

"Tell the whole story," Kenzie insisted. "Tell him she had terminal cancer and was under a doctor's care. Her doctor said it was natural causes. That's why it never came through here."

"Doctors can be wrong. Everybody says it was too early. She was expected to live for months yet. She wasn't dying. She was still fighting it and it wasn't her time to go."

"It was a doctor-attended death," Kenzie snapped. "It was his responsibility to report it if he thought there was anything suspicious about the circumstances of her death. People die before they are expected to all the time. They're not all murdered."

"She treated her boyfriend like trash. She kicked him to the curb, and not forty-eight hours later, she was dead."

Dr. Wiltshire studied Zachary, head cocked curiously. "Do I know your face? Who are you?"

Zachary thought he should stand up and introduce himself properly, shaking Dr. Wiltshire's hand. But he was still so shaky, he didn't know whether his legs would hold him. Collapsing in the middle of the floor was really not the best way of convincing the medical examiner that he had logical, reasoned arguments with respect to Robin's death.

"My name is Zachary Goldman. I'm a private investigator."

"A private investigator. And you were hired to look into this case?"

Zachary nodded.

"His ex-wife asked him to look into it," Kenzie interposed, trying to sway Dr. Wiltshire from thinking that someone had thought the case had enough merit to actually put the money into hiring Zachary to investigate.

"*Ex*-wife?" Dr. Wiltshire repeated. "And you took the case?" His opinion had clearly been swayed the wrong direction by Kenzie's argument. "I wouldn't take a case from my ex-wife if she was holding a gun to my head!"

They both laughed at the good-natured joke, but Kenzie's glare at Zachary was poisonous. She did not appreciate being shown up in front of her boss. Zachary could guess that the next time he wanted her opinion on a case or an explanation of medical terminology, she was not going to be so eager to help.

"Do we have a file on this case?" Dr. Wiltshire asked Kenzie.

"No, sir. Like I said, the doctor attending said it was a natural death. She was terminal."

"We can't rule out foul play even if she was dying anyway. The timing was unexpected?"

Kenzie looked at Zachary again. "I don't know a lot of the details of the case. You'd have to ask the private *dick* here."

Zachary swallowed. She was definitely not happy with him.

Dr. Wiltshire considered. "Why don't you come into my office," he invited Zachary. "Kenzie, please open a file and bring me the initial intake form. How long ago did this happen? Do we know where the body is?"

"It was last Friday," Zachary contributed. "The funeral home collected her body. I don't think there's been any service yet, but I don't know whether she's still... what state the body is in."

"You know which funeral home?"

"No."

"Find out from the hospital or care center," Wiltshire told Kenzie, "and tell them to put a hold on the remains as a courtesy, until we contact them with further instructions."

Zachary tried not to look at Kenzie as he got unsteadily to his feet to go with the medical examiner into his office.

10

***

D r. Wiltshire looked back when he realized that Zachary wasn't keeping up with him.

"Sorry," Zachary apologized, growing even more conscious of his legs and how they were not moving properly. "I had a spinal cord injury and sometimes it takes a minute to remember how to walk…"

Dr. Wiltshire nodded and waited for him, then walked more slowly to his office to allow Zachary to get control of his gait, which still felt unnatural. They sat down, Dr. Wiltshire behind his desk and Zachary in one of the guest chairs before it. Dr. Wiltshire took off his glasses and laid them down on the desk.

"You're the private investigator who challenged my findings on the Declan Bond case and proved that he was murdered."

"Uh, yes." Zachary nodded, hoping this wasn't going to get him kicked right back out of the office without a further interview.

"How is his mother? My daughter-in-law loved *The Happy Artist*. Is she going to start the show again? Or have they canceled her contract?"

"Her return is going to air in a couple of weeks. It's been a hard time for her, but I think she's looking forward to getting back again."

"Good." Dr. Wiltshire smiled. "Her audience will be thrilled. She has quite the following in these parts."

"She does," Zachary agreed politely.

"And you were the one who was involved in that nasty business at Summit too, weren't you?"

Zachary swallowed. He shifted in his seat and tried not to think about the nightmare that had turned out to be. Clarissa haunted his dreams regularly with her electric shock devices and her sadistic smile. At least the nightmares about Annie were fading.

"And now you're looking into another death in my jurisdiction."

Zachary felt like he should apologize, but he held his tongue. He wasn't trying to discredit the medical examiner. It hadn't even crossed Dr. Wiltshire's desk. Zachary was just trying to find the truth. He was just doing his job.

"What have you discovered so far?" Dr. Wiltshire asked. "Start at the beginning."

Zachary did his best to give a coherent narrative of all that he had discovered so far. Bridget's impressions that Robin was not near death and had not given up the fight. The medical professionals' concurrence, even though they didn't think it meant anything. Robin's symptoms before her death, the availability of insulin and her IV.

Dr. Wiltshire listened carefully, asking the occasional question. Zachary was aware that it didn't add up to much. It was all circumstantial and there was no evidence that anything had been done to harm Robin. But there wouldn't be any evidence unless an autopsy was conducted.

Dr. Wiltshire picked up his glasses from the desk. He cleaned the lenses, scratched his ear with one of the arms, and tapped them against his desk thoughtfully.

"This is unusual," he said eventually. "I have to say, we don't take on the case of every crackpot who walks in off the street or every family member who wants an investigation started. But you do have a track record. And there is enough to suggest that someone might have shortened Robin Slater's life…"

"You'll look into it, then?" Zachary asked, hardly daring to hope.

"I'm sticking my neck out here, so I hope you're right and there is something to it. Not that we ever wish foul play on anyone. But we are in the business of uncovering the truth."

There was a tap on the door and Kenzie entered. She didn't look at Zachary, but approached and put a new folder down on Dr. Wiltshire's desk, looking at him questioningly.

The medical examiner nodded his thanks and opened the folder up to fill out the first form. "You asked the funeral home to hold the remains?"

"Yes."

"Has she been embalmed?"

"No. Not yet."

"Well, that will help. This is going to take a little finessing, Kenzie. It's going to take some work to smooth the feathers we ruffle by getting involved in a case this way. I'll need to file a report with the police department to start a proper death investigation. The evidence has already been compromised."

Kenzie nodded jerkily. Zachary wished he could just sink into the floor. She was going to be furious with him. He hadn't intended to do an end-run around her, but now her boss had overridden her, and if Zachary knew Kenzie, she was truly pissed about that.

"Okay. Let's get the remains scheduled for a post as early as we can. Some of the evidence will have already broken down." He glanced over at Zachary. "Some substances break down after death. Insulin breaks down within forty-eight hours, for example, which is one of the reasons it is preferred by killers. It looks natural, it's fast, and it's almost impossible to detect."

"If it was insulin… is there any way you'll be able to tell?"

Dr. Wiltshire sighed and rocked his chair back. It let out a long squeal. "By starting a death investigation, there will be police involvement. They can get copies of the patient's records and inventory to cross-check them, get surveillance videos, shift schedules, that kind of thing. They'll do interviews and maybe someone will confess."

Kenzie shook her head. Zachary knew she was holding back. She wanted so badly to blast him and tell him how bad they were all going to look when there was no evidence of anything but a natural death. That turned his thoughts in the opposite direction.

"If there wasn't foul play and it was the cancer, will you be able to tell that?"

"Possibly. We may get lucky and be able to see that a mass cut off blood flow to a major organ or shut down liver function. Though the staff probably would have seen signs of that."

"But don't hold my breath."

"The result of my investigation will likely be that there is no evidence to indicate it was anything other than a natural death. I don't want to mislead you. The chances we will find anything are very slim." Dr. Wiltshire smiled at Kenzie. "But I do like a challenge! And you and Mr. Goldman have a history of being able to untangle things."

Kenzie opened her mouth to protest. Zachary looked at her. He hadn't said anything about Kenzie helping him out with previous cases, so anything that Dr. Wiltshire had divined had either come from something Kenzie had said to him, or just from the fact that Zachary had gone to her for help.

"I'm reading between the lines," Dr. Wiltshire said, "but I don't think I'm wrong, am I?"

Kenzie shifted her stance, looking uncomfortable. "It's mostly Zachary," she said. "He's like a bulldog with a steak. I help him a little with forensic knowledge, but... he's the brains behind it."

Zachary was stunned. He had grown up with everyone telling him how stupid he was, how easily distracted and impulsive, how he couldn't ever just focus on one thing and get the job done. He had no schooling past twelfth grade except for what he had taught himself. He hadn't even earned a diploma. Growing up in foster care had meant going straight into the work-force once he was eighteen.

"I'm..." He wasn't sure what to say to this. "I'm stubborn, that's all. I just... stick with it until it's done."

"There's much to be said for being stubborn. And now... Kenzie and I have some fires to light and some to put out. You know how to get ahold of each other?" His grin widened.

"Uh, yes, sir," Zachary agreed, getting to his feet. Though he still felt awkward, his legs had gained some strength, and he was able to walk back out of Wiltshire's office without looking too much like a penguin on crack.

He had accomplished the impossible. A death investigation was going to be opened into Robin Salter's death.

But what were they going to find?

11

Zachary's heart was thumping as he approached the house. It wasn't like there was a restraining order against him. Bridget had threatened to get one in the past, but Zachary had never been served with one and it wasn't like she didn't know where he lived. She was the one who had been coming to see him lately. She had been the one who needed him. He rolled the word around in his mind. It made him feel stronger, more virile. She *needed* him.

He rang the doorbell and in a few minutes, Bridget opened the ornate white front door. She raised her eyebrows, looking at him and then looking behind him as if he might have brought someone else with him. Who would he bring? Kenzie? The police? Lawrence Long?

"Hi."

"What are you doing here?" She didn't know how to react to his presence. She couldn't be angry with him, even though she'd previously told him to stay away, because he was doing what she wanted him to do, and she didn't want to alienate him. She didn't know whether to be concerned about his health and well-being, her usual fall-back position. Or was he there for something else?

Zachary smiled, feeling warm. He had done it. She had needed his help, and he had succeeded. At least with the first step.

"I did it, Bridget. We did it."

"Did what?"

"We got them to open up a death investigation into Robin Salter's death. They looking into it."

"Who is? What are they going to do?"

"A proper investigation. Doing an autopsy to determine cause of death. Interviewing witnesses. Reviewing the hospital records. The whole bit."

She stared at him, stunned. "Are you kidding me?"

He shook his head. "No. They're looking into it. The medical examiner's office has opened their file and requested her remains from the funeral home. They're starting on the arrangements right away."

"I can't believe it."

Zachary wanted to step forward and take her in his arms. He wanted to assure her that it was true and comfort her in the loss of her friend. He wanted to be the one who was there for her again. A partner. Her other half.

He took a step toward her. Bridget took a step back, maintaining the distance between them. Zachary stopped.

"So this is real," Bridget said.

Zachary nodded, though he was uncertain what she meant.

"This is really happening. I wasn't just imagining things."

"We don't know yet whether there was any foul play, or whether she did just die," Zachary clarified. "We have to wait and see."

"But there was enough there for them to look into it. They believed that there might be something wrong."

"Yes, you were right."

Zachary reached a hand toward her to take her by the arm. She seemed a little unsteady on her feet, and he was suddenly worried about her. Maybe he shouldn't just have shown up at her door and announced it without any lead-up. Maybe he should have told her to sit down first.

"Who is it?" a male voice boomed, and in a moment, Gordon stood behind Bridget.

Gordon Drake was not a bad guy, other than the fact that he had moved in on Zachary's territory and was now living the life that should have been Zachary's. For that, Zachary strongly resented him. He knew that it was just an emotional reaction, and not a fair one. Gordon hadn't come into the picture until after Zachary was gone. He hadn't been fooling around with Bridget while she and Zachary were still married. Zachary had checked into his background, and Gordon didn't seem to have any major skeletons in the closet. As far as Zachary knew, he didn't complain when Bridget called or dropped in on Zachary, even allowing their holiday plans the previous Christmas to be delayed while Bridget checked up on Zachary's wellbeing. Gordon was, to all appearances, an all-around good guy. But that didn't mean Zachary had to like him.

"Zach," Gordon greeted cheerily. "What are you doing here? You're looking good." He looked at Bridget. "Anything I can help with, my dear?"

She gripped his arm, which irritated Zachary, as he had been about to take her arm and to steady her, but once again Gordon had stepped right in between them. Gordon looked down at Bridget with an expression of concern. "Are you alright?"

"She might want to sit down," Zachary said. "I was just talking to her about Robin Salter. The developments in her case."

Gordon raised his brows, bemused. "Robin Salter...?" He looked back at Bridget. "Isn't she that woman you were in treatment with?"

Bridget nodded. Zachary was interested to note that Bridget had apparently not talked to Gordon about what had happened. It wasn't immediately apparent whether Gordon even knew that Robin had died. Bridget had not told him anything, but she had gone to Zachary for help.

Score one for Zachary.

"Do you want to sit down?" Gordon asked Bridget. He indicated Zachary with his eyes, clearly not sure what to do about him.

"Yes... come in, Zachary, and tell me about it."

Gordon made a grand gesture for Zachary to enter. For the first time, Zachary was allowed in through the front door. Any other time he had shown up at Bridget's door, he'd been run off the property with threats of the police and getting restraining orders. But things were changing. He was once again part of Bridget's circle.

It was a spacious house, lots of classically beautiful art pieces. Nothing abstract like Lawrence's work. Not the kind of place that you had kids in, so Zachary could only guess that Bridget was sticking to her guns about not wanting to have a family. She had done as the doctors had said to and had her eggs frozen before radiation in case she ever changed her mind about that, but Zachary imagined that ten or twenty years down the line, the eggs would reach their expiration date and be quietly destroyed without anyone ever using them.

He would have loved to have had children with Bridget. He had imagined it from the first day they had met. But she had been adamant that she wanted a career before family. She *didn't* want family almost as much as Zachary *did*.

Gordon and Bridget led the way to a cozy living room decorated almost entirely in white. They sat down together on a long white couch and Zachary chose one of the few pieces in the room that was a deep rich red instead of white. Even though he had put on clean clothes that morning, he would be humiliated if he'd left one smudge of dirt on one of the pristine white pieces of furniture.

"I asked Zachary if he would look into the circumstances of Robin's death for me," Bridget explained to Gordon. She was pale, but each cheek had a red flush in the middle. Or maybe it was her makeup, still tinting the skin that had gone as white as the room's decor.

"Robin's death?" Gordon echoed. "Bridget, what happened? Why didn't you tell me?"

Bridget dabbed at dry eyes with a tissue. "It was… I don't know. I didn't want to tell you about it until I knew what had happened. I wanted to know first."

"And… what did happen?"

Gordon looked at Bridget and Bridget looked at Zachary. Gordon turned his head to look at him as well.

"What did happen?" Gordon repeated.

"We're still sorting it out," Zachary explained. "They've now opened a death investigation, which means they'll actually be collecting evidence and doing an autopsy. Trying to establish the cause of death instead of just relying on what the doctor attending her said."

"But it was cancer, surely."

Bridget shook her head.

"It still might have been," Zachary cautioned, repeating what Dr. Wiltshire and Kenzie had tried to drill into him. "It may be that they do the autopsy and find that it was the cancer, it was just more advanced than the doctor thought. Or a blood clot caused by the cancer. Or some other complication. But they're going to check."

"What did you find out about Lawrence?" Bridget asked. "He didn't do it. I know that. But what did you find out?"

Zachary leaned forward, his elbows on his knees. "I found out that Robin dumped Lawrence the Wednesday before she died."

"What?"

"That was the secret. That's what he was trying to hide. They didn't have the perfect last date because she wanted to do those things before she died or wanted to give him the gift of a perfect day together to remember her by. She wanted to have one last date with him, and then she broke it off. Told him that she wanted him out of her life."

Bridget opened and closed her mouth. "But that's… cruel. They were always so good together. Why would she even break up with him?"

"I guess they weren't as perfect as you thought." Zachary thought back to their own relationship and how Bridget had jettisoned him once things got to be too difficult. "Maybe she needed space. Maybe he was just dead weight."

Bridget's forehead wrinkled. Zachary couldn't tell whether she recognized herself in his words or not.

"So she broke up with her boyfriend," Gordon summarized, eager to hear the rest of the story, "and then…?"

"That was Wednesday night. Thursday she was very tired from the long day and mostly slept. Lawrence did show up at some point, but he didn't stay long. And the next morning, Friday, the nursing staff found her dead."

Bridget and Gordon both stared at Zachary.

"You think he killed her?" Gordon asked. "You think he put something in her food, or smothered her with the pillow…?"

"He didn't smother her," Zachary said. "I think the nurses and the doctor who signed her death certificate would have noticed if she'd been smothered. But poisoning… I think he might have. It wouldn't even have to be in her food. It could be straight into her blood, through the IV."

"Lawrence didn't do it," Bridget said. Her voice was weak, less sure than it had been the last few times she had insisted it couldn't have been Lawrence. She was starting to see that he was the one who had the most motive and opportunity. "I know how much he loved her. When they were together, he couldn't take his eyes off of her. It was like…" She looked at Zachary and stopped. Was she remembering how besotted he had been with her? How she would look up and find his eyes on her, just drinking her in? "He just couldn't have, Zachary."

"Extreme love can turn quickly to hate when spurned," Gordon said wisely. "It's a story as old as time. If I can't have you, nobody can. If you won't have me, you won't have anybody. Jealousy has turned many a lover's hand against his former mistress."

"Don't, Gordon," Bridget murmured. She looked at Zachary again, as if hoping that he hadn't heard Gordon.

"Anyway…" Zachary decided to fill Bridget in on the few other bits she didn't know, telling her about meeting with Dr. Wiltshire and his agreement to open a death investigation for Robin. "They're going to audit the insulin prescriptions against the inventory to see whether there are any missing doses. I guess they'll do that with any of the medications they think could have been used to kill her. And they'll look at all of her records, and at all of the shift logs and the surveillance cameras. Make sure she wasn't given something she should not have been."

"You're not going to find anything on the surveillance. I don't believe anyone killed her intentionally. She was probably given a wrong dosage, or the wrong medication…"

"I don't know what it was. I told Dr. Wiltshire everything I knew. He couldn't tell from the symptoms what it might have been… she was sick. She was going to die anyway… just maybe not that fast."

"It still doesn't make it right. She should have had more time with her family. I want whoever is responsible for taking her away from her family and friends so soon to pay. They shouldn't just walk away from this. It shouldn't just be an 'oops' like if you added the wrong cells in a budget spreadsheet. We're talking about someone's life here. Her last days were just taken away from her."

Zachary could hear the pain in Bridget's voice. Survivor's guilt? Because she had overcome cancer and Robin had not? Because Bridget still had days and years ahead of her, and Robin was gone?

Bridget still had time to make things up to Zachary and be reconciled with him. Robin would never have that chance with Lawrence. That ship had sailed.

12

Nurse Betty wasn't nearly as happy to talk to Zachary as she had been on the previous occasions. She gave him a glower that would have curdled cream.

"You sure stirred up a crap-ton of trouble. I thought you were a nice guy. Quiet, not pushy, just a nice guy helping out his wife. But now... we've had police all over this place. I have been run off my feet trying to get them all of the records they want. We have patients to care for. We can't be running around dealing with all of their demands!"

"I'm sorry it's all landed on you. I never meant for that to happen. I didn't realize how much extra work it would be for you."

She looked a little mollified, unsure whether to keep complaining or not. She hadn't expected any sympathy from him.

"It's just that for Bridget and for Robin's family... they had to know the truth. They had to know what it was that went wrong, if anything. What it was that took Robin away from them so suddenly. I certainly never intended to target you or any of the other staff."

"Well, of course we want to know what went wrong too," Betty agreed. "But we've all seen it happen before. Some people just go before you think it's their time. It doesn't mean anyone did anything wrong or anything malicious. Sometimes a person's time just comes before you expect it."

"I'm sure that's all it will be in this case," Zachary soothed. "Can I get you anything? Can I bring you a coffee or a sandwich from the cafeteria? You're probably sick of cafeteria food; is there a restaurant nearby that you like? I can bring you whatever you want."

She blushed and patted at her hair. "Oh, you don't need to do anything like that. I'm just doing my job. These things happen sometimes and you just have to go with the flow."

"I know, but it's been such a burden for you..."

"No, no." She waved his concern away. "It's something interesting to break up the long stretches of boredom. At least being called on to photo-copy records means that I wasn't the one who had to take care of Mrs. Groucho's diaper this morning." She rolled her eyes dramatically. "Oh, but that woman can..." She pressed her thin lips together primly. "Treatments can be very hard on the digestive tract, and she is no exception. And the way she starts yelling the second she makes in her diaper, you'd think the woman was on fire! Honestly, some of the patients around here think they are the only one you have to take care of. Believe me, if I only had to take care of one woman, it would not be her."

Zachary chuckled sympathetically. "I can only imagine. It must be very trying to deal with some of the patients."

"They ain't called *patience* for nothing." She shook her head.

"You'd rather deal with someone like Robin?" Zachary suggested.

Betty raised her brows and cocked her head slightly. "Robin Salter?" she said. "No, I should think not!"

"Oh. She wasn't one of the better patients?"

"Oh, no."

Zachary remembered Lawrence confiding that Robin sometimes over-dramatized and complained about the care she was getting at the treatment center. Maybe he was being generous. A woman that could string a man along like Robin had, only to dump him hard at the end of the day was probably not the nicest one in the unit.

"I didn't realize. Her boyfriend did say that she often found reasons to complain, but he didn't think she had any reason to. He thought the care here was very good."

"Well, thank you for that."

"I know I never found any reason for complaint when Bridget was here," Zachary said. Which was truthful. He hadn't been around to hear any complaints from her or to have any himself. If Betty thought about it, she probably knew that, but she wasn't about to turn down a compliment.

"I suppose they have a right to be miserable," Zachary said. "But taking it out on the staff... that's not very fair."

"You know, we get some patients through here who are angels on earth. They could be coding and they would smile and apologize for making you hurry. But some people, the women in particular... honey, the sooner they are out of here, one way or the other, the better."

And Robin had been one of those patients. Zachary was glad that the police department was already looking at the staff at the care center. It saved him the trouble of trying to sort out which of them might have had a reason to put an early end to Robin's suffering. It sounded like they all did.

Zachary had decided that he was going to pop over to the cafeteria and pick something up for Nurse Betty anyway. She might have said that she didn't really want anything and that she had been happy to have to do paperwork for the police rather than take care of irritable patients for a while, but he knew he had still inconvenienced her, and that even after that, she had given him more insight into Robin and what it was like to deal with her while she was there. The more he knew about Robin's personality and the dynamics, the better.

"Leave me alone! Just get your hands off!"

Zachary froze at the words. He stopped stock-still in the middle of the hallway. If someone had been walking behind him, they would have walked right into him. Zachary looked around.

"No," the voice repeated. "I said to stop."

The sound came from one of the small visitor rooms that branched off from the main hallway. Small rooms for families to meet in, some with a TV or toys, some with plants, toys, or books; there were different kinds of surroundings to suit different visitor personalities or needs. Zachary stepped into the doorway ready to stop whatever assault was going on.

A man bent over a woman in a wheelchair. He was standing at an awkward angle beside it, as if he had been behind it to push it, but had to step around it to take care of a problem. The problem seemed to be his attempt to sponge off a layer of drool that coated the woman's chin and stretched down to her chest, where she wore a bib to soak it up. Her hands, stiffened into claws, battered at his, trying to make him stop

Zachary didn't know what to do or say at first.

The man avoided the woman's awkward movements and patted at her throat and chest, blotting the spittle with a thin hospital towel. It was obvious from his smock that he was part of the staff. The woman's movements became more frantic, her words dissolving into a sob of protest.

"Leave her alone," Zachary finally worked up the courage to say.

The hospital worker turned around to look at Zachary. He sneered, but he took a step back from the patient as if he had been caught doing something he wasn't supposed to.

"Who are you? This is none of your business." The oft-repeated refrain of an abuser.

"She asked you to leave her alone, so leave her alone."

"She needs help. I'm just taking care of her."

"She said no."

"She doesn't get to say no."

"I say she does," Zachary insisted. He stepped into the small room. He wasn't physically imposing; he was smaller than the man, and yet the man stepped back again, looking around the room to measure his escape.

"You don't work here. You don't have to spend your days carting around people who are so broken down by disease and treatment that they can't do anything for themselves. She should be thanking me, not fighting me."

"She doesn't owe you anything."

"I need to take her back to her room."

"No, you don't."

"I'll call security on you! You don't have any right to be ordering me around. Who are you to walk in here and act like you're my boss?" The man was inching toward the door. It was obvious he was on his way out. He was just using the words to cover himself, like a man caught with his pants down.

Zachary just stood there and watched him retreat. He shifted his body sideways to allow the man to make a swift exit without blocking his way. Zachary wasn't about to get punched in the nose by an animal desperate for escape.

Zachary stood there and listened to the whisper of the man's soft-soled shoes down the hospital corridor.

He turned to the woman. He didn't know if he should apologize to her for interfering or maybe push her back to her unit.

She was younger than he had first realized. The clawed fingers and reedy voice had made him think she was an elderly woman. But he saw that in spite of her boniness and air of frailty, she was younger than he was. Her expression was a mixture of relief and dread. Did she think that he was going to do something to her? That he'd gotten rid of the man just to have her to himself?

Zachary sat in one of the visitor chairs, lowering himself to her eye level. "Are you okay?" he asked gently, "What else can I do for you?"

She gave an odd, choking laugh and tears brimmed up in her eyes.

"They think they have a right to your body," she said. "They think that being in a wheelchair or being weak means they can do whatever they want. But I'm still in here! I still have the right to choose who touches me and how!"

Zachary nodded. "Yes. You do."

"It may be his job to take me from one place to another, but it's not his job to touch me. And even if it was, I can still say no!"

Her voice was getting stronger and more strident.

"I'm sorry," Zachary said. Apologizing not for himself, but for what had happened to her. All of the times people had made presumptions and thought they had the right to control her.

The woman was quiet for a few minutes, breathing and trying to get her emotions under control. Tears brimmed over her lids and down her cheeks, and Zachary made no move to try to stop them or wipe them away. He made a soft, calming noise.

"Sh, it's okay."

After a couple of minutes, she attempted to bring her hand up to her face. Zachary saw that she had a balled-up tissue or cloth in her grip that she was trying to dab at her face with. A way for her to have control over her own spit and tears. Her arms shook and the muscles in her hands and arms grew taut as she tried to perform the simple task. She touched the tissue to her cheek, but that was all she could manage. More tears flooded down her face and soaked into the tissue. Keeping her hand up appeared to be too great an effort for her, and it sank down into her lap until both hands lay there still, side by side.

"You put a person in a wheelchair," she said shakily, "and they suddenly become an object. Something to be acted upon. People grab the wheelchair and push you around without asking, like just because you have some impairment, you no longer have a will of your own. You complain, and they say they are just *helping*." Her hands shook in her lap. "And it doesn't stop there. Some of them say vile things. They touch you without permission. You can't do anything to stop them. They can do whatever they want to and get away with it. Because even to the police or the staff or people out in public, you are just an object. You lose your personhood when they put you in this chair."

"That's..." Zachary couldn't think of language strong enough. He remembered what it was like after the accident that had left him paralyzed and needing to learn how to walk and take care of himself again. People coming in and out of his room, moving him around, transporting him from the bed to the chair, down to physio, or wherever else they wanted him. It wasn't as serious as what the woman was describing; he'd never had anyone take advantage of him. Not really. He'd felt minimized and less than a real person, but he hadn't had to deal with all of the things she was talking about. It was probably worse for a woman, and his convalescence had not been long. "That's not right. I'm sorry. People don't have the right to treat you that way."

She snuffled, snorting back tears and phlegm and swallowing. The choking, gagging noise made Zachary feel sick. He wanted to help her, but he knew there was nothing he could do. Even to offer seemed insensitive when she was so worked up about people treating her as an object.

Zachary felt guilty for his instinct to help. Was he any better than the others? If he had worked there, how long would it have taken for him to stop listening to the objections and asking or waiting for consent? With so many people needing so much help, could they be blamed for moving in and doing what needed to be done, even if the patient didn't want help?

It had been a complaint he had often heard from Bridget, even before she was sick. *I don't need help. I don't need you to do things for me.* He had wanted to do things for her, to be the strong one, the provider. But she was strong-minded and independent and didn't want him to rush in and take over when a jar needed to be opened or the groceries carried in.

How much of a toll had it taken on Bridget to approach Zachary and ask him for help in finding out what had happened to Robin?

"Who *are* you?" the woman asked. "I don't think I've seen you here before."

"My name is Zachary Goldman. My wife was in treatment here a while back, but right now I'm looking into the death of Robin Salter."

"Robin?" Her head had been sinking down and it bobbed up at his explanation.

"Yes. Did you know her?"

"I know who she was. Didn't know her very well. We weren't in the same unit. Are you a policeman, then?"

He considered whether to fudge his answer. People sometimes felt more comfortable talking to someone they thought was a police officer rather than a private investigator. But his rapid assessment was that the woman had been mistreated by authority figures and was more likely to trust an individual than an official.

"No. I'm a private investigator. Bridget knew Robin and asked me to look into it. The police are involved now, but I'm not part of the department."

She gave a small nod.

"I'm Ruth. Ruth Wick." She lifted her left hand, the one not holding the tissue, and offered it to him, fingers still hooked. Rather than trying to fit his hand into hers in a traditional handshake, Zachary folded his fingers around hers to give them a comforting squeeze, then let go.

"Pleased to meet you, Ruth."

"Thank you… for that." She made a small gesture in the direction of the door the hospital worker had left through.

"No problem. You think he's really going to call security on me?"

"Why would he? You didn't do anything wrong. He doesn't have any reason to have you kicked out. It would just backfire and put him in the spotlight. Cowards like him don't want the attention."

"Are you okay now?"

"Getting there. Being like this," she nodded toward her lap to indicate her condition or the wheelchair, "it makes you very vulnerable. You depend on other people for all of your needs. Most of the nursing staff is pretty good, but it's like walking around naked." She gave a short laugh. "I feel like I spend half the day naked as it is. I don't want to feel that way the rest of the time."

Zachary nodded. "I had an accident," he confided to her. "I had a spinal cord injury. Not serious, but enough that I was paralyzed for a few days and had to work to get my mobility back. It is invasive to have other people handling your body and acting like you are a thing instead of a person."

Ruth nodded. "And I've heard them talk about the patients who are worse... ones who can't respond at all or are in a vegetative state... talking about them like they are plants in a garden instead of people. Even if they can't move at all, they are still people," she said explosively. "Talking about watering the vegetables is disrespectful! It's depersonalizing." She sniffled again. "And I'm going to be one of them, one day."

There was a lump in Zachary's throat. "I'm so sorry."

"What am I going to do when I can't even tell them to stop anymore? What am I going to do when I can see and feel what is going, and I can't even say a word?"

"I don't know." He didn't suggest assisted suicide. He was sure that she knew all of the options and had already looked into that. But if she had religious or other ethical objections, or if she was looking at being completely disabled but not considered to be terminal within six months, it wasn't an option.

Ruth took a long, shuddering breath. She swallowed and lifted her chin. "Okay. I'm done feeling sorry for myself now. Enough self-pity. Where were you headed? Were you on your way in or out?"

Zachary shrugged. "Both, actually. I was talking to one of the nurses in Robin's unit, and I thought I would get her something from the cafeteria before doing anything else."

"Ah. Okay."

"Did you want to come with me?" Zachary offered. "Or if you wanted, I could take you back to your unit or wherever it was you wanted to go next. If you don't want to stay here." He was worried about offending her with his offer. She had just been complaining about people moving her around, and he was offering to do just that. He had no idea whether she was capable of getting around on her own. Her hands didn't appear to be dexterous or strong enough to control the wheelchair, which was not one of the electric ones with a joystick. But he could be completely wrong. He didn't know anything about her condition.

"I'd love to go to the cafeteria," Ruth said, brightening.

"Great!" Zachary didn't get up from his seat right away. "Do you want me to push you, or...?"

"Yes, please."

Zachary got up. He positioned himself behind her and checked the brakes on the wheelchair. They had already been released, so he gave a little push and got Ruth on her way. She was very light and pushing the chair was effortless.

Once in the cafeteria, they discussed what the best treat to get for Nurse Betty would be, neither of them knowing any of her preferences. After settling on a chocolate puffed wheat square and hoping Betty wasn't gluten intolerant, Zachary took a look around at the other offerings.

"Can I get you something?" he suggested. "Would you like coffee or a piece of pie?"

"Oh, you don't have to... are you having anything?"

Zachary could see that he wasn't going to be able to get her anything without buying something for himself. Otherwise it would be seen as a pity offering. The last thing that Ruth needed was for him to show her pity. She was trying to be strong and independent, and he needed to support that.

"Hm. I'm thinking maybe... apple pie. You're not going to make me eat alone, are you? Just me, and my pie, and Nurse Betty's chocolate square?"

Ruth giggled. "I don't know. It could be difficult. I'm really not up to eating by myself."

"I could manage it, if all you need is a steady hand. If you need a tube, we're going to need some help..."

"I'm not quite to tube feeding yet," Ruth said, with an appreciative smile. "But I am on a liquid diet, so..."

Zachary considered the options. "Maybe yogurt or pudding? Would that work?"

Ruth shifted back and forth in her seat, trying to see what was on the higher glass shelves. "Are there Jell-O parfaits?"

"Red or green?"

"Red!"

Zachary added a piece of pie and a red Jell-O cup to a tray and slid it along beside him as he pushed Ruth forward. "Do you mind if I pick up the tab?"

"I seem to have left my purse at home."

"Good." Zachary checked them through and picked up a plastic spoon and fork at the cash register, then found a place for them to sit and eat.

571

13

After a leisurely snack, Zachary pushed Ruth's chair back to her unit, following her directions. They arrived to find the unit in an uproar, with nurses squawking loudly and police officers questioning the man who had been harassing Ruth.

"Ruth! Oh, thank goodness you're okay!" exclaimed one nurse, hurrying over to them. "What happened?" Without waiting for an answer from Ruth, she looked at Zachary. "Where did you find her?"

Zachary waited for Ruth to answer, but before she could, the hospital worker interrupted.

"That's him! That's the man who threatened me!"

"Threatened you?" Zachary echoed, raising his eyebrows.

"Sir, I need you to step back from the wheelchair," one of the cops said, straightening to his full height and moving toward Zachary, hand on his holster.

Zachary wasn't sure whether he was going for a taser, a gun, pepper spray, or something else, but he wasn't going to wait to find out. He released the wheelchair, putting his hands up.

"There's been a misunderstanding," he said, looking at the hospital worker. "I don't know what this guy has been telling you, but I never threatened anyone."

"Step back please. When you are clear of the wheelchair, I want you to lie face-down."

"Seriously?" Zachary took a step backward, and then another. Walking backward was not something he had practiced very much and he teetered, worried for a moment that he was going to topple over before he regained his balance. He put his hands on his head to get down to his knees, and then to lie down. "You're making a mistake listening to this guy."

But the police had to do what they had to do. The cop patted him down and removed the contents of his pockets. There was nothing of particular interest for them to find.

"Zachary didn't do anything!" Ruth protested, her voice high and reedy. "He just went with me down to the cafeteria and we had something to eat. He didn't do anything wrong. *Lucas*," it was the first time she had put a name to the hospital worker, "he's the one you ought to be arresting."

"Nobody is being arrested at this point," one of the other officers said smoothly. "Just tell us what happened and we'll take it from there. No need to get upset."

"I am upset! Zachary was a good Samaritan who came and helped me out, and you're treating him like a criminal. Let him get up and stop being ignorant!"

The police officers exchanged looks with each other. No one looked directly at Ruth. Finally, a heavyset officer nodded, and the one who had frisked Zachary helped him politely to his feet. He looked at Zachary's pocket contents, unsure whether he should be giving them back. The one in charge picked up Zachary's wallet and opened it up to have a look.

"Zachary Goldman," he read. "What is your relationship with Miss Wick?"

"I had dessert with her in the cafeteria. We don't have a previous relationship."

"Zachary Goldman," someone repeated behind Zachary. "Private eye?"

Zachary turned his head and saw Joshua Campbell. Zachary didn't turn all the way around or make any attempt to greet him, not wanting to alarm the officers who were contemplating him.

"Well, I'll be," Campbell said, grinning. "What's up, Zach?"

"Uh…" Zachary wasn't sure what to tell him.

"You here on an investigation?"

"Mind if I get my stuff back, now?"

Campbell motioned for him to help himself, and Zachary picked up his possessions and put them back in his pockets. Everyone seemed to be waiting for him to say something. Zachary realized he hadn't answered Campbell's question. "I'm investigating the death of Robin Salter."

"The way I understand it, *we're* investigating the death of Robin Salter," Campbell countered.

"The police didn't get involved until after I reported to the medical examiner. I don't give up a case just because the police decide to investigate as well."

"No. Stubborn that way," Campbell agreed. He sighed and looked around at the other police officers. "Nothing left to see. I take it this is the young lady who disappeared?"

Everyone nodded.

"You weren't kidnapped?" Campbell asked Ruth. He was the first of the officers who had deigned to talk to her directly. "You were not held or taken anywhere against your will?"

"No," Ruth said tartly. "I was not."

"Then I'm guessing that all of this alarm was a simple overreaction."

There was a lot of grumbling from the other officers, and Lucas did his best to avoid answering any questions directly and to brush the whole thing off as a misunderstanding. Campbell remained nearby as everyone dispersed. He cocked his head at Zachary.

"No trouble, Zach?"

Zachary looked at Ruth, wondering how she wanted it handled. Ruth sighed and shook her head. Zachary guessed that she didn't want any additional harassment that might come from accusing one of the hospital staff of acting improperly. Especially when all she had to complain about was that Lucas was trying to mop up her spittle before returning her to her unit. Just doing his job.

Zachary pressed his lips together, considering whether there was anything he could say that would give Campbell a heads-up, but not go against Ruth's wishes.

"Did you run him to see if he had a record?" Zachary questioned, tilting his head in the direction Lucas had been standing up until a couple of minutes before.

"He wouldn't be able to work here if he had a record."

"Nothing?" Zachary persisted.

"I'd have to check to see if there was anything else… dropped charges, a sealed juvenile record. But there's no warrants outstanding and no convictions."

"Might be a good idea," Zachary said.

Campbell looked toward Ruth, wanting more details.

"Just a feeling," Zachary said, not giving him anything else. "Something setting off my alarms."

Campbell nodded. He was a cop. He understood all about trusting those niggling little feelings.

"I'll take a closer look. You're okay now, ma'am?"

"I'm tired."

"Of course. I don't need anything else from you."

Ruth looked at Zachary, then looked around at the medical staff. She indicated one of the nurses with her eyes. Zachary got the woman's attention.

"Ruth would like to go back to her room," he explained. "She's worn out from visiting."

"Well, we'll take care of that, dearie," the nurse said, taking hold of the handles of Ruth's wheelchair. "Time for a nap, Ruth."

Ruth's head wobbled in what wasn't quite a nod. The nurse wheeled her away.

Campbell and Zachary watched them go.

"Another case?" Campbell asked.

"No. Just met her today. I just want to make sure… she's taken good care of."

"They have a very good reputation here," Campbell assured him. "Try not to let your view be colored by what happened to Robin Salter."

"I'm not. She's just… very vulnerable."

Campbell nodded his agreement. "Well, I suppose if I'm not going to arrest you for kidnapping, we may as well get on our way. You're here on the Salter case?"

"Yes. I wanted to talk to a few more of the people who knew her. Maybe some of the other patients might have some insight."

Campbell let out his breath and made a face. "Look, Zach, we know each other. You know I've got no problem as long as you're operating within the law. But remember we're just starting on this case, and you investigating it simultaneously… I just don't want anyone's toes being stepped on."

"You can't stop me from asking people questions."

"Well, I could strongly discourage you. But that's what I'm talking about... we're both professionals. We can work this out so that no one is getting in anyone else's way."

Zachary walked along beside Campbell. It was true; Campbell was one of the cops Zachary had never had to worry too much about. He didn't automatically get his back up whenever he saw Zachary or heard he was involved in one of their cases. There were certainly enough cops around who did, doggedly territorial of their own investigations.

"I've already talked to the main doctor and nursing staff. That's probably who you're focused on, isn't it?"

Campbell nodded. "They have not been happy with all of the questions and extra work we've been making for them, believe me!"

"I know," Zachary agreed, and held up the puffed wheat square. "Peace offering for Nurse Betty."

Campbell chuckled. "Keeping the wheels greased with sugar and chocolate. Yeah, she's a bit of an old battle-ax, that one. Wouldn't want to be a patient stuck in her care."

"I don't think she's a bad nurse. She's just trying to keep things running smoothly. Hospitals don't run well with cops and private investigators shaking everything up."

They got to the unit. "Bridget was here?" Campbell questioned, looking around. "That's how you got involved in this case?"

Zachary nodded. "Yes. This is where she was, where she got her treatments. Not a place you want to be... but the best place, if you're trying to fight that fight."

"Well, just glad she's in remission, Zach. That's good news."

"You bet."

They stood there for a minute longer, then went their separate directions without further comment. Zachary tracked Nurse Betty down and offered his bribe, and she told him which patients would be able to tell him the most about Robin.

Zachary's first interview was with Chenka Redneslav, Robin's roommate at the time she died. She had been moved to another room so the crime guys could properly process Robin's room and see if there was any evidence to be turned up a full week after Robin's death. Chenka was grumpy about having been moved and let Zachary know she didn't appreciate it.

Chenka was a blonde with classic Russian features and an accent just heavy enough to be romantic. She was slim, but not emaciated like some of the women in the unit. Like Robin, she had retained her good looks. Even in a hospital bed with no makeup on, she was stunning.

"I don't know why you have to come in here and start stirring things up. You're making everybody miserable with all of your questions and bringing the police into this. Everything was fine, I don't understand why you had to stick your nose in and interfere."

"I'm sorry it's been such a problem," Zachary apologized. "But I'm sure that if it was you, you would want people to know the truth. You wouldn't want everyone thinking it was just a natural death when it was not."

"You don't know that."

"No, but it needs to be investigated."

"It's ridiculous." She folded her arms across her chest and looked out the window. She hadn't had a window in the room she had shared with Robin.

"I know. And again, I apologize. I'm just trying to find out the truth. You believe it was Robin's time, I gather? You didn't think she was going to last much longer?"

Chenka pursed her lips. "I didn't think she was going to die *then*," she admitted. "But she had cancer. We all have cancer. Any of us could go at any time."

"Sure. Any time. *You* could go tomorrow," Zachary agreed.

She frowned fiercely at this. "Why do you say that? I am not... I am not going to die tomorrow. They're going to keep giving me medicine, and they will kill all of the cancer. Then I will be well again."

"You could go at any time," Zachary echoed what she had said.

"No, not any time. Those who are ready. Those whose time it is."

"Like Robin."

Chenka looked uneasily over at the call button for the nurse. She wanted to get Zachary out of there, but what would happen if she succeeded? Would it be over, or would he tell people that Chenka had lied to him? Would she be taken to the police station to be questioned, instead of being questioned in the comfort of her room?

577

"I did not know it was Robin's time. I *know* it is not my time. But I did not know it was Robin's time."

"Robin didn't know it was her time either. My wife was visiting with her just before she died, and she didn't know. She didn't have any idea she was going to die soon. She thought she still had months left."

"Your wife?"

"Bridget Downy. She was a friend of Robin's. They were both in treatment together. You probably know her too?"

"Bridget Downy isn't your wife."

She was the first one to challenge Zachary on the fact.

"Bridget is my ex-wife," he agreed. "But we are still very close. She asked me to look into Robin's death. She doesn't believe it was Robin's time. She thinks something happened."

Chenka chewed on her lip, her eyes fastened on Zachary's. "What happened?"

"You were there. Maybe you need to tell me."

"I did not do anything. I did not see anything. I have nothing to tell you."

"Nothing unusual happened Thursday evening or Friday morning?"

"Nothing. No."

"Robin seemed just like her usual self. No change in her condition."

"Obviously, there was a change in her condition on Friday morning."

"Yes. You weren't aware she had passed?"

"No. She died sometime in the night. I don't know when."

"And the nurses didn't discuss it on their night rounds?"

"They don't go around waking everybody up if they are sleeping. They only give prescribed medications or help if patients are having trouble."

"Did Robin have any trouble?"

"She was restless. But she slept."

"She didn't call the nurse for anything that night?"

"Pain meds. She said she was in a lot of pain."

"Was that normal?"

"Cancer can be painful."

"But for Robin. Had she been in a lot of pain before that?"

"For a few days."

"But not before that?"

"No. Before, she was still pretty good. She had energy and able to get

578

around. But then she got pain in her joints and her stomach and chest. She was afraid it was the cancer spreading. I guess it must have been."

"We'll find that out in the autopsy. After she had the pain meds, she slept okay? Did she talk to you at all?"

"She didn't talk to me."

"Not at all? It would be strange to be in the same room as someone and never to have any conversation."

"I was not her friend. She was only here for treatment, not to make friends."

"But she was friends with Bridget," Zachary pointed out.

"I guess... she only needed one friend, then," Chenka said, shrugging. "She had plenty of family. They came to see her all the time. And that boyfriend of hers. Lawrence."

"But she broke up with him."

Chenka looked at Zachary sideways. "What makes you think that?"

"Didn't she tell you? That she dumped him on Wednesday night, after their big date?"

Chenka shook her head adamantly. "She never told me that."

"She told Lawrence. Was that before they came back? I thought it was after the date, when they were back here."

"I don't know. I don't listen to other people's conversations."

Like with Lawrence, Zachary knew Chenka was lying. Of course she had listened to their conversation. Of course she knew what had happened. Two people couldn't have a conversation like that in a hospital room without someone on the other side of the curtain hearing. Zachary considered. Was she trying to protect Lawrence? Or to protect Robin's reputation? Which one of them was she concerned about?

"Who came to see Robin on Thursday? The nurse said that she had a number of visitors, though none of them stayed very long."

"She was too tired for them. So everyone just said hello and then left again."

"Lawrence came by. Did he think he was going to be able to talk her into getting back together? Did he think she'd only been joking the night before and would have changed her mind?"

"How do I know what Lawrence was thinking?" Chenka scoffed. But her next words belied the assertion. "Lawrence was a nice man. He just wanted to make sure she was okay. He wasn't going to abandon her just because she had broken up with him."

"She wouldn't exactly want him to visit, though, would she? She must have told him they weren't a couple anymore and he should leave." Zachary didn't have to imagine what Bridget would have said to him in similar circumstances. He'd lived it. Zachary had been afraid she was just trying to spare him the horrors of cancer and the treatments. He had vowed to stand by her anyway, to be there as her friend even if she was breaking up their marriage. He had been in denial about just how bitter she was toward him.

Chenka shrugged. "She said she did not want him there."

"Did Lawrence have the opportunity to put anything in her IV?"

"The curtain was pulled across. I could not see."

"What do you think? Was there time? Could he have done it without Robin seeing him? Was she asleep when he got there?"

"Lawrence would not have hurt her. He was a nice guy."

"Even a nice guy can be pushed over the edge when he is treated unfairly."

"He did not do anything to her. He wasn't here for long enough."

Zachary nodded slowly, wondering if it were true. Even if Chenka were telling him the truth, would she have been able to judge if Lawrence had the opportunity to put something in Robin's IV? How long would it have taken? Had Robin been awake or asleep when he arrived? If Robin had been given something Thursday, it wasn't something fast-acting. Any fast-acting drug would have to have been administered by someone at the hospital during the night or early morning.

"Who else was here?" he asked. "Were her other visitors here before or after Lawrence?"

"After. He came during the day. Her family didn't come until late afternoon, when school and work were out."

"Her mother and her sister?"

"And that poor boy."

"Her nephew, Rhys?"

Chenka nodded. "Rhys. Yes. Gloria's son."

"Why do you call him a poor boy?"

She raised her eyebrows at him. "Because of what happened to him." When Zachary continued to look at her blankly, she went on to explain. "His grandfather's murder."

"Murder?" Zachary couldn't pick his jaw up off the floor. "Vera's husband was murdered?"

"Yes, of course." Her eyes were wide. "You didn't know that?"

"Nobody happened to mention it. Did this happen recently?" Even as he asked it, Zachary was running through what he knew about Vera and her family from talking to Vera. Her husband hadn't died recently, but years before. *And Rhys had never been the same.*

"No, when Rhys was a little boy. You don't know anything about it?"

"No. What exactly did he die of? What did it have to do with Rhys, other than that they were close?"

"I don't know all of the details," Chenka lowered her voice as if someone might overhear them. "It was a violent death. Shot or stabbed. Rhys was there. He and his grandfather were home alone."

"Did he see it, then? He knew who did it?"

"They think so."

Zachary cocked his head, puzzled, waiting for more.

"That's when they *lost* Rhys." Even in the quiet of the hospital room, Chenka's words were difficult to make out. He leaned forward to hear better and communicate to her that he was engaged. He wanted to hear more. "The boy was never the same after that. He wouldn't talk. He was sent away for a while, to some institution."

"I didn't know that. So he probably saw, but he could never tell what happened?"

Chenka nodded. "Exactly. He withdrew completely. Like a nervous breakdown. He came back to live with his grandma again after a while, but they couldn't ask him about what had happened without setting him off again, so they had to let it go."

"And he's never talked about it since?"

"He's never talked since."

"Oh. Wow." So Vera was right. He was *special.*

"And now this," Chenka said. "It was bad enough that his aunt was dying of cancer. But now that you've started this investigation... to be saying she was murdered too... I can't imagine how the poor boy—and the others—must be feeling now."

Zachary refrained from pointing out that it wasn't his fault that someone had taken Robin's life. All he was doing was trying to find out the truth.

"We don't know if it was murder," Zachary said. "It might have been an error on the part of the doctor or someone else involved in Robin's care. Or it still might have been the course of her cancer or the chemotherapy. We won't know until the medical examiner has had a chance to complete the autopsy and whatever lab tests they have to order."

"But you made it worse. Worse than if you just let them believe it was cancer."

Zachary gave a helpless shrug. "I'm just trying to uncover the truth."

"Maybe sometimes what is hidden should stay that way."

Zachary redirected the conversation. "Did she have any other visitors? Lawrence, Vera, Gloria, and Rhys? Is that it?"

"I don't know." Chenka closed her eyes and rested her head back. "I don't remember. She was tired and the nurses discouraged anyone from visiting."

"Any nurse in particular?"

"What?"

"Which nurse discouraged visitors?" Maybe someone had wanted visitors out of the way in order to give Robin something that would ease her pain permanently.

"I don't know. They said she'd be feeling better in a day or two."

"Who did?"

"Nurse..." Chenka trailed off, trying to recall which one it had been. "Was it Rachelle? I don't remember for sure."

Chenka appeared to be getting pretty tired herself. In another minute or two, she was going to be snoring.

"What is she like? Nurse Rachelle?" Zachary tried to remember which nurse that was. He thought she was the heavy redhead he had already spoken with. She hadn't been able to tell him much about Robin or the events of her last day on earth.

"She's a sweetie," Chenka said. "Always very happy and kind, even when she's run off her feet. Not like some of the others."

"Do you have complaints about the care here? Or did Robin?"

"It's a hospital. You can't expect them to take care of you like your baba. It's not an easy job."

Chenka went quiet and Zachary didn't pursue the conversation any further. He'd gotten everything out of Chenka that he was going to.

14

Zachary sat in his car and turned the key again, to no avail. He didn't know much about cars, so he wasn't sure whether he had a dead battery or something more serious. All he knew was, it wasn't starting. He called his mechanic and told him where it was and what it was doing, and Jergens agreed to pick it up and have a look.

Zachary tapped his foot lightly on the gas pedal, considering who to call next. He could try Kenzie or Bowman; either of them would give him a ride if they were available, but both were probably working and wouldn't be free for a couple more hours. He could call a cab, walk, or take the bus.

He took out his phone and instead called Bridget.

"Zachary!" She always sounded surprised and a little disapproving when he called, even though he had been doing his best to help her out. There had been too many times in the past when she'd had good reason to be angry with him, and it was something of a habit. "What's up?"

"My car broke down at the hospital. I'm sort of stranded and I wondered if you'd pick me up. We could go back to the apartment and discuss the case. Kill two birds with one stone…"

"Can't you just have it towed?"

"I am. But then I still need to get home. I don't know how long it will be until it will be fixed."

Bridget sighed, but to Zachary's surprise, she agreed. "Fine. I'll be a little bit. I have some work to do before I head over. Maybe… half an hour? With traffic, that means it might be an hour before I get there. You might be better off getting a cab."

"No, that's fine. I can keep busy for that long. Just give me a call when you're here. You want to pick me up on the east side, the emergency entrance?"

"I never like to pull in there in case someone in a hurry rear-ends me. There's an entrance just south of there, where the elevators are. You know the one with the statue?"

"Sure. I'll head over there and be ready in about an hour."

Bridget acknowledged this and hung up the phone.

Zachary got out of the car, locked it up, and headed for the other side of the hospital. He hadn't picked the east side just to give himself some exercise, but he did think it would help him kill a little time. He strolled along looking at the artwork on the walls, stopping to read plaques, and listening in on private conversations that caught his attention.

The hospital housed not only a small gift shop with the requisite flowers, stuffed animals, balloons, and candy, but it also had a well-equipped pharmacy. Zachary considered the gift shop, wondering about buying something for Bridget to thank her for the lift, but decided against it. She would probably take it the wrong way. She would decide it was a romantic gesture and overreact, reversing all of the ground that Zachary had been able to gain. It was too soon. He'd just have to take it a step at a time and wait until he was sure she was ready for that step. Not wanting to tempt himself, he chose the pharmacy instead.

He wandered up and down the aisles, impressed with the amount of merchandise they stocked. He would have thought that, being a hospital, there wouldn't be a great need for over-the-counter drugs, but they appeared to do a brisk trade.

It occurred to him that it wouldn't hurt to get some kind of immune system booster with the amount of time he was spending at the hospital. Not that he was going to catch cancer, but there were plenty of other bugs and viruses floating around the hospital that could be really nasty. Zachary's diet and sleep habits were not conducive to a strong immune system, so a supplement might be a good idea, even if it were just vitamin C.

He found the supplements aisle and walked along it slowly, running his eyes along the shelves and trying to determine what kind of order had been used to shelve them. The supplements appeared to be arranged by function rather than alphabetically, so he looked over each group. He might get a sleep remedy too. They rarely did anything for him, and he would have to research anything to make sure it wasn't contraindicated by his other medications, but Zachary always had his eyes open for anything that might help him through the long, restless nights.

There was a group of bottles in pinks and pastels, with women's silhouettes on them. Multivitamins for women, herbs to ease cramps or increase fertility. Pregnancy multis, iron, and laxatives. Moving farther along the shelves, he came upon digestive aids of all sorts, then a shelf of various supplements and formulations for balancing emotional issues. Zachary paused to look at them for a moment, but didn't feel like ending up with worse problems, so he continued to look.

There was a big section devoted to boosting immune function as well as treating cold and flu symptoms. The staff had thoughtfully added tissues, wipes, and disinfecting gels to the display. Zachary picked through the various vitamins and formulae, eventually deciding on one bottle of vitamin C and one supplement that was supposed to help protect against cold and flu. He decided to add hand sanitizer as well. He'd use it as soon as it was paid for to eliminate any nasty hospital bugs he had picked up. He had touched a lot of different surfaces during the day. Who knew how many millions of bugs he'd managed to pick up.

Bridget called Zachary to advise him she was pulling up to the statue, and Zachary hurried out to meet her, not wanting to keep her waiting. He sat down in her overly-warm car and smiled in appreciation.

"Thanks so much for the ride, Bridge. Sorry to take you away from your work."

He was curious as to what work she was doing. She'd had a full-time job when they had been married, before she had been diagnosed with cancer. She'd taken a leave of absence for her treatments, then eventually given them notice. Having gotten together with Gordon had changed her financial situation. Instead of pooling her resources with Zachary, whose income was sporadic and, at best, middle class, she could just rely on Gordon to provide her with everything she needed. A big, beautiful home, which

Zachary assumed came with maid service so that Bridget wouldn't be run ragged taking care of it, and a life of leisure. She still had the yellow VW she had driven when she'd lived with Zachary. She loved that little car and would probably never give it up until it fell apart. Any work that she was doing was a choice, something that she wanted to do for herself, rather than for survival.

Bridget glanced over at Zachary as he fumbled trying to join the ends of the unfamiliar seatbelt buckle around his coat, which kept ballooning out to block his vision.

"I'd better not find any electronics in that seat or under the mats," she warned. "You put a bug or a tracker in this car, and believe me, you'll never get another rescue from me."

The thought hadn't occurred to Zachary. He was so happy to be sitting in the same car as she was, he hadn't even thought of the opportunity it presented. He could have put some tiny electronic device inside of it. It wouldn't be easy with her watching closely or checking the obvious locations once he was out, but he could still have hidden it pretty well.

After finally clicking the seatbelt into place, Zachary held up his hands to show they were empty. "No electronics," he promised. "And I had no idea I was going to be in your car in the first place. I don't even have anything on me."

She gave him a hard look, then nodded. "Good." She turned the radio up, which discouraged conversation, and headed back to Zachary's apartment.

"Will you come up? So we can go over the case?"

Bridget considered. "I don't know if that's a good idea. I should probably be heading home. Gordon…"

"He wouldn't let you?" Zachary asked. He knew Bridget wouldn't like to think someone else was controlling her.

"I can go where I want," Bridget asserted. "I was just thinking I should get home soon. I've been out for quite a while today, and he doesn't like—"

Zachary raised his eyebrows.

"It's not like that!" Bridget bristled. "He doesn't like me to do too much. I still get tired faster than I used to. He worries about me."

"Ah." Zachary nodded.

They caught the elevator up to Zachary's apartment, not speaking to each other on the way. Zachary didn't want to get her more worked up. He wanted her to be nice and comfortable and loose. Like they used to be when they were together.

Zachary let himself into the apartment. It occurred to him that Bridget didn't have the keys for the new place. She'd had keys for his old apartment. He wasn't sure he wanted her to have keys, but he wasn't sure he didn't, either. It would be a nice gesture to let her know she was always welcome and that he trusted her. But he'd already called the police once when he thought he had a burglar and it had only been Bridget. He didn't want a repeat.

Bridget heard the distinctive rattle of pills in bottles when Zachary put his pharmacy bag down on the kitchen counter. Her head snapped around.

"What's that?" she demanded. Without waiting for an invitation, she grabbed the bag and opened it.

"Immune system," Zachary explained. "I'm trying to take care of myself. Make sure I don't pick something up at the hospital with all of the time I've been spending over there."

She put the vitamin C down on the counter and examined the other bottle. "What's in this? Are you sure it's safe for you?"

"No, I haven't checked yet. But I will before I take any."

"You know you have to be careful. There could be contraindications with your meds. They could cause a reaction or make something you're taking stop working."

"I know."

She put the second bottle down on the counter. "That's good," she approved, forcing a smile. "I'm glad you're trying to take care of yourself. Good for you for thinking ahead."

She fished the hand sanitizer out of the bag and put it on the counter with the supplements. Crumpling up the bag, she opened the cupboard under his sink, and frowned.

"You don't have a recycling container?"

"Not yet. I'll get one when I'm at the grocery store."

With a scowl, she stuffed the bag beside the garbage can. "I'll just put it here for now, then. Instead of mixing it with the trash." She closed the cupboard door and looked at her watch. "You should have something to eat." She opened the fridge to survey the contents.

"Uh... you don't need to do that, Bridge. I can feed myself. Are you hungry? Can I get you something?"

Her expression as she looked at the food that had been sitting in the fridge for almost a week told him that she was not impressed.

"I don't have a lot of time to prepare anything," Zachary said. "I've been busy with this case. There's frozen meals in the freezer. I did go to the grocery store."

She didn't trust his word, but opened the freezer door to check. Lips pressed tightly together, she closed it again. "So... I gather you had something to tell me about the case?"

"I was at the hospital most of the day today," Zachary said. He hadn't prepared for what he was going to say to her, in spite of the fact that he'd had an hour to wait for her. He should have thought through what he wanted to say while he was waiting. "I talked a bit more to the hospital staff. Some of the patients. Just spent the time going over Robin's last few days, her mood, how she interacted, who was there to visit her..."

Bridget nodded and sat down at the table. "That sounds good. Find out anything interesting?"

"The police were over there today too. They've started in on their investigation. Looks like Joshua Campbell is supervising the evidence-gathering at the hospital."

"Joshua was always nice," Bridget approved. "He wasn't automatically prejudiced against private investigators like some of the police."

Bridget seemed to be able to make friends with everyone, and she and Zachary hadn't been together long before everyone Zachary knew seemed to be friends with her. People he had known for years were suddenly best friends with Bridget, without Zachary ever being sure how they had happened to get to know each other so well.

"Yeah. He was pretty good. Called off the dogs when they wanted to arrest me today..." Zachary grinned.

"To arrest you?" Bridget repeated. "Why would they want to arrest you? Because you were getting in the way when they were trying to investigate Robin's case?"

"No, actually. Campbell headed them off there. Told me not to step on their toes, and they wouldn't step on mine. They were more interested in arresting me for kidnapping."

"Kidnapping?" Bridget's voice shot higher.

Zachary related his chance meeting with Ruth and spending time with her. He kept it light, but Bridget was still frowning, little lines appearing on the bridge of her nose.

"That was very kind of you," she admitted. "You've always been very concerned about other people. The champion of the underdog. That's why I knew you would want to find out what really happened to Robin."

"But…?"

"Nothing. Just that. It was very kind."

"You think I was neglecting Robin's case? Because I wasn't. The whole thing didn't take more than an hour. Even with the police take-down."

"No. I didn't say there was any problem with it."

But her voice certainly did. She definitely had something more to say. Zachary shrugged and waited. Push her, and she would just push back and get angry and defensive.

"I don't know this Ruth, but she sounds very nice."

Zachary nodded again. "She was. She was having a pretty rough time of it."

Bridget's eyes grew distant. She didn't talk a lot about her time at the hospital. She'd rarely said anything to him about her treatments there, what kind of torture she had gone through to kill the cancer and still survive. Zachary knew the doctors pushed as close to the edge as they could. Kill the cancer but not the patient. Kill it so that it would never come back. Zachary lived in dread that it would reoccur. That in a few more weeks or months, Bridget would mention that she was having symptoms. Or she would go to the doctor for her regular scans and they would tell her the cancer was back, and twice as bad. Eventually, Gordon would call Zachary to tell him that Bridget had fought the good fight, but was gone.

"It must have been hard for you too," Zachary offered.

"Of course it was. I wouldn't want to put my worst enemy through what I had to go through. It was horrible. I was so sick. So tired I could barely move or speak. I begged them to stop the treatment and just let me die. But they always talked me back into it. Just two more cycles. Just one more. Another one just to be sure."

Zachary shook his head. "I wish… I'd been able to be there for you."

"I couldn't manage it. I couldn't deal with anybody else while I was going through that. I just needed to take care of myself."

"Of course. I know. I'm just saying. I wish… things had been different."

"I needed all my strength and focus to get through it. There wasn't anything left for anyone else. That's just the way it is. It was the same for Robin."

Zachary thought about Robin and the way she had dumped Lawrence, the same as Bridget had dumped him.

"Was there anything else? What other problems were taking Robin's mind off of her recovery?"

Bridget's eyes wandered around the kitchen as she considered her answer.

"She had some family issues. I told her she should try to resolve them. Get them out of her life so that they weren't pulling her mental energy."

"Resolve them."

"Yes," Bridget said evenly. "If you have all of these toxic people pulling away the energy you need for healing and recovery, you have to cut them off."

"You told her to cut off her family?"

"I didn't say that."

"I'm asking. It's important to the investigation, Bridget. Did you tell her to cut off her sister and mother? Because if she did, they would be suspects too."

"She said her family was too important to her." Bridget's face was stony. "That was her business, not mine. If she thought she was getting what she needed out of the relationships, then that was fine. If they were giving her more benefits than deficits, then maybe she should keep them around her. But... I didn't see her getting a lot out of it. I don't think they were helping her healing." Bridget sighed. She got up and got herself a glass of water. Leaning against the counter to drink it, she added, "Maybe that's why she died."

"You think one of them had something to do with her death."

"I didn't mean it that way. I just think the cancer grew and spread because there was so much negativity in her life. If she had gotten rid of those toxic relationships and only fostered positive, beneficial ones... maybe she could have beaten it."

Zachary nodded. His mouth was dry too. "So... I gather you didn't think much of her family."

"Everybody has good and bad traits."

"Her mother seemed quite nice to me. You didn't think so?"

"I think she was one of the people sucking all of Robin's energy away.

She spent all of her time mourning her husband and making sure that everyone around her did too. He died ten years ago, and she still walks around making sure that everyone knows that he died. Her poor murdered husband. Her poor family, losing him like that for no reason. Her poor, damaged grandson. Some people always carry a cloud around with them. The negativity clings to them. You can't be around them without feeling worried and depressed."

Zachary figured that was pretty much how Bridget saw him. Now that she was getting her health back, she could afford to put a little energy into being decent to him. But she still saw him just the same way. As someone who always needed support and extra time and energy. Someone hopelessly negative and toxic. If he was going to win her back, he needed to show her he could change. He could be upbeat and give her back positivity instead of negativity.

"And her sister…" Zachary said, moving through the people in Robin's family, "…I got the feeling she was pretty stubborn and single-minded. She and Robin were probably always competing and butting heads."

Bridget nodded. "Good guess. Yes, they always seemed like they were on opposite sides of everything. If one of them said the sky was blue…"

"Yeah. And from what Vera said, I gather Gloria hasn't always been there. They raised Rhys, rather than Gloria having full-time custody of him."

"Robin always talked about Gloria like she was the bratty baby sister. The one who always wanted to take the spotlight and got away with whatever she wanted to because she was the baby in the family. Robin said that if she'd been the one who had gotten pregnant, she would have been out on the street. But instead of kicking Gloria out, they took her back in. Coddled her and took care of the baby and let Gloria get away with leaving him there all the time and going out to party or do drugs."

"I would think that was better for the baby than letting Gloria try to take care of him on her own."

"Maybe. Or maybe that would have forced Gloria to take some responsibility for her actions and grow up."

"Seems like she did, eventually."

"Not until it was too late. Not until after their father was killed and Rhys was in an institution."

Zachary closed his eyes, fighting back images of his own institutional stays. How many times had he daydreamed about his mother changing her mind and coming to get him and put their family back together again? But it had been too late for his family. There was no going home.

"Zachary."

Her fleeting touch on his hand, so familiar and comforting, and then it was gone. Zachary forced himself to breathe, drawing air in and pushing it out. He opened his eyes, swimming through the memories and emotions to get back to her.

"Sorry. So…" He cleared his throat and tried to get back on track. "Was there more bad blood between Robin and Gloria, or just some leftover sibling resentment?"

"I think they were pretty good. They didn't generally fight when Gloria came by. I didn't hear a lot of sniping between them. But then… I always left when the family arrived, too. Sometimes I'd stay for a few minutes, if Robin asked me to, but not any significant length of time."

"Did Robin resent her mother? Because of the way Gloria was favored? Because she spent more energy mourning her dead husband than she gave to Robin?"

"Robin kind of did, yeah. But that's pretty normal." Bridget spoke in a light tone. "Relationships get strained when you're sick like that. Some people get closer to each other, but if there are problems with the relationship, a stressor like cancer, it magnifies them. Splits people apart."

Zachary nodded. He didn't need to draw a line to connect Robin's issues with her family to Bridget booting Zachary out of her life.

"I'd like to talk to them more in depth. But I think that's going to be harder now that the police investigation has started up. Do you think you could talk to them and get them to meet with me?"

"I don't know. I can try, I guess. What do you want to talk to them about?"

Zachary tapped the pads of his fingers on the table, working through what he knew so far and what his next step should be.

"I don't want to wait until we get the results of the autopsy back. Who knows how long all of the lab work will take and if it will show anything significant. I feel like we're already behind. If we wait until we know whether it was cancer or an accident or euthanasia, it might be too late to find anything out. Especially if the police scare everyone into being quiet. I want to get a better feel for the family and to find out if anything important happened the last couple of days of Robin's life."

"Are you saying they're suspects?"

"I'm not saying that they're *not*..." Zachary scratched the back of his head. "Just tell them... I need background, Robin's history, to talk to them about anything that happened at the treatment center."

"They're not going to like it."

"Tell them... that I think it was just the natural course of Robin's illness, and I won't believe you that it might have been medical error."

"Make it look like I'm the bad guy and you're on their side," Bridget said baldly.

"Uh... yes. They're more likely to let me talk to them if they think I'm trying to prove their case rather than yours."

Her eyes snapped. "You *are* on my side, though, aren't you?" she demanded.

"Yes." Zachary nodded. "I'm completely on your side."

15

Late in the evening, there was a sharp rap on Zachary's apartment door that had him jumping to his feet, heart thumping, before he even thought about it. He tried to slow his breathing to get the wild thundering of his heart under control, and went to the door.

No one had his address. Only Bowman and Bridget. And Kenzie. Maybe a few other people who needed to know where to direct his mail or new furniture. And the landlord. Maybe he wanted to discuss the damage to the wall and doorframe the movers had caused and when it was going to be fixed.

He applied his eye to the peephole and looked out. The lighting in the hall wasn't great. Something he would have to address with the landlord to ensure that he knew whether it was safe to open his door to visitors. Maybe Zachary would install a discreet surveillance cam in the hallway so he could get a proper look at anyone at his door. But as it was, he didn't need much more than a glance at the shadowy figure in the hall to tell that it was a police officer or security guard.

He opened the door even as his brain rang alarm bells that anyone could get a security guard uniform and it didn't mean that his visitor was someone who could be trusted. But the door was open and it was too late to change his mind.

"Zachary," Campbell greeted with a booming voice. "Glad you're still up."

As if Zachary could have slept through the loud knocking on the door.

"Hey. Come on in."

Zachary ushered Campbell into the apartment and shut and locked the door behind him. They went to the living room, where there were at least two places to sit even if there was still an empty hole where the couch should have been. He was going to have to find something sooner or later that would actually fit through the door without being cut into pieces. They each selected an easy chair and sat down.

That eased Zachary's mind a little. He had been sure that Campbell was going to tell him he was off the case and to stay out of the way. He'd been warned away from too many police investigations in the past; he knew that was how such things were handled. If Campbell wanted to warn and threaten him, he wouldn't have sat down. He would have wanted to stay in a position of power over Zachary, using his greater height and heft to intimidate.

"Nice place," Campbell said without sincerity. "I gather you've just moved in?"

"Yeah." There were still a few moving boxes around, so even if Campbell hadn't heard that already, it wouldn't have taken a genius to figure it out. "You probably heard the last place got burned down…"

"Yeah, seems to me something like that might have come across the desk at some point." Campbell's smile made it obvious this was a joke. He settled into the chair with a tired sigh. "Don't happen to have any beer, do you?"

"Uh… no, sorry. A glass of water…?"

"No, I'll get something when I get home. Just on my way there now, but I thought I'd give you a little heads-up on the case."

"You found something already?"

"No, no evidence that points to any medical malpractice or foul play. Just… background."

Zachary leaned forward. It was rare for the police to be so forthcoming. They had privacy policies that prevented them from telling certain things to members of the public.

"I heard today that Robin's father was murdered ten years ago," Zachary said. "Is it something to do with that?"

Campbell nodded. "That was one of the things that came up," he agreed. "An interesting coincidence, but it doesn't appear, on the surface, to be related."

"Did they ever catch the murderer? What exactly happened?"

"The man was attacked in his home. Appeared to be a burglary gone wrong. The thief thought the house was empty, or maybe they had the address wrong and were looking for something else. He was shot. Killed instantly. Turns out there was a child in the house as well, the grandson. But he was unable to testify as to what he had seen."

"Rhys. Yeah, I heard about that."

"They never found the perp and the case went cold. I'm having the boys review the details just in case there is any connection, but I don't think there's anything there."

"Any chance I could see the file?"

"Go through normal channels. I won't block any request."

"Is that it, or was there something else?"

Campbell grinned. "You haven't done a full background, then."

"Uh… no. Just some interviews. Checking to see whether there was anything to the claim that Robin's death might not have been natural causes. What did I miss? One of the hospital employees? Lawrence Long?"

The policeman shook his head. "Nope. Although we haven't finished backgrounds on everybody who might have had access to her at the hospital. That will take a while. But there was a history of domestic violence."

Zachary mentally berated himself for not doing police and courthouse searches of all of the individuals close to Robin. "Lawrence? He certainly didn't seem the type."

"It wasn't Lawrence. There were several police incident files and a protective order. You'll have to search them up yourself, I can't divulge any details."

"I was so focused on medical error or euthanasia, it didn't even occur to me to look at domestic violence."

"They are probably completely unrelated," Campbell said. "More than likely, you're right. You don't usually see domestic violence turn into poisoning, or whatever else happened here. It's just not the natural progression. But… things may turn out to be different in this case."

"Yeah. It's been a curious case from the start. Bridget getting so wound up over Robin dying when she did… it's not like her. She has pretty good intuition, so I had to check it out."

"What are you onto tomorrow?"

"I'm hoping to talk to the family again. But maybe I should search up these cases first, so I have the background…"

"No. I'd go ahead and interview the family members first. The public records can wait. It's not like they're going anywhere, and like I said, they're probably not related at all."

Zachary was baffled. "You're not going to tell me to stay away from the family until your officers have had a chance to talk to them?"

"No. You're a good investigator. If you find anything suspicious, you can pass it on to me. If my officers go in there asking questions… the family's backs will be up before they even start. They'll be guarded. They might have to be Mirandized at some point. But a private citizen doesn't have to worry about Miranda warnings. Things can move more naturally and might leak out. I know you're good at worming your way in." Campbell cleared his throat. "My officers will still need to interview them, but they might just have to be busy with other things tomorrow. You'll tell me if you find anything significant?"

Zachary did report to the police when he had to, but normally he kept information to himself. Robin Salter's case was not a collaboration with the police, and he needed to make sure that was understood.

"If something is reportable," he hedged.

"Come on, Zachary. You can do better than that."

"I can't promise to tell you everything I find. I don't know if anything will be relevant to Robin's case. But if I find evidence of a crime, I'll let you know."

"I came here tonight, without any prompting, to let you know what was on my radar. You wouldn't have found out about this history otherwise. I scratch your back, you can't return the favor?"

"I appreciate the information. I'll follow up on it after I interview the family." Unless, of course, Campbell was trying to push Zachary into interviewing the family while he followed the case in another direction, like wherever those domestic violence charges led. He might have to pursue them both simultaneously, splitting his time and attention in two different directions. "I'm just saying that I'm a private investigator. Not one of your cops. You can't expect me to report back to you like that."

Campbell wrinkled his nose and made a sour expression. He pressed his hands to the arms of the chair to push himself up. "That's not being very cooperative, my friend. I expected a little more gratitude from you."

Zachary stood up as well. "I'll do what I can," he hedged. "But I don't work for you."

Zachary always dreaded car problems. Having no real understanding of anything other than the basic maintenance required to keep the metal beasts running, he was always worried that the mechanic's bill was going to run to the thousands and something huge like the engine or the transmission would need to be replaced. Maybe he should have had Ray-Ray take a look at it for him. At five years old, Ray-Ray's knowledge of the inner workings of cars far outstripped Zachary's, and probably that of a lot of mechanics too.

So in the morning and with a tight knot of dread in his stomach, Zachary called Jergens to see when he was going to be able to get his car back and what the bill was going to be like.

"Oh, Zachary, I was going to give you a call." Jergens always sounded hoarse and secretive, like he was doing something dishonest and was afraid someone was going to overhear him. But he was as honest as the day was long, and Zachary trusted him not to run up the bill despite Zachary's ignorance of all things automobile related.

Was it a good thing or a bad thing that Zachary was already on his list of people to call? It couldn't have taken too long to figure out what was wrong with his car. That could mean the engine or transmission was totally wrecked.

"Uh-oh. Is it bad?"

Jergens chuckled. "Oh, yeah, Zach. We're going to have to completely replace your... spark plugs."

Zachary let out his breath. Even he knew that replacing spark plugs was not expensive or complicated. "Whew. I was really worried about it. What's wrong with the old ones? Are they just... worn out?"

It was a pretty new car, and while he had bought it used he hadn't expected to have any big bills in the near future. It seemed odd that the spark plugs would be worn out already.

"They're missing."

"Missing? How could they be missing? It was working earlier yesterday. They can't just… fall off, can they?"

"No. Definitely not. Somebody would have had to remove them. Someone sabotaged your car."

Zachary swore under his breath. He started considering the possibilities. It wasn't just random vandalism. Someone who didn't know him and was just out to commit mischief might key his car or slash his tires, but they wouldn't go to all of the work to get his hood open and remove his spark plugs. That was targeted. Someone sending him a message. Somebody was telling him that they didn't like what he was doing and wanted him to get lost.

While he always had several cases on the go, and it could be any number of disgruntled husbands, employees, or insurance claimants, there was really only one that prominent. Cheating spouses rarely went after the private investigator, rarely even knew who it was. And if they did, it was yelling, a slap in the face, something confrontational.

Spark plugs pulled from his car while he was doing interviews meant someone was unhappy with the Robin Salter investigation. One of the hospital staff? One of the police officers who didn't like him being involved? Lawrence Long or someone from Robin's family?

"Zachary?"

Zachary looked at his phone, disoriented for a moment. "Oh, Jergens. Sorry, I spaced."

"I said if you can catch a cab or bus over here, it can be ready for you this morning. I just don't have time to drop it off to you."

"Yeah, that would be great. I can find my way over there."

"Great. I'll see you later, and you can tell me about the case you're on."

16

It was Gloria who answered the door, her mouth an angry red slash across her otherwise stony face. It was a pretty good indicator right from the start that they didn't want Zachary sticking his nose into their business.

"Mr. Goldman," she greeted stiffly, and motioned him into the living room, where he had visited with Vera before. "My mother will join us in a moment. She's just getting Rhys settled."

It seemed strange to be talking about getting a teenager settled like she would a fractious baby or toddler. From everything Zachary had heard, Rhys was emotionally traumatized, not mentally handicapped or developmentally delayed. But Zachary had yet to meet Rhys face-to-face, so he wasn't able to make any judgments.

Zachary browsed over the pictures on the mantel again. This time, he wasn't trying to identify the members of the family and their relationships to each other. He was looking for bruises or any other signs of abuse. He was looking for the way they stood together, touched, and looked at each other, searching for subtle clues showing who had been afraid of whom. Who had been abused and who had been the abuser. He saw no bruises on either Robin or Gloria. None on Rhys either, for that matter. Zachary was a good observer, but he didn't spot anything out of place in the pictures.

Vera came into the room, her head slightly down, feet shuffling across the floor.

"I really appreciate you seeing me again," Zachary told both women. "I know this isn't easy for you."

"I don't know what you're here for," Gloria complained. "I don't understand why the police are getting involved. All of this is just nonsense. Robin died of cancer. They can't go around exhuming everyone who has died of cancer, complaining that someone must have done it on purpose. People die. Especially people who are as ill as Robin was."

"I know," Zachary soothed. He kept the role he was playing planted firmly in his mind. He was supposed to be supporting their position, trying to prove to Bridget that there was nothing to be concerned about. No accident. No intention to kill. Just a woman who had come to the end of her natural life. "I'm sorry for disturbing you again like this. If we can just work through a few questions, I'm sure this will be the end of it and you can just go on with your lives and getting through the grieving process."

They all sat down. Zachary looked for a natural starting point.

"You've been talking to the police?"

"No, not yet, but I'm sure that's coming," Gloria declared. "They've been talking to the staff at the hospital. We've had reporters calling here. Reporters!" She said it like it was the most incredible thing she'd ever heard. "Calling here and asking questions about why the police would be opening an investigation into Robin's death. We had to keep telling them that we had no idea. Why would the police be looking into the death of a cancer patient?"

He wasn't about to tell them that he was the one who had prompted them to open a death investigation.

"One of them asked me if Robin had committed suicide," Vera said, shaking her head in confusion. "Why would they think that?"

"It's probably just a natural conclusion. She was terminally ill and she died before the doctors expected her to. Some patients do choose their own exit time."

"Robin would never have done that," Vera insisted.

"Even if she did," Gloria said, "it wouldn't be anyone's business but the family's. It's legal in Vermont. There wouldn't be any need for a police investigation into something legal."

"No, of course not," Zachary agreed. "If Robin had applied for physician assisted suicide, there would be a paper trail. The doctor would just show the paperwork to the police."

"That isn't what happened," Vera insisted.

"No," Zachary agreed. "I know it isn't."

"Your wife thinks it was a medical error." Gloria leaned forward, looking at Zachary intently. "She said that's what you're trying to find out. But that you don't believe it was."

"I don't know..." Zachary rubbed the back of his neck, attempting to look sheepish. "I don't like to second-guess my wife. She's the one who knew Robin. She's the one who lived at that hospital like Robin did... but," a regretful head shake, "I just don't see it. I think she's jumping at shadows."

"Exactly," Gloria agreed. "If Robin had decided to end her own life, she would have told us. She would have said something. And the doctors and nursing staff doing something to her...? They were nothing but gracious and helpful. Heaven knows Robin could be difficult!"

"Gloria," Vera objected. "Don't talk about your sister that way."

"It's not going to change anything now, is it? It's true. The way she complained and ran those nurses off their feet sometimes! But they were very kind and patient with her."

Zachary nodded. "They all seemed very professional there. I don't imagine it's an easy place to work."

"Not a job I would want," Gloria agreed.

"Especially a unit like that, with terminal patients. I don't think I'd be able to function, knowing so many of them were going to die. Unable to do anything to stop the progress of their disease. Not able to do anything for their pain, in the end."

Vera dabbed at watery eyes. "Even just having Robin there was so difficult. Seeing so many other people, some of them whose disease was even more advanced than Robin's, knowing she was going to go through that... it was so difficult."

Gloria sent a warning look toward her mother. "I imagine you would get used to it if you worked there," she said briskly.

"Maybe," Zachary said. "I'm not sure if I ever could."

Vera sniffled. "You wife is lucky that she went into remission. She might have still had to go through the pain of treatment, but she didn't have to face death the same way as Robin did when she was told the cancer had metastasized."

"Ma," Gloria warned again.

"You didn't ever wish… that there was something you could do to make Robin feel better?" Zachary ventured.

"Of course, all the time," Gloria said. "Who wouldn't? But there wasn't anything we could do. The doctor could give her pain prescriptions and stuff to help her sleep, but they couldn't take away the cancer. And if they couldn't do that, she knew she was going to die sooner or later."

"None of the staff ever suggested that they could give her higher doses of painkillers or sleeping pills? Or that you could?"

"No." Vera spoke the word sharply, almost making Zachary jump with her sudden vehemence. "No one ever said anything like that."

"Okay." He made a calming motion with his hands. "Sometimes it is done that way. Making a patient comfortable, even at the expense of their body's ability to keep functioning."

"No. We would never do that."

Zachary nodded that he understood.

"Gram?"

Zachary startled. He whipped his head around to find Rhys standing there, looking at them. Vera stood up immediately

"It's okay, sweetie. It's okay, it's nothing you need to worry about," she soothed. "Come on, why don't you show me your homework? You didn't get everything done that fast, did you?"

He shook his head. Zachary watched the skinny, sad-looking boy until they were back out of sight. He turned and looked at Gloria, trying to control his shock.

"It's a school holiday," Gloria advised, misinterpreting his surprise.

"I thought he couldn't speak."

"He can, physically," Gloria said. She took a deep breath and let it out. She rubbed at the fatigue lines on her forehead. "Obviously. He'll often go days without a word, and when he does, it's usually like that. Just a one- or two-word request. If you push him for more, he'll just shut down. They call it selective mutism, but that doesn't mean he can choose to talk or not. There are times when he is able to talk and times when he is not. Some kids with selective mutism are little chatterboxes at home but then can't get anything out at school. For Rhys, it's not like that. One word or phrase, or no words. Usually."

"How does he communicate with you? Does he sign? Write?"

"No. He… doesn't usually attempt any kind of direct communication. He is capable of speech, writing, gesture… but he just withdraws into himself. It's been like that ever since my father passed."

"How does he do his homework, then?" Zachary indicated the direction Rhys and Vera had gone with a jerk of his head.

"It depends what kind of work it is. He's best at math. No need for words, it's just like solving a puzzle. In other subjects, he's pretty good with short answer or multiple choice. Long answer…" Gloria shook her head. "He just can't seem to be able to tell us what's in his head, to communicate what he's thinking. He does modified assignments in place of essays or creative writing."

"Poor guy," Zachary said. What had happened ten years before that had traumatized him so much that he couldn't share his own thoughts, even about completely unrelated subjects? "It must be very difficult to parent a child you can't communicate with or understand."

He was thinking about the children he had met at Summit Learning Center, autistic or non-speaking, and how difficult it was for their parents to know what was bothering them or what else was going on in their heads. He had heard stories of children who were non-speaking and had no way to communicate more than the most basic needs for the first twenty years of life, but when introduced to alternative communication or assistive devices, were discovered to be capable of complex reasoning and deep self-reflection.

"I can communicate with him," Gloria disagreed. "He understands everything I tell him. That doesn't mean he listens to me all the time. Just like any teenager, he's got a mind of his own and he doesn't always want to do what mom tells him to. I can communicate with him just fine."

"But just because he understands you, that doesn't mean that you can understand what he is thinking and would want to tell you, if he could."

She shook her head in irritation. "You don't know anything about my boy, Mr. Goldman. Just because *you* don't know what he's thinking, that doesn't mean his own mama can't. I know what's going on in his head. I know my own boy."

But she wasn't the one who had responded to Rhys's call and left the room to help him. She wasn't the one who had been 'settling' him at the beginning of their interview. Zachary didn't want to antagonize her, so he shifted the conversation.

"How has Rhys been handling Robin's illness and death? It must be pretty hard on him."

"Why?" Gloria demanded.

"She's his aunt… part of his family. You all lived here together, before Robin got sick, didn't you? She's always been part of his household."

Gloria snorted and rolled her eyes. Zachary was taken aback by her response.

"They… weren't close, then?"

"My mother is close to Rhys. He idolized Papa. But Robin? No. She didn't have much use for him and he didn't have anything to do with her."

"You took him to the hospital to visit her, didn't you?"

"Yes, of course. That was the right thing to do."

What had Rhys thought of that? Had he been happy to go see her? Had he understood that she was dying? There was no indication that he was slow, so he must have understood that she was dying of cancer.

"That wasn't difficult for him? He didn't object to going?"

"Of course he didn't want to go. But that doesn't mean he was going to get away with not going. If I told him he had to come to the hospital with us, he had to come to the hospital with us. Sometimes he had homework or other things he had to do and I'd let him off, but most of the time… he came with us. He could sit quietly and patiently and visit like a grown-up."

"He could visit with her?" Zachary was getting more confused about Rhys's condition and abilities rather than less.

"He could sit with her. Hold her hand. Get things for her. Answer basic yes or no questions. I expected him to do his part, just like anyone else."

"I'm sorry for acting like a dunce," Zachary apologized. "I was told that he couldn't talk at all, and I had formed this picture in my mind about what his capabilities were… I don't mean to insult either of you by asking stupid questions."

Gloria's expression softened a little and she attempted a reassuring smile. "Of course not. They're not stupid questions. You're just trying to understand. Think of any teenage boy. You know how they tend to give closed, one-word answers to everything you ask? How was your day? Fine. How was the math test? Good. Did you do your homework? Not yet."

Zachary had to smile. "Yes."

"Well, Rhys is just the same, except most of the time he doesn't bother with the answer. You know what it is anyway. Just like you know that the average uncommunicative teenager is going to say 'fine' when you ask him how his day was. But you ask it anyway."

"Does he understand why Robin's death is being investigated?"

Gloria shook her head slightly, scowling. "I'm not sure *I* understand why it's being investigated. We haven't talked to him about it."

"I'd like the opportunity to talk to Rhys, if I could. I'd like to see what he thinks of all of this."

Her expression was immediately closed. "I don't see what good that would do you. How would talking to Rhys help you? He can't tell you anything. He doesn't know anything about what's been going on. No. There's no reason for you to talk to him."

Vera shuffled back into the room.

"Is he okay?" Gloria asked. But she didn't, Zachary noted, make any sign she would check in on him.

"He'll be fine," Vera assured her. She looked at Zachary. "It's all been very hard on him. He's already had to deal with one murder in his young life, so all of this is very disturbing. He doesn't like everything being so disrupted."

"Nobody *likes* it," Gloria snapped. "I wish they would just say everything is fine and send her back to the funeral home, so we can have her cremated and have the funeral. At this rate, who knows how long it will be before she's released? It could be months or years before we can lay her to rest." This comment was aimed at Vera, obviously intended to get her wound up.

"Years?" Vera reacted immediately. "How could it take years? They can't just keep her for that long. That's not right! How are we supposed to deal with this if we can't move on?"

"It won't be that long. Probably just a couple of days. The medical examiner is doing the autopsy right away," Zachary reassured her. "They'll release… her remains back to the funeral home very quickly."

"Can you guarantee that?" Gloria challenged. "You're not in charge of the police department or medical examiner's office. They don't answer to you."

"I'm just telling you what's likely to happen. They don't keep bodies for that long."

"But they *could.*"

Zachary squared his shoulders and didn't argue with her any further.

"I wonder if you could tell me some details about your husband's murder," Zachary said to Vera.

"His murder?" She looked confused, peering at Zachary and then looking uncertainly over at Gloria. "Why would you need to know that?"

"I know there probably isn't any connection between his murder and Robin's death, but it's just one of those things that I try to explore. You don't want there to be any loose ends."

"Robin was not murdered," Vera said.

"I didn't say she was. I just want to know the history. The big picture. Then I can tell Bridget that I've looked at everything. I haven't left any stones unturned."

"I don't know." Vera again looked at Gloria, trying to determine what she was supposed to do. "It was so long ago, I don't see how it could help you."

"I'm sure there's probably no connection," Zachary repeated. "I just want to cover all of the bases."

"Well… Clarence… that was my husband… he was home one night with Rhys. Just the two of them. Gloria and I were out. Clarence was babysitting. I mean, not that it's babysitting when it's your own grandson. When we got home… well, it was Gloria who discovered Clarence… Clarence's body."

Zachary looked over to Gloria to see what she had to contribute. She shook her head.

"It was the most awful thing I've ever seen," she said, her voice flat and unemotional. She could have been announcing the weather or the moves in a chess match. "He was there, at the kitchen table. He'd been shot at close range. The police said that he was probably startled by a burglar who thought the house was empty."

"Sitting at the table?" Zachary repeated. "No struggle?"

"No." Gloria shook her head. "Papa didn't hear too well. They were probably in the house and he never heard them… until they walked in on him."

"And Rhys? Where was he?"

"He was in his bed. He didn't see what happened."

Zachary frowned. If Rhys hadn't seen anything, then why had he been so deeply affected by it? And how did Gloria know if he saw anything or not if he had been uncommunicative since then and withdrew any time they asked him about it?

"Just stop it," Vera said. "That's all Rhys would say for days after it happened. *Just stop it. Just stop it.* Any time anyone tried to ask him about it, that was all he would say."

"But eventually, he stopped saying that too," Gloria sighed.

Zachary let a few moments of silence pass, waiting to see if there was anything else Vera or Gloria might have to offer. He let out his breath slowly. He wasn't sure he'd made any forward progress.

"There was one other thing I wanted to follow up on." He looked from one face to the other, watching them for any change. "I understand there were some domestic violence reports and a restraining order."

Their eyes widened and they turned toward each other simultaneously. Fear and anxiety. This was not something they had been expecting. Gloria recovered first.

"That was a long time ago," she said. "Ancient history."

"I see."

"I don't know why you're bringing it up. It doesn't have anything to do with Robin's death."

"Maybe not," Zachary said. "Just covering all bases. Was Lawrence abusive toward Robin?"

"Lawrence?" Gloria was incredulous. "No, no, certainly not Lawrence. All of that business… that was when she was dating Stanley, not Lawrence."

Zachary remembered the family picture with Stanley in it. "Robin's fiancé."

"Yes. They were engaged, but then they broke up. Probably a good thing."

"Was that before or after Clarence's death?"

Gloria frowned in concentration. She looked over at Vera. "Ma, do you remember? It was after, wasn't it? Stanley was still around when Papa passed."

Vera's eyes were vague and misty as she searched the past. Eventually, she nodded. "Yes. It was after Clarence died."

"Was there something particular they broke up over? Was it because of abuse?"

"People change," Gloria said obliquely. "Robin wasn't the same person before she died as she was… ten years ago when she was with Stanley."

"A lot of women keep picking the same kind of men over and over again. They get rid of one abuser, only to pick a new one. But Robin straightened things out? She didn't pick another abuser?"

Gloria and Vera again exchanged a look.

"No, Lawrence wasn't abusive," Vera assured Zachary. "He's gentle as a kitten. He would never have hurt anyone. He is an artist."

"Sometimes people hide their real personalities, bury them deep down, so you don't see it unless you do something that triggers them. They might seem perfectly normal and reasonable on the surface, and it isn't until you're close to them that you discover their demons."

Zachary should know, he'd been there enough times.

"No. Not Lawrence. He doesn't get angry."

"What about emotional abuse? A woman might move from someone who is physically abusive to someone who is verbally and emotionally abusive and not understand that they're living with someone who is unreasonable and just perpetuating the cycle of abuse. Because he doesn't hit her, she thinks he's different, and that she's just not adequate."

Vera and Gloria shook their heads. Zachary watched them closely. They were hiding something. Those looks had meant something. But if Lawrence had been abusive, why would they hide the fact? If there were any chance she had been killed by an abuser, wouldn't they want it to be known? Wouldn't they want him to be put in jail?

Abusers could be charming to everyone outside their immediate family. They could fool everyone into thinking that the victim was lying or exaggerating about the abuser's behavior. Vera and Gloria might think that Lawrence was perfect, but the chances that he had never lost his temper were slim. Just because they hadn't seen it, that didn't mean he had never gotten angry and physically or verbally abusive.

"That all happened a long time ago," Gloria repeated. "It doesn't have anything to do with Robin's death."

Maybe. Or maybe it was a pattern. But Zachary agreed in order to put their minds at ease. "I understand. Sorry, I just have to make sure everything has been investigated. I want to be able to tell Bridget conclusively that Robin died as a result of the cancer, there was no outside interference. That's what you want too, isn't it?"

They both nodded, relaxing as he abandoned the topic.

"Those last days in the hospital... have you thought of anything that happened that was unusual? Any little thing that concerned you, even if it was just for an instant?"

Vera shook her head, staring vaguely into the distance. Gloria gave an exaggerated shrug. "Nothing. Don't you think we would have told the police?"

"Sometimes the things that bother us can be so small that we think they're not of any value. Or we think that no one will believe us or will think anything of it. So we just brush it off." He looked at both of them carefully, looking for any flicker of doubt.

"No," Gloria insisted.

"None of the nurses did anything that concerned you? None of them treated you like they didn't want you there?"

"We would have told the police."

Zachary nodded his understanding. He prepared to get up.

"Do you mind... could I use your facilities before I go?"

Gloria scowled and seemed to be about to deny him access, but Vera nodded, always the gracious host. "Of course you can. The bathroom is just in this hallway," Vera gestured, "to the left. Last door."

"Thanks. Too much coffee today, I'm thinking!"

Zachary headed for the bathroom before Gloria could try to override her mother and tell Zachary he'd have to find a public restroom on his way home. He found the bathroom, shut and locked the door, and turned on the exhaust fan to help muffle any noise.

He opened the medicine cabinet behind the mirror and scanned the rows of bottles of liquids and pills. It had occurred to him that even if all of the hospital's insulin was accounted for, Vera or Gloria could be diabetic and have their own insulin prescriptions. A few bottles had prescription labels, most of them in Vera's name, but he didn't see any insulin. Zachary had no idea if any of the prescriptions would be poisonous in the wrong dose. He had to assume that they would be.

He turned a few of the bottles so that all of the labels were facing out, then used his phone to take pictures of a few at a time. There were some nonprescription sleep aids, painkillers, vitamin and mineral supplements, and one of the same immune boosters as Zachary had picked up from the hospital pharmacy. Nothing unusual. Nothing he wouldn't find in any other medicine cabinet in any other home. Zachary closed the cabinet quietly and turned on the water.

While he ran the tap, he opened and closed the drawers of the vanity. Bandages, tweezers, toothpaste, razors, feminine products. Nothing unexpected or unusual. Not that he'd expected to find a prescribed lethal dose or anything with a skull and crossbones on it. There was no sign of rat poison, household cleaners, or any chemicals that would have made more sense stored in a garden shed.

He hadn't expected to find anything, but he was still a little disappointed. It would have been nice to turn the murder weapon over to the police. A big ego boost.

But that wasn't going to happen.

17

Zachary checked his voicemail as he got back into his car to see whether Bridget had called. He was also hoping for a call back from Bowman. Zachary had left a message for him early in the morning before he actually got on shift, asking him about the police incident files on Robin. If the records went back ten years, they would have to pull files back from storage. They wouldn't still be on site. There were computer files, or Campbell wouldn't have known any details. Hopefully, Zachary could get printouts of those. But he wanted the physical file too. He knew from experience that there could be important reports or notes on the file that hadn't made it to the computer. A computer record from ten years before would only be a summary, not the full documentation.

There were no messages from Bridget or from Bowman. But there was one from Kenzie's work number. Did they already have preliminary results from the autopsy?

Zachary got comfortable in the car, then listened to the message, which only told him to call Kenzie back, with no hint of what she wanted to talk about.

Zachary tapped to call back, and Kenzie answered in a couple of rings, obviously not in the middle of assisting with an autopsy.

"Hi, Kenz. It's Zachary."

"Where've you been?"

"Uh… interviewing witnesses. Joshua Campbell visited last night last night and—"

Kenzie cut across him. "I was trying to get ahold of you."

"Did you find something?"

"Well, we can't be sure yet. There are still plenty of slides and fluids to be tested. We didn't identify anything that confirmed foul play on gross visual examination. There are some organ abnormalities; we have to test to see whether it is cancer or something else."

"Okay. I guess we didn't really expect to find anything until the labs are done. But insulin wouldn't show up, right?"

"No. For that, you'll have to wait for the results of the hospital inventory against the charts."

"I checked in the family's medicine cabinet in case they had insulin." Zachary was proud of himself for thinking of this. "But there wasn't any in the cabinet."

There was silence for a few seconds from Kenzie before she broke the news to him. "Insulin wouldn't be in the medicine cabinet. It would be in the fridge."

"Oh." Zachary's face grew warm, and he was glad she couldn't see him. "I didn't realize that." He looked at the house. Did he dare go back and say he needed a drink? Even that wouldn't get him access to the fridge. He'd need some other ruse, and he couldn't think of any that would work. "I guess we'll have to wait to see if the police can get a search warrant."

"Yeah," Kenzie agreed. "But so far there isn't any reason to suspect the family of anything, so I doubt they will."

"So that's why you called me? Just to let me know the autopsy was done and you were waiting on the labs?"

"Yes… and I wondered if you wanted to do something. Maybe take in a movie…?"

Zachary was startled. Usually, the most he could get Kenzie to do with him was to go to dinner. And then only when he had medical documents to go through with her. It seemed that it didn't rain, but it poured. On one hand, he had Bridget back in his life, however peripherally, and the chance that he might somehow be able to get her back, and on the other he had Kenzie, suddenly interested in more than just a free meal and friendly chat. He was reluctant to lead Kenzie on, in case he could work things out with Bridget.

"I'm not sure when I'll be free. I've got this case to work, and I still have some other surveillance and insurance jobs I need to put some time into."

"You still need to eat."

"Well, yes, you just said… a movie."

"If you don't want to do a movie, we can do dinner, like usual. That would be okay, wouldn't it?"

"Uh…"

"What? Come on, Zachary. You're breaking for dinner at some point."

"No, probably just grabbing something on the run. I have a lot of work to be done."

"Fine. I get the message. I guess we'll talk again when one of us has something to say." Her tone was hard and brittle Zachary couldn't fail to hear her disappointment and confusion over being turned down.

But he couldn't lead her on when he might still have a chance to get somewhere with Bridget.

Having told Kenzie that he had a lot of other investigative work to do, Zachary decided he'd better do it. He didn't want to get too far behind on his other cases, especially when he wasn't getting paid to investigate Robin's death. If he wanted to be able to pay for his apartment, he needed to be making money. So he went home and tackled the mountain of paperwork he'd been ignoring, did some background searches, and filled out some final reports and invoices on cases he had completed but not yet been paid for.

After a couple of hours, his brain was feeling wrung out. Zachary pushed the pile of paper aside and logged into one of the social networking sites he had an account on. He told himself he was only there to work background on the subjects of his current investigations, but his eyes were caught by a red-flagged icon. A connection request. He clicked to see who it was, and stared at Rhys Salter's name and photo.

It would seem that Rhys was a little more communicative than Gloria had led Zachary to believe. True, Zachary hadn't asked whether he was active in any online communities, but he'd assumed by her description of his communication abilities that he wouldn't be interested in messaging with friends.

Zachary accepted the request, and once he was connected with Rhys, clicked through his profile to see when it had been set up, who he was friends with, and what he had posted on his timeline recently.

Was it really Rhys? Or was it someone masquerading as him? Anyone connected with the case could have set up a dummy profile for the boy, working on the assumption that Zachary would want to talk to him, which of course, he did.

Everything seemed to be real. The profile was a couple of years old, and most of the friends who had connected with Rhys were boys his age, some at the school Rhys would attend, and some international, who maybe he had met through online gaming or some other shared-interest group. He posted to his timeline sporadically. Nothing with verbose introductions. Usually, just sharing someone else's material, sometimes with a keyword or a friend's name.

There was a colored tag on Rhys's profile that indicated he was currently online. Whether he really was, or whether he had just left his phone or computer on with the app running, Zachary didn't know. He clicked on the chat icon.

"Hi, Rhys, thanks for connecting with me."

There was no immediate reply. Zachary left the tab loaded and switched to another site, forcing himself to work instead of staring at the chat window with Rhys waiting for an answer. When he allowed himself to switch back for a look, he saw a picture of a dog.

"Is that you? He looks sad." Zachary included an arrow pointing up to the basset hound, who did look worried and seriously depressed.

Rhys responded faster this time, with a sad face emoticon.

Zachary typed back, "I'm sorry about you losing your aunt."

There was another long delay. Zachary decided to tackle his paper filing, which he could do while keeping an eye on the screen so he would know the next time Rhys posted. When he finally did, it was a picture of the three women with Rhys. Vera, Gloria, and Robin smiling, arms around each other, with Rhys in front of them. He had been younger in the picture. Below the women's chins. Now, he was probably at least as tall as his grandma, maybe taller than his mom too.

Zachary studied the picture. As with the ones in the photo album Vera had shown him, Rhys was not smiling. Maybe he was incapable of smiling. Zachary could only imagine how many photographers might have told him to smile for a picture. And still, Rhys didn't. He just stared at the camera.

Though the women were all smiling, Zachary wasn't sure they were genuine. Their stances looked awkward and separate, even though they were holding each other. Like they had just been posed that way and wouldn't have touched each other otherwise.

Or was he just reading what he wanted to into the picture?

"She was pretty," Zachary posted. "You must miss her a lot."

There was no response from Rhys.

It was almost the end of the day when Bowman called Zachary back.

"Running into some problems with these incident reports, Zach."

Zachary stopped what he was doing on the computer to give the phone his attention. "What kind of problems?" he asked, thinking of failed searches or database corruption. Bowman knew his way around the system and didn't usually run into any problems.

"I've got brass that don't think you need access to these records."

"What? Campbell said I should have a look at them. He said he wouldn't block them."

"Then it must be someone further up the food chain. I'm not sure who it is, but I'm getting a lot of push back. They want the death investigation closed and they want you shut down."

Zachary swore under his breath. Up until then, he'd been pleasantly surprised at how well the police investigation was going. He hadn't dared expect that they would think he had enough to open an investigation in the first place, and then having Joshua Campbell running the investigation at the scene meant he could continue to investigate without fear of running into cops who thought they had the exclusive right to investigate and to use Zachary as a punching bag.

"I should have known it was going too smoothly."

"Yeah, it should never be easy," Bowman agreed with a laugh. "If it's easy, we obviously aren't doing our job. So what do you want to do?"

"What are my options? Are you telling me you won't give me the information? Were you told to turn down my request?"

"I was told to put you off. Stall you. Make it take longer. If they can close the death investigation and stall you for long enough, it will all just go away."

"How can they shut down the death investigation? There hasn't been a determination yet."

"They're rushing the medical examiner. Don't ask me, I'm not privy to all of the details. They're saying if he hasn't found any evidence of foul play, they should close the file."

"But all of the evidence hasn't been processed. They're still waiting on lab results."

"It's obviously political, Zach. My guess is that the family has reached out to someone and is threatening to go to the media. Not everybody is of the opinion that there was enough evidence to recommend opening an investigation in the first place. They don't like seeing your name on a case."

"Incredible," Zachary growled. "Well, they can't close it without the agreement of the medical examiner, so get me my files. Or I will go to the press myself with how the police department is participating in a cover-up."

He could hear the grin in Bowman's voice. "I'll see what I can do, Zachary. We certainly wouldn't want any bad press."

"Thank you."

"Just remember, there is a family out there who can't bury their dead yet, and that doesn't play well either. They're not going to stay quiet for long, and they want her cremated."

"Which means we can't exhume her later to finish what we started."

"There's only so much you can test for once the body's been burned."

18

It had taken Zachary some time to track down Stanley Green, Robin's ex-fiancé. There were too many Stanley Greens around, too many of them the right age or race. But eventually, he was able to whittle the list down and identify the correct Stanley Green.

Zachary anticipated that Stanley would not want to set up a meeting with him, so he hung around at the building that housed the offices of the copper mining company Stanley worked for and watched for him to come out. It was getting late, and he wondered whether he had missed Stanley or maybe he hadn't been scheduled to work that day, when he finally spotted the face that he had memorized.

"Stanley Green?"

Stanley turned around and looked at Zachary. Maybe it wasn't the best idea to be coming up on a man unexpectedly in the gathering dusk, but Zachary was sure that when Stanley Green compared his height and bulk with Zachary's, he wouldn't be concerned. Stanley looked him over, tried to place him, then shook his head.

"Do I know you from somewhere?"

"No. I just wanted to talk to you for a few minutes. I'm taking part in the investigation of the death of a woman you used to be engaged to." He saw comprehension starting to form in Stanley's eyes. "Robin Salter."

Stanley shook his head. "Robin died? How did that happen?"

"Well, the how is what we're currently trying to figure out. She was in hospital. She had terminal cancer. But as it turns out, someone might have hurried the process along a little." It was a stretch, but the main points were correct, so Zachary didn't worry about it.

"Who would do a thing like that?" Stanley shook his head. "Well, I haven't had any contact with Robin for a long time. I don't think I can help you."

"I'll buy you a drink. Just a short chat and then you can get on with your evening."

Stanley considered this. Zachary was surprised he was so reluctant, given his size. He could probably break Zachary in two. It wouldn't be much of a fight, even if Zachary had been inclined to show off his rather limited physical prowess.

"Alright," Stanley finally agreed. "There's a bar about six blocks down this street." He pointed. "Big orange sign outside. Meet me there."

Zachary couldn't be sure Stanley was going to meet him there, he might just as easily be giving himself an opportunity to skip out and avoid the talk. After watching Stanley head into the employee parking lot to get his car, Zachary hurried to his. He rolled up to the Farmhouse Tavern at about the same time as Stanley, and hurried to catch up with him, feeling like a toddler on his short legs when compared with Stanley's.

They got a table and Stanley took a careful look at Zachary. Apparently unworried by his interrogator, he leaned back, relaxing after a long day of work. A waitress came by and they ordered their beers. Zachary didn't try to talk to him until they both had their drinks. Zachary took a sip of his. It had been far too long since he'd had beer. He would have to limit his intake to one, and that wouldn't be easy. He took another swallow and put it down, a few inches farther away than was comfortable. Stanley's eyes took this in, but he wasn't concerned by Zachary's strange behavior.

"What was your name? Who are you?"

Zachary slid a business card across the table to Stanley. "Zachary. Goldman Investigations."

Stanley looked at the card and considered it for a while before sliding it into his shirt pocket. "How did Robin die?"

"That's under investigation. She died in her sleep at the hospital, but the timing was unexpected. It looks like something might have been administered to her IV." Not strictly true, maybe, but it was enough to hook Stanley.

"Somebody gave her something in her IV? That seems rather…" Stanley searched for a word. "Brash."

Zachary nodded. "It's a strange case."

"And what do you want me for? Like I said, I haven't seen her in years. I wouldn't have any reason to track her down after we were both out of each other's lives."

"Well, from what I hear, there was a restraining order. It seems like you did need something to keep you apart back then."

"Restraining orders don't last forever. If I remember right, it was only for six months. And it was never violated. We *were* able to go on with our lives."

"Good for you. Well… I didn't come here because I thought you did anything to her. I mean, it's always a remote possibility, but I don't think anyone seriously thought you might have something to do with it. I think you would probably have drawn attention at the hospital, and no one claimed to have seen you there."

"That's because I wasn't."

Stanley took a long drag on his beer. He eyed it, probably wondering if he should just down it all at once and then get out of there, saying nothing more to Zachary. But his curiosity kept him there.

"Then what are you looking for from me?"

"Background. You knew Robin back at a very difficult time in her life. You were accepted as a member of her family. Who better to talk to about the personal dynamics?"

"Her family."

"You knew her father before he was killed?"

"Yes. He was still alive when we got engaged." Stanley stopped and said nothing more, even though Zachary gave him plenty of time.

"What was he like?"

"He was… the patriarch… he dictated how things were to be run in the family. No one ever really challenged him."

"What kind of things?"

"Pretty much everything. He's the one who decided to take Gloria and her baby in. He set the house rules. Mealtimes, curfew, bedtimes."

"Robin would have been in her twenties, wouldn't she? He gave her a curfew and bedtime?"

"Look what happened to Gloria. He had to be sure."

"What happened to Gloria...?"

"Her pregnancy."

"Oh." Zachary nodded. He'd lived in his share of homes with seemingly bizarre, arbitrary rules. He never did understand how they were supposed to keep him from getting into trouble. He got into trouble for not being able to follow the rules. It seemed like the only reason they were imposed was so that families would have a good excuse to punish him or to send him on to the next place. "I've noticed they're somewhat... religious."

Stanley shrugged.

"And I have met Vera," Zachary said. "Seems like she might be getting a little forgetful. Or is that just part of her personality?"

"Forgetful? No, I don't think so. She never seemed to have any trouble when I was around. But that was a while back, now."

"How did you and Robin meet?"

"She was temping at the company I worked for. Not Copper," Stanley jerked his head the direction of the building they had come from. "Another company. We saw each other a few times.... I asked her if she wanted to go out... things progressed."

"What was she like? I've heard descriptions from a few different people, but I never knew her myself."

"She was a strong woman. I found that attractive. Good-looking and well-dressed. Not wishy-washy like other women I had dated. You ask them what they want, and they ask what you want. Can't answer a question or express an opinion. Robin wasn't like that. She had definite opinions and she wasn't going to keep quiet because she thought someone else might be of another opinion."

Zachary thought about Bridget. "It can be exhausting to have to make all of the decisions for two people. Having someone who is willing to take charge and not just be blown around... that can be a big relief."

"Yeah. Robin did everything well. I thought she was an amazing person."

"I heard from the hospital staff that she sometimes complained. She was irritated by things that weren't quite the way she wanted them. Does that sound like the way she was when you were together?"

Stanley took a pull at his beer. "Robin was never afraid to lodge a complaint. If we were at a restaurant and the service or the food wasn't top notch, you can bet she would have something to say about it. She knew what she wanted. And she knew how to persuade other people around her to do things the 'right' way."

"And after a while, that started to get old and to grate on you." Zachary knew how relationships worked. A difference that initially brought a couple together could quickly turn into a rift that separated them. Stanley had been attracted to a strong, opinionated woman, but then he had started to dislike the fact that she was so strong and opinionated all of the time. He started to crave someone who was softer and more moldable.

Stanley frowned at his beer. "She got more extreme. More... angry."

And it had become a power struggle. Robin getting angry when she didn't get exactly what she wanted, Stanley trying to change her mind and bend her to his will. The anger had escalated. The violence had escalated and that was how they had ended up with their names on multiple domestic violence complaints and a protective order.

Zachary backed off. He didn't want to make Stanley defensive.

"And Gloria? She was another hard-headed woman?" he suggested.

Stanley shook his head. "She was messed up. She could clean up nicely, put on a good show for a few hours, but she was an addict. A party girl. She was living at home most of the time, but she hadn't settled down. Vera and Clarence were mom and dad to Rhys. Gloria wasn't there most of the time. She didn't know how to be responsible and take care of her baby."

"That must have been hard on them. You don't expect to be raising a child again at that age."

"Plenty of people do, though. They loved Rhys, just adored him. And he loved them right back. They'd only raised girls, not boys, so they could suddenly do things that the girls had never been interested in. Woodworking, hunting, fishing. Guy stuff. Rhys was the little man of the house."

And now Rhys was surrounded by women, his voice literally silenced. Did he pursue any of those interests at school? So many school programs were getting cut, Zachary didn't know if they had shop anymore.

"When Clarence died, Rhys was about five?"

"Yeah. About that."

"And you were still together with Robin for a while after that. So you saw how it affected Rhys? How it affected the different members of the family?"

"Poor little guy." Stanley stared intently at his beer. "Rhys just worshiped Clarence. He loved him to bits. After the shooting…he became like a different person. He went from a smiley, fun-loving kid to being… broken and withdrawn. No one could reach him. And I tried. I really did. I was the only other man around, not counting Gloria's one-night-stands. I tried, but I couldn't help him."

Zachary nodded. Rhys was still suffering ten years later. That wasn't something that a sometimes father-figure could have fixed with a few visits.

"Do you have any idea what might have happened to Robin? I know you haven't seen them, I just mean as someone who knew the family dynamics at one time… could you see anyone stepping in and… intervening? For any reason. It might have been a mercy killing or assisted suicide. I'm just wondering if anything like that made sense to you."

Stanley raised his glass to take a drink, blocking Zachary's view of his face for a few seconds. He set it down firmly on the table. "I was lucky to get out of there when I did. There were things happening in that family… it was very unhealthy. People… are not always what they seem. Relationships that look healthy from the outside… sometimes they aren't."

Zachary thought about Clarence. He seemed to be at the center of everything. The patriarch set the example for the home. He was the one Rhys had been so attached to. He was the one who had been murdered. If he had been abusive, it would explain Gloria's rebellious years and Robin choosing an abusive partner. Both behaviors were common patterns in abused children. Had he been physically abusive? Verbally? Sexually?

"Clarence's murder was never solved," Zachary said.

"No? I didn't follow it after Robin and I broke up. It's too bad they never caught the killer."

"Did you have any suspicions at the time about how it might have gone down?"

"No. An unknown intruder. Burglar, they speculated at the time." Stanley shrugged.

"You don't think it was anyone in the family?"

Stanley just stared at Zachary.

"The wife is always the prime suspect, isn't she?" Zachary suggested. "If the family dynamics were toxic... maybe someone decided to take matters into their own hands."

"Why don't you ask the police that? That's their job, isn't it?" Stanley picked up his glass, drained the last of the beer, and stood up as he put the glass down. "You want my advice?" he asked, leaning aggressively into Zachary's personal space. "Get out of this case. Don't walk; run away. Get as far away from it as possible, because nothing good can come of you sticking your nose into it."

Zachary sat there, frozen, for several minutes after Stanley was gone.

He should have expected the intimidation tactics. Stanley was a big man, used to throwing his weight around. He'd been violent with Robin. If Zachary looked into Stanley's background, he'd probably find a long line of abused girlfriends.

Stanley Green would be a dangerous man to cross.

When Zachary got home, he threw a frozen dinner into the microwave to heat and sat down at the computer to check his email. He'd have to be sure to check his social networks for anything further from Rhys. He didn't want to push the boy, but he was really hoping that if Rhys had something to say, he'd make contact again.

Thinking back to the conversation with Stanley, Zachary shuddered. If Clarence had been abusive, then maybe it hadn't been a chance burglary. Maybe it was just set up to look that way. Was Rhys really so traumatized by his grandfather being killed while he slept? Or had he actually seen what had happened? Vera and Gloria could be lying through their teeth.

It was even conceivable that Rhys had been the killer himself. Gun accidents happened. It seemed like not a week went by that Zachary didn't hear some horror story about a two-year-old shooting his mother in the back of the head after taking her gun out of her purse. Something like that was far more likely to cause Rhys's trauma than just being asleep in his bed. If he hadn't seen or heard or been a part of what had happened, then why was he so damaged?

Zachary took a quick glance at his direct messages, but he didn't have anything there from Rhys. The boy hadn't posted on his own timeline either. Maybe he'd been grounded from using the computer or had been too busy with homework or extra-curricular activities to check in. Or maybe he was dealing with the emotional fallout of Robin's death.

Zachary retrieved his dinner from the microwave before checking his email. Way too many times he just left a dinner in the microwave, completely forgotten, until it started to stink or he opened the microwave to warm something else up. He sat down at the computer and opened his email inbox.

There was an email from Kenzie with a red flag beside it. Zachary opened the message and scanned it quickly.

"You're not answering your phone again. Found something. Call me."

His heart started pumping twice as hard and fast. Zachary put his hand on his pocket, but his phone wasn't there. He looked quickly over his desk and nearly flipped his dinner right off looking under papers for his phone. He jumped up and carried the dinner with him back into the kitchen. There his phone lay on the counter waiting for him. He turned on the screen and saw missed calls and a voicemail from Kenzie. The voicemail would say the same thing as her email. *Call me.* She wouldn't tell him in a voicemail what they had found. Zachary stabbed his finger at the screen to call her back, and decided abruptly it was time to sit down. His legs were shaking so badly that if there hadn't been a kitchen chair right there, he would have ended up sitting on the floor. He put the phone to his ear and waited for Kenzie to answer. It rang through to voicemail. He looked to see which number he had called, and switched to her cell phone instead. It too went to voicemail.

"Come on," Zachary urged. "Come on, answer!" He tried the call again, praying she would notice her phone ringing and pick it up. It wasn't late enough for her to be in bed yet, but she could be having a bath to relax or be out with friends for dinner. She hadn't asked him to dinner; but then, he hadn't answered her calls.

"Zachary."

"Kenzie, hi! I'm sorry I missed your call. I was in the middle of an interview. I didn't even notice it ringing. It was pretty intense..."

"Well, maybe it doesn't matter to you what we found out. I mean, the woman is dead, after all."

"No, of course it matters. I was continuing my investigation. Bowman told me Dr. Wiltshire was getting a lot of political pressure to close the case. I know he's not going to do that prematurely, but I want to make sure that I've done everything I can to—"

"You really run off at the mouth when you're in trouble, did you know that?"

Zachary closed his mouth and tried to stop giving her excuses. He needed to be businesslike. He wasn't a fourteen-year-old trying to explain why he didn't have his homework assignments to hand in yet again. He was a professional. He hadn't been neglecting the case. He wasn't sure why Kenzie was so pissed at him, but he was just going to have to deal with that. Like a professional.

"That's better," Kenzie snapped, though she sounded irritated that he had stopped talking. He just couldn't win. "We had something show up in the labs that may be cause of death."

"What kind of thing?"

"I told you that some of the organs had irregularities that needed to be checked out. We prepared a number of slides of the pancreas, heart, and liver. And of course, we ordered whatever we could think of to test the blood for."

"Uh-huh."

"It isn't unusual for a cancer patient to have irregular results in their blood tests. Low white blood cell count, red blood cells, platelets, anemia..."

"Right. And blood sugar. Nurse Betty said that Robin's blood sugar had been high. That's why she was getting insulin."

"Who's telling the story here, you or me?" On another day, Kenzie would have said it in a flirtatious, teasing voice. But her cutting tone told Zachary that he was treading on thin ice and had better shut up.

"Sorry. I didn't mean to interrupt."

"She had diabetes because most of the insulin-producing cells in her pancreas had died," Kenzie told him.

"Ouch."

"The whole point of chemotherapy is to kill cells. We just want to kill more of the cancer cells and fewer of the body's healthy cells. It's a delicate balance."

Zachary made an encouraging noise, determined not to interrupt her flow again.

"So it's not unusual to cause something like this. It's one of the risks that patients are warned about. There's probably a waiver somewhere that Robin had to sign saying that she understood all of the risks."

"Right." Zachary tried to demonstrate that he was listening and fully engaged. "Is that what happened to the liver too?"

"The liver is a really important organ. It performs a lot of functions that we don't know how to replicate artificially. With other organs, even though they are vital for survival, we can replicate artificially for some time to prolong life. We can pump blood through a bypass machine, clean it with dialysis, inflate the lungs with a respirator. But liver function is very complicated. We can't replace a liver artificially. Once cancer reaches the liver, the patient's days are numbered."

"Robin's cancer had gotten into her liver?"

"No. Dr. Wiltshire knew there was something off with the liver when he examined it, but it wasn't cancer. There were no masses and the slides didn't show any cancerous cells."

Zachary held his breath, not sure whether he should prompt her to go on, or just wait for it.

"What the liver showed us was iron overload," Kenzie finally finished.

"Iron?"

"When there is too much iron in the blood, the liver tries to store it. But it can only store so much before it becomes overloaded. The stores of iron damage the liver, and if the iron is not removed from the body quickly enough, it results in death."

"How would she get too much iron in her liver? Or her blood? Was that because of her cancer?"

"No. Cancer often causes anemia, which she had been diagnosed with, but that is too little iron, not too much."

"And it's treated by administering iron?" Zachary guessed.

"Bingo. It's going to be harder to figure out if they overdosed her with iron than with insulin. It isn't controlled the same way. I'm not sure there will be any way for them to tell if she was given the wrong dosage or concentration."

Zachary let his breath out in a slow stream. "So it *was* medical error."

"Looks that way."

"Was liver failure the cause of death?"

"Maybe. She also had damage to her heart. Cardiomyopathy was observed. She probably tired quickly with exertion. She may have had chest pain or skipping beats."

"She did. I remember that." It was her roommate, Chenka, who had mentioned chest pain. Surprisingly, her family and the medical staff hadn't been specific about the kind of pain she was having. "Does that mean she might have had a heart attack?"

"Hard to tell whether her liver or heart failed first. They were both in bad shape."

"What other symptoms would iron overdose have?"

"Joint pain. Stomach and digestive issues. Bronzing of the skin, but that's difficult to discern on someone who is already dark-skinned. Diabetes."

"The iron caused the diabetes?"

"Possibly. We can't really tell whether it was the chemo or the iron. We didn't find any cancerous cells in the pancreas."

Zachary's brain was churning through the possibilities. "How long does iron take to kill? It must have been given to her before that Wednesday."

"Two to five days. That matches up with her chart. There was a significant increase in her pain meds beginning the Monday before she died."

"And was the hospital giving her iron then?"

"They started her on an iron protocol the week before."

"Doctor error," Zachary repeated. "Bridget was right all along."

Kenzie sniffed.

"I'll have to give her a call." Zachary looked at the time on his phone. "I'll call you back, okay? I'm going to see if I can get her before bed."

Kenzie didn't even say goodbye before cutting the connection.

Zachary dialed Bridget's number. He tapped in the numbers manually, not looking up her contact record. He knew all of her contact details by heart. It was satisfying to punch them in one at a time. He savored the moment. He was no knight in shining armor, but he had accomplished what he had set out to do. He had fulfilled her quest and earned her gratitude.

"Hello?" Bridget obviously answered without checking the caller ID beforehand. "Oh, Zachary. Can I call you back? I was just going to—"

"No. No, this will just take a second, but it's important."

"Well?" She was impatient. "What is it?"

"Robin Salter didn't die of cancer. You were right. She died of iron overdose."

"Iron? I thought iron was good. It can kill you?"

"I guess more isn't always better. Your body can only handle so much, then the liver starts to store it. If there's too much for the liver to store, it can result in death."

"Wow. I remember they gave me iron when I was there. They said I was anemic from the treatments."

"Robin was too. But it looks like they gave her too much."

"Is this official? Does that mean they change her death certificate?"

"I... guess so. I just got this from the medical examiner's office—"

"From Kenzie, you mean."

"Kenzie is at the medical examiner's office."

"Yes, luckily for you." There was a hint of a sneer in her voice.

"Lucky for you too," Zachary countered. "I would never have gotten the death investigation opened without her."

There was a call waiting alert. Zachary pulled his phone away from his ear to look at his screen. It hadn't been his call waiting, but Bridget's.

"I have to take that," Bridget said. "Can we talk later?"

"Sure. Of course. You know how to reach me—"

But Bridget had already hung up.

19

Zachary decided the next morning that a courtesy visit to the Salter family was probably in order. The medical examiner's office or the police department would undoubtedly contact them at some point, but Zachary's investigation had started everything and he wanted to be sure that they were told what had been discovered, rather than waiting for the information to get to them through the grapevine or at some press conference.

Vera was the only one home. Still in a bathrobe, she looked at Zachary blearily, as if she'd just gotten out of bed and wasn't sure who he was.

"Zachary Goldman," Zachary reminded her. "I'm the investigator who has been looking into Robin's death."

"Oh, yes," Vera nodded and motioned Zachary into the house. The front entryway and living room were somewhat in disarray, as if caught between a weekend binge and Monday cleanup that had never been completed. Zachary detoured around what appeared to be Rhys's book bag and a chip bowl and sat down with Vera.

"Are you here by yourself?" He was a little concerned about her being left to her own devices. Presumably she could be trusted on her own, but Zachary was uncomfortable with how distant she appeared to be.

"Yes. Gloria had to take Rhys..." Vera trailed off, clearly unable to remember the details. To school, probably, or maybe a therapy appointment, and then off to work herself. There wasn't really anyone available to keep an eye on Vera if Gloria had to work during the day.

"Are you okay here on your own? Is there anything you need?"

"Oh, of course. I've been on my own for years. I can manage. The kids will be home after school."

Zachary took a quick look at the time on his phone. That wouldn't be for hours yet. But that was presumably the same every other day, and if Vera were unable to take care of herself, they would have found other arrangements for her.

"I wanted to let you know that I heard back from the medical examiner's office with preliminary details of what they had found in the lab work they did for Robin." He intentionally did not use the word 'autopsy,' which would probably just upset her. 'Lab work' sounded much less invasive.

"For Robin?" Vera repeated. "Why?"

"To find out why she died."

"It was the cancer, wasn't it?" She seemed confused, as if she'd been unaware until then that there was any question of Robin's cause of death.

"That was what the doctor thought initially," Zachary agreed. "But we have looked into it further and done some testing, and it turns out that there were actually some other issues to be considered."

"Oh?" Vera cocked her head.

"When will Gloria be home?" Zachary looked down at his phone again.

"I don't know. She usually gets home after Rhys."

"Maybe I should wait until then. So there's someone here with you."

"What is it? What did you find out?"

"Well… it looks like the medical staff made a mistake on the amount of iron she was to be given. I don't know whether the wrong amount was prescribed, or if they gave the wrong dosage. But Robin died of an overdose of iron, not the cancer itself."

"Iron?"

"Yes. Her liver couldn't process the amount that was given to her, and she…"

"She was anemic," Vera said, demonstrating that her grasp of the situation was better than Zachary had anticipated. "They had to give her iron for her anemia."

"Yes. But it looks like they might have given her too much. They *did* give her too much."

"She needed iron."

"Yes, she did."

Vera shook her head. "Gloria should talk to them."

"I'm afraid it's too late. They already gave Robin too much. You remember... she passed away, don't you?"

"How could I forget?" Vera demanded.

"Okay, I just wasn't sure. Yes, maybe Gloria should talk to the medical examiner's office. They can confirm their finding and give her the details."

Vera nodded. She looked around. "Where are they? When is she going to get home?"

"After school." Zachary refrained from looking at his phone again. "Is there anyone who checks in on you during the day?"

"No. I'm fine here by myself. I've looked after myself all my life."

Zachary was still uncomfortable leaving her there alone. He turned on his phone and pressed redial on Bridget's number. Bridget knew Robin's family; maybe she would want to visit with Vera for a while and make sure she was okay. Or maybe she knew someone who could be called to deal with it. It was outside of Zachary's usual experience.

He waited for Bridget's impatient answer, but it went instead to voicemail and Bridget's light, pleasant greeting. Zachary hesitated, then suggested that she call him back. He hung up and looked at Vera again.

"Just one more call," he promised.

This time, he called Joshua Campbell. He might not be exactly the person to contact, but he could probably put Zachary on to the right person.

Campbell picked up after a few rings. "Campbell."

"Hey, it's Zachary. I'm at Mrs. Salter's house, and—"

"What the hell are you doing there?" Campbell demanded. "Didn't you get the message that the case is closed?"

"Well, not exactly... Kenzie told me the preliminary findings—"

"Then you know it was medical error and the file is closed. Why are you still questioning the family? It's no wonder I've got the brass on my back! You never know when to leave things well enough alone!"

"I... wasn't questioning them. I just came over to make sure they knew what was going on, and..."

Campbell sighed in exasperation. "And what?"

"I'm a little worried about Mrs. Salter being here alone. Her daughter is away and I'm not sure she's okay to be here by herself."

"She's upset?"

Zachary looked at Vera sitting there on the couch, staring at one of the pictures nearby. He got up and walked into the kitchen so that she wouldn't overhear him. Similar to the living room, it looked as if nothing had been cleaned up since the weekend.

"No," he said in a low voice. "She seems forgetful and maybe not capable of looking after herself if something was to happen."

"Call the daughter."

"The daughter already knows and is the one who left her alone like this. If I call her, she's just going to tell me that her mother is fine and to butt out of something that's not my business."

"Not bad advice."

Zachary didn't say anything. Maybe Campbell hadn't been the best person to call for advice.

"Okay, Zach," Campbell acquiesced. "I'll get a couple of officers over there for a welfare check. If they think she shouldn't be left alone, they can make the necessary calls to have her cared for until something can be arranged with the family."

"Great. Thanks. I appreciate it."

"But you know the case is closed now. So I don't expect to be getting any more calls from higher up telling me that you're still poking around and causing trouble."

"I'm not on the force," Zachary reminded him. "I'm a private citizen, so you can't tell me what to do unless I'm breaking the law. And I'm not."

It wasn't like he had planned to do any more investigating. The answers from the medical examiner's office seemed pretty conclusive. But he bristled at the order to stay off the case. He hated being told what to do, especially by someone who had no real authority over him.

"I can charge with you impeding an investigation."

"An investigation that's closed?"

"Zachary, I'm helping you out with the Salter woman. So can't we get a little bit of reciprocation here? There's nothing left to investigate."

"I'll be the one to decide that."

Before Campbell could say anything else, Zachary hung up.

When he got back into his car, Zachary checked his phone to see if he'd missed a call back from Bridget. She was usually on her phone all of her waking hours, so it was unusual not to be able to reach her or at least get a call back pretty quickly. But she still hadn't responded. There was, however, a direct message from Rhys, continuing their conversation from earlier.

Zachary frowned as he studied the moving gif of a fat dog stuck in a toilet bowl, looking out with bulging, glistening eyes. It was captioned "help me."

Rhys had used a dog picture for his greeting the previous chat session as well. Zachary didn't know how much to read into it. He considered the little dog for a few minutes before messaging back.

"Hi, Rhys. I was just at your house. Is everything okay?"

The reply that came eventually was a cartoon character, from Disney maybe, surrounded by walls of fire. The caption said "everything is going to be just fine."

Zachary didn't know what to make of the sarcastic meme. Did Rhys mean everything would be okay? Did he mean he was in danger? If it was just the first option that came up when Rhys typed in "everything fine," then did he really mean he was fine? Or was it intended to be sarcastic?

"Does that mean you're okay or not?"

He waited, but no answer was forthcoming. Zachary stared down at the short exchange on his phone, trying to figure it out. It seemed clear that Rhys wanted something, but Zachary didn't know what. He didn't think he could go to the authorities and get them to agree that the memes might mean Rhys was in some kind of trouble. They were pictures. Maybe they had meaning and maybe they were just random. And the words on the last one said that everything was going to be fine. The police wouldn't interpret it as meaning anything else.

There could be plenty of reasons Rhys had stopped messaging. He might have been using his phone between classes, but had to put it away when the next period started. His phone might have been taken away because he was caught using it in class. The whole thing might have been a pocket dial and randomly selected messages.

He'd just have to wait and see if he got anything else from Rhys.

20

Having returned home to work on other files, Zachary looked in his fridge, decided that he'd just have a cup of coffee, and sat down in front of his computer to work. He tried to focus, but his thoughts kept getting dragged back to Rhys and Bridget. He kept looking at his phone for any more messages from Rhys, but nothing materialized. He tried reaching Bridget by phone several times, and kept just ringing through to her voicemail.

It figured.

She had come back into his life, acting like she was ready to take him back again, and he had fallen for it. He had taken the case for her because he would do anything for her. He still cared about her and if there was any chance he could get her back, he would take it.

But she didn't feel the same way. All she wanted were his services. She had said she would pay him, and maybe that should have been the first tip-off. She wasn't looking for a favor or a relationship, just for his investigative experience. Any investigator would do, but he was the one she knew, and he came cheap.

Now that he had shown that Robin's life had, in fact, been cut short by a medical error, Bridget was satisfied. She could go on, knowing that justice had been served. She didn't have any lasting attachment to Zachary. Now that it was all sorted out, she didn't even have the time to answer a call from him. Not even to tell him to take a hike.

It was a good thing he didn't have any alcohol around, because he would have downed a whole bottle and maybe washed down a few pills while he was at it. He couldn't believe he had let himself be used by Bridget. Hadn't he figured out by now that she was the worst thing for him? How many times was he going to let himself be hurt by her?

Zachary considered throwing his phone across the room, but he couldn't be bothered to have to replace it. He placed it face-down as punishment for not being useful to him and resolved to ignore it. Even if Bridget decided to call him back, he wasn't going to answer it.

He looked back at his computer, but instead of navigating to his file system to work on reports, he clicked on the tab to see if Rhys had messaged him back again.

At ten o'clock, Zachary was crawling out of his skin. He was so anxious and agitated he couldn't stay in his apartment, even pacing, so he went out for a walk.

It maybe wasn't the best time of day to go out to burn off some steam, but his new apartment was in a reasonably nice neighborhood and it wasn't *really* late. It was still before midnight. The bars were open, so rowdies were still occupied and weren't wandering around looking for excitement. He walked in well-lit areas and kept his eyes open for signs of trouble.

All the while, his heart was pounding out an angry rhythm. Bridget didn't want him. Rhys hadn't posted again. The case was closed, but he didn't feel the sense of satisfaction and resolution he usually did when a case was resolved. Instead, it felt like an open wound. Something that needed to be properly treated and bandaged before he would feel better. It didn't make much sense. He hadn't known Robin. He had been hired—or asked as a favor—to find out why she had died so soon, and he had done that.

But Vera had been left alone and Rhys was asking for help. Gloria obviously wasn't dealing with her responsibilities to either one of them. Maybe he should go back to the house to make sure Gloria had gotten home and everybody was okay. She could have fallen back on old addictions and be out somewhere completely wasted, while her mother and son struggled to care for themselves.

Of course, it was Bridget's behavior that was really bothering Zachary. Even at their worst, darkest times, she had still called him back. Maybe she had only done it to yell at him and threaten to take out a restraining order if he didn't leave her alone, but she had still called him back.

Zachary turned back after an hour and headed back the way he had come. That way he would be back at his apartment at midnight. He could take some pills to help him sleep, and maybe in the morning, he'd be able to move on and deal with his other cases.

As Zachary approached his building, he saw a stealthy figure in the parking lot. Somebody hanging around, trying to keep to the shadows and not be seen. Zachary had done it enough times himself on surveillance to immediately recognized the movement pattern. The figure was definitely male, taller than Zachary, as most men were, broad across the shoulders. Zachary hung back and watched him, seeing what he could learn. The man put his phone to his ear and looked up at the windows of the apartment building. Watching for a figure to cross the window or a phone screen to light up the room? Or calling to report to someone on the movements of his quarry?

Zachary ducked back as the man turned around to scan the parking lot. He thought he got back behind an electrical box quickly enough that the man didn't see him. But Zachary had been able to get a full view of his face, well-lit by the phone screen.

What was Stanley Green doing hanging around in his parking lot?

Zachary never did get to sleep that night.

Eventually, it was late enough in the morning that he wouldn't be waking Kenzie up. If he'd timed it correctly, he figured she should be getting her coffee on her way to work. But by the way she answered the phone, he figured she hadn't had any caffeine yet.

"Case is closed, Zach. Why are you still bugging me?"

"Um…" Zachary tried to come up with a snap response and failed. He needed more time to compose an answer that would make any sense or satisfy her. "Sorry?"

"Brilliant. You're sorry. Sorry for what, should I ask?"

"I didn't… I wasn't calling to bug you about the case… not really."

"Not really. And what does that mean? Either it's about the case, or it's not."

"I was just going to tell you… about last night… nothing to do with the case, not really."

"Why should I care about it, then?"

Zachary stopped trying to explain and backed off. "What's wrong?"

"Maybe I've got my own life to deal with. My own job and my own personal problems. I don't need to deal with yours too."

"No."

"You're always wanting something from me. But what happens when Bridget shows up playing damsel in distress?"

"I fall for it," Zachary admitted. "I know I did… and now she won't even answer my calls. I gave her what she wanted and she doesn't want anything else to do with me."

"You see? I warned you. I told you not to think she was going to get back together with you. It was just a trap. That's how she gets you. She's still got you wrapped around her little finger. All she has to do is give it a little pull and you'll dance for her like a marionette on a string."

"Yeah."

"I warned you, and you didn't listen and got your hopes all built up. Now she drops out of sight, and I'm the one left to pick up the pieces."

Zachary took in a deep inhale, trying to keep his emotions under control. He sat at his desk, elbows on the table, covering his eyes. On the phone, Kenzie swore.

"You're a grown man, Zachary. Why don't you try acting like one instead of a lovestruck teenager? Your crush has moved on. Time for you to let her go."

"You're right."

There was silence from Kenzie. Zachary waited. He didn't trust his own voice. She obviously needed to blow off some steam. He hadn't registered before how irritated she'd been by Bridget's reappearance in his life.

"Okay. I'm done," Kenzie conceded. "So, what's this about last night?"

"It's not important… just… Stanley Green was hanging around my parking lot," Zachary explained, happy to move on to a less personal topic. "Robin's fiancé of ten years ago."

"Well... that's a little weird. I gather he knew you were investigating the case."

"Yes, I interviewed him Tuesday."

"Then if he wanted you, why didn't he just give you a call? That would have been easier than stalking you, surely."

"Exactly," Zachary agreed.

"What did he have to say for himself?"

"I didn't talk to him. I just called the police to say this guy was lurking around in the parking lot. I didn't say I knew who it was."

"Why not?"

"For one thing... I didn't want him to have confirmation that I lived there. Or that I had seen him. Better if he just gets the idea that it's not a safe place for him to loiter."

"Are you safe? What if he comes back and you don't see him the next time?"

"I'll keep a close lookout. If he does show up again, I'll have to get a restraining order."

"I'd feel a lot better if I knew you were carrying a gun. All of the private eyes on TV do, why don't you?"

"Because this is real life. Real private investigators don't go around shooting everything up."

"Well, not everything, maybe, but if someone is stalking them..."

"I'll take pictures. Proof that he's following me."

Kenzie sighed. "How am I supposed to admire you for your manliness when all you do is take pictures?"

Zachary allowed himself a smile. "You'll have to take my rugged good looks instead."

Kenzie snorted.

Zachary was checking for any messages from Rhys when his phone rang. He startled so badly that he almost threw the phone in the air. He didn't recognize the number, but he answered it anyway. Maybe it would be a new client to distract him.

"Goldman Investigations."

"Zachary?"

Zachary grasped for the identity of the voice, but couldn't quite place it. "Yes, this is Zachary."

It wasn't Stanley Green, that was the important thing. Or Joshua Campbell.

"It's Gordon Drake. Uh... Bridget's... *friend?*"

"Oh. Uh, hi Gordon. What can I do for you?" Zachary hung on to the hope that perhaps Gordon had a big corporate espionage investigation he wanted to hire Zachary for. Those could be quite profitable, from what he understood.

"I know this is going to sound a little strange, but... I was on a business trip, and when I got home today... well... Bridget isn't with you, is she?"

Goosebumps prickled up Zachary's arms. "With me? No. Why would she be with me?"

"Well, it was the only thing I could think of. I can look up her call records online, and I saw that you had phoned her a few times..."

"I've been calling her since Tuesday. I had a short conversation with her, but she had to take a call. I haven't been able to reach her since."

"That's a little odd, don't you think? She's pretty good at returning calls."

"I just figured she was avoiding me."

"She wouldn't do that," Gordon's voice was painfully frank, "not when you're conducting an investigation for her."

"That's just the thing... when I talked to her last, it was to tell her that we had figured it out. That Robin died of an iron overdose, probably the result of medical error. Bridget had to hang up to take another call, and that was the last I heard from her. She didn't... tell you where she was going? Leave you a note?"

"No. There's nothing. I've called the appointments on her agenda yesterday... she didn't get to any of them."

Zachary felt panicked and vindicated at the same time.

Bridget wasn't just avoiding him. Bridget was missing.

21

In the time Zachary and Bridget had been together, it seemed like Bridget had gotten to know half the police force. She knew at least as many of them as Zachary did, maybe even more. She made friends far more quickly and naturally than Zachary, and fast became the darling of the force. By the time Zachary made it over to Gordon's and Bridget's house, at least a dozen police cars were pulled in all along the driveway and the street, both marked and unmarked cars, a testament to her many warm relationships.

Zachary pulled his car over down the block and hurried to the house. He was stopped before he even got close to the door.

"Crime scene, you can't go in there."

"I'm family," Zachary snapped at the unfamiliar police detective. "I need to get in to talk to Gordon and whoever is in charge of the investigation."

"No one is allowed past—"

"Oh, Zachary!" Jonathan Bailey spotted him and intervened. "You're here. Come on through."

The policeman who had stopped Zachary scowled in irritation, but he let Zachary past and focused on the observers that he could keep back. Zachary didn't have time to smooth over bad feelings. He allowed Bailey to escort him to the door and announce him to the crime scene investigators who were busy inside the house.

"This is Zachary Goldman. Get him in to see Lashman right away."

One of the investigators instructed Zachary to glove up and put paper booties over his shoes, and then escorted him in a circuitous route that avoided the main walking paths through the rooms, to Bridget's study. It was a bright room, lush with green plants in planters and cut flowers in a vase on the desk. That was where he found Detective Lashman and Gordon Drake. They too were wearing protective gear, and a tech was paging through her appointment calendar in front of them with gloved fingers.

"Zachary. Thanks so much for coming," Gordon welcomed him.

The investigator escorting Zachary directed him around the perimeter of the room, and Zachary joined Gordon and Lashman.

"Have you found anything?"

"So far, just eliminating possibilities," Lashman said, with a wave at the calendar. "It looks like you were the last person to talk to her. She didn't take any other calls or attend to any other responsibilities."

"She hung up on me to take another call."

"Just her maid service. Nothing there."

Zachary's hope that the call that had interrupted them would guide the direction of the investigation vanished. He felt a stab of anger that Bridget would hang up on him and his news that Robin had died because of a medical error to deal with something so routine and unimportant. He had hoped it would be a clue to what had happened to her.

"Tell me about this case you were investigating for her," Lashman said. "Mr. Drake said you had found something?"

"The medical examiner found something," Zachary corrected. "It turns out that Robin Salter didn't die of cancer, as her physician had believed. She died of an iron overdose."

Lashman's bushy black eyebrows furrowed. "Murder?"

"Medical error. Someone at the hospital gave her the wrong dosage for her anemia."

"And you had just informed Miss Downy of that fact."

"Yes. I had just told her, and she said she had to answer the other call coming in. Said she'd call me back. But then she never did. I called her back several times, but couldn't get through to her."

"You weren't concerned about her sudden unavailability?"

Zachary looked at Gordon and then looked down. He looked around the room, trying to focus on any clues it might provide as to Bridget's whereabouts instead of his own guilt and embarrassment.

"Well... no. I didn't think that anything had happened to her. She's my ex-wife, and I figured... she had the information she needed from me and didn't want to talk to me anymore."

"How would you characterize your relationship with your ex-wife?"

Zachary's stomach tied in knots. He knew his answer would make him a suspect, but lying would only make it worse.

"Well... rocky. She had been pretty angry and bitter toward me. But she still helped me out sometimes. She asked me to take this case. I thought maybe she was softening toward me." Zachary's cheeks burned at having to admit this in front of Gordon. "It wasn't a... an amicable divorce."

Lashman looked at Zachary for a long moment, then looked at Gordon for confirmation. Gordon nodded, looking as uncomfortable as Zachary felt. "Bridget's relationship with Zachary was... complicated. There were a lot of resentments. On both sides, I think."

"And you thought you would invite him to the crime scene?" Lashman challenged. "He shouldn't be in here."

"I know it sounds like the height of stupidity, but I trust Zachary. I don't believe he had anything to do with Bridget's disappearance."

"Did she ever have a protective order against him?"

Gordon cleared his throat and didn't look at Zachary. "It was discussed. But no, she never officially pursued one. And there were never any allegations of abuse."

"Then why would she want a protective order?"

"Zachary was following her. Tracking her car. Generally being obsessive about where she was and what she was doing. Bridget wanted it to stop."

Lashman looked at Zachary. "And did it?"

Zachary nodded. "I've been getting counseling. Changed my meds. I knew... if I kept it up, she was going to charge me. I was doing my best..."

"Doing your best. That sounds like maybe you weren't quite as pure and innocent as you suggest."

"I..." Zachary swallowed. He looked at Gordon. "I sometimes drove past the house. Or other places she liked to go. I didn't make contact and I didn't track her, but..."

Gordon shook his head. "Right now, I'm wishing you *had* put another tracker on her car. Then we'd know where she was."

"How did these trackers work?" Lashman asked.

Zachary explained about the app on his phone, and Lashman held his hand out.

"I want to see it. Unlocked."

Zachary complied, pulling his phone out and unlocking it. He handed it to Lashman and watched as he first reviewed the call history and texts sent and received. Lashman found the tracker app and found that access was locked. Zachary told him the password. Lashman looked at the flashing triangles on the map.

"Does it say which triangle is whom?"

Zachary nodded. "Just tap them. You can label them whatever you like. You'll want… independent confirmation that none of them are her."

Lashman looked up at Zachary briefly and agreed. "Does it keep a history?"

"In my online account. I'll give you the login. You can erase information, though. I don't know if their server keeps a backup of what's been deleted somewhere."

Lashman nodded.

"I can tell you her usual routines," Zachary said. "Where she usually went and when." He glanced at Gordon. "I haven't been tracking her lately, I just know from before."

"Empty your pockets," Lashman directed.

Zachary looked at Lashman as if he might not have heard properly. But of course he had. If he'd been a police detective, he would have asked for the same thing.

"Detective, please don't arrest Zachary," Gordon begged. "I know it looks bad, but he didn't do anything to her. He couldn't. If anyone can find her, it's Zachary. Please."

"I'm not arresting him yet. But time is of the essence here and I'm not going to be *that guy*. The stupid official who didn't see what was right in front of his own nose and didn't take all of the proper evidence. I want the contents of your pockets, Mr. Goldman. Now."

Zachary didn't like it. "Can we go to another room? Maybe the kitchen? I don't want to contaminate this scene."

Lashman scowled, looking down at Bridget's desk. Then he nodded. They moved to the kitchen, as Zachary had suggested, and laid a plastic sheet over the table so that he had somewhere clean to put the contents of his pockets without compromising any prints or evidence that might be on the table itself.

As Zachary knew he would, Lashman picked up Zachary's keys. "We have your permission to search your car?"

Gordon started to protest, but Zachary held up his hand. "No. He has to. We don't want to waste time while he gets a warrant."

Lashman gave a curt nod and took the car keys off of the ring. He handed them to another officer. "We need a search of Mr. Goldman's car. Check the interior and trunk first, then get it towed to the lab for full forensics. What is it and where is it parked, Mr. Goldman?"

Zachary told them where to find it. Lashman looked down at the rest of the items that had been in Zachary's pockets.

"What are the pills?"

"They're prescription." Zachary indicated each in turn and told Lashman what they were.

"You know better than to be carrying pills around without the prescription bottle. You could be arrested for possession of controlled substances."

"Yes, sir."

Lashman could undoubtedly see how ridiculous it would be for Zachary to carry that many bottles of pills around with him. He apparently didn't see anything else suspicious in the miscellany that had been in Zachary's pockets. He opened Zachary's wallet with his gloved hands.

"Is this your current address?" He indicated Zachary's driver's license.

"No. I've just moved."

"You know you're required to update your records with DMV."

"Yes. I will."

"You'll consent to a search of your house? What's the address?"

Zachary sighed and gave it. Gordon was red-faced with outrage.

"I called Zachary for help because he knows Bridget and is a good investigator. He is not a suspect!"

"Everybody is a suspect," Zachary told him. "But especially me. And you."

"Me?"

"The spouse or significant other is always the prime suspect. And the ex-spouse."

"But I'm the one who called the police!"

Zachary shrugged. "You had to. It would look pretty suspicious if you didn't."

Lashman nodded his agreement. "This doesn't mean that I think either one of you did it," he assured them. "But I would be negligent if I didn't treat you as suspects. We can't afford to let any evidence fall through the cracks. She's already been missing more than twenty-four hours. If we don't get a lead pretty quickly..."

The florid color drained out of Gordon's face. Zachary grasped his arm and steered him into one of the kitchen chairs.

"It will be okay," he told Gordon. "We'll find her. It's going to be okay."

Gordon's bearing, previously stoic, was breaking down. He put his hands over his eyes, trying to hold himself together.

"It doesn't make any sense, Zachary. She wouldn't just leave. Somebody must have taken her."

"I know," Zachary agreed. "We need to work through this. We need to figure out who took her and why. The police can collect all of the evidence, but you and I are the ones who know her."

Gordon nodded. He wiped moisture from his eyes. "She would think it's hilarious that I'm the one who broke down instead of you."

Zachary took a long breath in and let it out. "I'm just trying to focus on what needs to be done. Can't afford to be emotional right now."

"You're right. So. What do you need? I already showed Detective Lashman her schedule. He'll follow up with everyone she's talked to the last few days."

"Is there... anyone she's had trouble with lately? Arguments? Strange phone calls?"

Gordon shook his head. "Nothing I'm aware of. But she didn't tell me everything. As you probably gathered the other day... she hadn't even told me about Robin's death. That was a pretty big deal and she didn't even mention it."

"Did she talk to you during the day yesterday? When is the last time you heard from her?"

"Tuesday when I left. I tried her a couple of times yesterday, between meetings, but I thought I was just calling at the wrong times. While she was having her hair done or was in a meeting."

"No bedtime call?"

Gordon rubbed his forehead. "Er... no. I had clients to entertain until late. She goes to bed pretty early. She needs a lot of sleep." He looked at Lashman. "She had cancer. Did I tell you that? It's in remission and she is building up her strength, but she still needs a lot of rest. I wouldn't call her after eight and risk disrupting her sleep for the night. If I woke her up, she might not get back to sleep again."

Zachary nodded.

Lashman spoke up. "So, we don't know whether she disappeared Tuesday after Mr. Goldman's call with her, or sometime Wednesday or even early today. We know she didn't show up for any appointments yesterday, so that suggests yesterday, but we can't be sure. She might simply have felt under the weather..."

"She wasn't here yesterday," Zachary told him flatly.

"How would you know that? You know she didn't answer your calls, but you said yourself she might just be avoiding your calls."

Zachary shook his head adamantly. "The flowers in her office."

"What about them?"

"The water in the vases is low and murky. Some of the flowers are starting to wilt. She didn't look after them yesterday morning and she certainly didn't change the water today."

"She might have forgotten. Been too busy."

"No. She wouldn't have neglected them."

"She might have been too sick or tired."

It was Gordon's turn to disagree. "We have a girl. She comes in and covers anything Bridget can't manage. If Bridget was too tired, all she had to do was make a phone call. Zachary's right. She wouldn't have neglected the flowers."

"It was that important to her?" Lashman was skeptical.

"They're a symbol of life and growth. Of her recovery. Neglecting them would be like..." Gordon struggled for the words.

"Like letting death into the house," Zachary suggested.

"Yes." Gordon agreed. "Like that. She would not let death into the house." He looked at Zachary. "Not knowingly."

They were both overcome for a moment.

"She's not dead," Zachary said. "I don't know what happened, but she's not dead."

"Okay." Gordon cleared his throat. As if by both of them agreeing to the fact, they could keep her alive. "She's not. She's okay. We just need to find her."

"Was your wife accustomed to taking walks? Or going off on her own to visit… I don't know… museums or craft fairs or some other interest."

"No. Bridget is very social. She isn't the type who sought out solitude. She liked to have people around her."

It had been a whole different world for Zachary. He had enjoyed it at first, having so many friends around. Being with Bridget and a coterie of admirers helped fill the empty space inside him. He'd led such a lonely existence for so many years. But it had also worn on him. Having people constantly around them. Not getting any time to just regenerate on his own. When he turned down invitations, he felt guilty and Bridget would be irritated with him. She would go on her own and he wouldn't hear the end of how she'd had to be there dateless. Bridget needed someone at her side. She needed people around her.

"How much do you know about their relationship?" Lashman asked Gordon, with a nod at Zachary. "When they were together?"

Gordon looked at Zachary uncomfortably. "Well… as much as you can know about someone else's relationship."

"Was their relationship abusive?"

Gordon's eyes avoided Zachary's and Lashman's.

"No. Not in the way you mean."

"In *any* way?"

"Zachary never did anything to harm Bridget…"

"Verbal or emotional abuse? I don't like the way you're avoiding the question, Mr. Drake."

"No, there was no verbal or emotional abuse… by Zachary."

Lashman stared at Gordon, his eyebrows drawn down, not comprehending.

"Gordon," Zachary protested.

Gordon shook his head unhappily. "If there was verbal abuse, then it was by Bridget, not Zachary."

2 2

It hadn't taken Lashman very long to decide he had reason to take Zachary in to the police station for questioning. Zachary didn't protest. He knew all of the indicators were there. He was an ex-spouse. They'd had a dysfunctional relationship when they were together and since then. Zachary was the last one to talk to her. All of those things were big red flags.

He sat alone in an interrogation room for what seemed like a long time. He was impatient to get out of there to investigate. The longer it took the police to let him go, the more time passed with Bridget gone, and the less likely it was that they'd be able to find her alive and well.

Eventually, Lashman returned to the room to continue the interview. He sat down and thumped a stack of papers down on the table in front of him.

"We've had someone looking at surveillance tapes taken in Bridget's neighborhood the past few days for any suspicious activity. Cross-checking license plates."

Zachary's stomach coiled as tightly as a spring.

"Maybe you'd like to guess at what we found."

Zachary gulped. "My license plate." His voice was strangled.

"Bingo. Your license plate. Your car. You in your car in the wee hours this morning, driving around Bridget's neighborhood. You want to explain that to me?"

He could have said it was because he had a surveillance job in the neighborhood. But there were probably enough cameras in the area that both his entrance and exit would have been well-documented, and they'd know that he hadn't been there for hours watching a certain house. He'd been there just long enough to cruise by her house a couple of times to reassure himself she was okay. Or maybe long enough to let himself in while Bridget slept and to take her away from there. Drug her, stuff her in the trunk, and take her out of there.

"I couldn't sleep. I was wound up. I was anxious. After a while, I started to worry about Bridget. If she was okay. So... yeah... I drove by her house."

"And what did you find?"

"There weren't any inside lights on. Just the usual security lights. I didn't see anybody hanging around."

"Except you."

"Only for a few minutes. I never went in. I just... checked."

"What made you think she might be in danger? It seems to me to be pretty coincidental that you would go to check on her around the time as she disappeared."

"I was worried. After seeing Stanley hanging around my apartment, it got me worrying about Bridget... if he knew who she was or where she lived—"

"Hold on." Lashman held up a hand. "Who is Stanley? What are you talking about?"

"Stanley Green. I got home at midnight, and he was loitering around the parking lot in the dark. I called the police, got them to move him on. There will be a record of it."

"Stanley Green."

"He was Robin Salter's fiancé ten years ago. Then they broke up. I talked to him about Robin and her family for some background. But then he showed up at my place..."

"Was he a suspect?"

"I... not really. He hasn't been around. He didn't visit Robin in the hospital, as far as I know, so he couldn't have given her anything."

"But then he was hanging around your apartment after that? Last night?"

Zachary nodded.

"And what did that have to do with Bridget?"

"Nothing. It just... wormed its way into my brain. I didn't know why he was there, and I started to worry about if he would go after Bridget, because she was the one who hired me." Zachary shook his head. "He didn't know Bridget. It was just... paranoia."

"You don't think he has anything to do with Bridget's disappearance."

"No. He didn't know anything about her."

"Unless he talked to someone else."

Zachary thought about that. Would Stanley have called the Salters after his interview with Zachary? To warn them about the investigation or to ask them why he was involved in it?

"I guess... but the medical examiner found cause of death, so there wasn't anything else for me to look into. I wouldn't have been investigating Stanley or anyone else any further."

Sitting in a jail cell shouldn't have been a problem for Zachary. It wasn't like he hadn't done it before. He'd been in the detention cells at Bonnie Brown, he'd been picked up by the police or put into custody while they tried to figure out what to do with him as a teenager. As a private investigator, he wasn't the type to break the law for a case. Not usually. But occasionally, he got run in anyway because of a cop who didn't like his involvement in an investigation or had some other beef with him.

But having been detained before didn't help him. Bridget was out there somewhere and he was being kept from the investigation. He should have been out there looking for her. Asking about her. Listening to the word on the street. Instead, he was stuck in a cell for just one reason: the fact that he had once been married to her. Everything else was just a nail in the coffin. His real crime was having been married to her.

Zachary paced back and forth across the small cell, which ended up being more like spinning in a circle because he couldn't take more than a couple of steps one way or the other.

"What the matter with you?" one of the other inmates demanded. As if Zachary needed to justify himself to a man whose yellow track suit made him look like a dirty banana. If wearing a getup like that wasn't a crime, it should have been. "This your first time in a cell?"

"No, it's not my first time. I'm just trying to think."

"What did you take? You're seriously amped up, dude."

"Nothing. I haven't taken anything."

"Yeah, right," the banana shared a laugh with the rest of the jailbirds. "You're that juiced but you didn't take a thing."

"Shut up and let me think."

The banana tried a few more lines, but when nothing was getting a rise out of Zachary or a laugh out of the rest of the inmates, he gave up and left him alone.

Who would want to hurt Bridget? Who would want to make her stop talking about Robin Salter? One of the medical staff? Surely they knew by now that the medical examiner had discovered Robin's iron overdose and there was no point in trying to keep Bridget quiet. Was it Stanley Green? He'd had nothing to do with Robin's death, there was no reason for him to go after Bridget. Lashman would have someone bring him in, but Zachary was confident it wouldn't amount to anything.

Maybe it was nothing to do with the investigation. Even though it was the first thing that came to Zachary's mind, there was no evidence that Bridget's disappearance had anything to do with the Salter investigation. Nothing at all.

Had a predator been watching her, observing her habits and figuring out the best time to strike?

Or was it an acquaintance or a business associate she had crossed and who wanted to get back at her? Bridget had a sharp tongue and Zachary was sure he wasn't the only one she had ever used it on. She wasn't afraid to voice her opinions. Especially after facing down cancer. *Life is too short to waste on being tactful and polite.* If people were going to be hurt by a few misplaced words, then they were going to go through life being wounded. Bridget didn't have time to be sensitive and politically correct. As numerous as the people who loved her were, she had her share of enemies or injured parties as well.

Gordon would know better than Zachary who Bridget might have had a falling out with lately. Hopefully, Gordon was telling them everything he could. Or maybe it was a business associate of Gordon's...

"Zachary."

He was so focused on his own thoughts, it took a few moments before he was able to take in Mario Bowman, standing in the corridor outside Zachary's cell, holding a folder and looking at him.

"Bowman? What are you doing here?"

"Zachary," Bowman stepped closer. His voice was low and confidential. "I had to bring these to you. I thought they might be important."

Zachary looked down at the file. Why would Bowman have any paperwork that would be important to him? His concern was with Bridget. That was where he had to stay focused. Zachary made a motion to wave him away.

"I heard about Bridget," Bowman said. His eyes were wide.

Zachary stared at Bowman hard, trying to determine whether he knew anything more than Zachary. *Was he sorry because they had found Bridget? Was she hurt? Dead?* He couldn't bear it if she were dead.

"Whoa, there." Bowman reached through the bars and held Zachary steady. "It's okay, brother."

"Have you heard something?"

"No. No one knows anything. They're looking for her. They're putting bulletins out on the TV, internet, everything. Drake has money. He'll spare no expense. They'll find her, Zachary."

Zachary nodded. He grasped the bars of the door to keep himself from shaking.

"I thought you needed these," Bowman said, proffering the file folder. "I thought they must be important."

Zachary automatically took the file folder, though he had no interest in anything except figuring out where Bridget was. He opened it and looked at the printed reports inside. Incident reports. He vaguely remembered asking Bowman for them, though all of the reasons had been driven from his mind. His hand was shaking too badly to make out the words. He sat down on the bunk and put them in his lap to hold them steady. He stared at the reports, trying to make the words stop swimming so that he could read them.

A domestic violence incident report between Robin Salter and Stanley Green. Zachary looked down the page to the description of the incident and only got a couple of lines in when he looked up at Bowman in disbelief.

"Stanley Green was the *victim?*"

Bowman nodded. "It happens more often than you might think. Sure, the majority of domestic violence reports are male on female, but there are still plenty that are women beating on men."

"Robin was the perpetrator."

"Yeah. Some of these women can be hellcats, you know." He opened his mouth to make a wisecrack, but then apparently thought better about what he was going to say and closed his mouth. "There are more in there."

Zachary flipped through the stapled reports, noting the parties on each. Robin Salter and Stanley Green. Robin Salter and Gloria Salter. Robin Salter and Vera Salter and Gloria Salter.

Zachary sat there on the bunk, his vision going white. Everything around him dissolved.

Robin Salter wasn't the victim of domestic violence. She was the abuser. The things Stanley had told Zachary came into sharp focus. *There were things happening in that family... it was very unhealthy. People... are not always what they seem. Relationships that look healthy from the outside... sometimes they aren't.* Zachary had thought that Stanley meant Grandpa Clarence was abusive. But he hadn't. He'd meant Robin.

She knew how to persuade other people around her to do things the 'right' way

She got more extreme. More... angry.

How had Zachary missed what Stanley was really trying to tell him? Zachary had taken one look at the big, broad man and assumed he was the abuser. It never occurred to him that the small, sick woman whose death Zachary was investigating had once terrorized him.

Zachary's head whirled. He pressed his fist to his forehead, trying to keep it all in logical order.

Where had Robin been when Clarence had died? Clarence and Rhys were at home, and Vera and Gloria were out, but where was Robin? Her name had been left out of the story completely. Had she been at Stanley's house? Out partying? Were the two of them out to dinner or running errands?

Someone had gone into the house and shot Clarence as he sat at the kitchen table. There hadn't been a fight. A burglary gone wrong, the police had suggested. But what would it take to make it look like a burglary? Move the electronics into a pile. Leave a few drawers open. A broken window would help to set the scene, but wasn't necessary. A high percentage of burglars simply entered through unlocked doors.

"Bowman."

The jail cell reformed around him. Bowman was still standing there, wide-eyed at Zachary's reaction to the reports.

"Yeah, I'm here, Zachary."

"I need Lashman. I need him right now."

"I don't think he's here. He's running the investigation into Bridget's disappearance…"

"I know. But this changes everything. I was wrong."

"About what?"

"About everything. Nothing is what it looked like. I need to tell him what's going on. Right now."

Bowman seemed to finally be getting the urgency of the situation. "This is something to do with Bridget?" he asked, pointing at the file folder.

"Yes. We need to get to her before it's too late." Zachary clutched the file. "If it's not too late already."

"Okay. I'll get ahold of him. I know who to call."

If anyone would know who to call, it was Bowman. He was the only person in the world who understood all of the politics and inner workings and motivations of the police department. It didn't matter if Lashman had said he wasn't to be disturbed, Bowman would find a way to get to him.

23

W hen Lashman got there and gave Zachary the stink-eye before unlocking the door to the cell, he wasn't prepared for the earful he was about to get.

"It wasn't Stanley," Zachary said urgently. "It wasn't Stanley and it wasn't a medical mistake. It was retribution. She had to make Robin suffer. She couldn't just let her die of natural causes. That wouldn't have served justice."

"What the hell are you talking about?"

Zachary waved the file folder at him. "I thought Stanley was abusive of Robin, but the domestic violence incident reports show that *she* was the aggressor, not him."

Lashman's eyes followed the folder. "Quit waving it in my face and let me see it," he growled, opening the cell door and taking the file folder from Zachary. "Slow down and start at the beginning."

Zachary let him have the folder. He blathered away to Lashman as they walked down the hallway, and it wasn't until they reached the end of the corridor that he realized the detective hadn't heard a word he had said. Zachary closed his mouth and waited. Lashman skimmed through the incident reports and then looked at Zachary, nodding.

"Okay, Robin Salter was the abuser, not the abused. Why does that matter?" Lashman led the way to an interview room. He motioned for

Zachary to take a seat, but Zachary couldn't sit down, not with everything bubbling up inside him.

"She was physically violent. It wasn't just verbal abuse, there was physical violence." Zachary tried to find the place in one of the incident reports. "She broke bones. She used weapons. If she didn't like the way you were doing something, she would show you the light. She wasn't a nice person."

"And you think that means what? I don't follow what it has to do with Bridget's disappearance."

"Her father was murdered."

Lashman blinked at him. "Mr. Goldman… those pills that you had with you earlier today…?"

"What?" Zachary didn't understand the segue.

"You missed taking something, didn't you?"

"No. I don't want to take anything. I need to stay clear."

"You're not making sense. I know you think you are, but you're not. I think you're… getting yourself confused."

"No." Zachary scowled. "You need to listen to the rest. This is bigger than anything we ever thought."

"Okay… tell me the rest. But realize that while you are explaining, you're keeping me from finding Bridget."

Zachary blew out his breath in exasperation. "You're not going to find her without me. I'm the only one who has put it together."

"Go." Lashman made an impatient motion. "Let's hear it."

"Robin's father was murdered. Clarence. At the time, the police thought it was a burglar, but it wasn't. Robin wanted everything done her way, and if it wasn't, she got mad. She got violent. I don't know what her father did that day, but she killed him. It wasn't a burglar. It was *Robin*."

"What's your evidence?"

"Her family knew. Maybe they were the ones who made up the burglary story in the first place. They covered for Robin. But they didn't know how it was going to affect the family. How it was going to *keep* affecting their lives for the next decade."

Lashman shook his head, but he was following Zachary so far.

"Gloria's son, Rhys, was home that night. He must have seen or known what happened. He had a nervous breakdown. He was just a little kid. They probably told him he dreamed it. They thought he would just forget it and that everyone could just go on as they had before."

Lashman swore. Zachary knew exactly how he felt.

"Yeah. They all stayed together. Rhys had to keep living in the same house as his grandfather's murderer. By now, maybe he's completely forgotten what happened, but the feelings aren't gone. He's still mute. He hasn't been able to deal with the fear and betrayal."

Zachary started to pace. He knew Lashman wanted him to sit down and take some kind of tranquilizer to settle him down, but it was suddenly all clear, and he couldn't waste one extra second explaining it.

"They were all still living together. Gloria started standing up for herself and her son and got her life together. But it was too late for Rhys, he was already damaged. Vera was starting to get forgetful. Maybe to the point where she couldn't remember what had really happened anymore."

"You don't know that, though. You're only speculating."

"I *know*. I can see it. I need my phone. Can someone get me my phone?"

"It's in evidence."

"I need it. I'll show you. You'll see."

Lashman shook his head in irritation, but he popped out the door to flag down another officer and explain what he needed. He returned to his conversation with Zachary.

"And how does this explain everything? It seems to me that you're just muddying the waters further. This doesn't bring us any kind of clarity."

"Robin was diagnosed with cancer. Whatever Gloria had been dreaming of doing to make things right, it was too late. She couldn't turn Robin in and expose her to the world. Robin would be dead before she could get to trial. There wouldn't be any justice. Robin would never have to pay the piper. Gloria had to think of something else to do instead."

"And you think she poisoned Robin," Lashman sighed, connecting it up at last.

"I know she did!" Zachary insisted.

The officer eventually returned with Zachary's phone. Zachary powered it on.

"Look. Look at this." Zachary went through his photographs. He found the ones he had taken of the Salters' medicine cabinet. "I took this picture before we knew what it was that had killed Robin. I was looking for insulin —which I now know would actually have been in the fridge. There were other prescriptions, so I took a picture of them... just in case. I thought maybe one of them had tried to stop Robin's suffering. A mercy killing. Euthanasia. Maybe even assisted suicide, without a physician's involvement. But it wasn't. Her death was meant to be painful. The hospital had to keep increasing her painkillers because of the damage the poison was doing to her system."

Lashman looked at the small screen. "I'm sorry, I'm supposed to be looking for…"

Zachary zoomed the image in. A pink and blue bottle from the hospital pharmacy. The silhouette of a woman on the front. 'Fe' in big block letters

"Iron."

Seconds ticked by while Lashman processed this.

"I'm sure a lot of women have iron supplements."

"It's clear liquid," Zachary pointed out. "Not pills. It could be injected directly into Robin's IV. No one would be the wiser."

"That's not proof."

"You need to get someone over to the house. Find out whose fingerprints are on the bottle. See if there are any syringes around. Find out if either Vera or Gloria was anemic. Find out if there was enough iron in that bottle to kill Robin, when added to the amount the hospital was giving her."

Lashman picked up his own phone and talked quietly to some assistant at a desk somewhere about getting a warrant for the Salter house to search for evidence that Vera or Gloria had given Robin a fatal dose of iron. He hung up.

"Now then; what does that have to do with Bridget?"

Zachary looked up from his phone. "Bridget stuck her nose into it. She wouldn't believe that Robin's death was natural. She asked me to investigate. The Salters all knew I was there because of Bridget. Gloria needed me to stop asking questions and knew I was only asking questions because Bridget was pushing me."

"But if Bridget disappeared, you wouldn't have any reason to keep investigating."

"Right."

"Wouldn't Gloria know that you would look into Bridget's disappearance? You would still be investigating, just from the other end of the problem."

"She must not have thought I would see the connection between Robin's death and Bridget's disappearance."

Lashman gave a grim smile. "Well, she was wrong there, wasn't she?"

Lashman returned and put a cup of coffee down on the table for Zachary.

"There's no one home at the Salters' house. Search team says it looks like they packed up and left in a hurry."

Zachary had been holding out hope that they would still be at the house, that maybe they would be holding Bridget there tied up in the basement. All they would have to do was search the house, Bridget would be found, and that would be all the proof they needed that Gloria had been involved in Robin's death and Bridget's kidnapping.

"What happened the last time you were there?" Lashman asked.

"At the house?" Zachary frowned. "I went over there after I heard what the medical examiner had found. Yesterday."

"To ask them about the iron in the medicine cabinet?"

"No. To tell them it had been a medical error. I didn't realize then that it had been intentional. I didn't know it was Gloria."

"If they knew the medical examiner thought it was accidental, why would they run?"

"Gloria wasn't there. She was at work. Rhys was at school. It was just Vera home alone. I don't know if she really understood what I was trying to explain to her. She was a little... distant."

"Do you think Gloria had already run?"

"No, they hadn't run yet, Vera was still home."

"There was a notice left at the house that Social Services was taking Vera into care. Dated yesterday."

Zachary swallowed and nodded. "I asked for a welfare check. The officers who came by said they would talk to Social Services and get ahold of Gloria. They told me to hit the road. I just assumed they would call Gloria home from work to deal with it..."

"Apparently they weren't able to contact Gloria. She hasn't been home or answered any calls."

"Then Gloria *had* already run when I went there. Monday or Tuesday. That would make sense... she knew an autopsy had been ordered, but didn't know the results yet. She was still ahead of the game." Zachary closed his eyes, concentrating on a mental image of the house that day. He reviewed the memory as if it were a photograph he had taken. "Rhys's book bag was on the floor. I thought he was at school, but he couldn't have been at school without his books. The house was a mess... like Vera might have been left alone to fend for herself for a couple of days..."

Lashman nodded. "Long enough to track Bridget down and to make a plan to take her. I'll get an APB out on Gloria's car."

24

The door opened, and instead of Lashman, it was Kenzie. Zachary blinked at her.

"Kenzie...? What are you doing here?"

"A mutual friend asked me to check in on you."

For just an instant, Zachary's mind went to Bridget. It made perfect sense, in that split-second leap, that it had been Bridget who had called Kenzie. But of course, it hadn't been. Bridget was gone and she had no way of even knowing where Zachary was, let alone that he could use a visitor.

"Bowman," he guessed.

"Yeah. He didn't want to make a second appearance in case there was trouble, so he asked if I would stop in." Kenzie looked around the bare interview room, as if looking for something to talk about. But of course, there wasn't anything. "Are you okay?"

Zachary gave a wide shrug. He didn't know how much she already knew about what was going on and he didn't know where to start

"Bridget is missing?" Kenzie said softly.

"You heard... yeah. I think she was kidnapped. I *hope*," Zachary's voice hitched on the word, "she was kidnapped."

Because the alternative was just too awful. If Gloria had murdered her sister, would she hesitate to kill again to cover it up? Zachary shut this thought away, pushing it out of his mind and refusing to consider it.

"Do you know who? Where she is?"

"It was Gloria Salter."

"Robin's sister?"

"Yes. Because she's the one who killed Robin." Zachary raised his eyes to Kenzie's. "It wasn't a medical error. It was intentional."

Kenzie's mouth hung open. She didn't argue and say that it wasn't possible, as Zachary had expected. Finally, Kenzie shook her head and spoke. "Are you sure?"

"It's the only thing that makes sense. And she's missing. Gloria. Looks like she ran a few days ago. Then took Bridget… Tuesday night, Wednesday morning… It's Thursday afternoon now." He swallowed, but it didn't get rid of the lump in his throat. "Bridget will think I don't care. She'll think I'm not coming."

"She knows you care," Kenzie assured him. "There can't be any doubt of that. She knows you'll be looking for her and you won't give up until you find her."

"How am I going to find her? I can't even get out of here. I can't do anything." Zachary smacked his palm down on the table, frustrated.

"If they know it's Gloria Salter who took Bridget, then they've got to release you."

"Tell Lashman that. I wasn't arrested as a suspect. He's holding me as a material witness."

"We both know that's just semantics. I'll go talk to him."

Zachary hadn't expected that Kenzie would actually talk to Lashman, but Kenzie ducked back out of the room and went to find him. Zachary watched the clock on his phone, getting more and more wound up, until he again couldn't sit still and got up to pace.

Lashman returned with Kenzie. He scowled at Zachary. "I don't want you getting in the way of this investigation."

"I'm not going to get in your way."

"What are you going to do? Because I don't believe for a minute that you're just going to drop it and leave finding Bridget Downy all up to us."

Zachary chewed on his lip. "Vera, I guess. She's the only one who might be able to tell us where Gloria would go."

"I've already had officers talking to her. She's too confused to be of any help."

"With all due respect," Kenzie said aggressively, "the odds that your officers will be able to drag information out of a senile old lady and the chances that Zachary can sit down with her and tease something useful out are not even in the same league."

Lashman bristled at this. "We can't have him contaminating a witness."

"If she's too confused for your officers to get the story out of her, then what's the problem with me talking to her?" Zachary asked. "You can't exactly get *less* than nothing out of her."

Kenzie snorted and covered her mouth.

Lashman glared, but Zachary thought he saw a hint of a smile on Lashman's lips as well. "I doubt she has any idea where Gloria went. Gloria wouldn't have told her and then left her behind."

"I'm not going to ask her where Gloria went."

The police detective gave Zachary a look like he was crazy. A look Zachary had seen plenty of times before. "Then what are you going to ask her?"

"I'm just going to have a chat with her. I might not ask her anything at all."

Kenzie laughed at Lashman's perplexed expression. "You've got to trust the process, detective. Come on. What's it going to hurt to let Zachary out of here? If he can find Gloria or Bridget, then that's good for everyone, isn't it?"

"What are people going to say if you don't let me?" Zachary played on the weakness Lashman had already shown, his worry about being the stupid cop. The one who let something important just slip through his fingers. "They'll say that you just let a resource go to waste. Someone who knew Bridget and was a skilled investigator. Someone who was more invested than anyone else in finding her. And instead of using me, you just kept me locked up."

"I don't know…" Lashman was softening. "If I screw this up by letting you go…"

"What if I stay with him?" Kenzie suggested. "I can keep an eye on him, make sure he's not going to run or screw up your investigation…"

Zachary glanced over at Kenzie, surprised. Did she want to be with him? Or did she just want to give Bridget the best chance at survival? Did she care about her rival? She'd been pretty chilly toward Zachary since he had taken Bridget's case on.

"Fine." Lashman growled. "If you think you can crack this case before the police department, you're welcome to it. But if I get word from my officers that you're getting in the way, or you mess with any of my witnesses and end up screwing up the case, don't think there won't be consequences."

Zachary was on his feet, nodding his agreement. "Yes, sir. I'm not going to screw anything up. Thank you!"

He didn't wait for Lashman to tell him they had to fill out a bunch of paperwork to get released. He didn't ask for the possessions he had turned over to the detective to be returned to him. He had his phone and nothing else was worth worrying about.

"Uh… I guess I need to know the facility they put Vera into, if you're willing to give it to me. And I wonder if I could go by her house and get a few things…"

"I can't have you touching things and contaminating evidence."

"Someone can go in with me. I won't touch anything important. I just want to get a few things that might help her to feel more at home. The more comfortable she is, the better the chances are that she'll be able to tell me something helpful."

"You're a pain, you know that? This is why we don't like private detectives."

Kenzie opened her mouth to protest.

"Yes, sir," Zachary agreed, motioning Kenzie to silence.

The detective looked sourly at the two of them. "Fine, then. She's at the East Side Care Center and I'll have someone meet you at the house. Are you going straight over there now?"

"Yes."

"Someone will be waiting for you."

Zachary took his leave before Lashman could think of anything else to delay them. "You can drive?" he asked Kenzie.

"You don't want to take your car?"

He shook his head quickly. "It's… unavailable right now."

"Oh." She paused, considering whether to get more details, then decided not. "Well, you know I love to drive, so that's fine. And it's been in the police parking garage, so I know it hasn't been tampered with."

Zachary was thinking about his spark plugs being pulled as he folded himself into Kenzie's little red sports car.

"So, what are you picking up at the house?" Kenzie asked, after getting the address.

"Just some things to make her comfortable," Zachary repeated.

Kenzie kept looking at him expectantly when the police officer let them into the Salters' house. Like she was expecting him to suddenly find Bridget or an important clue, or maybe to do a back flip. She didn't believe that he was just there to pick up items to make Vera more comfortable and at home.

Zachary didn't want to take too long, but he didn't want to rush it, either. It was probably his only opportunity to look through the house, so he didn't want to miss anything important.

"Take pictures of each room," he suggested to Kenzie, motioning to her phone. "Just in case we miss something."

"What do you want me to take pictures of?"

"Everything you can."

"Hey," the policeman objected, when Kenzie started to do so. "You can't do that."

"We're not tampering with anything," Zachary said. "And we're not sending them to anyone. They're just for reference in the investigation."

"You don't have permission to do that."

"I have permission to be here. No one said we couldn't take pictures."

The house was just as Zachary had left it on Wednesday when he talked to Vera and had the police check on her welfare. They had taken her out of the home, and no one had been there until the police arrived to execute their search warrant.

It was obvious that Gloria had left in a hurry. There was a lot of stuff thrown around the rooms in the whirlwind of packing in both Gloria's and Rhys's rooms. Vera's and Robin's did not appear to have been touched.

The police had processed the house. The iron supplement was gone from the bathroom and the mirror and other surfaces had been dusted for prints. They didn't appear to have touched much else.

Kenzie studied each of the items Zachary picked up and showed to the police officer to get permission for their removal. A quilt. A sweater. A photo album.

"I don't really understand this. Why are these things important?"

Zachary glanced at the policeman. "They're not. They're completely unimportant." He looked through the living room and kitchen to find Vera's favorite mug. She'd had it on the table beside her both times he had visited her. He found it in the kitchen and showed it to the officer.

"Can I take that? It's dirty, I'll need to wash it."

The policeman inspected the mug, then shrugged. "Go ahead."

"Why don't you find the tea while I'm washing this?" Zachary suggested to Kenzie. "It smelled like peppermint."

Kenzie didn't move. Zachary cleared enough space in the sink to wash the mug, and while he scrubbed it, she finally did as he asked and looked through the drawers and the canisters on the counters until she came up with a tin of tea bags. The peppermint smell wafted over Zachary when she popped the lid to have a look inside.

"That's it," he confirmed.

"Okay. We've got her mug and her tea. And her blanket, sweater, and photo album."

"That should do it."

The police officer had one more look through everything before allowing Kenzie and Zachary to take them out of the house. Zachary packed everything but the photo album carefully into the small trunk of the sportster. He put the photo album in his lap and paged through it as Kenzie drove them to the care facility.

2 5

Vera sat in a bed in a hospital-like room at the care facility, looking anxious and confused. She didn't remember who Zachary was and snapped at him about when she was going to be able to go home.

When Zachary brought out the quilt and spread it over the bed, she patted at it, making soothing sounds. She pulled it close and snuggled into it.

"You probably don't need this," Zachary displayed the sweater. "Not with the quilt on. But if you decide to get up and walk around, you might want something to put on."

"No, I want it now," Vera disagreed. "Help me put it on."

She leaned forward away from the pillows and Zachary helped her to thread her arms into the sleeves and straightened it out. She lay back again, and he did the zipper up.

"There. That's very pretty. It's a nice color on you."

Vera smiled and patted at her hair, making sure it was all neatly in place. Zachary reached back to take the mug of hot tea from Kenzie. One of the nurses had been kind enough to let him use the electric teakettle in the staff kitchen to prepare it.

"Here, it's very hot, so you'll have to be careful and let it cool down for a few minutes."

Vera held the mug under her face and inhaled the peppermint scented steam. "Oh, this is my favorite," she said happily. "How did you know that?"

Zachary sat down on the visitor chair, which put him closer to her eye level. "There, that's better, isn't it?"

Vera nodded. She reached out for Zachary, and when he extended his hand, she patted it. "You're such a nice boy. How did you know just what to do?"

Zachary shrugged. He'd been moved around enough times to understand how much a few precious possessions could mean. "How are you feeling? Are you okay?"

"Oh, yes. I feel fine. I don't know why they brought me here. I'm not sick."

"I think they were just worried about you being alone, with Gloria being away."

Vera thought about that for a minute. "But where did she go? This is all so sudden!"

"I know. She and Rhys had to go, didn't they? It must have felt strange, being all alone in the house."

"I'm used to being alone. During the day, anyway. The girls work, and Rhys goes to school. Clarence is long gone, so it's just me there during the day. At night..." She frowned and shook her head. "I'm not used to that. It's a little bit *scary*."

"You must be glad that you were here last night, where you didn't have to be alone."

Vera brightened at that. "Yes. It was much better."

Zachary didn't look at Kenzie. They had both heard the staff talking about how Vera had whined and complained all night that she just wanted to go back home. It was better if Vera remembered being happy to be there at night, even if it wasn't true.

"I brought some pictures." Zachary pulled out the photo album and rested it across Vera's lap. "I thought you could tell me about your family. About Clarence, and the girls when they were younger. And Rhys."

Vera squealed in delight. She ran her hands over the ornate cover as if she hadn't seen it in years, instead of having looked at it with Zachary only a few days earlier. "You brought my pictures! You are in for a real treat. Let me show you..." She opened the photo album reverently. Zachary scooted closer to look at it. It was the same album as he'd looked at with Vera before, but he knew more about the family this time. He wasn't going into it blind like he had at the beginning. If he was right, Clarence had been murdered by his own daughter, not killed in a burglary. And the others had covered it up. Gloria, at least, knew what had happened. Maybe she knew at the time, and maybe she had learned since, but she hadn't gone to the police and told them what she knew. Her son had suffered for years and the resentment between Robin and Gloria had grown.

"Here is me and Clarence." Vera started at the beginning, with what might have been an engagement photo of her and her husband. As much as Zachary wanted to race on ahead, he looked at their faces and their body language and tried to put together the story that they told without words. Vera took him through the births of the two girls.

Zachary looked at them together, looked at them with their father. He was still suspicious of Clarence abusing the girls. That was the story he was accustomed to hearing. Robin must have had a good reason for killing him. Women didn't just go around killing their fathers out of the blue. Had Clarence abused them as little girls? Had he been too strict? Molested them? Zachary wouldn't have guessed it from the pictures. The girls were usually smiling or laughing. They didn't seem awkward or afraid when Clarence was in the same picture.

"What was Clarence like as a father?"

"He was a good daddy." Vera sighed. "I know he wished that he could have been home more to spend more time with them. He worked a lot when they were little. Long hours. They barely saw him during the week. Just on the weekend, when he got a break. And he'd be so tired he'd just fall asleep in front of the game on the TV."

"Did he get mad when they bothered him? Yell at them?"

"Everybody yells sometimes. He was a good daddy."

Vera reached for her mug. Zachary handed it to her and watched like a hawk to make sure she was steady enough to take it and that it wasn't too hot. He didn't need her dumping scalding tea all over herself. When she'd had a sip, he took it from her and put it down on the side table.

"And then when they were older, he didn't have to work so much?"

Vera was looking at pictures of the girls as they got older. Graduation pictures. Boyfriend pictures. The pictures of Gloria with Rhys, looking awkward and posed.

"How did Clarence feel about Gloria getting pregnant? I'll bet that was a shock."

"Well, neither of us was happy about it, I'll tell you that. But shocked? No. Gloria was wild. She wouldn't listen. Sneaked out at night. Who knows how much drinking and drugging she was doing. She wasn't a nice girl. Not like Robin."

"Robin didn't run wild like that?"

"No. She was more careful. The older one is always the perfectionist. Tries to show Mom and Dad that they can do everything right. Gloria was never like that. She was always looking for her own way to do everything."

"But you took her and the baby back."

"How could we not? She couldn't take care of a baby by herself. That child would have been abandoned in a garbage can or on the street. We had to look after him. And we hoped that she would learn to take some responsibility, get back on track. Turn her life around."

"I guess it worked," Zachary offered. "She seems much better now."

Vera frowned for a moment, then her brow smoothed again. "Yes, she's a very nice girl now. Very responsible. A good mom to Rhys. It took her a long time to get there, but she got herself turned around."

Zachary looked down at the page. Gloria with Rhys. Grandpa Clarence holding Rhys, laughing. A couple of random shots of Robin or Gloria by themselves. Robin and Vera making Christmas cookies.

Zachary's stomach tightened, thinking of Christmas preparations. He still couldn't think about getting ready for Christmas without a feeling of panic.

"How did Gloria and Robin get along, after Rhys was born? Robin was older, it must have been strange for her to have a little sister with a baby."

"Yes, they didn't get along too well together." Vera's lips twitched. She was looking at the pictures, her eyes far away. "Robin was going through a difficult time."

"Oh?" Zachary glanced over at Kenzie. She sat quietly, listening to the stories, staying out of Zachary's way and not attracting Vera's attention. Vera might not have even been aware that Kenzie was in the room. "What was she having a difficult time with? I'll bet it was boys."

Vera chuckled. "Robin never had problems with boys. She always had a boyfriend, and others waiting in the wings for her to break up and give them a chance. She was my social butterfly. Always getting ready for this party or that dance. She knew everybody in her school. She even ran for school president."

"She seems like a very capable woman. So what was bothering her? You said she was going through a difficult time."

"You know how it is." Vera sighed. "When they go through puberty, things can get a little crazy. Teenage girls are so emotional. They can get quite unbalanced."

"What did she do?"

Vera turned over the next page slowly. "It wasn't one thing... it was a build-up over time. We just didn't know what to do with her. She would get angry over the littlest thing. Hysterical tears. All kinds of drama. Everybody was out to get her. Nobody understood her. Everybody was talking about her behind her back."

"Was she just hormonal? Or mentally ill?"

"There wasn't anything wrong with her," Vera assured him. "She's a very nice girl and everything is good now. She just went through that little stretch as a teenager. It was hard for her after Rhys was born. Here was her sister getting all kinds of attention and Robin, the perfectionist, wasn't getting any. We were too busy trying to raise Rhys and get Gloria onto a better track. We didn't have any time to give to Robin." Vera raised her eyes from the photographs and looked at Zachary. "It was a matter of life and death," she said. "Robin didn't understand that, but it was true. She couldn't see that we were trying to keep Gloria from doing something that would harm Rhys, or harm herself. She thought Gloria was just being a bratty little sister."

"Did she... get any treatment? Counseling?"

Vera turned the page. Rhys older in these pictures. Sitting in his mother's lap. Sitting in Robin's. A round-faced, smiley little toddler, beaming at the camera.

"She needed some help," Vera admitted. "She needed someone to talk to. It was hard for her. She didn't understand that what she was going through was normal. Everybody has a hard time. Growing up isn't easy."

"No. Is that what the doctor said? That she was just acting out?"

"Oh, what do doctors know?" Vera asked irritably. "They put us off for years. There's nothing wrong, it's just hormones. Try these antidepressants. Try tough love. Make her do things for her sister. She tried. We all tried."

Zachary looked down at the pictures. Robin's smiling face, carefully posed for the camera, gave nothing away. She had put up walls. She had tried, like Zachary had tried, to deal with the meds and their side effects and the doctors with conflicting opinions, and with parents who couldn't understand what she was going through. And she'd put on a brave front and tried to pretend to be normal for everyone else. While under the surface, the anger bubbled away.

Was it the first time she had been violent? All of the incident reports Zachary had were after Clarence's murder. Had they been afraid to do anything before that? Afraid that if they reported Robin, it would ruin her life? So they kept ignoring it and sweeping it under the carpet, until everything exploded and it was too late to put Humpty Dumpty together again.

"Robin fought with Clarence, didn't she?" he suggested.

"All kids fight with their parents. It's part of growing up. They need to learn to be independent."

"She wasn't a teenager anymore," Zachary pointed to a picture of Robin. "She must have been out of school at this point. She should have been past all of the rampaging hormones and been settling down."

"She was trying. I know she was trying. She struggled so hard to be what everyone wanted her to be. The perfect student. The perfect daughter. The perfect worker. I told her she didn't have to be perfect for me. It was okay for her to make mistakes and to let us know when she was feeling down. She didn't have to be happy and gracious all the time for everyone."

"Wearing a mask."

"That's what she said. She always had to wear a mask. She could never show anybody what she was really like underneath. Because it was too awful. I didn't believe that. I knew she was mixed up. Things were messy inside. But she was my daughter. I knew she was a good girl. No matter how hard it was for her to do the right things, she was really a good girl inside."

Vera turned a couple more pictures. Zachary knew they would soon reach the end of the pictures of Clarence. Clarence most often was with Rhys. Fishing with him, doing woodwork or other kinds of handyman work. The boy obviously idolized his grandpa and spent as much time as he could with him.

"Grandpa's little shadow."

Vera nodded, a sweet, sad smile on her face. "Oh, yes. Grandpa's little shadow. They were inseparable. I always said to Clarence, 'what are you going to do when he has to go to school? How is he going to be able to go by himself when you spoil him all the time?' He always just shook his head and said it would all work out in good time. Who knew how long he had to spend with his grandson?"

Tears started to leak out the corners of her eyes. Because Clarence had been right. He had been right to spend as much time as he could with his grandson, because in the end, he was going to be taken away long before his time.

"And then you came home one day, and you saw what Robin had done."

Vera didn't disagree. She continued to dab at the tears, mourning her departed husband.

"Did you know before then that she might hurt someone? Had she ever hurt anyone before that?"

Vera sniffled. "Not… like that. She would get out of control. I knew it wasn't her fault. She couldn't help it."

"And what would happen? She hit you?"

Kenzie shifted in her seat, distracting Zachary's attention. He darted a look over at her, and saw her wide, worried eyes. He pushed them out of his mind and focused on Vera.

"She'd hit you," he suggested. "Probably more than once. She'd left you with bruises."

"It wasn't her fault. The doctor kept saying that if he could just get her medications right, she would be fine."

"She'd broken bones. You didn't tell anyone?"

"We said… they were accidents. And they were, because they were out of her control. She never meant to hurt anybody."

"And Rhys?"

Vera shook her head slowly. "You have no idea what it was like trying to raise that boy. His mother running around all over town, acting like a little hussy. Coming home drunk or as high as a kite. So irresponsible. And Robin… she was trying so hard. She wanted so badly to be a good girl. She really did. But no matter what they gave her…"

"It never worked."

"She didn't deserve to be punished." Vera blinked her big, dark eyes at Zachary. "Gloria said she should be punished for what she did. Put in prison. Gloria was the irresponsible one. Robin shouldn't have to be put in prison when she was trying so hard."

"You all knew she was the one who had killed Clarence. You knew there was no burglary."

"We didn't know what had happened," Vera insisted. "We didn't see it. We could only piece it together, we could only guess."

"What about Rhys? Was he a witness? Grandpa's little shadow?"

"He was in his bed, curled up tight in a little ball. *Just stop it. Just stop it.*"

"Stop what?"

"It was Robin's voice. What Robin would say when someone was 'driving her crazy.' Chewing too loudly or fidgeting or doing something else she couldn't stand. Rhys kept repeating it over and over. *Just stop it.*"

Vera reached to turn the page. Zachary put his hand out to stop her from turning it. He wanted to hear more about that day. To understand why Clarence had died and why everyone had covered it up.

Vera glared at him and with a force he hadn't expected, pulled the photo album away from him and turned to the next page.

"Poor little Rhys," she said in a faraway voice. "He was so sad after Clarence died."

"He had to go to an institution."

"You don't put a little boy in a place like that... but we didn't know what else to do. He was falling apart."

"And Robin? Did you send her away?"

She wasn't in any of the pictures on that page, nor on the next.

"I couldn't," Vera said. "People would know what had happened. We had to make things look normal. She was different after that." Vera's brows furrowed, and she shook her head. "She had changed."

"How had she changed?"

"She wasn't my sweet girl anymore. She wasn't... innocent anymore."

Or maybe Vera had stopped seeing her as the little girl trying to be good and saw what she had become; a jealous woman who had to have everything her way. Who had taken her own father's life over some petty bother.

"You started calling the police when she got out of control."

"She was very angry about that. Stanley left her, said he couldn't deal with it anymore. Up until then... I had thought she would settle down with him. She would get married and she'd have someone giving her all of the attention she needed. She would be out of the house and we could live in peace."

"You must have found something that worked eventually. The calls to the police stopped. Rhys came home and you were all living together again."

"It was a hard time." Zachary was sure that was an understatement. "Making sure that Rhys was safe... Robin knew if she ever did anything to hurt him, she would go to jail. We didn't talk about it, but we never left him alone with her. Never left her to watch him."

Zachary couldn't imagine what it had been like for the boy. To have had to live in the same house as a woman he knew to be a murderer. Unable to tell anyone what had happened. He looked at the boy's sad face in all of the pictures after Clarence's death. Gloria had finally grown up and taken responsibility, but she couldn't fix the damage that had been done. She lived every day with the knowledge that Robin had never been punished for what she had done. Then she was faced with the fact that Robin was going to die without ever being punished. Poisoning her must have seemed like such a small satisfaction. A few days of suffering, after all that they had suffered over the years. One tiny retribution; depriving Robin of her last few months of her life.

Zachary wondered whether Vera knew what Gloria had done. Had Gloria told her? Had she watched Gloria inject the iron into the IV? Approved of it? As much as he wanted to know and to get a clear picture, that wasn't the most important thing. It was more important to keep Vera talking. If she clammed up, there was no chance of finding out where Gloria might have gone with Bridget. Zachary studied the pictures as Vera turned the pages. Rhys's growing-up years. Moving from boyhood to a gangly teenager. His face always worried or sad.

There was a candid shot of him looking down, intent on something in his hands. Playing an electronic game or texting with a friend.

Zachary's sudden movement startled Vera. She looked at him, eyes wide as he dug the phone out of his pocket. "Did you get a call? I didn't hear it ring."

Zachary shook his head. "Does Rhys ever send you messages on your phone? Maybe pictures or a text message?"

26

Vera's eyes were wide.

"Rhys sent me a few messages," Zachary said. He was working out the timeline in his head. The friend request from Rhys had come Monday after Zachary had been at the house. Rhys had come out to see his grandma while Zachary was there and had been hustled back away to his room. After Zachary had left, Rhys had tracked down Zachary's social media account to connect with him. Vera must have told him who Zachary was and why he was there.

Zachary looked at those first messages. Sad faces. First the basset hound and then the emoticon. Zachary had thought that Rhys was sad about Robin's death. But Rhys had been sad a lot longer than that. He was sad about losing his grandpa. About the horrible situation he found himself in, living with someone who might cause him harm if given the opportunity. Unable to make his voice heard and to be safe.

When Zachary had said he was sorry about Robin's death, Rhys had responded with a picture of his family. The three women together, with him posed in front of them. What had he been trying to tell Zachary? Not that he missed Robin and was sad she had died, but that this was how he had lived, trapped in a home built of secrets, lies, and abuse? How had he felt looking at that picture, with the women's plastic smiles trying to hide what had happened all those years ago? Did Rhys remember what had happened?

Or had they managed to erase that night from Rhys's conscious memories, leaving him with just a feeling of dread and danger and deep unhappiness day after day.

"You must miss her a lot," Zachary had written back, not understanding, and Rhys had not responded.

Were they already on the run? Was Zachary the one lifeline that Rhys had reached out to, hoping a private investigator would understand and be able to help? But Zachary had not understood.

"What did he send you?" Vera asked, her head turned to try to see the messages Zachary was looking at.

Zachary thumbed to the next message. Wednesday. The day Gloria had taken Bridget. Zachary held the phone where Vera could see the picture of the moving gif of a fat dog stuck in a toilet bowl. *Help me.*

"Oh, look at that," Vera said, with a catch in her throat. "Isn't that funny."

But she didn't say it like it was funny. Did she know that Rhys really had been begging for help? She had known the boy since he was born. She had communicated with him throughout all of his mute years and had probably seen similar pictures or messages. She had the insight into Rhys's mind that Zachary lacked. She probably knew that, far from simply sharing a funny picture with Zachary, Rhys had been reaching out, begging for help.

And then the last picture Rhys had sent to him. He didn't show that one to Vera. A cartoon character surrounded by walls of flame. *Everything is going to be just fine.*

Knowing what he did now, Zachary had a chill at the ominous picture. Where was Rhys? What hell was he going through? Did he know that Gloria had killed Robin? Did he understand why Gloria had taken Bridget? Did he know what was going to happen next?

Zachary had waited patiently for responses from Rhys. He had not wanted to push Rhys away by being too nosy. He had just accepted that Rhys would message him back again when he was comfortable doing so, sending him another amusing picture or cryptic message.

But he couldn't wait any longer. Zachary tapped the field to enter his own message to Rhys.

Where are you?

He looked over at Kenzie. She inched her chair a little closer to him. "Rhys has been messaging with you?"

"Just twice," Zachary said, looking down at his phone and willing Rhys to message him back again. "On Monday and on Wednesday."

"And Wednesday…" Kenzie trailed off.

Zachary nodded.

Vera was watching them, looking troubled. Zachary drew her attention back to the photo album. "Did you ever go somewhere on vacation?" he prompted. "Somewhere you went with the whole family? Or maybe somewhere you and the girls and Clarence went, when they were young? Before Gloria started getting into trouble."

Vera looked back down at the album. She turned a couple of pages slowly. "We didn't have a lot of money. There was no Disneyland or anything like that."

"No," Zachary agreed. "Maybe a road trip? A cabin in the woods or somewhere Gloria really loved?"

Vera's expression was vague. Her eyes went over the pictures of Rhys and her daughters. "A cabin?" she echoed. Zachary watched her eyes, trying to read whether she was remembering something or just repeating his words.

Zachary's phone vibrated in his hand and he looked down at it. There was an answer from Rhys, but again, it was in the form of a picture. Zachary stifled a groan. Rhys was capable of writing a short answer, that's what Gloria had told him. So why couldn't he give Zachary a word or two pinpointing his location instead of making him interpret a picture?

"What is it?" Kenzie asked.

"A fish." Zachary showed it to Vera. "Where would Gloria and Rhys go that there were fish?"

Vera smiled. "Rhys used to love to fish."

"He used to go with Clarence, didn't he?" Zachary encouraged. "Where did they like to go?"

"They went lots of different places. There are many good fishing spots around here."

"Yes, there are," Zachary agreed. He had never been fishing in his life and had no idea where the popular fishing spots would be. "Did Gloria ever go with them?"

Vera shook her head. "Gloria didn't like fishing. Neither of the girls did. They were city girls, both of them."

"They never went somewhere there was also fishing?"

Vera looked blank.

Frustrated, Zachary tapped a message back to Rhys.

Need more. Want to help but don't know where u r.

Zachary pictured Rhys, hunched over his phone in some McDonalds or somewhere else with public wifi, pretending he was playing a game while Gloria ordered their dinner. Or closeted in a bathroom out of her sight, with only a few minutes to get his message to Zachary.

The phone vibrated. Zachary stared at the picture of Snoopy from the Peanuts comic strip. Smiling and dancing with his feathered friends.

"Come on, Rhys," he murmured. "I'm not getting it. Kenzie, can you think of anything? Vera?"

He showed the picture to each of them. Vera smiled and said "Snoopy!"

"Does Snoopy mean anything? Did Rhys go somewhere with Snoopy as a kid? Did he have a Snoopy toy? A dog? A beagle?"

"No. We never had a dog, though Rhys has always liked them. We couldn't have one; Robin was allergic."

Vera's forehead wrinkled and she looked to the side, giving off clear signals she was lying. She reached for her tea and Zachary again guided her hands to make sure she was steady with it. Though it was cooling now and would only be uncomfortable if she spilled it.

"Robin wasn't allergic to dogs," he said.

Vera's lip stuck out in an exaggerated pout. Kenzie looked at Zachary. "How do you know that?"

"Because she wasn't, was she?" Zachary directed it back at Vera again, who shook her head and didn't fill in the rest of the details. "But maybe it was Robin that prevented you from having a dog even though Rhys loved them." He searched her eyes. "Did Robin not like dogs, so Rhys couldn't have one? Or maybe you were afraid she would hurt a dog. You couldn't get one in case it got underfoot and Robin hurt it. It was hard enough keeping track of Rhys and keeping him out of her way."

Vera looked at Zachary in dismay. Zachary pursued it, not because he wanted to hurt her, but because he had to figure out where Gloria had gone with Rhys.

"Was there a place they would go to get a dog? If Gloria decided it was okay to have a dog now that Robin wasn't around anymore, was there a farm or supplier that they might have gone to?"

"No."

"Rhys never had a dog? Even for a few days? A stray he had to get rid of?"

"No," Vera insisted. "We never had any animals. It just wouldn't have been good. Things upset Robin. Things irritated her. Animals... you can train a dog, but you can't make sure it never does anything to irritate her"

"What do you think of when you look at this picture?" Zachary showed it to them each again. "Snoopy... happy... dancing..."

"Peanuts, Charlie Brown," Kenzie contributed. "Charles Schultz. Chuck."

"Flying, birds," Vera said, getting into the spirit of things. "Yellow. Flapping. Woodstock."

"Woodstock!" Zachary said. "That's it. That's gotta be it. Did Rhys or Gloria ever go to Woodstock?"

"The music festival?" Kenzie asked, puzzled.

"No. Woodstock, New Hampshire." Zachary looked at Vera. "Did any of you ever go to Woodstock, New Hampshire?"

"Rhys went fishing there with Clarence," Vera said slowly, seeming uncertain. "Is that... is that what you meant?"

"Yes. Tell me about that. Where did they go in Woodstock? Where did they stay? In a hotel? Did they camp?"

"I don't know..." Vera touched the photo album uncertainly.

Zachary reached over and turned the pages, running the clock back until he saw a picture of Clarence again. "Is there a picture in here? Of Woodstock?"

"Maybe..." Vera's voice wavered.

Zachary scoured the pages. He pointed to a picture of Rhys standing with his grandfather, green leaves behind them.

"What about that? Is that in Woodstock?"

"It might be..." Vera leaned over it to study it more carefully. "Yes... I think it might be..."

Kenzie got up from her chair and leaned over the picture as well.

"Where did they stay?" Zachary prompted again. "This looks very rustic." He could see just the corner of a building, gray weathered wood. "Did they have a cabin here? Was there a fishing lodge?"

Vera nodded. "I don't remember the name of it. Clarence rented it from an Indian fellow. He wanted a real fishing experience with Rhys. Getting up before the dawn. Frying their own fish over the fire for breakfast. It was supposed to be a *guys'* vacation."

Zachary cocked his head at her wording. "It was *supposed to be*. But then what happened?"

"Gloria decided that Rhys was too young. He couldn't go with Clarence without Gloria or me there to supervise. Clarence was wonderful with Rhys, but he wasn't a mother. A mother knows when her child is sick and what to do about it. And doesn't let him get caught on a fishhook. Or fall in the lake and drown. She didn't think that Clarence would be responsible enough. And she thought that Rhys might miss her and get homesick. Then they would have to come back and not have their special weekend."

"She wanted to go along," Zachary summarized.

"Well, what woman would want to go along on a fishing trip like that? She didn't want to, but she didn't think Rhys was old enough to go on his own. So she insisted she had to come along too."

Zachary exchanged looks with Kenzie. "So she went. She knows where this cabin is."

"Cabin!" Vera made a noise. "It wasn't anything more than a shack. Gloria said it had running water, but no electricity, no shops within walking distance. It was in the middle of nowhere."

"Do you know exactly where it was? Do you have a map? The name of the fellow Clarence rented it from?"

"No… I don't know. I wasn't there, so I don't know, exactly. But it was Woodstock," Vera nodded definitely. "I know that for sure."

"We'll find it," Zachary said. "Woodstock is no bigger than a postage stamp. There could only be a handful of people renting out cabins there. I might be able to get more details from Rhys once we're there and he can tell us what's close by."

"You did it," Kenzie breathed. "I can't believe you figured it out. We should call Detective Lashman and let him know."

Zachary swore.

Kenzie looked at him, frowning. "What? What's wrong?"

"They crossed state lines."

"Is that a problem?"

"Not only is it out of Lashman's jurisdiction, that makes it an FBI case."

"That's good. FBI has great resources."

Zachary looked at the time on his phone. If he told Lashman and

Lashman told the FBI, they would start looking Saturday morning. Bridget would have been missing for four days. Being past the first forty-eight hours, the FBI would assign it a lower priority. There was less likelihood of retrieval. If Gloria had not been taking care of Bridget's needs, death was a real possibility.

He wished he'd been able to ask Rhys more questions and that Rhys had been able to answer him more clearly.

"We have to go. We'll call Lashman on the way and give him a heads-up. He can call the feds, and if they get there before we do, more power to them. But I can't sit and wait on them."

"I don't know…"

"If you're afraid of getting in trouble, I can take your keys and go without you. Just give me a head start before you call and report it." Zachary stood up.

"Oh, you're not driving my baby without me!" Kenzie shot back.

"Then let's go. If you really don't want to come, then drop me at a car rental. But if you're just afraid of what the cops or Dr. Wiltshire will say, I'll happily agree that I coerced you. Or that you were worried about my stability." He gave her a hard, forced smile. "You *are* worried about my stability, aren't you?"

"I'm always worried about your stability," Kenzie agreed. "Especially wherever Bridget is concerned."

"Then let's hit the road."

Vera was looking at them, a puzzled crease in her forehead. Zachary bent over and kissed her cheek.

"Thank you, Vera. You were a big help. We're going to go now, to go help Rhys."

"Okay," Vera agreed, giving him an uncertain smile. "Thank you."

27

They hit the road. It was probably a good thing that Kenzie was the one who was driving, because once Zachary sat down in the car, he found himself shaking all over. Kenzie didn't say anything at first as they headed east on the highway. But after a while, she looked over at him.

"Are you okay?"

"How could I be? Bridget could be hurt or sick. She could be dying. She's going through who-knows-what hell, and I'm sitting around having tea and looking at pictures with an old woman. Do you know how that feels?"

"But it worked. You never would have been able to figure it out without getting Vera to talk to you. You did the right thing."

"I should have figured it out sooner. I should have figured out that Bridget was missing on Tuesday! How could she be missing for three days before I knew it?" Zachary's voice rose. He knew it wasn't Kenzie's fault. He shouldn't be yelling at her. But he was feeling bad. Overwhelmed and inadequate and too late.

"Because you thought she was just avoiding you. You thought she had what she needed and just didn't want to talk to you."

"How could I think that about her?"

"Because it's probably true," Kenzie said calmly. "That's exactly what she would do. Why feel guilty for that? You're doing everything you can to help her. You've been able to get further than Detective Lashman with all of his personnel and resources. That's why Gordon called you."

"He called me to find out if Bridget was with me."

Kenzie turned her gaze away from the highway to look at him. "Do you seriously think he thought Bridget was with you? When he realized that she hadn't been home in a day or two, he thought maybe she had shacked up at your place? Or maybe the two of you were out having brunch? Gordon Drake didn't get to where he is today by being stupid. He called you because he knew you were the best man for the job. He called the police to cover all his bases, but he called you first."

It was hard for Zachary to believe. He shook his head and looked out the window, wishing that they could get to Woodstock faster. Should they have gone to the airport instead? Would that have gotten them there any sooner? Probably not. They would have to make arrangements, wait for flights, deal with security and delays. Maybe the FBI would block him from flying in an effort to keep him out of the case. Driving was better. Short of setting up road blocks, there was no way the FBI could stop him from driving there.

Rhys lay as still as he could, listening to his mother breathing. Gloria was restless, and stayed up late muttering to herself, watching reruns of American Idol on her phone, and frequently going to the windows to peer outside and make sure no one was going to sneak up on them.

A few times, Rhys had dozed, the restless kind of sleep he experienced when he had to sleep somewhere other than his own bed. He would stay awake late into the night, and not until he became convinced that he was not going to sleep at all would he finally drift off into restless dreams about coyotes and Grandpa Clarence and things that had happened when he was little.

But it had been several days, and his body wanted to sleep, even though he was trying to stay awake.

It was a long time before Gloria's breathing finally settled into a long, slow rhythm and Rhys was sure she was asleep. He counted to one hundred slowly in his head. If she made any noise or movement, he would start over again, so that he could be sure she was soundly asleep.

Then he left his blanket on the floor and crept over to where the other woman, Bridget, moved around restlessly. She wasn't trying to sleep and she had no blanket or warm jacket or anything else to make her comfortable. He had seen her fall asleep sitting up several times during the day, her chin gradually lowering to her chest until she startled and sat up again.

She saw him moving toward her but didn't make any sound. Not a single whisper or movement that might rouse Gloria out of her restless sleep. Rhys drew up close to her until they were nearly touching. Bridget's white skin seemed to glow in the moonlight.

Rhys worked the paper-wrapped half hamburger out of his pocket. It was squashed flat, but Bridget didn't seem to take any notice. She eagerly took it from him and took a bite. In a few moments, it was gone. She licked at the wrapper. Rhys dug into his other pocket and pulled out the remains of a cookie. His stomach was grumbling, but he knew Bridget was in worse shape than he was. He could only save so much for her without Gloria noticing. The bit of cookie was polished off just as quickly as the hamburger. Bridget looked at him to see if there were anything else. Rhys shook his head regretfully.

She drew a finger down her throat. *A drink?*

Rhys looked over at Gloria. She hadn't moved. He stood up and tiptoed over to the bathroom. He didn't turn on the light, but he knew where everything was in the tiny bathroom. He felt for the cup he'd left there earlier in the day. He positioned it under the faucet and trickled water into it. If Gloria woke up, he would just drink it himself. She couldn't prove he was getting it for Bridget unless she caught him giving it to her.

Since his stomach was growling, he downed a glass himself first, and then refilled it for Bridget. He stopped in the bathroom doorway and listened for Gloria's breathing to reassure himself she was still asleep, then went over to Bridget with the water. She gulped it down. Rhys could tell by the way she pressed her hand over her stomach that she had eaten and drunk too fast. She pressed the cup back into Rhys's hand, smiling her thanks. Her lips were rough and cracked.

Rhys pulled out his iPod and navigated to the games folder where he'd hidden his messaging app. He tapped on the message thread, positioned the messages, and turned it around so Bridget could see. Her eyes darted over the contents, then went back to Rhys, questioning, hopeful. He nodded. Then he deleted each one so that if Gloria ever looked at it, there would be no evidence of his communication. He met Bridget's eyes one more time, imploring her to be careful and not do anything to upset Gloria.

Then he went back over to his blanket and lay down.

P inpointing the cabin where Gloria was likely to have taken Rhys and Bridget was not as easy as Zachary had hoped. He had imagined that with the small population of Woodstock, he'd be able to find out who had cabins that might have been used as fishing lodges in the past ten years, who was still renting them out, and quickly narrow down which one Gloria was using.

But he wasn't a native of Woodstock and hadn't been prepared for the suspicion that he would face as an outsider.

"I just want to find out who owns the cabin that my father rented a few years ago," he told yet another resident. "He said he got it from a native fellow. He kept talking about how remote it was. Not even any electricity, just running water pumped by a generator. Very rustic."

But the woman selling ice cream cones was having none of it. "I don't know," she said stubbornly. "Everybody in these parts has somewhere they go. The woods are littered with 'rustic' shacks and shanties. Anyone who rents one of those deserves what they get!"

"No, he liked it," Zachary protested. "I wanted to find the place he stayed... take some pictures..."

The woman just shook her head and continued to scoop ice cream. Zachary and Kenzie cycled through various different stories, trying to find something that would gain the trust of the Woodstock residents.

"They think they're going to get into some kind of trouble," Kenzie said. "They're getting cash and not declaring it as income or they're afraid you want to sue them. Asking questions is just making people more and more suspicious, no matter what kind of story you have about a relative who came here once and stayed there."

"Then what are we going to do? If I had the time, we could just surveil the area, watch the main services and wait for Gloria to show up. But we don't have the time. In the amount of time it would take to find her, Bridget could…"

"Well, then… we're not looking for a specific cabin. We're just looking for one we can rent. Somewhere no one will bother us. If someone has something promising, we go take a look. If they say it's already rented…"

"Then we see who rented it," Zachary finished, "and if they match Gloria's and Rhys's descriptions."

"And if we happen to find a Native renting out his old shack, one that was old and falling down ten years ago, we take a look at that one for sure. Whether he remembers an old black man coming out here with his grandson ten years ago or not."

Zachary nodded his agreement. "Do we stay together or split up?"

"Let's split up… we've both got phones and can reach each other if we get a promising lead. Cover twice as much ground."

"Okay. But if you get a bad vibe from anyone… we get back together. I don't want you running into any danger alone."

"Or you," Kenzie declared. "You're the one who keeps landing in hospital."

"Uh… or me," he agreed.

"And you promise me you won't go off on your own or do anything stupid. As soon as you get a lead, you let me know."

Zachary nodded.

"What about calling the authorities?" Kenzie suggested. "Do you think it's time?"

"When we find out where they are. Right now… if you fill this town full of FBI agents… word is going to get back to Gloria in two seconds. I don't want to put Rhys or Bridget in danger."

"Have you messaged Rhys? To see if you can get any details from him? It would be a lot easier if we had some better clues as to where they are."

"I've messaged him, but I haven't gotten anything back. I'm thinking that if they don't have any electricity, he might not be able to keep his phone charged. Or they might be out of cell range some of the time. It seems like he can only message me once a day, so I'm thinking that might be when they go into town for something else."

"Well, we'll keep our eyes open. I take it you don't want me to ask the restaurant owners whether they have seen a black boy and his mother...? You have that picture on your phone you could show around."

"Too dangerous. I can't risk tipping them off. We have to find out where they are staying. If they come into town and someone says there's been people asking questions about them... they may take off without going back to get Bridget, and if we don't know where they're staying and she's being kept, then..."

Kenzie nodded, conceding the point. "Then I'm off to see if someone has a cabin I could rent for a couple of days."

"We need to leave today," Gloria told Rhys.

Rhys was sitting on his blankets on the floor. He stared at her and shook his head, not understanding.

"We've been here long enough," she told him. "People are going to start to ask questions. It's a small town. They're used to tourists coming through for a few days and then leaving again. We can't stay here forever."

Rhys looked over at Bridget.

"We'll leave her here," Gloria said. "That should make you happy. We'll leave her here and she'll be fine. We'll find another house and start a new life, just you and me."

Rhys closed his eyes and tried to picture it. How many times over his life had he dreamed of just that? Being able to leave Aunt Robin and his old life behind. He would be like a new person, undamaged, able to talk like anyone else and not plagued by nightmares.

But Gloria had brought him new nightmares. He would never be able to forget the pretty, blond Bridget and how her eyes had become more dull and sunken with each passing day. Her features would be burned into his brain for the rest of his life, just like Grandpa's face. He'd always seen Aunt Robin as the monster, and his mother as his protector, but that had changed. When Aunt Robin died, Gloria had changed and had taken her place, angry and snapping at Rhys and taking this woman who she saw as a threat. He would never have predicted that his mother would have done those things.

"I think maybe we'll go south," Gloria suggested, "settle down somewhere it doesn't snow. How would you like that? No heavy coats and gloves and traipsing to school through all of that ice and snow."

Rhys looked away from her. He took out his iPod and tapped through the screens to find a game to play.

"Rhys!" Gloria's voice was sharp. "Look at me. Don't ignore me!"

He didn't look up. Gloria strode across the room toward him. Rhys tensed, bracing himself against her anger, but still didn't look up at her. Gloria snatched the iPod out of his hand and flung it to the side, making it clatter across the floor. She grabbed his upper arm and shook him.

"I said look at me!"

Rhys did as he was told, his heart beating hard and fast, a lump in his throat.

"I'm doing this for you!" Gloria shouted. "All of this is for you! You think I'm doing it for my own good? I'm doing it to give you a life. You deserve to have a real life!"

Rhys shook his head and blinked out tears. That wasn't what he wanted. Not if it meant hurting other people and losing his mother. He wanted her to be the woman she'd always been for him.

Gloria shoved Rhys, pushing him over. She turned her back on him, isolating him to emphasize her anger.

Rhys didn't move for a long time, just lying on the floor where she'd discarded him. She picked up her coil notebook and started to write notes furiously. After her attention had been distracted from him for a while, Rhys reached out for his iPod. It was a few feet out of his reach, so he crawled over to it, then pulled it to him and held it protectively against his body. He stayed there motionless for a long time, just curled up on the floor, watching Gloria. Out the corner of his eye, he saw Bridget shift her position, silently and very slowly. So she was awake, even though she'd pretended to be asleep or unconscious when Gloria had checked on her earlier.

Rhys sat up and moved so that his back was against the wall. He looked down at his iPod. The screen was cracked, two long lines that angled toward each other and joined in a V at the edge. Rhys woke it up with the press of a button and was relieved to see that it still powered on and was readable in spite of the damage.

He wished that Gloria would take him back into town so he could get a wifi connection and see if Zachary had sent him any more messages. He wanted to send Zachary a few words or a picture to make sure he knew where to find them. Zachary had to find them before Gloria decided to leave Woodstock. Rhys didn't know if his mother planned to do something to Bridget to make sure she couldn't follow them or give them away, or if she just planned to leave Bridget chained up there to starve to death before someone found her. If Rhys hadn't been surreptitiously giving Bridget food and water, he was pretty sure she would already be dead.

He had one other option, and that was to try to tether his iPod to Gloria's new phone. She had given it to him to set it up for her, but he hadn't had the nerve to piggyback it. If he could connect to it and it had a strong enough signal, he might be able to contact Zachary without going back to town. But he ran the risk of Gloria realizing what he was doing and taking measures to make sure he couldn't do it again.

He watched her writing in her notebook and tried to decide whether to attempt it.

It was almost lunchtime when Zachary and Kenzie got back together at a rustic-themed diner to compare notes. Zachary ordered a coffee for himself and a sandwich for Kenzie, knowing she would be hungry after their busy morning.

"I've got a couple of possibilities," Kenzie said. "Nothing that immediately felt like 'this is the one,' but they fit the profile closely enough."

Zachary nodded. "Me too."

"But the trouble is, they either aren't rented or the person who rented them doesn't match Gloria's description. You don't think she's working with someone else, do you? A boyfriend...?"

"I don't think so. Other than Rhys, and he couldn't pass as an adult. The thing is, she might *not* be renting it. She might have just found it empty and used it."

Kenzie nodded. She took a big bite of the sandwich and didn't say anything else while she chewed.

"I found a couple." Zachary pulled up the notes he had made on his phone. "They might be the same ones as you found…"

He put the phone on the table and slid it across to Kenzie. Kenzie leaned over it to read the details, nodding.

The phone gave a short vibration. Kenzie looked up at Zachary. "It's him."

"Rhys?"

Zachary grabbed the phone and turned it back around to look. The banner announcing Rhys's message disappeared, and Zachary switched apps to find it. He could see the last message he had sent to Rhys.

We are coming to Woodstock. Where r u staying?

And then Rhys's reply, a picture that appeared to be a photo he had taken himself rather than a meme or gif available within the app. It was a low angle, showing a wood plank floor and a steel bed frame, with just a piece of Robin sitting on the thin mattress covered with a gray wool blanket.

"Okay, we're right, it is a cabin," Zachary said, showing it to Kenzie. "Do you think there is enough for anyone to recognize?"

"Maybe for whoever owns it. But they're going to be suspicious about why we're asking."

Zachary concentrated on the problem, then texted back.

Did Gloria rent it?

The reply came back quickly.

No.

"No," Kenzie repeated aloud. "Then it could be Old Bear's cabin. It's supposed to be empty right now."

Before they could send anything back to Rhys, another message came in. Another photo Rhys had taken himself. There was a heap of clothes in a corner, difficult to see in the dim lighting. Zachary studied it, trying to make out the details to see what else Rhys was trying to tell him. Obviously, Rhys had to be careful and could not use his flash and attract Gloria' attention.

Zachary realized it wasn't a pile of clothes. It was the shape of a woman.

Bridget.

R hys deliberately moved slowly. *Where was Zachary?* Rhys thought Zachary had understood where they were, but maybe he'd gone to the wrong cabin. There had to be dozens of them in the wilderness surrounding Woodstock.

If Zachary had gone to the wrong one, all hope was lost. Rhys was convinced Gloria intended to do something to Bridget before they hit the road. Gloria hadn't told Rhys so, but Rhys was afraid of what was in the first aid kit Gloria brought with her and kept eyeing as she waited for Rhys to get ready to go.

Gloria had become more and more obsessed with medical matters since Aunt Robin had been diagnosed. She got thick texts out of the library and spent hours researching different therapies and medications that might help Aunt Robin. But as it had turned out, all of her research was for naught, since Aunt Robin had ended up dying even sooner than the doctors had predicted.

"Come on, I told you it's time to go," Gloria urged.

Rhys hesitated. He could squeeze a few more minutes out with a trip to the bathroom, but that would also mean leaving Gloria alone with Bridget, and Rhys was worried about what Gloria might do.

He walked to the cabin door with his bag. He opened the door and scanned the clearing for any sign of Zachary or someone who could help him. All was quiet. Rhys offered his bag to his mother with a head-jerk toward the car, then hooked his thumb back toward the bathroom indicating that he wanted to use it before leaving.

Gloria sighed in exasperation and took the bag from him. "Honestly, Rhys. I wanted to be on the road an hour ago!"

He waited until he was sure she was on her way to the car to put their bags inside before heading to the bathroom. Bridget lay in the corner of the cabin, unmoving. Rhys pulled out his iPod as soon as he was through the bathroom door, looking for an update from Zachary. But there was nothing, and with Gloria out at the car, she was too far away for Rhys to piggyback on her signal again.

He filled the cup he had left on the edge of the sink, thinking that he might have enough time to give Bridget one more drink before Gloria returned. But when he opened the door to check her position, his heart jumped. Gloria was bending over Bridget.

"Ma—no!"

Gloria whirled around at the sound of his voice, dropping what was in her hand with a clatter. Her eyes were wild. "Go out to the car, Rhys!"

Rhys shook his head. His mouth moved as he tried to form words again, but his exclamation had drained his speech reserves.

"Go on. Go sit down and get yourself settled. You've done everything you need to do to get ready at least twice."

Rhys couldn't find any more excuses. But he couldn't let her do anything to Bridget. He shook his head again, refusing.

Gloria marched across the room to him. Rhys stubbornly stood his ground. She slapped him across the face, the blow so hard it made him see stars. His mother had never before hit him. He could see the shock and horror in her own face at what she had done, but she didn't apologize.

"Look what you made me do!" Her voice cracked. "You do what I tell you, Rhys. This is important. I know you don't understand what's going on, but you need to listen to me. Now go out to the car."

Rhys shook his head. He held his hand up in front of his face to block her from slapping him again. Gloria grabbed his wrist and wrenched his arm to the side.

"The car!" she insisted.

Rhys's face throbbed. Hot tears leaked out the corners of his eyes and a lump formed in his throat so big that he could barely breathe. He tried to get words out, but between his brain and the lump in his throat, he knew he couldn't speak. He grasped her hands. Not violent, like she'd been toward him, but soft and gentle. He lifted each up and kissed it, begging her with his eyes. Gloria was his mother and she knew him almost as well as Grandma, all of his facial expressions and body language. He silently begged her for all he was worth not to hurt Bridget. She wavered.

"Rhys..." she murmured. "I just want to protect you."

He continued to hold her hands, warm and smooth in his, praying for her to listen.

Finally, Gloria turned toward the outside door. Rhys let her pull her hands out of his and followed her out of the shack. She had nearly reached the car when an authoritative voice shouted over the stillness of the clearing.

"Freeze! Federal agents! Stay where you are!"

Gloria's head snapped around to look at Rhys to make sure he was okay. Rhys lifted his hands in surrender. How many times had she lectured him on how to behave if he were ever stopped by the police? How many times had she warned him about the hazards of being a young black man, especially one who couldn't say 'yes, sir' to a policeman? Gloria stared at Rhys for a minute, then mirrored his movement, raising her hands.

The peace of the forest clearing was broken by a swarm of black-uniformed men with big guns, overwhelming the unarmed woman and youth. Rhys kept his body soft, letting them pat him down and move him without resistance. They handcuffed Gloria, but not Rhys. When the all-clear had been called, Zachary entered the clearing.

Rhys let his breath out with a soft puff. Zachary approached him, both hands extended to either hug Rhys or give him a two-handed handshake. But Rhys moved away, taking hold of one of Zachary's hands and leading him into the cabin. There were already a couple of FBI agents there, bending over Bridget. Zachary rushed over; calling her name, swearing, and apologizing to her all in a jumble. The agents moved out of the way to allow Zachary to see her. One of them had picked up the syringe Gloria had dropped. Rhys retrieved the cup from the bathroom and inserted himself beside Bridget as well. Her eyes were open and she was attempting to smile at Zachary and reassure him. Her lips were cracked and swollen and her eyes deeply sunken. Rhys put the cup into her grasp and Zachary helped steady her shaking hands and raise it to her mouth. He kept the angle low, forcing her to sip it slowly instead of gulping it down.

Bridget licked her lips and cleared her throat. "He's my hero," she whispered. "She was going to kill me. Rhys wouldn't let her kill me."

Zachary put an arm around Rhys and pulled him close. Tears were streaming down his face.

"Thank you, Rhys. Thank you so much."

Rhys didn't try to squirm out of Zachary's hold. He just let Zachary hold him tight, both of their faces wet with tears.

30

One of the police officers held a cup of coffee in front of Zachary's face. He looked up from the chair in the hospital waiting room and saw that it was Joshua Campbell. He nodded his thanks and took the coffee, taking a sip of the hot, rich blend to steady his nerves.

"Another feather in your cap," Campbell observed, sitting down in one of the other chairs. "You're getting quite a reputation for being the guy to solve murders that weren't supposed to be murders."

Zachary gave a self-deprecating shrug. "Sometimes the family—or friends—know instinctively what the police or medical examiner could never have known. I'm just following the direction they point me."

"Well, I've known you were a good investigator for a long time. Nice that you're getting some recognition."

Zachary's ears got warm. He was tongue-tied for a moment. He never had gotten the knack for graciously accepting a compliment.

"These murder cases," Campbell said, "that woman principal a few months back, the abuses at Summit…"

Zachary nodded and took another sip of coffee. "Yeah, I guess. Sometimes it feels like it's all skip tracing and cheating spouses, but there have been a few more interesting cases lately."

"And Lucas at the hospital," Campbell added to his list of Zachary's cases.

Lucas. Zachary had to think for a minute before he remembered the hospital worker who had upset Ruth Wicker during the Salter investigation.

"Lucas. I forgot about him. You looked into him? Did you find something?"

"Nothing we can charge him with, but enough to drop a word to the hospital on the QT that they might want to find a reason to let him go."

Zachary thought back to the way the hospital worker had behaved. Ignoring Ruth's protests, trying to bully his way through when confronted by Zachary, insisting he had the right to do whatever needed to be done for Ruth and that she owed him her gratitude for it. Then the way he had reported that Zachary had threatened him and kidnapped Ruth, which could very well have landed Zachary in jail if Ruth hadn't been able to verify his story and Campbell hadn't shown up when he did.

"That weasel," Zachary said. "What did you find out?"

"He's had various assault charges against him in the past. Not by hospital patients... but his work history is very checkered. He doesn't stay anywhere for long, and his previous employers say things like 'we cannot comment on that matter.'"

"They're gagged. They told him he could leave quietly and they would keep whatever had happened confidential."

"That's my impression," Campbell agreed. "In a case like this, if you fire the guy and refuse to give him references, then he sues you for termination without cause. That blows up into some big media circus and a legal case that costs thousands of dollars, if not hundreds of thousands. Cheaper to pay him out, give him a reference, and keep quiet."

"Especially when you can't prove he's done anything illegal or harmful to a patient."

"Exactly."

"Is the hospital going to send him on his way?"

"They're talking to their legal department."

So Lucas would be gone and no longer be a danger to vulnerable patients like Ruth.

Until he got another job.

Zachary wasn't able to see Bridget that first day, but when she asked him to visit her at the hospital the next, it sent his heart soaring. He knew she wasn't calling him about Robin's death, because she already knew Gloria had been the one to give Robin the iron that had caused her death.

That meant that Bridget wanted him for something else.

Maybe she had realized, when her own life was in jeopardy, that she really did love Zachary and wanted to get back together with him. Her relationship with Gordon could be no more than a sham when compared to the love Bridget and Zachary had shared together, the love that had driven Zachary to find Bridget and bring the forces of the FBI to bear just in time to save Bridget and apprehend Gloria before she could run again.

Zachary thought everything through before he went to see her. He showered, carefully shaved, and put on clean, neat clothes, a good notch or two higher than his usual jeans-and-tee combination. He went to a flower store. Not the hospital flower store with its sad little arrangements, but a real flower store. He didn't buy her red roses. Instead, he picked from the varieties of flowers that he had seen at the house, having the florist design a bright and cheerful arrangement in an elegant vase. He didn't buy her chocolates. That would be going too far, and he knew that since the chemo, she eschewed sugar and would not want to compromise her health. She needed to heal from her ordeal and overloading her system with sugar would just lower her immunity.

Then he headed to the hospital. He had her unit and room number, and followed the hospital color and letter codes to get to the right place.

When he walked into the room, his heart sank. Gordon sat beside the bed, talking with Bridget in a low voice, holding hands with her. They both looked up when Zachary arrived. Bridget pulled her fingers out of Gordon's grip.

"Gordon, dear, would you mind…?"

Gordon nodded briskly and stood up. "I'll give the two of you some time alone."

Zachary strove to keep his expression blank as Gordon left the hospital room. He didn't want to sneer at Gordon or to give him a gloating look over Bridget's dismissing him. Zachary could be gracious whether he were the loser or the winner. For once, he was actually going to be the winner.

With Gordon out of the way, Zachary walked the rest of the way into the room. He showed Bridget the flowers and let her smell them, then put them down where she directed. Bridget stared at the arrangement for a few long seconds, giving no sign of what she was thinking. She motioned for Zachary to sit in the chair that Gordon had just vacated so he could sit at eye level with her. He could still feel the warmth from Gordon's body there.

"How are you feeling?" Zachary asked.

"I'm doing much better. So good to get properly hydrated and to be able to eat at regular intervals. It really is amazing how we take food for granted! We've always had what we need, so we don't understand what it is like to want."

Zachary nodded his understanding. He had experienced plenty of lean times as a child. Times when they simply didn't have food to put on the table and the children went to bed with empty stomachs. But Bridget wasn't thinking about that. She wasn't asking him whether he had ever experienced it. She was just sharing her experience with him.

"You're looking a lot better." It was amazing how much of a difference one day could make. Her color was better. The hollows in her skin had filled in. Her eyes were bright and alive with interest. He'd been afraid when he'd seen her at the cabin. She had looked so close to death. She had not been able to sit up or to raise the cup of water to her mouth on her own.

"I hope so!" Bridget patted at her hair. "I must have looked a fright…"

"No. Just… sick. I was worried about you."

"I wanted to thank you for everything you've done. For investigating Robin's death and figuring out what had happened. And then for searching for me and tracking me down. You really are… an amazing investigator."

Zachary smiled sheepishly, his face getting warm. "I had to find you. When I knew how long it had been, and that you would be waiting for me, wondering why I hadn't come…"

"It was the only thing I had any hope for. The police and the FBI…" She shrugged expressively. "I trusted your investigative skills and your… passion."

Zachary hadn't thought it was possible for him to blush even more, but he did, his ears and cheeks on fire. He reached for Bridget's hand.

"I care about you, Bridge… I couldn't live without you. If I had let something happen to you…" he trailed off. He wanted to tell her that he loved her. But the last few times he had said it, she had brushed his feelings off, even mocked him for making such a ridiculous statement in the midst of the dissolution of their marriage. *You don't even know what love is. You don't want a wife, you want a mother.*

"Zachary... no. Don't say anything else."

He was quiet, waiting.

"I care about what happens to you too. But... let's not go too far here. You and I... we're never going to be a couple again."

He felt like she had just stabbed him in the gut. She lay there and smiled sweetly as she twisted the knife.

"Gordon and I are not breaking up. I don't want to be with you again. We weren't good for each other."

"But—"

She shook her head. "You come here all cleaned up, with your flowers and your company manners... it's obvious what you're thinking. But we're over, Zachary. I can't ever be with you like that again."

Zachary took a long, shuddering breath. He nodded stoically. "Okay. Got it."

He stood up. He didn't know whether to shake her hand or kiss her on the cheek. He ended up doing neither.

"I'll, uh, see you around, then."

She reached toward him, eyes soft and concerned. "Are you okay, Zachary? Will you be okay?"

"Sure. Of course. Don't you worry about me."

EPILOGUE

Zachary had been holed up in his apartment for some time. Long enough that he'd lost count of the days and frequently had to look at the date on his phone or computer to orient himself. He had plenty of computer work and other desk work that he could do without going out or having to talk to anyone, so that was what he worked on.

Some friends or clients had called him and left messages. Zachary replied to them by email so he wouldn't actually have to speak to anyone. He'd finally ordered a couch for his living room that fit through the apartment door, and that was where he was spending his nights, watching TV until he fell asleep, the nights he actually managed to fall asleep.

There was a persistent knocking on the apartment door. Zachary ignored it for a good ten minutes, but whoever was there was not taking no for an answer, so they probably knew he was home and had not left the apartment in days. Zachary went to the door and looked through the peephole. He sighed and opened the door, stepping back to let Kenzie in.

"Hey," Kenzie said brightly. "I wondered where you'd gotten to. Glad to see you're still around."

Since he'd texted her answers to her voicemails, she really couldn't complain that he hadn't responded or that she thought something had happened to him.

"Hi. Yeah. I've been busy with work."

"Any interesting cases?" She followed him into the living room and sat down on the new couch, testing it out. "Oh, this is nice! Comfy?"

"Sure."

Kenzie glanced over at the TV, which had pretty much been playing 24/7 for however long it had been since Zachary had gotten home from visiting Bridget at the hospital. He didn't like it when it was too quiet. "Are you watching something, or could we shut that off?"

Zachary wasn't even sure what time of day it was, let alone what program was on. He slipped out his phone and covertly checked the time and date on his way over to shut off the TV.

"Are you out of work early, or didn't you have a shift today?" he asked.

"I've been working overtime, so I took off early today."

"That's good," Zachary said without enthusiasm. "It's important to take care of yourself."

Kenzie snorted. He sat back down and glanced over at her.

"It's time to pick yourself up and dust yourself off, Zach."

"I'm fine."

"No, I don't think you are. I think you're spending your life holed up over here, moping over Bridget again. I told you from the start she wasn't interested in getting back together with you. She wanted your investigative services. She should have just hired someone out of the phonebook. That would have been a lot kinder."

"Someone else would not have dug down deep enough to find the truth. They probably wouldn't even have taken the case."

"And what would that matter? I'm sure homicides like this usually go undetected. Robin was dying anyway. All Gloria did was hurry things along. If you hadn't been digging into it, Gloria would never have gone after Bridget. She would have just stayed home with Rhys and gone on with her life."

"But that wouldn't have been *right*," Zachary pointed out. "That wouldn't have been justice."

"By whose definition? Robin was a killer, don't forget. She had ruined their lives. Especially Rhys's. Would her just living out her normal lifespan without ever having to confront what she had done be justice?"

"Turning her in ten years ago would have been justice. What Gloria did wasn't justice. It was revenge."

Kenzie shrugged. "Whatever. You still need to get past this and go on with your life." She raised a finger when Zachary opened his mouth to respond. "And that is not what you are doing."

"Maybe I'm not ready."

"Then it's time to see your psychiatrist. Get some help."

Zachary drew in a deep breath. It wasn't the first time he'd fallen into such a depression. Kenzie was probably right.

"Fine. I'll make an appointment."

"And start taking your meds."

He looked for an argument, then shrugged, conceding.

"Let Bridget go. She's with Gordon Drake now. So you're not getting her back, no matter what she led you to believe. You need to let that whole notion go."

"That's not as easy as you think. I made vows. I promised…"

"She's released you from them. So go on."

Zachary shook his head and didn't try to explain how impossible that was for him.

"You're taking me out for dinner tonight," Kenzie informed him. "You choose the place."

"I'm not hungry."

"Then just order an appetizer. We'll head over there after. Maybe you'll be hungry in a couple of hours."

"After? After what?"

She shook her head, her hair bouncing around her face, bright red lips curved in a smile. "After we go see Rhys."

Once again showered, changed, and dressed in fresh clothes, Zachary headed out with Kenzie. She wouldn't give him any details about where Rhys was or how he was doing. She told him to just go with her and see for himself, and he couldn't argue with her logic. It was the first thing that had interested him since seeing Bridget at the hospital. Bridget would be back home and completely recovered. Since Zachary hadn't left the apartment, he hadn't even driven by her house since she'd been released and could only assume that everything was back to normal for her.

"Good to feel the sun on your face and the wind in your hair?" Kenzie asked, winding through the streets with the top down. Zachary brushed his hand over his hair with one hand, but it was short enough that the wind couldn't mess it up.

"Yeah, it's nice," he agreed.

She turned up the radio to eliminate the need for more conversation. Zachary watched the streets pass by, his arm resting on the window ledge.

He was surprised when they pulled up to the Salter house. He had assumed that Rhys would be in foster care, maybe even institutionalized, given his mutism and the trauma of the kidnapping and his mother's behavior. He'd had to go to a facility once before, after Clarence's death and, in Zachary's experience, one institutionalization led to another.

"But who's...?" Zachary shook his head, not even finishing the sentence, because he knew Kenzie wouldn't answer it. There must have been some other relative willing to move into the house to look after Rhys. Some cousin.

Kenzie just smiled and walked up the sidewalk, using her fingers to comb her hair back into shape after the ride in the convertible. She rang the bell.

Zachary nearly fell over when Vera answered the door. He hadn't expected to ever see her outside of a care facility again.

How could they have released her? She couldn't possibly be taking care of Rhys, and Rhys couldn't be taking care of her.

"Mr. Goldman, I'm so glad you could come. Come in, come in."

Kenzie and Zachary entered.

The house was spotless, everything put away in its proper place. Even the shoes at the door and Rhys's skateboard were neat and tidy. Zachary sat down on the couch with Vera. She put her arm around his shoulders and gave him a hug.

"I wanted to thank you for everything you did. I don't know what would have happened if you hadn't stepped in."

Zachary looked at her and shook his head. "I don't understand. The last time we talked to you, you were..." he trailed off, not sure of a tactful way to say that she'd appeared to have dementia. When now, she obviously didn't.

"Gloria again," Kenzie said. "It looks like she was intentionally giving Vera drugs that would make her muddled. So she wouldn't understand what was going on or be able to tell anything to the police."

Zachary blinked. "That's... I don't know. That's *devious*."

Kenzie laughed. Vera sighed and shrugged. "I guess so. I really don't know what to think of this all. I started to feel better after a few days off of those pills. Like myself again. I'm still not sure of everything that happened while she was giving them to me, or how long she was doing it for. She was always in charge of dividing up my pills into daily doses for me. I just... took what she gave me."

"So, you're better now... and you can take care of Rhys."

Vera nodded. "That's right." She raised her voice. "Rhys? Where are you? Are you going to come in to see Mr. Goldman or not?"

Zachary looked up at a heavy approaching footfall. But it wasn't Rhys he saw, it was Stanley Green. Tall and broad and looking like he owned the place.

Zachary's jaw dropped open. He looked at Vera and Kenzie, but neither of them seemed to be surprised or alarmed, so obviously they had already known that Stanley was there or was going to be. Both women looked at him expectantly.

"What... what are you doing here?" Zachary asked, fumbling his words. "I thought... what?"

Stanley scratched his ear, a slightly sheepish grin on his face. "After you told me about Robin's death... I couldn't get it out of my mind. I wanted to reconnect with Rhys, see if I could help him out. I was very close to the family, once. If Robin hadn't been so..." Stanley looked over at Vera. "...uh, so volatile..."

Vera nodded. She looked down at her hands. "It wasn't Stanley's fault," she reassured Zachary. "He was never the one who started things."

Zachary nodded. "I know. I read the police incident reports. That's when it all came together."

They were all silent, not sure where to go next.

"I'm sorry about scaring you that night," Stanley said, looking down in embarrassment. "I never meant to freak you out. You weren't even supposed to see me."

"Why would you even come by?" Zachary asked. "Why didn't you just call me? Set up a meeting? Or email me?"

"I didn't really know what else to say to you. I didn't want to leave things where they were... I realized that you thought I was abusive toward Robin, when that wasn't the way things were. I wanted to straighten things out. But what could I say?" Stanley gave a shrug. "Here I am this big guy...

who's going to believe that Robin was the aggressor? Or that I couldn't make her stop?"

Zachary thought about Mrs. Phipps at Ptarmigan House, one of the group homes he had been in. She was a little, wizened old woman with a bad leg, but she could whale the hell out of a boy with her cane if she caught him disobeying the rules. At fourteen, even with his stunted growth, Zachary had been bigger than she was, and logic dictated she was the one who should fear him. But the *thunk* of her cane on the floor and the drag of her bad leg was all it took to send his heart racing wildly, even if he couldn't think of anything he'd done wrong. Especially if he didn't know what he'd done wrong.

"It's okay," he told Stanley. "I get it."

"I was trying to think things through. Sometimes… I have to physically go somewhere to make sense of a thing. I thought if I was there, where you lived… I could figure it out. Decide what to do next."

Like Zachary's compulsions to drive by Bridget's house. Even though he couldn't see her car in the garage and couldn't see if she were sleeping soundly in the house, it comforted him to be there. He had to go by there to settle his brain down and reassure himself she was okay. Nothing else would work. He had gone to Bridget's the same night as Stanley had come to his apartment, both of them driven to put themselves in a specific place to work through their thoughts.

"I get it. Sometimes… you just have to do something."

Zachary looked up when he heard another set of approaching feet, and this time it was Rhys's familiar lanky figure. Rhys gave a little wave and a nod to Zachary. He stood there looking at Zachary, then looked at his grandmother.

"Rhys wanted to see you," Vera said. "He wanted to thank you for helping him. For finding him and saving him and Bridget."

Zachary met Rhys's eyes and nodded. Rhys still looked sad, but there was something looser and more comfortable about him. Like a great weight had been lifted off his shoulders.

"Thank you for helping me to find you," Zachary told Rhys. "And for helping Bridget. She would have died if you hadn't helped look after her." Zachary swallowed. He wasn't sure he could express to Rhys how much Bridget meant to him and how much he appreciated what the boy had done. Faced with being loyal to his mother or with helping a woman he'd never even met before, Rhys had done what was right, even though it meant his mother had to go to jail.

Rhys nodded. He held out a hand to Zachary and they shook.

"I tried to do the right thing for our family," Vera said quietly. "When Clarence died… it felt like the most important thing to do was to shelter Robin from the consequences. I couldn't bear to think that she could go to prison for what she had done. She really wasn't well." Vera looked over at Rhys. "I guess… that's what I told myself. It was something she couldn't control. But…" She grimaced. "She could have, couldn't she? She made her choices. And we chose to protect her."

Rhys gave a shrug. Not an 'it doesn't matter' shrug, but one that said that what was done was done. They couldn't undo the past.

"How are you, Rhys?" Zachary asked, searching Rhys's face for the answer. "Are you okay?"

Rhys cleared his throat. He looked at his grandma for reassurance before answering. "It's gonna be okay."

It was a long utterance for him. Zachary took in a deep breath and let the words wash over him.

Was it?

Was it going to be okay for Zachary, too? Was he going to be able to get out of the funk he was stuck in and move on?

There were other cases to be solved, other questions left unanswered. And supper with Kenzie. Rhys was safe with Vera, with Stanley Green around to lend a hand and be there when he needed a man's guiding hand. Thanks to Rhys, Bridget had survived her ordeal. Zachary couldn't imagine the darkness he would be in if she hadn't.

But Bridget was alive and happy. So Zachary would go on, just as he had before.

It was gonna be okay.

HE WAS WALKING ALONE

ZACHARY GOLDMAN MYSTERIES #4

To those who walk alone, no matter what they have done to get there

1

Zachary was standing staring out his window at the businesses across the street from his apartment building, where an old man with a ladder was stringing up Christmas lights when his phone rang. He was startled out of his trance and nearly did a face-plant into the window before he regained his balance.

He put his hand on the glass to steady himself and pulled his phone out of his pocket with the other. A glance at the screen showed him that it was Mario Bowman, and he didn't hesitate to answer it. Since moving out of Bowman's apartment, the two of them had usually gotten together every couple of weeks for a drink. A year ago, they had been acquaintances, just friendly after the various times they had met while Zachary had worked cases the police were involved in, but after the fire that had destroyed everything Zachary had owned for the second time in his life, that had changed. Bowman had graciously allowed Zachary to stay with him until he got back on his feet, which had turned into months rather than the 'few days' they had initially talked about. Bowman had never complained about Zachary being underfoot, and even after Zachary had moved into his own place again, they had continued to get together, cementing the friendship.

Years before, Zachary had accepted the fact that he would never have any real friends. Moving constantly from one foster family or institution to another, battling with learning disabilities and childhood trauma, he had not found it easy to break into the circles of already-established friendships and had remained on the outside. Not having developed those skills as a child, he had remained a loner as an adult. He'd never expected to have a 'best friend' like Bowman.

"Mario!"

"Hey, Zach. I didn't get you up, did I?"

Zachary pulled the phone away from his ear to look at the time to better compose his answer. After ten o'clock in the morning, a time even night owls were normally up by. "It's halfway through the day. You know I don't sleep that late."

"I know you don't usually sleep," Bowman admitted. "You're like a vampire. Except, I guess they sleep during the day, and you don't do that either. You could have been asleep though, if you had some kind of surveillance job last night."

"Well, I didn't. I've been up for hours. I thought you had night shift this week; aren't you heading to bed?"

"Yeah, I'd better knock off before long. But I have a possible case for you."

"Oh! What kind of case?"

Zachary worked everything from skip tracing and insurance fraud to money laundering and, in a few cases, death investigations. While he was trying to avoid the cheating spouse cases, he always seemed to have a couple of them on his plate.

"Why don't we get together later to discuss it? I'll introduce you to the potential client and you can see what you think."

"Uh, sure." It sounded like a much bigger case than just a background check. "When and where?"

"Old Joe's before I go back on shift? Say, seven?"

Zachary didn't know how Bowman could eat a steak dinner for what was essentially his breakfast. Zachary had a hard time with heavy meals at the best of times. His meds tended to suppress his appetite, and the most recent mood stabilizer added to his cocktail left him nauseated most of the day. But he knew that dinner at the steakhouse wasn't about the food. Bowman would enjoy being treated, as Zachary would pick up the tab for a client dinner. Hopefully, his client would feel at ease at the town's iconic steakhouse. And Zachary was going for the case, not the food.

"Yeah, that sounds good." He didn't need to check his calendar. He knew he wouldn't have anything that couldn't be moved. "I'll see you there."

"Perfect. See you tonight, then."

Zachary thought about it after he hung up. It was late for Bowman to still be up when he would have to be up again at six. He would not get a full eight hours in, and when he was working shift he was very careful to get the sleep he needed so that he wouldn't get worn out and sick. Despite asking Zachary if he'd been asleep, he knew that Zachary was normally up before dawn and he could have safely called hours before. That suggested that he'd worked past the end of his shift, which meant a big case. If that was what they were having dinner to discuss, Zachary might be looking at quite a profitable file. Something he could really dig his teeth into to help him to forget about the holiday season.

The man across the street was working diligently at getting his Christmas lights on. They would make a festive display for Zachary in the coming weeks. He drew the curtains to shut out the sight.

The client who accompanied Bowman was a woman. That was the first surprise. And not just a woman, but an attractive one. At first glance, he would have put her as college age, but on closer inspection, the dim lighting at Old Joe's had softened the lines of her face. She was probably in her forties, like he was. Taller than Zachary. A dark blonde, rather than the almost-black hair that Zachary kept cropped close to his head. She wore no makeup as far as he could tell, and grief was plain on her face. It was no corporate case. Whatever Bowman had brought him, it was personal.

"Zach, this is Ashley Morton. Ms. Morton, Zachary Goldman."

Zachary shook hands. "Nice to meet you, Ms. Morton."

"It's Ashley," she informed him. "Thanks for agreeing to meet with me on such short notice. You must have a busy schedule."

Zachary glanced over at Bowman to gauge his reply. "I've always got cases on the go, but I can make room when something important comes up."

She nodded, looking relieved. "Good. Mr. Bowman said you'd be able to fit me in, but..."

Bowman motioned to an empty booth. "That's our table, shall we sit down? Did you want a drink, Zach?"

"No." Bowman knew he wouldn't have alcohol for a case meeting. Even when they got together to watch a game, Zachary was mindful of his alcohol consumption.

They made their way away from the bar to the quiet corner. Bowman and Ashley slid in with their drinks. Zachary sat across from Ashley.

Bowman took a sip of his beer and talked to Ashley about Zachary's qualifications. He touched on the cases Zachary had worked in the last year or so that had made it to the media. The drowning of Declan Bond, the only son of local TV celebrity *The Happy Artist*, the institutional abuses at Summit Learning Center, and the death of Robin Salter. While Robin's death had not been particularly newsworthy, the subsequent kidnapping of Zachary's ex-wife, socialite Bridget Downy, had been.

Ashley nodded solemnly throughout Bowman's recounting of the cases, her wide eyes going from Bowman to Zachary and back again. She didn't seem inclined to jump in immediately with her story. They ordered their dinners and discussed the menu for a few minutes. Zachary looked at Bowman, waiting for the signal that it was time to talk about Ashley's case. Bowman took a long draught of beer and wiped his mouth with the back of his hand.

"You want to tell Zachary about Richard's case?"

Ashley chewed on her lip.

"Do you want me to give him the broad strokes?" Bowman prompted.

She nodded. "That would be good," she said in a weak, watery voice.

Zachary hoped she wasn't going to cry. He was never sure what to do about tears. A lot of the women who engaged him to catch their cheating husbands cried. He had come to realize that the best thing to do in those cases was just to nod and push through for the details. Trying to comfort them didn't help. It seemed that those tears came from anger rather than sadness, and trying to be sympathetic just caused increased anger and outrage, putting him in the crosshairs in place of their husbands.

But he didn't think Ashley's case was for infidelity. She seemed too brittle, stretched too thin. Grief, not anger.

"Ashley's partner, Richard, was the victim of a fatal hit and run," Bowman said, confirming his suspicion. "It's a little more difficult to investigate than your usual MVC, since there were no witnesses, no cameras, and the body wasn't even discovered immediately. That has all made it very diffi-cult for Miss Morton—Ashley—to deal with."

Zachary nodded. The waitress had brought him a glass of water. He took a sip, waiting for the rest of the story. Bowman sounded confident of the facts, so Zachary suspected he wasn't looking for Zachary to do an accident scene reconstruction. The police had probably already done their own, or had plans to, depending on how long they'd had to work the case.

"They're calling it an accident," Ashley said. "They said the driver isn't at fault." She shook her head, sputtering for words. "There's no way it was accidental."

Zachary considered. "What were the conditions? Was there alcohol involved?"

"All they have is the driver's word for it what time it was. There aren't any witnesses. No proof. The police couldn't do a breathalyzer three days later."

"No," Zachary agreed. He pulled a notepad out of his pocket. "Do you mind if I make some notes?"

She nodded her permission.

"Your boyfriend's name was Richard...?"

"Harding. Just how it sounds."

"And the date of the accident?"

"Well, we don't know, do we? All we have is his word for it. And it *wasn't* an accident."

"Sorry. Incident. When did this allegedly happen?"

She was mollified and gave him more details. It had been a week since she had seen her boyfriend last and the police suggested that it had been that night he had been killed on the side of a rural highway.

"But you don't believe that's when it happened?"

"Well... I guess I do. I mean, Richard just dropped off the face of the earth, and that's not the kind of thing that he did. He was very reliable."

"So it probably was that night."

She nodded. Zachary wrote down the location and the date. He could look up weather conditions, sunset and sunrise, and any surveillance camera locations later on. The police might have missed something. They were usually pretty thorough, but every now and then, Zachary managed to tease out new information from a suspect or the available evidence.

"And you didn't know that anything had happened to him, just that he had disappeared."

"I knew something was wrong. I reported him missing in the morning when I woke up, but they said I would have to go to the police station and make a proper missing persons report once he had been missing for twenty-four hours. I know they can start an investigation sooner than that." She flashed a glare at Bowman.

Bowman shrugged. "In the case of a missing child, or someone we have evidence was kidnapped or in danger. But just a routine missing person... no. They tend to show up on their own and we don't want to waste precious police resources on someone who just went out on a drunk."

"He didn't go out drinking! He was hit on the road!"

"Yes." He had a sip of his beer, which was almost empty. "We know that now, but we didn't know it then. To start with, it was just a routine missing person with no evidence of violence. No ransom. No sign that there had been a fight. No witnesses that he'd been taken by force. He just disappeared off of his property."

"His car was still there. Did you think he just walked away? Off of a property twenty miles from the nearest town?" Her voice rose accusingly.

"It's just policy, Ms. Morton," Bowman reassured her. "You were not wrong to suspect that something had happened to him. Your instincts were right on."

She nodded, seeming appeased by his words. She fiddled with her drink for a minute, making tracks in the condensation on the side with her finger.

"So, they started an investigation after he had been missing for twenty-four hours," Ashley said. "They got people out searching the property, even though I had already looked everywhere for him. And they got scent dogs out to see if they could track him."

Zachary nodded. "And that's when they found him?"

"He was in the ditch beside the road, but you couldn't see him because it was overgrown with weeds and grass and bush. They just covered him up." Her voice was cracking like an adolescent's.

Zachary gave her a sympathetic smile. He didn't reach out to take her hand, too awkward when he had only just met her. "I'm sorry. Do you need a minute?"

At that point, the waitress came with their meals, a welcome distraction.

The plates were delivered and they each took a few bites of their dinners before attempting to continue the conversation.

"Why don't you tell him the police findings?" Ashley suggested.

Bowman nodded. He took a big bite of steak and chewed it vigorously for a few minutes before offering any comment.

"Date of death was the night he disappeared. Exact time unknown. Gross examination suggests he was hit from behind and to the left, which is consistent with him being found in the right-hand ditch if he was walking away from the farm, toward the highway. As Ms. Morton said, the body was hidden by the overgrowth. Both she and the police had driven by the location several times without seeing him from the road."

"Any tire tracks?"

"It's a rural road, but it is paved and gets a fair bit of traffic because it joins two highways. If you know it goes through, you can use it as a shortcut. But there was no fresh rubber along the stretch of the highway before the collision to indicate an attempt to stop. There was a minor skid mark and tire tracks where a truck had pulled over after the point of collision. Since it's just a rural road, there's really no shoulder to pull onto and it isn't a safe place to stop in the dark."

"So someone might have stopped after hitting him."

Bowman agreed. He glanced at Ashley and continued. "The driver says he got out of the truck, looked at the damage on the truck, and looked for any sign of an animal he had hit along the side of the road."

"But he didn't see the body because it was hidden in the ditch." Zachary pushed the food around on his plate. "Is this the driver who hit him, or someone who just happened to be along? I thought you said it was a hit and run."

"As it turns out, it was more of a 'hit and stop and have a look around and then leave'," Bowman said with gallows humor. "As he didn't know he had hit a person, he didn't call it in. He got back in his truck and drove away."

"He really didn't know what he had hit?"

"Apparently."

"He knew very well!" Ashley insisted. "It was no accident!"

"You asked me to talk about the police findings. That is the police finding."

Ashley closed her mouth, pressing her lips into a thin, straight line.

Bowman gave her a moment in case she wanted to say something else, then went on.

"The driver self-reported. Not for a couple of days, but later when he got suspicious that maybe it wasn't just an animal he had hit out there."

That seemed a little suspicious to Zachary, but he nodded and made a note of it. "You don't think that he was just waiting until he would be clean of any drugs or alcohol before reporting it?"

"We followed up with his insurance company. He had filed an insurance report the morning after the accident—er, MVC—saying that he had hit an animal and giving the pertinent details."

"That could have just been a complete cover-up," Ashley broke in.

"Sure," Zachary agreed. "I would have to look into it further to see how well his story held together. But he could be telling the truth. If you hit a person in a small car, you're going to get a lot of damage and know for sure what you hit. But a bigger truck... it wouldn't do as much damage to the vehicle."

"It was a semi taking a shortcut," Bowman informed them. Zachary nodded. A lot of inertia behind something like that. He would have to hit something pretty big to make a big impact on a truck of that size.

"And you've interviewed this driver and decided that you believe his story. It was just an accident."

"I didn't interview him personally. But interviews were conducted. The final autopsy results are not in yet. They'll want to run a tox screen and see if there is anything else suspicious, but chances are, it's going to be ruled an accident pretty quickly. There are, as yet, no indications of foul play."

"Richard didn't drink," Ashley said.

Zachary smiled politely at her. "What?"

"They aren't going to find anything on a tox screen. Richard didn't drink. He didn't take drugs. He didn't take anything. He was very careful."

"Did he have some kind of history of alcohol abuse?"

"No, of course not!" Her reply was vehement. She shook her head and put her fork down loudly on her plate. "He did not have anything to do with alcohol. Not ever."

"Religious? Personal decision? No family history...?" In Zachary's experience, people weren't teetotalers for no reason. It was the society norm to have a drink now and then, particularly on social occasions, and people didn't fall outside the norm without a conscious decision.

"He just didn't think it was a good idea," Ashley said primly. She took a sip of her own drink and picked up her fork again. "There's nothing wrong with that."

"No," Zachary agreed, glancing down at his own glass of water. "Nothing wrong with that."

"So would you take the case?" Ashley asked him tentatively. "Would you look into it, dig down deeper than the police did, and prove that it was really an intentional homicide, not an accident?"

"I can't guarantee the results," Zachary said. "I can't tell you what my findings are going to be or whether you're going to agree with them. Is there really a case to be made for intentional homicide? What are you reasons for thinking it wasn't just an accident?"

Ashley took a bite of her salad and chewed it slowly. "The driver got out of the truck and went to have a look," she said. "That tells me that he knew exactly what he had done. He got out to make sure Richard was really dead."

"Or he got out to look for the animal he had hit, but not seeing one, decided to go on his way."

"I know Richard. He would never be careless like that, walking with his back to traffic. He would have walked on the other side of the road so he was facing oncoming traffic. He would have gotten off of the road if there was a truck coming. He was very careful to avoid traffic accidents. He would never have let something like that happen."

Zachary scratched down a couple of notes and closed his eyes, thinking about it. "Were you there that night? Did the two of you live together?"

"I have my own place, but I stayed over with him a lot. It just depended on what our schedules were like. That night... I went home."

"Because you wanted to? He wanted you to? Whose idea was it?"

"I don't know... I don't think either one of us said specifically. It was just one of those things... mutual. I had things to do, he had things to do. So I went home."

"And you realized he was missing when? The next morning."

"Yes." Without prompting, she went on to give him the details. "I called him every morning. We always chatted for a few minutes over coffee. Just touched base, talked about how our days were going to be. Couples stuff. It didn't matter whether we were together or apart, we always had that talk."

"So you called and he didn't answer."

"Right."

"How often had that happened before?"

"It wasn't unusual... he would be getting breakfast ready or shaving and he would call me back once he was free."

"But he didn't."

"I waited a while, then called again. Over and over. He still didn't answer. I texted him. I didn't know what else to do. I went to work for the morning, but I couldn't keep my mind on my work, I was so worried about why he wasn't answering. So I took the afternoon off and went to see him. I thought... maybe he was sick in bed. I really couldn't think of anything else. It never occurred to me that he might have left the house."

"He didn't normally go for a morning jog or walk?"

"No. We both thought that was a little silly. Not that there's anything wrong with it if that's how you choose to get your exercise! But we both had fitness equipment and club memberships. No need to brave the weather and the traffic if you could just take a spin on the stationary bike while watching the morning news. It just seemed a lot more... civilized."

Zachary looked at Bowman. "How was he dressed?"

"Comfortable, casual. Not dressed for the office, but not dressed for bed or for a jog either. Jeans, t-shirt, warm jacket. Sneakers, not loafers."

"Where did he work? Did he have a stressful job?"

Ashley gave an uncomfortable shrug. "He was... a janitor. Well, somebody has to be! It was a good, steady job. It paid his expenses and he was putting a little away. I bring in good money from my job, so if we got married..." Ashley swallowed hard and didn't finish the thought. She was still in the process of figuring out how to manage without him. She still thought of him as being there, present with her, and the thought that they didn't actually have a future together anymore was startling and tragic.

"Nothing wrong with a good, honest job," Bowman asserted. "We checked him out and there were no indicators that he was into anything illegal on the side. One hundred percent legit."

Zachary was glad that the police investigation bore out what Ashley had to say about her deceased partner. But that didn't mean he wouldn't find something more when he had a chance to really look for any issues. He smiled and nodded at Bowman.

"Good. It helps with an investigation when I'm told everything."

He looked at Ashley. She didn't jump in with more details. He had a feeling she was holding back, but he didn't know what kind of information it was she was holding back. She claimed that Richard was clean, no drugs or alcohol, holding a custodial position. No problems with the law.

"What was Richard's background?"

"What do you mean?"

"Custodial jobs are usually entry-level. People don't stay there unless they don't have a choice. Did he have any education? Did he grow up with his family or in the system? It doesn't sound from his name like he was an immigrant whose qualifications were not accepted here."

"No. He just... I don't know. That's what he could get, so he stayed there. He and his family grew up in Minnesota."

"Are they still around?"

"No."

"Hobbies?"

Ashley's brows drew down. "I don't understand what that has to do with anything."

"I wonder how he spent his time. If he wasn't doing something he enjoyed for work, then I assume he was getting satisfaction from something else he was doing at home."

She gave a helpless shrug. "No... no hobbies. I guess he just... we did things together. Went out to eat or watched TV. Nothing... special."

Zachary tried to think of what else to say. He still didn't know what made her so sure that it hadn't been an unfortunate accident. Was she in denial? He didn't like to take a case just based on the fact that she was in shock over Richard's death. She'd come around to it and then wouldn't want to pay him.

"I'll need a retainer," he said. "If you really want to go ahead with this. But I don't hear anything that leads me to believe it wasn't an accident. I'll need money up front, and you need to be prepared for the fact that I might not find anything that supports your feeling that it was accidental. The police are pretty thorough..."

"But you've solved cases before that they thought were accidental when they were really murder."

"Yes. I have."

"That's why I need you. I need someone who is willing to suspend disbelief and not just follow what the police say. If you come back with it being an accident... I guess I'm going to have to live with that. But I'm not going to find out anything if I don't pursue it. I really need to know. I need to know what happened to Richard. He wouldn't have just gone out walking in the middle of the night and gotten in an accident like that."

"Okay." As Zachary's dinner got cold, he outlined the financial terms and conditions for Ashley, and she nodded and ate her meal and didn't blanch at the rates he gave her and the upfront retainer. Eventually, Zachary had given her all of the warnings he could think of. "Well, if that sounds okay to you, I'll write it up. You sleep on it tonight and make sure it's really what you want. If you wake up in the morning and have changed your mind, no harm done. Just let me know. If not... I'll start in on what the police have gathered, and see what else needs to be done." Zachary looked at Bowman. "Can I get access to the case files?"

"You know how it is. It's an active investigation, so no. But talk to the right people and push the right buttons, and that could change. Your friend Joshua Campbell is on the case, so it probably won't be too hard. He was happy with the work done on the Salter case."

Zachary nodded, relieved. There were plenty of cops at the police station who didn't like him or didn't want anything to do with a private investigator, but Campbell was not one of them. He'd always been civil toward Zachary. Sometimes, like in the Salter case, he had even given Zachary a tip or given him leave to investigate in a direction he knew his own officers wouldn't be able to pursue.

"That's great. He won't give me any trouble."

"Good," Ashley approved. "You always hear stories about how cops and private eyes can't get along together, or cops and the FBI. I'm glad to know that's just pulp fiction."

Zachary exchanged looks with Bowman. "Oh, it's not always fiction. But it shouldn't be a problem on this file."

2

The first thing for Zachary to check, once he had his retainer from Ashley and was sure that he was okay to go ahead and begin his investigation, was what Richard had been wearing the night he had been killed. There was a big difference between a jogger out with a headlamp and reflective vest and a man walking down the shoulder wearing black pants topped by a black hoodie. In the middle of the night, with no streetlights, a vehicle would be almost on top of him before their headlights picked him out, and then it would be too late. It was easy for a quickly-moving vehicle to outrun its headlights, especially a big, heavy, fully-loaded rig with a deadline to meet.

After talking to Joshua Campbell, Zachary sat down in a meeting room with the first file from the case box, and read through the description of the body and the initial evidence gathered at the scene.

Richard Harding. White, six foot one, one hundred sixty pounds. Body found in the ditch of a secondary highway that ran along his property line. Probable cause of death, pending the autopsy results, blunt force trauma from an MVC. The pictures of the body at the scene did not show a lot of bleeding or bruising. Death had probably been instantaneous.

He was in stocking feet. One shoe had been recovered at the scene and the other was missing. Fashionable red sneakers. Zachary didn't want to guess what they had cost him. Dark blue jeans, white t-shirt, dark green winter coat. The coat would have covered up the white t-shirt and didn't appear to have any reflective embellishments.

The evidence suggested that he had been hit with a powerful force, which had blown him right out of his shoes. Zachary knew from his past investigations and accident scene reconstructions that it indicated a fast-moving vehicle. Had Richard not even heard it coming? Zachary didn't see anything in the file indicating that he'd been wearing earphones that might have blocked the noise of the approaching vehicle. His phone was in his pocket. If he'd been wearing earbuds, they had been torn from his body by the force just the same as the shoes had been.

What reason would he have had to be walking or standing on the road at that time of night? Had he been meeting someone? Walking to a neighbor's? Had he pursued a trespasser or burglar from his property out to the highway? Was he investigating a sound or an animal? Or had he just been out for a walk, unable to sleep and hoping that the exercise and fresh air would help him to reset and get some sleep?

It hadn't sounded from his discussion with Ashley at Old Joe's that walking outside had been a normal activity for Richard. He did his workouts inside where there weren't big rigs to mow him down.

Then what *had* made him decide to go out the night he had died? Zachary made a note in his notepad to check later and see if there had been any trouble Ashley wasn't aware of. Threats or a break-in. Any previous police reports or alarms with his security company. Just because Ashley said there wasn't anything going on, that didn't mean it was true. Richard might have hidden it from Ashley or Ashley might be hiding it from Zachary. He never could understand why a person would want to hire a private detective on a case and then keep secrets from him. But everyone seemed to hold something back.

In the evening, he was transcribing his notes from his notepad to the computer. He supposed he should make notes on his phone or get a tablet or a notebook that he took to the police station or other research sources with him, but he preferred the notepad. It was idiot-proof, the batteries didn't run down, and he hadn't yet lost his notes taken in a physical notepad, other than the ones he lost in the fire, along with everything else.

If he'd taken those notes on a cloud-connected app, he wouldn't have lost them, and would still have been able to get them back. But he hadn't had anything backed up to the cloud. Not his computer, not his photography, nothing. He was happy to find that his phone had automatically saved his contacts, and he'd had his email, but that was about it. Everything else had been lost in the fire, and Zachary had once again been left vulnerable and homeless, just like after the first fire, when his mother had decided that she couldn't take it anymore and had kicked him out of her life.

Zachary's phone buzzed. It was a few moments before he could tear his eyes from the computer screen to look at the display on the phone. His heart leapt when he saw Bridget's name. He swiped quickly before picking it up, to catch it before she hung up.

"Bridget?"

"Oh, you're there. I was beginning to wonder, Zachary."

"Sorry. I was just in the middle of writing reports. Needed to finish my thought."

"Are you home, then?"

"Yes."

"Mind if I stop over for a few minutes? I have something to give you."

Something to give him? While she still sometimes tried to take care of him, monitoring whether he was taking his meds and eating properly, he couldn't think of what it was that she might want to give him. But he didn't really care. He still welcomed any opportunity to see her again. No matter how many times Kenzie told him that he needed to just cut off contact with his ex, he couldn't do it. Bridget was a big part of his life, and even as an ex, she still had a place in his life.

"Sure, Bridget. I'm around all night."

"Great. I'll pop by a little later, then. Maybe an hour or so."

"I'll see you then."

The call had completely broken his concentration and he wasn't able to focus on the case notes again. He tried for another twenty minutes to get back into them and eventually gave up.

He went to the fridge and looked for something he could serve Bridget when she stopped by. But he didn't entertain much and he didn't think she'd be interested in a frozen dinner. He should start keeping a few bottles of her favorite drinks on hand so he'd always be prepared in case she decided to stop by.

He could just hear what Kenzie would have had to say about that plan.

It wasn't much past the predicted hour when Bridget got there. Zachary could hear her footsteps in the outside corridor and looked out his peep hole to make sure it was her, then opened the door as she drew closer. Bridget raised her eyebrows.

"Well, you didn't need to wait right at the door for me," she said dryly.

"I just happened to be there. I was looking to see if I had any drinks." He motioned to the fridge, giving a little shrug. "Not really anything interesting... maybe some tea?"

"No, I'm not going to be here for that long."

That was one of the reasons Zachary had been hoping to have something for her. Having a drink would encourage her to stay longer than she would otherwise.

"Oh. Well, come on in." He led her to the couch and the two of them sat down side by side. Zachary was careful not to crowd her too much. He didn't want to make her uncomfortable.

Bridget settled into the couch, taking a minute to look around the room for something to compliment or comment upon.

"It's starting to look lived-in," Bridget said. "Not like you just moved in."

"You mean it's a mess?" Zachary tried to keep his possessions orderly, knowing that they would quickly get out of control if he wasn't disciplined about putting things away where they belonged. But his home didn't have the decorator-magazine look of Bridget's home with Gordon. He couldn't function in something that was so antiseptically neat. He would find it just as distracting as an apartment with clothes and food wrappers on the floor.

But he didn't always succeed at keeping everything tidy, especially if he were working on a major case.

"No, I don't mean it's a mess. I mean it looks... like it's yours. Like you've settled in a little bit."

Zachary nodded. "Yeah. It's starting to feel like home."

"That's good. I didn't like it when you were at Mario's. I mean, it was nice to know that there was someone around to keep an eye on things and notice if you were going off the rails, but I think it's important for you to have a place of your own. It really is important for you to..." She shook her head, wrinkling up her nose as she fished for a way to explain her thoughts. "It's important for you to have a home base. An anchor."

Zachary nodded his agreement. He had lived so many years with uncertainty and unstable living arrangements, it was one thing that he craved and really couldn't live for long without. With his own place, he felt better mentally and was better at taking care of himself. Relying on someone like Bowman had allowed him to let things slip, and that wasn't good. He didn't have a lot of room to slip before hitting bottom.

He looked at Bridget, waiting for her to announce the reason she had showed up. She had said that she had something to give him. Bridget stiffened her backbone and reached for her purse.

"This was sort of strange. I didn't know what to make of it."

She inserted two fingers into the mouth of her purse and came out with an envelope. Not a number ten envelope, but the personal size, like grandmothers used when they wrote long rambling notes on flowery stationery. Bridget hadn't opened it, and Zachary's eyes immediately narrowed, wondering if she was worried about a letter bomb or harassing note. She handed it across to Zachary. He held it by the edges, not wanting to get his fingerprints on any evidence.

The envelope was made out in Zachary's name, not Bridget's. At an address that was a couple years old, from when they had been living together in wedded bliss. Or not so much bliss.

"I still have the mail forwarded," Bridget explained. "I know I shouldn't keep paying for forwarding from an address that neither of us has used in years, but then every time I think of letting it expire, I end up getting something that wouldn't have reached me otherwise. Or... you."

Zachary looked over the envelope to see what other information he could gather from it. His name and address were printed. Not exactly neatly, but clear enough to read without a problem. A hand that he would have identified as male rather than female, when women were the ones who usually sent personal notes by postal mail. Handwritten mail—did anyone really do that?

There was a return address, printed in tiny letters, but not so small that Zachary needed a magnifying glass to make it out.

T. Goldman.

Zachary's heart started to pound. He looked at Bridget in disbelief. "T. Goldman?"

"I know, I saw that. I didn't think... well, you haven't had any contact with anyone, have you?"

P.D. WORKMAN

"No." Zachary hadn't had any communications with anyone in his family since that fateful day when the social worker had insisted that Zachary's mother come to the hospital to see him before making the decision to dissolve the family and relinquish them all to foster care. Mrs. Pratt had hoped that by bringing Zachary and his mother together again one more time, she would see the error of her ways and would agree to look at other solutions. There were other social programs, other ways the family could be given support and help. But Zachary's mother had been adamant. She had called him incorrigible. She had looked him in the eye and told him, "You don't deserve to be part of a family. None of you do, but you most of all. Every time I turn around, you're getting into some kind of trouble. Don't give me those sad puppy dog eyes. You know I don't want you."

Her words cut him to the heart. He had tried so hard. Even after that, he had tried to be well-behaved in the hopes that she would change her mind and take him back. He wanted to prove to everyone how well he was doing. Show them that he could be a good son and a good brother. They could reunite him with his siblings. Maybe once their mother had had a bit of a rest, she would feel strong enough to take them again. She'd see that he could be a help to her instead of causing her more stress. But that wasn't the way it had turned out. She had never changed her mind and, in spite of Mrs. Pratt saying that he would be able to see his siblings again, he had never laid eyes on any of them since the fire that had burned down his childhood home.

"Zachary." Bridget touched his arm to try to bring him back to the present. "Zachary. Why don't you open it? See what they have to say." She hesitated, searching his face. "Do you know who T is? Is that a brother or a sister? Or a more distant relative?"

"Tyrrell. Younger brother. His nickname was T. At least, that's what I called him sometimes."

"Remind me of the names of the others. I know you've told me before, but I don't remember. There were two girls...?"

"Two older girls," Zachary corrected. "The oldest kids were Jocelyn—Joss—and Heather. They were like... they were supposed to take care of the rest of us. Like... second mothers."

"And then you?"

"Yeah. Me, I was ten. And then T was... I think he was in first grade.

Six years old. Then Vincent. And Mindy. She was just little. Not a baby anymore, exactly. A toddler. Maybe two. Not quite two, I don't think."

It was hard to remember back that far. So many things had happened in between. His memories of those early years with his family felt like a dream. Not a happy one, but distant and blurry.

"Wow, that's a lot of kids. You haven't had contact with any of them?"

"No. I don't know where they are."

"Well, apparently you do now," she indicated the address on the envelope. "Besides, you're a private detective, you could find them anytime you liked, couldn't you?"

"I don't know. They might have changed their names. Been adopted. Moved out of the country."

"But you've never looked for them?"

"No."

She sat there looking at him. She didn't pry, but it was obvious she wanted more from him. They'd been married for two years, and he hadn't told her any more than the absolute minimum about his biological family. It would be easy to say he had forgotten about them, but he hadn't. He'd been ten. He'd held as tightly to those memories as to his own name and identity. They were all he had left of his family.

"I'm afraid," he admitted. "If I contacted one of them, and they said they didn't want anything to do with me, I don't know if I could handle that. And if they blamed me for breaking our family apart and ruining their lives… well, I did. It was all my fault. Everything that happened to them from that Christmas Eve when I started the fire until now. It's all my fault."

"You never intended to start the fire. And I don't think you can say that you were the reason your mother and father decided to split the family up. That's on them, not you. There have been other families that have gone through worse tragedies and toughed it out together. None of you were killed in that fire. None of them were even injured, were they? Just you."

"Yeah." He'd spent weeks at the hospital recovering from the burns and the damage done to his respiratory system. But everyone else had gotten out of the house without any injuries, he had been told. "But she told me. She said it was my fault, and that it was because of me that she couldn't do it anymore."

"If it was because of you, then why didn't she raise the other kids and just have Social Services take you away? That doesn't make any sense."

Zachary shook his head. He looked down at the envelope in his hands.

"Open it," Bridget prompted.

"I can't."

"Then give it back to me and I'll open it."

He didn't. It was his. It wasn't Bridget's to open. It wasn't even hers to read or to insist that he open it in front of her. Just because it had gone to her house, that didn't give her any claim over it.

"So... you're just going to sit here looking at it. You're not going to open it."

"Uh-huh."

"Because you're afraid of what he'll say."

Zachary nodded. He flipped the envelope over in his hand, turned it back around again, and studied the postmark and stamp as if they were important evidence in a case.

"You think that he's waited thirty years to tell you how much he hates you for something that wasn't your fault."

"It *was* my fault."

"He was a little boy. He's trying to reach out to his big brother. It isn't about blame. He wants to get in touch with you."

Zachary pressed his lips tightly together and shook his head. He looked at the clock on his DVD player across the room. "I didn't realize how long I've kept you," he said. It wasn't a total lie because he was surprised at how much time had passed. He must have withdrawn into himself for a long time. He shook his head, as if that would clear his sense of disorientation. "Gordon will be wondering what happened to you."

Bridget recognized a dismissal when she heard it. She stood up slowly, looking down at Zachary on the couch.

"I'm here because I want to help, Zachary."

"Thank you for bringing the letter. I appreciate it."

Kenzie had said to cut his ties with Bridget. This was exactly what she had meant. Bridget thought that she had the right to be involved in Zachary's life and to make decisions for him. She thought that he owed her something because she had put up with him for two years and had brought him the letter. But she was the one who had chosen to break up. That hadn't been Zachary's decision.

Bridget huffed out an exasperated breath and headed for the door. "Are you just going to sit there looking at it all night?"

Maybe. Probably.

"Thanks for bringing it," he repeated.

Bridget's heels clicked all the way to the door, and she pulled it shut behind her with force that wasn't quite a slam, but not exactly a sedate departure either.

Zachary put one hand over his face, elbow braced on his knee, and tried to figure out what to do.

3

Rusty Donaldson was the trucker who had hit Richard. Zachary didn't know if Rusty was his birth name or a nickname due to his orange beard and hair. He was a pleasant man, around Zachary's own age, but much bigger, his chest twice as thick as Zachary's, towering over him by a least a foot. A hearty man's man.

"Uh, hi." Zachary forced a smile and offered his hand. Big men made him nervous. Sure, he'd known a few gentle giants, but more often he'd been bullied by the bigger boys as he grew up. There was lot of competition in foster homes and institutions, lots of opportunities for physical and emotional torture by the boys who were bigger and stronger.

Rusty took Zachary's hand and shook it warmly, without squeezing the life out of it. Though he had a naturally cheerful face, it turned grave as he looked at Zachary.

"I'll answer whatever questions you might have," he said. "I'm just sick over this thing. I'd never intentionally hurt someone, much less kill them. I feel awful for his family, and I'll do whatever I can to... make some sense of this for them."

Zachary nodded. Rusty had picked out the meeting place, the lounge of a truck stop. It was clean, quiet during the day, and upholstered in a dark red. They sat down and Rusty leaned in, eager to get started with the questions. Zachary felt a little disconcerted, used to witnesses who were a little more reticent.

"Why don't you tell me in your own words what happened that night, and then we can go over some additional details as questions come to me. You don't mind if I take notes while you're talking?"

"No, man. Go ahead."

"Thanks." Zachary opened his notepad and nodded for Rusty to begin.

He started off with a lot of technical information about the run he'd been doing, which meant little to Zachary, but he wrote down the details he thought were pertinent. Rusty's deadline and destination, the route he'd followed until he got to the secondary road where Richard had been killed.

"You'd been on that road before?" Zachary asked. "You're familiar with it?"

"Oh, sure. Been on it a dozen times before. A good shortcut, if you know the road goes all the way through. A lot of experienced truckers take it."

"And you'd never run into any trouble before."

"Nah. It's quiet. No accidents, no mechanical problems. The road itself is in good condition; paved, no potholes or ruts to deal with."

"But no shoulder, either, if you did run into any problems."

"No, you're right. Have you been on it?"

"I'm going to drive out to take a look at it after I have your story. No point in going out without knowing something about what happened."

"So you can check out my story," Rusty said with a bit of a grin.

Zachary returned his smile. "Of course."

"Good man. So… there's not really that much to tell. I was flying along, no obstacle or problems, nice straight stretch of road. Then I hear a bang and feel the truck take some kind of impact. So I hit the brakes and pulled over the best I could, in the dark with no shoulder. Got out the old Mag flashlight and scouted around the truck to see what had happened. Figured maybe I hit a deer. Not like it hasn't happened before."

"And what did you see?"

"A new dent and a bit of blood on the front right. No significant damage, lights were all intact. Maybe an animal smaller than a deer. A coyote or something."

"Did you have a look around to see if you could see it?"

"Sure. Walked back along the road maybe half a mile, sweeping my light across the road and off the side into the ditch. But I couldn't see anything suspicious. Couldn't find the place where I'd hit it, couldn't find any sign of a hurt animal. Sometimes they just run off into the woods and there's nothing you can do. I looked again on my way back to the truck, still couldn't see anything. So I got back in and kept going."

"And you had to have your load delivered the next morning," Zachary said, looking at his notes. "So you must have driven all night."

"We've all pulled an all-nighter now and then. I'm sure you have too."

Zachary hadn't slept a wink the night before. He nodded. "Yes, a few."

"Company's got rules about night driving and the number of hours you can drive at a time, all aimed to keep sleepy drivers off the road. Most guys are pretty good about following them."

Zachary noticed that Rusty didn't exactly say that he had followed them.

"I dropped my load and headed for home. I was just a couple of hours further on, then I could flake out in my own bed."

"Right. The police said you reported the possible collision to your insurer that morning?"

"Sure. You have to get these things taken care of as quickly as you can. No one is going to give you any breaks if you put it off. I called, told them I figured I hit a coyote, all the details, and went to bed."

"But it was a few days before you called the police."

Rusty nodded grimly. "I got my sleep in, took a couple of days' break, just like the company policy states. I was lined up for another run, so I went out to check out my truck, make sure I hadn't missed any damage in the dark that night."

Zachary cleared his throat and waited. Rusty was scowling, his bushy eyebrows drawn down fiercely over his eyes.

"There was a dent and blood spatter on the front, like I said. I took a picture with my phone and grabbed the high-pressure washer to clean it off. While I was washing it off, I was looking for any other damage or clue to what I had hit. There was a torn bit of cloth in the fender. It could have gotten there some other time. I didn't know for sure. But it seemed... out of place. Like it wasn't just someone who had brushed by it in the parking lot and got their jacket caught."

"So that's when you called the police."

"Yeah. Didn't get much response when I first called it in. It was just kind of a routine report, they didn't seem to think there was anything to be worried about. But then I got a call back from the police detective who was in charge of this Harding case. Told me I'd better come in and give a statement. Answer some questions." Rusty sighed. "So that's what I did. You might think that all truckers are naturally law-breakers, always in trouble with the police, but we're not. There are some rowdies out there, and everybody's had a traffic citation at some point, but most of us, we do our best to stay out of trouble and just live our own lives."

"Sure. So you were pretty anxious about having to go in and tell them about what had happened. You wondered why they had called you back after the reception to the initial call was so cool."

Rusty nodded earnestly. "Yes. Exactly. That's it exactly. I go in, thinking they want me to just write down in triplicate what I had told them on the phone, and it turned out that they had found a body in the ditch. I'd actually hit a person, and I had no idea." He blew out his breath noisily. "You have no idea how that feels."

"The police followed up on the call you made with your insurer. They examined your truck, even though you had already washed it off."

"I guess there was still some blood that I hadn't gotten off. In cracks. They charged me with hit and run, but released me, and the DA is reviewing it now... I guess deciding whether I did everything right, or whether there was something else I should have done. I swear I looked in the ditch, but it was dark, and I must have missed him. If there was something I could have done..." He had a haunted look. "I can't imagine him, lying in the ditch there, dying, thinking that nobody cared and that I had just gone on..."

It was a macabre thought, and Zachary didn't envy Rusty his nightmares. He had done everything right as far as Zachary could tell. He hadn't known that he had hit anyone.

But Zachary had been hired to look into Richard's death from the other angle. To look into the possibility that Rusty Donaldson had intentionally killed Richard on the road that night.

"Did you know Richard Harding?"

"Know him?" Rusty shook his head. "No way. I'd never heard of the guy before the police told me he was dead. I guess I'd driven down his road before, past his farm, but I had no idea. I don't know anyone who lives along that route. Not that I know of."

"His girlfriend doesn't think it was an accident."

"Not an accident? What, she thinks…" Rusty's florid color drained. "She thinks that I ran down her boyfriend on purpose?"

"Yes."

"Why would she think that?" He seemed truly astonished. Apparently, the police hadn't told him about Ashley's theory.

"I haven't quite figured that out yet. There may be something she isn't telling me. Maybe he got threats or had something on his mind. Maybe it's just the shock and grief. I don't know. But that's why she's hired me."

"She hired you to prove that I killed Harding on purpose?"

"Yes."

Rusty's expression changed so rapidly Zachary was reminded of a board game spinner cycling through options. Where was it going to land? Anger, astonishment, regret, fear, more anger, directed at Zachary this time, confusion, guilt, more wide-eyed fear. Finally, he just stared at Zachary, blanking all expression out, staring at him with lifeless eyes, as if Rusty himself had left his corporeal form and gone far away.

"I never met Harding before in my life. I don't know what he was doing out on the road that night, but if I'd seen him, I would have avoided him. I would never have hit him on purpose. The thought that I hit and killed a man… it just makes me sick. Whenever I think of the thud that night, my stomach is all in knots."

"As far as you know, you never talked with him, never emailed or texted him, never ran into each other at some social event."

"No. Nothing. I've never heard of the guy before in my life."

"You never dated his sister or his girlfriend."

"Uh…" Rusty shook his head. "I have no idea who his girlfriend is. How would I know that?"

"Do you know an Ashley Morton?"

"Is that her name?"

"Do you?"

"No. No, I don't know anyone named Ashley Morton. I don't date a lot, and when I do, it's usually ladies who… hang out around the truck stops. If your girlfriend is one of those gals, then maybe we've hooked up before. But I don't remember an Ashley."

"I'll try to find any connections between you. And I'm a good investigator, you should know that. If you've had any contact with Richard Harding or Ashley Morton before or after the accident, you should just tell me now."

"No. I swear, I've never heard of either one of them before."

"Would you mind giving me all of your contact details? Any phone numbers or email addresses that you use? Your home address, anywhere you use computers regularly?"

"Why would I do that? You could set me up!"

"I'm not trying to set you up. If you haven't had any contact with him, then you have nothing to worry about."

Rusty motioned for Zachary's notepad and pen. Zachary flipped to a fresh page and slid it across to him. Rusty wrote down several lines of information.

"Anything else?" he demanded. "Social security number? Blood type?"

"If you want to include those, and your birth date, that would make things easier for me," Zachary agreed, keeping his voice and expression flat.

Rusty looked up at Zachary in surprise, then broke into a grin again, the mask of indifference falling away. "It's not in my best interests to make your job easy." He looked down at the information he had written down. "So why am I giving you all of this?" He pushed it back across to Zachary as if he were afraid that he might tear the page out and crumple it up. "If I had contact with Harding, do you really think I would give you that address or phone number?"

"No. I don't. I don't think I'll find any of these numbers or addresses on anything with Richard Harding's name on it. But eliminating them is one more step. One more thing I can do for my client."

Rusty shook his head. "Helluva job you've got there, Goldman. Helluva job."

Zachary knew that if he wanted to avoid another sleepless night, he was going to have to open the letter from Tyrrell. Bridget hadn't called him or contacted him to see if he'd opened it yet, but he was sure she was thinking about it, wondering how long it would take him to pull himself together and simply rip the envelope open.

He wore gloves and slit it carefully with a knife, treating it as if it were important forensic evidence. And it could be, couldn't it? There might be DNA in the saliva that was used to seal the envelope, if it wasn't a self-sealing envelope and if the sender hadn't used a sponge-top bottle to seal it.

There could be fingerprints on it. There could be other evidence that he wasn't aware of. A hair stuck in the seal. Skin cells. Other transfer evidence.

He slit the end rather than the top, and then pressed the top and bottom of the envelope to make it pop open in a tube shape to examine the contents.

It appeared to be a single sheet of paper. No unknown powders or other contaminants. No letter bomb. Just one piece of paper.

He used a pair of tweezers to snag the letter and pull it out onto the table. Just a plain white piece of paper, torn off a tablet, slightly jagged at the top. Not a densely-written letter, just a few loose lines of print, the same printing that had appeared on the outside of the envelope.

Dear Zachary,

I am looking for my brother.

Do you remember me?

If you are the right Zachary Goldman, please get in contact with me.

T

He had followed with several lines of contact information. An email address, a cell phone number to call or text. A repeat of the return address written on the outside of the envelope.

Zachary read the words over again hungrily, like a starving man who, expecting a feast, had been given only a single cracker. Tyrrell—assuming it was Tyrrell who had written the letter—wanted to get in touch with him. But he had left it up to Zachary.

There were no declarations of love or hate, leaving him to wonder how Tyrrell felt about him. Sorry they had been separated? Angry for what Zachary had done? Maybe he didn't care about reconciling and just needed a kidney. Would Zachary give him a kidney if he asked?

Zachary carefully put the envelope and letter into a plastic bag before taking off his gloves.

4

Zachary ran a full background check on Rusty Donaldson. Criminal record, courthouse search, credit check, past residences, family members, all of the public records he could think of. He owned his truck and rented his house. He didn't have any criminal charges. No DUIs. A few speeding tickets, but none of them at crazy speeds and none of them at night. He'd had stable employment. No marriages, divorces, or paternity suits. All in all, a guy who had been living quietly within the law for many years.

The next task was to check out Harding's phone and laptop, which Ashley had supplied Zachary with. The police had looked at his phone and not found anything of interest, but Zachary knew they didn't usually look at electronics too closely unless there was a compelling reason, and in the case of a man accidentally hit from behind on a dark road at night, there wasn't a reason to give them more than a cursory look. Zachary had called Gerry Birch, his usual tech guy, who had cloned the computer's hard drive to preserve any data. Gerry had also broken the news to Zachary that the drive was encrypted, which meant that a simple boot hack like he'd used in other cases would not be helpful.

The first thing he thought odd was that Harding's phone didn't have any social media on it. No profiles, no instant messaging apps, nothing. The apps built in by default had been removed. The email address that was attached to the phone was a new address that had just been set up within the last year and had only a few non-spam messages in it.

Even the text messages had been wiped. Zachary had looked at dozens of phones that still had every text message since the beginning of time stored on them. People hardly ever deleted text messages, and if they did, it was just a few here and there. The ones that were incriminating. Harding's text messages had been completely wiped. There were only a few messages exchanged with Ashley, in the day or two before he had died. Then the increasingly worried and frantic texts that Ashley had sent when she couldn't reach him the morning after the accident. Zachary followed the progression from casual and routine to really worried, demanding Richard call her.

The phone itself was a recent purchase, within a few months of Harding's death. For anything earlier than that, Zachary would have to see what he could get from the phone company. Getting call logs, text logs, and old voicemail messages from phone companies could be complicated. It sometimes took weeks or even months to get everything. Even a police warrant didn't always get an immediate response from one of the big providers.

Ashley had known the unlock code for the phone, which had saved Zachary the effort of trying to hack it. The computer was another story. Zachary tried a few different passwords, hoping that the computer didn't have any kind of software on it that would automatically destroy data once the limit of password retries was reached. Variations of Ashley's name, Harding's birthday, anniversaries of when they had met and started dating. The phone unlock code had been a simple pattern, but trying to replicate it on the computer didn't work.

Zachary searched through the phone for any note or password keeping app. He glanced at the computer screen and noticed an unlock icon. He turned the phone screen off, sending it into standby mode, and the lock icon disappeared. He could have kicked himself. The phone was a key to unlock the computer. A proximity auto-unlock. Zachary unlocked the phone again and clicked the unlock icon when it appeared on the computer screen. The laptop whirred and the screen came to life. He was in.

At first look, the computer was much the same as the phone. It was of recent vintage and didn't have a lot stored on it. The email address was the same as the one attached to the phone and all messages and messaging apps had been removed.

When he opened the browser, it booted automatically into a private window instead of the usual browser experience. The kind that didn't leave electronic footprints showing what sites had been visited. In Zachary's experience, it was rare that the average computer user even knew about private browsing modes, much less had their default browse mode set to private. He dug into the computer's connection details and found that it was also set up to connect through an IP anonymizer, making it more difficult to track where the computer was logging in from. It was some serious online security, which was surprising considering how easy it had been to get onto the phone and computer in the first place.

Private mode on the browser was set to automatically wipe the history of the sites visited. Zachary switched over to regular browsing, and found that the history had been deleted there.

He switched over to the built-in operating system app that could save and autocomplete passwords, and found that it had not been cleared out. Zachary went methodically through the list. All of the main social media sites. Some news sites. Harding's email address. But there was another email address too, one that neither the computer nor the phone were logged into. Zachary typed the webmail URL into the browser and accepted the autofill suggestion. The inbox had obviously not been checked in some time and was overflowing with unread messages. Zachary stared at the bold black subject lines.

How could you live with yourself?

You are a piece of s***

You should be ashamed of yourself

You should die

Zachary swore to himself under his breath. He had begun to suspect that there was something strange going on with Harding. The lack of social apps and texts on his phone, the private browser, and a brand-new email address were not exactly red flags, but had made him curious. If Harding was being electronically stalked and harassed, that would explain why he had started taking countermeasures to cover up his online activity.

Zachary started to read through the accusatory emails. They were, unfortunately, vague and rambling and did not outline exactly what the writer believed Harding had done. The accuser had known and had assumed that Harding also knew exactly what he was talking about.

The emails came from a number of different addresses with odd combinations of letters and numbers, obviously from a system that generated one-off addresses. The kind you could use when you wanted to download a free guide without getting spammed by the company afterward. Chances were the email addresses themselves would be untraceable.

Zachary logged into each of Harding's abandoned social media accounts in turn. It didn't take long to find the vitriolic messages in the direct mailboxes of each of them too. It was no wonder Harding had stopped using them. There was no escaping the messages. Harding's banned, muted, and blocked user lists were long, but his stalker had obviously just kept creating new identities and harassing Harding relentlessly.

After spending hours going through Richard's social media and poison pen messages, Zachary was almost afraid to look at his own phone when it buzzed to indicate that he'd received a text message. He knew it was silly, because he wasn't the one who had been getting the harassing messages. The only unusual contact that he'd received recently was the letter from Tyrrell. But after seeing how the stalker had hounded Richard, Zachary couldn't help feeling a little vulnerable himself.

As a private detective, he knew how easy it was to find out all kinds of supposedly private details about the average person, but he had never been particularly careful about protecting his own information. Maybe in the back of his mind, he had hoped that by leaving a trail, one day some member of his family would come along and track him down. If he made himself too difficult to find, then there was no chance he would ever be reunited with his loved ones.

Zachary picked up his phone, and instead of seeing a message from Richard's stalker or from Tyrrell, he was almost surprised to see a message from Kenzie.

Hear you're on the Harding case. Give me a call when you're free.

Zachary stretched and yawned noisily. He unfolded himself from his chair at the desk and made a trip to the bathroom and then to the fridge before calling Kenzie back. If they ended up having a longer discussion, he didn't want to be interrupted by inconvenient physical demands. He'd been hunched over the computer for hours, which was not good for his body or his mind. He walked briskly around the apartment for a minute to get the blood flowing and to clear his head.

He sat on the couch and gave Kenzie a call. He closed his eyes and visualized her masses of dark curly hair and her bright red lipsticked lips as the phone rang. He felt a rush of warmth when he answered and heard her "Hi, Zachary."

"Hi. How are you?"

"What's this I hear? You get a new case out of my office and you don't give me a call? What's going on with you?" Her voice was teasing, not really angry with him. Usually, she was irritated when he asked about a case that she believed was clearly accidental but he thought might just be something else.

"You hear it from Bowman?" he asked.

"Where else? You apparently didn't think it was important enough to call me."

"I don't need you yet," Zachary returned, teasing her gently back.

"Ha. Exactly! I know how it is. The only reason you're interested in me is to get someone to interpret pathology reports for you."

"Kenzie, you know that's not true... I'm getting pretty good at reading them by myself."

She chuckled. "Well, your friend is in autopsy right now, so I thought maybe you'd like to get together for supper to go through initial findings. Full report won't be ready yet, of course, but I can hit the high points."

"Yeah, that would be great." Zachary looked at Richard's phone and computer, and thought he might want to show Kenzie what he had found there. Which meant that a restaurant wouldn't be the best place to meet. The two of them huddled over a laptop at a restaurant would be awkward, even if he waited until after they had eaten. "How would you like to come over here and we'll order in?"

"Oh," she was obviously surprised at the invitation. They really didn't stay in. Most of the time, she was trying to make sure he got out of the house for something other than surveillance. "Sure, that sounds fine."

5

Kenzie showed up on schedule and she and Zachary went through a few takeout menus before settling on pizza and placing their order. They talked in general terms about work and the weather and current events while they waited for the pizza.

"Are you getting ready for Christmas?" Kenzie asked.

Zachary tried to figure out how to respond to her. She didn't mean anything by it, she was just making more small talk, the events of the previous year and what she knew of his past far from her mind.

Kenzie lifted one eyebrow, waiting for his answer. Then he saw realization enter her features, and her mouth formed a small 'O' of surprise. "I wasn't even thinking, Zachary! I forgot that Christmas is a hard time for you. I'm sorry."

"It's okay." Zachary tried to brush it off and move on to other topics. "It's just my thing, you shouldn't have to tiptoe around me."

"Well, since I already put my foot in it, how are you doing with it? Does your therapist have any tips for getting through holidays and anniversaries of bad things happening?"

"I… never thought to ask."

"You know that you're seriously depressed every Christmas, and you haven't addressed it with him? Don't you think that might be a good idea?"

Zachary shrugged. "I've had so many psychiatrists and therapists in the past… none of them have ever been able to do anything about my state of mind around Christmas. I'm just used to… trying to get through it on my own."

"I don't think that's a good idea. You need to get help and not be left alone with your own thoughts at a time when you know you're likely to be suicidal."

Zachary scratched his jaw, his face and ears burning. "Uh…"

"I'm sorry if being blunt embarrasses you. But it's not a topic to be delicate about. Do you know how many people end up in the morgue because they didn't talk openly about being depressed and having suicidal thoughts?"

"I guess more than would if they talked about it. I'm just… not used to it. People just usually don't want to hear. It makes them uncomfortable." He was aware that he was echoing Bridget's words. How many times had she chided him that talking about depression or mental illness in front of their friends made them uncomfortable, and he should never do anything that he knew would make them uncomfortable. He had grown up knowing this rule in the back of his head and knowing that talking about depression and suicide was taboo, but he'd never had anyone tell him that explicitly before Bridget. It just *wasn't* discussed in polite company.

"Taking care of yourself means letting other people help and explaining when there is a problem," Kenzie said. "If you push everyone away, then you're going to find yourself alone and that's going to be a problem."

"Yeah. I know you're right, but over the years… people have their own family traditions at Christmas. I don't like to impose on anyone."

Kenzie pulled her phone out. "Look, let's start planning now. Christmas Day, you and I are going to get together for dinner. My place." They never went to Kenzie's apartment, so this news startled Zachary. He figured since she had never invited him to her apartment, that she was protecting her own safety. She didn't want someone else in her space. She didn't want someone else to have access to her living quarters. It was a matter of keeping safe. She knew she could always leave Zachary's apartment, but she couldn't leave her own. Kenzie didn't seem to notice Zachary's consternation, tapping the details into her phone. "Don't expect a big turkey dinner. I'll do a two-person version. Turkey breast, gravy, mashed potatoes. But I'm not doing a whole bird, there's no point in that." She looked up from her phone, raising both brows.

"Okay," Zachary agreed. "Sure. Thanks, that's really nice of you."

"Aren't you going to put it into your phone or planner?"

Zachary's guts knotted tightly. He could barely breathe. "I'll do it later."

"You might forget later. Just put it in now."

Zachary looked for a way out of it. He knew that he'd never be able to put anything on his calendar past Christmas Eve. That was always the way. He couldn't plan anything past that cliff.

He swallowed hard and pulled a sticky note out of the dispenser on his desk. Putting it on the desk, he hovered his pen over the note for a few seconds, with no idea what to even write. Finally, he forced himself to scratch out the words, "Kenzie X-mas?" He unstuck the note from the desk and stuck it to the edge of his monitor. Kenzie looked satisfied with this process.

"Good. You know what can really help around Christmastime when you're feeling really overwhelmed with everything?"

She really didn't have any idea how paralyzing it was for him. He didn't just feel stressed at Christmas. He didn't have problems with Christmas lists and trying to buy presents for loved ones. He didn't worry over baking cookies for Santa or some community potluck. For him, it wasn't overwhelming because there was too much to do. It was overwhelming because he couldn't stop thinking about his family and how he had ruined their lives and his and how the pain would stop if he just chose to put an end to it.

He shook his head in response to Kenzie's question. "No. What helps?"

"Doing something for someone else. Taking the focus off yourself and thinking about how you can help someone else to have a good Christmas."

Zachary grunted noncommittally.

"I know. You think it sounds cliche. But it isn't. Reaching out to someone else, taking the focus off of your own problems, it really does help."

"Yeah, maybe."

"You know what would be a really good idea?" Kenzie's voice rose excitedly as the thought came to her. Zachary shook his head. "What about doing something for Rhys?"

Rhys was a young black boy whom Zachary had met on a previous case. Rhys's mother had ended up in prison, which meant he really was going to have a bad Christmas, his first one without her. Or maybe going to the prison to visit with her on Christmas. Not quite as bad as Zachary's experience of burning the house down and losing everything he had on Christmas Eve, but it was a contender. Rhys had selective mutism, which had developed after his grandfather was murdered when he was still just a child. If anyone could compete with Zachary for rotten childhoods, it was Rhys.

Zachary swallowed, his throat dry. "Yeah. He's going to have a pretty sad Christmas this year."

"So let's do something for him. Think about it, okay? We'll brainstorm, and maybe talk to Vera and see what she suggests."

"Yeah." Despite his misgivings, Zachary found that his heart did lift a little at the thought of doing something for Rhys so that his Christmas could be a little better. He forced a smile for Kenzie so that she would see he agreed it was a good idea. "Thanks."

There was a knock on the door and Zachary peered through the peep hole at the pizza deliveryman before opening it. The spicy and sweet smell of freshly-baked pepperoni pizza wafted into the apartment. Zachary settled up the bill and tipped the deliveryman, then put the box out on the table and opened it up.

"That smells great! I could eat a horse!" Kenzie declared.

Zachary had disposable plates and he had nipped across the street to pick up some beer before Kenzie's arrival. He put out the extra items. Kenzie twisted off the cap on a bottle of beer.

"You having anything tonight?"

He considered the possibility, then shook his head. He hadn't slept the night before, and if his thoughts turned to Tyrell's letter he might want to take something to help calm his thoughts and help him to sleep. He wasn't supposed to mix alcohol with his medications, so if he didn't want to eliminate the possibility of taking pills later, he'd have to pass on beer at supper.

"I'll just have water."

"You know, I admire you being careful not to mix your meds and alcohol," Kenzie commented as she took a couple of big slices of pizza from the box and slid them onto her plate. "Too many people just ignore those problems and end up with liver damage or a really bad reaction. Or a toxic combination. I'd rather not see you on Dr. Wiltshire's table."

Zachary shrugged and looked for the smallest piece of the pizza. "It's not a big deal."

"Actually, it is. I'm proud of you for not allowing yourself 'just one' or saying you'll have burned it all off by the time you need to take anything. A lot of people ignore those warnings."

"Well... thanks."

They sat down in the living room to eat. Kenzie lounged comfortably against the armrest and closed her eyes to savor the pizza. "This is great. I'll have to remember them next time I'm ordering in."

As disgusting as it might seem to outsiders, Zachary and Kenzie often talked over autopsy results while they ate, so once they were settled, Zachary started to think about Richard Harding and his sudden death on the side of the road that night.

"So you have some initial autopsy findings on Harding?"

Kenzie took another big bite and nodded while she chewed it. "Yeah. Nothing shocking. Blunt force trauma that shattered everything down his left side. Consistent with what would happen if he was walking down the right side of the road with his back to traffic. Death was probably instantaneous. Not a lot of bleeding despite the trauma."

"That will make Rusty Donaldson feel better."

"Who is Rusty?"

"The trucker who hit him. Having nightmares about Harding slowly dying in the ditch because he didn't see him in the dark, even when he went back and looked."

"Oh. That sounds pretty awful. I didn't know they'd caught the guy. But yeah, Harding didn't likely suffer."

"And there wasn't anything out of place or unexplained?"

"Tox screen was clean. He wasn't drunk or high, so I have no clue why he was out walking on the road in the dark."

"Wearing dark clothing and walking with his back to the traffic."

"A lot of people don't seem to know they're supposed to walk on the left. They're so used to driving on the right, that's what they automatically do. But dark clothing... that's pretty stupid. From what I understand, there's a fair bit of traffic on that road."

"Yeah. It's not exactly a quiet farm road, from what I gather. I'm going to go out and take a look at the scene in a day or two."

"Well..." Kenzie shrugged. "Who knows what his reasons were. Maybe he was out looking for his dog. Or checking on a strange noise. Or a UFO."

Zachary chuckled. He nibbled at his slice of pizza. Kenzie had already worked her way through one big slice and was starting the second.

"The girlfriend thinks it wasn't an accident. She thinks that the driver hit Harding on purpose."

"Is that why you're on the case? Looking to prove intentional homicide?"

"Yeah. I mean… not trying to prove it, but investigating whether it's a possibility. I don't have any intention of railroading the guy."

"I hope not. Not the Zachary I know. Why does she think it was on purpose?"

"She didn't give me a cogent reason. But I might have found it without her help."

"What?" Kenzie inquired, mouth full.

Zachary motioned to Richard's computer. He crossed the room to sit at the desk, putting his plate to the side so it wouldn't be near any sensitive equipment. He hated the feeling of crumbs crunching under the computer keys.

"I've got his computer. A lot of stuff has been deleted from his phone and computer. All of his social media apps. He had been using a new email address recently, but I did get into his former email address." Zachary beckoned Kenzie over. She stood behind his shoulder, keeping her pizza well back from the computer. Zachary switched back to the email screen he'd been looking at previously and waited for Kenzie's reaction. She leaned forward to read the subject lines and her mouth dropped open.

"Holy crap!"

Zachary nodded his agreement. "He tried to block the guy, but nothing worked, he just kept rotating email addresses. So Harding created a new email account and stopped opening the previous one. And he started using IP anonymizers and private browser windows to keep from leading the stalker to the new email address."

"That's pretty hard core."

"The stalker was sending stuff to all of his social media accounts and probably his phone number, and was harassing him through whatever means possible. I mean… look at these."

Kenzie was looking at the subject lines. She shook her head. "Things were really bad. Poor guy. You think this is why the girlfriend said it was intentional homicide? Because she knew he was being stalked?"

"He must have told her about it, right? I can't imagine him just going on with his life and not even mentioning it to his partner."

"You're right. He'd need to tell someone. He couldn't just deal with it without anyone else even knowing."

Zachary nodded. He held a lot of things in. He put up with the pain and didn't tell those closest to him. He thought he could deal with it himself. But keeping the extent of the harassment Richard was dealing with a secret seemed impossible.

"So does the girlfriend think that this Rusty, this truck driver, is the one who was harassing Harding?"

"I don't know. She didn't say anything about it. But that's going to have to be my next step. Trying to trace the cyberstalking back to Rusty. Matching up his schedule with the IP locations of the emails. He's a long haul trucker, so these emails should originate from all over the area he covers."

"Yeah. Good thinking. Unless he's been masking his IP addresses, which I certainly would if I was stalking someone. If he knows how to track Richard's email address and other details, then he wouldn't leave himself open the same way. He'd cover them up so no one could get back to him."

"Even if he did, there should still be a pattern to the timing as well. No emails when he was actually driving from one place to another. More during his down times. And some kind of connection between the two of them, because he needs to have a reason for this. They must have belonged to the same club, gone to the same church, something. And they don't exactly live in the same neighborhood. They must have some kind of shared history. This sounds personal, don't you think?"

"Have you read through them to see what they're talking about? What it was that triggered this guy?"

Zachary randomly clicked on one of the subject lines, opening the email. The subject line was "you should be too ashamed to even live," and when the email opened, it was filled with dark and violent moving gifs. Kenzie winced and pulled back.

"Oh. Yuck."

"There is text in some of them." Zachary closed the email and clicked on another. There were a couple of lines of rambling text. Zachary, staring hard at the words to make them stay still and make sense, ended up just shaking his head. "I can't make heads or tails of it. You'd think that with my experience, raving lunatics would make at least some sense."

"Don't put yourself down. If you're going to catch this guy, you're going to have to outsmart him. You've done that before and you can do it again. He'll have made a mistake somewhere, we just have to find it."

Zachary closed the email again and just stared at the flickering screen. "Do you think it's the trucker? Or do you think it's coincidence that he was being stalked and then got killed?"

"I don't know… Obviously, the girlfriend would disagree with me, but this doesn't have the hallmarks of a stalker or a crime of passion or insanity. It feels like an accident. Like the truck driver was just lighting a cigarette or changing the radio tuner, and looked away from the road in the instant that he might have caught a glimpse of Harding. Night driving, going a bit too fast, Harding is all dressed in dark colors. Rusty wouldn't have been able to see Harding until he was on top of him, and then it's too late."

Zachary nodded. So far, he didn't see anything that suggested otherwise. The fact that Richard had a cyberstalker did not mean that the stalker had killed him.

6

 - - - - - - - - - - - - -

Ashley griped and groaned about having to meet Zachary at suppertime out at Harding's house, and Zachary wondered if maybe she thought he was fishing for a date or even just a free meal. That wasn't what he had been doing, and he tried to explain to Ashley without saying anything that might disturb her.

"I'd like to see the road while it's still light enough to see where they found Richard's body and scout around a little. But I also want to see it at night. How dark it is, how busy it is, how far ahead a truck would have been able to see. I don't want to have to put you out twice, so I thought if I could catch the daylight and the nighttime both in one visit, that would work the best."

"Oh." Ashley thought about this. He didn't know if she were looking for an argument, a way to talk him out of his logic, but if she were, she didn't seem to find it. "I guess… I can see your point."

"You don't need to feed me. I realize it's suppertime and it's inconvenient. I don't want to put you out, so you just go about your business and have your meal like you normally would. I'll want to look around the house about that time. You don't need to entertain me."

"I wasn't thinking that."

"If you were concerned about it, you don't need to be. I'll be around for a few hours, but other than a few questions, I won't need you most of the time."

"Well... okay, I guess. I'll have to get out there to tidy things up for the real estate agent anyway. May as well do it all at once."

"I'm sorry to put you out..."

"No, like I say, I have to get out there anyway..."

So he got his way and showed up at Richard Harding's home after a slow drive down the road Harding had been killed on, looking for anything out of the ordinary. There was no sign of the accident that had occurred there, no marker showing where he had been struck or where his body had been found. Zachary didn't see any significant marks on the pavement, though there were occasional light skid marks, some of them perhaps made as cars avoided wildlife, and one by Rusty Donaldson after something bounced off his front fender, when he pulled his rig over to have a look.

Ashley stood in the open doorway of the house watching him as he pulled into the gravel pad to park. She didn't greet him, but simply asked, "What do you want to see first?"

"I'd like to have a look at where his body was found. I have the GPS coordinates from the police report, so I don't need you to go with me."

"Why didn't you just look at it on your way in?"

Zachary hesitated, trying to work it out in his own mind. It just hadn't seemed like the right thing to do.

"I didn't want to be poking around without checking in with you first." He gave an awkward shrug. "I guess you probably don't care, but it didn't seem proper."

Ashley didn't disagree with his assessment or say it was stupid. She just looked at him for a minute. In the afternoon sun, her complexion was washed out and she seemed older and more worn than she had at Old Joe's.

"You don't need to come with me," Zachary told her again. "But if you want to be there to supervise or... be where it happened... we can go out together."

"Okay," she conceded. "Should we take my car or yours?"

Zachary grimaced. "I know it's not environmentally conscious, but we should probably take both. I have cameras and other investigative equipment in my car that I might need and you might want to come back before I'm done. If you have your own car, you can decide how long you want to stay."

Ashley headed over to her own car, a shiny blue VW Bug, and got in. It was a far cry from Kenzie's beloved red convertible or Richard's nondescript black four-door Cavalier. He pondered what it might say about her personality. Fun loving? Artistic? Outgoing? It was hard to reconcile in her current grieving state. He slid back into his white compact, which looked exactly like hundreds of other white compacts in the county, commonly used in rental and courier fleets and by people who were concerned with maintaining a good resale value. A private detective's car, intended to be invisible and unmemorable.

He let Ashley lead the way rather than relying on the GPS coordinates, though one thing he would do when he got there was to verify the location against the police records. He couldn't think of any reason Ashley would have to lead him to the wrong location, but people's memories could be faulty. The record the police had made was unlikely to be.

The irrigation ditch was close to the road, so there wasn't much space to pull over. He did the best he could and hoped that the passing traffic would take care and not hit his car.

Ashley motioned to the ditch, her motion languid, her shoulders slumped and head bowed.

"This is where they found him, down there in the grass and undergrowth. You couldn't see him, even standing here and looking down during the day. Certainly not from a car driving by. He wouldn't have been found if we hadn't been looking for him. It isn't exactly a place that hikers come through."

He could see glimpses of black water and mud through the dense grasses and brush. There was brown grass beside the road that was trampled into the dirt, but it had snowed on and off in the past week and he couldn't see a lot of footprints. Zachary could picture it as it would have been while the investigation was ongoing. Pylons with yellow tape stretched between them. Evidence markers wherever they had found anything that might have to do with the investigation. Examining and taking pictures of the body while it was in situ. Then it would be carefully loaded into a body bag and carried away. He hoped that Ashley had not seen any of these activities close up.

"Thanks. This is going to take me a while. You can stay or go, it's up to you."

It appeared she was going to stay. Zachary did his best to ignore her and go about his investigation like he would without any supervision.

He used a handheld GPS to record a few reference points, drew a diagram, measured the distances between the reference points and various landscape features. He had been involved in accident reconstruction scenes before. He was no expert, but he knew the basics and would collect enough information that he could consult with an expert later if he had to. The police had already done their best estimates, but it was difficult, given that they were out there several days after the collision had occurred and they had little evidence to rely on.

He walked back on the road, keeping a careful eye and ear on the occasional vehicles that approached to ensure that he didn't end up in the same position as Harding had. He walked the side of the road as Harding must have done, feeling the evenness of the pavement, the pitch of the slope, the way the road crowned and then sloped off at the edge. He kept a sharp eye on the ditch, his attention jumping from the road to the traffic to the ditch in rapid succession over and over again. They hadn't found both of Harding's shoes, so the other had to be out there somewhere.

After walking the road both approaching and departing from the site where the body had been found, Zachary geared up and descended into the ditch. There was a crust of ice over the sludgy water and mud. He slogged down its length; it was much harder than walking the road, and he was glad he had thought to bring hip waders. If someone were out there at night, they would definitely have to walk the road rather than the ditch. It would have been far too dangerous and difficult to get through in the dark. Even in daylight, it took at least four times as long to traverse the ditch as it did the road.

He watched for any sign of snagged clothing, anything that Harding might have been holding or wearing and any sign that someone else had been there. Had Rusty descended into the ditch to check on whether Harding was alive or dead? Had there been someone else with him? Had Harding been running away from someone or chasing after someone? What had made him go out there so late at night?

Even after Zachary figured he had gone past the point of collision, he kept going. He started to see trash in the ditch, which meant he had gone past the perimeter the police had established. The police would have collected every piece of debris they had found within the perimeter in case it were relevant to the case. The sun was getting lower in the sky. It would be dusk before too long. Zachary pressed on, slowed by the muck and vegetation and having to stop to examine the bits of garbage. Food wrappers, straws, unidentifiable clothing ground with mud. A "For Sale" sign. Curled black hunks of tire. Shredded plastic of every description. His foot caught on something in the ditch. Probably another piece of tire or a shelf of ice. Zachary bent down to pick it up, glad he was wearing industrial rubber gloves.

What he came up with was a very muddy red high-top shoe. The mate to the one the police had found.

Zachary clambered up the side of the ditch to the road. From his pocket he pulled a large glow stick and snapped it along its length to activate the chemical reaction that would start it glowing. He placed it on the side of the road, then placed a second one for good measure. Zachary briskly walked the road back to his car. Ashley had, at some point, left him alone there, taking her car back to the house. Zachary was glad she wasn't there to see the sneaker. He put it directly into a plastic bag and left it in the car. He grabbed a small orange pylon and walked it back to the glow sticks and placed it as well.

Another walk back to his car to add the new location to the hand-drawn map. He measured the distance between the shoe and the body, taking a careful GPS read and using a laser sight to get as accurate a distance as possible. He pulled out his phone and searched through his contacts for Joshua Campbell.

Apparently, he was in Campbell's contact list as well, since Campbell recognized his caller ID and greeted him by name.

"Zachary Goldman!"

"Hey. I'm out at the Harding scene."

"You've seen our file, so I'm not sure I'm going to be able to help you with anything further."

"No, I've got something for you."

"Oh." Campbell gave a rumbling laugh. "What did you find?"

"I've got the other shoe."

"Hell! How did you find that? We searched and searched. Even had the dogs out, but they were useless at finding any kind of trail after a couple of days had passed."

"It was outside of your search radius. And underwater."

"Hmm." Campbell cleared his throat and thought about that for a few minutes. "That's going to have an impact on the reconstruction wonks' calculations, isn't it?"

"Yes. The rig was heavier or going faster than they figured."

Campbell swore. "You're on the scene now?"

"Yes. I planned to go through the house next, then come back out here after dark. Maybe seeing the scene like Harding would have seen it that night will trigger something else."

"It will be the same, except dark."

Zachary laughed. "Well, yes. And the traffic patterns will be different. Animals coming out. I don't know what else, because I haven't seen it yet."

"If you're going to be out there after dark, do me a favor and light yourself up. Like a Christmas tree. Lights and reflectors from head to toe."

His mention of a Christmas tree made Zachary remember the other tree. The tree that had blazed with fire. Whenever anyone said 'lit up like a Christmas tree,' that was what he remembered. It had been bright; like a burning torch. He gripped the phone hard and tried to focus on the feeling of it in his hand. He took a deep breath of the chilly air. "I'll be sure to be visible," he agreed weakly.

"Just leave the shoe where it is. I'll have a couple of guys come out to take photos and forensics. They can bring out the big lights. If you just give me the geocoordinates—"

"I already moved it," Zachary confessed, after a split-second consideration of whether to toss it back into the ditch. "Uh, sorry. It was underwater, stuck in the mud. I pulled it out to see what it was, and when I saw... I figured I'd contaminate it more by putting it back. Maybe wash off something that was stuck to it."

"So now it's got your fingerprints and transfer on it," Campbell growled.

"I was wearing gloves. I put it directly into a plastic bag without letting it touch anything else. I've done my best to mark the location for you."

Campbell grumbled, but couldn't come up with an argument for that. "Alright. My guys will come by. Beam me your coordinates. They'll have to find it in the dark."

"I've got glow sticks out. As long as they slow down when they're getting close, they should be able to see it. I'll be back here once it's dark."

"Is it safe to leave the scene unsecured?"

Zachary took a slow look around. He didn't see any other houses close by; it was pretty isolated. There were occasional vehicles, but no one had paid any particular attention to him. Without his car there attracting attention to the scene, there was nothing there to indicate it was a crime scene. No reason for anyone else to be poking around.

"Yeah, I think it's fine. The only person of interest around is the girlfriend, and she'll be in the house with me. If she suddenly decides to go out to run an errand, I'll keep an eye on her, make sure she's not tampering with anything."

"Don't tell her that you found anything. She's not watching you now?"

Zachary looked back toward the house, but he couldn't see it clearly. "Not unless she's got a pretty good telescope."

"Okay. Thanks, Zach. I'll be in touch."

Back at Harding's house, Zachary had to knock on the door to be let in. He had divested of his boots and gloves and was fairly presentable. Ashley looked him over warily, as if she'd never met him before or he was someone she thought might be dangerous. Did she have something to hide? He knew she wasn't telling him everything. Like the reason she thought Harding's death was not an accident.

"If it's okay with you, I'll take a look around the house... see if there's anything that jumps out at me."

She didn't react for a few seconds, then stepped back from the door, nodding and opening it the rest of the way. "Did you find anything out there?"

She was his client, but Zachary wasn't ready to divulge everything he knew yet. If he told her about the shoe and she decided to go out for a look, Campbell would not be happy about it. "That remains to be seen," he said obliquely.

Ashley bit her lip. She looked around the living room of the small house. "I don't know exactly what you want to see."

"I'll just wander, if that's okay with you."

"Well... I suppose."

She didn't go back to whatever it was she had been doing, but stood there looking at him. Zachary did his best to again pretend that she wasn't there and just focus on his investigation. It was his chance to get to know who Richard Harding was and what kind of a person he was. Zachary didn't have a good picture of him, only an amorphous impression of a man who had walked off down the road and been hit by a truck. He was a colorless sort of person. A custodian, non-drinker, steady girlfriend, owned or rented his own place, kept to a regular routine. No hobbies or interests, nothing that seemed to set him apart from the rest of the human race. Other than his stalker.

Zachary had seen pictures of Harding, but only after his death, and that was never a very good representation of what someone looked like in real life, especially after a few days decomposing in a ditch. So the first thing Zachary did was look for pictures.

The paintings on the walls were cheap reproductions, mass produced and purchased in some home decorator store. There were no pictures of Harding's parents, or of himself with Ashley. No pictures of his brothers, his college friends, or bowling buddies. Either he lived a very solitary life, or he kept the evidence of his relationships somewhere else. Maybe he felt that they were not for public consumption. Not everyone felt the need to show everything off in the living room.

Zachary circulated around the room, glancing at magazines and books on the shelves, opening drawers in the side tables to poke through an assortment of pens, pencils, rubber bands, and junk. A few phone numbers scribbled on a piece of paper. Pizza delivery, a couple of first names, nothing that looked very interesting. The phone numbers were not ones he had gotten harassing text messages from.

Zachary went on. Ashley was in the kitchen, so he walked past it, leaving her to herself, and checked out the bedrooms. There were two of them. The one Harding used as his bedroom was immediately identifiable. His clothes were in the closet and drawers; the bed was made, but wrinkled; there was a picture of him with Ashley. Zachary picked it up and looked at it. Ashley appeared to be happy and relaxed. Harding did not. He was smiling unnaturally, looking anxious about having his picture taken, as if he might dart over and take the camera out of the hand of the photographer. Zachary didn't like posed pictures. Even before he had become a private investigator, he had preferred candid shots. The pictures that showed people in unexpected moments, looking natural.

"He hated having his picture taken."

Zachary jumped and looked up at the doorway, where Ashley was looking in on him. "Some people do," he acknowledged.

"I had to beg him to get that one. I told him I had to have a picture of him. It was a dealbreaker. So he finally agreed. But I think you can tell, looking at the picture, that he really didn't like it."

Zachary gave her a small smile of acknowledgment. "Yes, I can see that."

"So, this was his room," she made a small gesture to present it to him. "This is where he slept. Where we slept when I stayed over. But there's not really anything... no secrets, nothing that was really... special to him." She looked around the room critically. "I never realized how little he had."

"What was his childhood like? He grew up with his family?"

"Yeah, sure." Her manner was dismissive.

Zachary put the picture down and continued to look. There were no pictures of Harding's family. "Are his parents still living? Did he keep in contact with them?"

"No, they passed a few years ago."

Richard had been forty-five. It was possible that both of his parents had already passed away, but unlikely. Zachary opened and closed drawers, pushing clothes around to look behind and under them. Ashley was right, he had few possessions. She had almost as many clothes in the closet and drawers as he did. And more dresser space for her cosmetics and jewelry.

His clothes in the closet were uniformly nondescript. T-shirts, blue jeans, a couple of blazers. Nothing really dressy for church or funerals. One pair of loafers on the floor of the closet, placed neatly together.

Zachary approached the door and Ashley moved out of the way to let him back out of the bedroom. "I'll just hang out here until you're done."

"Wherever you want, I don't want to put you out."

She picked up a book from the dresser and sat on the bed. Zachary went to the second bedroom, which was a multi-purpose room. A small computer desk and chair, a couch that undoubtedly folded out into a spare bed for guests. An exercise bike and some free weights. Zachary could see by the wires that the desk was where Harding's computer normally resided. Zachary took a slow look around the bleak room. Richard Harding really was an enigma. Had he even existed before he had died? There was nothing of his personality in the house. He could have been someone that Ashley had made up, except for the fact that the police had found a body.

Zachary spent a couple of minutes in the bathroom, looking through Harding's toiletries, which weren't much more revealing than the rest of his house. He did not use generic bath products, but the more expensive brand names. He used a manual razor with a disposable head. The medicine cabinet contained all of the usual products—toothbrush and toothpaste, pain pills, cough syrup, antibacterial spray. But also a few over-the-counter sleep aids, and several prescription bottles.

Zachary was well-versed in the pharmacopeia of mental illness. A glance at the labels showed him that Richard Harding was being treated for anxiety and depression. Not just one of each, but several different types, which meant they had been struggling to find the right cocktail for him. Zachary reviewed the dates of the prescriptions and could see Harding's treatment plan take shape in front of him.

He closed the medicine cabinet and checked under the sink for anything Richard had preferred to keep out of sight. Nothing more interesting there than cleaning products. The last room to check was the kitchen. He didn't expect to find anything enlightening. With the way Harding had kept the rest of his house, Zachary didn't think he'd find a secret stash of booze or evidence of some other vice there. He looked anyway, methodically going through the drawers and cupboards. Ashley returned to the kitchen as he finished up.

"Did you find anything?"

"You didn't mention he was suffering from depression."

She bit her lip, thinking about that. "I don't know if he really was. I thought he was being a hypochondriac. He didn't *act* depressed."

"People who are depressed don't necessarily go around acting sad all the time."

"Then why do they call it depression?" she challenged.

"They may feel depressed without looking depressed. They might be silly and clown around. Look at Robin Williams. It's a way of covering up what they're really feeling, or trying to connect with the world in spite of it."

"Well… Richard didn't seem depressed to me, and we were together. We shared everything."

"He may not have had it before. It might have been the result of the harassment."

Ashley's brows went down. "What?"

"He was probably having such difficulties because of the harassment."

"What harassment? Did something happen at work?"

Zachary searched her features for any sign that she was trying to mislead him. Could she really have not known about the unrelenting harassment her boyfriend had been going through? Could Harding have kept that a secret? If Ashley had known, that would explain why she thought Harding had been intentionally murdered. If she didn't know, where did that leave him?

He couldn't see any deception in her face. She really didn't know what had been going on in Harding's life. It must have consumed him, but he'd kept it from her. He'd continued to go to work and to do things with her, acting like there was nothing wrong. He told her he was depressed—just a chemical thing—and that he'd be straightened out as soon as the medication kicked in. And she hadn't known how some lowlife was driving him to distraction.

Zachary indicated the chairs at the table. Ashley sat down, and Zachary pulled out a chair and sat across from her, making sure he wasn't too close, wasn't crowding her.

"Richard was being cyberstalked. It was… very brutal. Very threatening. He was doing everything he could to keep out of this stalker's reach. He closed all of his social media accounts, changed his phone and his email."

A light went on in Ashley's face. Suddenly, it all came together for her. "I didn't know! He said he was spending too much time online and that's why he was shutting down his accounts. He dropped his phone in the water and had to get a new one. He said he was getting too much spam email and needed to start fresh… I never connected them all. He spread it out, it wasn't all in one day, and I never… I didn't realize what he was doing. He never said a word about being stalked."

"Men tend to feel like they should be the strong ones in a relationship. That they should be the protector, keep bad things from happening. He was probably embarrassed and didn't want you to think that he was weak for trying to avoid this guy instead of 'being a man' and 'taking care of it.'"

"I never would have expected him to act like that. We never had gendered roles or felt like we had to follow those societal pressures. I told him I liked a man to be sensitive and to have real emotions." She shook her head. "He never should have felt like he had to play the big, strong man for me. That's not the way we were."

Zachary nodded slowly. He pulled out his notepad and jotted down a few thoughts and things to check before they could flit away from his churning brain.

"So he never told you anything about this."

"No. I'm sorry. He should have. I would have supported him. He knew I'd support him through anything."

Did he? It seemed to Zachary that their devotion to one another hadn't really been tested. It didn't seem like a passionate relationship, but like a partnership of convenience. Something warm and comfortable, where they could cuddle up and watch a movie together, but didn't have to be totally devoted to each other all of the time. They each kept their own residences, their own jobs, their own vehicles. They were still themselves more than a couple. How could Harding have known how Ashley would react to the news that he was being hunted and harassed?

"Is there anything you need to tell me?"

Ashley looked at him for a long time, her eyes swimming in tears, looking helpless and uncertain. But she didn't offer him anything. It wasn't the depression. It wasn't the stalking. She was still holding something back from him.

"If you don't tell me everything, how do you expect me to find out what really happened?"

Ashley shook her head. "I've told you all I can. I know it wasn't accidental, and this proves it. He was being stalked by someone. That person caught up with him in real life and killed him!"

"You think the trucker was his stalker? Why turn himself in to the police?"

"I... I don't know. Maybe he wasn't the one who really hit Richard. Maybe he hit a deer and someone else hit Richard. Or maybe when he hit Richard, he was already dead. I don't know. But whoever was stalking Richard, *that's* who killed him."

"I'll pursue it as far as I can," Zachary promised. "But you need to tell me the rest if you want me to sort it out."

7

Z achary looked at the letter from Tyrrell, still in its protective sleeve on his desk. Was it really from Tyrrell? His Tyrrell?

He remembered his little brother. So anxious to please, so trusting of everything his parents or teachers told him. The perfect little man, always trying to be well-behaved and follow the rules. More like a firstborn than one so far down the line in the birth order.

Tyrrell cried when their parents fought and often crawled into bed with Zachary to cuddle, too afraid to go to sleep on his own. Zachary would hold him gently and hum to him, trying to drown out any noise from their fighting parents and lull the little boy to sleep. And then he lay awake himself, staring into the darkness, listening to Tyrrell and Vincent breathing, waiting for sleep to come and take him, but it always took hours to come. He couldn't sleep when their parents were still up. He had to wait until they had stopped fighting and had gone to bed, and everything was quiet and peaceful with no danger of the argument blowing up again. Then he could start to relax, but the process still took a long time.

The nights when the police were called were the worst, and they were a relief. It was humiliating for the whole neighborhood to see what was going on in the Goldman home. He hated for the kids at school to know that his parents didn't get along. If it was just arguing, he could have laughed it off. But not when the neighbors saw his mother or father being put into handcuffs to be carted off to jail for assault. The next day, when it had all blown over, the arrested parent would be back, and things would go on as usual, but that didn't stop the teasing and bullying at school.

And on the other hand, it was a relief to have the police come and break it up. Zachary would be able to get to sleep sooner, knowing that the fight was over. While they had sometimes threatened to put both parents in jail, they never had, always picking out the one who they thought had been most at fault and leaving the other at home so they didn't have to call Social Services to find emergency homes for six children.

Tyrrell. Zachary touched the plastic bag. *Do you remember me?* How could Zachary ever forget? He couldn't forget any of his siblings, not ever. He longed to call Tyrrell or to write him back. But he couldn't bring himself to. Not when Tyrrell might blame him. It had been Zachary's fault that they had all been taken away. Tyrrell had been old enough to understand that.

He closed his eyes and tried to remember everything Mrs. Pratt had said about the other children back in the beginning. They hadn't been able to keep the other five children together. It was just too many for one home to take. Joss and Heather had been put in one home, and the littles in another. Had they stayed there? Had they been good homes where they were treated fairly and the parents were interested in adopting them permanently? Or had they been emergency placements that had never been meant to be anything but temporary?

Mrs. Pratt had said it was best to let them settle into their foster placements to start with. Not to disrupt them with visits by Zachary. That meant that they had been meant to stay in those homes permanently. Or at least long-term. Every time Zachary had asked about being allowed to visit them, the answer had been no, and eventually, he had stopped asking, though he had never stopped thinking about them.

Joshua Campbell was a busy man, but he agreed to meet and spend a few minutes with Zachary on the Harding case. Zachary had, after all, managed to dig up additional evidence, so maybe he merited a face-to-face conversation when Campbell would normally expect a PI to just be happy to get access to the paper file.

He graciously offered Zachary coffee, which he accepted, even knowing it was likely to be hours old and bitter as grapefruit. He took a sip without wincing and put it down on the offered coaster as he sat down on the other side of Campbell's desk.

"How is the case coming along then?" Campbell asked genially. He stretched and leaned back in his chair as if he were ready for a nap. He'd probably started his day pretty early.

"It's intriguing," Zachary said slowly. "There may be something to the girlfriend's claims, but she's not been completely open about her reasons, so I'm still a bit in the dark."

"Why would someone hire you and not tell you all of the reasons why?"

Zachary gave a shrug. "It's actually not as unusual as you think. People usually hold something back. Maybe it's something inconsequential, maybe it's a secret, or maybe they just want to see if you can find it, so they know you're really putting some effort into the investigation."

Campbell nodded. "I know they hold back from the police, but it never occurred to me that they'd hire you and then not produce."

Zachary leaned forward. "I'm wondering whether Richard Harding ever filed a complaint with the police."

Campbell raised his brows. "A complaint? For what?"

"Criminal harassment. Cyberstalking."

"No... something like that would have shown up when we opened the missing persons report and when we started the investigation into his death. You think he was being harassed?"

"I know he was. Email, social media, texts, calls. I don't know whether he got snail mail or any face-to-face harassment, but he was the victim of some of the worst cyber-harassment I've ever seen."

"You need to turn those records over so we can have a look at them. How did you get access? I'm sure my guys must have taken a look at his electronic footprint."

"He'd closed his social media and replaced his phone and his email address. Recently, he'd been anonymizing all of his online activity. Trying to keep this guy from tracking him down again."

"Okay. Yeah. Pass on what you've got so we can investigate it further. We'll see whether there is any connection between Rusty Donaldson and this cyberstalker."

"None that I can find. I've been through everything with a fine-toothed comb, and it doesn't follow the patterns you'd expect to see from a long-haul trucker. The times he is sending his messages follow more of the pattern you'd expect to see with someone with a nine-to-five job or school schedule. Little or nothing from nine until noon or one until four. A lot more in the early morning, noon hour, and evening. A long-haul trucker... wouldn't follow a distribution like that."

"Unless he was smart enough to use some kind of scheduler."

Zachary shrugged. "I suppose. In my experience, people take a lot of care to cover up the things that can be traced back to them electronically—burner phones, anonymous accounts, stuff like that—but they don't think to cover up behavioral patterns."

"I'll see what we can find. We might be able to trace some of the messages back to the source. I assume you've already done the preliminaries."

"The obvious stuff. With the amount of harassment that went on, it's impossible for me to check everything, but with a few more people following the trail, maybe you'll be able to."

"Might call on the feds for help. They have a lot more manpower and some pretty slick technology."

Zachary nodded. "You'll let me know what you find?"

"Usual answer." Campbell took a sip of his coffee. "It depends. If we have enough for an arrest, we're just going to move in and do it, and you won't be involved. If the feds find something, we might be prohibited from sharing it with you. If it's a rat's nest that I can't do anything with... you're welcome to it."

Zachary grinned. He liked Campbell's open, honest manner. He knew the strengths of the police department, and he knew Zachary's strengths, and he had no problem with feeding information to Zachary if he thought that Zachary had a better chance of coming up with an answer than his own staff.

"Fair enough."

Campbell took another drink, his eyes distant as he thought things over. "Do you think this stalker had anything to do with his death?"

"Right now... I can't see a connection. I don't believe Rusty Donaldson has any connection with the stalker. It just doesn't feel right. Does that mean that the stalker didn't have something to do with why Harding was out there on the road that night? I can think of a few different scenarios that could connect them… but nothing that feels right yet. So far, it still seems like an accident."

"Well, you've proven to have a pretty good instinct for these things, so I'm glad to hear it."

"You haven't heard anything back from your accident reconstruction guys yet…?"

"Early days. They want confirmation of the weight of the truck, so we're in the process of getting a warrant for the weigh station records and looking into the possibility that Donaldson might have added something to his load without telling anyone. Truckers sometimes supplement their incomes by carrying extras they don't tell their employers about."

Zachary wasn't a math guy, but most of the things he could think of a trucker transporting for extra money didn't weigh enough that he thought they would make a difference.

"How much extra weight would it have taken? Would a passenger have made up the difference?"

"A passenger." Campbell looked at him sharply. "Do you have anything to suggest that he had a passenger?"

"No. I'm just spitballing. Could we put the stalker in the truck? I'm not sure that makes any sense even if the answer is yes…"

Campbell shook his head. "What's he going to do? Tell Rusty Donaldson to run down the guy walking by the side of the road?"

"Probably not. Unless it's a woman and she tells him that the guy is trying to kill her or did something to her in the past. More likely… distracts him at the key moment, grabs the wheel without warning…"

"I'm sure he would have been eager to tell us something like that if it was his passenger's fault. He wouldn't have a reason to protect the passenger."

"Unless they knew each other." Zachary sighed and blinked his eyes a few times, trying to refocus. "No evidence, just trying to think of what would fit."

"Chances are, he was just going faster than he wants us to believe."

Zachary nodded.

Campbell sat up and leaned forward over his desk, his body language indicating that the interview was over and he had other work to do. "Good luck. Get us the information you've got, and we'll see where the evidence leads us. How is Bridget doing, by the way?"

Zachary swallowed and attempted a smile. "She's recovered from the kidnapping, seems back to her usual self." Which was to say, she still had no interest in getting back together with Zachary and hadn't had much reason to call him since the Salter case was closed. While Zachary might occasionally run into her around town, he couldn't make direct contact with her or she might just call up Joshua Campbell or one of her other friends in the police department and take out a restraining order against Zachary.

"Good. It was too bad things didn't work out between the two of you. Cancer is a bitch. I think the two of you might have had a chance if that hadn't thrown a wrench into the works."

Little did Campbell know that things were already bad between them before the cancer diagnosis. It had been the straw that broke the camel's back. It was nice to think that they might have worked things out without the cancer, but seeing the relationship Bridget had with Gordon Drake, Zachary had to face the fact that he could never have been the kind of spouse that Gordon was. Women like Ashley might say that they liked sensitive men who weren't afraid to cry or wear their hearts on their sleeves, but in his experience, they just liked the idea of that kind of man. Bridget's declarations of love had quickly faded as she came to realize just how broken Zachary really was. That he had real problems that weren't just going to be healed by their relationship or her no-nonsense advice.

"Zachary."

Zachary tried to force himself back to the present. He had picked up the cup of coffee as he prepared to leave. He put it up to his lips, letting the bitterness of it shock his senses and help to ground him. He didn't want to get swallowed up in the past. Not even his past with Bridget, where the memories started out sweet but quickly descended into something even more bitter than the stale coffee.

"Sorry," he told Campbell, pushing himself to his feet. "I'll be getting on my way."

"No, I'm sorry. I didn't mean to reopen old wounds. I thought you were over it…"

Zachary tried to say that he didn't think he'd ever be over Bridget. But he couldn't get the words out. He just nodded and fled as quickly as he could.

Kenzie had suggested that Zachary could conquer his own depression by helping someone else. Zachary decided to put it to the test. Maybe he could head off the rapidly descending darkness by making a difference in some one else's life. After checking with Vera Salter, Zachary sent an instant message to her grandson Rhys, asking whether he would like to go out for a burger.

Following his usual protocol of answering with a gif rather than words, Rhys sent back a picture of a chihuahua nodding eagerly, the bold text "yes!!!" superimposed on top of the picture. Zachary chuckled. That seemed clear enough. He sent back the details and confirmed that Vera had already approved the activity. Rhys returned a thumbs-up, and they were on.

He was at the school waiting when classes let out for the day. He watched the waves of teens leaving the school, some singly and some in groups, feeling that same knot of dread in his stomach that he used to feel whenever he was at school or thinking about being at school. It was hard to fathom that even after so many years, just watching students at school brought back that same anxiety. He was glad not to be a teenager anymore. Glad to be on his own and independent and no longer to have to follow all of the rules of a foster home, school, or other facility. There were still societal rules, but he could live his own life without fear of being beaten, humiliated, or locked up.

His eyes were drawn to a thin black boy with a familiar loping stride, and reached over to unlock the door for Rhys.

Rhys climbed in, giving him a nod and a shy sort of smile.

"Hey, Rhys!" Zachary greeted, holding out his fist for Rhys to bump. Rhys was quick to do so, his smile broadening to show a few teeth. He put on his seatbelt as Zachary backed out of the parking space he had been occupying.

"Find something on the radio if you like," Zachary suggested, not wanting Rhys to feel like he was going to have to hold a conversation while they drove. Rhys ran through Zachary's presets quickly, then scanned for something more acceptable. Zachary let the pounding beat of the station Rhys picked fill him up and block out any worries he had about meeting with Rhys or about the approaching Christmas season. Maybe he should listen to music more often. It wasn't something he usually thought of when he was having a bad turn.

The burger joint was conveniently close to the school, prime real estate for a place that targeted kids as its customer base. It wasn't until they got inside that Zachary realized it might not be the best place for them to meet. Rhys's friends and peers would be there. Would they think it was odd that he was meeting with an older white guy for dinner? Would he be teased and bullied for it?

"Uh... is this okay? Do you want to eat somewhere else?"

Rhys waved the question away with an unconcerned gesture.

"Yeah? You're sure? You aren't going to to get a bunch of questions about what you were doing here with me?"

Rhys shook his head.

Zachary scanned the menu on the wall without much interest. He'd get some kind of small combo. He wasn't really there because of the food, he was there to see if he could help Rhys. Rhys touched Zachary's arm and then tapped the poster beside him.

"Is that what you want? Bacon cheeseburger?"

Rhys nodded.

"Combo, supersize?"

Rhys grinned.

They waited for the teens in line ahead of them to place their orders, and in a few minutes were choosing a table and sitting down to eat. Zachary ate slowly, watching Rhys put away his supersized combo as if he hadn't eaten all day. He was long and lanky, his teenage frame not yet starting to fill in. It would be a few years before he might have to start watching what he ate.

"Do you know these other kids?" Zachary asked, taking a look around the restaurant and classifying which were likely to be the same grade as Rhys. There were not very many non-white students; Rhys would definitely be in the minority.

Rhys gave his hand a side-to-side rocking movement. *So-so.*

Zachary nodded. Knowing who people were wasn't the same as being friends with them. Or actually *knowing* them.

"I guess Christmas is coming." As if Zachary were only casually aware of the fact. "I was wondering if you wanted to do something. It will be kind of different for you, not having your mom around." Or his aunt Robin either. Rhys was probably happy about that.

Rhys nodded.

"Will you be going to see your mom on Christmas Day, do you know?"

Another nod.

"You know what time?"

Rhys shook his head. He made a motion backward over his shoulder, a questioning look on his face. Zachary looked behind Rhys to see if he was motioning to someone. Rhys shook his head and pulled out his iPod. He tapped a couple of words and slid it across the table to Zachary.

Xmas Eve?

Zachary shook his head. He tried not to betray his feelings to Rhys. "I... I can't do anything on Christmas Eve."

Which made him wonder why he was even trying to set something up for Christmas Day. What if he wasn't even around on Christmas Day? What if he slid down that hole and didn't come back up this time? It had been Kenzie's idea to set something up with Rhys, not his, and he should have just left it to her. What kind of service was he doing Rhys if he set something up for Christmas, and then didn't make it? The kid was going to have a bad enough day without that adding to his troubles.

Rhys's eyes were on Zachary, sharp and intelligent. He touched Zachary's arm and again indicated the iPod screen.

Xmas Eve?

"I can't."

Eyebrows up, inquiring. *Why?*

Zachary didn't want to tell Rhys about it. He didn't share the experience with anyone but his closest friends or therapists. Rhys was only a kid. He couldn't understand the full impact of what Zachary had been through.

But Rhys had been through awful experiences of his own. Zachary didn't want to talk about his, but Rhys *couldn't* tell his even if he wanted to. They strangled his voice and kept him from communicating anything but the most rudimentary thoughts.

"I had... some really bad stuff happen to me on Christmas Eve," Zachary explained awkwardly. "There was a fire... my family... the anniversary always gets me... in a really bad place."

Rhys clasped Zachary's hand in a strong handshake, holding it firmly and nodding.

We'll help each other. We'll be strong together.

Zachary gave a little squeeze, then pulled out of Rhys's grip. "I don't think I can."

Rhys studied him for a long moment, his face once again sad.

"We'll figure something out," Zachary promised. "Maybe closer to the time, when our plans have solidified…"

Rhys picked his burger back up and resumed eating. A knot of guilt tightened in Zachary's stomach.

"I'm sorry Rhys. I know it's stupid. I'd change if I could. I've been… it's something I've been working on for a long time."

A shrug. That just made Zachary feel worse. He knew Rhys couldn't understand just how difficult Christmas, and especially Christmas Eve was for him. Zachary concentrated hard on how to explain it.

"It's like with your speech."

Rhys looked up, raising one eyebrow.

"You'd change it if you could, wouldn't you? You'd want to just be able to talk like yours friends can?"

Rhys gave a small nod.

"And you've been working with doctors and therapists since you were little. They've tried helping you in all different ways."

Rhys nodded agreement, his eyes bright and piercing.

"It isn't like you're lazy. It isn't like you just can't be bothered or don't want to talk. It's something inside that's… broken."

Was it offensive for him to suggest that Rhys was broken? Was it too personal for him to compare his psychological problems to Rhys's? He looked away from Rhys's eyes, worried about the anger and insult he'd find there. Rhys held his hands together in front of him as if he were holding a horizontal stick, and then snapped them downward.

Broken.

Zachary breathed out, nodding. "You want to be fixed. You want to fix yourself. But so far… no one has figured out how."

Rhys nodded his agreement. He picked up his iPod and slid it back into his pocket, hiding the offending words away again.

Zachary ate a couple of fries. He wasn't hungry and hadn't even put ketchup on them, but it was something to do, to try to make things more comfortable between them. As if they weren't discussing what messes their lives were, but were just a couple of friends having a meal together.

"Do you remember when you were little, after your Grandpa Clarence died? When you had to go away for awhile, to a hospital?"

Rhys nodded, his eyes downcast. He was ashamed of being in hospital for his trauma and depression. Like he should have been stronger. Should have been *not broken.*

"Well, that's what it was like for me, too. I spent a lot of time in places like that. Hospitals, institutions, therapeutic care centers. Especially around Christmas, but other times too. There were years when I spent more time in crisis than out."

Wide eyes. *Really?*

"Yeah. So... if I can, we'll get together at Christmas. Or maybe New Year's. But not Christmas Eve. I'm not sure where I'll be Christmas Eve."

Rhys nodded and gave Zachary a thumbs-up. *Okay.*

"Okay," Zachary agreed, sighing. He ate another fry, even though his churning stomach did not want anything.

They sat in silence a bit, but it was comfortable. Zachary felt like they had come to an understanding. He no longer felt so guilty. Zachary's phone buzzed in his pocket and he pulled it out to look at the screen. When he put it down on the table to watch for any further text messages, Rhys made a palms-raised query.

What's up?

"It's a client." Zachary hesitated, wondering how much to stay to Rhys. It wasn't like the boy was going to blab it to anyone. He couldn't be much more safe. "She wants to know if I've managed to find out anything else about the man who was stalking her boyfriend."

Rhys's interested eyes begged for more.

"He was killed in an accident, but we're trying to track down this cyber-stalker in case it was somehow related."

Rhys nodded.

"They probably weren't. We know who it was who actually hit him—in this accident—and I can't find a connection between him and the stalker." Zachary took a sip of his soda. "The funny thing is, he never even told his girlfriend that he was being stalked. She had no idea what was going on. She knew he was on medication for depression, but she didn't think he was actually depressed. He hadn't told her anything about this guy who was sending him hundreds of harassing messages."

Rhys's mouth formed a circle. *Wow.*

"I don't even know what it was that triggered this harassment. The stalker thought the boyfriend had done something wrong, something terrible, but he never said what it was. Not in any of the messages I read. So I don't know where to look."

Rhys was easy to talk to. Unlike most of Zachary's acquaintances, who would have peppered him with questions, Rhys just listened and let him talk. Zachary shook his head. He thought about his observation to Ashley that someone who was depressed could just as easily appear to be a clown, putting on a happy front while hiding the pain.

"How are *you* doing, Rhys? And I mean for real, not just 'fine, how are you?' For real."

Rhys lifted his hands in a shrug. He gave a pronounced frown, then blinked the expression away. He flicked his hand toward Zachary. *You?*

"You're sad," Zachary deduced, and fished for the words to match Rhys's body language. "But you're okay? You said before, 'it's all going to be okay.'"

Rhys nodded his agreement.

"You still feel like that? That it will all work out and be okay?"

He continued to nod.

"Are you still seeing a therapist? You don't have to answer me, it's private. I just wondered."

A nod.

"Are you on antidepressants? Or something that helps?"

Rhys rocked his hand back and forth. *So-so.*

"You'll tell someone if it gets worse, won't you? It doesn't have to be me. But your grandma or your doctor? A guidance counselor at school? If the depression gets worse, or you start having suicidal thoughts, you'll tell someone?"

Rhys grimaced and nodded. He again flicked his finger back toward Zachary, holding his gaze. *You?*

Zachary sighed. It was hard to pull away from Rhys's intense stare. He looked down at his fries. "I don't know. I've talked to doctors, tried everything already. If I have to check myself in somewhere... I guess I will."

Rhys raised his brows slightly and pointed at Zachary firmly. *You do it. For sure.*

"Okay," Zachary said. "I will. And I told my... *friend...* that I'll talk to my therapist. About Christmas Eve."

Rhys gave a grin and pulled out his phone. Zachary wasn't sure what he was doing, until Rhys slid the phone over to him, and he saw that Rhys had a picture of Kenzie.

"Uh, yeah. Kenzie."

Rhys pursed his lips and made a smacking sound. Zachary's cheeks got warm.

"I wouldn't say she's my girlfriend... not yet. Maybe someday. We get together... have dinner... consult on cases. But we're not... serious."

Rhys's smirk said he wasn't buying it. Zachary rubbed his chin, trying to hide the flushing of his cheeks. Rhys took the phone back, nodding his approval.

8

Kenzie called shortly after Zachary got back from his dinner with Rhys, and he couldn't help wondering whether Rhys had messaged her, prompting her to call Zachary to check in on him. There was a growing network of people around Zachary who kept in touch with each other, trying to keep watch over Zachary's emotional wellness, and maybe Rhys had added himself as a node. *Check in with Zachary. Make sure he's not going to do anything stupid.*

Of course, Rhys wouldn't use that many words. His communications were much more succinct, but Zachary wouldn't put it past him to shoot Kenzie a brief *Zachary OK?* or to just send her his picture.

"You doing anything tonight?" Kenzie asked.

"I don't have anything planned. Was going to do a bit more work on the Harding case tonight, but there's no urgency."

"Why don't I just come over and we'll watch a movie together? You can do simple stuff while we watch, right?"

He could spend some more time trying to analyze the harassing messages, trying to crack the patterns, to parse the words, to trace IP addresses in case the stalker hadn't always remembered to use an anonymizer service. "Yeah, sure. I'd be up for that."

"Great. I'll bring some munchies. Maybe some soda."

He noted that she did not suggest beer as she often did, which meant

781

she probably already figured he wouldn't be able to have any due to his night meds, which he'd been increasing recently.

"Sounds good. Whenever you want to come by is fine, I'll see you then."

She didn't put the movie on as soon as she arrived, but visited and wandered around the apartment restlessly and asked if he'd gotten any further on the Harding case.

"Not much," Zachary admitted. "Still working on it." He related the finding of the shoe and checking to see whether Harding had filed any complaints against the stalker. Kenzie rolled her eyes at the news that Harding had been on antidepressants. "Well, duh! I think any sane person would be. Who could handle that kind of pressure without some kind of aid?"

"His girlfriend didn't think he was depressed. She though he was just a hypochondriac. But he didn't tell her about the harassment, so…"

"He didn't tell her?"

Zachary shook his head. "No." He narrowed his eyes, looking at Kenzie. Something about the way she asked the question suggested that she had a thought about it.

"Maybe he didn't tell her because he figured she already knew."

"You mean he thought she was the stalker?"

"He might have. Why else wouldn't he say anything about it to her, even just in passing? Maybe he was watching her to see if she was the one cyberstalking him."

Zachary shuddered. "That's horror movie material."

"Psychological thriller," Kenzie corrected. "But really, I wonder."

"I think he just didn't want to look weak. Guys are like that, you know. They want the girls to think they're perfect and don't have any problems. That they're strong enough to take all comers."

Kenzie snickered. "You don't say."

"It could be as simple as that. He was too macho to tell her."

"Could be," Kenzie agreed. "But I like my theory better. It has more… dramatic potential."

Zachary nodded. He clicked through a few more messages on Harding's computer, letting his eyes just skim over the words. They got redundant after a while. The stalker hadn't had a lot of creativity, but tended to use the same words and phrases over and over again. And what stalker sending dozens of messages in a day would have been any different? If he didn't settle on a standard set of half a dozen accusations and threats, he'd wear himself out. He'd have writer's block or a nervous breakdown trying to figure out how to make all of the messages unique.

"Oh, snail mail too?" Kenzie asked, and picked up a paper from beside him.

Zachary was hyperfocused on the screen, and it was a minute before her words reached him, and several more before he realized that he didn't have any hard copy threats from the stalker. By the time he realized what Kenzie was looking at and turned to take it from her, it was too late, she'd already read the message, flipped it over to look at the envelope, and was staring at him with open mouth.

"Where did this come from?"

"It's…" Zachary pulled the plastic bag away from Kenzie gently, taking care not to just snatch it rudely. "That's just a note…"

"From your brother? You told me you had siblings, but I didn't know you were in contact with any of them."

Zachary looked down at the inquiry. *Do you remember me?*

"I'm not. I just got this… a few days ago. It's the first contact I've ever had from any of them."

"That's fantastic, Zachary! How exciting for you!" Her smile was shockingly bright, and Zachary wasn't sure whether it was excitement or dread that welled up in his chest at her exuberance. Her smile remained for only a few seconds, then started to fade.

"But you're not excited."

"I am… and I'm… scared…" He paused, awkward and not sure how she would take his declaration. He remembered Ashley's declaration that it was okay to be sensitive and to have an honest emotional reaction. But he wasn't sure all women felt that way, or that they would still feel that way once they saw their man dissolve in front of them.

Kenzie leaned against the corner of the desk, frowning. "Why would you be afraid? This is your brother! Or are you afraid that it's not? That it could be someone else?"

"I don't know." Zachary's hands had started shaking too much to work the mouse, so he held them in his lap under the desk, squeezing them together. "If it is Tyrrell… I ruined his life. I don't know why he would want to see me again, except to tell me that. Just how much I messed him up."

"Why do you think he would feel that way? What happened when you were kids was just an accident. Kids can't be blamed for things like that. They're not responsible. Whatever happened to your brothers and sisters after that... it probably would have happened anyway. If you hadn't been taken away from your parents that day, it would have been a few days or weeks later. Believe me, they were not going to be ideal parents and raise you right. This didn't happen because you were a bad kid. It's because they were bad parents."

"I burned the house down!"

"I'm aware of that," she said calmly. "And you weren't the first kid to ever light a fire by accident. Do you think every kid who lights a fire by accident should be taken away from his family?"

"No."

"Then why do you think that your parents were justified in doing what they did to you?"

"That wasn't the only thing I did. I was in trouble all the time. At school, at home, in the neighborhood. I was always getting in trouble for one thing or another."

"Uh-huh." She still didn't sound convinced of anything. Zachary stared at her, trying to figure out a way to impress on her just how bad he had been.

"Zach... those kids that you met at Summit...?"

Zachary blinked and nodded. "Yeah?"

"Those kids were trouble, right?"

"Well... no. They did put some kids in there just for behavioral issues, but mostly it was kids with autism. You know that."

"So they're still pretty bad, right? I mean, they won't follow instructions, they hurt people and cause property damage, they're too disobedient to be able to stay with their parents anymore."

"No. Their brains don't work the same way as other kids' brains do. They learn differently. They express themselves differently. The world can seem very threatening to them. They're just reacting in the only way they know how."

"That's why they need to be zapped. Because they're like animals. They are children who are so wild that they need to be trained like dogs to do what they're told."

Zachary knew she was intentionally pushing his buttons, but he couldn't stop the outrage and anger that welled up in him at her words.

"No!"

"If you can understand that they are wired differently and can't be held responsible like a normal child or an adult, then why are you still blaming yourself and repeating the lies that your mother told you?"

If Zachary hadn't already been sitting, he would have fallen into his seat. As it was, his head spun with blinding speed and he couldn't slow it down enough to allow for logical thought.

"What?"

"Tell me what you know about your own diagnoses."

Zachary cleared his throat. "I don't see..."

"Don't you? Humor me."

"ADHD."

"Impulsivity, difficulty maintaining focus, hyperactivity. Right?"

Zachary nodded.

"That's not something you can just change by deciding to, is it?"

"No."

"You have learning disabilities to go along with that?"

"Dyslexia. Dysgraphia. But that's not—"

"And PTSD, right?"

"Yes."

"Before or after the fire?"

Zachary swallowed. His mouth was like cotton. He looked around for a drink. "They think... before."

"Why?"

"My parents' fighting... and... abuse..."

"If I took one of those kids from Summit and told you that he had ADHD, learning disabilities, PTSD, and a history of abuse, and that he'd knocked over a candle and burned the house down, injuring himself in the process, would you say he was just a bad kid? That he had to be institutionalized because he was irredeemable?"

"No. I'd feel bad for him. But I didn't knock a candle over—"

"No, you just lit them."

"I shouldn't have. I wasn't supposed to be out of bed or to use the matches."

"You were trying to do something nice for your family. Trying to make it so they could all have a nice Christmas Day."

"But I was breaking the rules. My mother said I was incorrigible. I would never follow the rules."

"So any child who can't follow the rules is incorrigible?"

Zachary pressed his lips closed. He didn't need to be told that his feelings were illogical any more than he needed to be told he was broken. Too broken to ever be fixed.

Kenzie's color rose when he refused to engage any further in the debate. Then she covered her eyes and blew out her breath, relaxing her body. She dropped her hands from her face and looked at him.

"I'm not trying to prove you wrong, Zachary. I'm just trying to show you... that *you* wouldn't blame yourself for what happened to your family if it was any other child but you. You are a compassionate person. You try to help people. You get inside and try to understand them. You wouldn't blame yourself, and I don't think your brother would either." She gestured to the letter. "I don't think he'd write to you if he just wanted to blame you for the bad stuff that happened in his life. I don't think he'd reach out just to lash out at you when you answered."

"But you don't know that."

"Of course I don't know that, but you don't know that he will either. Is that the kind of person he was? A mean, angry kid?"

Zachary remembered the sweet, concerned, helpful boy Tyrrell had been. So earnest.

"No. But things can change. I met a lot of kids in foster care and institutions who had turned bad. Bullies and sadists of the worst kind. If he ended up in a bad home... or a few of them... even the sweetest kid can turn into a monster."

"Obviously I'm not going to talk you into anything. You're going to have to work through this yourself. But don't shut him out just because you're scared. Being reunited could be the best thing that could ever happen for both of you. It could be a wonderful experience. You could have family back in your life, and the two of you could help each other and share memories."

Zachary swallowed and nodded. "Yeah. It could be really good."

"So don't block him out. Take a chance."

He looked down at the handwritten note. "I will," he agreed, "just not yet."

"Does that mean not today or not this year?"

Zachary cleared his throat. "Maybe after the holidays. When everything is back to normal."

"Do you think it's a coincidence that he sent that before Christmas? He wants to be with family. Christmas is probably a difficult time for him too, and he's trying to reconnect."

"I just can't deal with it right now."

She opened her mouth to argue.

"I just can't, Kenzie."

She gave a frustrated sigh. "Fine. I'll stop pushing you. You know what's best for you."

9

Having so far run into dead ends identifying the cyberstalker, Zachary decided to change tack and run background on Harding. Sometimes, profiling the victim could provide an investigation with a new direction to go. He wasn't getting anywhere on Rusty Donaldson or the stalker, so he needed a fresh avenue to investigate. Ashley had said Harding didn't have any family, but that didn't mean it was true.

A lot of the background he could run online from the comfort of his own apartment, but the police check required actually going to the police station to fill out request forms. Zachary was pretty sure they would come up clear, since the police would undoubtedly have checked to see if their victim had any prior history, but he wasn't going to assume anything. He would run everything, as if he were just starting the investigation and the police had had no involvement.

Bowen was at the information desk and gave Zachary a big grin, as if Zachary had gone there just to see him.

"Zach, my man! How is the investigation going?"

"Not going very far in any direction," Zachary admitted. "What little I've found hasn't gone anywhere. I thought I'd run police record checks on Harding."

Bowen rolled his eyes. "He was clean."

"Did you do the police checks?"

"I don't remember. Probably. You don't think Campbell and his boys would have forgotten something like that, do you?"

"Not everyone runs background on the victim."

Bowman passed Zachary the requisite forms, still rolling his eyes and griping over the duplication of effort. But he was the one who had suggested that Ashley hire Zachary in the first place, and he knew that meant Zachary going over the same ground as the police had already done.

"How are you and Ashley Morton getting along?" Bowman asked, after he had worn out the topic.

"Alright." Zachary shrugged. "I've certainly had worse clients."

"She's quite the looker, don't you think?"

Zachary focused on filling the search forms out neatly, his printing painfully slow. If Bowman was the one who had done the search, Zachary didn't particularly have to worry about it being legible, as Bowman knew all of the details himself. But if it went to someone else to do the search, they might toss it in the garbage if it was too hard to read. Or misspell Richard's name on the search, even though both names were pretty standard. It was best to get it right the first time.

"Ashley. She's a pretty lady," Bowman persisted, not getting the response he wanted from Zachary.

Zachary looked up from his form, distracted. "What?"

"Where are you, Zach? I was talking about the girlfriend. The client. She seemed like a nice girl."

His words started to filter into Zachary's brain. He frowned. "Her boyfriend just died. You think she's going to want to go on a date with you?"

"With me?" Bowman guffawed. "No, not with me. I thought maybe you and she…"

"Me?" Zachary was getting even more confused. In the past, Bowman had encouraged him to pursue Kenzie, saying that she was interested in him and all he had to do was declare his intentions more clearly. His ears got hot. "But Kenzie and I…"

Bowman raised his brows. "You and Kenzie have been lukewarm for a year. She's a girl who likes to go out and have some fun. I think you're stuck in the friend zone with her, and good luck ever getting out of it."

"Oh." The thought had never occurred to Zachary. They were friends, and he thought that if he just allowed the relationship to unfold naturally, if he and Kenzie were meant to be together, things would work out.

"I told you before you needed to be proactive," Bowman said. "A girl likes to know where she stands."

Zachary looked back at the form that he had come there to complete. "Okay. Good to know." He struggled to focus on filling in the lines on the form. "Is she seeing someone else, then? She hasn't mentioned anyone…"

If he were "just a friend," then she would tell him if she started dating someone, wouldn't she? But she hadn't said so, and when they talked and she was busy and couldn't get together, it was usually because she had friends to meet up with, or work, or she had something to get done. Had those just been excuses? Was she just trying to let him down easy?

"I don't know," Bowman admitted. "No one from here, I don't think. But you have to understand, if you're not meeting her needs…"

"Uh… yeah. Okay. Thanks." Zachary handed Bowman the forms back. "Thanks for that."

Bowman shook his head and pushed the papers back at Zachary. "You didn't sign them."

Embarrassed, Zachary scribbled his signature at the bottom of each page and slid them across to Bowman again. "Just let me know when the results are in."

"Zachary…"

Zachary walked away without another word.

Zachary sat in his car, waiting for his heart to stop pounding and his head to stop spinning. He'd never been good at relationships, but he had thought that he and Kenzie were doing well. They were connecting, they enjoyed doing things together, and they each called the other regularly. It seemed, for the most part, to be a balanced, two-way relationship, with both of them getting something out of it. Even though Bowman had told him he should push harder for a more intimate relationship, it had never felt right to Zachary and he had resisted. Did that mean he'd lost out?

He turned the key in the ignition to warm up the cold car. There was an icy bite in the air. Winter was starting to assert itself. He turned the radio on. It was still on the station Rhys had tuned it to and the heavy beat shook the car. Zachary couldn't help smiling a little as he turned it down. Rhys was a good kid, and Zachary hoped he'd be able to grow and mature and not be kept down by the traumas he had suffered through so young.

Zachary pulled his phone out of his pocket to check for messages. There were no urgent messages. He tapped on the email icon to make sure there wasn't anything in his inbox that he needed to act on. There were a couple more emails from the stalker, which he trashed, and nothing else of importance in the inbox. Everything else could wait until he was at his computer later.

He slid his phone back into his pocket and put the car into reverse to back out of the parking space. He was backed most of the way out when he was hit by a lightning bolt.

Emails from the stalker? In his own inbox?

Stomping on the brake, he pulled his phone back out and quickly navigated to the trash. He opened the first one.

What you did was criminal.

They should have locked you up and thrown away the key.

You should have just died in that fire.

Zachary stared at the words in horror. Of course it wasn't Harding's cyberstalker, in spite of the similarities between the poisonous messages. Harding's stalker would have no idea of Zachary's past and no reason to start harassing him.

But someone connected to Zachary's past had tried to make contact with him recently. If Tyrrell was able to find Zachary's old address from when he and Bridget were living together, then it followed that he'd be able to find Zachary's email address. Zachary ran a business, he didn't exactly keep it a secret. When Zachary had failed to answer the letter, Tyrrell had gone looking for another way to get ahold of him, and had vented his anger through email.

Zachary closed the first email and opened the second. They were in reverse chronological order with the most recent at the top, so the second email had actually arrived first. Zachary stared at the contents of the email, gobsmacked.

Someone laid on the horn behind him and Zachary realized that he was still sitting in his car in the police visitor parking lot, his car at an angle from pulling out, blocking the aisle completely. He threw the phone on the passenger seat beside him and shifted into drive. Without looking at the car behind him, he drove out of the parking lot and all the way home without picking up his phone again. The radio blasted out music he didn't even hear and he couldn't remember any of the drive home once he found himself sitting in the parking lot of his apartment building.

He picked up his phone, woke it up again, and looked at the screen.

10

It was Pat who answered the door. He stared at Zachary in surprise.

"Zachary! I didn't know you were coming by. Lorne isn't home. Did he know...?"

Zachary had driven for several hours to get to the home of Mr. Peterson, an old foster father, fully believing that he would be there when Zachary arrived. It seemed inconceivable that Mr. Peterson would not be there when Zachary needed him.

"No," he admitted. "I didn't... I just came. Is he coming back? He didn't move, did he?" Already mired in the past, Zachary couldn't help but remember the day he had arrived on the Petersons' doorstep expecting to be able to develop pictures with Mr. Peterson, only to be told by his wife that he had moved out. That had been when Mr. Peterson's relationship with Pat had come to light, predictably ending the marriage.

"Of course he's coming back," Pat assured Zachary. "Come in." He took Zachary by the arm and tugged him inside. "You're white as a sheet, Zachary, what's wrong?"

Zachary leaned on Pat for support. Though a good ten years older than Zachary, Pat was taller and his muscular chest almost twice as broad. With his help, Zachary managed to get to the couch and sit down. He buried his face in his hands, elbows braced on his knees. "He's coming back?"

"I promise, he's coming back. He just went out to pick up some groceries."

Pat didn't tell Zachary that he should have called ahead to arrange something. Mrs. Peterson had always criticized Zachary for showing up unannounced, when he had been told repeatedly that he needed to call and set up appointments ahead of time. In contrast, Pat and Mr. Peterson had always told him that Zachary was welcome anytime, so he hadn't hesitated to go there when everything in his world had suddenly gone sideways.

"Let me give him a call," Pat said. "I'll let him know you're here, see how long he's going to be."

He walked out to the kitchen to make the call out of Zachary's hearing. Zachary couldn't make out his words, but did recognize the low tones of concern. Pat looked back over his shoulder at Zachary once as he talked, then looked back away. After he hung up, he turned back around and stood in the doorway between the living room and the dining room.

"He's on his way. Ten, fifteen minutes."

"Okay." Zachary nodded, his movements feeling awkward and wooden. "Thanks."

"Just relax and make yourself at home. I'll bring you a drink in a minute."

Zachary turned his head to look out the living room window, watching for Mr. Peterson's return. He could hear Pat moving around in the kitchen, but the sounds didn't really enter his conscious thoughts. He was in limbo, drowning in memories, waiting for someone he could share them with to try to get them out of his head.

Pat walked in and placed something on the glass-topped coffee table.

"Zachary."

He tried to travel the long span of time back to the present, but it took a couple more prompts from Pat before Zachary could get there. He turned his head and focused on the older man. Still handsome and fit, looking fashionable even in a t-shirt. Pat motioned to the coffee table.

"Have some tea," he urged. "It will help."

Zachary leaned forward and, with a shaking hand, picked up the white mug with a cat picture on the side and forced himself to drink a few tiny sips of the hot tea. It was an herbal blend Zachary wasn't familiar with, but it was pleasant enough. It had been sweetened with a generous amount of honey. *Good for shock.*

"Thanks."

He put the mug back down. It rattled against the coaster as he set it down.

Pat sat down in one of the upholstered chairs. "It's good to see you. You know Lorne would love to see more of you. Any time you want to make the trip, we'd love to have you. Take a week off and have a real vacation."

Zachary nodded wordlessly. Just a reflex reaction, keeping the flow of the conversation.

"It was nice seeing you at Thanksgiving, but we'd be happy to see more of you."

Zachary turned his head and looked out the front window again, catching a movement out the corner of his eye. But the car continued to drive on past the house. Not Lorne Peterson.

"He'll be coming through the back," Pat advised, following his gaze. At that moment, Zachary heard the grinding of the garage door motor in the attached garage.

Zachary turned toward the kitchen and watched as Mr. Peterson entered with a couple of grocery bags. He put them down on the counter and joined Pat and Zachary in the living room without putting his purchases away.

"Zachary, it's so good to see you!" He sat down on the couch with him. "How are you? Is everything okay?"

"No. I don't know. No." Zachary shook his head, not sure what to say.

"Okay! That's a little confusing. Tell me what's up."

Zachary pulled out his phone and brought it to life. It was still open to the email. He handed it over.

Mr. Peterson looked at the phone screen. He put on a pair of glasses, looked at it again, and took them off. "I really can't see those little phone screens worth a darn. Can you bring it up on my computer? Or just tell me what it says?"

"Uh, yeah." Zachary swallowed and nodded. "Sure. Where's your computer?"

Mr. Peterson led him to a bedroom that was being used as a study, and motioned to the computer on the desk. Certainly not the latest model, but it had a big screen, and it would do. Zachary sat down in the swivel chair and brought up the browser, logging out of Mr. Peterson's email and into his own account. There were several new emails in his inbox, but he didn't look at them, navigating to the deleted mail to open the email with an attachment. He clicked the jpg and it filled the screen.

It was even more disorienting to see it on the big screen than it had been on the phone. Mr. Peterson gazed for a moment at the picture of the family on the screen. Mother, father, and six children, apparently at a Christmas party in the late eighties. Mr. Peterson lifted his hand so fast it made Zachary jump. He pointed at the third child, the oldest boy. "That's you!" He looked at Zachary's face and then back at the screen again. "It is, isn't it?"

"Yes."

"This is your bio family?"

Zachary nodded.

"Where did you find it?"

Zachary closed the picture and pointed with the mouse to the text of the email.

This was your family before you destroyed it.

It's hard to believe that kind of evil can be allowed to exist.

"Oh, Zachary…" Mr. Peterson breathed. "You can't believe that. Who sent you this?"

"Tyrrell." Zachary clicked on the photo again and indicated the smiling six-year-old. "There."

"Are you sure?" The older man shook his head. "I really can't see something like this coming from a member of your family. I know there were issues with your mother, but the other kids…? They wouldn't do this."

"You never even met them. How could you know that?"

"It's just… it doesn't make sense. He was just a little boy. He wouldn't have blamed you. I don't know if they even would have told him any details of what had happened. Social Services wasn't too keen on sharing that information, even with foster parents who needed it."

"He was old enough to remember. He was six."

Zachary had to admit that the little boy in the picture looked closer to three than to six. But he could remember their ages. They had probably all been small for their ages. Zachary knew he had been endlessly teased and bullied for being so small. But that was normal for children who were neglected and malnourished. Then, years of meds that stunted growth had ensured that Zachary would remain shorter than average as an adult too, even though he had been fed better in later years.

"It's not signed. What makes you think it was Tyrrell?"

"He sent me a letter. I didn't answer it, so he sent these."

"He sent you a letter? Snail mail?"

"Yes. I guess I should have answered, like Kenzie said. Maybe he wouldn't have resorted to this."

Mr. Peterson shook his head. "I'm so sorry this happened. The boy obviously has some lasting problems. To blame you for everything thirty years later… maybe he has some kind of psychosis…"

Zachary couldn't envision Tyrrell as a man. In his mind, Tyrrell was forever that six-year-old who had cowered in Zachary's arms as their parents fought. Tyrrell would always be a little boy in his memories.

"But something good did come of this," Mr. Peterson offered.

"Good?"

"You got a picture of your family. You've never had anything to remember them by."

Zachary hadn't. He hadn't had anything after the fire. Had that one picture survived? Had there been anything else that had been saved from the fire? He scrutinized it, looking for any signs of scorching or smoke damage, but it seemed to be in good condition.

"Yeah."

"Why don't you print a copy out?"

"I should adjust it first." Zachary studied the lighting and color in the old photo. "Balance the lighting and fix the color…"

"You can do that later. Just print a copy for now. We'll go sit down and you can tell me about them."

Zachary downloaded the picture and sent it to the printer. He and Mr. Peterson waited while it printed.

"You should report him to the police," Mr. Peterson commented.

"No. I couldn't do that to him."

"He could be unbalanced. He could do something to harm you."

Zachary thought about Richard Harding, getting struck down on the road that night. What had happened? Had his stalker shown up? Had he been running away from someone or chasing after them? From what Ashley had said, he wouldn't have been likely to have chased after the man. Running away, then. Running right into the pathway of a speeding semi? Maybe he had been trying to flag Rusty down for help and had turned away at the last moment to protect himself when he realized the truck wasn't going to stop.

Mr. Peterson put his hand on Zachary's shoulder.

"I'm okay," Zachary told him, his voice hoarse. He leaned forward and plucked the photo from the printer. Holding it in his hands somehow made it more real than just looking at it on the phone and computer screens. He felt like he could reach out and touch each one of them. It was like the fire had just happened the day before. Or like it had never happened.

Mr. Peterson squeezed, then let go of Zachary. "Let's go sit back down."

He shuffled a little when he walked. Mr. Peterson had always seemed so big and solid; it was only in the last couple of years he had started to show some frailty. The fact brought a lump to Zachary's throat. Mr. Peterson was his only family. Zachary had thought that he would be around forever, even though he knew it wasn't true. Maybe his thoughts of the end of his own life had prevented him from seeing that Mr. Peterson would die one day too. Zachary had never been able to see more than a year ahead in his own life. Never past the next Christmas.

Zachary sat back down in the spot he had vacated. He took a sip of the tea, which had cooled enough to drink. He hesitated, then handed Pat the family picture. Pat was family too. He'd been with Mr. Peterson for almost thirty years.

"That's my bio family. Back... before."

Pat handled the picture carefully. He gave a little laugh. "Is that you? Man, look at how young you are!"

Zachary ducked his head. "Yeah."

"How old were you when we first met? Fourteen? You're a lot younger here."

"Ten. Before I went to the Petersons'."

"Wow. Where did you turn this up?"

Zachary looked at Mr. Peterson, not sure he could explain it himself.

"Zachary has been getting... some disturbing letters. This was with one of them. Maybe from one of his brothers."

Pat looked again at the picture and then handed it back to Zachary. "*That's* what happened. That's why you came here."

Zachary nodded. "I just... it's the only place I could think of. I couldn't go to a therapist or group... I needed... somewhere grounding."

"Family," Pat said firmly.

"Yeah."

Zachary held the photo, staring down at it. Mr. Peterson's eyes were on it as well.

"It's hard to believe that's just before you came to us. When the social worker brought you… you were a very sad little boy."

The children in the picture were happy. They were all together and their eyes sparkled with the excitement of the party. There was something else different too; the arm Zachary had around Tyrrell was unscarred. No burns from the fire. No cuts on his wrists. There were a couple of visible bruises, but all active boys had bruises on their arms and legs. And Zachary had been very active.

"No scars."

Mr. Peterson squinted and nodded. "The fire must have been just a few days after this."

Zachary held his breath, waiting for the images to subside. "I guess. I don't remember this party."

"Maybe this is the year before. You don't look ten."

"No, I was."

"How soon did you go to Lorne's?" Pat asked. "Right after?"

"I was in hospital… then Bonnie Brown. It was a few months."

They didn't discuss how long he'd been at the Petersons'. That he'd been too much for them to manage and Mrs. Peterson had insisted that he be reassigned to another foster family within a few short weeks. But even so, Mr. Peterson had become an anchor for Zachary. He had given Zachary his first camera for his birthday and allowed him to keep in contact after he had been moved. They had processed hundreds of photos together and Mr. Peterson had never made him feel unwelcome.

"I want you to tell me about your family," Mr. Peterson said, though of course he'd heard their names and what stories Zachary could remember before. "But first, I want you to tell me what you're going to do. About the letters."

"I don't know."

"It should be reported to the police."

"If I don't respond, he'll stop."

"There's no guarantee of that. Something must have happened to trigger this behavior. You don't know what it was. If he's just been through some kind of breakup or tragedy... you don't know how much it might have affected him."

"I can't report Tyrrell."

"If he starts making threats..."

"He hasn't. Let's just wait and see if it blows over."

11

Zachary had never stayed over at Mr. Peterson's house before. He was close enough that he could drive over in the afternoon for dinner, then drive back home for bed. There had been invitations, but he'd never accepted them. But Mr. Peterson refused to take 'no' for an answer.

"I want to make sure you're okay. This has been very upsetting for you."

Zachary's moods had been all over the map as he'd tried to process both the hate-filled messages from Tyrrell and the precious picture of his family. He'd had several vivid flashbacks, and more than once had excused himself to the bathroom because he didn't want Pat and Mr. Peterson to see him cry. He hadn't been able to touch anything at supper.

In the end, Zachary was too exhausted to argue about it. Mr. Peterson wasn't giving him a choice and it was immensely easier to just accept the edict than to try to fight him on it.

"We have everything you need," Pat assured him, "and we have the space. You're not in the way; you know we've been trying to get you to stay over for years."

"I don't like to impose…"

"Good grief, Zachary. Sleeping on the guest room bed is not imposing. Listen to Lorne."

"Okay." Zachary held up his hands. "Fine. Okay. I'll stay."

And then came the invitations for Christmas. They'd always invited him to join their observance, other than the couple years he'd been with Bridget, but Zachary was always physically unable to accept.

"We might get a visit from my family this year," Pat offered. "Fingers crossed." He held up his hands with this index and middle fingers crossed on both. "One can always hope."

Zachary had rarely heard Pat even acknowledge that he had any family other than Mr. Peterson. He looked at Pat curiously. "Who's coming? Your parents?"

"My dad passed last year. Maybe my mother and sister will come. For years, they've all refused to come anywhere near here."

"They wouldn't have anything to do with me," Mr. Peterson said wryly. "They were fine with Pat going home for a visit, but I'm the person who corrupted him." Mr. Peterson looked at his partner affectionately. "Apparently, I'm very persuasive."

Zachary felt a flush creeping up his neck. He'd never been comfortable talking to them about their romantic relationship; how they had met, what had attracted them to each other, or what other relationships they might have had other than each other.

Pat laughed. "They always hoped I'd decide it was a big mistake. That it was just a phase I was going through. My dad was very religious about this one thing. He was never particularly concerned with any of the other Biblical teachings, but he believed our relationship was unnatural and a sin and he wouldn't do anything that might be taken as condoning it."

"Too bad he missed out on spending time with you," Zachary said. He wanted a family so badly, it was hard to believe anyone would choose to push their child away.

Pat nodded, looking pensive. "We could have had some good years together. But that was his choice."

After a couple of days at Mr. Peterson's house, Zachary was feeling a lot calmer and more stable. Pat and Mr. Peterson repeated their invitations for him to return for Christmas, invitations which, again, were met with fumbling silence.

"You know you're always welcome," Mr. Peterson assured him. "Any time you want to come join us, just do it. I don't need a commitment ahead of time."

Zachary nodded and got back into his car. Heading back home, he had mixed feelings. It would feel good to get back to work and his own apartment and just put the incident behind him.

But he knew that it wasn't over. Tyrrell had demonstrated that he wasn't going to just send one letter and then wait for a response. He had a deep-seated anger and resentment toward Zachary, and he was going to continue to vent it, just the way Harding's stalker had not only continued his harassment, but escalated it. Zachary continued to send the messages to his email trash, but he also found that he couldn't just ignore them and leave them alone. Instead, like picking at a scab, he kept digging back into the trash to read and re-read the messages. Like if he could just figure out what to say to Tyrrell, he could stop the influx of poison pen emails. Even though he knew it was impossible, he couldn't stop himself from obsessing over the contents of the emails and what responses to give.

Probably, there wouldn't even be a way for him to reply if he wanted to. The anonymous email service Tyrrell was employing wouldn't even accept an answer. But knowing that fact logically and being able to stop the obsessive re-reading of the vitriolic emails were two different things. He had put on a mask of dispassion for Mr. Peterson and Pat. *Oh, it's nothing. As long as he's not making threats, I'll just delete them.* But he suspected they didn't believe that for a minute.

As he entered the city limits, work started to call to Zachary. He could hyperfocus on his files and push everything else out of his mind. That would be a relief, and would bring in some extra cash. His phone rang and Zachary answered it on Bluetooth.

"Zachary, are you okay?"

Zachary took a deep breath. He had answered Kenzie's various messages while he'd been at Mr. Peterson's, but he knew she wouldn't believe he was really okay until she'd had a chance to see him face to face.

"I'm fine, Kenzie. Just got back into town."

"Thought you might want to go over the details of the Harding autopsy."

"Oh!" He hadn't been expecting that, and it was a welcome surprise. "Sure, that would be great. Take you out this time? Buffet?"

"Why is it always buffet when we're reviewing autopsies?"

Zachary thought about it. It wasn't like he had taken that many homicides. But Kenzie might be right. "I didn't realize we did that. Do you want to go somewhere else instead? Somewhere nicer?"

There was a moment of hesitation. "I don't know if it would be kosher to pull out autopsy photos somewhere nicer."

Zachary thought about her response. "We don't have to look at the photos while we're there. We can have a nice dinner and then go back to my place to look at them and go over the results."

"Maybe…"

So perhaps Bowman had been right about Kenzie being interested in a deeper relationship. But maybe it wasn't too late to advance it. As long as she was still calling him, there was a possibility.

"You want to try the Inn? It's been a while since we've been there."

Not since New Year's the previous year. The night that they had been in a serious wreck after someone had cut Zachary's brake lines.

"It was really nice last time, wasn't it? I wouldn't mind that."

"I don't remember much about it," Zachary admitted. His memories of the dinner had been clouded by everything that had happened afterward.

Kenzie laughed. "Then I guess it's about time we went back. And this time, you don't have a psychotic killer stalking you."

Zachary's mouth went dry. He hadn't even thought to check his car for tampering before he'd gotten into it at Mr. Peterson's house. He would have to be sure to check it before and after they ate. He wasn't about to have another accident.

"Zachary?"

"Yeah, I'll make the reservations. Was there anything interesting on the autopsy?"

"I'm afraid not, no. You can look, but I don't think you're going to find much enlightenment in this one."

"He seems to be quite the enigma," Zachary said. "I should be getting the rest of the background reports today, but so far I haven't turned up much of anything."

By the time they met for dinner, Zachary had followed up on the background searches, and not only had they not turned up much of interest, they had come back almost blank. He was used to being able to find at least a few points of interest on a subject, but Harding was different. He didn't seem to have a history. Even his electronic footprint only went back a few years. Before that, he might not even have existed.

"Have you ever had that happen before?" Kenzie asked. "I mean, he could just be a really boring person, right?"

"It's not just that he's boring. Or law-abiding. There's just nothing there."

"So..." She took a polite bite of her salmon. "Are we talking witness protection program?"

"I guess that's a possibility. More likely he was in the country illegally. Or he created a false identity."

"And which do you think it is?"

Zachary poked at his potatoes. "I need to talk to the girlfriend. Ashley. See if she knows anything about it. I know she's been holding back on me. She never could explain *why* she couldn't believe it was an accident."

"She knows, then," Kenzie decided. "How about her? Did you run any background on her?"

"Well..." Zachary was hesitant, wondering whether she would approve or whether she thought it was an invasion of privacy. He didn't usually run background searches on his clients. Not without a good reason. "I did do some preliminary searches on her. Hers come back more normal. Credit history, mentions of awards and scholarships in school, work history on her LinkedIn account. Interests, hobbies, and family on her social media accounts. She comes back as a real person, but he doesn't."

Kenzie pondered this and had a sip of wine. "It's fascinating to hear how it's all done. It really is."

Zachary smiled. Most people, finding out how mind-numbingly boring private investigation could be, were let down. Real private investigators weren't Dick Tracy or Nero Wolfe. Real private investigations work involved a lot of paper, thinking time, and waiting around.

Back at Zachary's apartment, Kenzie unpacked her portfolio briefcase while Zachary got out drinks and ducked into the bathroom to take a couple of pills unobserved. When he sat down on the couch with Kenzie, she turned the bottle around to look at the label.

"Sparkling white grape and peach," she read. "Sounds nice." She poured it into the two brand-new champagne flutes and had a taste. "It's good. This is really nice, thank you for a great evening."

"It's not over yet," Zachary pointed out, smiling a little, "there are still autopsy photos."

Kenzie laughed. She pulled the written report out from under one of the pictures and started to tell him the findings, outlining Harding's numerous broken bones. Zachary listened closely.

"Can you tell by the broken bones how fast the vehicle was going when it hit him?"

"Not with any accuracy, no. The breaks are sharper and there is more shattering the faster the vehicle is going, but we can't say 'this was a truck going fifty and this was a truck going sixty.'"

Zachary nodded. "And you can't tell what he was doing—whether he was walking or running, what position he was in when he got hit...?"

"Not much more than that he was standing and he was hit on the left side."

"Is there anything that doesn't make sense? Anything that stands out? Inconsistencies?"

"It's a pretty straightforward MVC."

Zachary nodded. He hadn't really been expecting anything different, but he had hoped that there would be something illuminating. Just one or two little facts that would point him in a different direction. He took a sip of the sparkling juice Kenzie had poured for him. While he would have preferred a Coke, the sparkling juice was to help set a romantic scene. He thought too late about putting on some background music. It might seem awkward to get back up and do it while they were discussing dead bodies. And there were no candles. Never any candles. He had been relieved that the flickering candles on the tables at the Inn had turned out to be little electric lights rather than the real thing.

"How about this..." he said slowly. "You've seen the body. Say it's a John Doe. You don't know anything about him. What does the body tell you about what kind of a person he was? Where he lived, what he did, health issues, medical history..."

"Interesting question." Kenzie considered. She stared up at the ceiling as she thought about it.

Zachary looked through the photos as she thought.

"Caucasian male in his thirties. He was in good shape," Kenzie said, "Body Mass Index put him at a healthy weight for his height. But not really muscular. A bit of stooping in his shoulders and back, which says he was probably sedentary, sitting for long periods of time. Maybe a computer gamer. Hands would suggest some manual work, though. Some dental work that wasn't really up to first-world standards, so maybe he had lived out of the country for a while."

Zachary picked up one of the photos. "He had tattoos." He didn't know why that surprised him. A lot of people had tattoos, even forty-something stay-at-home moms and minor children.

"Yeah, a few of them." Kenzie shuffled through the pictures to pull a couple more out. "I thought this one a little odd." She handed him a picture of a snake tattoo. "It looks like it was applied over broken skin, which is a big no-no. You see how the ink tones are uneven."

"Trying to hide a scar?" Zachary suggested.

"Maybe that was the idea, but any self-respecting tattooist would wait until it was properly healed over, so you don't end up with these color shifts."

"Why put a tattoo over broken skin, then? Wouldn't that be painful?"

"I would expect it to be quite a painful process." Kenzie took a sip of her drink, then suddenly frowned. "Actually, you may be onto something there…"

"What?"

Kenzie looked at her written report, and then tracked down a photo. She handed it to Zachary. He saw an expanse of skin, with a little group of parallel cuts.

"What's this from?"

"We weren't sure when we looked at it to start with. But now I'm wondering… if he was self-harming. You see cutting more often with girls, but some guys still do it. You said he was on meds for depression. Maybe he was cutting too."

"And the tattoos were to cover the areas he'd been cutting? To hide them?"

"Maybe… or maybe to amplify the pain."

Zachary grimaced. "Ouch. You think?"

"Sometimes body modification aficionados are addicted to pain or using it the same way as someone who self-harms. Tattoos or other mods could be socially acceptable ways to harm himself."

"Maybe. He was depressed; if the meds weren't giving him any relief or he was looking for something that would work faster…"

Kenzie looked sideways at Zachary and didn't agree or disagree.

"What about this one?" Zachary held up the initial tattoo picture he had grabbed. "I don't see any scarring in or around this tattoo."

Kenzie studied it. "This one looks different. Like maybe a homemade tattoo instead of a professional one."

"You think he did it himself?"

"I don't think he could have done it alone. He would have needed help, even if he was trying to do it at home."

"Another question to ask Ashley."

"I think you should definitely talk to her. Maybe this is enough ammunition to get her to open up."

12

Zachary met with Ashley at the police station. He hoped that if he talked to her there, she would be uncomfortable and off-balance, and more likely to talk about what it was she had been keeping a secret. Since he wasn't a police officer himself, it had taken a little finessing to get the use of one of their meeting rooms. In the end, Bowman had reserved it in his own name, and insisted on being present for the interview since his was the name that was on the record.

He started with a disclaimer that Zachary was not the police and that she wasn't required to answer anything he asked. Ashley nodded, but her eyes went back and forth around the room, anxious at the unfamiliar setting.

"Some things have turned up in my investigation," Zachary explained.

"What things?"

"You haven't been completely honest about who Richard was, have you?" Zachary pressed, keeping his language vague. "You thought it didn't make any difference, but I need all of the details if I'm going to sort this out."

She chewed on her lip, uncertain. "I just want you to prove that the truck driver intended to murder him. You don't need to know every little detail about Richard's life for that."

"I do need to know. Keeping it from me doesn't help."

"What did you find? You said you had turned things up in your investigation."

Zachary studied her, waiting for her to fill the silence. She was sweating and squirming uncomfortably, but she didn't break down. He put down a copy of the photo of the DIY tattoo that Kenzie said Harding would have needed help with. Maybe Ashley had been the one to assist him. If not, he was sure she would at least know the history of such a thing. She wouldn't just see tattoos on her boyfriend's body and not ask about them.

Ashley wiped her forehead and grimaced. "I promised never to tell anyone," she said plaintively.

"I think he would have made an exception for when it would help convict his killer."

"But I don't see—it can't help you. And if you already know, then me telling you would just be betraying him for no reason!"

"I need the details. I need you to explain it to me."

He waited. He had certainly attacked the right weakness on his first try. There were several ways the conversation could have gone and he was happy it had worked right away. There *was* something about that tattoo. Something that had made Richard different. Something that explained it all.

"I told him he should get it removed," Ashley said. "I told him it could come back to bite him if the wrong person saw it. But he said... no one but me was going to see it, because it was covered up normally. He said no one else would ever see it."

"And maybe they didn't. While he was alive. But now we've seen it. I'm still waiting for an explanation."

Ashley sighed. She looked over at Bowman, as if asking whether she really had to tell Zachary. Bowman just lifted his eyebrows and waited, arms folded.

"He got it while he was in prison," Ashley finally admitted.

Bowman shifted. Zachary was careful not to look at him. He kept his eyes on Ashley. He nodded, showing no surprise, as if she were only confirming what he had already known. And maybe he should have figured it out. A prison tattoo. That's why it was lower quality. That was why it looked homemade.

"How long ago did he get out of prison?"

"Three years."

"Around the time you guys met."

"Yes. I was one of the first people he met when he moved to Vermont. He figured that here, he'd be able to start a new life. He'd be able to be a normal person instead of someone that everyone knew was a convict. You can't live a normal life when everyone knows you've been to prison. They judge you. They don't treat you the same way."

"No," Zachary agreed. And it was true of other facilities as well. A psych hospital, juvie, drug rehab, residential care. People looked at him differently when they knew. They looked at him like he was an alien, a completely different species. "Why didn't you just tell the police that when they started the investigation? Instead, you've had everybody running around not knowing where to look."

"Where to look for what?" Ashley challenged. "You already know who it was that ran him down. You just need to prove that it was intentional instead of accidental."

"How can we do that without being able to tie him to Richard's earlier life? Or even to his original name?"

"He wasn't that person anymore. It was a tragic accident, and he paid for it. He wanted to leave that chapter of his life behind and be able to leave a normal life as Richard Harding."

"But it isn't that easy, is it?"

"No. He was always paranoid someone would recognize him or would be able to track him down in spite of the name change. I told him that was silly. No one was going to be stalking him. Everyone else was just going to go on with their own lives, and he could to."

"Except that it did catch up to him." Zachary thought about the words in the accusing emails and messages. *People like you. What you did. Unforgivable.* "Someone did run into him or track him down and was sending him those emails."

"He never told me. Did he think I wouldn't believe him? Why wouldn't he trust me with that?"

"Maybe because it was from a part of his life that you hadn't had anything to do with." Zachary thought about how he had instinctively gone to Mr. Peterson when he got the first few messages from Tyrrell, not to Kenzie or Bowman or another of his friends. Zachary had been sent to the Petersons' house after the fire, when he had been put into foster care for the first time. He associated them with that time in his life. Sharing information with Kenzie about his early life wasn't easy. She had not been a part of it. "Is there someone he might have gone to? Someone from his previous life that he would have gone to with his problems?"

"No, he'd completely cut himself off from his former life. His therapist suggested changing his name and moving away. His family didn't really want anything to do with him. So he figured, why not? He didn't want to be punished over and over again for something that wasn't even his fault."

"How much do you know about his life before, when he was—what was his name?"

"Brandon Powers."

Zachary wrote it down in his notepad. "Did he give you his version of what happened when he was Brandon Powers? What it was he went to prison for?" Zachary said it as if he already knew the details, and just wanted to check to see if Ashley did.

Ashley sighed. Zachary could see that even though she had been fighting against telling him, trying to keep the secret she had promised to keep for Harding, she was relieved to have someone to tell it to. She wanted to get it off her chest, to have someone to share the burden of knowledge with.

"It was an accident. He had half his life taken away from him because of a car accident."

Zachary couldn't suppress a shiver. Harding had been convicted because of a car accident and then he had been killed in one? He could already begin to see the parallel that had convinced Ashley that it must have been an intentional homicide.

"Just tell me about it in your own words," he told her. He didn't want to have to drag each individual statement from her. He didn't want to be left with a hodgepodge of unconnected statements and with no overall picture. He wanted to know the story, as if it had happened to him.

"He was in college. He and some of his friends had been out to the bar, and Richard was driving them home. He was the designated driver. But then a girl stepped out in front of the car, coming from nowhere, and he couldn't stop in time."

Vehicle versus pedestrian. Just like Harding's death.

"Did he kill or injure her?" he asked, pushing her to provide the lynchpin. Everything else would be easier to tell once she had gotten that part off her chest.

"She was killed. Instantly, I guess. Richard… wasn't really clear telling that part."

"Was he arrested at the scene?"

Ashley swallowed. "No. Not exactly."

"Not exactly." He waited for the rest. What, exactly?

"He was woozy. He hit his head during the accident. He couldn't really be responsible for his actions after the accident."

Zachary knew what she was trying to avoid saying before she managed to get it out.

"He sort of… wandered away from the scene. He was disoriented and didn't know what he was doing."

"Hit and run."

"Yes, that's what they called it." She looked straight at Zachary for the first time. "You see? You see why him getting killed in a hit and run just couldn't be an accident? You understand why I'm sure it was intentional?"

"I see your point. It stretches the bounds of plausibility."

"Yes. It does. I don't know what happened out there that night. I don't know how the trucker is connected. But I know it wasn't an accident."

"I'll do my best to find the connection. But for that, you have to tell me the truth. The whole truth, without covering anything up because you don't think it's relevant."

She nodded, eyes down.

"Good. It's time to hear the real story. Do you know why he was out on the road that night?"

"No. None of that has changed. I still don't know why he went outside and why he'd be out on the road. Like I said, he didn't go outside for walks, he exercised at home on the bike. He didn't spend a lot of time outside the house. He was afraid someone would see him and know who he was."

Zachary thought of what Kenzie had said. At a healthy weight, but not muscular. As if he'd done a lot of sitting, hunched over for long periods of time. The curse of prison life. Free time. Time to sit and think and do nothing else. Waiting for the seconds, minutes, hours, and days to pass. Waiting for the time to tick slowly away, until his release day finally arrived.

Then he'd been released, but he'd been afraid to go out. Whether it was paranoia or agoraphobia, Zachary didn't know. Harding's stint in prison had damaged him. It had affected him for the rest of his life, even though he had tried to put it behind him.

"He was the designated driver the night of the accident." Zachary repeated what Ashley had told him.

"Yes."

"He hadn't had anything to drink?"

Her eyes darted to the side, trying to decide whether to tell him the truth or not.

"He said he'd had a couple of beers. He wasn't drunk, but if the police had tried to test him that night, he would have had some alcohol in his blood. Just a little. It would for sure be below the limit, but it wouldn't be zero."

"Is that why he didn't stick around the accident scene? Because he didn't want to be tested?"

"I told you. He was disoriented."

"I think there might have been more to it than that."

"I know Richard. He wasn't lying about that."

"Even if he'd had no alcohol in his blood, he still killed this pedestrian. He's still responsible."

"And he paid for it. He served his time."

"Which was how much?"

"Eight years in prison."

Zachary nodded. It computed. And the length of time confirmed that the court had convicted him of first degree vehicular homicide, not a misdemeanor. There was more to it than just misjudging the distance of the pedestrian from the car. Leaving the scene of the crime hadn't helped. Neither had drinking, if there had still been alcohol in his system when they caught up with him.

"What was the victim's name?"

"How do you expect me to know that?" Ashley demanded.

Zachary just gazed at her steadily. She turned red.

"Hope Creedy."

Zachary wrote it down. There, at last, were two more names to feed into his searches in trying to find a connection between Richard Harding and Rusty Donaldson. Brandon Powers and Hope Creedy. Hopefully, one of them would lead him to the answer to the puzzle.

"Was there anyone specific Richard didn't want to run into or be tracked down by?"

"What do you mean?"

"Was there anyone from Hope's family who had been threatening him? Anyone sending letters to him at the prison? A specific person that he never wanted to hear from again?"

Ashley's brow wrinkled as she considered the question. "No... I don't think so. He didn't say there was one person, just that he didn't want anyone to know his old name or his history. I wasn't allowed to tell anyone."

"Did you?"

"Did I what?"

"Tell anyone. It's a pretty big secret to keep. Did you tell a girlfriend? Your mother? Your hairdresser? Someone who you thought would keep the secret and would never be a threat to Richard?"

"No!" she looked offended that he would even think such a thing. But in Zachary's experience, people always told someone. A secret just kept itching away and the secret-keeper had to scratch it somehow, by telling at least one person they considered safe and trustworthy.

"A therapist? Someone who was required under law to keep it a secret?"

"No."

But he thought he had seen a shadow cross her face. Who, then? A spiritual confessor? Ashley was keeping tight-lipped. She had no intention of telling him who she had spilled the beans to. Had her indiscretion led someone from Richard's past to him? Or was it just one of those things? People were getting easier and easier to trace. It wasn't just Zachary's growing expertise; there were more tools out there. More electronic trails. Saying one thing online...

"Did Richard ever have any contact with anyone from Hope's family? Did he ever go back to try to apologize?"

"No. He wasn't required to do that. And he hadn't done anything wrong. It was an accident. He didn't see her coming. It was unavoidable."

That hadn't been the court's determination, but Zachary couldn't be sure if she knew that or not. Either way, she was just going to go on repeating Richard's own rhetoric, no matter what Zachary tried to get out of her.

"So as far as you know, he didn't contact them and they didn't contact him."

"No." Ashley looked around the bare-walled meeting room. "So is that it? Can I go now?"

"Did Richard have any papers? Anything from the trial, a legal name change, anything like that?"

"I got rid of it all. Burned it."

Too bad the police hadn't reacted faster than they had. Maybe they would have been able to get their hands on Richard's papers before she'd had the chance. But there would still be public records. She couldn't do anything about those.

13

N ice job," Bowman commented, as they watched Ashley's departure.

She wasn't happy, but at least she hadn't fired him for doing what she had hired him to do. That just bolstered his opinion that she was relieved to be able to share the burden of Richard's secret. She didn't have to be the only one who knew about it anymore.

"Thanks. I knew from the start she wasn't telling me everything, but I didn't have a clue what it was. Not to start with."

"How did you get that from a tattoo?"

"I didn't... not the whole story. I just knew that it didn't fit. It didn't match the others, and there was no explanation for him having a homemade tattoo. I figured he must have given her some story, even if it wasn't the truth."

"But who would make up something like this? It had the ring of truth, right?"

"Mostly."

"You're saying you don't believe that he was sober?" Bowman gave him a sardonic grin. "Now why would you not take the lady's opinion for that?"

"Because he wouldn't have told her the truth. Maybe he didn't even tell himself the truth about that one. He was the designated driver, but he thought it was okay to have a couple of beers? That's not the way it works."

"Nope."

"And I don't believe the pedestrian jumped out in front of the car, either. I think I'll find a different story when I order the court documents."

"You mean like that he was driving recklessly and under the influence? But that would mean it was his fault, and the lady just told you it was not his fault."

Zachary appreciated Bowman's sense of humor, but at the same time didn't feel it was appropriate for him to be laughing at someone else getting killed. Or even about Richard having to go to jail or Ashley trying to cover for him. It was a tragedy all around. Even a pure accident could change someone's life forever. And one that was Richard's fault because of a stupid choice he had made... Zachary could empathize with that.

He didn't have to wait for the court documents to get started on the investigation into Brandon Powers's hit and run in New Hampshire. A few internet searches of Brandon's and Hope's names brought up the old news stories, and Zachary browsed through them for details of the accident and for the names of Hope's family and friends. Enough of them had spoken to the media to get started on his investigation. The news stories had similar details to what Ashley had told him. Harding, aka Powers, had been driving the vehicle with three passengers, college buddies who had been out drinking together. One of his friends had also been killed in the accident, a Kyle Corcoran. He hadn't been wearing a seatbelt and had been ejected through the windshield. The two friends in the back sustained only minor injuries.

Hope Creedy had been waitressing; not at the same bar as the young men had visited. She had finished her shift and was walking back to her apartment just a few blocks away.

The police had determined that speed had been a factor. With Powers having walked away from the accident, they were unable to test his blood alcohol levels. It had taken them a few days to identify and track him down. But they had tested vomit found near the body, which Powers admitted was his, and it did contain alcohol. Powers eventually conceded to having had a couple of beers, but insisted that he was not drunk. The police nevertheless believed that alcohol had been a factor in the accident, and he was charged with manslaughter, conduct after an accident, and DWI.

Zachary made a list of the names of the people he hoped to interview and started to search for their current contact information. When he had everything assembled, he threw some clothes in a bag. While most of his subjects were only a couple of hours away, it would probably take several days to get interviews with them all, and he wouldn't want to be wasting time traveling back and forth every night. He added some toiletries and pills to the bag, his computer, camera, and any electronics that might come in handy. He stopped and considered whether there was anything else he was going to miss. Anything he really needed, he could buy on the way. He had plenty of experience surviving on the bare necessities. He'd already packed more than he normally had going from one foster home to the other.

He waited until he was on the road to make his phone calls. He wasn't sure whether he would be able to catch Kenzie at her desk or not, but she answered after just a couple of rings.

"Zachary. Bowman said you put that tattoo to good use."

"Sure did. Helped us to get a break in the case. He told you it was a prison tattoo?"

"Yeah. That also explains the dentistry and sedentary lifestyle. I don't know why I didn't think of it when I saw the quality of the tattoo. It just didn't click in."

"You can't know everything. You gave me enough to figure it out. Though you shouldn't have had to—the client should have told me everything she knew when she hired me."

"Crazy to expect you to be able to solve a case without giving you the most important details."

Zachary nodded his agreement, not thinking that she couldn't see him.

"So, what's your next step?" Kenzie asked. "I assume you're going to have to look into this old hit and run, see what the parallels are...?"

"The parallels are already pretty obvious. He killed someone else in a hit and run, and then he was killed in a hit and run. If they're not connected, that's a pretty big coincidence. I'm going to see if I can talk to the first victim's friends and family, see if I can figure out if one of them was somehow involved in Harding's death."

"How long will it take you to get that?"

"I'm on my way now."

"On your way... where?"

"To talk to the family. That's why I called you. To let you know that I wouldn't be home. I'll be in New Hampshire. So... don't be worried."

"How are you already on your way?"

Zachary grinned. The expression felt unnatural, like it had been a long time since he had last smiled. "It doesn't take me that long to get a few names and addresses."

"No kidding. You just found out about this other MVC this morning."

"The internet is your friend."

"It must be better friends with you than with me! It takes me time to find the information I want to."

Zachary gazed at the road ahead of him, enjoying the comforting sensation of gliding over the highway. Long-distance driving was one of the few times his thoughts slowed and he felt calm and focused. Maybe he should have become a long haul trucker like Rusty Donaldson, spending most of his days in a rig. It had a certain appeal.

"When will you be back?" Kenzie asked.

Zachary had almost forgotten she was still on the line. "It depends how long the interviews take. If no one will talk to me, it might be a pretty quick trip. But I think it will be a few days."

"Okay. Anything you need? Water the plants? Pick up the mail?"

"I don't have any plants and I only pick up postal mail once a week anyway."

"You should get some plants."

"Why?"

"They improve your environment: clean and oxygenate the air and lower stress levels... and it would give me something I could do for you when you're out of town."

"I don't like to have anybody or anything depending on me. I think it's best that way."

There was no immediate response from Kenzie. The silence grew uncomfortable. Zachary swallowed and licked his lips.

"Why do you say that?" Kenzie asked.

"It's just... I wouldn't want anyone depending on me, because if something happened to me... I would want to know that everyone was okay. That I hadn't left any unfinished business."

"Are you planning on leaving us any time soon?"

"No, I don't mean that…" But Zachary realized too late that that was exactly what he had meant. She'd nailed it. He liked to keep his affairs neat and tidy so that when things got to be too much for him, he wouldn't have to feel guilty about anything he had left undone. He mentally reproached himself for letting it slip out like that. "I'm sorry, Kenz. I really… I just like things to be uncomplicated."

"Yeah." Her tone was hard and biting. "Uncomplicated. Fine. I guess I'll see you when you get back."

She didn't say anything else. When Zachary glanced over at the Bluetooth display, he saw that she had terminated the call.

14

He wasn't sure, to start with, how to approach Hope's family. Whether he should show up in person or call or email them first. Whether to tell them that he was a private investigator, or to suggest that he was a policeman, lawyer, or reporter doing some kind of follow-up on Hope's death.

Eventually, he decided to stick as close to the truth as he felt he could, and that he would make a cold approach. If they had too much time to think about it, they might decide they didn't want to talk to him. If he caught them off-guard, he was more likely to get an honest reaction.

He figured that evening was the best time to catch Hope's parents at home. They were a middle-aged couple who had suffered a terrible tragedy and had been forced to live in the public eye, and he was hoping that meant they wouldn't be out partying, that they would want to relax after work or would be semi-retired.

Their home was a nice brick bungalow. Not the height of luxury, but very comfortable. The home they had raised their children in. Zachary looked at himself in the mirror before getting out of the car. He had shaved carefully before he left the apartment, wanting to look clean-cut and trust-worthy, not like some bum who had just wandered in off of the street. His hair was cropped short enough not to have to spend any time worrying about it. He had on a fresh button-up shirt, electing not to go with a tie or blazer. Professional, but not stuffy.

He took a few deep breaths. The anxiety had started to seep back as soon as he got off the highway. He forced himself to get out of the car, go up to the house, and press the doorbell.

It was only a short wait, and then a woman was standing at the open door, looking out at him curiously. Her hair was a sort of dark strawberry blond. It tapered around her face with minimum fuss, but looked polished rather than plain. She was taller than he was, and the step up into the house made Zachary feel even smaller, like he was a kid being dropped off at yet another new foster home.

"Mrs. Creedy? My name in Zachary Goldman." He paused, waiting for her to ask what he was there for, but she didn't. "I am working with the police in Vermont, consulting on a case that has an old connection with your family. I'm wondering if I could come in for a few minutes?"

She frowned slightly, then turned her head to look back into the house, directing her call back over her shoulder. "Mike?"

Her husband didn't show up immediately, and Mrs. Creedy stepped back from the door, motioning Zachary in.

"Mike, can you come here?" She lowered her voice to speak to Zachary. "Just... come have a seat, Mr...."

"Goldman," he repeated.

He sat down in the living room at her instruction. It was an awkward minute of not speaking to each other before her husband joined them. Mr. Creedy was taller than his wife, dark-haired but balding, with glasses. He was wearing a sweater with a few buttons done up.

"Who was at the door? Oh, excuse me..." He looked at Zachary, raising his brows.

"Zachary Goldman," he introduced himself again, electing not to stand up and shake Creedy's hand. "I'm working with the Vermont police..."

Creedy shook his head, not understanding. But his wife had already invited the unexpected guest in, and there wasn't much he could do about it until he knew why exactly Zachary was there.

"I don't really understand what this is about. Investigating what?"

Zachary studied his hands. "I don't know whether you heard about what happened to Richard Harding."

"Richard Harding?" Mrs. Creedy looked at her husband, but neither of them seemed to make any connection with the name. "Who is that?"

"You would know him by his former name. Brandon Powers."

There was an instant reaction to that name. Anger, pain, and frustration mingled on both of their faces. The anger was stronger in Mike Creedy's face, but that didn't necessarily prove anything. Women tended to be better at controlling their facial expressions.

"Brandon Powers is the monster who killed our daughter," Mr. Creedy spat. "Whatever happened to him, I can assure you it is not enough."

Zachary studied both of their faces, trying to memorize everything he saw, before letting slip the next bit of information.

"He was killed in a hit and run."

Both mouths opened in shock. Mr. Creedy's face drained of all color, making him look like a ghost.

"He's dead," Mrs. Creedy said, a blank statement rather than a question. Repeating the words that she was too shocked to believe.

"Yes," Zachary agreed. "A couple of weeks ago."

"Why didn't anyone tell us? Why didn't we hear about this?"

"Like I say, he was going by the name Richard Harding. No one connected it with his previous name."

"Nobody even knew who he was?"

"I just discovered it myself. His girlfriend knew, but no one else in Vermont, as far as I know."

Mr. Creedy shook his head. "Someone should call the papers. Let everybody know. This is the best news I've heard in years!"

His wife looked at him with wide eyes. "You can't say that about someone dying. He has a family too. How do you think they're going to feel? How many times have we said we wouldn't wish what we went through on our own enemies?"

"Turns out that wasn't true. I did wish it on my own enemy, and I'm happy it happened. Like I said, he deserved what he got."

Mrs. Creedy wasn't so sure. She was a lot more cautious about her reaction to the news. She looked at Zachary, giving a little grimace to tell him that her husband wasn't always like that. He was a good person, he was just bitter about his daughter. And she wasn't sure how she felt about it. Her eyes were tortured hollows.

"How exactly did it happen?" she asked tentatively. "It's so bizarre that he was killed the same way as Hope."

"That's one thing that we're looking into," Zachary said authoritatively. "It is a big coincidence. That's one of the reasons I wanted to talk to you. To see whether you know of anyone who might have been threatening Brandon or who might have wanted to hurt him."

"It serves him right," Mr. Creedy reasserted. "It's not very often you see real justice done in this world. But that… that might be the exception."

Mrs. Creedy was dabbing at the corners of her eyes. She looked at Zachary, waiting for his answer. Zachary tried to replay the conversation to see what he had missed.

The details. She wanted to know how Harding had died. It wasn't enough for her to know that he was dead, or that he had died in a hit and run like her daughter. That was enough to satisfy her husband, but Mrs. Creedy wanted the details. She wanted the whole story.

"I'm afraid I can't tell you very much. He was walking near his home and he was struck by a semi."

"Just like Hope," Mr. Creedy said with relish. "You see?"

"His body was thrown into the ditch and he wasn't discovered for a couple of days. They had to have scent dogs out to see if they could find him. Search parties. For a couple of days, his girlfriend had no idea what had happened to him; where he had disappeared to, or why."

Mrs. Creedy's eyes were seeking to connect with her husband's. "You see? We didn't have to deal with that. We knew right away what had happened, we didn't have to wait for days to find out."

But Mike Creedy apparently didn't care about that.

"Do you know anyone who might have had reason to harm Brandon?" Zachary pressed. "Or someone who might have threatened to?"

"Besides us, you mean?" Mr. Creedy challenged. "You want to know who other than us wanted to kill him?"

Mrs. Creedy put her hand over his, trying to quiet him. "Mike…"

"It's true and I'm not going to deny it. If I ran into that monster on the street, I would have done my best to kill him. He should not have been out walking free. He should have been behind bars for the rest of his life. He knew what he was doing when he got into that car, and he should never have been given the opportunity to do it again. People like that cannot be allowed to walk around in free society."

"He served his sentence," Mrs. Creedy said.

"His sentence. They could have given him thirty years. Why didn't they? If Hope was still alive today, she would have been thirty-two. She might have been married. She might have had babies, given us grandchildren. She could have been living a happy, fulfilling life with a family and a career. But he took that away from her. He took that away from all of us. And he should have had to pay. Not just eight years. Forever. He should have had to spend the rest of his life behind bars."

Zachary thought about the sentence. Harding had killed two people because he was drinking and driving and stunting. Why had the sentence been so light? He could understand Mike Creedy's bitterness and venom. Brandon Powers might not have planned to kill anyone that night, but he had still caused their deaths. He had chosen to drink when he was supposed to be the designated driver. He had chosen to speed. He had chosen to leave the scene of an accident where two people had been killed, to run away from his dead and injured friends and the stranger he had struck down in the night.

"I imagine that your extended family members probably feel the same way," Zachary suggested, trying to nudge the couple back to the question at hand.

"I'm sure everyone felt the same way," Mrs. Creedy agreed. "We all loved Hope dearly. She was the light of our lives."

"You have another daughter and a son...?"

"Yes. Noelle and Luke. They are twins."

"I imagine this was just as devastating for them as it was for you."

"It was," Mrs. Creedy agreed, eyes filling with tears for her children and the trials they had been through. "They were young teens at the time of the accident and the trial, old enough to understand everything that was going on and to know that they were never going to see Hope again. To be in the public eye all the time, everybody watching them for their reactions, reporters wanting to interview them, and the daily torture of the trial and sentencing... to have to go through that while their brains were still developing..."

Zachary nodded his understanding.

"I can't help but think that it damaged them... that things would be different now if we had been a whole, happy family, instead of having had to go through all of that."

"How are they now? You think it affected them permanently?"

"Oh, they're fine..." Mrs. Creedy looked at her husband, soliciting his opinion. "They're not drug addicts or homeless. But they both struggle with depression, and I think that if Hope had been able to finish college and go on, she would have been such an example for them. They would be motivated to further their educations and to be... more successful in life."

"They've done just fine," Mr. Creedy said. "You don't give them enough credit. And becoming successful in a career takes years. I didn't get to where I am in a year or two. I had to work at it for a long time."

"Yes. They're doing well, really," she said, retracting her previous comment. "It's so hard for kids to get ahead in today's world."

"They've got their own places?" Zachary suggested, though he already knew this to be the case. "They're not living at home anymore?"

"Oh, yes, of course. Let me get you their information."

Mr. Creedy looked like he would stop her, but then shrugged and let her get her address book to write out the information for Zachary.

"They really are good kids," he said to Zachary, not even looking at him.

"I just need to cover all of the bases," Zachary assured him. "None of you are suspects. Like your wife says, it is a huge coincidence. I don't think I need to tell you, the police don't like coincidences."

Mrs. Creedy focused on writing the addresses, phone numbers, and email addresses down for her two children.

"Did you know that Harding—that is, Brandon—was out of prison?" Zachary asked.

Mr. Creedy nodded. "Of course we knew. We knew the day and the hour they released him. We were doing everything we could to block his release, but there was nothing we could do. We spoke to the review board and everything, but it didn't do any good. They didn't care about us or our family or what damage Powers could do if he was unleashed on the public again. It was all just a sham."

"I suppose they thought he was young and had made a youthful mistake," Zachary suggested. "One that a lot of kids make... but not usually with such devastating consequences."

"He killed our daughter. He should have had to give his life for hers. He should have had to stay in prison for the rest of his life."

So far, Mr. Creedy hadn't repeated the same words as the stalker. He hadn't said that Harding shouldn't have been allowed to live. He didn't say that Harding should have died, or killed himself, or been executed. The stalker had repeated those phrases hundreds of times. If the cyberbully were Mike Creedy, Zachary didn't think he could have avoided saying those things when he was angry. They would have been part of his speech, like an auditory fingerprint.

Mrs. Creedy had kept quieter than her husband, so Zachary couldn't be as sure of her. She might have been saying less and keeping calmer in an effort not to make Zachary suspicious.

They had both seemed genuinely shocked when Zachary had told them about Harding's death. He really didn't think they had been faking it.

He met her eyes briefly as she handed him the addresses, and again Zachary saw the deep wells of sorrow. But he didn't see guilt there. He didn't see the stalker or a killer.

1 5

Zachary had only just begun his interviews. There were other people to talk to. Noelle and Luke were already on his list, and he added the additional details Mrs. Creedy had provided to his list. Mr. and Mrs. Creedy probably called the children as soon as he left the house, so he decided to give them a chance to talk with each other and decide that it was in their best interests to help Zachary, then he would follow up with them later.

Hope's old best friend, Suzie Markell, would probably be harder to catch in a surprise visit than Mr. and Mrs. Creedy had been. She was younger and more likely to be out, either running children around or spending time with her friends, depending on what direction life had taken her. So Zachary called her to set up a meeting. He was encouraged to be able to meet with her the same day as the Creedys. If all of the interviews could be lined up so quickly, he would not have to spend as much time in New Hampshire and would be home a lot sooner. Maybe with the case laid to rest.

Suzie Markell's house was chaotic. It was not in as nice an area as the Creedys, not as big a house. It looked like it had rolled off the assembly line with all of her neighbors' houses. There were a number of children running around making noise. Zachary wasn't actually sure how many there were. At least four, maybe more. He found it hard to ignore them and to focus on

Suzie, distracted by noise and activity around him every few seconds. If he'd had it to do again, he would have topped up his ADHD meds before going to her house. He was used to keeping the dose as low as possible, but that just wasn't sufficient for the Markell house. It was, like some of the homes that Zachary had lived in, a hub of activity, and there wasn't anywhere he and the busy mom could escape to for a quiet word.

"Have a seat," Suzie offered, sweeping toys from the couch to the floor to make space for him. There were cracker crumbs between the cracks of the cushions, and Zachary sat down gingerly, wondering about what else he was going to sit down in.

She made space for herself in an easy chair and flopped into it with a sigh. She straightened up, pulling some more toys from behind her, and leaned forward to talk to Zachary.

"So tell me exactly what this is about? Something to do with Hope Creedy's death all those years ago? Poor Hope. I felt so badly for her family. It was a terrible, terrible thing."

"Yes," Zachary agreed. "I can see that they're still suffering from it. I'm helping the Vermont police with a possibly-related incident. Did you hear anything about the death of Richard Harding?"

"Richard Harding." Suzie shook her head. "That name doesn't ring a bell. Who is he?"

Zachary watched her face for any tells, but there was a crash like a bookcase falling over somewhere above his head, and he nearly jumped out of his seat. Suzie didn't turn a hair.

"Just ignore it," she advised. "If there's no blood, we don't worry about it."

"You're sure it's okay?"

She made a motion to brush it away. "Really. Don't worry."

"I..." Zachary tried to pick up the thread of the conversation.

"Richard Harding," Suzie prompted. "Who is that?"

"Oh. Richard Harding's former name was Brandon Powers."

"Brandon? The guy who hit Hope?" She covered her mouth. "Oh, my goodness. I didn't even know he'd changed his name. I knew he got out, of course, but he just kind of disappeared, so I didn't know whether he had left the area or what. I thought he should go to some South American country and just start a new life. How could you keep living in the same neighborhood when people knew you had done a thing like that?"

"He'd didn't go as far as South America. Just to Vermont."

"I guess if you like snow…" Suzie laughed.

"Mommy!" One of the myriad children rushed into the room and directly for Suzie so fast that Zachary looked around to see who was chasing her. "Mommy, I need to know where the alligator is. I must know where it is *right now!*"

"Later, sweetheart." Suzie kissed the urchin on the forehead. "Mommy's busy right now. Don't you have some homework you should be working on?"

"But I can't do it without the alligator!"

"Then do something else for now. Don't bother Mommy when she has a visitor."

The little girl turned and looked disdainfully at Zachary. "Who are *you?*"

"I'm… er…"

"Leave him alone. Go study your spelling words."

The girl pouted and marched out of the room.

"You said he died?"

Zachary looked back at Suzie in consternation.

"Brandon Powers. You're looking into his death? What happened?"

"He was the victim of a hit and run."

"No!" Suzie's eyes were dramatically wide. Was she putting on an act? Just dramatizing for him? "That has to be the most bizarre coincidence I've heard since… oh, I have no idea. How could he have been in a hit and run? He wasn't the perpetrator again, was he?"

"No. He was the victim. He was walking and was hit by a truck."

"How awful. I remember how sick I felt when I heard about Hope. I just couldn't believe it. I felt like throwing up. It was such a horrible thing."

Another child came into the room. He was Asian, and the rest of the children Zachary had seen had been white. Probably a friend to one of Suzie's own children or someone she was babysitting. He was about four. He walked into the room with a little pair of scissors and a stack of paper. He sat down on Suzie's feet and proceeded to fold and cut a snowflake out of the first piece of paper. Zachary stared at him, mesmerized by the triangular and diamond-shaped bits of paper that fell from the little boy's scissors every few seconds.

"Do you think there is some kind of connection between Hope's death and Brandon's?" Suzie prompted. "I can't see how there could be."

"No… I haven't been able to find a connection either." There was another crash and a squeal from overhead. Zachary felt like his head was going to explode. He closed his eyes, taking deep breaths.

"I mean, the only way they could be connected that I can think of is if someone who knew Hope had tracked Brandon down and then hit him in revenge." Suzie gave a sharp laugh and shook her head. "I don't think that's realistic."

"You can't think of anyone who would be angry enough to do that?" Zachary was forcing the words out, but they sounded wrong in his own ears. Flat and emotionless. Distant.

"No. Unless you mean—no. Nobody would do that!"

"Unless who?"

"I just… I mean, her father… he was so angry. But I know the man and he really is a lovely person. Of course he was angry. Any father would have been. I don't think he was *too* angry. I can't see him doing anything like that. For someone to hunt Brandon down and run him over, that's just… it's sick."

Zachary nodded his agreement. His eyes darted around the room, looking for any other approaching children or disasters. He was perched on the edge of his seat, ready to spring up at the slightest warning. His muscles quivered and adrenaline was surging through his veins, his heartbeat loud to his own ears.

"I really can't think of anyone who would do anything like that," Suzie said. "And I think I've met all the major players."

"Do you know Hope's brother and sister?"

"Yes, but they're just kids."

"They were just kids eleven years ago. They're not anymore."

"No… I guess not. Funny how you think kids don't grow up while you're gone. In your mind, they will always be the same age as they were the last time you saw them. Or when you really knew them well."

A red plastic ball went whipping across the room for Zachary's head, launched with the click of a trigger and the force of a spring somewhere behind Suzie, where Zachary couldn't see. He batted the ball down and jumped to his feet.

"Ari!" Suzie's voice was stern. "What's the rule about throwing balls in the house?"

"I didn't throw it," a disembodied voice replied.

"What is the rule about shooting people?"

"It wasn't a bullet, it was—"

"Okay, Mr. Lawyer. You lose the gun for the rest of the day and your name goes up on the fridge. Go put it up."

The little boy voice groaned, and there was a dragging noise as he scooted out of the room, never becoming visible to Zachary. Zachary stayed on his feet, unwilling to sit down again.

"Can you think of anyone else who was close to Hope at school? Or anyone who organized protests at the court house?"

"It was so long ago now. I tend to have other things on my mind these days! You may not have noticed, but..." She broke off laughing.

"Any names at all?" Zachary prompted, trying hard to stay focused just a few minutes longer.

She thought about it and offered a couple of names, but they were people who were already on Zachary's list, so he just nodded and didn't ask for their details.

"Thanks for taking time to meet with me. I can see you're a busy mom..."

"Oh, any time. I crave adult conversation."

Zachary got out of there as quickly as he could.

The visit at Suzie's had wound up and exhausted him. Zachary decided he'd had enough for the day. He'd compile his notes and follow up with more people on his list the next day.

There was a place near his hotel that sold pizza by the slice, so Zachary bought himself a piece and went back to his room.

So far, he hadn't seen any signs that any of the people he had seen were involved in Harding's death. They had all seemed genuinely surprised. While Mr. Creedy had expressed a lot of anger, Zachary didn't think he was the author of the poison pen messages. With a release valve for his anger, he didn't let the pressure build internally. His wife was a more likely suspect.

Did her more calm and empathetic demeanor hide what was actually going on under the surface? Was it all an act?

When he logged on to his computer to write up his notes, Zachary was distracted by the new emails in his own inbox. Adding to the general clutter of messages were several new messages from Tyrrell. Even though he had determined to simply delete any negative messages from Tyrrell, he found he couldn't do so without opening them first, and was again assaulted by the red-hot spewings of hate from his little brother.

How do you think your brothers and sisters felt waking up to fire and smoke and sirens?

If it wasn't for you everybody would have been fine.

You would still have a family if you hadn't destroyed it.

Zachary closed his eyes and tried to push the images back, but he couldn't. He was flooded with the sensations of what Tyrrell described. The fire had started while he slept and he had awakened in a room engulfed in flames. The smoke burned his lungs and made him cough uncontrollably. It burned his eyes, and billowed so thickly through the room that he was disoriented and didn't know which way was out. He had crawled under the couch for shelter, trying to protect himself from the hellfire that burned around him, but it didn't block the heat of the flames from reaching him. His flesh seared and his throat was on fire. Even so, he screamed warnings to his family, trying to raise the alarm and to get them out of the house. He knew he was going to die, and his only thought was to save the other children.

Zachary gasped for breath. He could feel the tears flooding down his cheeks. He tried to tell himself that he wasn't still in the fire, but he couldn't pull himself out of the whirlpool of memories. The hotel room around him morphed into a burning inferno, and he saw Suzie and her multitudes of children.

"You have to get out! There's a fire! Get the children out!" His voice was a croak and he couldn't shout the words to her as the children screamed in terror and huddled and cried for him to save them.

Zachary's phone was in his hand. He fumbled with it, trying to launch the emergency call feature with fingers swollen as fat as sausages. The heat of the fire was so strong his fingers felt like they were going to explode.

Why wasn't the smoke alarm going? Could he get out to the hallway to pull the red fire alarm? It was so far away, and by the time he got there, the children would all be burned. The smoke was so thick, he didn't know which way to go.

"Zachary? Are you there?"

Zachary's hand shook as he held the phone to his ear and tried to croak out an answer.

"Zachary, it's Lorne. Are you okay? What's wrong?"

He sobbed with relief as he tried to answer Mr. Peterson's questions. If Mr. Peterson was there, that meant the fire was over. The ashes were cold and everybody was out. When he had been taken to the Peterson's house, it had been months later.

"It was—the fire." He tried to croak the words out in an order that made sense.

"Focus on where you are, Zachary. Tell me where you are."

He blinked, trying to see through the tears and orient himself. "Hotel."

"You're in a hotel," Mr. Peterson repeated in a calming voice. "You're not in the fire. Look around the room. Tell me about it. How many beds are there?"

"One. Just one."

"One bed. Can you tell me the color of the carpet?"

Zachary wiped his eyes, looking down at the muddy shades of the carpet, designed not to show the dirt, but looking dingy and worn.

"No. I don't know."

"You're an artist," Mr. Peterson reminded him. "Describe it."

Zachary struggled. "Greeny brown, like goose poop. With flowers... sort of brownish pink."

Mr. Peterson chuckled. "How pleasant. I must have Pat talk to their decorator."

Zachary tried to laugh at that, but it was still all coming out as sobs.

"How's the smell?"

It was musty and stale. He could smell the chemicals they used to clean the bathroom, body odor, and old cigarette smoke. For a few seconds, the cigarette smoke triggered a panic response, but he was able to stay in the present, shifting his focus to the bathroom cleaners.

"The bathroom... bleach and Lysol..."

"At least you know they cleaned it."

"Yeah."

"What hotel are you in?"

835

Zachary had to look at the receipt he had left on the table, but he could see what was actually in front of him instead of billowing smoke and flames. He instantly recognized the logo of the chain, and when he got that out, knew the name of the city.

"What are you doing in New Hampshire?"

"Interviewing." Zachary sniffled and wiped tears from his face. Hie eyes had stopped streaming. "My hit and run case—the victim used to live here, under another name."

"Got any suspects?"

He cleared his throat and looked around the room again. Everything was perfectly normal. There was no smoke, no fire, no burning children.

"What?"

"Suspects in your hit and run."

"Uh… hard to say. We know who hit him, but not if he was somehow connected to Harding."

"You're sounding better. Are you okay?"

Zachary took a deep breath in and let it out slowly. It didn't hurt to breathe. Everything was returning to normal.

"Yeah. Better, thanks."

"Do you want me to come? I'll stay with you if you need me to."

"No. I'll be okay now."

"Can you talk about what triggered this flashback?"

"An email from Tyrrell." Zachary reached over and closed the laptop without looking at the screen. "An email about the fire."

"I thought you weren't going to read anything from him."

"I know… but… what if he calms down? What if after he's got it all out, he feels better and he just wants to talk?"

"Do you want to have an attack every time you get an email from him? I think it's time to report him to the police. This harassment is causing damage. You don't want to go backward in your treatment."

"No. I can't. You're right, I just won't read them. Like I said to start with. I'll just delete them."

"Can't you report him to his email provider? They could close his account."

"He's using a program that generates unique email addresses for every email. I can't trace him back to his real email account."

"What he's doing is criminal. Cyberstalking is against the law. You can't bully people online and get away with it."

"Tyrrell's just… trying to express himself. He was damaged by the fire too, and by being in the system. He's just trying to heal."

"I don't think so."

Zachary wasn't going to be persuaded. "He's my little brother. He's hurting."

"He probably is," Mr. Peterson agreed. "But that doesn't give him the right to hurt you."

"I'm okay. It was just a stupid flashback. I've had plenty of flashbacks without his help."

Mr. Peterson was quiet for a minute. "You're sure you don't want me to come?"

"No, no. I'm okay now. It's passed."

"Take care of yourself. Make sure to get a good sleep tonight. Have you eaten? Do you need to talk to your therapist?"

"I ate. I'll take a Xanax and go to bed. It will be fine."

"Call me again if you need me. You know I'll be here."

"Yeah, thanks." Zachary blew out his breath. "You really helped."

1 6

Zachary's first interview with someone friendly to Richard Harding was with Devon Masters, one of the young men who had been in the car with Harding when Hope Creedy was killed. They met at a coffee shop near the university. Devon was a handsome man, though he looked older than Zachary had expected. He had dark hair and a narrow build. Their eyes met across the shop, and they gravitated toward each other.

"Devon?" Zachary asked.

"You must be Zachary Goldman."

They shook hands briefly. Devon smiled and waited while Zachary got his coffee, then motioned to a table near the window.

"I like to sit in the sun and watch my students walk to class."

"Sure."

They sat, and Devon eyed Zachary curiously. "I have to say, I'm not sure at all what this is about. You said you are investigating… what?"

"I'm investigating the death of Richard Harding."

Devon raised an eyebrow. "And who is Richard Harding when he's home?"

"You knew him as Brandon Powers."

"Brandon?" Devon's eyebrows went up and his eyes widened. "I had no idea! He died? How?"

"It was a hit and run."

"No! I'm guessing you know about… his history."

"I do now, or parts of it, anyway. It took a while for me to get this far, though. He had changed his name, moved out of the state, and started over. But his girlfriend knew who he was."

And did anyone else?

Zachary lifted his coffee cup to his lips, watching Devon's face. Devon stared out the big window. It was a chilly day, so there wasn't a lot of foot traffic. Mostly students running from one place to another, not dressed warmly enough, laughing and rubbing their arms, like it was a big surprise that it was so cold on a winter day.

"Wow." Devon shook his head. "The end of an era. We didn't talk to each other, obviously, but I thought about him sometimes. Wondered how he was getting along."

"He didn't call when he got out of prison?"

"No. We haven't had any contact since the trial. It didn't really… it wasn't a bonding experience, I'll tell you that. I see Fulton every now and then, but we don't really do anything more than nod and wave."

Fulton was the other man who had been in the car. The other survivor.

"It must have been pretty traumatic," Zachary suggested. "First the accident and then the trial."

"And being ostracized. For years, I was identified as one of the boys who had been in that car. One of those boys who had gotten drunk and killed a girl. We were all painted with the same brush, even though Brandon was the one behind the wheel." Devon leaned forward. "He was the one who was supposed to be sober. The rest of us were drinking, but he was the one who had agreed to drive us."

"And you didn't know he had any alcohol while you were together?"

"I guess I was too far gone at that point. I don't remember him having anything to drink. Just Coke."

"So what are your feelings toward Brandon? Do you blame him for that reputation?"

"I've worked hard to dig myself out and overcome that stigma. And I think I'm a better person for it. We had to grow up fast. We were adults, and you would think that we would know better, but we really didn't. They say at that age your brain is still developing… We were still acting like kids, irresponsible, not thinking about the consequences of our actions. I can't put all of the blame on Brandon. I don't remember a whole lot about *that* night, but other nights... we encouraged each other to drink too much, to drive too fast, to do stupid and dangerous stuff. We were an accident looking for a place to happen."

"So you don't resent him."

Devon spread his hands. "How can I resent him if he's dead?"

Zachary's brain echoed the question. If Zachary were dead, Tyrrell couldn't resent him. He would be able accept that Zachary had finally gotten his due and Tyrrell could go on with his life again. Maybe he could let the bitterness go and live the life he'd been meant to. He tried to refocus on the case.

"Did you get any accusatory emails about the accident? Not back then, but recently?"

Devon visibly shrank back. "What?"

"Brandon was getting some pretty awful harassing emails. If you were all painted with the same brush, I'm wondering if you got some too. Did the same person made contact with you?"

"I've had some emails," Devon admitted cautiously.

"Do you think I could see some of them? Maybe you could forward them to me and I can analyze whether they are from the same person?"

"I deleted them."

"You can probably still forward them—"

"No, I nuked them. Permanently deleted. I didn't want to see them again. I didn't want to be tempted to go back and reread them afterward. They were trash. Once I got a few, I set up filters to catch them and permanently delete them before I could even see them."

"That's smart." Zachary wondered for a moment why he and Harding hadn't done the same thing. Zachary was tech savvy enough. But he hadn't, because he wanted to read them all no matter how they hurt. They were the only contact he'd ever had with his family and even if they pierced him to the heart, he couldn't delete them without ever seeing and reading them.

What about Harding? Had he thought to do something like that? Did he even know it was possible? A lot of people didn't bother tweaking their computers to work the way they wanted them to. They didn't know what they could and couldn't do. He hadn't asked Ashley how good Harding's grasp on technology was. Harding had learned to use anonymizers, but someone might have helped him with that.

"Sorry." Devon shrugged. "I didn't want them taking over my life. I have enough to do without having to deal with something like that."

Zachary nodded his agreement. "And the other man who survived the crash—Fulton—you don't talk?"

"Not really, no. We've all gone our different directions. That happens as you get older. All those things that once held you together—school classes, social circles, shared interests—they fade as you grow up and take on different responsibilities."

"Right. And there was another man with you who also passed away."

"Kyle Browne."

"Did you keep in touch with his family at all? There wasn't really anything in the news articles that I read that talked about Kyle. Brandon wasn't charged with manslaughter in his case, which I thought was a bit odd, considering the way they went after him for the rest of the charges."

"You'll have to talk to Fulton about that. I don't remember much… but he said that Brandon made Kyle put his seatbelt on before they started, but at the time of the accident, he wasn't wearing it, so he was…" Devon made a helpless gesture, choking up. "He was thrown from the car. If he'd been wearing his seatbelt, he probably would have been okay, like the rest of us. Fulton clearly remembered Brandon forcing Kyle to put his seatbelt on before leaving. He must have taken it off again after."

Zachary nodded. "Well… one thing in Brandon's favor. You didn't keep in touch with his family?"

"No. I never knew them. I knew Kyle from school. I didn't have any reason to have anything to do with his family, other than to say how sorry I was for what had happened. We didn't have any contact after the funeral. Nothing during or after the trial. I don't know what happened to any of them."

"Do you know of anyone who held a grudge against Brandon? Someone who was still bitter toward him, even though he had served his time?"

"I don't know. Hope Creedy's family, I guess. I did have a confrontation with her brother once."

Zachary's interest was immediately piqued. "Really? When was that?"

"It was a few years ago, I think Brandon was still in prison at the time. The kid was maybe nineteen, twenty."

"And what did he want? He confronted you?"

"Yeah. He was pretty messed up. Wanted a fight. Wanted to punish the guys who had killed his sister. Like it had just happened the day before. It was weird, facing a specter from the past when I had done my best to put all of that behind me."

"So what did he do?"

"Ranted on about it. Told me he was going to kill me. But he couldn't even get one punch in. He was drunk and so agitated... I don't think he could have hit the broad side of a barn."

"What did you do?"

"Bouncers threw him out. I told him I'd call the police if he bugged me again. Or I'd call his mother. He never showed up again. If he remembered it the next day, I suspect he was so embarrassed he never wanted to mention it again."

"You were in a bar?" Zachary wasn't sure why that surprised him so much. He'd half-assumed that after having been in a drunk driving accident, Devon would swear off of drinking. Social drinking, especially.

"A club," Devon said. He looked at Zachary defiantly, like he knew what Zachary was thinking. "It's my life. I didn't die in that accident. I can choose whether to drink or not. That's up to me."

Zachary nodded, not disagreeing. "Luke is on my list of people to follow up with, so I'll see what he has to say. Did you ever have any trouble with his father? Hope's father?"

"No. I mean, the guy was angry, but at Brandon, not us. Brandon was the one who was driving. He couldn't very well blame us for drinking when we weren't driving."

Zachary felt like he was on a see-saw with Devon flipping back and forth between whether they were partially responsible for what had happened or not. He seemed most intent on insisting that he didn't have any responsibility, but had given that little speech about needing to grow up and how they had egged Harding on in the past.

"Is there anyone else you can think of? Ideas of who might have sent those emails?"

Devon shook his head. "No. I never really... there were so many of them to start with, back when the trial was on. Emails, phone calls, people on the street holding signs and trying to tell us how we were going to hell for what we had done. I didn't really attach any particular face or personality to them, I was just... surprised that so long after the trial, anyone still remembered."

There were plenty of people who would never forget what had happened to Hope and that Harding and his friends had been responsible for her death.

17

Noelle and Luke had obviously been waiting for Zachary's call.

"Mom told us about you," Luke told him. "And about that creep Powers being killed. Good riddance to him, I don't know why you expect us to help you out. He deserved what he got."

"I understand you feeling that way. I'd really appreciate a chance to talk with you, even if it's just for a few minutes. I'm just trying to tie up some loose ends, and then I'll be able to report back to the police that there's no connection between the two deaths. Just coincidence."

"Why should we waste our time?"

"Maybe it will give you some closure on Hope's death. But even if it doesn't, I'd really appreciate your help. This is my job, you know, and if I go back to them saying that no one will talk to me..."

Zachary had gathered from what his mother and Devon had said that Luke's circumstances were not ideal, and he was hoping to trade on Luke having some empathy for someone else who could lose his job if Luke didn't give him just a bit of his time.

There was a moment of silence while Luke considered this. Zachary was afraid it was drawing out too long and Luke was going to come back with the fact that he couldn't care less if Zachary got himself fired, so long as it didn't inconvenience Luke.

"Well, fine," Luke grumped. "You can come see us at two o'clock. At Noelle's apartment." He gave Zachary the address.

"Great, thank you for helping me out. I really appreciate it."

Luke muttered something and hung up.

Zachary hadn't really needed to convince anyone; they had clearly agreed ahead of time on where and when they would meet Zachary.

Since he had a few hours to kill before he'd be able to see anyone else, Zachary decided to visit the scene of the crime. He had no illusions about finding evidence that would somehow shed light on the case. The MVC that had killed Hope had been years before. The police had fully investigated it at the time. Zachary wasn't looking for evidence, he just wanted a feeling for the location. How it would have looked to the boys, to Hope walking home, to the police investigating it. He wanted to see the space himself rather than just relying on the descriptions and diagrams that he had seen and that would be in the court files.

He drove the route that Harding had taken. They had flown along the empty streets, exceeding the speed limit, but Zachary took his time. There was traffic during the day and he wanted a chance to look around. As he approached the intersection where Hope had been killed, he slowed down, drawing irritated honks from the cars behind him. He scanned for a parking space, and pulled over.

Getting out, he walked the intersection, circling through all four crosswalks and taking pictures of the road, the approaching cars, and the light standards. Harding had hit one of them after hitting Hope, perhaps making a last-second attempt to miss her. It was that collision that had thrown Kyle Browne from the car. The news articles reported that Brandon hadn't even seen Kyle after the accident. He knew that his friend had been thrown from the car, yet when he got out of the car, he hadn't seen or looked for him. He had gone to Hope, trying to rouse her, hoping beyond hope that he'd just clipped her. But she was dead, and there was nothing he could do about it. Brandon had done nothing to help his friends sitting unconscious in the back seat, or Kyle, lying broken on the pavement somewhere close by, and had just left the accident scene.

The prosecution had said that Brandon didn't care about anyone else, that he didn't have any concern for anyone but himself, and had left to hide what he had done, to try to escape punishment. Brandon had explained that he was disoriented. He'd hit his head and hadn't known where to go or what to do. He didn't understand what he had done. It never occurred to him to call for help or to give some assistance to his friends. It was all just a blank.

The truth probably lay somewhere in between. He'd been panicked. He was under the influence, had killed at least one person, and he'd hit his head. He wasn't thinking rationally. If he had been, he would have known that the police could trace him from the car he had left behind. They knew exactly who they were looking for and that at some point, he would return home. Where else was he going to go? He was a stupid kid, not a master criminal who had carefully planned an escape route.

"You lost?" demanded a homeless man sitting on a stack of flattened boxes to insulate him from the cold sidewalk. He had apparently been watching Zachary pace around the sides of the intersection.

"Oh. No, I was just taking a look around."

"At what?"

"Just at the intersection. How it's laid out. What it feels like."

"You a surveyor? Planning on building something here?"

"No. A private investigator. Looking into an accident that happened here years ago."

"How long ago? You weren't here."

"No. I wasn't here."

"She was a pretty girl."

"Did you see her? Hope Creedy?"

"No, I never did. You think I was sleeping out here on the road where I could see anything? No one sleeps out here by the traffic."

"No, I guess not. But you might have seen something. Maybe the crash woke you up and you came out for a peek, to see what had happened. The police never identified any eye witnesses."

"That's because there wasn't none. No one saw what happened 'cept those kids in the car."

"So how do you know she was pretty?"

"From her picture."

"In the paper?"

"No!" The man shook his head at Zachary's stupidity. "There!"

Zachary followed his finger and realized that in trying to get a big picture view of the intersection, he had missed the little things. A little homemade wreath strapped to one of the traffic light posts. Inside the circle, a picture of Hope Creedy protected by a plastic bag, the same picture as

Zachary had seen in a number of the news stories. A beautiful young lady, struck down in her prime. So full of promise, wiped out by one person's carelessness and disregard.

Looking at the little memorial, Zachary felt anger rise up inside him at Harding. He had been feeling sorry for the man, killed after being stalked relentlessly. A life that had been destroyed by a mistake, by years in prison, and by the person or people who just wouldn't let him carry on. In Zachary's mind, Harding had been the victim. But he *had* killed Hope. Just as certainly as if he'd pulled a gun and shot her. Mike Creedy was right; eight years in prison wasn't nearly long enough for killing both her and Kyle Browne.

"Did you live here then?" he asked the homeless man. "Were you around when it happened? I understand you didn't see it, I'm just wondering if you lived here when it happened."

"I don't know nothing," the man asserted. He spat on the sidewalk. "I ain't the one who put the wreath there. I never knew the girl."

"Who did put the wreath there?"

"A young man."

"So you were here. You saw that."

"I see him when he takes it down and puts a new one up. That one hasn't been around for so many years."

Zachary looked at it again. Of course not. It had been over ten years since the accident, and the wreath was not tattered and stained by the weather. It had been there for a while, but not ten years.

"What does this young man look like?"

"I don't know." The homeless man didn't like being pinned down with more detailed questions and was clamming up. "Young."

"How young? Thirty? Older? Younger?"

"I never asked him how old he was," the man said saucily. "How would I know?"

"Younger than me?"

The man studied him. "You're not so young."

"No, I'm not. So, younger?"

"Yes. Maybe."

"Twenty?"

"No. He wouldn't be old enough to have known her."

Hope would have been thirty-two if she had lived. Her younger siblings in their mid to late twenties. So someone Hope's age. Zachary got close to the wreath and tried to see the back of the photo to see if there was a date or inscription.

"You leave that alone. That's desecration. You can't take it!"

"I'm not taking it. I just wanted to see if it had anything written on it."

"It doesn't."

"No," Zachary agreed, having gotten a good look at it. "It doesn't."

Eventually, it was time to move on. He needed to get back to Noelle's apartment to see her and Luke.

He assumed that they had picked Noelle's apartment because it was nicer, and that made Zachary wonder just how miserable the place that Luke was living must have been. While he didn't see any evidence of rats, it was small, and it was obvious that Noelle split the rent with other people. There was a communal living room to sit and visit in, but the place smelled like reheated dinners and sweat and uncleaned toilets.

The twins favored their father more than Mrs. Creedy, dark-haired with narrow faces, both of them tall. They looked remarkably alike, more so than most siblings. Zachary knew that fraternal twins didn't share any more genetic material than the average sibling pair, but Noelle and Luke looked like male and female versions of the same person.

When Zachary sat down on the saggy couch, he had the uncomfortable feeling that someone had been sleeping there. His skin crawled as he thought of lice and bedbugs. He wanted to get up and brush off his clothes and wash his hands. Instead, he concentrated hard on giving the twins a pleasant smile, and not being obvious about evaluating and judging the kind of place where Noelle lived.

"Thank you again for agreeing to meet me. I know that you aren't really getting anything out of this, though I hope maybe it helps you to know that your sister's killer isn't out there roaming the streets anymore."

"You think it helps us to know that he's been put out of his misery?" Luke demanded. "He should have had to suffer longer. Just like we have."

Luke's words didn't fit with the stalker's, "Why don't you just die?"

"I'm sorry for what you've had to go through. It couldn't be easy growing up in the shadow of Hope's death and the trial."

"Everything was about her," Noelle agreed. "Not just in the news and every time at school or on the street that someone stopped to talk to us. And not just Mom and Dad being sad and mad about the trial. Everything was about her." Noelle brushed her dark hair back from her face, tucking it behind her ear. "Curfews because we couldn't be out on the street after dark like she had been. Not knowing who really wanted to be our friends and who just wanted to get to know the sister of the dead girl. People watching the news and wanting to talk about it. We didn't just mourn Hope, we had to relive her death. Constantly."

Zachary remembered how it had been for him in the years after the fire. People who were morbidly interested in his burn scars and who wanted to hear his story. Parents and social workers who thought that, given a chance, he would burn another house down, when nothing could be further from the truth. People were fascinated by death and grief. It had kept the pain raw and fresh when he should have been able to put it behind himself long before.

"That must have been very difficult. The two of you were how old when she was killed?"

"Fifteen." It was Luke who answered, his tone still aggrieved.

"And you knew when Brandon got out of prison?"

"Sure everybody knew when he got out. All of the reporters were hounding us again, wanting to get our *reactions* to his release. What did they think our reactions would be? Overjoyed?"

"There was quite a media circus over it?"

"Yeah. It was a circus, alright."

"Did Brandon contact either of you?" Zachary switched his gaze between the twins, looking for any changes in their expressions. They were mirror images, pouting over injustices done years ago.

"Why would he contact us? We didn't want anything to do with him."

"But he might have wanted to make an apology to you, ask for your forgiveness."

"No," Noelle shook her head. "He never contacted us. Or Mom and Dad."

"Did you have any contact with any of the passengers who were in the car?"

There was a quick glance between Noelle and Luke.

"None of them ever contacted us," Luke said.

"And you didn't ever run into any of them and have a conversation?"

Luke stared at Zachary, suspicious. "Why would you ask if you already know the answer?"

"I like to see how people react. Whether they tell the truth."

Noelle was looking at her brother. A warning, telling him to shut up.

"Sure, I ran into that one guy, Devon. Would have beat the hell out of him, too, if it hadn't been for a couple of bouncers. I would have wiped that look right off his face."

"What look?"

"That fake concern. The pity. He helped ruin our family and he thought he could be all sympathetic and I'd think he was a good guy? I would have wiped that smug look right off of his face!"

Zachary nodded. "It bothered you that he never had to serve any time?"

"Well, he wasn't the driver," Noelle put in, before Luke could answer.

Luke looked at her.

"It wasn't his fault," Noelle pointed out. "The only person they could blame for the accident was the person behind the wheel. It wasn't the fault of the passengers."

"They were all out drinking together. If they hadn't been drinking, it wouldn't have happened."

"You don't drink?" Zachary asked. "What were you doing at the club when you met up with Devon?"

"I don't drink and drive," Luke shot back, "and I don't get in the car with a drunk driver. Anyone who let him have his keys and get into that car should have been punished. The bartender, whoever was serving him drinks, all of his friends. They should all have to be punished for letting him drive drunk!"

Noelle gave Zachary a little shrug. "We have issues," she said with a little laugh.

Luke glared at her.

Noelle raised her eyebrows dramatically. "Well, what do you want me to say? That you're a miserable jerk all of the time?"

"I'm glad you know better than to drink and drive," Zachary inserted, trying not to let the conversation degenerate further. "Devon says he doesn't remember Brandon having anything alcoholic that night. His memory of the events of that night seem to be pretty clouded."

"He's lying."

"Maybe he is. Most people will lie to protect themselves even if they consider themselves honest people."

"I'm not sure how any of this is helpful," Noelle said.

"No," Zachary agreed. "Can you tell me whether you know of anyone else who had a grudge against Brandon? Someone who might have stalked and threatened him, even though he had changed his name?"

They looked at each other, but not a covert look this time. Blank faces. Nobody who jumped immediately to mind.

"Anyone who knew Hope," Noelle said. "Who could *not* be outraged by what happened? We didn't know her friends from school. We got to know some people during the trial, but I don't think Mom and Dad have kept in touch with anyone, do you?"

Luke shook his head in response. "Hope wasn't the only one killed, either. It could have been someone who was related to the other victim. His family or friends. His girlfriend."

"Did you meet his girlfriend?"

"No, not that I remember." Another look between the twins, checking in with each other. "No."

"And Hope didn't have a boyfriend?"

Just a fraction of a second too long before Luke and Noelle shook their heads in unison.

"No."

Zachary gave them a few beats to think about it, not jumping in with any accusations, but waiting for them to grow uncomfortable with the lie and either say more to cover it up or to back off.

"No? No boyfriend?"

They didn't admit it.

"Girlfriend?"

Again, a negative response, Luke giving a little grin of amusement at that. Not a girlfriend, then.

"Was she seeing someone your parents didn't like?" 'Seeing someone' instead of 'dating,' to give them a little more wiggle room. 'Seeing someone' could be more casual. Boyfriend made it sound serious, more committed.

Noelle looked at Luke, asking for permission. He shrugged like he didn't care if she spilled it.

18

S he was seeing someone," Noelle admitted. "Mom and Dad didn't disapprove, but only because they didn't know."

"She was afraid to tell them about him? What was wrong with him?"

He was expecting her to say that he was black, or Muslim, or maybe he was unemployed or had been in trouble in the past. People had frequently judged Zachary by his class or social standing, his prospects, or other things he had no control over. Zachary wasn't responsible for his parents' poverty, his learning disabilities, or that there had been no pathway to higher education for him. He was a foster kid, and he'd had to support himself once he'd aged out of foster care, or end up homeless.

"It was... their age difference," Noelle said hesitantly.

Maybe she had gotten together with one of her professors. A May-December romance that she knew her parents would not approve of.

"An older man?" Zachary prompted her for more details.

Luke snorted. "A younger one!"

Zachary *was* surprised by that. He blinked at them. "Younger?"

Noelle nodded, her cheeks getting pink. She looked at Luke, giggling, and then looked away again. This was apparently something they had laughed about in private before. Their big sister dating a younger man.

"How much younger?" Zachary demanded. Hope had been a young

college student herself. How much younger could a boyfriend have been? A year? Two? Did she think that would be scandalous?

"Seventeen."

Not even an adult. No, her parents would not have been happy to hear about such a thing. She should have turned him down and dated someone more suitable.

Zachary gave his head a shake. "Where did she meet this guy?"

Noelle shrugged. "She didn't know at first how young he was. She said he looked a lot more mature. And acted more mature. She didn't see what could be wrong with it and why people made such a big deal when he was more mature than his age."

"She never considered breaking up with him because of it?"

"She wouldn't exactly tell me if she did. We weren't even supposed to know about it, but we had friends who knew him. He was closer to our age than hers!"

"And your parents never found out about it?"

"No."

"And his…?"

"Nothing ever came out after she died. He hung around the courthouse a little. I would see him there, standing out on the sidewalk, with the protesters. But he didn't come into the courtroom. I don't think he could. Or maybe he just didn't want to be seen there and have anyone ask him questions."

"Do you know his name? What became of him?"

Noelle looked at Luke, not sure whether she should tell Zachary or not. He made a little motion. *Go ahead.*

"Roper. Jonathan Roper. He's still around, but I don't know what he does or where he lives."

"You've seen him around?"

"Yeah. I think he does something at the university, but I'm not sure what."

"A teacher?"

"I don't think so. What other kinds of jobs are there at universities? Maybe some kind of counselor. Like, careers or special needs accommodations. I don't know."

Zachary wrote it in his notebook. It was a name that he hadn't picked up from the news or public record. Somebody that maybe the police had never known about. What difference would it have made if they had? They were trying to track down and gather evidence against the man who had killed her. There was no connection between Roper and Harding.

"Harding—that is, Brandon—and his friends. I gathered from what I read that they went to school together. And Hope was going to university, right? Did they know each other at all? Did they have any personal connection with Hope or with Roper?"

"No." They checked in with each other to confirm their responses. "No, nothing ever came out in court. They weren't friends, they didn't share classes. I don't know if they ever saw each other in passing, but they didn't know each other."

"And Roper, he didn't go to university? He wasn't on some kind of accelerated track?"

"No," Luke was definite about this. "He was still in high school, same as us. That was part of what made it so weird."

Zachary was back in his hotel room in the afternoon to do some research on Jonathan Roper. He hadn't heard of the man before, but if what Noelle and Luke said was true, that wasn't particularly surprising. He would have been forced to stay under the radar or risk bringing outrage down on Hope when it was important that she be seen as an innocent victim.

He had forgotten to ask Luke whether he was the one who had put up the wreaths in the intersection, or whether that was Roper. The homeless man had said that it was a young man, not a young man and woman, and Zachary assumed that the twins would have done something like that together; it wouldn't have been Luke alone.

He tracked down Jonathan Roper's contact details pretty quickly and decided to do a quick background on him while he was at it. He wanted to know what kind of a person Roper was or how he had spent the past decade.

He was, as Noelle had suggested, working at the university. If Zachary had known that, he could have gone to see Roper after interviewing Devon. Roper was a "student services counselor," whatever that was. He'd been doing it for several years, maybe since he'd graduated from university himself.

Zachary's phone rang but he kept his eyes on the computer monitor for the first few rings, absorbing what he could, before tearing himself away from it and picking up the phone to see who it was. It was an unexpected name.

"Bridget. What's up?"

"I was just checking to see how you are."

Zachary thought about it for a moment. When he was fully immersed in a case, the time passed quickly and he didn't think as much about himself or his situation. Delving into the background of a new suspect was a good way to leave his own troubles behind for a while.

"I'm having a pretty good day," he offered. He didn't want to mention any of his recent panic attacks or depression to her, so he just focused on the positive. "Making progress on an investigation."

"Good. I know how this time of year… well, it's good that you're having a good day and have something to keep you occupied."

"Yeah." Zachary was silent for a few seconds before he realized he wasn't holding up his part of the conversation. He fished for something to say. "Are you going to Gordon's family's again this year?"

"At some point. Maybe not on Christmas Day, maybe for New Year's. We're going to have a little party for our friends…"

The Christmases that Zachary had spent with Bridget had been different from any others in his life. He'd actually had something to look forward to and someone to hold on to. That didn't stop the depression, but it made a difference. He'd thought that he might be able to make it through to the other side, instead of seeing nothing but blackness. He'd been very low, but not suicidal.

Nevertheless, his depression had been hard on Bridget. For someone who was used to celebrating the season, to being happy and optimistic and spending time with friends and family, it had been difficult to deal with a husband who just couldn't do all of those social things. The first year, they'd gone to a few quiet events, but then she'd had to explain to friends why he couldn't be in the same room as candles, or why they had to leave when they'd just barely arrived. She told him to get over himself, to cheer up, to quit acting like a baby and embarrassing her.

The next year she'd tried having people over instead of going out, but that had been worse. People didn't know what to do when the host of the party withdrew from the party and took to his bed, unable to deal with anything. She told them he had a migraine and wanted them to go on without him, but people had still left early, marring her plans.

Zachary realized that Bridget had been talking and he'd lost track of the conversation. "What?"

She was silent in response.

"I'm sorry. Just zoned out, thinking about this case. What was the last thing you said?"

"You didn't want to come to the party, did you?" she asked doubtfully. "I mean, there will be a lot of people you know there, and it's just a casual affair, but you…"

"No," Zachary agreed. "You guys have your party. I'll be doing my own thing for Christmas."

"Are you going to see your family?"

"What?"

"Your family. You did get in touch with your bio family, didn't you?"

"Uh… no. Not yet."

"For someone who wants a family so much, you sure aren't doing much to connect with them! Why not?"

"I just… I'm very busy with this case right now, and the Christmas season… I'll connect with them another time. In the new year."

"What exactly *are* your plans for Christmas?" she demanded.

"I'm not sure yet. Kenzie and I are going to have dinner together. And we're trying to set something up with Rhys." Rhys had saved Bridget's life; he didn't have to explain to her who he was, or why he would be having a hard time his first Christmas without his mother home. "Lorne and Pat really want me to come spend it with them. Pat's family might come."

"Really?" Her voice was cautiously interested. It wasn't the answer she'd been expecting. Zachary's Christmas plans were usually solitary. Put on a classic movie and have a drink. Celebrate the fact that he'd survived another Christmas Eve. Telling Bridget he was going to spend it with other people was a surprise.

"Pat's family has never met Lorne. They've never gone to the house. It will be a memorable year for him, if they do."

Bridget *tsked.* "I can't believe that in this day and age people can be so silly about relationships. Pat and Lorne have been together for twenty years. More than that. It's obviously the real deal."

"You would expect them to get used to it before this," Zachary agreed.

"Okay… well… you know how to get me. If you do need someone…"

He knew then just how concerned she was about him dealing with the Christmas season. She never encouraged him to call her. Just the year before, she had torn up one side of him and down the other for still having her listed as his emergency contact when they'd called her after the car accident.

"I'll be fine," Zachary told her. "Don't worry about me."

19

J onathan Roper might have been a mature-looking seventeen-year-old when Hope had started seeing him, but his boyishly round face and curly hair made him look more like one of the current university students than one of the staff.

Zachary had told him as little as possible about the reason for seeing him, not wanting to scare him off by announcing he knew about his relationship with Hope Creedy.

Roper shook Zachary's hand with an open, friendly manner and motioned him into a chair. His office felt something like a psychologist's office that had been decorated in an attempt to make visitors feel comfortable and relaxed. Just the right furniture, a few books on the shelves, a plant that was real instead of plastic. A picture on Roper's desk that showed him with a young woman and a little girl with a mop of blond hair who was smiling fit to burst. Zachary's background had not turned up a marriage, so the woman and the girl were probably a sister and a niece, just a bit of show to make people think he was actually a family man.

Roper saw Zachary studying the picture and raised his eyebrows questioningly.

"You have a very nice-looking family," Zachary said.

"Thank you," Roper accepted the compliment politely. He smiled, and just a bit of a flush started at his neck above his collar. This was an implied lie that he was practiced in making, but his body still reacted to it. Not as effective as a lie detector, but his body's psychological reaction would make things a bit easier for Zachary.

"I'm here about Richard Harding," Zachary told him.

"Richard Harding? Is he a student here?"

Zachary couldn't see any change in the flush. He should have made small talk and waited for it disappear before mentioning Harding's name.

"No. It's the name Brandon Powers took after he got out of prison."

The flush rose up Roper's neck. "And who is Brandon Powers?" he asked, choking a little on the words.

"You know who Brandon Powers is. Do you think I would be here if I wasn't sure of that?"

"Maybe I heard his name in the news. It sounds sort of familiar, but I'm really not sure."

"You were dating the woman he killed."

Roper opened his mouth to deny it again.

"Isn't it obvious that I know?" Zachary challenged. There was no point in Roper wasting time in denials. They needed to get past the lies and have a real conversation.

Roper swallowed. His eyes rolled up toward the ceiling, either searching for another lie or trying to hold back tears. Maybe both.

"Okay," Roper said in an unsteady voice. "I knew Hope Creedy. I know who Brandon Powers is."

"You were more than a casual acquaintance."

"We were... close."

"How close?"

"I don't see how that's any of your business."

"Maybe not. I guess I'll just have to imagine."

"There was nothing wrong with us dating. We were only four years apart. Plenty of people who are further apart than that in age have long, successful marriages."

"Yes. But not usually the ones that start while the younger partner is still a minor. Hope shouldn't have been dating you."

"There was nothing wrong with us dating."

Zachary let it go. He said nothing for a minute, considering the possibilities. If Roper had been forced to keep their relationship a secret for all of those years, it was certainly possible that the pressure had built too much and he had turned his anger and resentment outward, taking it out on Richard Harding and the other men who had been in the car.

"It must have been very hard on you to mourn her passing when you couldn't tell anyone about your relationship. All these years, you've had to keep it from your family and friends in case it was to get out in the public and damage Hope's reputation. You didn't want anyone to think less of her for falling in love with you." Zachary looked at the picture on the desk. "Does your wife know about her?"

Roper sighed, looking at the girl in the photograph. "That's my sister and her little girl."

Zachary had been right on the money. "And I'm guessing she probably doesn't know."

"She was a few years younger than me. I don't know if she even remembers the accident and the trial. It was big news around here, but news fades fast. A few years in prison and they can let a murderer go free."

"You know it wasn't intentional murder."

"No. But he still killed her."

"Not like Brandon's death."

Roper shook his head. "I don't know anything about it. I didn't even know he was dead."

"He was killed in a hit and run. Just like your girlfriend. Only the driver wasn't drunk, was he?"

"How do you expect me to know anything about it?"

"You're used to keeping secrets."

"I've kept them quiet for a lot of years, yes... but that doesn't have anything to do with Brandon Powers, or whatever else you called him. I never knew the guy. Never spoke to him. Didn't keep track of what happened to him after he got out of prison."

"Someone did."

"Who?"

"Someone was stalking him."

"If you know anything about it, then you know it wasn't me. I haven't had any contact with the guy ever."

"How about the other men who were in the car?"

"The other men?" Roper looked puzzled for a moment. "I remember... there was a passenger who was killed, wasn't there? Were there others?"

"They testified in the court case."

"I couldn't go to that. I couldn't do anything that would suggest that I knew Hope. I had to pretend that nothing had happened. I had to just go to school and pursue my normal activities and not give away that she had meant anything to me. It was awful. You can't know what it did to me."

"You were seen at the courthouse. Outside, where the protesters were."

Roper looked stunned. "By who?"

"By people who knew who you were and that you were in a relationship with Hope."

"But nobody knew. I didn't tell anybody. Hope didn't tell anybody."

"Maybe you mentioned it to a best friend. Or maybe someone saw the two of you together. Maybe Hope told one of her friends. But the two of you didn't keep it quite as quiet as you thought you did."

Roper sat back in his chair, shaking his head in disbelief. "All these years... I never thought anyone else knew." He tilted his head thoughtfully. "Whoever it was... they didn't leak it. I never had anyone approach me about it. Not a single reporter."

"Maybe they had reason not to tarnish Hope's reputation either."

There was a flash of understanding across Roper's face, and Zachary thought he might have figured out who had known.

"Just why are you bringing all of this up now?" Roper asked. "Why not just let sleeping dogs lie?"

"Because I'm investigating Brandon's death."

"What does that have to do with me?"

"There are a lot of people who had reason to want him dead."

"And you think I'm one of them?" Roper shook his head. "I'm not some psychopath who thinks that I can bring Hope back by taking revenge on her killer. What good would that do anyone? Like you said, Brandon never intended to kill her. He made stupid choices. Choices he could never take back or make amends for. The court decided what the penalty for that was, and he paid it."

"And you're not at all bitter about him walking away from prison eight years later."

"On one hand, it seems like it happened just yesterday. But on the other hand... it feels like it was a whole lifetime ago. I was a different person then than I am now. I can't live my life being bitter about what happened over a decade ago. It would be a waste."

Zachary studied him for any sign that he was just putting up a smoke-screen. He had to assume that Hope had been Roper's first girlfriend. The first person he had ever fallen in love with and maybe been intimate with. It wasn't so easy to forget a relationship like that. But Roper sounded sincere.

Zachary's eye was drawn back to the photo of Roper and his sister again. "You never married."

"Not yet. That doesn't mean that I never will."

"Do you have a girlfriend? Are you dating?"

Roper's eyes slid to his computer. "I have a pretty busy life. Not a lot of time left for socializing."

Zachary rolled his eyes. "Plenty of busy people have time for a private life and relationships. People get married, have kids, raise families while they're pursuing busy careers. It isn't like you're a surgeon or working eighteen-hour days. Unless you choose to."

"Then maybe I'm just not ready yet."

Zachary took a deep breath and let it out slowly. "Can you think of anyone who is still bitter toward Brandon? Bitter enough to want him dead?"

"I wasn't in touch with anyone involved in the case. Look at Hope's family and close friends. I don't know what any of them are thinking and feeling now."

"Well, if you think of anyone… if anything comes up that you think might be worth looking into, give me a call." Zachary slid a business card across the table.

"Don't count on it. I've moved on with my life."

Max Fulton was the fourth man in the car the night that Brandon Powers had mowed Hope down, killing her in the middle of the street. Zachary had been expecting a clone of Devon Masters. They had been friends back in the day. They had drunk together, had been sitting in the back of the car together. They could have died together, if they hadn't been wearing seatbelts or if Brandon had driven into the river or been hit by a train instead of hitting Hope Creedy. But Fulton was not like Devon. He was quiet and reticent, a contemplative man. He took his time in answering Zachary's questions and kept the inner workings of his brain hidden from observers.

Zachary had a feeling that people didn't know much more about Fulton than he was willing to let people see.

"Explain to me what it is you wanted to see me about?" he asked Zachary. "I don't like this. I don't like being kept in the dark about people's motives."

"I'm investigating the death of Richard Harding."

"Richard Harding," Fulton repeated with a frown. He didn't say it in that same blank way as everybody else had. It seemed to mean something to him. "When did he die?"

Zachary was surprised. "You know who that is, then?"

"I assume that's why you want to talk to me. There wouldn't be much point in questioning people who'd never heard of him."

"Most people have disclaimed knowing Harding's name."

"He told me before he moved. Said he was hoping to make a fresh start. I thought he deserved that. He'd suffered through a lot. I didn't know if he'd ever be able to put it behind him, but why not try? I didn't begrudge him that."

"I'm sure the accident made your life harder too. He wasn't the only one in the car, and I imagine people partially blamed you as well."

Fulton was quiet for a while. "I had my fair share," he agreed eventually. "But I wasn't the one who was driving. I didn't have to live with that on my conscience. Brandon did. When he got out of prison, he was a different person than he had been when it happened. That guilt over having killed an innocent person through his own carelessness and poor choices... he had to live with that for the rest of his life. However short that might have ended up being." He scratched his ear, staring off into the distance. "He didn't contact me again after he moved to Vermont. Did it happen right away? Or was it just recent?"

"It was more recent. He had a few years to try to start a new life."

"Did he find any peace?"

"I haven't looked too deeply into his history... but I would say no. He did his best. He was dating. He was working. He hadn't been in any trouble. But someone had been stalking him, and he was very agitated and depressed over it."

"Stalking him?" Fulton's voice went up several notes.

"Yes, I'm afraid so."

"In person? Or on the computer?"

Zachary watched Fulton's face for what he was thinking, but he wore a mask, keeping it to himself. But he had brought up the cyberstalking immediately.

"On the computer and phone. Emails, texts, messages. Devon said he's had a few messages as well. Have you?"

Fulton nodded slowly. "It's been very disturbing. I've done my best just to ignore it, but those times when things are quiet and my mind is looking for things to think about... when I'm going to bed at night or having a quiet drink... I can't stop thinking about it."

"Do you know who is sending the messages?"

"No. It's all fake addresses. Nothing that you can respond to or trace back to the sender."

"Have you talked to anyone about it?"

"No... I don't really want to remind people about that part of my past. I'd rather not bring all of that up again."

"You didn't mention it to Devon?"

Fulton's eyes flicked to the side. "I might have."

"He set up his mail so that the messages are automatically deleted and he doesn't even have to see them."

"That would be smart. I'll have to see if someone can help me set that up..."

Zachary noticed he didn't say he'd get Devon to help him set it up. Obviously, as Devon had said, the two of them were not close friends. Fulton didn't think to ask Devon to help him set up the same thing.

"That might be a good idea; help ease your mind a little."

"You don't think that Brandon's death and the stalking are related, do you? I mean... I don't have to worry about this guy coming after me next?"

Zachary had wondered that briefly himself. He didn't want to tell Fulton that there was no danger, in case there was and Zachary's advice made him less cautious. But he didn't want to scare Fulton unnecessarily either.

"I've been looking for a connection between the stalker and the motorist who killed Brandon, but I haven't been able to find anything. None of the messages were overtly threatening. Nothing that said 'I'm coming after you' or 'I'm going to kill you.' It looks like a coincidence, but I can't tell you for sure."

"I appreciate that." Fulton sighed. "I didn't report it to the police. I don't really want to bring myself to their attention. Do you think I should?"

"Cyberstalking is a crime. I'd like to catch this guy, and if law enforcement can help to track him down…"

Mr. Peterson's words came back to him. His repeated advice for Zachary to report Tyrrell to the police for his similar activities. But like Fulton, he was reluctant to take it to the police. Not because he was worried it would tarnish his reputation, but because he didn't want to hurt Tyrrell. Not when he had already ruined his life. It was Zachary's own fault Tyrrell was sending those messages, and they were all true, however painful it was to admit it.

He realized that Fulton was saying something, looking at him with a pronounced frown.

"Oh, sorry. What was that…?"

"Something more important on your mind?" Fulton asked sarcastically.

"Not more important. Just… distracting. I'm sorry. I didn't mean to zone out like that."

"I guess… I'll report it. But are they going to want my computer? I can't really function without it."

"They might want to look at it, but I think mostly they'll want your login information for your email address, so that they can examine the messages and try to trace them."

"I hate the idea of someone going through my email…"

Did he have something to hide? Some other secret that he would rather they didn't know about?

"I know," he assured Fulton. "We don't like people poking around in our private lives. But if you want to help them to find this guy, to get him off your case…"

"I don't suppose I'm the only one he's doing this to. There are other people out there who are more vulnerable. People who would take it more seriously or are more suggestible. Children. If he's harassed all three of us, what are the chances that he's never done this before and would never do it again?"

"If it's someone who was hurt by Hope's death, they wouldn't be targeting anyone else, I don't think. The three of you were the only ones in the car."

"Do you really think so? They could decide to go after our families. If they're unstable enough to go over the deep end about an accident that happened over a decade ago, what's to say that they won't flip out over something else? Especially if they are getting satisfaction out of it? I don't think this is someone who is going to be stopped by logic."

He was right. An obsessive personality didn't just go away. It would find a new direction. Was the same true for Tyrrell? Was there any danger he would start harassing someone else too? Zachary knew Tyrrell. He wasn't that kind of a person. He'd always been a very sweet and sensitive boy. His anger toward Zachary was justified. He wouldn't carry that over to someone who was innocent. Tyrrell understood the difference between right and wrong. He wouldn't hurt someone else.

"So you think I should go to the police?" Fulton pressed.

"Uh… yes. I think it would be a good idea. You want to stop this guy. I don't see any way for them to stop him without the evidence. I have some idea of who it could be… but we don't have any proof connecting them yet."

"I hesitate to do anything that would harm anyone from Hope's family. They've gone through so much already. Do you think it's one of them?"

Zachary thought of the people he had interviewed. Mike Creedy, with his vitriol for the person who had killed his daughter. Mrs. Creedy's suppressed emotions, kept carefully under wraps. The twins, Luke trying to keep Noelle from saying too much to Zachary, with an explosive temper when he'd been drinking. Suzie didn't seem like a viable suspect. Zachary couldn't even imagine her finding the time to send that many emails. And Jonathan Roper, the boyfriend who could never be acknowledged, forever excluded from Hope's circle of mourners, looking in from the outside.

"I suspect it probably is," Zachary admitted. "I'm going to have to spend some more time on it, now that I've had a chance to meet everyone. And I should probably meet Kyle Browne's family as well."

Fulton looked surprised at the mention of Kyle's name. "I don't think he has anyone left around here. His parents have passed away. There was a sister, but she moved years ago. Even before the trial concluded. She just couldn't handle being in the spotlight."

"Do you know where she went?"

"No… I really have no idea. It wasn't the same for them as it was for Hope's family. They didn't get much public sympathy, and Brandon wasn't even charged in connection with Kyle's death."

Which could have left them feeling very bitter toward the man who had taken Kyle away from them. If Kyle's parents were dead, then it wasn't them, but it could be the sister.

Zachary decided he'd done all that he could in New Hampshire. He was feeling increasingly anxious in the hotel room and wanted to be back home in familiar surroundings, so rather than stay one more night, he checked out and hit the road, pointing the nose of the car west. He could have sworn that it knew they were going home and was as eager to get there as he was. Traffic was good and the trip uneventful.

At home, he showered off the dust of the trail as if he'd been riding in an open coach. After so many years without a permanent residence, it felt good to have a place of his own. He plugged the computer in and opened it up. He had more notes to compile, research to do, and theories to think about. He was distracted by the email notifications counter and clicked through to see what was awaiting him.

Of course, he knew in the back of his mind that there would be another email or two there from Tyrrell. Should he make contact with him, like Bridget said he should? Should he turn the matter over to the police like Mr. Peterson suggested and like he had advised Fulton? He hated to do that. Tyrrell was hurting. Maybe venting all of the poison would get it out of his system, and he'd be able to move on, if he just thought someone was listening to him.

He clicked on the latest message from Tyrrell, trying to brace himself mentally. He was just there to listen, to hear what it was Tyrrell had to say. He didn't have to take it personally and let it affect his mood.

You have done nothing but cause pain to everyone who knows you.

Why don't you just kill yourself?

Zachary swallowed. A pain started in the center of his chest and radiated outward, making it hard to breathe. He knew it was true. He'd brought pain and suffering to his family. To other families he had lived with. He had brought it into his marriage with Bridget and into other relationships. He brought it to the Creedys and other families he had questioned in the cases he investigated. Everywhere he went, he dragged his own pain and sorrow with him and infected everyone around him.

His head throbbed with the heavy beats of his heart.

Why don't you just kill yourself?

He rubbed his eyes and looked at the words again. He'd seen the same phrase repeated a number of times in the cyberstalker's messages to Richard Harding. It was hardly a unique phrase; he had seen it in other incidents of cyberbullying before. He read through the other recent messages, analyzing the language and repeated phrases clinically instead of reading them as personal attacks. He did a search and looked at the list of results.

The pattern of send times was similar to what he'd observed in the messages from Harding's stalker. Most of them before nine, over the lunch hour, after three or four. Like someone fitting them in around a work or school schedule. That didn't mean anything by itself; a high percentage of the population followed a similar schedule. It wasn't the same person just because he used a few of the same stock phrases and worked a similar schedule.

Zachary *knew* that his emails were coming from Tyrrell. No one but someone in his family could have had that picture. They were not from Harding's stalker. There was no connection between Tyrrell and the cyberstalker, other than their style and the timing of the messages.

That twigged another thought for Zachary. He logged in to Harding's account and looked at the messages the cyberstalker had been sending Harding. He double-checked the dates.

For a few minutes, he just sat there, thinking things through. Then he called Campbell.

20

Zachary," Campbell greeted cheerfully. "How goes the battle?"
"I don't know how much progress I'm making with this, but I had another thought."

"Yeah?"

"When Harding died, he stopped getting emails from the stalker."

"Well, yes, that makes sense."

"No, it doesn't."

"What do you mean?"

"How did the stalker know that he was dead?"

There was silence while Campbell thought this through. It was a more complex question than it sounded like.

"When, exactly, did the emails stop coming?" Campbell asked.

"The last one was the night he died. Nothing after that."

"And he'd been getting them pretty regularly up until then. There weren't any other gaps in the timeline when the stalker took a break and stopped sending them for a day or two?"

"No. They were coming in several times a day, faithfully."

"The stalker knew there was no point in sending any more messages. That means that he knew Harding was dead. But no one else knew Harding was dead. Not the truck driver, not his girlfriend, not the police."

"No."

"Does that mean he was there? Does that mean that Rusty Donaldson was somehow involved and could report back to the stalker, or was the stalker himself?"

"You might want to get him back in and look into it further."

Campbell grumbled. "This was supposed to be an open-and-shut case, Zachary. What are you doing to me?"

"Sorry. I didn't expect to find anything, but…"

"First you find out he was being cyberstalked. Then you find out he'd been in prison for killing someone in a hit and run himself. Then that the stalker knew almost the instant he died. This is turning into a much more complex case than it was supposed to be."

"I know. There's more going on under the surface than I would ever have expected."

"It could all be coincidence. His stalker might have just decided to give up at that point. He might have had enough. Or something else came up in his life and he couldn't keep it up. Maybe his computer died."

"I don't like coincidences. I'll see if I can find any connections between the people I interviewed in New Hampshire and Rusty Donaldson. Another possibility is Ashley herself."

"You think the girlfriend is the stalker?"

"She could be. Kenzie suggested it. Ashley is the only one who knew that he was missing the morning after he died. Did she tell someone else? Or was she the one who had been sending him the messages all along?"

"You have a devious mind, Zach. That's very… disturbing."

"I know. But it had to be someone close to him. I just don't know how to explain it otherwise. Either the stalker has a connection with Rusty Donaldson, or he was out there to see the accident, or it was Ashley or someone she talked to that morning. I can't think of any other scenarios, can you?"

"No… that's all I can think of. Would she give you access to her phone records if you asked?"

"I might be able to get them out of her. See who she called that morning. And the night before."

"Get her to show you whatever you can get out of her, it will be easier than us trying to get a warrant for them. If she is the stalker… then I'm guessing she won't show you everything. Or she'll have an alternative phone or email that she won't show you."

Zachary grunted his agreement. He couldn't quite wrap his mind around why Ashley would stalk and harass her own boyfriend, but that didn't mean she hadn't done it. She might have a motive buried deep beneath the surface. She might have gone to school with Hope, she might have had a sister who had been killed in a hit and run, or she might be mentally unbalanced. There was no telling what her motives were. But Zachary didn't have to know the motive, not initially. If he had proof, or at least strong evidence, that she had been the one harassing Harding, that would be a start. Enough, at least, for the police to question her and look into it further. As things stood, they didn't have any reason to insist she submit to further questioning.

"I'll find out what I can."

"Thanks, Zach. Appreciate you keeping me apprised—"

"Actually, there was something else I wanted to mention." Zachary raised his voice, trying to grab Campbell's attention before he could hang up.

"What?" Campbell questioned from farther away, then held the phone to his mouth again. "I didn't catch that?"

"There was one other thing."

"Oh, boy. Am I going to like it?"

Zachary thought of the news that Hope had been dating a younger man, and a minor at that, carefully keeping it a secret from his parents and their friends. But that wasn't what he had stopped Campbell for.

"Around the time I took this case... I started getting some nasty emails."

"You don't think they're from the same guy, do you? Harding's stalker?"

"No, I was pretty sure they were from... a family member I've been estranged from. But the similarities between them are marked. I don't know what to think. I can't see how they could be related."

"Can't you?" Campbell was amused. "If it's Ashley..."

Ashley knew when Zachary had taken the case. She knew his email address and phone number and other details of how to contact him. Had she seen him as a replacement target for her boyfriend? Harding was gone and she couldn't tease and taunt him anymore, so she had needed a new victim?

"But the things that she—he—has said to me have been very personal, things that someone outside of my family wouldn't know."

"Things that you've never told anyone else about? Can you be sure that your estranged family members have never told them to anyone else? Once you put something out there, you lose control of it."

Zachary considered. The accusations that had come to him from Tyrrell or the anonymous stalker were not actually that specific. The mentions of what he had done were vague, sometimes focused on the fire and sometimes not. While he had not shared the story of the fire with many people, there were others who knew not only that he had been in a fire when he was young, but that he had been the cause of it, and that his family had broken apart after that. Dozens of doctors, therapists, social workers, foster parents, foster kids, teachers and school administrators. And the few people he had told the details to, like Bridget and Kenzie. Someone running background on him could have found out from many different sources. Despite the fact that his privacy was supposed to be protected by social services, Zachary knew of plenty of cases where confidentiality had been breached. Foster parents gossiped with each other. Professionals discussed difficult cases among themselves. The foster brothers and sisters he had lived with hadn't been under any legal requirement to keep his story to themselves. They were taught to respect each other's privacy, but that didn't mean they did.

"Zachary?"

"Just thinking about it. I guess… there were people who knew, alright. But he sent me a photograph. One of my family, right before… that had to come from someone else in my family. No one else could have had it."

"Maybe someone in your family posted it online somewhere. Have you done a search to see if you could find it? Asked your family about it?"

"No. Not yet."

"Someone in your extended family could have shared it. It might have been placed in a public archive for some reason. Hell, you know all this, Zachary. You're a photographer. You're a private investigator. You know what happens once a picture is circulated. It never goes away."

"Then…" Zachary's mood lifted a little. "Maybe it wasn't Tyrrell. But he did send me a letter, to our old address. It ended up being forwarded to Bridget's."

"How do you know it was him? Did you contact him?"

"Well… no. Not yet. I thought that maybe—" Zachary cut himself off. He didn't need to share any more details than that. He didn't need to say where or when he thought he was going to see Tyrrell, or if he was really going to follow through. "No. But it was before I took the case…" Zachary trailed off. "Actually... I don't think it was. It arrived after our first meeting."

"After being forwarded in the mail? Forwarding tends to add a day or two to delivery time."

"Wait... I still have the envelope." Zachary shuffled through the papers on his desk and pulled out the letter and envelope that had come from Tyrrell. He studied the postmark, trying to make out where and when it had been mailed. He was relieved to see that it had been mailed from Vermont, not New Hampshire, and the mailing date was several weeks back, before he'd been hired to investigate Harding's death. "Yeah. It was mailed before I took the case. So this one is from Tyrrell..."

"But you're right, the emails might not be. They follow the same patterns as the ones to Harding?"

"Same phrasing in a lot of places. Same distribution of times, like the person has an office job or goes to school."

"And Ashley Morton, what is her schedule like?"

"I'm not sure... I think she's been on leave since Harding died. But the emails I've been getting are still in the same distribution pattern. So either she's very careful to follow the same schedule as before, or it's not the same person."

"Right," Campbell agreed. "I want you to send them to me anyway. We have someone working on the communications with Harding. They can look at your emails too and see if there is anything comparing them side-by-side can reveal. Maybe if they have two reference points, it will help to triangulate this guy's location. I don't know if that's something they can do with emails."

"Uh... I don't really like the idea of someone else reading these. There's personal stuff..."

"You want me to get a warrant for your whole email account or your computer? If there's a couple you don't want anyone to see, then hold them back, but we need a stack of them to do a proper analysis. These guys aren't going to be reading them for their own entertainment or to hold over you. They're trying to solve a case, that's all. The point is to learn everything they can about the stalker, not about you."

"Yeah. Okay." If he could hold back the ones with the more personal references, that helped. He didn't want Campbell's department having full access to everything in his email or on his computer.

"That's more like it. We're on the same side here. We both want to find out who the stalker is. Or who they are."

"Thanks. I appreciate your help."

"Is there anything else?"

Zachary thought about Jonathan Roper. "N-no."

Campbell heard his hesitation. "On the case or personally. It sounds like there's something else."

"I don't know whether it's relevant or not yet. I have to process my New Hampshire interview notes."

"Is it time sensitive? Are we going to miss something if we put it off?"

"No. I don't see him going anywhere."

"Alright. We both have plenty to look at, then. Let me know if you find anything in Ashley's records and I'll tell you if we can get anything from the email comparison."

21

In spite of being back in his own bed for the night, Zachary found he couldn't sleep. He tried lying down a few times, but each time his brain started chattering, processing all of the disparate clues, and he'd think of something he had to get up and check, or to write down so he wouldn't forget it in the morning. Eventually, he gave up and went back to his computer, carefully sorting through everything he knew and trying to make sense of it. He ran deeper background on the suspects in New Hampshire, looking for any clues in their past and trying to tie them to Rusty Donaldson or Ashley Morton.

It struck him that while he had tried to find a connection between the stalker and Rusty Donaldson, he hadn't spent much time trying to find a connection between Donaldson and Ashley. Maybe Ashley was the stalker and maybe she wasn't, but what if she knew Donaldson? What if she put him up to killing Harding?

The trouble with that was that he couldn't think of a motive. They hadn't found any evidence that Harding was abusive or that Ashley would benefit from killing him. He was a blue collar working stiff without any money, without even a life insurance policy. She wouldn't get anything material from his death. There wasn't any sign that he'd been cheating on her. Despite having changed his email address and phone number, there was nothing on the old accounts to incriminate him. Zachary was an expert at spotting signs of infidelity.

By the time it was what could be considered a decent hour to call Ashley to see if he could meet with her, his eyes burned from staring at the computer screen for too long. He rubbed them and showered and put in eyedrops, then made himself a cup of coffee and sat down. Ashley still sounded like he had dragged her out of bed. Zachary explained that he wanted to get together to talk, to follow up with her on what he had learned in New Hampshire.

Ashley yawned unenthusiastically. "Couldn't you just make a report to me over the phone? I really didn't want to have to deal with anyone today."

"There are things I don't like to discuss over the phone. I'd like to come see you at your house. Would that be okay?"

"At Richard's, you mean?"

"No, no. There's no need to drive out there. I'll just come to your house. Why don't you give me the address, and I'll be there as soon as I can? Then you're free to do what you want the rest of the day."

She gave a noisy sigh. "Did you find something?"

"I need to talk face to face," he insisted. "I'd like it to be today, if possible... do you have work or another commitment?"

"Fine." She gave him the address that he already had for her and advised that she would need to shower and dress before he arrived. "So don't get here too fast."

"An hour?"

"I suppose."

Zachary did his best to soften her up, stopping at the donut shop to pick up some pastries and some good coffee before swinging by her house. Her hair was still wet from her shower, but she did manage a smile when she saw that he had brought her breakfast.

"Well, at least I get something out of this," she grumbled. As if Zachary weren't doing anything else for her.

They went into the kitchen to put the pastries and coffee on the table. Zachary had thought through his approach with Ashley, so he had his story all prepared. "I'm sorry I couldn't really say anything to you over the phone, but I'm concerned that someone might be monitoring your communications."

"Monitoring... you mean someone has my phone tapped?"

"I don't know whether it's your phone or your computer, but I'd like to look at both of them. And what about in here or your car? Have you had anyone out of the ordinary in your house lately?"

Ashley looked around her eyes wide. "You think the house is bugged?"

"It's a possibility, but probably not. It's easy to tap a phone or computer remotely. Not so easy to arrange to have a bug physically planted in a house or car that's in a different state."

"You think one of these people you saw in New Hampshire might have bugged me?"

"I can't say they did without looking at your equipment. And if you could get me a printout from your phone company of all of your call and text logs that they give you access to, that might be helpful."

"Why?"

"Chances are, if someone bugged you remotely, they sent you a trojan. I'll look at what I can find on the phone and computer, but if it was attached to a text that was since deleted, or if the stalker called you first to make sure that your phone was turned on..."

Wide-eyed, Ashley unlocked her phone and handed it to him without a word. She grabbed one of the pastries from the box and ate it as she walked into the living room to retrieve her laptop, scattering crumbs along the way.

"I'll print out what I can while you look at the phone," she said. "Then you can look at it. Unless... should I not be doing that?"

"If there's a key-logger installed, you'll need to go through your various online accounts and change the passwords after I clean it off anyway. I don't think it will hurt to print out those logs."

They sat down. Zachary went to Ashley's texts, and started flicking through them. "You don't recall getting any strange texts lately? From someone you didn't know or who normally wouldn't be sending you something? A video or gif or song?"

"Uh... maybe, I don't know."

Zachary went through each sender, scrolling back to when Richard Harding had died. If she had any brains, she would have deleted any incriminating texts she had sent; but criminals made mistakes all the time. That was how they got caught.

He stopped when he got to a sender that had sent only one text, apparently a video of a cat. Zachary turned the phone around to show her the screen.

"Who sent this?"

"Uh... I don't know. I thought maybe it was a school friend of mine. I ran into her at the store, and she said she would connect with me. But I don't know," Ashley shook her head, looking at that one lonely message. "She never sent anything else or responded to my texts..."

Zachary turned the phone back around to investigate further.

"Do you think that's it?" Ashley asked in a low, nervous voice. She looked around. "Do you think that's some kind of virus that bugs my phone?"

One of the problems with phones was that they were always on. Even when she turned off the screen, that didn't turn off the phone or its broadcasting abilities. A clever hacker could use it like a baby monitor, to listen to anything that was going on, even when she wasn't making a phone call. Zachary held his finger to his lips to silence Ashley. He turned the phone to airplane mode and removed the SIM card. He put the tiny black chip on the table.

"I'll need to spend some more time with it, but for now, no one can monitor you through the phone. If that was a trojan, I would suggest getting a new phone. I can't be sure he hasn't done something that will give him permanent access whenever it is online. Even with a system wipe... I can't give you any guarantees. You might have backed up the trojan. It may have attached itself to some other app or file that you've saved to the cloud. You should probably do like Richard did, get a new phone and a new email address. Don't try to retrieve anything from this account."

Her eyes were wide. "But my whole life is on that little thing! All of my contacts, my plans..."

"I can convert contacts and calendars to CSV files and reimport them on a clean phone. That should be safe."

She just continued to shake her head. "How could this happen? I thought phones couldn't get viruses?"

"People can hijack them. This wasn't just a random virus."

Ashley stared at her computer for a long time, then logged in. "Do you still want this log, or do you not need it anymore because you already found it?"

"Uh..." Zachary thought it through. The reason he had asked for the logs had not been to track down spyware, but to see if Ashley had any connections with anyone else on his list. He hadn't actually expected to find spyware. "Yes, to be safe, if you could still print them out. We want to be thorough."

Ashley nodded and went to work. Zachary focused his attention on the phone, seeing if he could track down a suspicious program in the app list. It was probably lurking in the operating system, not visible to the user, but sometimes they still left traces in the visible interface.

As Ashley printed off pages of phone and text logs, he found a calculator app that seemed to be more than it appeared to be on the surface. It wasn't the built-in calculator app, though it was certainly intended to mimic it. But Zachary's keen eye picked out a few discrepancies. He pulled out his own computer and, being sure to tether it to his phone rather than to Ashley's potentially insecure network, he searched up the app and confirmed that it was spyware.

"It is infected," he confirmed to Ashley.

She looked at him with wide eyes and said nothing. She left the room, and came back a few minutes later with a thick stack of print outs.

"Can you do anything with it?"

"I'll do my best, but like I say, if it's sophisticated… that might not be enough."

"And my computer?"

Zachary reached across the table and turned her computer around. "That may take longer."

But it didn't. The malware seemed to be fairly unsophisticated. Checking for open ports, it was quickly obvious that Ashley's computer had been infected as well. He blocked each of the spyware programs and down-loaded his preferred app to clean it. While he was working on it, his mind was churning through all of the possibilities and implications. He had told Campbell that the stalker was quite possibly Ashley or someone she had told that Harding was missing. That was no longer the case. Whoever had had access to her phone and computer via the spyware knew about all of her phone calls and messages. They had read and listened in on her increasingly worried messages to Harding, and then to the police. They knew everything that she knew in real time. It was back to square one, unless they could figure out who had been monitoring her.

The chances that Ashley was the stalker had gone down considerably. But they hadn't been eliminated. She still might have infected herself as a cover, or someone else might have infected her for some other reason.

Maybe a friend of Harding's had been suspicious of her and had investigated her. For that matter, maybe Harding himself had suspected her.

"How long had you and Richard been dating?"

Ashley looked at him, eyes narrowed. "What?"

"I don't even know how long you had been together. You met him when he got out of prison. I assume you had been dating for a while. But you were not living together, so maybe that was a wrong assumption."

She considered him for a minute before answering. "Two years," she said finally. "But I don't see what living together has to do with it. Plenty of people know each other for years and years and never move in together. You have different kinds of relationships. Some people don't want to give up their own independence."

"Was it your decision or Richard's? Were *you* someone who didn't want to give up your own independence?"

Again, Ashley weighed her answer carefully before saying anything. Zachary didn't like how cautious she was. Her answers were not natural, unplanned replies. They could easily be lies.

"I admit I didn't want to give up my own place," she said, looking around. "I don't like to be... subsumed in a relationship. I don't like the idea of only being a part of a couple, instead of an individual. I don't like how at the end of a relationship, someone has to move out, and all of the belongings that you had together have to be divided. You give up some of your own stuff to combine households, and then when you break up again, you don't have it anymore. Unless you left it in a storage locker or your parents' house."

As a foster kid, Zachary understood the loss of status that went along with losing his home and his material possessions. While he was at a foster home, he had stuff. He had a bed and clothes and books and toys. He had access to a TV and fridge and closet space. When it was time to go, he would get his toothbrush and a change of clothes in a plastic bag, and the camera he kept on his person at all times, and everything else was stripped away.

But as far as relationships went, his experience with the dynamics of two people becoming one couple was the opposite. He had loved the feeling of being a part of a completed whole. He had felt like for once he was a full person instead of one that was damaged and missing vital parts. He had been absorbed into Bridget's life. Her full, engaged life. He wasn't just Zachary anymore, but Zachary, Bridget's husband.

Her name was like a password that had opened up a magical world he could never had been a part of before. People knew her, admired her, and wanted to please her. Everywhere she went, she made friends. Even in places that were previously Zachary's domain, like the police department, Bridget quickly knew and was friends with more people than Zachary. And while they had been together, he had been a part of that.

Zachary forced himself back into the conversation with Ashley. "That makes sense." He saw her shoulders dip, her body language relaxing. "So you didn't know Richard in New Hampshire."

"No. I never met him until he moved to Vermont."

"When did he tell you about his past? That he had been in prison and had unintentionally killed someone in a hit and run?"

"I don't know when, exactly. We started getting serious. I knew that he avoided some topics, social situations, that he had problems with his health and with sleeping. It didn't all come out at once. Little revelations that he'd lived in New Hampshire, that he'd been involved in an accident, that he'd served time for his fault in it... it was difficult for him to talk about, so I didn't push to know everything at once. Just a little bit more every now and then, until I had the whole story."

"So you know everything?"

She pursed her lips, looking at him. "What do you classify as 'everything'? He was driving, he'd had a couple of drinks, he hit and killed a girl. He was disoriented and left the scene."

"There were others in the car."

Ashley nodded. "Yeah. He was driving the others."

"Did you know that one of them died too?"

No indication of surprise on her face. "Well... yes."

"Did he ever have any contact with anyone else involved in the case? Hope's family or friends? The other guys who survived the collision?"

"No. Except, I guess, whoever was stalking him. But I didn't know that before he died."

"So he might have had contact with any of them without you knowing it."

"Yes. But you've looked at all of his phone records and emails, right? So you'd know if he'd had contact with them."

"In the last couple of months, yes. We haven't gone three years back in phone records. Where did you live before?"

She raised her eyebrows. "Before what? I live here."

"Before you moved here."

She obviously hadn't lived there forever. It wasn't her family home. She complained about losing her home during a previous relationship or relationships. She must therefore have had several addresses before the current one. The fact that she wasn't answering automatically made him wonder why she wanted to hide it. Had she lived in New Hampshire? Did she have connections she didn't want him to know about?

"I'm not sure what you mean. I grew up in Burlington."

"And you came here from Burlington?"

"No... I've had a few other residences. But I've been here for three years."

About the same time that Harding had gotten out of prison. Zachary pretended to be occupied with Ashley's computer, clicking through a few screens to see how the virus scan was progressing and giving her time to relax between questions.

"You like it here?"

"Sure. It's a nice town. I've got a good job. No reason to leave any time soon."

"It has a nice atmosphere," Zachary agreed. It had felt like a good place for him to settle down too. After spending his life moving around, it had seemed like a good place to put down his roots. Big enough for there to be plenty of work for him, but small enough that it felt like a community instead of a big metropolis. "How about Richard, what did he think of it?"

"Well, he lived where it was more rural... I don't know if he really liked it, though. Most people choose to live on rural properties because they want gardens, or animals, or to be out in nature. But I think Richard just wanted to be away from people. He got anxious when he had to be in the city. He was... I'm not sure what the best word for it is. He was always watching, like something was going to happen. And in the city, he had to watch everything at once, all the different directions at the same time."

"Hypervigilance," Zachary supplied. That was something he knew plenty about.

Ashley's expression cleared. "Yes, that's the perfect word. When he had to be in the city, whether it was out on the street or in a grocery store, he was hypervigilant. He was okay for a while if he was here, in a house, but after a while, he'd get... jittery and want to go back home."

"Was he afraid of being in another accident?"

"Yes... but I don't think that was the only thing. He didn't like being around a lot of people. I don't know if he thought people were going to recognize him, or maybe bad things had happened to him in prison that had affected him... he was happier when he was at home, or just with a small group of friends."

"Did the two of you have shared interests? How did you spend your time together?"

"Like I said before. Just watching TV together, talking, relaxing. Maybe it doesn't sound like much, but it worked for us."

Zachary nodded. "And you weren't aware of it when the stalker started harassing him?"

"Thinking back... maybe... he said he was depressed. He started shutting down different accounts, saying that he needed to spend more time IRL—in real life—instead of so much of it online. I didn't really think anything of it. I thought he was exaggerating about being depressed. Maybe he was a bit down about things, but not really depressed."

Harding was probably just good at hiding his feelings. His time in prison had probably taught him that. Like Zachary's time in Bonnie Brown had taught him to mask his anger and pain, to keep anyone from thinking he was weak and a good target. If Harding's feelings about the cyberstalker's messages had been anything like Zachary's, he had probably been seriously depressed. The cutting and antidepressants were pretty big signs that he hadn't just been trying to get attention.

"So you couldn't narrow down the timeframe when the stalker first made contact."

"You can tell from his emails, can't you?"

"He deleted them and emptied his trash, so I can't be sure exactly when he started getting them." He watched Ashley's expression closely. "You don't know when the stalker started to send them?"

She shook her head. "So, sorry. And I don't understand why it's important."

"Don't you want the cyberstalker to be caught and punished?"

"Yes, of course..." her voice was uncertain.

"I would think you would want his stalker punished just as much as the person who killed him. After all, the person who killed him didn't cause any suffering. The person who stalked and harassed him did."

She didn't offer anything up. If she was the stalker, she didn't seem to be experiencing any regret or sorrow for it. If she wasn't, she didn't seem to have any comprehension of how much pain those words could cause. She acted as if it were nothing, instead of something that could have led to Harding's death just as surely as being hit by a truck.

22

As he got back into his car to return home, Zachary called Campbell to give him a heads-up on the latest developments, aware that it unraveled all of the progress they thought they had made with the realization that the stalker had stopped harassing Harding immediately after his death. Campbell wasn't as dismayed about it as Zachary was. Zachary could practically hear his heavy shoulder-shrug over the phone. "That's one mystery solved, anyway. You got the number that sent this suspected malware? We'll see if we can chase it down."

"He'll have thrown it out."

"Undoubtedly. But we still might be able to figure something out."

Zachary gave him the number. Campbell didn't hang up immediately. "And you're okay? You sound discouraged."

"I'll be fine. Just tired. Haven't slept much the last few days."

"Make sure you get it tonight, then. You need to get enough sleep for optimum brain function. If we're going to close this case, we need you at your best."

"Thanks." Zachary wasn't sure anymore there was any chance in bringing it to a successful conclusion. He hadn't been able to provide anything that showed that Rusty Donaldson hadn't just killed Harding by accident, just as the police had initially determined. "I'll try."

"Take care of yourself. We're going to need you on other cases. Got to have someone keeping us honest."

Zachary tried to laugh at the suggestion of him keeping the police in line. "I don't think this was anything other than an accident," he admitted.

"No. Neither do I. But at least we'll have independent confirmation of that."

Zachary grunted. After a bit more casual conversation, they hung up. Zachary put the car in gear and drove for a few minutes before calling Kenzie.

"Thought I'd let you know I'm back in town. Got back last night."

"Oh, good! How did it go?"

"Well... there are still a lot of bad feelings for Harding. No one was too sorry to hear he'd died. But I haven't been able to connect any of them to Rusty Donaldson or the cyberstalker."

"Maybe it just was a coincidence."

"That's what I'm thinking."

"Well, maybe you'll be able to close this case before Christmas."

"Yeah." And then what? He had plenty of little jobs to keep him busy, but they wouldn't occupy his attention like the Harding case had. And he needed something to distract him from the poisonous email messages. If they were from Harding's stalker, would they just go away when he had closed the case? Or had the stalker transferred his obsessive interest to Zachary, and would just keep taunting him? And if it wasn't Harding's stalker, if it was Tyrrell like Zachary had originally thought... then what was Zachary going to do about it?

"Still there, Zachary?"

"Yeah. Just thinking. Sorry. What are your Christmas plans again?" He was pretty sure she had told him, but he tended to withdraw from any conversation about Christmas.

"I thought we were going to have dinner together and go see Rhys."

"Rhys. Right. Did you manage to get something set up with Vera? Rhys said he was going to see his mom on Christmas Day."

"You were supposed to talk to Vera to hammer out the details."

"I was?" Zachary searched his memory, but couldn't remember anything of the sort. Had Kenzie told him to do that? Had he offered? Did Kenzie just think she had mentioned it? "I... guess I forgot."

"You'd better call her and find out. It's just a few days away, Zach."

"Uh, yeah. I will. I'm sorry."

"Are you going to do it?" She gave him a few seconds to answer, in which Zachary tried to formulate an answer, but failed to find the right words. "Don't tell me you're going to if you're not."

Zachary swallowed. "I don't think I can."

"Fine. I'll call her. But that means you'll have to abide by whatever plans I make."

"Yeah. Sure. No problem."

"You are nothing *but* problems," Kenzie complained, blowing her breath out in a sigh. But she didn't say it in a mean way. It was lighthearted, just a bit of teasing between friends.

Zachary pulled into the parking lot of his apartment building and headed toward his parking space. He hit the brake and swore.

"You okay?" Kenzie asked. "Did something happen?"

"Uh—fine. Everything is fine."

"It sounded like something was wrong."

Zachary tried to breathe long and slow. If he breathed slowly and calmed his body, then his heart would stop racing like it was going to drill right through his chest and everything really would be fine. There was a beep behind him. Zachary glanced into the rearview mirror and saw one of the other tenants trying to navigate to his own parking space. Zachary was stopped right in the middle of the lane, blocking him from entering. He eased his foot off the brake and crept forward, steering slowly, driving like he was a hundred and three and half blind. He managed to get into his spot and put the car into park. He was okay. There was nothing to worry about.

"What's going on? Should I hang up so you can focus?"

"No. I'm here. Just got home."

A few seconds of silence passed. "What happened? A black cat cross your path?"

Something just as ominous for Zachary. He swallowed.

"Apparently... the manager of my new building decorates."

"Decorates... for Christmas?"

"Yeah."

"That's nice. I like it when businesses take part in the festivities of the season. It's nice to look around and see everything looking Christmas-y."

Zachary's mouth and throat were too dry to agree.

"Okay, well, if you're back home, I'll let you go. Have a good night."

Zachary whispered a hoarse goodbye and hung up the call.

He took the key out of the ignition, gathered his things together, and got out of the car. He stared at the Christmas display inside the lobby apartment. Twinkle lights, a couple of decorated Christmas trees with fake presents underneath, and garlands around the windows.

He could deal with it. Every year, there was no avoiding Christmas decorations completely. He stuck to the stores and restaurants that did not usually decorate, didn't accept Christmas invitations, and was generally a Scrooge. But there would always be a few times when he had to walk past decorated trees or window displays or when he couldn't avoid Christmas music piped into a store. He still managed to do it.

The longer he took, the harder it would get, so Zachary forced himself to walk down the sidewalk to the building's doors, to push them open, and to use his security card to unlock the inside door. There was no one else in the lobby. He aimed his body toward the elevator doors, closed his eyes, and started walking, hands held slightly in front of him so he wouldn't walk right into the wall.

But his brain knew where the trees were and the fact that he was focused on them meant that he course-corrected to walk into them instead of past them. He felt the prickly needles and stopped. He didn't want to open his eyes, but he wasn't going to be able to get back on track without looking. The sharp smell of pine filled his nose. He opened his eyes and it was like he was inside the tree. His face was only inches from the upward-reaching branches, lights, and decorations. Zachary backed up, found the elevators again, and shuffled toward them, hands still held out in front of him in spite of the fact that he could see the trees and the walls and wasn't going to walk into anything. When he reached the wall, he put his hands flat against it. He bent his head forward slightly and rested his forehead against the cool wall.

He heard the lock on the lobby doors beep and then swoosh open. Trying to avoid looking like a complete idiot, Zachary managed to find the up button and push it. One of his neighbors fell in behind him to wait and didn't ask him what he was doing worshiping the wall.

When the elevator bell dinged, Zachary peeled himself away from the wall and shuffled into the elevator. He didn't turn around immediately.

"Floor?" the neighbor asked helpfully.

Zachary cleared his throat and gave it hoarsely, turning himself around as the elevator started up with a stomach-dropping lurch. The other man's eyes flicked over him.

"A bit too much Christmas cheer?" he suggested.

Zachary nodded, his head swimming. Definitely too much Christmas cheer.

"Do you need a hand or can you get there yourself?"

Zachary held to one of the hand rails inside the elevator. "I'm okay."

"You're sure? It would only take a minute. I don't mind."

"No. No, I'm good. Thanks."

He took a few deep breaths. Out of sight of the Christmas trees and decorations, the panic was starting to subside. He'd touched one of those trees. Actually touched it. It had been years since he'd done that. It hadn't been on purpose, but he hadn't fainted or thrown up in response. It had just been prickly.

The elevator stopped. Zachary checked the number to make sure it was his floor, and moved forward. The other man reached his hand out, tracking Zachary, making sure he wasn't going to topple over. His other hand pressed the 'open' button, making sure Zachary had lots of time to navigate through them without a problem.

"Thanks," Zachary told him, stepping over the gap into the corridor. He kept moving, showing the other tenant that he was able to manage on his own and didn't need to be physically escorted to his door.

The doors swooshed closed. Zachary stopped and stood still, one hand on the wall, waiting for the nausea the elevator had induced to calm back down. Then he walked slowly down the hallway to his door and let himself in. No lurching, no need to hold on to the wall, just a normal walk like it was any other day. He closed and locked the door and sat down in a chair in his kitchen, the closest piece of available furniture. He put his shoulder bag with his laptop and other items on the floor and took a few more breaths.

His phone buzzed, and Zachary took it out to look at it. A text message from Kenzie.

I just remembered how Christmas decorations bother you. Sorry. U ok?

Zachary blew out his breath. He was fine. He'd made it on his own with no ill effects. Just like a normal person.

Fine. Thanks for checking.

He watched the screen for a few minutes, waiting for her response.

Good. Call if you need to talk.

He texted back a thumbs-up emoji and turned the screen off.

The rest of the evening should have been fine. He was winding-up the file. Write out his conclusions. Put them together in a coherent report. Collect the rest of his fee.

His mind kept going back to the Christmas decorations in the lobby. He was going to have to walk by them every time he went out and returned. Unless there was an alternate route out of the building. Freight elevator? Stairs? Loading dock or emergency door? He'd never explored the building; he just walked in and out the same way every day like anybody else. But surely there was another way out. There had to be emergency exits in the event of… any sort of emergency. He'd figure it out. Then he wouldn't have to look like a fool every time he had to get through the lobby.

But the decision to find another way in and out of the building didn't help him to write his notes. He got hung up on the twins' names. Noelle and Luke. They must have been Christmas babies, with Mrs. Creedy marking the occasion by giving them Christmas names.

He was glad that Kenzie had agreed to take over the arrangements with Rhys and Vera. Zachary just couldn't manage it on his own. One day, maybe. After all, he'd touched a Christmas tree without any ill effects. But he wasn't ready for it yet.

Around and around his brain went, like a hamster on a wheel. While he'd been aware that Christmas was getting closer and closer, he'd been avoiding focusing on the exact date. When Kenzie had said it was only a few days away, it had sent his brain into overdrive. It was all coming back. The blackness and despair that he had to swim through every year never seemed to get any easier. Knowing ahead of time that the depression would worsen was no help at all.

He finally put his notes and unfinished report aside. If he couldn't distract himself with work, then maybe it was time to just veg out in front of the TV. While the networks were full of seasonal offerings, he had a streaming account that was full of non-Christmas shows and movies. He could start on a new series and binge watch until he fell asleep or Christmas Eve was over, whichever came first.

But he couldn't settle on anything to watch. That hamster kept running and running around the wheel. Kenzie was going to talk to Vera and set something up. Rhys had already said he wanted to do Christmas Eve instead of Christmas Day, and what if Kenzie set that up instead? She said that Zachary had to go with whatever she set up. Or what if she set it up for Christmas Day and Zachary was no longer around? It wouldn't be fair to put Rhys through something like that, especially on his first Christmas without his mother. If something happened to Zachary, it would be on Christmas Eve. Just like the fire.

The previous year, he had been in the emergency room. Not for himself, but for Isabella, waiting to see if she would pull through after her own suicide attempt. It was ironic that her attempted suicide had pulled Zachary away from his own contemplations. Without knowing it, she had saved his life.

Zachary went to the bathroom and opened the medicine cabinet. While he tried to keep things in his life neat and orderly to combat his distractibility and anxiety, the medicine cabinet was one area that he could never seem to tame. Maybe because he was so often at the end of his rope when he finally decided to take something, the bottles never got put away in proper order.

He started to turn each pill bottle around to read the prescription label and see how many pills he had left. His doctors thought it best not to dispense too many pills at one time, to try to discourage an overdose, but the different prescriptions could still be combined.

Zachary's hand brushed against something on the back of the mirrored door that hadn't been there before. He opened it farther and looked at the index card taped to the inside of the door. At the top of the card was the stern instruction "Call somebody!" And on each line was a name and number. Emergency hotline. His therapist. Bridget, Kenzie, and Bowman. Mr. Peterson. Hospital.

There was a lump in his throat. The printing, he knew, was Kenzie's. She must have put it there the last time they had gotten together, and he hadn't even noticed.

He closed the medicine cabinet. It snicked softly into place against the magnetic latch. Zachary went back out to the living room and picked up his phone. He launched the phone app and tapped on Kenzie's name.

"Zachary." Kenzie was mid-yawn as she said his name. "How's it going?"

"Can you come over?"

Her yawn cut off in a tiny squeak. "What?"

"Could you come over. Now."

"It's kind of late."

"I know. If it's too late for you… I can call someone else."

"Wait." She no longer sounded sleepy. "Are you saying you need help? Are you having a bad night?"

"I was just in the medicine cabinet… counting pills."

She swore. "You're having suicidal thoughts?"

"I just can't… shut it all off."

"I'll be right over. Do you need me to stay on the line with you?"

"No. I'll be okay for that long."

"Are you sure? Don't play the macho card here. I'm not going to get there and find out that you couldn't wait?"

"I won't do anything. I'm sitting on the couch. I'm going to stay here, right where I am, until you get here."

"Okay. I'll be right over. Hang in there."

Zachary was true to his word and sat there on the couch, browsing again through the options on the TV, trying a game of solitaire on his phone, and staring out the window at the lights of the city, streetlights mixed with traffic lights and multicolored Christmas lights. No matter what he did, Christmas would keep coming every year, plunging him into the unwanted memories.

Kenzie knocked at the door, calling out his name right away, as if afraid he wouldn't be there anymore. But he had told her he would be. He got up and went to the door to unlock it. She looked at him, relief flooding her features. She wrapped her arms around him and pulled herself tightly against him. He squeezed her gently, but she didn't release him. She kissed him urgently, and Zachary wriggled out of her grasp, overwhelmed.

"I'm sorry," Kenzie apologized. "I'm just so relieved to see… that you're okay."

"I know. I don't mind." Zachary's ears got hot. "I just… we're in the doorway… and I can't breathe…"

Kenzie gave a flustered laugh. She stepped the rest of the way into the apartment and shut and locked the door behind her.

"Yeah. Well. Let's go sit down. Do you want to sit down? Or should we… go somewhere?"

Zachary made a gesture toward the living room and the couch. "Yeah, come in."

Kenzie put her hand on his arm as they moved into the room, comforting him or reassuring herself that he was really there and was still okay. When they sat down, he noticed she sat closer to him than was usual.

"Should we go somewhere?" she asked again. "Do you want me to take you to the emergency room? What can I do to help you?"

"No. I don't want to go out." Especially not if he had to go past the Christmas display in the lobby. And whatever decorations they had at the hospital, though emergency room decorations were usually pretty sparse. Going to the emergency room would mean sitting and waiting for hours on end, just to have some young intern advise him that he should have his doctor do a thorough med review and send him home with a brochure on available services. Or if he wanted, he could admit himself for an evaluation, and he would be there for at least three days, taking him into the black hole of Christmas Eve.

"You want to just talk?"

"I don't know." Zachary rubbed his temples, his head pounding. He wasn't sure how long it had been since had had slept more than a couple of hours.

Kenzie studied him, her expression earnest and concerned. They were both turned toward each other on the couch. She put her hand on his knee. "Did you take anything before I came here?"

"No."

"Are you sure? You don't look good. If you did take something, you need to tell me, so we can deal with it."

"No. I was thinking about it… but I saw your note… and I called."

"I'm glad you did. And you haven't hurt yourself?" her eyes searched his face. "When we were talking about Richard Harding cutting, I got the feeling…"

"No." Zachary shook his head. "I didn't. I just called you."

"Do you want to talk about the case? You haven't told me any details of what you discovered in New Hampshire."

Zachary's thoughts were scattered. He gave her a disjointed account of the people he had interviewed. She was more interested in his description of what he had found on Ashley's phone and computer.

"So this stalker had been spying on them? Watching them, listening in on conversations?"

"Looks like it. I passed the details on to Campbell. The more data they have, from Harding's and my emails, the phone number that possibly sent the trojan to Ashley, and any numbers that repeat in the call and text logs... the better the chances that they'll actually be able to find who did this."

Kenzie nodded slowly. Her brows were down and Zachary wondered if the words were coming out differently from what he had composed in his head. Sometimes they did.

"Your emails?" Kenzie asked.

"What?"

"You had emails with this cyberstalker as well? Did he answer you, or...?"

Zachary tried to sort through his memories. He had told Mr. Peterson about the emails when he'd been so shocked by the picture of his family. He had told Campbell about them in case they had been from Harding's stalker instead of Tyrrell. He couldn't remember whether he had told Bridget or whether she only knew about the initial letter. He apparently had not told Kenzie.

He cleared his throat. "I've been getting emails like Harding was. I thought... that they were from my brother. Tyrrell. But it's possible they came from Harding's stalker."

Her eyes got wide. "Why didn't you tell me about that before?"

"I thought they were from Tyrrell... until recently."

"How would Harding's stalker get your email address? How would he even know you were on the case?"

Up until then, Zachary had been puzzled by that point. But knowing the stalker had the ability to monitor Ashley's phone, the answer was obvious. He'd been able to hear their conversations. He knew that Ashley had hired Zachary. A two-second search on the internet was all it would take to find his email address.

"He could hear anything that happened in earshot of Ashley's phone. We don't know when he was listening and when he wasn't. From the arrival times of the emails he sends, he's busy during the day, but when we initially met, it was for supper, in the evening."

"So what was in these emails? How bad are they?"

Zachary swallowed. He couldn't repeat out loud the things that the anonymous emailer had sent to him. He picked up his phone from the side table and went into his email app. He tapped a couple of times to find one of the more recent emails.

Nobody wants you after the horrible things you've done. Why don't you just kill yourself?

Kenzie took it when he handed it to her and only took a couple of seconds to read it. She swore under her breath.

"Oh, this is just what you need right now. Is that why you're having such trouble tonight? Because of this pile of crap?"

The corner of Zachary's mouth twitched at her words. Even in the dark place he was in, she could still almost bring a smile to his face.

"I probably would be anyway... but it doesn't help. I can't get his words out of my mind. And they keep coming..." He should have set up a filter like Devon had. Permanently delete the messages before he ever saw them. But even knowing they might have come from Harding's stalker instead of Tyrrell, he couldn't bring himself to do that. He needed to read them. He needed to be sure. If they were Tyrrell's words, he couldn't just discount them. He needed to hear them even if they hurt.

Kenzie shook her head. "It's horrible. You know it's not true, don't you? People do care about you. People would be hurt if something happened to you, especially if you harmed yourself. You haven't been as efficient about avoiding *complications* as you would like to be."

I just like things to be uncomplicated. He had admitted to her that he tried to avoid letting anyone get too involved in his life because he didn't want to leave anyone behind to mourn him if he did someday take the path from which he could never return. He had broken that rule with Bridget. He had tried to keep friends like Kenzie and Bowman from getting too close. But they had become a part of his life. Complications.

"I'm sorry. That was a thoughtless thing to say." He shrugged uncomfortably. "Poor impulse control gets the better of me..."

"But it was the truth."

"Part of the truth."

"Do I want to hear the other part?"

Zachary swallowed. He wasn't able to look her in the eye, staring down at his hands instead. "Yeah... the other part is... I need you."

23

There was only silence in return. Zachary shifted uncomfortably, looking around for something else to focus on or to keep his hands busy. Kenzie took his hands in hers.

"Life is complicated."

"Yeah," he agreed. "It definitely is."

She moved in closer, until she was snuggled up against him. Her body felt good against his. He tried to store that feeling away, to take a snapshot of it to remember during the lonely nights. She moved in and kissed him, not so desperate and insistent this time. He wasn't sure how much time passed while they sat there on the couch, wrapped up in each other, exploring a new level of intimacy. But Zachary's exhausted body and agitated brain couldn't advance any further. Eventually, Kenzie withdrew. She gazed at him.

"You look like a zombie."

"It's been... a while since I've slept."

"Then let's get you to bed."

She got to her feet. Zachary didn't rise immediately. His arms and legs felt leaden. He knew he should jump at the suggestion, but he was incapable of jumping at anything, physically or emotionally. Kenzie reached down and took his hand, giving him a little tug. Zachary rose to his feet slowly and, at her insistence, he dragged himself to the bedroom. He looked at the bed, his stomach writhing with guilt and dread.

"I'm sorry," he said. "But some of the meds… and the way I feel… I don't think I can…"

"Shush." She gave him a little push. "You need sleep. I promise I won't take advantage of you."

Zachary felt removed from the situation, watching from a safe distance. Kenzie encouraged him to get comfortable and lie down. She kicked off her shoes and peeled off her socks. After shutting off the lights, she lay down behind him, wrapping her arms around him and holding him as he had held Tyrrell or one of the other children when they'd had a nightmare or were frightened by the yelling and fighting, helping them to calm down and feel safe enough to sleep. He could feel her warm breath on his neck. He tried to match his breath to hers, slow and deep instead of the quick, shallow breaths his anxiety-tightened diaphragm produced.

"Do you need to take something?" Kenzie asked after a while, obviously able to tell that he was still awake, still too rigid and agitated to convince his brain it was time for sleep.

"Yeah." He tensed to get up to go to the medicine cabinet, but Kenzie pressed his shoulder down.

"Stay put. Let me get it. What do you want?"

"Xanax and Ambien."

"Both?"

"If I'm going to get to sleep."

"Okay. Stay here, I'll be right back."

She brought him the pills and a glass of cold water. Zachary propped himself up on his elbow to wash them down, then lay down again in the warm pocket his body had created. Kenzie put the cup away and climbed into bed, again snuggling up behind him and putting comforting arms around him.

"Just relax," she whispered. "It doesn't matter whether you really sleep. Just let your body and brain rest for a few hours."

He tried to do as he was told, and some time in the early hours of the morning, his consciousness released its hold and he dropped off to sleep.

897

Zachary was groggy and disoriented on waking, conscious thoughts coming to him slowly as his brain sorted itself out. He was alive. He had been asleep and had awakened. He must have taken something to sleep or he wouldn't have such a heavy, groggy feeling.

He shifted his position and rubbed his eyes. It was light out. Not a filmy dawn light, but the full light of day, well into the morning. The movement he made was echoed by another body, and a hand landed on his shoulder, molding to it.

Bridget?

"Hey, how are you doing?"

Kenzie. Zachary was still trying to catch up to the present. He lay still, feeling her breathing and trying to recall all that had happened. He'd been feeling dangerously low. He'd called Kenzie. She'd spent the night watching over him and making sure he slept.

"Kenzie?"

"Yes, Zachary?" her tone was slightly mocking, good-humored.

"Nothing. Just... thanks."

"Of course." Her hand left his shoulder and she turned and stretched. "You want coffee?"

"Sure."

She got out of bed. He listened to the whisper of her bare feet over the floor. It was nice to have someone else there. It felt like she belonged there. She opened and closed cupboards in the kitchen. She knew where everything was and moved around confidently. Before long, he could smell coffee brewing. He rubbed his eyes. They didn't ache as much as they had, and were not scratchy and gritty like they were after a long sleepless night. He knew he wouldn't be caught up on sleep after just a few hours, but even just part of one night helped. His brain wasn't chattering quite so frantically and the anxiety was a notch lower than it had been.

Kenzie returned to the bedroom and handed him a cup of coffee. She sat on the edge of the bed. They both sipped, knowing the coffee was going to be too hot, but savoring the ritual anyway, each watching the other to make sure they were comfortable.

"You think you can get in to see your doctor today?" Kenzie asked.

Zachary hesitated. "I don't really know if..."

"You should talk to him about seasonal shifts. Have a plan for this. Take something stronger in anticipation to see if you can head it off. Have a safety plan. Maybe arrange for inpatient treatment ahead of time." She raised her eyebrows at him. "For next year. It's too late this year to bother raising your doses; by the time your blood levels are up, you'll be past the crisis. But you need to see him, to make sure you're safe for the next few days. I know you'd rather stay home, but if a professional says it's not safe…"

"He'll say I'm the best judge."

"Fine. But I want him to know about this."

Zachary shrugged.

"And your therapist? You've been seeing him? He knows about Christmas and then this email harassment?"

Zachary took another sip of his coffee, hiding his face from her. "Um… I've been busy with this case… I haven't seen him for a while."

She raised an eyebrow. Zachary cleared his throat and looked away uncomfortably.

"You know that when you are having issues, you should be seeing him more often, not skipping sessions."

Zachary nodded.

"So you need to see him too."

"I don't know if I can get appointments for today. They'll already be booked up or off for the holidays. I usually have to schedule at least a couple of weeks out…"

"Call and see."

"I…"

"You need to. I want to make sure you're taken care of properly. I'm glad that you called me last night. I don't want you stepping in front of a bus or something next time."

Zachary frowned.

"Zachary…" Kenzie said insistently.

"I wouldn't do that."

"That's what you say, but if you're not well and you had the impulse…"

Zachary didn't say anything, his mind working through possibilities, fitting pieces of the puzzle together. Kenzie cocked her head to the side.

"What's going on in there?"

"Richard Harding."

"Harding? What about him...?"

"Ashley said it couldn't be a coincidence that Harding was killed in a hit and run after what he had done. She was right. It wasn't."

Kenzie's eyes sparkled. "You figured it out?"

"It wasn't homicide. It was suicide."

24

For a minute, Kenzie was quiet, considering this. She nodded slowly. "He was depressed, he was being stalked and harassed. He felt guilty about what he had done."

"We kept wondering what he was doing out there on the road. If he had seen or heard something. The fact that it was a hit and run. Why he would be outside wearing dark clothing, no lights or anything reflective. Why he wasn't walking on the left side of the road, where he'd be able to see oncoming vehicles. It explains all of that. It was suicide by truck. He was walking in the dark, waiting for a vehicle to come along. And then he stepped in front of it."

"And that's why the driver didn't see him ahead of time," Kenzie agreed. "He didn't want to be seen. It didn't just happen to clip him. It didn't steer into him. He waited until the last minute and jumped in front of it."

Zachary was sure they were right. Everything fit. There hadn't been a note, but that wasn't unusual. A lot of suicides never left notes. Richard Harding had wanted out. He'd tried changing his name and moving away, but his troubles followed him. He'd been stalked relentlessly, and Zachary knew what kind of feelings those poisonous words stirred up. The stalker piled on the guilt and suggested suicide as the way out. After enough repetition, Harding couldn't get it out of his mind. It wormed its way down, burrowing into his brain, until he couldn't think of any other way to relieve the guilt and pain.

Kenzie touched his knee, but didn't say anything. Zachary swallowed and nodded. He put his hand over hers briefly. He looked around for his phone. "I should call Campbell."

"I think it's still out in the living room. Hang on."

When she came back and handed it to Zachary, she had a grin on her face. The phone was ringing, and Campbell's name was on the screen. Zachary swiped it on.

"Hey, I was just going to call you."

"You must be psychic."

"Richard Harding's death wasn't an accident. Ashley was right."

"Are you sure?" Campbell's voice was surprised. "You found a connection?"

"Not to Donaldson. It was suicide. He was depressed. He stepped in front of the truck on purpose."

Campbell hummed for a moment, thinking about it. "It fits, but there isn't a way to prove it."

"It's circumstantial," Zachary agreed. "But…"

"It's not going anywhere. If it was suicide, there's nothing more we can do on *that* front."

Zachary heard the implied "but."

"What did you find out?"

"Looks like we—meaning the feds—have a lead on the stalker's phone. It was a throwaway purchased at a shop in New Hampshire, like you figured. Near the university."

Jonathan Roper.

"It's her boyfriend. Hope Creedy's secret boyfriend. Got to be."

"The distribution pattern is suggestive of a school schedule."

"He would have been meeting with students the rest of the time. He's young, a technology native, probably knows his way around computers. I'm sure there are plenty of people at the university who could help him out if he needed any advice. Maybe even some of the kids he mentored."

"It will take a while for the feds to gather enough evidence to get a warrant on the guy for computer fraud and cyberstalking. They've got to have evidence that he was the one who bought the phone and sent the spyware, and that he was the one who sent the harassing messages."

"What if he happened to confess to a private citizen who happened to record him?"

Campbell chuckled. "That might help law enforcement along a little, if it's legally recorded. You don't know any private citizens who might happen to have a chat with him, do you?"

"I might."

Zachary and Kenzie made the trip back to New Hampshire together. Kenzie seemed to be concerned Zachary might do something impulsive if left to himself, and he couldn't really argue her logic. As he got closer to D-day, he grew more reckless, less likely to take precautions for his own safety. He might not intentionally step in front of a truck as Harding had done, but he might do something less overt, tempting fate, telling himself that if he was meant to die, it would happen anyway.

Kenzie had called Dr. Wiltshire to tell him she was taking a couple of days extra for her holiday, not explaining that it was to babysit Zachary, and promised to be back to work after Christmas to help with the influx of holiday homicides.

Though Kenzie loved to drive her car out on the highway, Zachary insisted on driving his own, needing to be the one in control of the ton of metal hurtling down that interstate.

"We need something less identifiable," he told her. "Yours stands out too much."

"You're just going to go see this guy in his office, aren't you? He's never going to see what we're driving."

"I can't predict what is going to happen. We should take precautions. And yours is too cold. Mine holds the heat better."

Kenzie shrugged irritably and gave in. So Zachary drove, the stereo playing summer songs from his phone rather than the holiday songs on all the radio stations, Zachary pretending that it wasn't snowy and almost Christmas outside the toasty-warm car. Kenzie kept him distracted with interesting stories from the morgue when he wasn't too zoned out to hear them.

They drove directly to the university. Zachary remembered where Roper's office was. He tried out different scripts in his head, trying to determine what approach was most likely to get a confession out of Roper. He didn't have much time to plan, but sometimes the unplanned, reaction-driven conversations were the most effective.

"You really think he'll confess to you?" Kenzie asked.

"With a little nudging… I think so. I didn't have anything to challenge him with before. This time, I have the phone that he bought and I can use the emails against him."

"You can't prove he was the one who sent the emails or bought the phone."

"That doesn't mean I can't tell him I have proof."

They reached Roper's office door.

"You stay here," Zachary advised. "I don't know how long I'll be… but I think he's more likely to confess if it's just me."

He rapped sharply on Roper's door, reached for the handle, and stepped forward smack into the door when the handle didn't turn.

Kenzie snickered. Zachary tried the handle again, as if he might have been wrong the first time and just not turned it hard enough or in the right direction. He turned and looked at Kenzie.

"Locked?" she inquired sweetly.

Zachary knocked a few times on the door, loudly, hoping that Roper was just inside with a student and would open the door to see what the racket was. But everything was quiet. No one came to the door.

"Maybe he's gone for the holidays?" Kenzie suggested.

"Maybe."

There was no schedule or sign up on Roper's door to indicate where he had gone or when he would be back.

With a sigh, Zachary headed back toward the car. Down the hall, a young woman was walking the other direction. She gave Zachary a warm smile.

"Are you looking for Professor Devon?"

Professor Devon. Zachary blinked at her, thrown for a loop. *Professor Devon?* He had done background on each of the people who he interviewed in connection with Hope's death, but he hadn't remembered Devon Masters being identified as a teacher.

He remembered Devon's words when he and Zachary had sat down at the coffee shop. "I like to watch my students." Not *the* students, but *my* students. He was a university professor. But Zachary's initial background had listed Devon as a lawyer. That was why it was important to verify everything.

"I saw you at the coffee shop with him," the young woman confessed. "I memorized your face."

Zachary forced his head to bob up and down in a nod. "Yes, that's right. Could you show me where his office is?"

"Sure. This way."

He followed her through a few turns in the corridor, until they stood in front of a closed door.

Professor Devon Masters, Criminal Investigation.

Posted on his door below the name plate were the class marks for an exam or class. Cyber Investigations.

The girl pointed to one of the top marks. "That's me," she said proudly.

She was a good student, bringing in a ninety-five percent.

"Good job!" Zachary told her. He tried the door handle, but found it locked as well. "Has everyone gone for the holidays?"

"Yeah, pretty much. Just a few of us floating around, getting the last few things done."

"I wonder if he left me a message," Zachary bluffed, taking out his phone as if to check. "I thought he said he would be here." He looked at the number on the door. "Room 232. That's just what he said, isn't it?" he asked Kenzie.

She nodded helpfully. "Yes, 232."

"Huh."

The student hovered, wanting to help, but not sure what she could do.

"He didn't say where he was going, did he?" Zachary prompted. "He didn't mention to you…?"

"No. I saw him at his car. He was loading some boxes into it. But he didn't say where he was off to."

Zachary tapped at his phone. Bluffing, he brought his email up and studied it as if looking for Devon's name among the senders.

His eyes were drawn to the subject of one of the bolded, unread messages.

You're too late, detective.

The email address it had come from was a random string of alphanumeric characters like the ones he had been getting from the cyberstalker.

Kenzie looked down at Zachary's phone when she saw his expression. "Too late for what?"

Zachary's hands started to shake. The criminology student looked at him, concerned.

"Is there something wrong? What is it?"

"Do you have any idea how I can get in touch with Professor Devon?"

"I have his phone number and email address…" she offered tentatively. Of course she would have. He would give all of his students his phone number and email so that they could get in contact with him when they had questions or concerns. When they needed to submit assignments.

While she pulled out her phone to look up the information, Zachary tapped the email message to open it, dread forming a tight knot in his stomach. Kenzie peered over his shoulder.

For the crime of accessory after the fact and harboring a fugitive.

There was a picture below the words. It was a high-resolution image that took a minute to load, signals blocked by all of the brick and concrete in the university walls. Zachary saw a pixelated image to start with, a couple of faces close together, before they resolved into something recognizable. Lorne Peterson and Pat, with an X through Mr. Peterson's face.

Zachary swore. "Back to the car," he told Kenzie urgently.

"Wait," the student stopped them as they turned to hurry back to the parking lot. "Don't you want his number?"

Zachary fumbled with his phone to open up the contact app to add the details. He had to erase and re-key the information again several times before getting it right.

"Thank you. This is really helpful," he told her quickly, and he and Kenzie raced to get back to the car.

Zachary tried to dial and run at the same time. He was sure it would go through to voicemail, but in a moment, he heard a familiar voice.

"Don't tell me you got it already?" Campbell's cheerful voice inquired.

"No. It's not Roper, it's Devon Master. He's in the wind. I have a phone number. You need to get the feds to find him. He's… he's threatened my family."

"What?"

"I'll get Kenzie to forward you the email. But here's the number." Zachary read it out. His voice was cracking. "You can't let him hurt them."

They raced for the car. Zachary's gait was awkward. His heart was pounding hard and he was out of breath. But he pushed through, made it back to the car and jumped in. Zachary passed the phone to Kenzie when they were both in. Kenzie said a few more words to Campbell and promised to send him the email, then hung up.

"Seatbelt," Zachary told her as he pulled his across his body and snapped the buckle into place, getting the car started out almost out of the stall by the time he was done.

"I will," Kenzie said irritably, "let me just forward this first."

"No. We're going to be moving fast."

Kenzie looked at him, and seeing his face, didn't argue any further but put the phone down for a second to get her seatbelt on. Zachary hit the gas. She hung on to the door for a moment as he accelerated and rocketed around a corner.

"Sheesh! Where did you learn to drive like that?"

"This is nothing. Wait until we get to the highway."

Kenzie shook her head. She tried to hold the phone steady in front of her face while she forwarded all of the pertinent information on to Campbell.

"Where are we going?"

"To make sure they're safe."

"But Devon's ahead of you. Maybe by an hour or two."

"Or maybe not. I don't plan on him being ahead of me by the time we get there."

He made sure the Bluetooth was connected and told the in-car system to dial Lorne Peterson. It went to voicemail.

"Lorne. It's Zachary. Call me back right away. It's urgent."

He tried calling Pat, but with the same results.

"Give those numbers to Campbell. Have them located too. We need to know where they are. Devon might already have them." His heart pounded so hard he felt like he was going to have a heart attack. Surely Devon wouldn't hurt an innocent person. He pressed the gas pedal down farther, swerving around slower-moving vehicles and getting angry honks in response.

"You don't think they're at home? They might just be occupied."

"They'd answer. Mr. Peterson knows... about Christmas. He wouldn't ignore a call from me this time of year."

"Okay." Kenzie complied with his order, calling Campbell back again to give him the two numbers to track. Zachary couldn't hear what Campbell was saying back to Kenzie, but she cut her eyes toward Zachary, and said, "We're on our way there making due haste... let me know as soon as you locate them, and we'll adjust our course if they're somewhere else." She held on to the door as they careened down the exit ramp to the interstate. "You're going to get pulled over for speeding, Zach!"

"They'll have to catch me first."

But he took her point. Getting stopped by the police was the last thing he needed. It would take time for Campbell to get what he needed from the FBI. Zachary didn't know how long it would take for them to figure out where Devon and Mr. Peterson and Pat were. He eased his foot off of the gas and let the car slow to the speed of traffic. As usual, the flow of traffic was somewhat over the speed limit, but not fast enough to soothe his nerves. He pressed the gas again, until he was going just fast enough to overtake the cars in front of him and pass them, but not fast enough for anyone to take notice and call 9-1-1 with reports of some crazy driver speeding down the highway at a breakneck pace. Kenzie settled back into her seat, blowing her breath out through pursed lips, like a whistle.

"You don't think he'd really do anything to Lorne, do you? He didn't kill Harding, just sent him messages. I think that words are his only weapon. He's trying to drive you crazy with worry, but he wouldn't actually do anything."

Zachary bit the inside of his cheek. He couldn't point to anything that suggested that Devon was a violent person. He wasn't the one who had been driving the night Hope was killed. He hadn't, as far as they knew, done anything physically violent toward Harding. He hadn't been the truck driver and hadn't hired Donaldson to do his dirty work.

There was nothing wrong with Kenzie's logic. Devon was a university professor. Not a killer. He could have been going home for the holidays, like everyone else. His taunt to Zachary could have just been hot air, intended to goad Zachary into doing something stupid like getting into a crash on the interstate or humiliating himself in front of someone he loved. Just a bluff to see how far he could push Zachary.

"I don't know. There's no way to know, so I have to assume it's true."

"I agree," Kenzie said, "I know you have to do something; I'm just saying, he probably won't actually do anything. We probably don't really have to worry."

Zachary nodded. She might be able to choose not to be worried, but he certainly couldn't. His heart was pounding as hard as if Devon were holding a knife to Mr. Peterson's throat. What if he got to their house and found them dead? What if Zachary were responsible for destroying the one long-term relationship he had managed to maintain?

He tasted blood and didn't care, switching to chewing the cheek on the other side instead. He stayed focused on the road, carefully snaking his way through the traffic, doing the best he could to get to his friends before anything could happen to them.

His phone rang. Kenzie answered it rather than letting him take it on Bluetooth, probably figuring he had enough to concentrate on with his driving. She spoke few words, mostly listening to what Campbell had to report, then hung up.

"What did he find out?" Zachary asked, when Kenzie sat there without a word to him.

"They're still working on it."

He navigated around a slower-moving SUV. "They couldn't get a location?"

"Apparently, his phone is turned off. So they only have his call history to go by, and his most recent calls were made from the university."

"We already know he's not there. What about Mr. Peterson? Where is he?"

"Campbell is still trying to talk them into tracking his phone. They're being cautious, not convinced there is any real danger to Lorne and Pat."

"Can't they track them anyway? Just to make sure they're safe?"

Kenzie shook her head. "Apparently not. Privacy concerns. Campbell's working on it. I think he'll convince them sooner or later. He just hasn't yet."

Zachary thumped the steering wheel with the heel of his hand, frustrated.

Kenzie didn't say anything else, but she took a sidelong look at him that communicated she was holding something back. Zachary gripped the steering wheel, breathing slowly.

"What else?"

She didn't answer.

"Kenzie. What else did he say?"

"I don't think I should get you any more upset while you're driving. You have enough to focus on."

"Holding something back is going to distract me more than telling me what it is. I need to know everything Campbell found out."

"Zachary…"

"Tell me."

Kenzie rested her head back against the headrest, giving in. "He has a concealed carry permit."

Zachary felt sick. It took all of his willpower not to stamp the gas pedal to the floor. It would do Mr. Peterson no good if he ended up having an accident or getting pulled over because he was driving recklessly. Kenzie was watching him, waiting for him to explode or melt down. Eventually, she looked away. Neither of them said anything about what it meant. So much for Kenzie's evaluation that Devon wouldn't do anything violent. Mr. Peterson didn't carry a gun. Zachary didn't carry a gun. They were going to rush into a confrontation where the only one with a gun would be Devon. Zachary had no idea how they were going to handle it.

Campbell would make sure they had police and FBI backup as soon as they located Lorne and Pat. Now that they knew Devon was likely to be armed, they wouldn't fool around.

But that wasn't true, because even knowing that Devon had a permit for a concealed weapon, they were still reluctant to track the phones of two citizens who might be in danger.

With anxiety and anger burning a hole in his stomach, Zachary narrowed his focus to a fine point. He could do only one thing, and that was to get to Lorne.

2 5

He didn't even hear Kenzie talking on the phone again. He was so narrowly focused on driving, shutting the rest of the world out, that it took Kenzie's persistent nudging and calling him to get his attention.

Zachary startled and glanced over at her. "What? What is it?"

"They tracked Lorne's and Pat's phones. They're okay, Zachary, they're just not at home."

He found he could barely breathe for a minute or two, like he'd been kicked in the gut and had the wind knocked out of him. He rubbed his eyes.

"Really? You're sure?"

"They're at some kind of spa. Probably one of these places where they have a rule about leaving their phones in their lockers so that they can relax properly."

"Someone talked to them?"

"No, just located the phones. If they're not at home, they're not in danger, Zachary. We'll just keep calling them, and we'll warn them when they answer. We'll tell them not to go home until Devon is found."

"We have to go there. Can't the FBI send someone just in case?"

"There's no danger. They won't waste the manpower."

"What about Campbell? He believes me, doesn't he? This guy's got a gun."

"But Devon doesn't know where Pat and Lorne are. They're safe where they are."

Zachary glanced over at Kenzie. She really believed it. She wasn't just trying to calm his anxiety, she truly believed they were safe.

"Didn't you see the paper on his door? Cyber Investigations. You know what that is, don't you?"

She sighed in exasperation. "Yes, of course I do. Computer research. Online and all that."

"And using other technology. Like the spyware on Ashley's phone and computer."

"Right."

"Don't you think he could tell exactly where Ashley's phone was once he had the spyware on it?"

Kenzie's irritation changed into uncertainty. She frowned. "Well... I suppose. But how would he have gotten something onto Lorne's or Pat's phone?"

"The same way as he got it onto Ashley's. Send them something that looks legitimate and wait for them to open it."

"But how would he even know their phone number or email address to send it to them?"

"How did he know Ashley's?"

Kenzie was stumped. She looked for a way to argue his logic.

"Did you get the name and address of the spa?"

"I got the name. Let me look it up."

She used his phone to look up the address and directions. "There's an exit in a couple of miles. We're about half an hour away."

That was better than Zachary had hoped. The spa was closer than Mr. Peterson's house, instead of farther away. For once, things were working in his favor.

"Can Campbell send someone? Just in case?"

"It's out of his jurisdiction."

Of course it was. Zachary knew that. "And he can't talk to the local police department? Or get the FBI to send someone?"

Kenzie bit her lip. "I'll see... but don't count on it."

She wiggled her own phone out of her pocket instead of using

Zachary's, which still had the GPS program running to direct him to the spa. Zachary listened to the half-conversation, Kenzie presenting his arguments and pushing for them to please send someone, anyone, who had some authority and could back them up.

When she hung up, she wiped her arm across her forehead. Zachary turned the car heater down, though he knew that wasn't why she was sweating.

"Well...?"

"He's going to make some calls, see what he can do."

"He's never going to get someone out there in time."

Kenzie shook her head. "Probably not. But hopefully, he doesn't need to. We're assuming an awful lot. That it was Devon and not the boyfriend. That he would actually approach Lorne. That he would do him any harm. We don't have any proof, just conjecture."

"We'll have proof when we see him."

"He won't be there."

"Then why are you nervous?"

She looked like she was going to try to argue that she wasn't nervous, then abandoned that plan. "Okay. I'm nervous because of the possibility. I'm nervous because you are so sure. But I don't really *think* he'll be there."

Zachary nodded and followed the instructions of his phone GPS. It wasn't smart, walking in there unarmed against a possibly armed threat. Maybe there would be security guards who could help. Maybe an off-duty police officer there with his wife for a little pre-Christmas cleanse. A spa just wasn't the sort of place that a person took a gun to.

"It will be okay," Kenzie assured Zachary as they pulled into the parking lot and scanned around it for any sign of disruption or trouble. It was, Zachary thought, more to reassure herself than him. He already knew it wasn't going to be okay. Things didn't turn out okay in his life. He ended up burning down houses, getting electrocuted, or putting friends in danger.

There was no sign of trouble. If Devon was there, he hadn't driven his car up onto the sidewalk or left it parked in a driving lane. If he was there, he had parked it neatly in its slot and walked in, acting as if nothing was wrong.

Zachary also parked his car, though he picked a handicapped parking slot right in front of the building. He knew it was wrong, but if Pat's and Lorne's lives hung in the balance, he wasn't going to waste time parking farther away in a legitimate space. He got out of the car, wiping his hands on his pants. The cold air was a shock, but a welcome one. It sharpened his senses and helped to wake him up. His adrenaline had been running too long to be effective anymore. It had sapped his energy while sitting in the car, unable to use it constructively.

They walked into a warm, humid lobby that was full of light, green plants, and trickling waterfalls. A complete change from the frigid weather outside. Zachary took a second to acclimatize himself, looking around to be sure that Devon was nowhere to be seen, and then walked up to the smiling, fresh-faced blond woman at the reception desk.

"Hi," he forced a smile that he hoped was at least a shade as warm as hers. "I'm supposed to be meeting my friends here. I don't know if they'll be finished yet. Lorne Peterson?"

"Oh, yes." She gave him another smile, as if she had been expecting him. "Let me just see…"

She tapped the keys of her computer. Zachary looked around, taking a few calming breaths. It was a peaceful, relaxing place. No indication of any threat. Maybe he could relax.

"It looks like they should be finished with their treatments," the receptionist told him. "So they're probably at the juice bar." She pointed a tapered index finger to a set of glass doors. "Just through there, and follow the blue signs."

Zachary looked at Kenzie. She smiled back, clearly comforted by their surroundings. But Zachary didn't like it. The place was wide open. Anyone could walk in. There was no security, no attempt made to screen visitors.

"Let's go." He clutched at Kenzie's elbow and walked more quickly than was comfortable. Since the car accident of a year ago, his physiotherapist had mostly focused on walking, but walking faster than his normal pace felt awkward and out of sync. He scanned the signs as they moved through the broad, brightly-lit halls with inspiring words painted on them and gorgeous landscapes on display.

"Nice place," Kenzie commented, as if they were there on a tour.

"Yeah."

They eventually made it to the juice bar. Spacious and well-lit, just like the rest of the facility. Zachary bypassed the service counter and looked around at the tables for his former foster father. They were almost safe. They were almost to the end of the journey.

With relief, he saw Lorne and Pat sitting at a table by the patio. They were partially blocked from view by a waiter with his back to them. Zachary hurried across the room toward them. The waiter turned slightly and Zachary saw his profile.

It was Devon.

26

Z achary swore. His foot slipped on the tiled floor, and the resulting lurch as he caught his balance attracted the attention of Mr. Peterson. When he focused on Zachary coming across the room toward them, Pat and Devon both followed his gaze.

"You can stop right there," Devon warned.

Zachary did. Devon stood with one hand in the large pocket of the apron he was wearing. He must have taken it off of a hook or a shelf on his arrival in order to blend in while he watched for Mr. Peterson and Pat. It was impossible to tell whether there was anything in the apron pocket, or whether the threat was only implied.

"Zachary?" Mr. Peterson said, "What's going on?"

Zachary bit his lip. Keeping his eyes on the three of them, he tried to scope out the room peripherally. There were too many people there, coming and going. But he hadn't seen any kind of security staff. No one appeared to be aware that anything untoward was going on. Would Devon dare to do something around so many other people? There was a big difference between sending someone bullying emails from an anonymous address and overtly committing violence in full view of a dozen people.

"Kenzie," Zachary murmured, very low so that only she would be able to hear him, trying not to move his lips as he spoke. "Get cops here *now.*"

She gave no sign of having heard him, fiddling with her phone and then turning around to look at the densely written columns of ingredients over the juice bar.

"This is a pretty cool place," she said. "Really relaxing atmosphere. We should come back here, you know? I should ask them about packages. You should ask Pat and Lorne which package they got."

He wasn't sure whether she really didn't understand the danger they were in, or was just acting for Devon's sake. But he couldn't repeat the instruction and draw attention to it. He kept his gaze trained on Devon.

"I don't understand why you're doing this. Explain to me... why you are even here. Mr. Peterson never did anything wrong."

"You're the one who needs to be punished. You're the one who thought he could get away with it without having to pay the piper," Devon growled.

"Get away with what? I'm not the one who killed Hope."

"Not that. This isn't about Hope. This is about you, burning down the house, putting all of those people in danger. They could have all died in the house because you were so stupid and reckless. Society has to weed out people like you. You shouldn't be allowed to hurt other people with your stupidity."

Zachary resisted the flashbacks. He had to stay present to help Mr. Peterson. He couldn't let Devon and the memories sweep him away.

"What does that have to do with Mr. Peterson? If you want to punish me for what I did, then punish me. Not him. I didn't even meet him until after that."

"He took you in. Instead of letting you rot in some institution somewhere, he was an accessory. He sheltered you and kept you from having to pay for what you had done."

Mr. Peterson sat there with his mouth open, shock on his features.

Devon sneered at him. "People who protect murderers and arsonists should be thrown in prison themselves. They should have to pay the price!"

Mr. Peterson closed his mouth, still staring at Devon. "Zachary wasn't a murderer or arsonist," he finally said. His voice was quiet and even, his most soothing, calming voice. Used to calm dozens of foster kids over the years. Used to calm Zachary himself during the weeks he had lived there and when he had returned for help over the years as a troubled child, panicked teen, and confused adult, always trying to escape a past he could never forget. "He was a scared child in need of a home. I was sorry he wasn't able

917

to stay with us for longer, but he turned out to be more than we were able to handle."

"He should never have been in foster care. Don't you know what he did? He ruined their lives! All of their lives!"

"No. He made a mistake that he's paid for a hundred times over. Are you…" Mr. Peterson looked at Zachary and mouthed the words, asking Zachary rather than Devon, "your brother?"

Zachary gave a tiny shake of his head. He wished he could explain to Mr. Peterson more clearly what was going on, but he wasn't sure what would set Devon off. He needed to understand what was going on in Devon's head, but he couldn't quite wrap his mind around it.

"Are you friends with Zachary? I don't understand how he hurt you."

"People like him ruin lives. They ruin the lives of everyone around them."

"Like Brandon?" Zachary asked. "Is that what you mean? Brandon ruined your life when he hit Hope? He prejudiced people against you and treated you like it was your fault?"

Devon nodded his agreement. "He killed Hope and he messed up our lives forever. He should have just killed himself."

"He did."

"Not until it was too late. He should have done it long before then. People who do things like that should die. Why are they allowed to pollute our population? They should *all* die."

"You can't kill everyone who makes a stupid choice," Mr. Peterson pointed out. "Everyone makes stupid choices at some point."

"It wasn't my fault!" Devon protested, his voice going up a note. "It wasn't Fulton's or Kyle's fault. It was Brandon's. You can't paint us all with the same brush!"

"I didn't say it was your fault." Mr. Peterson considered for a moment. "But maybe you're feeling guilty about it."

The light went on in Zachary's brain and he knew Mr. Peterson had hit the nail on the head.

"Maybe you feel like you should have been punished for what happened," Zachary said. "Maybe you feel like you never had to pay for your mistakes, and it's eaten away at you all of these years. You went into law, hoping to bring criminals to justice, but it didn't make you feel better the way you expected it to, and all you ever saw was your own guilt."

"For what? Because we rode with him? Because we were drinking and he wasn't supposed to? How could we control that?"

"You call a cab," Mr. Peterson said. "You take away his keys. You make sure everyone gets home safely."

"He didn't seem drunk. He only had a couple of beers. He wasn't staggering or slurring. They called it a DUI, but he wasn't drunk. He'd barely had anything."

"You still shouldn't have let your designated driver have anything," Zachary pointed out. "When you saw him drinking, you should have made new plans."

"I didn't remember anything afterward. I don't know if I saw him drinking. I don't remember him drinking." Devon gave a little shake of his head. His eyes were haunted.

"You said that other nights, you had egged him on. Encouraged him to speed or stunt."

"Not *that* night."

"You can't remember. Or was that a lie? Are you just afraid to tell anyone the truth about what really happened that night?"

"Brandon was driving!" Devon's hand moved in his apron pocket. "He's the only one who is responsible for what happened!"

Zachary took a tentative step forward, seeing if he could close the distance between them. "You feel awful about what happened. Whatever it was, you are sorry. You feel the guilt all the time, weighing down on you." Zachary knew what that felt like. "It's there all the time and you just want it to go away. You'd do anything to make it go away."

A nod from Devon. Zachary took a couple more slow steps forward. "You want it to end. You want someone to stop the pain. You think that maybe if you were punished properly, it would go away."

"I wasn't at fault," Devon whined. But Zachary knew better. Criminally liable or not, Devon was still guilty. He had taken that on himself. It wasn't something that any outside force could wipe away.

"You wanted Brandon to pay. You thought that if he had to pay more, you would feel better. Justice would be served."

Devon looked at him, his expression frozen.

"But when Brandon killed himself, you didn't feel better, you felt worse."

"It was his choice. I never touched him. We weren't even in the same state. I'm not responsible for him killing himself."

He had stalked and bullied Brandon relentlessly. Brandon had served his time. He had a new name and a new relationship. He had been on the way to healing and a new life. But Devon had refused to let him off. What Devon had done contributed to Brandon's death, as surely as if he'd put a gun into his hand and then badgered him to use it.

"You felt so guilty over what you had done to Brandon, you needed a new target. You needed someone else you could blame for what you were feeling. You wanted to punish someone else, but you're the one you think needs to be punished."

Zachary was almost within arm's reach of Devon. Devon startled suddenly, jamming his hand deeper into the apron pocket. "Stop it. Stay there. Don't you say another word."

Zachary swallowed. He had almost been there. He had almost reached Devon both physically and emotionally. He looked at Mr. Peterson, not knowing what to do. He couldn't open his mouth again without endangering their lives.

"Have a seat," Mr. Peterson invited. "It's been a long day. Why don't you have a drink?" He nudged his own drink toward Devon. "I haven't even touched it. Pat's always trying to get me to eat healthier, but I'm really just not a wheatgrass kind of guy."

Devon looked at the cup. Zachary wasn't sure he was even seeing it.

"You need to let it go," Lorne continued softly. "You've been holding onto this for too long. Hanging on to pain doesn't help anything. It festers and gets deeper over time. You need to forgive yourself. You and Brandon didn't intend to kill anyone that night. It was a horrible mistake. But hanging on to it all this time hasn't made things better."

Devon put his hands on the back of one of the other chairs at the table, hesitating about whether to pull it out.

"You can forgive yourself and let it go. Just let the guilt and the pain go. You were young and you made a choice that would impact your life forever. You couldn't have known how it was going to turn out."

Zachary eyed Devon's apron and the big pocket he had taken his hand out of. Did he have the gun or not? If Zachary tackled him, was he fast enough and skilled enough to get the gun away from Devon? Without hurting anyone else? The wrong choice could have an impact on both of their lives, just like the fire and Brandon's MVC. Make the wrong choice, and someone in the room could be dead.

"Sit down," Mr. Peterson coaxed. "Come tell me about it."

Devon drew the chair out. Zachary took another step closer while Devon was looking away from him. Devon looked back, but didn't catch Zachary moving. He hesitated for a moment before lowering himself into the chair. In his new position, Zachary could see down into the gaping pocket. He could see the gleam of the pistol inside.

27

Zachary swallowed, mouth as dry as cotton. He must have made some change in expression that Mr. Peterson caught. He looked at Zachary for a moment, then focused all of his attention on the young man who sat across from him. Elbows on the table, Devon covered his eyes and cradled his head.

"How could anyone forgive me?" he demanded in a choked voice. "I can't forgive myself, how could anyone else? That girl died. I saw her family in court every day. Her parents and her little brother and sister. They had to grow up without her. I knew I was responsible for what happened to her. I had to take some of the responsibility."

"It takes time, but don't you think it will be easier to forgive yourself than it has been to beat up on yourself all of these years?"

It was like Mr. Peterson was speaking to Zachary. They rarely spoken of the fire and Zachary's part in it. Mr. Peterson knew what the social worker had told him before bringing Zachary to them, and little else. But Mr. Peterson knew how guilty Zachary felt. He knew the pain that Zachary carried around with him and how he beat up on himself. Zachary had no idea how to begin to forgive himself. He didn't deserve forgiveness.

There was a buzz in his pocket. Zachary had picked up his phone and put it back in his pocket as he got out of the car. He stayed still, moving only his eyes to look around. Where was Kenzie? Had she managed to talk the police into getting them some backup? Kenzie was right at the edge of his vision. When his eyes met hers, she made a small motion, tapping her own pocket, then indicating Devon with her eyes.

Zachary curled up the pinky and fourth finger of the hand that Kenzie could see hanging at his side, forming a gun shape with his index and middle finger and thumb.

Her eyebrows went up. *Are you sure?* Zachary gave a nod, just a fraction of an inch.

Kenzie moved silently out of Zachary's vision, too far back for him to see.

"You need help. You need to talk to someone," Mr. Peterson told Devon. "A licensed therapist would be better, but since I'm the only one here, why don't you tell me what happened?"

Devon rubbed his eyes. He started to talk, telling Mr. Peterson the now-familiar story of the hit and run. Zachary looked down at the gun in Devon's pocket. While he'd learned some pickpocketing, figuring it was a useful skill for an investigator to have from time to time, he hadn't practiced enough to become skilled at it. The gun was heavy and Devon was likely to notice a shift in its weight if Zachary lifted it.

He caught a glimpse of Kenzie again, approaching an older couple several tables away and speaking to them quietly. They got up and moved out of Zachary's vision, toward the door they had come in. Zachary turned his head toward her. She gave him a tiny motion. *Back up.* Zachary slid one foot back, then the other, as silently and slowly as possible. Devon didn't take his head out of his hands to see what was going on.

A dark figure slid by Kenzie like a ghost. A black-uniformed cop. He crouched down behind the table Kenzie had just vacated. She moved back the direction she had come. The cop had everyone's attention but Devon's. He made a motion to indicate Mr. Peterson and Pat, and pointed to the floor. *Get down.* He held up three fingers, then two, then one.

Mr. Peterson wasn't as spry as he had once been, but getting down was easier than getting up, and Zachary was surprised at how quickly the two men hit the floor.

"Devon Masters!" an authoritative voice boomed.

Devon dropped his hands from his face and looked around, pale and wide-eyed. His face was wet with tears.

"Put your hands on your head!"

He didn't obey immediately. His hands hovered as he tried to decide whether to go for the gun. Zachary was still close enough to grab him. If Devon went for the gun, Zachary could grab him, wrestle and hold on to him until the cops could get close enough to get the gun away from him and get him under control.

Then Devon did the smart thing and put his hands on his head. Zachary breathed a sigh of relief. He made a motion toward Devon's apron pocket. "Do you want me to—"

"Just stay where you are, Goldman," the voice barked. "Don't move."

Zachary froze. He looked at the cop that he could see, sheltering behind a table, gun trained on Devon. He didn't know how many others there were behind him and around the room. He didn't want to step into the line of fire, so he stayed where he was, as motionless as possible.

"Masters, lace your fingers together!"

Devon did as he was told. In another moment, he was stretched out on the floor, belly down, as he was instructed. Finally, the police moved in, securing his hands and removing the gun.

"I have a permit," Devon protested. "You don't have any cause to arrest me or to take my gun. I'll sue you for false arrest."

"We're responding to a call placed by a citizen. We'll get all of the pertinent details now. If there's no evidence of wrongdoing, you'll be allowed to go," the officer who handcuffed him said reasonably.

He was removed from the room to be interviewed separately from the witnesses. The cop who appeared to be in charge turned to Zachary.

"You're Zachary Goldman?"

"Yes."

"Mind if I check you for weapons?"

Zachary raised his hands. "I don't carry."

They patted him down just to be sure. At the cop's request, Zachary showed him the email message from Devon with Mr. Peterson's face x-ed out. The cop compared it to Mr. Peterson's face when he'd managed to get up from the hard tiled floor and back into a chair.

"Well, that's the first spa day I've ever had end that way," he said cheerfully.

"It's your first spa day ever," Pat pointed out.

Zachary grimaced, thinking about how it could have been Lorne's first and last spa day, if things had gone differently. He slid into the chair that

Devon had vacated, across from his ex-foster father and longtime friend. It wasn't until then that he realized how much his legs were shaking.

"You're okay?" Zachary asked Mr. Peterson.

"The old ticker is apparently still working." He was all smiles, as if the whole thing had been nothing more than an interesting diversion.

"What did he say to you before I got here?" Zachary asked. "Did he threaten you?"

"He wasn't here much before you. Said he recognized me, was I Lorne Peterson, did I used to take in foster kids. I was trying to figure out if he was one of ours, but the face didn't seem familiar. I take it... this is the guy who was emailing you? Harassing you?"

Zachary nodded. "Yeah, I guess so."

"But he's not your brother."

"No." Zachary frowned, looking in the direction they had taken Devon. "So... where did he get the picture?"

"Maybe from the photographer. I don't know how he would track it down, but..."

"He was teaching criminal investigation at the university, so he's had some experience... and with a concealed carry permit, maybe he's been a private investigator. I ran an initial background on him, but I thought he was just a lawyer."

"If he's been an investigator himself, he knows how to cover his tracks. Do you remember where that picture of your family was taken?"

Zachary steadied himself on the table. Thinking back was dangerous. It could open a whole floodgate of memories that would quickly whirl out of his control. He tried to keep narrowly focused on the night of the Christmas party and not let his mind slip to Christmas Eve, a few nights later.

"I think it was a company Christmas party. For my dad's work."

"They might have kept a historical archive of some kind."

Zachary nodded. "Yeah... I guess they must have."

He'd never gone looking himself. If he had, maybe he'd already have had that picture. Maybe others. Maybe even social network pictures his siblings had posted of their growing-up years, so he could find out how they had done and whether their lives had been as traumatic has his, or whether they'd had good lives and grown up happy in stable foster homes.

"That was really amazing," Pat told Mr. Peterson. "I've always known you could talk to anyone, but it was really something to see you connecting with him." He smiled proudly.

"I dealt with a lot of damaged kids when we were fostering." Mr. Peterson met Zachary's eyes and gave a sad smile. "Deep down, they all want the same thing."

Zachary tried to swallow the lump in his throat. Mr. Peterson had been the one constant through his rocky growing-up years. The one place he could go for acceptance and a shared interest. When he was with Mr. Peterson, he wasn't a broken kid anymore. He was a photographer. A friend. Mr. Peterson was someone he didn't have to prove anything to or be anyone but who he was.

"You were sad when you had to stop fostering," he said. "You should get back into it... or Boys and Girls Club or another organization that mentors kids. You're so good at it."

"Unfortunately... I still don't think we're to the point where gay men are accepted in organizations with access to children. Even an old guy like me is still seen as a potential pedophile, just looking for my next victim."

Anger flared in Zachary's chest. He'd experienced his share of predators in foster homes and institutions, but Mr. Peterson had never been like that. "That's not fair. You're really good with kids and you'd never hurt one of them."

"In today's world, even a pat on the back is interpreted as a sexual advance. You're not allowed to touch kids. Hugs are out of the question. Kids with disrupted lives *need* physical touch and reassurance, but they're barred from getting it."

Kenzie was allowed to join them at the table. There were still police everywhere, but without any actual drama going on, the other spa customers and employees were going back to their own conversations.

"Hey," Kenzie smiled. "Everyone okay?"

"Kenzie," Zachary motioned for her to sit in the fourth chair. "This is Lorne and Pat."

Everyone nodded and exchanged handshakes.

"I've heard so much about you," Kenzie said. "I'm glad to finally meet you."

Mr. Peterson smiled. "I could say the same. Good to actually meet one of Zachary's friends."

Zachary's face heated. While Mr. Peterson had always made it clear he was welcome to bring anyone along with him on visits, Zachary never had. Except for Bridget. Lorne had met Bridget at the wedding, and there had been one or two visits in the time they'd been married. But in spite of Bridget being polite and friendly to his surrogate father, Zachary hadn't felt comfortable mixing those two lives.

"So..." Pat looked at Zachary and Kenzie, his brows down slightly. "How did you two happen to come here? For that matter, how did your friend know that we would be here? It wasn't just chance, was it?"

Zachary scratched his ear. "Uh... no." He turned his phone back on and slid it over to the space on the table between Pat and Mr. Peterson so they could both see the threatening email with Mr. Peterson's face crossed out.

Pat shook his head. "He's more than a little unbalanced. How does he know you? And I still don't understand how either of you knew where we were."

"Zachary *is* a private investigator," Mr. Peterson pointed out.

"We had help. When I got this," Zachary gestured to the phone, "and I couldn't get ahold of you, we got the police and FBI involved. Kenzie managed to convince them to track your phone locations. I'm sorry. I was worried he might have already done something... that you might be in real danger."

"Don't apologize," Mr. Peterson said, smiling and shaking his head. "You didn't do anything wrong."

"I invaded your privacy..."

"You did the right thing," he said firmly. "Pat's not accusing you of doing anything wrong."

Pat shook his head. "Just trying to understand how it all went down. I'm pretty good with technology, but I don't understand how someone goes from being a cyberbully to actually finding us in real life. When we're somewhere like this, away from home. You went through the police, with legitimate concerns, but that's obviously not what he did."

"Did either of you get any strange emails or texts recently? Something with an attachment?"

They looked at each other.

"No, I don't think so," Mr. Peterson said. "The most unusual thing I got recently was that new social networking site you sent me."

Zachary shook his head. "I didn't send you anything."

"It was some professional referrals network. 'Click here if you would recommend Zachary Goldman Investigations.' So I did, of course."

"Well... thank you... but I didn't send that and I haven't joined any networking sites lately. That must have been it. You clicked on the link, and it installed a tracking program on your phone. Told Devon exactly where to find you at any time."

"They can do that?" Mr. Peterson sat back in his chair, shaking his head. "Well. Isn't that something."

"I'm so sorry he targeted you. I never thought that anyone would ever try to use you to get to me."

"Not to worry. No harm done." The man shrugged.

"But he came here to punish you. He brought his gun. He wanted to hurt you."

"Maybe, but deep down, I don't think he could. He couldn't make the leap from anonymous bullying to actually meting out punishment face-to-face."

"He killed Richard Harding."

"Physically? Face-to-face?"

"Well... no. Bullied him until he committed suicide."

Mr. Peterson made a gesture that indicated Zachary had just confirmed his point.

The cop in charge approached the table. His name bar said Buck, and he had heavy jowls like a bulldog.

"I need a little move information from you folks, if I could." Though his words were deferential, his manner was aggressive. Clearly indicating he was in charge. They all nodded they would cooperate.

"When Devon approached you," he directed the question to Pat and Mr. Peterson, "did he threaten you? Did he tell you he had a weapon on him?"

Mr. Peterson shook his head. "No, he never made any threats. I didn't know there was any danger until I saw Zachary's reaction to him. When he said to stop, and Zachary froze there... I knew this wasn't just an old foster kid trying to reconnect."

"And to you?" Buck looked at Zachary. "Did he tell you he had a gun? Did he tell you he was going to shoot someone?"

"No. Just the email I showed you, with Mr. Peterson's face crossed out. I found out when I talked to the police that he had a concealed carry permit, and when I got here and he confronted me, he had his hand in the apron pocket, where the gun was."

"But he didn't tell you he was going to shoot or hold you at gunpoint."

"No. But he's involved in a homicide in Vermont. A man he was harassing online."

"He was involved how?"

"He was stalking him and sending him harassing emails, telling him that he should kill himself... until he eventually did."

"Well, that's not exactly homicide, is it?"

Zachary opened his mouth to argue, then closed it again. He looked at Kenzie. She was obviously reading the same thing in Buck's manner as Zachary—that as far as he was concerned, Devon hadn't broken the law.

"He's been stalking me too. Sending harassing emails and messages... telling me that I should die..."

"Anything related to stalking, you'll need to take that up with the police in your jurisdiction, which I understand is Vermont...?'"

"Yes."

"File with the local police. Because it's a cross-border thing, they'll get the FBI involved, and they'll decide whether any laws have been broken."

"He threatened to kill Lorne. I showed you the email."

"It's ambiguous. It doesn't actually say he's going to do anything. I doubt it would ever hold up in court as a death threat."

Zachary swallowed. "You're not going to arrest him for anything?"

"I don't see anything I *can* arrest him for. The fact that we've detained him will be enough for him to launch a suit against us already. It wouldn't go anywhere, but it would be an annoyance."

Zachary looked at Kenzie. He looked at Mr. Peterson and Pat. No one had anything to offer. Kenzie gave a shrug and shook her head.

"I don't know, Zachary. We can call Campbell, but... I can't think of anything else we can do."

"So he stalks my—my—friend, threatens to kill him, brings a gun, and it isn't anything? There's nothing to charge him with? He can just go?"

"They're going to let him go. Let's take some time to relax and calm down, and then we'll call Campbell and see if there is anything he can do. Okay?"

Zachary buried his face in his hands, unable to let them see his fury and grief at the injustice of it.

For a while he just swam in the darkness, the quiet conversation of the others going on around him.

When he finally got control of himself and pulled his hands away from his face, determined to remain cool and aloof, Buck was gone. All of the police were gone. Pat's and Mr. Peterson's drinks were finished. Kenzie sat with one foot up on her chair, knee bent. She turned her head to look at him, but didn't say anything or make a big deal of his meltdown.

After a while, Zachary cleared his throat. "Guess we should be getting on our way. We've probably already kept you here longer than you meant to be."

Mr. Peterson shrugged, looking around at their surroundings. "It's a nice peaceful place—at least most of the time we were here. It's not exactly a hardship."

"I never pictured you as a spa sort of guy." Even in his drained emotional state, Zachary couldn't help the little tug at the corner of his mouth. Mr. Peterson had never had the exaggerated effeminate mannerisms popularized by gay characters on television.

"It took some talking to get him to agree," Pat advised. "But I told him this was what I wanted for Christmas and I finally managed to talk him into it."

"It was actually okay, though." Mr. Peterson put his hand over Pat's on the table briefly. "Next time you won't have to work quite so hard to convince me."

"I hope not. Though, don't expect the floor show next time."

They both laughed. Zachary wasn't quite up to seeing the humor in the situation. He shook his head, worrying it over in his mind. If the police wouldn't arrest Devon, how could Zachary ever be sure that the people around him would be safe?

"Zachary, why don't you and Kenzie come back to the house for supper? It's much closer than going home," Pat suggested.

"I wouldn't want to put you out."

"It's not. We'll put a couple of frozen pizzas in the oven and use disposable plates. No fuss. Give you some time to relax and recover."

"That sounds good," Kenzie agreed. She nodded to Zachary to

encourage him to accept the invitation. "I don't want you driving all the way back yet. You must be exhausted, I know I am."

Zachary's body ached from holding every muscle tense and his brain felt wrung out. He could drive, but maybe it wasn't the best idea. If he had something to eat and some more time to relax before going any distance, that might be better.

"You really want to eat something like pizza after a spa day?" he asked. "Isn't the whole point to cleanse your systems or detox or whatever? Are you allowed to eat pizza?"

"We're allowed," Mr. Peterson said, so firmly it made them all laugh. He might give in to going to the spa at his partner's insistence, but he wasn't giving up his pizza.

"It's settled, then," Pat said. He glanced toward the juice bar. "You need something to boost your blood sugar before hitting the road, Zachary?"

28

The three of them talked Zachary into a strawberry mango smoothie to replenish the calories he had burned off with the adrenaline-fueled rush to get there and facing down his opponent over a gun. Zachary put it into the cupholder in his car and sipped it occasionally along the way. He wasn't hungry, but it was sweet and refreshing and everybody insisted he needed something. Zachary hadn't heard what was in the dark purple concoction Kenzie had chosen, but she seemed to enjoy it. It was all gone before they reached Mr. Peterson's house.

Kenzie looked over the brick bungalow and smiled. "What a nice little place. It suits them."

"You should see it during the spring when the flowers are out. Pat has pink tulips in the borders."

"That's great. They're a really nice couple, I can see why you get along so well."

Pizza suited everyone. Mr. Peterson, Pat, and Kenzie seemed to be completely relaxed and unworried, not even thinking about Devon, but Zachary found himself unable to sit still. He prowled around the house, looking out the windows and rechecking the locks on the doors.

"You should sit down and relax," Kenzie said. "What are you so worried about?"

"They just let Devon go. He could come here. He could be here now. If he decides he wants to do something to Mr. Peterson... he'll be a sitting duck."

"Devon is not going to come here. Not now, when everybody knows his identity. He met Lorne face-to-face and knows what a nice guy he is. Devon couldn't do anything to hurt him. You don't need to worry. It's over."

Zachary looked out the dark windows. There were Christmas lights on all sides of the house, which didn't help calm his anxiety at all.

"He could be out there now."

"He isn't."

Zachary paced the house, looking out each window. When he returned to the living room, Kenzie and Mr. Peterson were talking in low voices, and their glances toward Zachary told him they had been discussing him.

"I'm not being paranoid," he asserted.

"You're the expert," Mr. Peterson said, no hint of sarcasm in his voice. "I was wondering whether we could persuade you to stay overnight. I thought maybe you would feel better if you could stay and see that everything was okay."

Zachary considered. He thought initially that they were just trying to placate him, but he could detect no eye-rolling or false front. The last time, he had felt better after staying over, rather than being anxious at being away from his own bed. He paced restlessly into the kitchen and looked out at the back yard, but there was no sign of trouble.

"I guess we could stay, if Kenzie is okay with it." He looked at her with eyebrows raised. Kenzie nodded.

"Sure. I've already let Dr. Wiltshire know I'm taking a couple of extra days for my holidays. I'm game."

"Then... just one other thing..."

"If you think there's a problem, we'll listen to you," Mr. Peterson promised, trying to anticipate what the condition would be.

Zachary rubbed his forehead, trying to disguise his embarrassment. "Could you put the candles away?"

"Oh!" Pat looked around at the various decorative groupings, which included a number of red and white Christmas candles. They weren't lit, but they were still ratcheting up Zachary's anxiety. "Sorry, Zach! If I'd known you were coming, I would have had those cleared away earlier." He got up and immediately started removing the candles and readjusting the spacing of the decorations to make up for their lack. "What about all the rest? The tree...?"

Zachary eyed the brightly-lit tree. He'd been doing his best to ignore it, focusing on keeping everyone safe from Devon. But it was one of the reasons he couldn't sit down and be comfortable in the living room.

He folded his arms across his chest, the best he could do to put a barrier between himself and the tree.

"It's okay. But if we could... turn off the lights before bed. Just in case."

Mr. Peterson was the closest to the tree. He leaned over and fished around until he caught the cord for the lights. He pulled the plug. The tree went dark. Zachary breathed out a slow sigh of relief. A cold, dark tree was infinitely better than one all lit up, with hundreds of ignition points around the tinder-dry needles and branches.

"You could have said something earlier," Mr. Peterson admonished.

Zachary's cheeks warmed. "I don't like to ruin things for everyone else just because of my issues. I can still enjoy myself around a Christmas tree."

As long as it was after Christmas Eve. Or clear of all sources of ignition.

"You're okay to stay over?" Kenzie asked.

"Yes. Sure. That would be good."

He carried an emergency supply of pills with him just in case he ended up in a situation where he could not get back to his apartment to get them. The second fire, his apartment fire, had taught him that. If he had a panic attack or couldn't get home for some reason, he needed to have a few things with him, to make sure he could get through the night.

But he didn't take anything to help him sleep. He was too worried about Devon breaking in during the night. Mr. Peterson needed a burglar alarm. He didn't have anything, not even a door chime or broken glass detectors. Zachary would have to see to it that the situation was remedied. That could be his gift to Mr. Peterson. A security system that would help to keep him safe from lowlifes who might target him because of Zachary.

"You need to get some sleep," Kenzie urged. She had borrowed a t-shirt from Pat to wear as a nightshirt and was reading in bed, waiting for Zachary to settle down and join her. He had told her several times to just go to sleep without him, but she seemed to think she could outlast him.

"I can go one night without," Zachary countered. "It's not going to hurt me."

"I thought one of the reasons to come here and to sleep over was to make sure that you could get some rest. Prowling around the house isn't going to help."

"I need to be sure."

"You're planning on staying up all night?"

Zachary nodded. He waited for her to tell him that he was being ridiculous and nothing would happen if he went to sleep.

"Do you want to take turns, so you can at least get a few hours?"

He was pleasantly surprised. "I'd say yes, but... I don't think I'd be able to sleep anyway, so you may as well get yours. No point in both of us being short. I'll sleep during the day tomorrow when everyone is up."

But he knew he wouldn't. It was too late in the year. He was too close to the edge of the abyss.

Kenzie shook her head. "Are you sure it isn't just because you don't trust me to do a good enough job? You're afraid that I'll miss something or fall asleep during my shift?"

"No. There just isn't any point, when I'm going to be awake anyway."

"Okay." Kenzie gave a big yawn. "I guess I'd better knock off. If something worries you, will you wake me up? Or if you start feeling... bad."

"If it gets too bad," Zachary said, not quite confessing that he was already feeling pretty desperate. But he had purpose. He needed to stay awake and alive to look after his family. He couldn't let Mr. Peterson suffer because he was too self-absorbed.

Kenzie looked at him steadily for a minute.

"Why don't you leave your pills in here?" She motioned to the side table on her side of the bed. Zachary didn't bother to argue. He retrieved them from the bathroom, and put them beside Kenzie.

"Is there anything else I should be concerned about?" she asked.

"No. I need to keep Mr. Peterson safe. I'm not going to do anything."

"Your brain can do strange things when you get overtired. You come and wake me up, got it? If you start hallucinating or having suicidal thoughts or anything unexpected, you come wake me up."

"Okay."

"And stay off of the computer and email."

He nodded his agreement. He didn't need any extra nudges toward the edge. "My computer is in here." He gestured to it. "I'll leave my phone here… no. I'm going to keep my phone with me. If I need to wake you up and can't get back here…"

Kenzie nodded. "Fine. I'll keep mine on right here, in case you call or text." She picked it up and tapped the screen a few times. "I've turned off 'do not disturb.' So you can disturb me."

"Have a good sleep." He leaned down to her, pausing with their faces just an inch apart. He could feel her warm breath on his lips. "Sweet dreams."

He kissed her gently. Kenzie wrapped her arms around him and hugged him close, lengthening out the kiss.

"I was hoping for some action tonight," she said, indicating the empty space on the bed and giving a conspiratorial smile.

"I have to watch," Zachary said, looking toward the dark window. "I'm sorry."

She reached over and turned the reading lamp off. With the room in darkness, Zachary could see what was outside the window much more clearly. He walked over to it and stood looking out for a few minutes, watching for any movement or sign of anything that was out of place.

"Sweet dreams," he told Kenzie again, and left her in the bedroom alone.

29

When everyone was up in the morning, Kenzie and Zachary called Campbell to see if he had any ideas about what to do about Devon.

"Unfortunately, I agree with Buck. Devon has a permit to carry, so that in itself is not an offense. There is nothing overtly threatening in the email to you about your friend... I wish I could say there was, but you'd be asking a jury to agree that an *X* through a picture was the equivalent of a serious death threat. All you need is one juror who cut her ex out of all of their pictures without ever intending to do him any physical harm."

"He bullied and harassed Harding to death. He was the one who told him to kill himself. He was the one who said that Harding didn't deserve to live."

"But that's not the same as killing someone. Nobody is going to convict on that. Bullycide is an internet meme, not a legal charge."

"Do we have enough to get him for cyberstalking? There must be enough evidence to charge him with that."

"Yeah, I think we've got a lock on that one."

"What's the penalty for cyberstalking?" Kenzie asked eagerly, giving Zachary two thumbs up to encourage him.

Campbell sighed and didn't answer. Zachary closed his eyes. The one thing they could get Devon on, and Campbell was afraid to even tell them the bad news.

"First, we'd have to convince the FBI that it was worth their while to investigate him, since he was living in New Hampshire and harassing you in Vermont. If we could convince them to investigate him, charge him, and send him to Vermont… the sentence is two hundred and fifty dollars or up to three months jail time."

Zachary thumped his head down on the dining room table in disbelief. Kenzie touched his back sympathetically.

"Are you still there?" Campbell asked.

"I am," Kenzie said. "But I think we've lost Zachary."

He shook his head, still resting it on the dining room table. Two hundred and fifty dollars. That was what his life was worth. That was what Richard Harding's life was worth. A miserable two hundred and fifty dollars or up to three months.

"Zachary?" Campbell asked.

He didn't answer.

"Can we go ahead with it?" Kenzie asked. "Can you get the FBI to pursue it so that we can at least get him off the streets for a few months? Maybe?"

"I'll ask them, but I wouldn't expect anything to happen immediately. They'll only have a skeleton staff over Christmas, and nonviolent crime is not high on their priorities list."

Zachary decided that if he were ever going to be able to feel good about leaving Mr. Peterson alone, he was going to have to take matters into his own hands. He made a few phone calls, calling in what favors he could, in order to get a security system installed immediately. It meant extra money to get people in during the holiday season but, as far as Zachary was concerned, money was no object. He would do whatever it took to make sure Mr. Peterson and Pat were safe.

He worked on their phones and computers, cleaning off any suspicious programs, and added extra firewalls and security measures to keep them from being hacked again in the future.

"Don't open any email you aren't expecting," Zachary insisted. "Talk to the sender and find out what it is if you're not sure. Especially if it's from me or something to do with me. Don't click any links or attachments unless you are one hundred percent sure what they are and that it was really the person you think it was who sent it to you. I think you should get burner phones. Change your numbers so that he can't track you or get into your phone logs somehow. This guy is good. Really good."

"Maybe we should go back to wall phones with rotary dials," Mr. Peterson joked. "I never got a virus on one of those, and there was no need to track them, they were always in the same place."

"You'll be careful?" Zachary persisted.

"We'll be careful," Pat assured him. "You know Lorne is just joking. You don't need to worry about us."

But Zachary *was* worried. He took their car to a local shop and had them put it on a lift so that he could make sure no one had put a tracking device underneath. He checked for bugs at the house and in the car and found nothing, which just made him more sure he had missed something. He kept going at a frenetic pace all day long, getting everything done that he could. He ignored all pleas to eat or rest or sit down and visit.

When it was all done and he had nothing left to do, it was Christmas Eve.

Zachary sat on the bed in the spare bedroom, facing away from the door. Staring toward the window, but not actually looking out, his eyes unfocused.

"Everything is all set?" Kenzie asked Zachary brightly.

"Yeah."

"Do you think Mr. Peterson will be able to figure out the security system?"

"Pat's got it."

"Good. Well, you've had a busy day. Now you can relax."

"Uh-huh."

"You deserve a holiday."

Zachary drew in a shuddering breath. Everything was an effort, even breathing.

"And you told Ashley about it being suicide?"

"No."

Kenzie cocked her head, surprised. "I thought I heard you call her. Didn't you?"

"I called her. But I didn't tell her it was suicide."

"Oh. What did you tell her?"

"That it was an accident, just like the police said."

"Did she believe it?"

He nodded. "She paid for my expertise. I uncovered everything else. She believed me."

"That's good," Kenzie decided. "No point in laying that on her. Now she can start the grieving process."

"As long as Devon leaves her alone."

"I think he will, don't you?"

"If he doesn't, we know who he is. We'll put him away for another three months."

Kenzie chuckled. "Actually, if he's been convicted before, they can put him away for six."

Zachary didn't respond. What was the point?

Kenzie sat down on the bed beside him and took his hand. "Maybe Devon will decide to get help. Maybe his conversation with Lorne will convince him to look at therapy instead of transferring his guilt to everyone else."

"Yeah."

She looked into his face, trying to connect with him. "Where are you, Zachary?"

He blinked. Even blinking was exhausting. He wanted to go to sleep and never have to wake up again. He wanted something to take away the unrelenting pain in his chest.

Kenzie squeezed his hand. "I'm here, Zachary. You're not alone."

The Christmas lights on the neighbor's house came on.

Zachary heard the screaming. His chest burned with the smoke. He felt again the terror that he was going to smother and burn, all alone, trapped in the room that burned with the fires of hell. The sense of horror that he had done this to his family. That they were all going to die too. His throat was raw from screaming to them and from the superheated air of the room.

"Zachary." Kenzie squeezed his hand. "It's okay."

"I could never carry a gun."

"No," Kenzie agreed. She had criticized him for it before, saying that if he were going to investigate potential homicides, he should at least protect himself.

But he couldn't. Not because he was a pacifist or because he couldn't shoot, but because it would have been too big of a temptation.

"You're safe." Zachary's voice was a croak.

"We're all safe. Lorne and Pat have this fancy new security system. State of the art."

Zachary raised his head, not to look at the window sensor and motion detector, but at the smoke detector on the ceiling over the bed.

"Yes, we're safe from fire too," Kenzie confirmed. "There are no fire hazards, you know that."

"I need to see the tree."

"Come on, then." She stood up and waited for him to follow. Zachary rose slowly, every muscle in his body protesting. Kenzie put her hand on his back to encourage him. He felt like an old man walking out to the living room. A hundred years old, tottering and unsure of his feet. Mr. Peterson joined them in the living room when he saw that was where they were going. Zachary sagged into the couch and sat there staring at the decorated Christmas tree. It was still unplugged. The candles were all packed back away.

Mr. Peterson said something, all smiles, but Zachary couldn't process it. Lorne's smile faded away and he sat down across from them, saying something quietly to Kenzie. She rubbed Zachary's back. For a long time, Zachary just stared at the tree, the events of that night replaying over and over in his head. It wasn't going to happen again. He wasn't going to let it happen again. But he could never go back in time to correct his mistake or to make things right with his family.

He put his hands over his face and sat there with Kenzie and Mr. Peterson. After a while, he became aware of Kenzie shaking him, trying to get his attention. He pulled his hands away from his face, still dry-eyed.

"Zachary, why don't you call Tyrrell?"

He shook his head.

"He wants to hear from you. It might help you to get through this."

"Kenzie, no. I can't."

"Are you afraid of feeling *worse* than this?"

She did have a point. He was scraping rock bottom, it wasn't like anyone could make him feel worse than he already did.

"Not today. Not now."

"Tyrrell might need you tonight just as much as you need him," Mr. Peterson pointed out. "Do you think it's a coincidence that he wrote to you as Christmas was approaching?"

He hadn't thought of that. He thought of Tyrrell as angry, another cyberstalker like Devon, intent only on hurting Zachary, but Tyrrell had been through the Christmas Eve fire too. Maybe he was traumatized rather than angry. He had the same blood running through his veins. He had grown up, at least until age six, in the same family atmosphere. It was possible he suffered the same PTSD and depression as Zachary, especially at the time of year when he'd lost his home and half his family.

"One of us can call if you can't manage it," Kenzie said. "You don't have to do it yourself."

Zachary rubbed the tight band across his forehead. He nodded.

"Yes?" Kenzie asked eagerly. "You want me to call? Or Lorne?"

Zachary felt his pockets for his phone, retrieved it, and handed it to her.

30

It was probably a good thing that Zachary hadn't been eating. Waiting for Tyrrell to arrive, he felt dangerously nauseated.

"He sounded really nice," Kenzie assured him after the call. "He sounds a lot like you do on the phone."

So maybe Tyrrell wasn't angry. Maybe he was just looking to connect. But Zachary still wasn't sure that meeting on Christmas Eve was a good idea. He wasn't very good company. If Tyrrell was having a rough time, Zachary wasn't sure there was anything he could do to help.

The doorbell rang. Zachary got to his feet and moved to the door, no longer exhausted and in pain, but numb and disconnected from himself, feeling as if he were watching himself from a distance. He knew he should check through the peephole first to make sure it wasn't Devon, but he was afraid that any hesitation would keep him from opening the door at all. He drew in a deep breath and turned the door handle.

He expected to see a stranger, but Tyrrell seemed completely familiar to him. He looked just as he was supposed to. Taller than Zachary, but with many of the same features as Zachary saw when he looked in the mirror. His hair was longer and shaggier. He was clean shaven, whereas Zachary knew he was scruffy after a few days without shaving. And his eyes were Tyrrell's. Just exactly the same eyes as Zachary remembered in six-year-old Tyrrell.

Zachary just stood there, looking at Tyrrell, stunned after decades of not seeing any blood relations.

"Hey, Zachary," Tyrrell greeted, holding out a hand uncertainly.

Zachary automatically shook in response, then Tyrrell pulled him in and wrapped his other arm around him, hugging him tightly. He swore and laughed.

"Man, Zachary, it's been too long! It's been so, so long!"

Then they were both crying. Kenzie came over and closed the door and herded them into the living room. She was grinning fit to burst.

"Merry Christmas, Zach," she murmured, touching him lightly on the arm.

He didn't even look at her, completely wrapped up in Tyrrell. Tyrrell kept thumping him on the back, exclaiming things like. "Can you believe it? My big brother!"

Eventually, they both managed to land on the couch. Tyrrell stretched his arm around Zachary's shoulders, still holding him close. "I can't believe it!"

"You look good," Zachary managed to say. Tyrrell seemed healthy and happy. He was well-dressed and didn't look like someone who had spent his life barely making ends meet.

"And you look..." Tyrrell ran his hand over Zachary's head, the hair cropped close in a style that was easy to take care of with minimal fuss. "You look like crap, Zachary. Are you sick?"

Kenzie snorted, then laughed aloud. "He doesn't always look this bad," she advised.

"I just... haven't slept in a few days." Zachary rubbed his eyes self-consciously. He had seen in the mirror that morning how hollow they looked, and didn't imagine they were much better after a hard day's work. He'd avoided looking at the mirror again. And his long whiskers. He should have cleaned himself up before Tyrrell arrived, but he hadn't had the energy or will.

"You gotta sleep," Tyrrell said. He patted Zachary again on the back. "You gotta take care of yourself, you know."

Zachary sniffled and nodded agreement.

Tyrrell leaned back, letting out a long stream of air. "Oh, you don't know how long I've been waiting for this day. After the first year or two, I never thought I'd ever see you again. The social workers would never tell me anything about you. Or they'd say they didn't know. I imagine they could have found out, if they really didn't know. They just didn't want to tell me. They wanted me to just forget."

Zachary nodded.

Tyrrell looked around the room. "This is a nice place. I thought you lived farther north—"

"It's not mine." Zachary took in his surroundings. He pointed to Mr. Peterson, still sitting in an easy chair. "Lorne, this is Tyrrell. Mr. Peterson—Lorne—was one of my foster parents. It's his place."

"Oh, okay." Tyrrell nodded. "You kept in contact after all these years? That's amazing. You must have lived with him a long time."

Zachary shook his head. There was so much to tell, so much to explain. "I was only with him a couple of weeks. Not here, with him and his ex-wife."

"Zachary and I are both into photography," Mr. Peterson explained. "Zachary used to come over to develop his pictures, even after he was moved. So we kept in touch over the years, even after my wife and I separated. Pat and I bought this place just a few years ago."

"Ah. Well, you can tell her that it's very nice. Very homey."

"You can tell him that yourself." He raised his voice and directed it toward the kitchen. "You should come in and join the fun, Pat."

Pat poked his head through the kitchen doorway, grinning. "How about some Christmas cheer? Would everybody like drinks? Cookies?"

There were agreeable noises all around. Mr. Peterson got slowly to his feet. "I should help in the kitchen. What does everyone want? Egg nog? Cider? Mulled wine?"

"Wine sounds good to me," Kenzie said.

Zachary wasn't sure he'd be able to get anything down. It had been so long since he'd eaten or slept, any alcohol would go straight to his head.

"Something nonalcoholic," Tyrrell suggested. "The cider?"

"Cider it is," Mr. Peterson said. "Zachary, the same?"

Zachary nodded. He glanced over at Tyrrell.

"You don't drink?" Tyrrell asked.

"Not usually."

"I'm a recovering alcoholic," Tyrrell said frankly. "So I don't drink at all."

"Oh. I'm sorry."

945

"Should we not drink in front of you?" Kenzie asked. "Would that be a problem?"

"No, no," Tyrrell waved his hands at both of them. "You go ahead. And there's nothing to be sorry about," he told Zachary. "We all have our own challenges. I don't remember much about it, but I guess Mom and Dad drank, and there's a genetic predisposition for these things. I found my way through it, but I never want to fall down that hole again, so I avoid it."

Zachary nodded. He remembered them drinking. Remembered the voices getting louder and angrier as the nights wore on and they'd had more to drink. Alcohol was not something that ever brought back happy memories for him.

Tyrrell looked around. "We should turn the tree on! Old Saint Nick will be making his journey around the world soon."

Kenzie looked at Zachary. He looked at the tree, trying to decide whether he'd be able to tolerate it, since Tyrrell was there with him. But it was Christmas Eve. The tree could go up like a torch.

Even though he knew logically that history wouldn't repeat itself, he couldn't help the panic and vertigo that swept through him when he even considered the possibility. He shook his head at Kenzie and Tyrrell.

"I… I can't. I…"

"Zachary sort of has a thing about Christmas trees," Kenzie informed Tyrrell.

Tyrrell looked at Zachary, understanding dawning. "Oh. Hey, I get it. I still can't listen to *Santa Baby*. That's okay, no sweat."

Madonna's rendition of *Santa Baby* had been playing on Zachary's radio that night, just before Tyrrell fell asleep. Remembering it brought back a flood of memories. His parents screaming and fighting. Tyrrell cuddled in his arms, scared. Holding him and humming along with *Santa Baby* to put him back to sleep.

Tyrrell tightened his arm around Zachary's shoulders. "It's okay, big bro. It's all okay now."

Zachary nodded, but he didn't feel okay. Everything was closing in. He wanted to be alone, but was surrounded by people. He felt good about seeing Tyrrell, but that didn't change the fact that it was Christmas Eve and terrible things happened on Christmas Eve. He didn't want to bring tragedy down on his family and friends.

Mr. Peterson and Pat brought in the drinks, Pat also carrying a plate of Christmas cookies and treats. Zachary darted a glance at Tyrrell, worried about how he would react to Lorne and Pat's relationship. Society as a whole had grown more tolerant of gay relationships, but individuals could still be prejudiced and unkind, and he'd run into a lot of intolerant behaviors in the system.

Zachary and Tyrrell took their warm glasses of cider, and Tyrrell touched the glass to his lips and took a sip. "Oh, this is perfect! And I need one of those gingerbread cookies…" Tyrrell took one from Pat's serving platter. "Did you do all of this yourself?" he asked. "The food and the decor?"

"Mostly," Pat admitted. "Lorne's passion is for photography, like Zachary."

Pat was not the stereotypical gay decorator, with an effeminate voice and manner. Neither of the men fit the stereotypes on TV or in the media. They were just individuals, Zachary's foster father and his partner.

"You like photography?" Tyrrell turned back to Zachary.

Zachary nodded. He put his cup on a coaster on the coffee table. "Yes… but it's not my profession. Though I use it at work."

"Are you really a private investigator? I wasn't sure, when I was looking for you, if that was you…"

"Yeah. That's me. Not a lot of Zachary Goldmans around here."

"That's so cool. My brother, the private eye!"

Zachary forced a smile. "It's not glamorous like people make out. Mostly, it's sitting around watching people and writing reports."

"Don't let him play it down!" Kenzie jumped in, pointing her wine glass in Zachary's direction. "He's solved several murders in the last year or so. That's no accident. He knows what he's doing."

She and Mr. Peterson proceeded to tell Tyrrell all about Zachary's biggest cases. Zachary just rolled his eyes and sat back, knowing there was no stopping them.

Kenzie, Mr. Peterson, and Pat had all excused themselves as it got late, heading off to bed. Only Zachary and Tyrrell were left, sitting on the couch and talking quietly as the night drew on.

"You should probably go," Zachary told him. "You must have places to be tomorrow. You need to get your sleep."

"No." Tyrrell shook his head. "I'll make some calls to my friends with little kids who will be up early, then I'll have a nap. I don't have to be anywhere until dinner tomorrow afternoon."

Zachary looked at Tyrrell's hands. "You're not married?"

"Divorced. Two kids. Their mom has them this year. I'll get them for spring break."

Tyrrell had also been looking at Zachary's hands. He reached out and touched the biggest scar on Zachary's arm, tracing it gently. "Is that from the fire?"

Zachary nodded. He swallowed hard, trying to get rid of the lump in his throat.

"She said you got burned. The social worker. She said it wasn't bad, that you'd be okay."

"Yeah. I was in hospital a few weeks... probably longer than they needed to keep me, because they didn't know where to put me."

"You don't have any on your face." Tyrrell moved back and forth, staring at Zachary. "I can't see any, if you do."

"I covered my face. Trying to protect it. Trying to make a pocket of breathable air." His body remembered being trapped in the inferno, squashing himself under the couch to try to escape the flames. His muscles quivered and his heart raced.

Tyrrell squeezed his arm. "It's okay. I'm sorry. I shouldn't have brought it up."

Zachary pressed his palms over his eyes briefly. "I screamed at you to get out. All of you. Did you hear me? Did anyone get hurt?"

"I heard you. I woke up and you weren't there. You were screaming to get out and the room was full of smoke. I tried to go out to the hallway, but it was too hot and smoky. I went back and hid under the bed. Me and Vinny. They said it was good we got down low, where there wasn't as much smoke. When the fire engines came, the firefighters broke the window. They got us out. They kept asking who else was in the room, and I told them you weren't there and I couldn't find you." He stared at Zachary for a few minutes, and Zachary wondered if he too was trying to make his way through the flashbacks. Then he focused again. "No one else was burned. Just a little smoke inhalation. They got us out through the bedroom windows, then went in looking for you. None of us had to stay at the hospital. Just you."

"Did you see them all? You saw they were okay?"

Tyrrell nodded. "I don't remember a lot of the details after the fire. It was all pretty chaotic and I was only six. I remember them splitting us up; there wasn't any respite home that could take five kids. I was so scared we'd never see each other again. And we didn't. I've talked and video chatted with Joss and Heather, but we haven't gotten together to meet face-to-face. But me and the little kids stayed together until we were teenagers."

"Do you still talk to them? Vinny and Mindy?"

Tyrrell nodded. "Not as much as I should, but yeah, we have each other's numbers."

Zachary didn't ask whether any of the others wanted to meet him. He assumed that if they did, Tyrrell would have said so.

"So you're not going to go home tonight?"

"Do you want me to leave?"

Zachary shook his head.

"Then I'll stay." Tyrrell patted Zachary's leg and gave him another hug, smiling.

31

Eventually, the sky started to get lighter. Zachary let his breath out.

"It's morning," Tyrrell said. "It's Christmas Day."

Zachary closed his eyes, feeling the peaceful stillness of the house. No fire. No disaster. Just his family and friends around him, seeing him through the tunnel.

"Merry Christmas, T."

"Merry Christmas, Zachary."

They sat in silence for some time, talked out and comfortable with just letting the quiet surround them.

Zachary got up from the couch. His clothes were sweaty and sticking to him. He wasn't sure when he had last changed. Mr. Peterson and Pat had offered him a change of clothes, but he hadn't wanted to wear something that wasn't his. Too many years of hand-me-down clothes shared through dozens of foster children. He only wanted what was his.

He bent over and plugged in the tree.

"You're sure you're okay with that?" Tyrrell asked.

"Yeah. If something was going to happen, it would have happened last night."

Tyrrell grinned. "You know that's crazy, don't you?"

"I know."

"You know what we never did?"

"No. What?"

"We never built that snowman."

Zachary remembered holding Tyrrell and trying to calm him while their parents raged at each other, yelling and hitting and throwing things around.

"Do you think Santa will come?" Tyrrell had asked.

"No!" Zachary laughed and rubbed Tyrrell's head. "Santa doesn't come here, silly."

"But tomorrow's Christmas."

"Yeah. Tomorrow's Christmas. No school. Maybe we'll build a snowman."

Tyrrell snuggled against him. "A snowman? Will you help me?"

"Sure. We'll all do it."

"We'll make it so big. Taller than me."

Zachary shook his head at the memory. "I can't believe you remember that."

"You said we could build a snowman."

"I don't think I can make one taller than you anymore."

"It doesn't have to be."

They got on their coats and shoes and gear and went outside. When Kenzie got up, that's where she found them, building a snowman.

At breakfast, Pat managed to cajole Zachary into eating a Christmas orange and a few bites of freshly-baked cinnamon rolls. The bun was so sweet it hurt his teeth, and after barely having eaten anything in the days before Christmas, his stomach wasn't ready for anything so rich.

"It's really good," Zachary told Pat. "I just... can't eat much in the morning."

"You need to get some weight back on," Mr. Peterson observed. "You're skin and bones."

"It's not that bad. I'll bulk back up. Just not all in one day. Next time... I'll have dinner."

"You can't stay today? Pat already has the bird in the oven, and his family is going to be coming over this afternoon. The more the merrier."

"I need to get home and get showered and changed. I'm not going to make a very good impression on Pat's family if they think I'm some homeless person you just plucked off the street."

"They'd like to meet you."

"Next time."

"My mother said you're probably the closest thing to a grandchild she's going to get," Pat said, grinning. "I think that means she's finally accepted that I'm not going to switch teams."

"What about your sister?"

"She doesn't want to marry or have kids."

Zachary couldn't understand how anyone could not want a family of their own. It was funny to think of Pat's mother calling Zachary her grandchild. In a tortuous way, she was sort of right. Zachary was the former foster son of her son's partner. Pat had been more of a parent to Zachary than the former Mrs. Peterson, strange as that seemed.

"Tell your mom I'm looking forward to meeting her, but we have another engagement today." He looked at Kenzie, who nodded. "We set up a visit with... a friend of mine who is spending his first Christmas without his mother. I don't want to let him down."

Finally showered, shaved, and dressed in clean clothes, Zachary answered his door and let Kenzie in. She had done a better job than he of looking after herself when staying over at Mr. Peterson's, so she really didn't look that different from what she had when he had dropped her at her house. Different clothes and some makeup were the only changes he could spot.

"You look much better cleaned up," Kenzie approved. "Some concealer to hide the bags under your eyes wouldn't be a bad idea..."

"No, thanks."

She laughed. "I'm driving. I know how little sleep you've had lately, you're a menace on the road."

"Besides, you want to drive your car."

"A convertible isn't the most practical thing during Vermont winters, but she's closed up tight. We're not going far. We'll stay warm."

They did, and before long, they were at the Salters' home, where Zachary could smell roasted turkey and the fixings before they even opened the door. Vera greeted both of them with a hug and a kiss on the cheek. She called Rhys, who must have heard them ring the doorbell anyway and didn't really need to be told they had arrived.

Kenzie and Zachary sat down, and it was a few minutes before Rhys came into the room.

He was dressed in neatly pressed trousers, a white, collared shirt, and a Christmas sweater that looked both ugly and uncomfortable. He raised a hand in greeting. He was smiling, but his eyes were sad and bloodshot.

"Rhys! Merry Christmas!" Kenzie jumped up to give him a hug and a kiss on the cheek.

Rhys looked flustered and Zachary figured if it weren't for his dark skin, he would have been blushing furiously. What teenage boy wouldn't have a crush on Kenzie and get all embarrassed over a kiss?

Rhys reached for Zachary's hand, and instead of just giving him a polite handshake, he clasped Zachary's forearm and pulled him to his feet. He kept a strong grip on Zachary's forearm, a gesture Zachary took to mean *brother* and *stay strong*. He hugged Zachary with the other arm, held him for a moment, and then released him.

Rhys nodded and licked his lips. "Merry Christmas."

Zachary gave him a warm smile. Rhys was going through his own hard time, but he was holding up well. It was good that they had made an effort to be there for him. He would be strong for Zachary, and Zachary would be strong for him.

"Merry Christmas, Rhys."

Rhys nodded and looked Zachary in the eyes for a few seconds, clearly imparting that he was glad that Zachary was there. Zachary wasn't just another guest at the table, but someone Rhys needed. He remembered the conversation with Rhys, discussing how they were both broken, and the light that had come into Rhys's eyes when he understood that he and Zachary were both part of the same special club. Both broken inside, even if they looked normal on the outside. Rhys needed someone from that club there with him for Christmas. Someone who knew what it was like to miss his mother being there on Christmas Day and to mourn the life he might have had, if things had been different.

Zachary rubbed his stinging, gritty eyes.

"Let's sit down," he told Rhys. "You can show me what you got."

PREVIEW OF THEY THOUGHT
HE WAS SAFE

1

T he little family gathered around the dining room table was about as far from a traditional nuclear family as one could get. Lorne Peterson had been Zachary's foster father for a few weeks when he was young, following the house fire that had been the last straw in the break-up of his biological family. But Zachary and Mr. Peterson had kept in touch, connected in part by a love of photography and his former foster father's darkroom facilities.

Mr. Peterson—Zachary tried, but could rarely bring himself to call him Lorne—had gone through his own family dissolution a few years later, when his wife had become aware of his alternative relationships. They had lost their certification to foster, and separation and divorce followed soon after.

Zachary remembered the initial shock when he had stopped in to visit Mr. Peterson and get some film developed and he realized that Pat, the other man in the apartment, was not a neighbor who had stopped in for coffee, but Mr. Peterson's partner. He had known that Mr. Peterson was seeing someone named Pat, but had mistakenly assumed that Pat was a woman. More than twenty years later, Lorne and Pat were still together, and society had changed enough that they were able to live together openly in the mainstream rather than keeping their relationship quiet.

Pat was between Zachary and Mr. Peterson in age, still muscular and vital, though he was definitely looking more distinguished than he had in his twenties, gray creeping in at his temples and fine lines mapping his face. Mr. Peterson's deeper wrinkles all pointed up, ready to burst into a sunrise when he smiled. He was losing his hair, and the fringe that was left was almost pure white. But even as his body got older, he remained energetic and young at heart.

They had been a constant in Zachary's life for two decades and, despite the fact that Mr. Peterson had only been his foster parent for a few weeks and Pat never had been, they were the closest thing to family that Zachary had. He hadn't kept in touch with any of his other foster siblings or parents, and much of his adolescence had been spent in youth centers and group homes. With his severe ADHD and PTSD, he hadn't been an easy kid to parent.

Tyrrell's face at the table was a new one. In spite of the fact that he was Zachary's biological brother, they had not seen each other from the time that Tyrrell was six until he and Zachary had been reunited on Christmas Eve.

As Christmas Eve was the anniversary of the fire that had destroyed their family more than thirty years previously, it was always a dark time for Zachary. Some years he had almost not made it through the holiday. Being reunited with his brother had been the fulfillment of what he had thought was an impossible dream. He had been sure that he would never see any of his biological siblings again. Even being a private investigator, he had never looked for them, never daring to interfere with what might be happy lives to remind them of the horrible thing he had done in causing that fire.

Tyrrell's facial features were similar enough to Zachary's to recognize a family resemblance, though Zachary's face was still gaunt, not yet filled out following his pre-Christmas depression. Tyrrell's hair was dark like Zachary's, but longer and shaggier. He was clean-shaven. It was his eyes that Zachary found startling. In spite of the hard life that Tyrrell had been through, they were still the shining blue eyes of the six-year-old brother he remembered.

They gathered around the table to exchange stories of Zachary's and Tyrrell's separate lives, comparing notes and getting to know each other again. Zachary needed an environment where he felt safe to share in spite of any flashbacks or surges of emotion brought up by the retellings. A restaurant or bar would just not have worked. Some of their experiences were similar, and others were not. Tyrrell had been younger at the time of the family's dissolution, and therefore less damaged than Zachary, and he had been able to stay with the two younger kids for most of his childhood, so he'd had that constant in his life. Zachary had been alone, bounced from one family to another so quickly that he'd been known to return to the wrong family after school, forgetting where he was supposed to be.

But in spite of the smiles around the table, Zachary knew there was something wrong.

At first, Zachary hadn't been able to put his finger on it. He thought that maybe Mr. Peterson and Pat were just awkward having a new 'son' at the dining room table. They were used to Zachary and his quirks, but Tyrrell was a recent addition and they didn't know enough about his past to know what might trigger him, or about his interests to know what questions to ask to encourage his participation in the conversation.

But it was more than that.

There were a number of looks exchanged between Lorne and Pat that didn't seem to follow the rhythm of Tyrrell's participation in the conversation. Mr. Peterson put his hand over Pat's as they ate, something Zachary had rarely seen him do at the table. Their natural cheer was diminished, as if there were something pulling them away from the conversation to think sad thoughts. Like someone who had recently lost a loved one but was trying to act unaffected.

He watched the two of them more closely, but didn't call them out in front of Tyrrell. Obviously, whatever was going on was something they didn't want to share with Tyrrell. Maybe not with Zachary either.

Tyrrell didn't know Pat and Lorne like Zachary did, and didn't seem to notice anything amiss. He tried to catch Zachary's eye.

"Do you remember that?"

Zachary hadn't realized how distracted he had become from Tyrrell's story. He licked his lips. "Uh... sorry... I missed that."

Tyrrell looked at him for a minute, nonplussed. He shook his head. "About time to top up your Ritalin?"

"Uh... not taking any ADHD meds right now," Zachary admitted. "Sorry."

"I didn't mean…" Tyrrell flushed pink. "I wasn't serious. It was just supposed to be a joke. Because you were distracted."

Zachary flashed a look toward Mr. Peterson and Pat, noting that their hands were again touching, and Mr. Peterson was giving Pat a questioning look as he thought Zachary was occupied by a separate conversation. Zachary swallowed.

"I try to only take them if I really need to focus on something. I don't like to have to take them all the time, and they can interfere with other meds. So I just take them when I really need to."

"I didn't mean you to take it seriously…"

"What were you talking about? That I missed?"

Tyrrell looked like he didn't want to cover the same ground again. Mr. Peterson put down his fork and jumped in.

"It was about your sister Jocelyn. I gather she was sort of a second mother to you guys?"

Zachary nodded, glad to segue to something in the past rather than focusing on the issues he still battled. "Yeah, she was really bossy. I resented it, because… well, who do you think got most of that bossiness? It wasn't the little guys; she was pretty patient with them. But me… she figured I was old enough that I should have figured out how to behave myself. We were supposed to pay attention to her and fly straight, but… I was always going off-script."

Tyrrell chuckled. "Is that what you call it?"

Zachary felt his own face get warm. "I tried, but… I wasn't any better at following her rules than I was anyone else's." He included Mr. Peterson and Pat in his broad shrug. They had either experienced or heard the stories of some of his more disastrous choices.

"Joss was a little bossy," Tyrrell admitted. "But she really helped me to figure out what I was supposed to do. I really wished that we'd been able to stay together when we went into foster care. She would have been able to help me to figure out the rules when I was in a new home. I often heard her little voice in my head, telling me how to behave properly, when I was trying to sort it out."

Zachary often had too many little voices in his head, and they all told him different things. But it wasn't usually until *after* he'd impulsively done something that he actually heard them. The voices of Joss, his parents, his social worker, or some other authority in his life, telling him that once again, he'd done something exceptionally stupid and that there were going to be consequences.

Zachary shrugged and looked down at his plate. He ate a couple of bites, forcing himself to eat despite the bubble of anxiety in his stomach from trying to figure out what Mr. Peterson and Pat were so worried about. As he'd told Tyrrell, he was off of his ADHD meds, so he actually had an appetite, and Pat was a good cook, but the unspoken tension in the room was getting to him.

"Have you had any contact with her?" Mr. Peterson asked with interest.

"A little," Tyrrell said. "Mostly just email or social media, you know. We haven't gotten together face-to-face. I think… she's got her own life and isn't that interested in reconnecting. It can be hard… stirring up old memories. She's got her own family now."

"You guys should have a reunion, get everyone together. It sounds like you know where everyone is now."

Tyrrell nodded slowly. He glanced sideways at Zachary. "I have ways to contact everyone now. But I'm not sure if everyone wants to get together. They're all living their own lives."

"But you grew up with the younger ones. You guys must have a pretty good relationship."

"We were together until I was fourteen or something, so yeah, we have a lot of shared memories, but then we didn't have anything to do with each other because we were in different homes until we were adults. It's a real hodgepodge of relationships."

"I can't imagine what it must be like not to know where your siblings are," Pat contributed. "I just have one sister, and we've always been in contact, even if she didn't particularly approve of my 'lifestyle choices.' It would be hard, not even knowing where they were."

There was a suspicious crack in Pat's voice that set alarm bells ringing for Zachary. Pat didn't usually get emotional about his family. He laughed about their attitudes, mentioned them now and then, but even when his father had died, he hadn't cried about it. Not in front of Zachary, anyway. With the number of times that Zachary had broken down around Pat, Pat certainly shouldn't have felt awkward about shedding a few tears in front of Zachary.

Zachary studied Pat closely, and then Mr. Peterson. Lorne apparently caught the significance of the look. He made an infinitesimal shake of his head, which might have even been unconscious, and Zachary knew it wasn't the time to ask what was going on.

"I guess it's a different experience," Tyrrell agreed, "but I've never known anything else, so for me, that's just the way families are. You spend a few years together, and then you don't have any contact for a decade or more. Now with the internet, you have these opportunities to touch base again and find out what people have been occupying themselves with. We're all adults now, so it isn't like we're looking to live together as a family again."

"I'm glad you reached out to Zachary," Mr. Peterson said. "It's been really good for him to have contact with someone from his family again."

Zachary nodded reflexively.

"I think everyone needs to know that they have somewhere they belong," Mr. Peterson went on. "Not just somewhere like this," he spread his hands to indicate his home, where Zachary was a welcome part of the family any time, "but biologically, too. I've heard that a lot of people who are foster or adopted kids really miss that biological connection, even if they never met their biological family before. There's just a hole where they feel like they don't belong or aren't a part of the family who raised them."

Zachary let his eyes linger on Mr. Peterson for a few moments. It was only natural that, as a foster parent, he would be aware of the needs of foster kids to find some kind of genetic connection. But he didn't want Mr. Peterson to feel like he hadn't been a good enough parent or friend to Zachary.

Tyrrell gave a shrug. "I guess so. I always knew I had biological siblings out there. Even parents, if I wanted to look for them. But I was more interested in building a family of my own. Getting married, having kids. I guess that was my way of having a genetic connection with someone. My own kids."

Zachary felt a pang. He hadn't told Tyrrell his own history with his ex, Bridget, and the issues that she'd had with having children. Zachary had always thought that he would have a family, a house full of kids to remind Zachary of the family that he'd lost. To make up for the pain that he'd caused.

Even though Bridget had said from the start that she didn't want kids, he'd thought that she would change her mind. That biological clock would start ticking, she would see what a great father Zachary would make, and she would decide it was time.

He'd been sadly mistaken and things had not ended well.

Mr. Peterson flashed a look at Zachary, knowing the history. Maybe that too was part of what he had read. How kids with no biological heritage longed for children of their own. Maybe it was an established pathological desire.

2

They got through the evening. Zachary found the time went much more slowly than usual as he watched Mr. Peterson and Pat, waiting for a flash of insight into what was going on with them. He was intuitive, skilled at reading body language and facial expression, and he knew Lorne and Pat well, but he couldn't quite put his finger on what was going on.

After saying his goodbyes, he walked out to his car, and waited until Tyrrell got into his and drove away. Then he returned to the house.

Pat opened the door, looking at Zachary with surprise. "Forget something?" he asked, looking behind himself to see if Zachary had left a book or bag.

Zachary shook his head. He hesitated. "I just wanted to see if there was something I could do…"

Pat looked at him for a minute, then stepped back. "Come in."

Mr. Peterson came around the corner. "Oh, Zachary. What's up? I thought you were on your way."

Pat looked at him, communicating something by his manner. Mr. Peterson nodded slowly. "I guess I should know better than to try to get anything past you." He led the way to the living room and they sat down. Mr. Peterson normally liked his easy chair, and Pat was usually back and forth, preparing coffee or checking something in the kitchen, playing the part of the diligent host. But they both sat down together on the couch, holding hands again.

Mr. Peterson looked at Pat. "You want to start?"

Pat blinked, looked down, then nodded. "Sure." He cleared his throat. He looked at Zachary, gaze steady. "A friend of mine is missing."

"Oh." Zachary thought about that. "I'm sorry. How long has he been missing? Have you talked to the police?"

"I talked to the police... they weren't really that interested. They said that they would look into it, but as far as I can see, they haven't done much. They said they would get back to us if they found anything, but..."

"You haven't heard anything back from them," Zachary finished. "They can keep their investigations pretty close to the chest, sometimes. If you're not the next of kin, they don't have any requirement to report back to you. They haven't said anything?"

"They don't think there's any foul play. They think that he just... left town."

Zachary nodded. "Could he have?"

"He didn't," Pat said with certainty. "I know Jose, and he didn't leave town. He would have said something to me if he'd been planning on leaving. Even if it was something unplanned, he would still have called."

"Where do you know him from?"

Pat looked at Mr. Peterson, and then back at Zachary. "We know him from the community. He's gay. Someone we get together with now and then to do something with."

They didn't often talk about their social life, so Zachary didn't know how large their group of gay friends was, or how long they had known this Jose. Zachary had never heard either of them mention him before.

"How long has he been missing?"

Pat swallowed and rubbed his forehead. Mr. Peterson patted his back and filled in the details. "As far as we can tell, it's been a week since anyone has seen him."

"A week." Zachary didn't like that. He could understand the police not being too concerned if it had only been a day or two, but a week should have been raising some red flags. "Have you talked to his work? His family?"

"He doesn't have any family here. He has a wife and kids back in El Salvador, he sends money home to them. Here, he doesn't have anyone... steady. Just friends, casual encounters."

"He's gay but he has a wife and kids in El Salvador?"

Pat shrugged and nodded. "Sometimes it happens that way."

Mr. Peterson had previously been married to a woman and had foster kids, so Zachary supposed he shouldn't have been surprised. People chose to do the socially acceptable thing, and then later decided that they couldn't maintain appearances.

"And work? Does he have a job?"

Pat nodded and took over again. "He did day labor, cash pay, but it was with the same company every day, not going from one job to another. I talked with the foreman and he said that Jose just stopped showing up."

"Was he surprised about that?"

"No... but that doesn't mean that he was right. If you had a worker coming in every day and then they just stopped coming without a word, wouldn't you be concerned?"

"I would," Zachary admitted. "But I don't deal with day laborers. I guess they probably have a pretty heavy turnover. Is he... legal?"

"No. Undocumented."

"So if there was trouble, he might have just disappeared."

"He could... but like I said, he would have at least given us a heads-up that something had happened."

"If he could. But sometimes there isn't any warning, they just get arrested and put into a facility awaiting deportation. You don't know that he would be able to call you. Or that he would. He might have been limited in the number of calls that he could make, or he might have figured there was no point. You couldn't do anything for him, so why bother?"

"I still think he would have told us if he could."

"Did the police check in with ICE? See whether he had been picked up in a sweep?"

"They haven't gotten back to us. I think if they had found his name on a list like that, they would have at least said that he was okay, even if they didn't give us any details."

Zachary nodded. In theory. But sometimes the police dropped the ball and didn't call back, especially if it were just a random friend and not the next of kin. Sometimes they got distracted by other cases or bogged down, and just clearing the case was all they could do, without making a bunch of reports to the friends or family.

"You don't think he went back to El Salvador? What if his wife said she needed him to come back? She or one of the kids was sick. Something that sounded like an emergency."

"He would have let someone know." Pat shook his head. "He didn't live by himself. Most of these illegals don't make enough money to get a place of their own. Especially when they're sending as much home as they can. So he had roommates. He didn't tell them where he was going. He just didn't come home one day."

Zachary found himself pulling out his notepad to start making notes. His brain was grinding through the possibilities. If Jose hadn't gone home, then ICE was still the most likely possibility. Someone had tipped them off and he had been nabbed on his way home from work, at a bar, or even at the grocery store.

But there were other possibilities. He was mugged or had an accident, and was in the hospital somewhere. Maybe under his own name and maybe as a John Doe. Similarly, he could be in the morgue. Going home to El Salvador was less likely. He would probably at least have told his roommates what was happening if he were going back home. There would be no reason not to tell them. He would have had to make arrangements; he wouldn't have just been able to hop on a plane and fly back in a couple of hours. Zachary scratched down a few thoughts. He looked up to see Mr. Peterson and Pat watching him intently.

"Do you have the name of the officer who investigated it? A case number?"

"Yeah. Just a minute." Pat got up and retreated to the bedroom to get the details.

Mr. Peterson gave Zachary a smile. "Thanks for this, Zachary. We've been very worried."

"You should have told me. I could have gotten started on it earlier."

"You have a lot on your plate. One undocumented worker disappears… it's not exactly at the top of the priority list."

"Not for the police. It would have been for me."

Mr. Peterson smiled. "Thank you."

They waited for Pat to return with the information about the policeman. "He and Pat were pretty close?"

"They clicked. Sometimes you just meet someone that everything falls into place with. You start a conversation with them, and it's like you've known them your whole life. You know?"

Mr. Peterson didn't sound jealous, but Zachary couldn't help wondering just how far the friendship went. He had never seen any cracks in the relationship between Mr. Peterson and Pat, but people hid that kind of thing. Zachary hadn't known that Mr. Peterson and his wife were getting divorced until he had shown up at the house one day to be told by Mrs. Peterson that her husband didn't live there anymore. He had seen, before that, that the two of them were not terribly compatible. They had very different personalities and viewpoints. If Mr. Peterson had had his way, Zachary probably would have lived with them longer than he had. Maybe not for years, but a few more weeks. They would have tried for longer to work things out. Mr. Peterson understood Zachary and his issues better. His wife had only been concerned about Zachary's behaviors and how they might affect the other foster children. As a mother, of course that was something that she had to consider.

Pat returned with a piece of paper. He handed it to Zachary. Detective Dougan, a phone number, and a case number.

"Thanks. Tell me the information you can about your friend. His full name, where he worked, where he lived, anyone else in your group I can talk to."

Pat sat back down. He pulled out his phone. "His name is Jose Flores. He worked for A.L. Landscaping." He read off a phone number and address for Zachary. "The roommate that I talked to…" He tapped around on his phone for a minute. "His name was Nando Gonzalez."

"Do you know him?"

"No. I hadn't ever met him before. I hadn't ever been in Jose's apartment. But I knew where it was. We had picked him up before and I knew what the apartment number was. So I just went and knocked on the door…"

Zachary processed this. He tried to envision what had happened, and how Nando might have felt about the broad-chested white man showing up without warning at his door. He would have been nervous. Anxious about being turned over to Immigration. Suspicious of whether Pat were actually a friend of Jose's, or someone playing a part. Nando probably wouldn't have told Pat everything he knew. Even if he knew from Jose that he and Pat were friends, he probably would still have hung back. Illegals had to be wary even of friends. There was no telling what Pat's true motivation might have been.

"Do you mind me looking into it? Going back and talking to him?"

"No, of course. Go ahead. I'd really like to know what happened to him. I'm worried. He wasn't that kind of guy, you know, the kind who would just disappear. I know some people do that. But Jose… he was dedicated to his job. He wanted to make things work in America. He wanted to help his wife and kids come here."

"This roommate that you talked to, he wasn't someone from your community, then?"

"No. We didn't know him."

"The two of them were not a couple?"

"No." Pat gave a smile and shook his head. "I doubt that he knew Jose was gay."

"Why not? Had he not… come out?"

It seemed like an antiquated term in a society where sexual orientation was no longer supposed to be taboo and gay marriage was legal. Was there still a reason for men and women to be in the closet and hide their orientation from their families and friends?

"It's different for men of color," Pat said slowly. "There is a belief that the word 'gay' only applies to white men. That it's not just sexual orientation, but race and class as well. The type of gay men that you see on prime-time TV. White, limp-wristed, lisping, middle-to-upper-class, sweater-wearing men. And people like Jose… aren't that. So they tend not to even identify as gay."

"Really?" It had never occurred to Zachary that the term meant anything other than a same-sex attraction. "I… I had no idea."

"How would you?" Mr. Peterson gave a smile. "Unless you spend a lot of time in those circles, you don't really hear what people think or what their prejudices are."

"So how would he identify himself?" Zachary asked curiously. "If he wouldn't say that he is gay, because only white guys are gay, then he would say that he is…?"

"MSM is a term they have borrowed from medical literature. During the initial years of the AIDS epidemic, medical practitioners found that a lot of non-whites said that they were not gay, even though they were having same-sex relations. So they had to change their language in order to properly identify the risk factors. Not 'are you gay,' but 'have you had sex with men?' MSM was the medical shorthand. Or WSW for the women."

Zachary wrote MSM down so he wouldn't forget it when he started to talk to people that Jose knew who might be part of the gay—MSM—community. Language was a powerful thing, and he didn't want to risk offending someone who might have information to share. Say the wrong thing, and he might never hear anything more from a witness.

Pat handed Zachary a photo. A group of men around a table. Pat and Lorne and others Zachary didn't recognize. Pat pointed to the Hispanic man beside him.

"That's Jose."

He was well-dressed, not what Zachary would have expected for an illegal worker. He had on evening wear, like the other men, a suit or dinner jacket and blue tie. He had a wide, pleasant smile, and looked comfortable, part of the group. Zachary raised an eyebrow at Pat, and when he nodded, kept the photo.

"Have you talked to his wife?"

"I don't know how to reach her. We never talked about it. I don't know her name or where in El Salvador she lives."

"Did *she* know that he was... MSM?"

"I doubt it. A lot of men like him keep it pretty quiet. Other than the people that they hook up with, they don't tell anyone. They live two lives, and keep them very separate."

"How did you meet?"

Pat and Mr. Peterson looked at each other. Not in a way that suggested they had something to hide, but just that they had to think about it and might need a memory jogger.

It was Mr. Peterson who answered first. "I think... the first time we met up was at a club downtown. There was a very popular lounge singer who was doing a night there... it was very busy, a lot of people wanted to see him. We went well ahead of time to get a table. The place was so packed, they were asking patrons to share tables. Jose ended up at our table, and we struck up a conversation."

"That's right," Pat's face cleared. "I'd forgotten all about that. We've done so many other things together. It was just one of those cases where everything fits together, and it was such a comfortable conversation... by the end of the night, it was like we had always been friends."

"And you've spent a lot of time together since then? How long has that been?"

"About... four months... five?"

"And the three of you together, or just Jose and you?"

Pat raised his eyebrows. "I'm devoted to Lorne, Zachary. This was not a hook-up."

"So the three of you?"

"Yes, the three of us. Usually other people as well. A group of guys getting together at a bar or club, or even a museum or gallery. Christmas shopping together. Just... things that friends do together."

Zachary nodded, getting a more clear picture of the relationship. "Can I talk to one or two of your friends? Or would that be intrusive?"

There were several seconds of hesitation, the silence drawing out.

"I'll have to talk to them first," Pat said eventually. "I'll get you names and numbers once I've had a chance to."

"Okay. Did the police talk to anyone else?"

"I don't know who they talked to. They didn't ask for the names of any other friends. Just for his boss at A.L. I think that's where the investigation stopped."

Order They Thought He Was Safe at pdworkman.com

ABOUT THE AUTHOR

Award-winning and USA Today bestselling author P.D. (Pamela) Workman writes riveting mystery/suspense and young adult books dealing with mental illness, addiction, abuse, and other real-life issues. For as long as she can remember, the blank page has held an incredible allure and from a very young age she was trying to write her own books.

Workman wrote her first complete novel at the age of twelve and continued to write as a hobby for many years. She started publishing in 2013. She has won several literary awards from Library Services for Youth in Custody for her young adult fiction. She currently has over 50 published titles and can be found at pdworkman.com.

Born and raised in Alberta, Workman has been married for over 25 years and has one son.

Please visit P.D. Workman at pdworkman.com to see what else she is working on, to join her mailing list, and to link to her social networks.

If you enjoyed this book, please take the time to recommend it to other purchasers with a review or star rating and share it with your friends!

facebook.com/pdworkmanauthor

twitter.com/pdworkmanauthor

instagram.com/pdworkmanauthor

amazon.com/author/pdworkman

bookbub.com/authors/p-d-workman

goodreads.com/pdworkman

linkedin.com/in/pdworkman

pinterest.com/pdworkmanauthor

youtube.com/pdworkman

Lightning Source UK Ltd.
Milton Keynes UK
UKHW021848240123
415916UK00005B/132